Everyman, I will go with thee,
and be thy guide

Lucan

THE CIVIL WAR

Translated as Lucan's *Pharsalia* by

Nicholas Rowe

———

Edited by
SARAH ANNES BROWN
Newnham College, Cambridge

and

CHARLES MARTINDALE
University of Bristol

EVERYMAN
J. M. DENT · LONDON
CHARLES E. TUTTLE
VERMONT

Page 299

Selection, Introduction and other critical material
© J. M. Dent 1998

This edition first published in
Everyman Paperbacks in 1998

J. M. Dent
Orion Publishing Group
Orion House, 5 Upper St Martin's Lane,
London WC2H 9EA
and
Charles E. Tuttle Co., Inc.
28 South Main Street,
Rutland, Vermont 05701, USA

Printed in Great Britain by
The Guernsey Press, Channel Islands

British Library Cataloguing-in-Publication Data
is available on request

ISBN 0 460 87571 X

CONTENTS

NOTE ON THE AUTHORS AND EDITORS

NICHOLAS ROWE was born in 1674, the son of a barrister of the Middle Temple. Rowe was trained for the same profession, but the death of his father in 1692 put him in possession of an income of about £300 a year, allowing him to fulfil his literary ambitions. His first success came with the production of *The Ambitious Stepmother*, a blank-verse tragedy, at Lincoln's Inn Fields in 1700. Rowe was an ardent Whig, and became under-secretary to the Duke of Queensbury in 1708. In 1715 he was made poet laureate in succession to Nahum Tate, and in May 1717 he was appointed Clerk of the Presentations. He died on 6 December 1718. Among his best-known plays are *Tamerlane* (1702), *The Fair Penitent* (1703) and *Jane Shore* (1713). His most important achievements are his pioneering edition of Shakespeare's works (1709) and his translation of Lucan's *Pharsalia* which was published posthumously in 1719.

MARCUS ANNAEUS LUCANUS was born at Cordoba in Spain in AD 39. He was the nephew of Seneca the Younger, the most popular writer of the day and one of the most powerful men in the Roman empire. Lucan studied with the Stoic Cornutus in Rome and continued his education in Athens for a time before being recalled by the emperor Nero, who favoured him greatly, appointing him quaestor. However, he later incurred the enmity of Nero and was forbidden to write poetry or plead in the courts. This incited him to take part in a conspiracy against the emperor. He was arrested for his part in the plot against Nero's life, and forced to commit suicide in AD 65, aged only twenty-five. The *Pharsalia* is his only surviving work.

SARAH ANNES BROWN is a British Academy Postdoctoral Fellow at Newnham College, Cambridge. She completed her PhD thesis on the influence of Ovid on Renaissance literature at the University of Bristol and went on to spend three years as a Teaching and

Research Fellow at St Andrews University. She is completing a study of English Ovidianism which is to be published by Duckworth in 1999.

CHARLES MARTINDALE, Professor of Latin at the University of Bristol, is the author of *John Milton and the Transformation of Ancient Epic* (1986) and *Redeeming the Text: Latin Poetry and the Hermeneutics of Reception* (1993) and co-author of *Shakespeare and the Uses of Antiquity* (1990). He is editor of *Virgil and his Influence* (1984), *Ovid Renewed* (1988), (with David Hopkins) *Horace Made New* (1993) and *The Cambridge Companion to Virgil* (1998).

CHRONOLOGY OF LUCAN'S LIFE AND TIMES

Year	Life	Literary Context	Historical Events
BC			
60			First triumvirate of Caesar, Pompey and Crassus
53			Crassus killed at Carrhae by the Parthians
49			Caesar crosses the Rubicon and invades Italy, starting the civil war
48			Battle of Pharsalus; death of Pompey in Egypt
46		Suicide of Cato the Younger at Utica	
44			Assassination of Julius Caesar
42			Battle of Philippi: deaths of Brutus and Cassius
31			Battle of Actium; defeat of Antony and Cleopatra
27			Octavian receives title 'Augustus'
19		Death of Virgil; posthumous publication of *Aeneid*	
8		Death of Horace	
AD			
c. 1		Birth of the younger Seneca	
2		Ovid at work on *Metamorphoses*	

Year	Life	Literary Context	Historical Events
8		Ovid exiled by Augustus	
14			Death of Augustus; succession of Tiberius
17		Death of Ovid	
37			Birth of Nero; accession of Caligula
39	Birth of Lucan		
41			Accession of Claudius
54			Death of Claudius; Nero becomes emperor
c. 55		Birth of Tacitus	
60	Wins a prize for a poem in praise of Nero at the Neronia		
c. 61	Quaestor; at work on Pharsalia		
62		Death of the satirist Persius	
c. 63		Seneca at work on his Letters to Lucilius	
65	Commits suicide	Suicide of Seneca	Conspiracy of Piso
66		Suicide of Petronius, author of Satyricon	
68			Suicide of Nero
from 92		Statius' Silvae published (2.7 on Lucan)	
from c. 100		Juvenal active as a satirist	

CHRONOLOGY OF ROWE'S LIFE

Year Age Life

1674   Born in Bedfordshire, son of John Rowe, a London barrister

1688   14   Elected a King's Scholar at Westminster

1691   17   Became a student in the Middle Temple
1692   18   Death of his father
1693   19   Married Antonia Parsons

CHRONOLOGY OF HIS TIMES

Year	Literary Context	Historical Events
1627	Thomas May's translation of the *Pharsalia*	
1641–52		Civil War
1649		Execution of Charles I
1660		End of Commonwealth; restoration of monarchy under Charles II
1677	Dryden, *All For Love*; Racine, *Phèdre*	Popish Plot: Catholics accused of planning regicide and *coup*
1678		War with Holland ends
1680	Death of Rochester	
1681	Dryden, *Absalom and Achitophel*	
1682	Dryden, *Mac Flecknoe*; Otway, *Venice Preserved* first acted	
1685		Death of Charles II; succession of his Roman Catholic brother, James II.
1688	Birth of Pope	Glorious Revolution; James II flees on the invasion of William; William III of Orange and Mary accede; Toleration Act allows Nonconformists freedom of worship; Bill of Rights bans Crown to Catholics
1689	Birth of Richardson; death of Aphra Behn; Purcell, *Dido and Aeneas*	
1693	Dryden's translation of Juvenal	
1694		Death of Queen Mary

Year	Age	Life
1696	22	Called to the bar
1700	26	His first play, *The Ambitious Stepmother*, performed
1702	28	First production of his tragedy, *Tamerlane*
1703	29	*The Fair Penitent*, a sentimental tragedy, first performed
1704	30	His translation of an extract from the second book of *Pharsalia* published by Tonson
1706	32	Death of his first wife, Antonia Parsons
1707	33	*The Royal Convert* performed at the Haymarket
1708	34	Contributed a memoir of Boileau to a translation of Boileau's *Lutrin*; became under-secretary to the Duke of Queensbury
1709	35	Rowe's edition of Shakespeare's works published; further translations of Lucan, including the whole of Book IX, published by Tonson
1710	36	Published a translation of Quillet's *Callipaedia*
1713	39	*Jane Shore*, which Rowe wrote in imitation of Shakespeare's style, first performed
1715	41	His last tragedy, *Lady Jane Grey*, performed at Drury Lane; he succeeded Nahum Tate as poet laureate; was appointed one of the land surveyors of the customs of the port of London; married Anne Devenish
1717	43	Rowe's translations of parts of the *Metamorphoses* were included in Garth's edition of the poem translated by several hands
1718	44	Appointed clerk of the presentations by the Prince of Wales Died on 6 December and was buried at Westminster Abbey
1719		Posthumous publication of his translation of the *Pharsalia*, dedicated by his wife to the king

Year	Literary Context	Historical Events
1697	Dryden's translation of Virgil	
1699	Dryden, *Fables Ancient and Modern*	
1700	Congreve, *The Way Of the World*; death of Dryden	
1701		French invade Holland; death of James II; his son James III recognized by Louis XIV
1702		Death of William III; accession of Queen Anne
1704	Swift, *The Battle of the Books, A Tale Of a Tub*	Battle of Blenheim
1706	Farquhar, *The Recruiting Officer*	Union of England and Scotland
1708		Success for Allies under Marlborough in war of Spanish succession
1709	Pope, *Pastorals*; Johnson born	
1710		Fall of Godolphin ministry; Harley succeeds
1711	Addison and Steele, *Spectator* (runs until 1712); Pope, *An Essay on Criticism*	
1712	Diderot born; Rousseau born	
1713		Treaty of Utrecht
1714	Pope, *The Rape of the Lock*	Death of Queen Anne; succession of George I; fall of Harley
1715	Pope's translation of Homer's *Iliad*	Jacobite rising put down; death of Louis XIV
1717	Pope, *Collected Works*	Triple Alliance
1719	Defoe, *Robinson Crusoe*	

FOREWORD

In editing Rowe's translation we have endeavoured to produce a text which will be easily accessible to students and general readers as well as to scholars. Eighteenth-century poetry does not present the same problems as medieval or Renaissance texts for the modern reader. The proportion of archaic words, or words used in an unfamiliar way, is much smaller, and we have therefore glossed them at the end of the volume rather than in the margin. We have followed standard modernizing procedures which always involve compromises and the need to find pragmatic solutions to complex problems.

Eighteenth-century verse was printed with copious elision marks. These have been retained where otherwise the modern reader is likely to read the line unmetrically. 'Ev'n' and 'fall'n' need the elision marks in order to make them unambiguously monosyllabic, and phrases such as 'th'excuse' and 'th'avenger' would also probably be pronounced incorrectly if they were printed without the elision. Sometimes, as with a word such as 'dispos'd', it was equally clear that the mark could be dispensed with. In some cases the decision was not so straightforward. Participles such as 'threatening' and 'neighbouring' may seem to be trisyllables, yet the context in which they appeared often provided a sufficient signal to the reader to swallow the middle syllable without the need of an elision mark. 'Ivory', 'different', 'prisoner', 'general' and 'favourite' are among many other words that fall into the same category. Although our normal practice is to print these words without marked elisions, it should be noted that in many cases in modern English the elided syllable is lightly pronounced; 'watery', for example, does not contain three equal syllables. We have printed 'them' for ''em' throughout.

In eighteenth-century poetry it was customary to italicize proper names and capitalize other nouns. One effect of the latter practice is to create occasional ambiguities as to whether certain abstract nouns, such as fame, are personifications. We have modernized the text in this respect, retaining the capitalization in only one instance which is discussed in the notes.

Spelling has also been modernized throughout. Generally, as when 'bosome' becomes 'bosom' or 'scull' 'skull', this does not affect pronunciation. There are a few exceptions such as the archaic variant spellings 'burthen' and 'salvage' which have also been modernized unless rhyme is affected. Proper names have been altered to conform with familiar modern usage: Martia thus becomes Marcia and Sylla Sulla. Occasional anomalous spellings which are the result of the author's (or printer's) error rather than eighteenth-century conventions have been left unaltered and discussed in the notes. We have retained Rowe's paragraph divisions as they provide useful guidance for how the narrative is articulated. Punctuation practice has undergone substantial changes since the eighteenth century. We have lightened Rowe's punctuation and modified it in order to highlight syntactic structure in accordance with modern usage. Speech marks, not used by Rowe, have been added for clarification, and the somewhat haphazard use of apostrophes in the first edition has been normalized.

Many people have given generously of their assistance, including Alex Brown, Christine Gascoigne, Michael Liversidge, Ellen O'Gorman, Liz Prettejohn and Vanda Zajko. In particular we would like to thank David Hopkins, Duncan Kennedy and Tom Mason, who read through earlier drafts and suggested many valuable improvements.

INTRODUCTION

> And kis the steppes, where as thou seest pace
> Virgile, Ovide, Omer, Lucan, and Stace.

Thus Chaucer instructs his 'little book' at the close of *Troilus and Criseyde* (V.1791–2). Lucan's *Pharsalia* (to use the poem's traditional title)[1] describes the civil war between Julius Caesar and Pompey and the decline and fall of the Roman Republic. The *Pharsalia* is normally categorized as a historical epic, but we can also usefully think of it as a political poem, since it is, or appears to be, an impassioned attack on the unchecked rule of the state by a single individual. Lucan (if we hold for the moment to a Republican reading of his poem, a reading which has historically been the dominant one at least since the Renaissance)[2] writes to commend *libertas*, freedom, conceived of both constitutionally as the Republic overthrown by the Caesars and spiritually as the inner freedom of mind that can be obtained in any circumstances by the Stoic sage. Political liberty died at the battle of Pharsalia, where Caesar defeated Pompey and the Senate (though in VII.645–6 Lucan, in an extraordinary flourish, implies that a new civil war would be justified to regain it), whereas the other kind of freedom not infrequently entailed resort to suicide. The defender of liberty in the poem is the Stoic saint and martyr Cato the Younger, who struggles for the dying Republic and – although Lucan never reached this point in the story – himself dies heroically by his own hand rather than become a slave of Caesar. Perhaps because of ideological objections to the poem, or perhaps for more personal reasons, Lucan was forbidden to recite or publish; he joined a conspiracy to overthrow Nero which was discovered, and, on the emperor's orders, he committed suicide in AD 65, his poem apparently still unfinished. He was twenty-five years old.

This edition is predicated on two assumptions: first that Lucan merits the canonical status accorded to him in the passage from *Troilus* that he has lost only over the past two centuries; and secondly that Nicholas Rowe's posthumously published translation of 1718 is by far the best version of the *Pharsalia* in English, and indeed not wholly unworthy of Dr Johnson's description of it as 'one of the greatest productions of English poetry'. The fame of Lucan's poem and of its finest English translation declined together, so it will be necessary in this introduction to offer some brief apologia for both.

One indication of Lucan's merits and historical importance is the number of distinguished writers who have admired the *Pharsalia* and whose own work has been informed in various ways by it; the list includes Statius, Tacitus, Juvenal, Dante, Marlowe, Milton, Marvell, Corneille, Goethe and Shelley. The introduction to Rowe by the Whig writer James Welwood includes a conventional rhetorical comparison (*synkrisis*) of Virgil and Lucan, which assumes at least a rough balance of advantage and disadvantage between the two epics. The *Pharsalia* has often been described as an anti-*Aeneid*, or at any rate a poem which in significant ways exists in a relationship of contrast and even opposition to Virgil's. Today, despite the sharp decline in the knowledge of Latin, Virgil remains a canonical name, where Lucan has become the province of specialists only. Theodore Ziolkowski has recently argued that the twentieth century, particularly the inter-war period, has constituted a renewed *aetas Virgiliana*; in this phase of the *agon* between the two poets Lucan has certainly been the loser, in a way and to a degree that would have surprised earlier ages. Robert Graves, one of the few modern poets to have taken any interest in Lucan, called him 'the father of yellow journalism', and in his translation for Penguin (1956) perversely turned Lucan's taut rhetoric into the flattest of English prose. His version of the opening is typical:

> The theme of my poem is the Civil War which was decided on the plains of Pharsalus in Thessaly; yet 'Civil War' is an understatement, since Pompey and Caesar, the opposing leaders, were not only fellow-citizens but relatives: the whole struggle was indeed no better than one of licensed fratricide. I shall describe how, after the breakdown of the First Triumvirate, Rome turned the imperial sword against her own breast . . .

Lucan's untraditional, unVirgilian procedures were indeed controversial from the start, and the differences between the *Aeneid* and the *Pharsalia* became part of a debate, often renewed, about the proper nature of epic poetry. Statius, an epic writer of the later Flavian period, well describes the *Pharsalia* as a *carmen togatum*, 'a poem that wears the toga [the national garb of the Romans]', continuing 'the *Aeneid* itself shall do you homage as you sing to the Latin peoples';[3] certainly the *Pharsalia* could be seen as resolutely 'Roman' in its commitment to 'history' and its contempt for flowery mythological embellishment borrowed from Greece. But traditionalists censured Lucan's failure to achieve the requisite 'mythic transformation'[4] of his material, in particular by the jettisoning of the 'divine machinery', the intervention of the gods in the epic action (the issue was one of decorum, not theology) – for Servius, the famous commentator on Virgil, Lucan ignored 'the law of the poetic art', writing like a historian not a poet. But the argument could be turned on its head, as it was by Welwood–Rowe and by Horace Walpole in a letter to the Reverend H. Zouch dated 9 December 1758:

I am just undertaking an edition of Lucan, my friend Mr Bentley [son of the great scholar Richard Bentley] having in his possession his father's notes and emendations on the first seven books. Perhaps a partiality for the original author concurs a little with this circumstance of the notes to make me fond of printing at Strawberry Hill the works of a man who alone of all the classics was thought to breathe too brave and honest a spirit for the perusal of the Dauphin and the French. I don't think that a good or bad taste in poetry is of so serious a nature that I should be afraid of owning too, that with that great judge Corneille and with that perhaps no judge Heinsius [a famous Dutch classical scholar], I prefer Lucan to Virgil. To speak fairly, I prefer great sense to poetry with little sense – There are hemistichs in Lucan that go to one's soul and to one's heart – for a mere epic poem, a fabulous tissue of uninteresting battles, that don't teach one even to fight, I know nothing more tedious. The poetic images, the versification and language of the *Aeneid* are delightful, but take the story by itself, and can anything be more silly and unaffecting? There are gods without power, heaven-directed wars without justice, inventions without probability, and a hero who betrays one woman with a kingdom that he might have had, to force himself upon another woman and another kingdom to which he had no pretensions, and all this to show his obedience to the gods! In short I have always admired his numbers so much and his meaning so little, that I think I should like Virgil better if I understood him less.[5]

Walpole's comments touch on the issue of good and bad 'taste', which often features in discussions of what we might call Lucan's extremist poetics and which was already exercising Lucan's Whig admirers in the eighteenth century:

> What though thy early, uncorrected page
> Betrays some marks of a degenerate age,
> Though many a tumid point thy verse contains
> Like warts projecting from Herculean veins,
> Though like thy Cato thy stern Muse appear,
> Her manners rigid and her frown austere,
> Like him, still breathing freedom's genuine flame,
> Justice her idol, public good her aim,
> Well she supplies her want of softer art
> By all the sterling treasures of the heart,
> By energy, from independence caught,
> And the free vigour of unborrowed thought.

So wrote William Hayley in *An Essay upon Epic Poetry* (1782):[6] for him Lucan's 'faults' of taste (seen as in part the result of his living in a decadent age) were offset by his commitment to liberty and independence of mind.[7] Appeals to taste frequently occlude the ideological factors involved in the construction of an aesthetic sphere, felt to exist beyond history and its contingencies, and in the case of a poem as overtly transgressive as the *Pharsalia* it is particularly important to scrutinize supposedly 'literary' judgements to see what concealed cultural assumptions and political subtexts they may contain.

Above all we should keep in mind the implications of Fredric Jameson's famous injunction 'always historicize'; aesthetic judgements are made from within history. Part of the value of reception studies is that they may encourage us to relativize our own cultural preferences. Thus Dante would doubtless have been baffled by criticisms of Lucan's bad taste and amazed by the current neglect of the *Pharsalia*. For him Lucan was *quello grande poeta* (*Convivio* IV.28.13); so impressive was his Cato that he could become a figure for God Himself, and later in the *Divine Comedy* could be made into the guardian of Mount Purgatory, despite having been a suicide (within Christianity a mortal sin) and an opponent of Julius Caesar whom Dante supported, since he regarded him as the first Roman emperor – Brutus and Cassius by contrast are put inside the mouths of Satan as guilty of the greatest treason against the state, together with Judas who betrayed God Himself. In *Inferno* IV Lucan is among a small group of *auctores*, canonical classical poets, whom Dante encounters in Limbo and with whom, by implication, he claims equality. Indeed, after Virgil and Ovid, Lucan is the Roman poet most powerfully evoked in Dante's Hell; Lucan's *terribilità*, in the combination of wickedness, violence, horror, black humour and ostentatious verbal paradox, constitutes a dominant strand within the *Inferno*. Dante's chamber of horrors is constructed, to a large extent, out of puns and word-plays, creating a kind of Poundian *logopoeia*[8] in a way that recalls the style of Lucan; and he appears to have grasped that parts of the *Pharsalia* can be read as a form of sardonic humour, something which, among modern critics, only W. R. Johnson and Jamie Masters have recognized. When in Canto 25 Dante describes the transformation of some Florentine thieves into serpents, he bids the classical masters of metamorphosis be silent, in a striking version of what E. R. Curtius termed the outdoing topos[9] which Lucan himself had employed: 'Let Lucan now be silent with his tales of wretched Sabellus and Nasidius, and let him wait to hear what now comes forth! Let Ovid be silent . . .' Dante here recalls the extravagant sequence in *Pharsalia* IX where Cato's army is attacked in the African desert by a host of what Graves calls 'fantastically unzoological serpents', in a bizarre series of 'etymological deaths';[10] for example Nasidius, who is bitten by a prester (whose name is connected with the Greek words for 'to swell' and 'to burn'), is burned and swollen into a featureless mass (789ff.). The dissolution of the boundaries of the human body is an extreme manifestation of the breaking of boundaries which is civil war. Dante, whose reading of the *Pharsalia* shows an exceptional awareness of the text's possible implications, reworks the material, in a *tour de force* of imitative virtuosity, to exhibit the dissolution of personality that attends the thieves' destruction of the proper boundaries which divide self and other, what is mine from what is yours.

It is striking how often, as in this instance, the poets are most responsive to those parts of the *Pharsalia* that conventional modern criticism censures for their excesses, like this episode of the snakes which Rowe's argument to book IX calls 'perhaps the most poetical part of this whole work', or the 'beautiful picture of horror' (in the words of the Preface) of the account of the necromancy performed by the witch Erictho in Book VI. With the authors – as with anyone – we love we cannot separate 'faults' from 'virtues'; similarly

Dickens without his awkwardnesses, his sentimentality, his excesses, would simply not be Dickens. Lucan's snakes also caught the imagination of Milton (for the metamorphosis of Satan and the fallen angels in Book X of *Paradise Lost*) and of Shelley. Partly no doubt out of admiration for Lucan's Republicanism Shelley described the *Pharsalia* as 'a poem as it appears to me of wonderful genius, and transcending Virgil', and in *Adonais* Lucan, 'by his death approved', is one of the writers untimely dead who mourn for the loss of the youthful Keats.[11] In *Prometheus Unbound* a powerful image is made from a fusion of a particularly resonant and famous passage from *Hamlet*:

> O that this too too solid flesh would melt,
> Thaw, and resolve itself into a dew . . .

with the memory of Lucan's Sabellus (IX.762ff.), whose bodily dissolution follows from the bite of a seps:

> all my being,
> Like him whom the Numidian seps did thaw
> Into a dew with poison, is dissolved (III.i.39–41).

This particular conjuncture in the mind of a great poet suggests that Lucan's lines – which Macaulay found 'as detestable as Cibber's Birthday Odes'[12] – may have their own peculiar power.

The seventeenth century was much more sympathetic than later periods to the sort of hyperbolic rhetoric and extreme verbal ingenuity that we find in Lucan. Moreover the civil war unsurprisingly encouraged an interest in the *Pharsalia*. Marvell's 'Horatian Ode' artfully juxtaposes evocations of Horace and Lucan to create a richly nuanced reading of a key moment in English history. Two quite different configurations of the Roman revolution – one Horatian and Augustan, the other Lucanic and Republican – are recalled, both relevant to, but neither quite exactly fitting, contemporary occurrences. Abraham Cowley tried to revise Lucanic epic in the royalist interest, but had to give up his poem when history failed to deliver the expected victory. Cowley's *The Civil War* is hardly a great or fully achieved poem, but certain passages would give a Latinless reader quite a good idea of Lucan's style, for example the grisly effects of disease on Essex's army (II.159ff.) or the battle on the Thames near Brentforth with its fire and water conceits (I.325ff.):

Witness those men blown high into the air –
All elements their ruin joyed to share:
In the wide air quick flames their bodies tore,
Then, drowned in waves, they're tossed by waves to shore.

However, stronger evidence of Lucan's power is furnished by the greatest poet of the century turning to him for his greatest poem. Milton's Satan is inspired in part by Lucan's Caesar, together with various Elizabethan villains and overreachers of similar derivation, including Marlowe's Tamburlaine, while Addison observed one important technical similarity between *Paradise Lost* and the *Pharsalia* in the unAristotelian construction of a personal epic voice which constantly intervenes in the narrative. Like Lucan – and for analogous reasons – Milton on occasion, in connection with Satan, builds up massive narrative structures only to displace or defer the expected climax. At the end of Book IV Satan and Gabriel loom ever larger in their extended confrontation, preparing for a duel that never eventuates. As Dr Johnson, objecting to 'the conduct of the narrative', put it, 'Satan is with great expectation brought before Gabriel in Paradise, and is suffered to go away unmolested'. The Satanic narrative – an orthodox epic action sequence – comes into conflict with a quite different set of values. Similarly Lucan, describing a world turned upside down, punctures the teleological structures of orthodox epic and the expectations that go with them. For example the long Erictho episode in Book VI builds towards a climactic revelation that is never delivered: the ghost simply refers Sextus Pompey to a future disclosure by his own father, 'a surer prophet' (VI.812).

De Quincey found in Lucan 'an exhibition of a moral sublime',[13] which may help to explain how his work can be appropriated within a certain kind of Christian mentality. Thomas Browne ends *Urn Burial* with a powerful meditation on death and decay, capping it with a quotation from Book VII of the *Pharsalia*:

'Tis all one to lie in St Innocent's churchyard as in the sands of Egypt, ready to be anything, in the ecstasy of being ever, and as content with six foot as the moles of Adrianus.

—tabesne cadavera solvat
An rogus haud refert. Lucan.

Here, as in Browne's earlier evocation of 'that duration which maketh pyramids pillars of snow', the conjunction of the massive and the exiguous has a hint of that stylistic extremism which is a mark of Lucan's own writing, while the words cited come from one of the finest passages in the *Pharsalia* and one which exhibits this Lucanic sublime, as Lucan responds to Caesar's failure to allow the dead Pompeians burial after the battle of Pharsalus (VII.809–19):

> nil agis hac ira: tabesne cadavera solvat
> an rogus haud refert; placido natura receptat
> cuncta sinu, finemque sui sibi corpora debent.
> hos, Caesar, populos si nunc non usserit ignis,
> uret cum terris, uret cum gurgite ponti.
> communis mundo superest rogus ossibus astra
> mixturus. quocumque tuam Fortuna vocabit,
> hae quoque sunt animae: non altius ibis in auras,
> non meliore loco Stygia sub nocte iacebis.
> libera fortunae mors est; capit omnia tellus
> quae genuit – caelo tegitur qui non habet urnam.

(You achieve nothing by this anger – it does not matter whether decay or the pyre dissolve the corpses; nature finds room for all in her gentle arms, and the bodies owe their end to themselves. If fire does not burn these multitudes now, it will burn them later with the earth, with the surge of the sea. There remains a shared funeral pyre for the world that will mix the stars with the bones. Wherever fortune calls your spirit, Caesar, there the spirits of these men are also. You will not go higher in the air than they, you will not lie in a better place beneath Stygian darkness. Death is free from fortune; earth holds all she has created – he who lacks an urn is covered by the sky.)

Here philosophical themes achieve a terrifying yet exhilarating poetic intensity; the allusion to the Stoic doctrine of the periodic destruction of the universe by fire (*ekpyrosis*) produces an extreme but exact image in the intermixture of bones and stars.[14] The direct address to Caesar (apostrophe is perhaps Lucan's favourite trope) heightens the effect: distinctions of time and place dissolve, as the world becomes a theatre for Lucan and his characters to play and die in. The passage combines a certain plainness, even prosiness, of diction[15] with various rhetorical features of the grand style (iteration, the final stabbing *sententia* and so forth) to produce a kind of maimed sublimity that might plausibly be seen as religious or prophetic. Among ancient writers perhaps only Lucretius and Juvenal (together with Seneca at a lower level of poetic achievement) offer anything analogous. To adapt Samuel Johnson's judgement of Pope, if this is not poetry, where is poetry to be found?

As we have already seen, not all Lucan's admirers have held to a version of Republican politics. Dante, for example, was a committed imperialist who favoured a universal monarchy in which the emperor in possessing all would be free from all appetite and, therefore, just (he sets out these arguments at length in his *De Monarchia*). Nevertheless many have been attracted above all by Lucan's espousal of 'liberty' and hatred for autocracy. The Dutch scholar Hugo Grotius, whose notes on the *Pharsalia* Rowe consulted, called Lucan *poeta phileleutheros*, the freedom-loving poet, while Louis XIV excluded the poem from the classical texts to be edited *ad usum Delphini*, for the use of the heir to the throne. In particular during the seventeenth, eighteenth and early nineteenth centuries Lucanian aristocratic *libertas* proved easily recuperable for modern Liberty and Republicanism, at the hands of whole cohorts of Whigs, radicals, revolutionaries and Romantics. Thus according to Welwood 'it was the darling passion he had for the liberty and constitution of his country' that inclined Rowe to think of translating Lucan in the first place. Among many tributes one may cite these eloquent words of the nineteenth-century man of letters Pietro Giordani, friend of Leopardi:

> So it seemed to me really sacred, and to be preferred to any other, this poem which took as its matter not the foundation or the conquest of a kingdom, not some curious or rare navigation, not the gods of a people or an age, but the funeral of Liberty, universally and eternally divine, which even if it could be driven into exile from the world, could not lose its right to reign there.[16]

It is symbolically appropriate that a line from the poem, *ignorantque datos, ne quisniam serviat, enses* (IV.579; 'men are ignorant that the purpose of the sword is to save every man from slavery'), was inscribed on the sabres of the national guard of the First Republic in France after the Revolution.

This sense of the *Pharsalia* as the poem of freedom (that most emotive, and contested, of political signifiers) was strengthened by certain events in Lucan's 'life', or what we might call 'the Lucan myth'. The precociously talented poet becomes the 'standard-bearer' of a conspiracy against Nero and dies by his own hand, the youthful victim of tyranny, declaiming, as a last act of defiance and assertion of liberty, lines from the *Pharsalia*, the poem that

the jealous emperor had forbidden him to recite. Readers less
entranced by the poem often dwell on less reputable elements in
the story: Lucan's earlier successes as a courtier, his anger at
Nero's snub in walking out of a recitation and his supposed
attempt to escape the emperor's wrath by implicating his own
mother Acilia. Indeed the idea has been widespread among modern
scholars that the *Pharsalia*, if properly understood, and at least as
originally conceived, is in no sense a poem of political protest or
opposition and contains no serious criticism of the Principate as
such, even if the later books are coloured by Lucan's personal
resentment of Nero (it is sometimes even argued that Lucan
intended to finish his epic with praise of the imperial peace and of
the Principate as a restored Republic).[17] The Republican outbursts
are dismissed as mere rhetorical flourishes. Such attempts to mini-
mize the political radicalism of the *Pharsalia* are at odds with the
dominant strand within the poem's reception that I have been
describing; and we should certainly be alert to the often concealed
ideological presuppositions of these less favourable accounts,
something in turn bound up, as we have seen, with the question
of the relative standing of Virgil and Lucan.

Perhaps the most sophisticated attempt to read the *Pharsalia*
against the Republican grain comes from Jamie Masters, who
argues that it is not a committed poem, but rather a parody of
such a poem, 'a *reductio ad absurdum* of politically committed
writing': 'Its message, if it has one at all, may be irresponsible and
opportunistic (everything is fair game for the satirist) or nihilistic
(all existing systems are ripe for deconstruction in this senseless
world). Ultimately what we will "learn" from Lucan's propagan-
distic excesses is that truth is a matter of interpretation; history
means what you want it to mean.'[18] It is certainly useful to be
reminded that, when we contemplate Lucan's transgressive poetics
and politics, it may not be as easy as we might think to determine
which drives the other. And undoubtedly it is important to be alert
to the *aesthetic* impact of the poem, what Masters calls its
'uncanny and perverse brilliance'; the *Pharsalia* is not to be valued
simply because we share, or think we share, aspects of its political
vision. Masters seeks to ground his reading in the poem's original
context and in Lucan's intentions (both matters pretty speculative).
But what seems most obvious about his account is how redolent it
is of a certain phase of post-modernism, what we might call the
'post-political'. To the victims of tyrannies ancient or modern it

might not seem so deep a truth that history means what you want it to mean. Hazlitt characterizes the poetic imagination in general (and, we might add, aesthetic judgement and critical interpretation) as 'right-royal' so that it 'naturally falls in with the language of power';[19] its Republicanism – if we are not too swift to deconstruct it[20] – may be precisely what makes the *Pharsalia* both so unusual among epic poems and so precious, even if it means that the writing can appear partly to run against the grain of poetry. In what is one of the most terrifying portrayals in all literature of the totalitarian project (to use a rather different appropriation) Lucan's Caesar – the very type of the absolutist charismatic leader – swallows up the world, obliterating all distinction between state and individual, as one who 're-deploys around his name all meanings, fixes a new centre from which all discourse is oriented and enforces *his* signs absolutely':[21] as Lucan more succinctly puts it, *omnia Caesar erat* (III.108). Even the divide between god and man is dissolved in the figure of the universal ruler. Masters argues that Republican readings of the poem are 'misreadings', but Harold Bloom, from whom he borrows the idea, thought that *all* readings were misreadings, some weak but others (the minority and mostly achieved by successor poets) strong. To say, as Masters does, that 'the response of the "intelligent reader" to Lucan's political tub-thumping is to be amused by it'[22] is ultimately (in comparison with other responses we have examined) to trivialize the poem, to assert a 'weak' misreading.

The *Pharsalia* may not at the moment be a major influence on European literature, except through its presence in other texts. However – partly as a result of the questioning of institutional traditions in the 1960s and thereafter – its reputation within the classical profession is rising; and some of the ablest Latinists – Denis Feeney, John Henderson, Philip Hardie, W. R. Johnson, Jamie Masters among others – are again treating Lucan with the kind of respect that is shown to Virgil. Scholars such as these encourage us to read the poem as transgressive and as enacting a kind of deconstruction of epic forms and styles. Civil war involves not only the dissolution of boundaries but also the generation of mutilated forms (the poem abounds with shattered corpses that often evoke the gladiatorial arena).[23] Lucan frequently substitutes for the solemnities of earlier epic an absurdist mode which Johnson calls the 'comic-ugly'.[24] Nonetheless the *Pharsalia* as an epic of the losers is necessarily bound in to traditional epic even while it denounces or undoes it (is this always the way with any form of deconstructionism?).[25] In civil war, moreover, power is obviously contested, and this produces a fragmented narrative, at war with itself (in this sense one could argue that the measured rhetoric of Rowe's version is at times too orderly); in Masters' words 'It is . . . mimicry of civil war, of divided unity, *concordia discors*, that has produced this split in the authorial, dominating, legitimizing persona, this one poet many poets, this schizophrenia, the fractured voice.'[26] The *Pharsalia*'s resistance to Virgilian teleology (a teleology that entails the vindication of an end-directed history spoken in advance by fate and engineered by Jupiter, in which victory belongs with 'the right side') involves deferral, obstruction, delay, implosion; and in the end the poem peters out, unfinished, *mediis in rebus*, without satisfying closure – this non-ending, presumably the result of Lucan's enforced suicide,[27] has a sinister appropriateness, for the poet can offer us no satisfactory conclusions (except perhaps death, or the destruction of the cosmos) but only the unending gladiatorial contest between Liberty and Caesar: *par quod semper habemus/Libertas et Caesar* (VII.695-6).

In the *Pharsalia* one finds a contrast, at times extreme, between an excessive wordiness, a very torrent of words, and a refusal to narrate, an inclination to narrative pause, as when the poet declines to describe the deaths of individuals at the battle of Pharsalus (VII.552-6). To relate the story of civil war is in a sense to re-enact, repeat, and thus be implicated in Caesar's unspeakable crime: hence the poet both wishes and does not wish to tell the story. And indeed Lucan's work is in certain significant respects Caesarean, vast, excessive, wild. Hence the poet, like Pompey a reluctant actor, must seek delay. The tension is, in a sense, terminal. As Rome and the universe self-implode, so the text collapses in on itself, as its massive structures are massively blocked. Lucan's tendency to build large static structures is well illustrated by the poem's opening. The *Aeneid* begins with a seven-line *propositio* (statement of theme), followed by an invocation of the Muse: the *narratio*, the narrative proper, begins in line 34 with an imperfect tense ('hardly out of sight of Sicilian land were they spreading their sails seaward'). By contrast in Lucan we have a deferral of the narrative until line 183, by which time Caesar has already acted, thereby thwarting the poet's delaying tactics: 'Caesar had already crossed/overcome the frozen Alps in his rapid course' and begun civil war. Moreover there is a strong narrative content to Virgil's *propositio* as it charts a movement from Troy to Rome and from past to present, in which there is a clear sequence of cause and effect, a history of coherent advance, that links origins and beginnings to ends, to validate the present order of things. Is coherent narrative necessarily teleological, even when it seeks to contest official histories? Are fractured narratives parasitic upon more conventional narratives? Lucan struggles with such paradoxes in his *propositio* which attempts to replace narrative with something more like stasis:

> bella per Emathios plus quam civilia campos,
> iusque datum sceleri canimus, populumque potentem
> in sua victrici conversum viscera dextra,
> cognatasque acies, et rupto foedere regni
> certatum totis concussi viribus orbis
> in commune nefas, infestisque obvia signis
> signa, pares aquilas et pila minantia pilis.

(Wars more than civil over Thessalian plains and legitimacy conferred on crime I sing, and a powerful people turning on its own vitals with victorious right hand, and kindred battlelines, and, the compact of government broken, a struggle with all the strength of a shattered world to achieve a communal crime, and standards opposed to hostile standards, matched eagles and javelins threatening javelins.)

As in Virgil we have a seven-line opening period, composed with immense care, with cunningly varied pauses and clause lengths. Marcus Fronto, a critic of the second century AD and an enemy of the baroque style of Neronian literature, is highly critical, accusing Lucan of saying the same thing many times over: 'Annaeus, will there never be an end?'[28] A formalist defence is possible: what we have is a set of variations on a theme, to achieve emphasis (such themes and variations are commonly found in Roman poetry). Moreover if we look at the clauses what we find is not merely inert repetition but an anticipation of different themes. *Emathios* hints at the tyrannical overreacher Alexander the Great, precursor of the Caesars; *plus quam civilia* introduces the idea of excess; *ius datum sceleri* points to the contestation over words and meanings characteristic of struggles for power; the third colon characterizes civil war as an act of communal suicide, enlisting the authority of the imperial poem itself (*Aeneid* VI.833, *neu patriae validas in viscera vertite vires*); *cognatas* reminds us that the contestants were related by blood and kinship; the fifth colon relates microcosm and mac-

rocosm, *urbs* and *orbs*, while *rupto foedere* relates the implosion of
Rome to the self-destruction of the universe, an analogy that later
becomes an identity; the final phrases introduce personified weapons that achieve a sinister identity (*pares* points to the gladiatorial
arena) and usurp the space of human beings; and so we might go
on. Nonetheless Fronto has focused on a crucial point about the
poem – Lucan says 'civil war I sing' and then he says it again and
again and again. In this way narrative momentum is refused,[29] the
unspeakable (*nefas*) remains partly unspoken – but of course there
is still an implied narrative. Caesarism may be for Lucan a form of
chaos not a form of order, a hellish spiralling down an abyss of
non-meaning; but there is still no escape from history for the strong
poet of civil war. Lucan, as I have already suggested, could be seen
as writing against the grain of language itself. It is an heroic
endeavour, an exercise in deconstructing the self-validating nature
of historical narrative, but one that, like any such act of deconstruction, may be doomed to failure. And that returns us once more to
the very core of the Lucan myth: the myth of the glamorous young
poet who falls victim to worldly realities but whose fractured and
fragmented song remains to inspire opponents of that world with
impossible hopes and dreams.

CAM

Nicholas Rowe's Translation of the Pharsalia and its Predecessors

Despite Lucan's prominence in the Middle Ages and the Renaissance, no full translation of his only surviving work was available
until the seventeenth century. Both Barnabe Googe (1540–94) and
George Turberville (1540–1610) considered translating the *Pharsalia*, the latter claiming to have given up the task so that it might
be carried out by a worthier poet, Thomas Sackville, Lord Buck-
hurst. However, this recommendation was not acted upon and the
first published translation from his work did not appear until 1600.
This was Christopher Marlowe's blank-verse, line-for-line, rendition of the first book of the *Pharsalia*. It is hardly surprising that
Lucan's portrait of Julius Caesar as an impious and overreaching
tyrant should have appealed to the creator of Guise, Dr Faustus
and most particularly Tamburlaine, who is himself aware of the
resemblance, proclaiming that:

> My camp is like to Julius Caesar's host,
> Nor ever fought but had the victory;
> Nor in Pharsalia was there such hot war ...
> (1 *Tamburlaine* III.iii.152–4)

The apocalyptic violence of Lucan found an answering voice in Marlowe; his spare, metaphrastic translation of the comparison between Caesar and lightning is a representative passage:

> So thunder which the wind tears from the clouds,
> With crack of riven air and hideous sound
> Filling the world, leaps out and throws forth fire,
> Affrights poor fearful men, and blasts their eyes
> With overthwarting flames, and raging shoots
> Alongst the air, and, nought resisting it,
> Falls, and returns, and shivers where it lights.
> (152–8)

The way the marked caesuras fall in different places within each line gives the translation a taut energy akin to the vigour of Lucan's own verse. It is to be regretted that Marlowe, who had such a clear affinity with Lucan, pursued his project no further, leaving the task of producing the first complete English translation of the *Pharsalia* to Sir Arthur Gorges. This was published in 1614. Its clumsy eight-syllable rhyming couplets are quite incapable of conveying the power of Lucan's poem, and at times irresistibly recall the mechanicals' burlesque performance in *A Midsummer Night's Dream*. Gorges' weaknesses may be seen in the following passage, describing the reunion between Cornelia and the defeated Pompey. Tired cliché and redundant padding mar what ought to be a moving scene:

> Wherewith this poor astonished wight
> Was overcome with death's dark night,
> That from her eyes deprived the light.
> Faint sorrow did her sprites invest,
> Down right she sinks, life leaves her breast.
> Her limbs were stark, her heart grew cold,
> A deadly trance her hope doth hold.[30]

Although, as we have already seen, not all modern critics are convinced that the poem should be read as a Republican manifesto, the *Pharsalia* has often been associated with a strong distaste for tyranny. This connection is particularly apparent in the next full-length translation, that of Thomas May, completed in 1627. May was to become a partisan of the Parliamentary cause and worked on behalf of Cromwell's regime as Secretary of Parliament until his death in 1650. The significance of his decision to translate Lucan's poem of civil war was noted by John Aubrey, who wrote that his 'translation of Lucan's excellent poem made him in love with the republic, which tang stuck by him.'[31] Others, however, attributed his conversion to pique at missing the laureateship. May went on to compose a continuation of the *Pharsalia*, taking the story up to the death of Caesar. This was published in 1631 and reflects a temporary shift in the poet's political allegiances; it is dedicated to Charles I, and expresses considerably less approval of Republicanism.[32] May's translation of the *Pharsalia* was far more competent than Gorges' and went into several editions.[33] However, his verse is often clumsy, as can be seen in his translation of the simile comparing Caesar to lightning which is less successful than Marlowe's earlier version. The apparently endless succession of clauses too often eludes the reader's attempt to perceive the shape of the whole sentence, a problem which is compounded by the sometimes awkward rhythms of the verse:

> As lightning by the wind forced from a cloud
> Breaks through the wounded air with thunder loud,
> Disturbs the day, the people terrifies,
> And by a light oblique dazzles our eyes,
> Not Jove's own temple spares it; when no force,
> No bar can hinder his prevailing course,
> Great waste, as forth it sallies and retires,
> It makes, and gathers his dispersed fires.

Lucan's popularity, particularly within a political context, continued into the eighteenth century and his influence can be perceived in the Whig literature of the day, with the character of Cato providing the strongest focus for Whiggish enthusiasm. One celebrated episode, Cato's attack on superstition in Book IX, was translated by Robert Wolseley, John Dennis, George Jeffreys and George Lord Lyttleton as well as Rowe himself. And of course one of the most famous Whig authors, Joseph Addison, took the character of Cato as the subject of his best-known tragedy. Attempting the first new translation of the *Pharsalia* for nearly a century was an appropriate enterprise for an ardent Whig poet such as Rowe.

Nicholas Rowe was born in Bedfordshire in 1674. He was educated at Westminster School and entered the Middle Temple in 1691. His entry into the Whig literary circle was established when his tragedy *Tamerlane* was first produced in 1701. This was a political allegory, designed to praise the virtuous rule of William of England and attack the despotism of Louis XIV. Readers familiar with Marlowe's *Tamburlaine* may be surprised to learn that Tamerlane himself is the counterpart to good King William, Louis being represented by the Turkish emperor, Bajazeth. Marlowe's Caesarian conqueror has been transformed into a mild, equitable and quite unmemorable character. But certain aspects of Rowe's *Tamerlane* may be traced back to the *Pharsalia*. Bajazeth is an unmistakably Lucanian overreacher. He is described as 'that comet, which on high, / Portended ruin',[34] and he proclaims his ambition in a manner worthy of Caesar:

> Can a king want a cause when empire bids
> Go on? what is he born for but ambition?
> It is his hunger, 'tis his call of nature,
> The noble appetite which will be satisfied . . .[35]

Tamerlane was traditionally performed on the anniversary of King William's landing, 5 November. Although Johnson claimed that *Tamerlane* was the tragedy Rowe valued most, he is perhaps best known today for *The Fair Penitent* and *Jane Shore*. The plot of *The Fair Penitent* (1703) is based on Massinger's tragedy *The Fatal Dowry*, and it was an important influence on Richardson's *Clarissa*, with its dashing villain providing the model for the attractive but dastardly Lovelace, as well as making his name – Lothario – a generic term for rakes. Sentiment and melodrama are leavened with a 'Gothic' extravagance that looks forward to Rowe's evident relish for Lucan's Erictho. The fifth act opens with the heroine, Calista, sharing a cell with the corpse of Lothario while she sings a song summoning midnight phantoms from the tomb to hasten her own death. Despite this penchant for horror Rowe was particularly celebrated for his evocations of connubial happiness in plays which became known as 'She Tragedies' because of their focus on unfortunate and pathetic females such as Lady Jane Grey. His best-known work in this mode is *Jane Shore* (1714), which was written in conscious imitation of Shakespeare's history plays and takes for its subject the sufferings of Edward IV's repentant mistress after the king's death.

The character of Rowe's drama is suggested by the testimony of his contemporaries. James Hurdis refers to him as 'charming Rowe / Politest grace of the dramatic age',[36] and in his poem 'Upon the Death of Mr Addison' Nicholas Amhurst alludes to the recent demise of 'soft-complaining Rowe'.[37] A more weighty tribute is paid by Pope in his 'Epitaph on Mr Rowe':

> Thy relics, Rowe, to this sad shrine we trust,
> And near thy Shakespeare place thy honoured bust.
> Oh next him skilled to draw the tender tear,
> For never heart felt passion more sincere;
> To nobler sentiment to fire the brave,
> For never Briton more disdained a slave!
> Peace to thy gentle shade, and endless rest . . .
>
> (1–7)

Although less rhapsodic, Dr Johnson's summing up of Rowe's career as a playwright is judiciously approving:

> Whence then has Rowe his reputation? From the reasonableness and propriety of some of his scenes, from the elegance of his diction, and the suavity of his verse. He seldom moves either pity or terror, but he often elevates the sentiments; he seldom pierces the breast, but he always delights the ear, and often improves the understanding.[38]

Contemporary accounts of Rowe emphasize his sweet and amiable nature. The following extract from a letter written by Pope to Edward Blount, for example, reveals him to have been a peculiarly delightful companion:

> I am just returned from the country whither Mr Rowe accompanied me, and passed a week in the forest. I need not tell you how much a man of his turn entertained me, but I must acquaint you there is a vivacity and gaiety of disposition almost peculiar to him, which make it impossible to part from him without that uneasiness which generally succeeds all pleasures.[39]

However, on occasion his cheerful levity seems to have been almost too much for Pope who, in response to Spence's comment that he thought Rowe 'had been too grave to write such things', replied 'He? Why he would laugh all day long! He would do nothing else but laugh!'[40] This suggestion that Rowe was easily amused seems to be confirmed by a rather disarming anecdote about the play-wright's response to his own play, *The Biter*. This was his only attempt at comedy and was universally despised, Congreve calling it a 'foolish farce'; 'but it pleased the author, who sat through the first and only representation, "laughing with great vehemence" at his own wit.'[41]

Rowe was appointed under-secretary to the Duke of Queensbury and Dover in 1709, and his edition of Shakespeare, dedicated to the Duke of Somerset, was published on 2 June of the same year. This was a pioneering work and represented the first attempt to divide scenes systematically as well as provide scene locations and lists of *dramatis personae*. He was also the first to write a life of Shakespeare and the material he collected long remained part of a biographical tradition. On 12 August 1715 he became Poet Laureate.

Rowe's contemporaries were swift to connect his decision to translate the *Pharsalia* with his political leanings. His biographer James Welwood commented: 'He had entertained an early incli-nation for that author, and I believe it was the darling passion he had for the liberty and constitution of his country that first inclined him to think of translating him.' Rowe's first essay in translating Lucan was a short passage, II.232–325, the conversation between Brutus and Cato about civil war, which appeared in Tonson's *Poetical Miscellanies, the Fifth Part* in 1704. This choice is signifi-cant. Although Cato roundly condemns the unnatural evil of civil war, he asserts that it is impossible to remain aloof from the struggle, allowing Roman liberty to be destroyed. The political motivation behind this choice of passage seems to have been noted by Tory satirist William Shippen, for his pamphlet *Faction Dis-played* (1704) alludes to Lucan's Brutus in association with 'Whig-writers', although the jibe at Rowe is a veiled one. By choosing this particular extract from the *Pharsalia*, Rowe was providing a tacit contribution to the current political debate at a time of Whiggish anxiety about the future of the country under a Tory Parliament and a Queen who was the daughter of James II. Rowe may have been encouraged in his translation project by the Whig Lord Halifax, who was to lend him support in his career and to whom he dedicated *The Royal Convert* in 1707.

Rowe went on to publish further excerpts, VI.1–262, which includes the account of Scaeva's valiant exploits, and the whole of Book IX. Both of these translations appeared in the Sixth Part of

Tonson's *Poetical Miscellanies* in 1709. Rowe's decision to publish Book IX in full is probably explained by its focus on Cato, the defender of the Republic. A particular attraction of Book IX was the fact that it contained Cato's famous reply to Labienus' suggestion that he should consult the temple of Jupiter Ammon. Cato's condemnation of superstition chimed with protestant distaste for 'popish' practices. Rowe makes his own prejudices very apparent in his forthright note to this passage: 'But, thank God, the foppery of pilgrimages is out of fashion in England, or at least those who are weak enough to travel from one country to another in search of holiness are wise enough not to own it amongst us.' That Rowe should have shared Lucan's admiration for Cato is not surprising. But Rowe's notes also show that he was troubled by Lucan's apparent prejudice against Julius Caesar. It may appear curious that Rowe should wish to excuse a figure who was associated with tyranny and whose assassination seems eloquent of the Republican idealism which Rowe shared. Works such as Addison's *Cato* confirm that Caesar would have been held in opprobrium by Whigs, yet even here the tyrant's *clementia* is singled out as his one redeeming quality: 'His enemies confess / The virtues of humanity are Caesar's' (4.4.33–4). Rowe's own insistence on this one virtue – in contradiction of Lucan's apparent total condemnation – seems to be a sign of his wish for fair play and historical accuracy rather than a symptom of sympathy with Caesar's politics. As with his choice of the disputation from Book II, the significance of Rowe's selection of Book IX was not lost on his first readers. The wit and man-about-town Henry Cromwell wrote of his translation to Pope: 'He is so errant a Whig, that he strains even beyond his author, in passion for liberty, and aversion to tyranny; and errs only in amplification.'[42]

It seems that Tonson had projected a complete translation of Lucan by several hands, but this plan never came to fruition, and Rowe's translation appeared posthumously in 1719,[43] following his death the preceding year. His widow Anne dedicated the work to King George I, apparently in fulfilment of Rowe's own wishes, and James Welwood contributed a preface to the edition, included in this volume. In his 1950 dissertation on Rowe's Lucan, Alfred Hesse puts forward a convincing case for ascribing much of Welwood's preface to the hand of Rowe himself. As well as a striking correspondence in thought and expression between Rowe's notes and the preface, there is an additional stylistic affinity which gives weight to Hesse's claim that Rowe had prepared a life of Lucan before his death which was later incorporated into Welwood's preface.

Rowe clearly prepared his edition with care; although his notes reveal considerable reliance on the annotations of his forebears, he was not entirely dependent on earlier editions of the poem for his information. He was familiar with such works of contemporary scholarship as Dr Basil Kennett's *Antiquities of Rome* (1696), as well as a great many classical writers, including Herodotus and Plutarch, whose works were contained in his personal library. The principal Latin edition of the *Pharsalia* consulted by Rowe appears to be the variorum edition of 1669, edited by Cornelius Schrevelio and published in Leiden, which included the notes of the Dutch statesman Hugo Grotius – whose taste for Lucan was avowedly connected with his own hatred of tyrants – as well as the later notes of the English scholar Thomas Farnaby. Rowe also used the notes which accompanied Thomas May's own earlier translation.[44]

The translation was widely admired at the time of its publication. Although he had reservations about the extent of Rowe's amplification of the original, Pope expressed 'a very good opinion of Mr Rowe's ninth book of Lucan'.[45] Addison also praised the translation[46] and John Dennis even exalted it at the expense of Pope's Homer, although the force of his encomium is compromised by the enmity between Dennis and Pope.[47] But by far the most significant comment on the translation is the generous tribute paid by Dr Johnson in his life of Rowe:

> The version of Lucan is one of the greatest productions of English poetry, for there is perhaps none that so completely exhibits the genius and spirit of the original. Lucan is distinguished by a kind of dictatorial or philosophical dignity, rather, as Quintilian observes, declamatory than poetical; full of ambitious morality and pointed sentences, comprised in vigorous and animated lines. This character Rowe has very diligently and successfully preserved. His versification, which is such as his contemporaries practised, without any attempt at innovation or improvement, seldom wants either melody or force. His author's sense is sometimes a little diluted by additional infusions, and sometimes weakened by too much expansion; but such faults are to be expected in all translations, from the constraint of measures and dissimilitude of languages.[48]

It is not difficult to identify the most important poetic influences on Rowe. *Paradise Lost* was still the supreme model for epic writing in English and there are a number of Miltonic phrases in the *Pharsalia*. For example in Book IV, during the description of a sea battle, Lucan describes how Vulteius encouraged his men to kill one another rather than suffer defeat. Rowe refers to the death blows the men give their comrades as 'this last best gift', a presumably ironic echo of Milton's description of Eve (*Paradise Lost* V.90). But the more obvious models for Rowe were Dryden's Virgil (1697) and Pope's Homer, the first volumes of which had already appeared by 1717. Like these the *Pharsalia* is written in rhyming couplets, varied by the use of Alexandrines and triplets. A great many stylistic correspondences may be found between all three poets, at the level of diction, phrasing and rhetorical structure. Considering their shared epic subject matter, it would be surprising if there were not a high degree of similarity between these works. All three poets, for example, refer to the sea as 'liquid plain', 'purple flood' and 'crystal flood', the first of which phrases is also Miltonic. Although Dryden may be the most important source for such locutions, their absorption into the well-developed neoclassical idiom makes it perhaps inappropriate to talk in terms so specific as influence and imitation, although Rowe must of course have been aware of the relationship between his *Pharsalia* and the *Aeneis*.

Rowe is noticeably more expansive than either Pope or Dryden, sometimes amplifying passages to include information provided in a note in the edition he consulted. Pope cites his translation of IX.808–10 as an example of this tendency. As the literal Loeb translation demonstrates, the significance of these lines is somewhat obscure:

> And as Corycian saffron, when turned on, is wont to spout from every part of a statue at once, so all his limbs discharged red poison together instead of blood.

The historical information provided by the note to the 1669 variorum edition is incorporated into Rowe's translation:

> And as when mighty Rome's spectators meet
> In the full theatre's capacious seat,
> At once, by secret pipes and channels fed,
> Rich tinctures gush from every antique head,
> At once ten thousand saffron currents flow,

And rain their odours on the crowd below;
So the warm blood at once from every part
Ran purple poison down, and drained the fainting heart.

A further example of Rowe's expansive tendencies can be found in his translation of Book I, during an account of the beliefs of the Druids.

> longae, canitis si cognita, vitae
> Mors media est
>
> (I.457–8)

Thus life for ever runs its endless race,
And like a line death but divides the space,
A stop which can but for a moment last,
A point between the future and the past.

(I.802–5)

Here there is no real addition to Lucan's original meaning; the second couplet clarifies and amplifies rather than modifies the point made in the first couplet. Rowe's translation seems a more judicious solution than May's attempt at metaphrase, 'The midst 'twixt long lives (if you truth maintain) / Is death'.

If there is a Lucanian mode to which Rowe does not do full justice, it is perhaps his characteristic fondness for the pithy, contorted paradox. To some extent this is a problem faced by any English translator of a language which is capable of so much greater compression. To take a well-known example, 'Victorious Caesar by the gods was crowned, / The vanquished party was by Cato owned' translates one of Lucan's most famous lines – *victrix causa deis placuit, sed victa Catoni* (I.128) – which may be seen as the ultimate expression of Lucan's lack of faith in the gods as arbiters of mankind's destiny. At this point Gorges' translation is simply incoherent, 'The conquering part the gods avowes, / Cato the vanquished allowes'. May is rather more successful in his attempt to match Lucan's pithiness: 'Heaven approves / The conquering cause; the conquered Cato loves'. The expansion of one line into two in Rowe's version could be said to result in a diminution of force, yet within his own idiom, the rhyming couplet, Rowe has at least replicated the balance and antithesis of the original, using the rhyme to point the opposition and paradox, rather than the caesura – the terse astringency of the original is not altogether lost. Rowe's translation is less happy when he tries to copy Lucan's succinctness, as in his rendition of *etiam periere ruinae*, the hyperbolic expression of Troy's decay, as 'And ev'n the ruined ruins are decayed'. Although he attempts to go one up on Lucan, and add a further level of decline, the impact is weakened – if ruins which are already ruined can decay, the ruin is somehow less absolute and apocalyptic than it seemed to be in the original, and the passive participle 'decayed' lacks the force of Lucan's *periere*. But Rowe is also capable of effective compression, translating *omnibus incerto venturae tempore vitae* (IV.481) as 'all is but dying' (IV.812).

On occasion Rowe's amplifications appear to reflect his political views. In Book V, for example, he offers a close translation of Lucan's caustic description of Rome's capitulation to Caesar's tyranny – 'Then was the time when sycophants began / To heap all titles on one lordly man' (563–4), but then appends a couplet which is his own addition, 'Then learned our sires that fawning lying strain, / Which we their slavish sons so well retain' (565–6). And in Book IX Rowe offers an accurate translation of *et solus plebe parata / privatus servire sibi* (193–4) as 'When crowds were willing to have worn his chain, / He chose his private station to retain' (334–5), but goes on to cap it with a line whose sentiment has more to do with the second Augustan age than with the Roman Republic, 'That all might free, and equal all remain' (336). A later amplification in Book V reflects another characteristic of Rowe's, his predilection for pathos. 'Soft-complaining Rowe' may not have found much to gratify this penchant in Lucan, but the love passages between Pompey and Cornelia would certainly have struck a chord in the author of *Lady Jane Grey*. *Heu quantum mentes dominatur in aequas / Iusta Venus!* (V.727–8) is expanded to four lines by Rowe:

> Oh who can speak, what numbers can reveal,
> The tenderness which pious lovers feel?
> Who can their secret pangs and sorrows tell,
> With all the crowd of cares that in their bosoms dwell?
>
> (1043–6)

Rowe chose to improve upon those parts of his translation which had already appeared in Tonson's miscellany, and Kings MS 296, a manuscript copy of Book I, also demonstrates that Rowe was inclined to revise and refine his work. His draft of the first six lines illustrates his capacity for self-improvement tellingly enough:

> The slaughter of Emathia's purple plain,
> And fury more than civil, swell my strain.

> Of lawless wickedness, and daring might,
> Ranging at loose, and trampling o'er the right;
> A mighty people, once the earth's dread lords,
> Turned on themselves with their own conquering swords.
>
> (Kings MS 296, I.1–6)

This MS provides evidence that Rowe's editors rather than Rowe himself were responsible for the punctuation of the first edition. The manuscript is far more heavily punctuated and the spelling is more wayward than in the printed version.

The handful of alterations which he made to the Tonson excerpts are comparatively trivial, consisting of a few one-word discrepancies or the occasional reworking of a line or couplet. For example, IX.298 originally read 'Robes thrice to Capitolian Jove displayed', but appears in the 1718 text as 'Robes to Imperial Jove in triumph erst displayed'. Further evidence of Rowe's tendency towards perfectionism is provided by a long note to Book I.950, which shows his anxiety to provide an accurate translation:

> These *Feriae Latinae*, or Latin festivals, were performed by night to Jupiter at Alba. As I shall be always very ready to acknowledge any mistake, so I believe in this place I ought rather to have translated these verses thus:
>
> > The parting points with double streams ascend,
> > And Alba's Latian rites portentous end.
>
> But I was led into the error by not considering enough the true meaning of the Latin expression, *confectas Latinas*.

However, another note, to the necromancy performed by Erictho in Book VI, reveals that Rowe on occasion does not scruple to 'improve' on the sense of the original.

> In the translation of this passage I have taken the liberty to vary so far from my author's sense as to make the English quite contrary to the Latin. Lucan says, the corpse did not rise leisurely, but started up at once. I must own, I could not but think the slow heavy manner of rising by degrees, as in the translation, much more solemn and proper for the occasion. I have taken so few liberties of this kind, in comparison of what Mons. Brebeuf the French translator has done, that I hope my readers, if they don't approve of it, will however be the more inclinable to pardon what I have altered from the original here.

It has generally been assumed that the *Pharsalia* was left unfinished at Lucan's death. Rowe offers a brief continuation:

> What follows to the end of this book is a supplement of my own, in which I have only endeavoured to finish the relation of this very remarkable action, with bringing Caesar to safety to his own fleet, with the circumstances in which all authors who have writ on this subject agree.

As narrative, Rowe's conclusion is not especially successful, yet it does contain some noteworthy details, such as the epic simile which likens Caesar to a serpent, picking up on extensive serpentine imagery throughout the poem as well as the obvious plague of snakes in Book IX. Rowe appears to have been influenced by Milton's description of Satan, himself a descendant of Lucan's Caesar, in Book I, of *Paradise Lost*, where he is compared to Leviathan (I.192–224). Rowe also shows his awareness of one of the *Pharsalia*'s most striking characteristics, its lack of divine machinery. He invokes a picture of Venus begging Jupiter to have pity on 'the dear offspring of her Julian race', but scornfully refuses to indulge in such 'wanton fancy' himself. The rejected scenario most obviously recalls Venus' pleas for the safety of her son Aeneas (*Aeneid* I.223–304) and it seems that Rowe was well aware of Lucan's competitive relationship with his predecessor.

We inevitably compare Rowe's *Pharsalia* with the great translations of Pope and Dryden. Considering that these latter works are infinitely more celebrated, the consistently high quality of Rowe's verse may come as a surprise to the modern reader. Rowe is perhaps best known for *Jane Shore*, yet there the poetry, although competent, comes far below the achievement of the *Pharsalia*. At its best Rowe's translation attains a level of excellence worthy of his more famous contemporaries. The low ebb of Lucan's reputation during the last two centuries, the relative mediocrity of most of Rowe's other works, the comparative lack of interest in Augustan poetry as well as the diminished status of translation generally in the nineteenth century are all factors which have contributed to the astonishing neglect of this major work. Dr Johnson's concluding words on the *Pharsalia* are as apt now as they were two centuries ago: 'The *Pharsalia* of Rowe deserves more notice than it obtains, and as it is now more read will be more esteemed.'[49]

SAB

Notes

1. Lucan's own title was probably *Bellum Civile* or *De Bello Civili*, recalling Julius Caesar's prose account of these events to which the poem constitutes a rejoinder.
2. Other possible readings will be discussed later in this introduction. It is worth insisting, in view of what will then emerge, that there can be no summary of the poem's contents which is not also an interpretation and indeed a politicized one. Thus, while a Republican reading has been dominant, the poem can be, and has been, appropriated for other political positions. Modern scholars sometimes argue that Lucan's apparent Republicanism is merely for rhetorical effect; more subtly Jamie Masters sees the poem as divided between a Republican and a Caesarean voice.
3. *Silvae* II.7. 53, 79–80.
4. Feeney 1991, 264.
5. *Horace Walpole's Correspondence*, ed. W. S. Lewis (39 vols, London and New Haven), vol. 16 (1952), 22–3.
6. Gillespie 1988, 146–7.
7. Victorian critics and schoolmasters froze this view of Lucan as evincing the bad taste of a 'silver' age of decadence, and (in addition) as writing 'rhetoric' not 'poetry'. By the time aesthetic criteria shifted, it was too late for any popular recovery of Lucan's reputation – Latin was already in sharp decline, and poets, most influential of canon-makers, could no longer necessarily draw on a classical education.
8. 'Poetry that is akin to nothing but language, which is a dance of intelligence among words and ideas, and modification of ideas and words' (quoted in connection with Lucan by Bramble (1982), 541, from *The Little Review*, 1918).
9. *European Literature and the Latin Middle Ages*, trs. W. R. Trask (London and Henley, 1953), 162–6.
10. I owe this phrase to John Bramble.
11. For Lucan and Shelley see Dilke 1972, 104–5.
12. Duff 1928, xii.
13. Gillespie 1988, 147.
14. So Mayer 1981, 24; despite the negative slant Mayer's discussion of Lucan's style is not without insight.
15. *Cadaver*, for example, is an unpoetic word (epic poets favour *corpus*) – it appears thirty-six times in Lucan, only twice in the *Aeneid*. Similarly *mors* is preferred by Lucan to the more poetic *letum*, while *nil agis* was originally colloquial. For Lucan's diction see Bramble 1982, 541–2.

16. Quoted by J. H. Whitfield in *Classical Influences on Western Thought AD 1650 – 1870*, ed. R. R. Bolgar (Cambridge, 1979), 142.
17. For detailed arguments against such views see Martindale 1984.
18. Masters, 'Deceiving the reader: the political mission of Lucan *Bellum Civile 7*', pp. 151–77, in Masters and Elsner 1994, 168–9.
19. Quoted Quint 1993, 208.
20. Though we could say that the pathos of the *Pharsalia* is that its Republicanism is always already deconstructed – historically as well as politically and aesthetically. Moreover 'Republicanism' itself can be seen as falling in with the language of power, in the sense that the language of the Principate is an appropriation of the language of the Republic and indeed claims to be the 'same' language.
21. Henderson 1988, 134.
22. Masters 1994, 168.
23. Quint 1993, 147.
24. Johnson 1987, 56; cf. pp. xi–xii.
25. Quint 1993, 136.
26. Masters 1992, 90; cf. pp. 10, 214–15.
27. Masters, 1992, ch. 7, however, argues that the poem as it stands is complete.
28. See *The Correspondence of Marcus Cornelius Fronto* ed. C. R. Haines (Loeb Classical Library, London and New York), vol. 2, 104–7.
29. Rowe fails to achieve such a static quality; he introduces an increased element of narrative momentum by imitating the delayed main verb of the opening of *Paradise Lost*. See our note ad loc.
30. Cf. Rowe, VIII.77–82.
31. Aubrey 1950, 197.
32. May's body was exhumed from Westminster Abbey in 1661 as part of the reaction against Cromwell's regime. This event prompted the satire 'Tom May's Death', which is generally attributed to Marvell.
33. See Chester 1932, Norbrook 1994 and Smith 1994.
34. Rowe 1929, 78.
35. Rowe 1929, 82.
36. James Hurdis, *Tears of Affection* (London, 1794), 30.
37. Nicholas Amhurst, *Poems on Several Occasions* (London, 1723), 24.
38. Johnson 1932, I, 413.
39. Sherburn, 1956, 1, 329–30.
40. Joseph Spence, *Observations, Anecdotes, and Characters of Books and Men collected from Conversation* (2 vols, London, 1820), I, 109.
41. *Dictionary of National Biography*, XLIX, 342.
42. Sherburn 1956, 1, 102–3.

43. Although Rowe's translation did not appear until early in March 1719, 1718 is the date which is printed on the title page and the latter date is used to identify the first edition in this volume.

44. The sale catalogue of Rowe's library lists three additional editions of Lucan, as well as the translations into French and Spanish of Brebeuf and Oropesa (see Hesse 1950, 71).

45. Sherburn 1956, 1, 104.

46. In the *Free-holder*, 7 May 1716.

47. E. N. Hooker, ed., *The Critical Works of John Dennis* (Baltimore, 1943), II, 135.

48. Johnson 1932, I, 413.

49. Johnson 1932, I, 413.

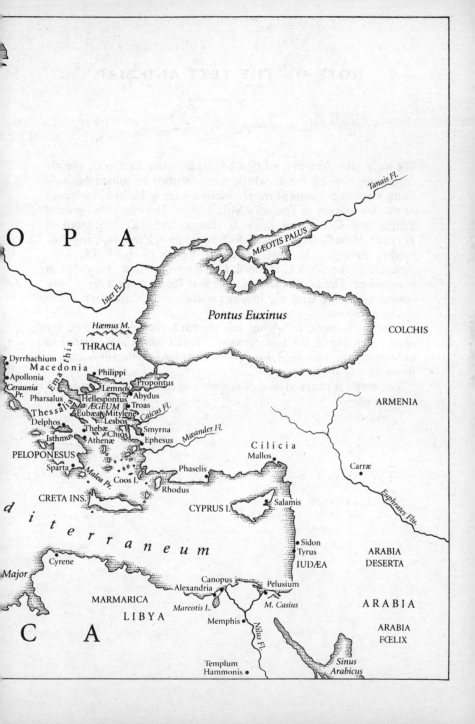

NOTE ON THE TEXT AND MAP

We have taken the first edition of 1718 as our base text, silently correcting obvious errors which were rectified in subsequent editions. Certain portions of the translation were published in advance of the first edition in Tonson's Miscellanies. The interview between Brutus and Cato from Book II (Lucan 232–325) appeared in *Poetical Miscellanies, The Fifth Part* in 1704, and in 1709 two further passages, VI.1–262 and the whole of Book IX, were included in the Sixth Part. Book I of the translation also exists in manuscript. The first edition reveals that Rowe made a few minor emendations; the more significant variant readings are discussed in the introduction.

Short references, following the Harvard system, are given for works included in the bibliography. Works which are referred to only once are identified by full bibliographical details within a footnote.

The map on pages xlvi–xlvii is a simplified version of the one in the first edition.

THE PREFACE

GIVING SOME ACCOUNT OF LUCAN*
AND HIS WORKS, AND OF MR ROWE

By James Welwood* MD, Fellow of the
Royal College of Physicians, London.

I could not resist Mr Rowe's request in his last sickness, nor the importunities of his friends since, to introduce into the world this his posthumous translation of Lucan with something by way of preface. I am very sensible how much it is out of my sphere, and that I want both leisure and materials to do justice to the author or to the memory of the translator. The works of both will best plead for them, the one having already outlived seventeen ages, and both one and t'other like to endure as long as there is any taste of liberty or polite learning left in the world. Hard has been the fate of many a great genius, that, while they have conferred immortality on others, they have wanted themselves some friend to embalm their names to posterity. This has been the fate of Lucan, and perhaps may be that of Mr Rowe.

All the accounts we have handed down to us of the first are but very lame, and scattered in fragments of ancient authors. I am of opinion that one reason why his life is not to be found at any length in the writings of his contemporaries is the fear they were in of Nero's resentment, who could not bear to have the life of a man set in a true light, whom, together with his uncle Seneca, he had sacrificed to his revenge. Notwithstanding this, we have some hints in writers who lived near his time that leave us not altogether in the dark about the life and works of this extraordinary young man.

Marcus Annaeus Lucan was of an equestrian family of Rome, born at Cordoba in Spain, about the year of our Saviour 39, in the reign of Caligula. His family had been transplanted from Italy to Spain a considerable time before, and were invested with several dignities and employments in that remote province of the Roman Empire. His father was Marcus Annaeus Mela, or Mella, a man of a distinguished merit and interest in his country, and not the less in esteem for being the brother of the great philosopher Seneca. His mother was Acilia, the daughter of Acilius Lucanus, one of the most eminent orators of his time. And it was from this grandfather that he took the name of Lucan. The story that is told of Hesiod and Homer, of a swarm of bees hovering about them in their cradle, is likewise told of Lucan, and probably with equal truth. But whether true or not, it's a proof of the high esteem paid to him by the ancients as a poet.

He was hardly eight months old when he was brought from his native country to Rome, that he might take the first impression of the Latin tongue in the city where it was spoke in the greatest purity. I wonder then to find some critics detract from his language, as if it took a tincture from the place of his birth, nor can I be brought to think otherwise than that the language he writes in is as pure Roman as any that was writ in Nero's time. As he grew up, his parents educated him with a care that became a promising genius and the rank of his family. His masters were Remmius Palaemon the grammarian, then Flavius Virgineus the rhetorician, and lastly Cornutus the Stoic philosopher, to which sect he ever after addicted himself.

It was in the course of these studies he contracted an intimate friendship with Aulus Persius the satirist. It's no wonder that two men whose geniuses were so much alike should unite and become agreeable to one another. For if we consider Lucan critically we shall find in him a strong bent towards satire. His manner, it's true, is more declamatory and diffuse than Persius', but satire is still in his view, and the whole *Pharsalia* appears to me a continued invective against ambition and unbounded power.

The progress he made in all parts of learning must needs have been very great, considering the pregnancy of his genius, and the nice care that was taken in cultivating it by a suitable education. Nor is it to be questioned but besides the masters I have named he had likewise the example and instructions of his uncle Seneca, the most conspicuous man then of Rome for learning, wit and morals. Thus he set out in the world with the greatest advantages possible, a noble birth, an opulent fortune, great relations, and withal the friendship and protection of an uncle who, besides his other preferments in the empire, was favourite, as well as tutor, to the emperor. But rhetoric seems to have been the art he excelled most in, and valued himself most upon, for all writers agree he declaimed in public when but fourteen years old, both in Greek and Latin, with universal applause. To this purpose it's observable that he has interspersed a great many orations in the

Pharsalia, and these are acknowledged by all to be very shining parts of the poem. Whence it is that Quintilian,* the best judge in these matters, reckons him among the rhetoricians rather than the poets, though he was certainly master of both these arts in a high degree.

His uncle Seneca being then in great favour with Nero and having the care of that prince's education committed to him, it's probable he introduced his nephew to the court and acquaintance of the emperor. And it appears from an old fragment of his life that he sent for him from Athens, where he was at his studies, to Rome for that purpose. Everyone knows that Nero, for the first five years of his reign, either really was, or pretended to be, endowed with all the amiable qualities that became an emperor and a philosopher. It must have been in this stage of Nero's life that Lucan has offered up to him that poetical incense we find in the first book of the *Pharsalia*. For it is not to be imagined that a man of Lucan's temper would flatter Nero in so gross a manner if he had then thrown off the mask of virtue, and appeared in such bloody colours as he afterwards did. No! Lucan's soul seems to have been cast in another mould; and he that durst, throughout the whole *Pharsalia*, espouse the party of Pompey and the cause of Rome against Caesar, could never have stooped so vilely low as to celebrate a tyrant and a monster in such an open manner. I know some commentators have judged that compliment to Nero to be meant ironically, but it seems to me plain to be in the greatest earnest. And it's more than probable that, if Nero had been as wicked at that time as he became afterwards, Lucan's life had paid for his irony. Now it's agreed on by all writers that he continued for some time in the highest favour and friendship with Nero, and it was to that favour, as well as his merit, that he owed his being made quaestor, and admitted into the College of Augurs, before he attained the age required for these offices; in the first of which posts he exhibited to the people of Rome a show of gladiators at a vast expense. It was in this sunshine of life Lucan married Polla Argentaria, the daughter of Pollius Argentarius a Roman senator, a lady of noble birth, great fortune and famed beauty, who, to add to her other excellencies, was accomplished in all parts of learning, in so much that the three first books of the *Pharsalia* are said to have been revised and corrected by her in his lifetime.

How he came to decline in Nero's favour we have no account that I know of in history, and it's agreed by all that he lost it gradually, till he became his utter aversion. No doubt Lucan's virtue, and his principles of liberty, must make him hated by a man of Nero's temper. But there appears to have been a great deal of envy in the case, blended with his other prejudices against him, upon the account of his poetry.

Though the spirit and height of the Roman poetry was somewhat declined from what it had been in the time of Augustus, yet it was still an art beloved and cultivated. Nero himself was not only fond of it to the highest degree, but, as most bad poets are, was vain and conceited of his performances in that kind. He valued himself more upon his skill in that art and in music than on the purple he wore, and bore it better to be thought a bad emperor than a bad poet or musician. Now Lucan, though then in favour, was too honest and too open to applaud the bombast stuff that Nero was every day repeating in public. Lucan appears to have been much of the temper of Philoxenus the philosopher, who, for not approving the verses of Dionysius the tyrant of Syracuse, was by his order condemned to the mines. Upon the promise of amendment the philosopher was set at liberty, but, Dionysius repeating to him some of his wretched performances, in full expectation of having them approved, 'Enough', cries out Philoxenus, 'Carry me back to the mines.' But Lucan carried this point farther, and had the imprudence to dispute the prize of eloquence with Nero in a solemn public assembly. The judges in that trial were so just and bold as to adjudge the reward to Lucan, which was fame and a wreath of laurel, but in return he lost for ever the favour of his competitor. He soon felt the effects of the emperor's resentment, for the next day he had an order sent him, never more to plead at the bar, nor repeat any of his performances in public, as all the eminent orators and poets were used to do. It's no wonder that a young man, an admirable poet, and one conscious enough of a superior genius, should be stung to the quick by this barbarous treatment. In revenge, he omitted no occasion to treat Nero's verses with the utmost contempt, and expose them and their author to ridicule.

In this behaviour towards Nero he was seconded by his friend Persius, and no doubt they diverted themselves often alone at the emperor's expense. Persius went so far that he dared to attack openly some of Nero's verses in his first satire, where he brings in his friend and himself repeating them. I believe a sample of them may not be unacceptable to the reader, as translated thus by Mr Dryden:

FRIEND

But to raw numbers and unfinished verse,
Sweet sound is added now, to make it terse.
'Tis tagged with rhyme like Berecynthian Atys,
The mid part chimes with art that never flat is.
'The dolphin brave,
That cut the liquid wave,
Or he who in his line,
Can chime the long-ribbed Appenine.'

PERSIUS:

All this is doggerel stuff.

FRIEND:

       What if I bring
A nobler verse? 'Arms and the man I sing.'

PERSIUS:

Why name you Virgil with such fops as these?
He's truly great, and must for ever please.
Not fierce, but awful in his manly page,
Bold in his strength, but sober in his rage.

FRIEND:

What poems think you soft? and to be read
With languishing regards, and bending head?

PERSIUS:

'Their crooked horns the Mimallonian crew
With blasts inspired, and Bassaris who slew
The scornful calf, with sword advanced on high,
Made from his neck his haughty head to fly.
And Maenas when with ivy bridles bound
She led the spotted lynx, then Evion rung around,
Evion from woods and floods repairing echoes sound.'

The verses marked with the commas are Nero's, and it's no wonder
that men of so delicate a taste as Lucan and Persius could not digest
them, though made by an emperor.*

About this time the world was grown weary of Nero, for a
thousand monstrous cruelties of his life and the continued abuse of
the imperial power. Rome had groaned long under the weight of
them, till at length several of the first rank, headed by Piso, formed a
conspiracy to rid the world of that abandoned wretch. Lucan hated

him upon a double score, as his country's enemy and his own, and went heartily in to the design. When it was just ripe for execution, it came to be discovered by some of the accomplices, and Lucan was found among the first of the conspirators. They were condemned to die, and Lucan had the choice of the manner of his death. Upon this occasion some authors have taxed him with an action which, if true, had been an eternal stain upon his name, that to save his life he informed against his mother. This story seems to me to be a mere calumny, and invented only to detract from his fame. It's certainly the most unlikely thing in the world, considering the whole conduct of his life, and that noble scheme of philosophy and morals he had imbibed from his infancy and which shines in every page of his *Pharsalia*. It's probable Nero himself, or some of his flatterers, might invent the story to blacken his rival to posterity, and some unwary authors have afterwards taken it up on trust, without examining into the truth of it. We have several fragments of his life where this particular is not to be found, and which makes it still the more improbable to me, the writers that mention it have tacked to it another calumny, yet more improbable: that he accused her unjustly. As this accusation contradicts the whole tenor of his life, so it does the manner of his death. It's universally agreed, that, having chose to have the arteries of his arms and legs opened in a hot bath, he supped cheerfully with his friends, and then, taking leave of them with the greatest tranquillity of mind and the highest contempt of death, went into the bath, and submitted to the operation. When he found the extremities of his body growing cold, and death's last alarm in every part, he called to mind a passage of his own in the 9th book of the *Pharsalia*, which he repeated to the standers by, with the same grace and accent with which he used to declaim in public, and immediately expired, in the 27th year* of his age, and tenth of Nero. The passage was that where he describes a soldier of Cato's dying much after the same manner, being bit by a serpent, and is thus translated by Mr Rowe:

> So the warm blood at once from every part
> Ran purple poison down, and drained the fainting heart.
> Blood falls for tears, and o'er his mournful face
> The ruddy drops their tainted passage trace;
> Where-e'er the liquid juices find a way,
> There streams of blood, there crimson rivers stray;
> His mouth and gushing nostrils pour a flood,

And ev'n the pores ooze out the trickling blood;
In the red deluge all the parts lie drowned,
And the whole body seems one bleeding wound.

He was buried in his garden at Rome, and there was lately to be seen in the church of S. Paolo an ancient marble with the following inscription:

Marco Annaeo Lucano, Cordubensi Poetae
*Beneficio Neronis, Fama Servata.**

This inscription, if done by Nero's order, shows that even in spite of himself he paid a secret homage to Lucan's genius and virtue, and would have atoned in some measure for the injuries and the death he gave him. But he needed no marble or inscription to perpetuate his memory – his *Pharsalia* will outlive all these.

Lucan wrote several books that have perished by the injury of time, and of which nothing remains but the titles. The first we are told he wrote was *A Poem on the Combat between Achilles and Hector, and Priam Redeeming his Son's Body*, which, it's said, he wrote before he had attained eleven years of age. The rest were: *The Descent of Orpheus into Hell, The Burning of Rome*, in which he is said not to have spared Nero that set it on fire, and *A Poem in Praise of his Wife Polla Argentaria*. He wrote likewise several books of *Saturnalia*, ten books of *Silvae*, an imperfect tragedy of *Medea, A Poem upon the Burning of Troy and the Fate of Priam*, to which some have added *The Panegyric to Calpurnius Piso*, yet extant, which I can hardly believe is his, but of a later age.* But the book he staked his fame on was his *Pharsalia*, the only one that now remains, and which Nero's cruelty has left us imperfect, in respect of what it would have been if he had lived to finish it.

Statius in his *Silvae* gives us the catalogue of Lucan's works in an elegant manner, introducing the muse Calliope accosting him to this purpose. 'When thou art scarce past the age of childhood', says Calliope to Lucan, 'thou shalt play with the valour of Achilles and Hector's skill in driving of a chariot. Thou shalt draw Priam at the feet of his unrelenting conqueror, begging the dead body of his darling son. Thou shalt set open the gates of hell for Eurydice, and thy Orpheus shall have the preference in a full theatre, in spite of Nero's envy,' alluding to the dispute for the prize between him and Nero, where the piece exhibited by Lucan was Orpheus's descent into hell. 'Thou shalt relate', continues Calliope, 'that flame which the execrable tyrant kindled to lay in ashes the mistress of the world, nor shalt thou be silent in the praises that are justly due to thy beloved wife, and when thou hast attained to riper years thou shalt sing in a lofty strain the fatal fields of Philippi, white with Roman bones, the dreadful battle of Pharsalia, and the thundering wars of that great captain, who by the renown of his arms merited to be enrolled among the gods. In that work', continues Calliope, 'thou shalt paint in never-fading colours the austere virtues of Cato, who scorned to outlive the liberties of his country, and the fate of Pompey, once the darling of Rome. Thou shalt, like a true Roman, weep over the crime of the young tyrant Ptolemy, and shalt raise to Pompey, by the power of thy eloquence, a higher monument than the Egyptian pyramids. The poetry of Ennius', adds Calliope, 'and the learned fire of Lucretius, the one that conducted the Argonauts through such vast seas to the conquest of the Golden Fleece, the other that could strike an infinite number of forms from the first atoms of matter, both of them shall give place to thee, without the least envy, and even the divine *Aeneid* shall pay thee a just respect.'*

Thus far Statius concerning Lucan's work; and even Lucan in two places of the *Pharsalia* has promised himself immortality to his poem. The first is in the 7th book, which I beg leave to give in prose, though Mr Rowe has done it a thousand times better in verse. 'One day', says he, 'when these wars shall be spoken of in ages yet to come, and among nations far remote from this clime, whether from the voice of fame alone, or the real value I have given them by this my history, those that read it shall alternately hope and fear for the great events therein contained. In vain', continues he, 'shall they offer up their vows for the righteous cause, and stand thunderstruck at so many various turns of fortune, nor shall they read them as things that are already past, but with that concern as if they were yet to come, and shall range themselves, O Pompey, on thy side.'

The other passage, which is in the 9th book, may be translated thus: 'O Caesar, profane thou not through envy the funeral monuments of these great patriots that fell here sacrifices to thy ambition. If there may be allowed any renown to a Roman muse, while Homer's verses shall be thought worthy of praise, they that shall live after us shall read his* and mine together; my *Pharsalia* shall live, and no time nor age shall consign it to oblivion.'

This is all that I can trace from the ancients, or himself, concerning Lucan's life and writings, and indeed there is scarce any one author, either ancient or modern, that mentions him but with the greatest respect and the highest encomiums, of which it would be tedious to give more instances.

I design not to enter into any criticism on the *Pharsalia*, though I had ever so much leisure or ability for it. I hate to oblige a certain set of men, that read the ancients only to find fault with them, and seem to live only on the excrements of authors. I beg leave to tell these gentlemen that Lucan is not to be tried by those rules of an epic poem which they have drawn from the *Iliad* or *Aeneid*, for if they allow him not the honour to be on the same foot with Homer or Virgil, they must do him the justice at least as not to try him by laws founded upon their model. The *Pharsalia* is properly an historical heroic poem, because the subject is a known true story. Now with our late critics truth is an unnecessary trifle for an epic poem, and ought to be thrown aside as a curb to invention. To have every part a mere web of their own brain is with them a distinguishing mark of a mighty genius in the epic way. Hence it is, these critics observe, that their favourite poems of that kind do always produce in the mind of the reader the highest wonder and surprise, and, the more improbable the story is, still the more wonderful and surprising. Much good may this notion of theirs do them, but, to my taste, a fact very extraordinary in its kind, that is attended with surprising circumstances, big with the highest events, and conducted with all the arts of the most consummate wisdom, does not strike the less strong, but leaves a more lasting impression on my mind, for being true.

If Lucan therefore wants these ornaments he might have borrowed from Helicon,* or his own invention, he has made us more than ample amends by the great and true events that fall within the compass of his story. I am of opinion that, in his first design of writing this poem of the civil wars, he resolved to treat the subject fairly and plainly, and that fable and invention were to have had no share in the work. But the force of custom, and the design he had to induce the generality of readers to fall in love with liberty and abhor slavery, the principal design of the poem, induced him to embellish it with some fables, fearing* that without them his books would not be so universally read – so much was fable the delight of the Roman people.

If any shall object to his privilege of being examined and tried as an historian that he has given in to the poetical province of invention and fiction in the 6th book, where Sextus inquires of the

Thessalian witch Erictho the event of the civil war and the fate of Rome, it may be answered that perhaps the story was true, or at least it was commonly believed to be so in his time, which is a sufficient excuse for Lucan to have inserted it. It's true no other author mentions it. But it's usual to find some one passage in one historian that is not mentioned in any other, though they treat of the same subject. For though I am fully persuaded that all these oracles and responses, so famous in the pagan world, were the mere cheats of priests, yet the belief of them, and of magic and withcraft, was universally received at that time. Therefore Lucan may very well be excused for falling in with a popular error, whether he himself believed it or no, especially when it served to enliven and embellish his story. If it be an error, it's an error all the ancients have fallen into, both Greek and Roman; and Livy, the prince of the Latin historians, abounds in such relations. That it is not below the dignity and veracity of an historian to mention such things, we have a late instance in a noble author of our time who has likewise wrote the civil wars of his country, and intermixed in it the story of the ghost of the Duke of Buckingham's father.*

In general all the actions that Lucan relates in the course of his history are true, nor is it any impeachment of his veracity that sometimes he differs in place, manner or circumstances of action from other writers, any more than it is an imputation on them that they differ from him. We ourselves have seen in the course of the late two famous wars* how differently almost every battle and siege has been represented, and sometimes by those of the same side, when*at the same time there be a thousand living witnesses ready to contradict any falsehood that partiality should impose upon the world. This I may affirm: the most important events, and the whole thread of action in Lucan, are agreeable to the universal consent of all authors that have treated of the civil wars of Rome. If now and then he differs from them in lesser incidents or circumstances, let the critics in history decide the question. For my part, I am willing to take them for anecdotes first discovered and published by Lucan, which may at least conciliate to him the favour of our late admirers of secret history.*

After all I have said on this head, I cannot but in some measure call in question some parts of Caesar's character as drawn by Lucan, which seem to me not altogether agreeable to truth, nor to the universal consent of history. I wish I could vindicate him in some of his personal representations of men, and Caesar in particu-

lar, as I can do in the narration of the principal events and series of
his story. He is not content only to deliver him down to posterity
as the subverter of the laws and liberties of his country, which he
truly was, and than which no greater infamy can possibly be cast
upon any name, but he describes him as pursuing that abominable
end by the most execrable methods, and some that were not in
Caesar's nature to be guilty of. Caesar was certainly a man far from
revenge, or delight in blood, and he made appear in the exercise of
the supreme power a noble and generous inclination to clemency
upon all occasions. Even Lucan, though never so much his enemy,
has not omitted his generous usage of Domitius at Corfinium, or of
Afranius and Petreius when they were his prisoners in Spain. What
can be then said in excuse for Lucan, when he represents him riding
in triumph over the field of *Pharsalia*, the day after the battle,
taking delight in that horrid landscape of slaughter and blood, and
forbidding the bodies of so many brave Romans to be either buried
or burnt? Not any one passage of Caesar's life gives countenance
to a story like this, and how commendable soever the zeal of a
writer may be against the oppressor of his country, it ought not to
have transported him to such a degree of malevolence as to paint
the most merciful conqueror that ever was in colours proper only
for the most savage natures. But the effects of prejudice and
partiality are unaccountable, and there is not a day of life in which
even the best of men are not guilty of them in some degree or other.
How many instances have we in history of the best princes treated
as the worst of men, by the pens of authors that were highly
prejudiced against them?

Shall we wonder then that the Roman people, smarting under
the lashes of Nero's tyranny, should exclaim in the bitterest terms
against the memory of Julius Caesar, since it was from him that
Nero derived that power to use mankind as he did? Those that
lived in Lucan's time did not consider so much what Caesar was in
his own person or temper, as what he was the occasion of to them.
It's very probable there were a great many dreadful stories of him
handed about by tradition among the multitude, and even men of
sense might give credit to them so far as to forget his clemency and
remember his ambition, to which they imputed all the cruelties and
devastations committed by his successors. Resentments of this kind
in the soul of a man, fond of the ancient constitution of the
commonwealth, such as Lucan was, might betray him to believe,
upon too slight grounds, whatever was to the disadvantage of one

he looked upon as the subverter of that constitution. It was in that quality and for that crime alone that Brutus afterwards stabbed him, for personal prejudice against him he had none, and had been highly obliged by him. And it was upon that account alone that Cato scorned to owe his life to him, though he well knew Caesar would have esteemed it one of the greatest felicities of his to have had it in his power to pardon him. I would not be thought to make an apology for Lucan's thus traducing the memory of Caesar, but would only beg the same indulgence to his partiality that we are willing to allow to most other authors, for I cannot help believing all historians are more or less guilty of it.

I beg leave to observe one thing further on this head, that it's odd Lucan should thus mistake this part of Caesar's character, and yet do him so much justice in the rest. His greatness of mind, his intrepid courage, his indefatigable activity, his magnanimity, his generosity, his consummate knowledge in the art of war, and the power and grace of his eloquence, are all set forth in the best light upon every proper occasion. He never makes him speak, but it's with all the strength of argument and all the flowers of rhetoric. It were tedious to enumerate every instance of this, and I shall only mention the speech to his army before the battle of Pharsalia, which in my opinion surpasses all I ever read, for the easy nobleness of expression, the proper topics to animate his soldiers, and the force of an inimitable eloquence.

Among Lucan's few mistakes in matters of fact may be added those of geography and astronomy, but, finding Mr Rowe has taken some notice of them in his notes, I shall say nothing of them. Lucan had neither time nor opportunity to visit the scenes where the actions he describes were done, as some other historians both Greek and Romans had, and therefore it was no wonder he might commit some minute errors in these matters. As to astronomy, the schemes of that noble science were but very conjectural in his time, and not reduced to that mathematical certainty they have been since.

The method and disposition of a work of his kind must be much the same with those observed by other historians, with one difference only, which I submit to better judgements. An historian who like Lucan has chosen to write in verse, though he is obliged to have strict regard to truth in everything he relates, yet perhaps he is not obliged to mention all facts, as other historians are. He is not tied down to relate every minute passage or circumstance if they be not absolutely necessary to the main story, especially if they are such as would appear heavy and flat, and consequently encumber his genius or his verse. All these trifling parts of action would take off from the pleasure and entertainment which is the main scope of that manner of writing. Thus the particulars of an army's march, the journal of a siege, or the situation of a camp, where they are not subservient to the relation of some great and important event, had better be spared than inserted in a work of that kind. In a prose writer these perhaps ought or at least may be properly and agreeably enough mentioned, of which we have innumerable instances in most ancient historians, and particularly in Thucydides and Livy.

There is a fault in Lucan against this rule, and that is his long and unnecessary enumeration of the several parts of Gaul, whence Caesar's army was drawn together, in the first book. It is enlivened, it's true, with some beautiful verses he throws in about the ancient bards and druids, but still in the main it's dry, and but of little consequence to the story itself. The many different people and cities there mentioned were not Caesar's confederates, as those in the third book were Pompey's, and these last are particularly named to express how many nations espoused the side of Pompey. Those reckoned up in Gaul were only the places where Caesar's troops had been quartered, and Lucan might with as great propriety have mentioned the different routes by which they marched, as the garrisons from which they were drawn. This therefore, in my opinion, had been better left out, and I cannot but likewise think that the digression in the sixth book, containing a geographical description of Thessaly and an account of its first inhabitants, is too prolix, and not of any great consequence to his purpose. I am sure it signifies but little to the civil war in general or the battle of Pharsalia in particular to know how many rivers there are in Thessaly, or which of its mountains lies east or west.

But if these be faults in Lucan, they are such as will be found in the most admired poets, nay, and thought excellencies in them; and besides, he has made us most ample amends in the many extraordinary beauties of his poem. The story itself is noble and great, for what can there be in history more worthy of our knowledge and attention than a war of the highest importance to mankind, carried on between the two greatest leaders that ever were, and by a people the most renowned for arts and arms, and who were at that time masters of the world? What a poor subject is that of the *Aeneid* when compared with this of the *Pharsalia*, and what a despicable

figure does Agamemnon, Homer's king of kings make, when compared with chiefs who by saying only 'be thou a king' made far
greater kings than him? The scene of the *Iliad* contained but Greece,
some islands in the Aegean and Ionian seas, with a very little part
of the Lesser Asia. This of the civil war of Rome drew after it
almost all the nations of the then known world. Troy was but a
little town, of the little kingdom of Phrygia, whereas Rome was
then mistress of an empire that reached from the straits of Hercules
and the Atlantic ocean to the Euphrates, and from the bottom of
the Euxine and the Caspian seas to Ethiopia and Mount Atlas. The
inimitable Virgil is yet more straitened in his subject. Aeneas, a
poor fugitive from Troy, with a handful of followers, settles at last
in Italy, and all the empire that immortal pen could give him is but
a few miles upon the banks of the Tiber. So vast a disproportion
there is between the importance of the subject of the *Aeneid* and
that of the *Pharsalia*, that we find one single Roman, Crassus,
master of more slaves on his estate than Virgil's hero had subjects.
In fine, it may be said nothing can excuse him for his choice but
that he designed his hero for the ancestor of Rome and the Julian
race.

I cannot leave this parallel without taking notice to what a height
of power the Roman empire was then arrived, in an instance of
Caesar himself, when but proconsul of Gaul, and before it's thought
he ever dreamed of being what he afterwards attained to. It's in
one of Cicero's letters to him, wherein he repeats the words of
Caesar's letters to him some time before. The words are these: 'As
to what concerns Marcus Furius, whom you recommended to me, I
will, if you please, make him king of Gaul, but if you would have
me advance any other friend of yours, send him to me.' It was no
new thing for citizens of Rome, such as Caesar was, to dispose of
kingdoms as they pleased, and Caesar himself had taken away
Deiotarus' kingdom from him, and given it to a private gentleman
of Pergamum. But there is one surprising instance more of the
prodigious greatness of the Roman power, in the affair of king
Antiochus,* and that long before the height it arrived to at the
breaking forth of the civil war. That prince was master of all Egypt,
and marching to the conquest of Phoenicia, Cyprus, and the other
appendixes of that empire. Popillius overtakes him in his full march
with letters from the Senate, and refuses to give him his hand till he
had read them. Antiochus, startled at the command that was
contained in them to stop the progress of his victories, asked a

short time to consider of it. Popillius makes a circle about him with a stick he had in his hand. 'Return me an answer', said he, 'before thou stirr'st out of this circle, or the Roman people are no more thy friends.' Antiochus, after a short pause, told him with the lowest submission he would obey the Senate's commands. Upon which Popillius gives him his hand and salutes him a friend of Rome. After Antiochus had given up so great a monarchy, and such a torrent of success, upon receiving only a few words in writing, he had indeed reason to send word to the Senate, as he did by his ambassadors that he had obeyed their commands with the same submission as if they had been sent him from the immortal gods.

To leave this digression: it were the height of arrogance to detract ever so little from Homer or Virgil, who have kept possession of the first places among the poets of Greece and Rome for so many ages, yet I hope I may be forgiven if I say there are several passages in both that appear to me trivial, and below the dignity that shines almost in every page of Lucan. It were to take both the *Iliad* and *Aeneid* in pieces to prove this. But I shall only take notice of one instance, and that is the different colouring of Virgil's hero and Lucan's Caesar in a storm. Aeneas is drawn weeping, and in the greatest confusion and despair, though he had assurance from the gods that he should one day settle and raise a new empire in Italy. Caesar, on the contrary, is represented perfectly sedate and free from fear. His courage and magnanimity brighten up as much upon this occasion as afterwards they did at the battles of Pharsalia and Munda. Courage would have cost Virgil nothing to have bestowed it on his hero, and he might as easily have thrown him upon the coast of Carthage in a calm temper of mind as in a panic fear.

Saint-Evremond* is very severe upon Virgil on this account, and has criticized upon his character of Aeneas in this manner. When Virgil tells us:

> Extemplo Aeneae solvuntur frigore membra,
> Ingemit et duplices tendens ad sidera palmas, &c

'Seized as he is', says Saint-Evremond, 'with this chillness through all his limbs, the first sign of life we find in him is his groaning; then he lifts up his hands to heaven, and in all appearance would implore its succour, if the condition wherein the good hero finds himself would afford him strength enough to raise his mind to the gods, and pray with attention. His soul, which could not apply itself to anything else, abandons itself to lamentations, and, like those desolate widows who upon the first trouble they meet with wish they were in the grave with their dear husbands, the poor Aeneas bewails his not having perished before Troy with Hector, and esteems them very happy who left their bones in the bosom of so sweet and dear a country. Some people', adds he, 'may perhaps believe he says so, because he envies their happiness, but I am persuaded', says Saint-Evremond, 'it's for fear of the danger that threatens him.' The same author, after he has thus exposed his want of courage, adds, 'the good Aeneas hardly ever concerns himself in any important or glorious design; it's enough for him that he discharges his conscience in the offices of a pious, tender and compassionate man. He carries his father on his shoulders, he conjugally laments his dear Creusa, he causes his nurse to be interred, and makes a funeral pile for his trusty pilot Palinurus, for whom he sheds a thousand tears. Here is', says he, 'a sorry hero in paganism, who would have made an admirable saint among some Christians.' In short, it's Saint-Evremond's opinion he was fitter to make a founder of an order than* a state.

Thus far, and perhaps too far, Saint-Evremond. I beg leave to take notice that the storm in Lucan is drawn in stronger colours, and strikes the mind with greater horror, than that in Virgil, notwithstanding the first has no supernatural cause assigned for it, and the latter is raised by a god, at the instigation of a goddess that was both wife and sister of Jupiter.

In the *Pharsalia* most of the transactions and events that compose the relation are wonderful and surprising though true, as well as instructive and entertaining. To enumerate them all were to transcribe the work itself, and therefore I shall only hint at some of the most remarkable. With what dignity and justness of character are the two great rivals, Pompey and Caesar, introduced in the first book, and how beautifully, and with what a masterly art, are they opposed to one another! Add to this the justest similitudes by which their different characters are illustrated in the second and ninth book. Who can but admire the figure that Cato's virtue makes in more places than one? And I persuade myself, if Lucan had lived to finish his design, the death of that illustrious Roman had made one of the most moving, as well as one of the most sublime, episodes of his poem. In the third book, Pompey's dream, Caesar's breaking open the temple of Saturn, the siege of Marseilles, the sea fight, and the sacred grove, have each of them their particular excellence that in my opinion come very little short of anything we find in Homer or Virgil.

In the fourth book there are a great many charming incidents, and among the rest that of the soldiers running out of their camp to meet and embrace one another, and the deplorable story of Vulteius. The fifth book affords us a fine account of the oracle of Delphos, its origin, the manner of its delivering answers, and the reason of its then silence. Then upon the occasion of a mutiny in Caesar's camp near Placentia, in his manner of passing the Adriatic in a small boat, amidst the storm I hinted at, he has given us the noblest and the best image of that great man. But what affects me above all is the parting of Pompey and Cornelia in the end of the book. It has something in it as moving and tender as ever was felt, or perhaps imagined.

In the description of the witch Erictho, in the sixth book, we have a beautiful picture of horror, for even works of that kind have their beauties in poetry, as well as in painting. The seventh book is most taken up with what relates to the famous battle of Pharsalia, which decided the fate of Rome. It is so related that the reader may rather think himself a spectator of, or even engaged in, the battle than so remote from the age in which it was fought. There is towards the end of this book a noble majestic description of the general conflagration and of that last catastrophe which must put an end to this frame of heaven and earth. To this is added, in the most elevated style, his sentiments of the immortality of the soul, and of rewards and punishments after his life. All these are touched with the nicest delicacy of expression and thought, especially that about the universal conflagration, and agrees with what we find of it in Holy Writ, in so much that I am willing to believe Lucan might have conversed with St Peter at Rome, if it be true he was ever there, or he might have seen that epistle of his, wherein he gives us the very same idea of it.

In the eighth book our passions are again touched with the misfortunes of Cornelia and Pompey, but especially with the death and unworthy funeral of the latter. In this book is likewise drawn, with the greatest art, the character of young Ptolemy and his ministers; particularly that of the villain Pothinus is exquisitely exposed in his own speech in council.

In the ninth book, after the apotheosis of Pompey, Cato is introduced as the fittest man after him to lead the cause of liberty and Rome. This book is the longest, and, in my opinion, the most entertaining in the whole poem. The march of Cato through the deserts of Libya affords a noble and agreeable variety of matter, and the virtues of his hero amidst these distresses through which he leads him seems everywhere to deserve these raptures of praise he bestows upon him. Add to this the artful descriptions of the various poisons with which these deserts abounded, and their different effects upon human bodies, than which nothing can be more moving or poetical.

But Cato's answer to Labienus in this book, upon his desiring him to consult the oracle of Jupiter Ammon about the event of the civil war and the fortune of Rome, is a masterpiece not to be equalled. All the attributes of God, such as his omnipotence, his prescience, his justice, his goodness, and his unsearchable decrees, are painted in the most awful and the strongest colours, and such as may make Christians themselves blush for not coming up to them in most of their writings upon that subject. I know not but Saint-Evremond has carried the matter too far, when in mentioning this passage he concludes, 'If all the ancient poets had spoke as worthily of the oracles of their gods, he should make no scruple to prefer them to the divines and philosophers of our time. We may see', says he, 'in the concourse of so many people that came to consult the oracle of Ammon what effect a public opinion can produce, where zeal and superstition mingle together. We may see in Labienus a pious, sensible man, who to his respect for the gods joins that consideration and esteem we ought to preserve for virtue in good men. Cato is a religious, severe philosopher, weaned from all vulgar opinions, who entertains those lofty thoughts of the gods which pure undebauched reason and a truly elevated knowledge can give us of them; everything here', says Saint-Evremond, 'is poetical, everything is consonant to truth and reason. It is not poetical upon the score of any ridiculous fiction, or for some extravagant hyperbole, but for the daring greatness and majesty of the language, and for the noble elevation of the discourse. It's thus', adds he, 'that poetry is the language of the gods, and that poets are wise; and it's so much the greater wonder to find it in Lucan', says he, 'because it's neither to be met with in Homer nor Virgil.' I remember Montaigne, who is allowed by all to have been an admirable judge in these matters, prefers Lucan's character of Cato to Virgil, or any other of the ancient poets. He thinks all of them flat and languishing, but Lucan's much more strong, though overthrown by the extravagancy of his own force.*

The tenth book, imperfect as it is, gives us, among other things, a view of the Egyptian magnificence, with a curious account of the then received opinions of the increase and decrease of the river Nile. From the variety of the story, and many other particulars I need not mention in this short account, it may easily appear that a true history may be as delightful as a romance or fiction, when the author makes choice of a subject that affords so many and so surprising incidents.

Among the faults that have been laid to Lucan's charge, the most justly imputed are those of his style, and indeed how could it be otherwise? Let us but remember the imperfect state in which his sudden and immature death left the *Pharsalia*, the design itself being probably but half finished, and what was writ of it but slightly, if at all, revised. We are told, it's true, he either corrected the three first books himself, or his wife did it for him, in his own lifetime. Be it so, but what are the corrections of a lady, or a young man of six and twenty, to those he might have made at forty, or a more advanced age? Virgil, the most correct and judicious poet that ever was, continued correcting his *Aeneid* for near as long a series of years together as Lucan lived, and yet died with a strong opinion that it was imperfect still. If Lucan had lived to his age, the *Pharsalia* without doubt would have made another kind of figure than it now does, notwithstanding the difference to be found in the Roman language between the times of Nero and Augustus.

It must be owned he is in many places obscure and hard, and therefore not so agreeable, and comes short of the purity, sweetness and delicate propriety of Virgil. Yet it's still universally agreed among both ancients and moderns that his genius was wonderfully great, but at the same time too haughty and headstrong to be governed by art, and that his style was like his genius, learned, bold and lively, but withal too tragical and blustering.

I am by no means willing to compare the *Pharsalia* to the *Aeneid*, but I must say, with Saint-Evremond, that for what purely regards the elevation of thought, Pompey, Caesar, Cato and Labienus shine much more in Lucan than Jupiter, Mercury, Juno or Venus do in Virgil. The ideas which Lucan has given us of these great men are truly greater, and affect us more sensibly, than those which Virgil has given us of his deities. The latter has clothed his gods with human infirmities, to adapt them to the capacity of men; the other has raised his heroes so as to bring them into competition with the gods themselves. In a word, the gods are not so valuable in Virgil as the heroes; in Lucan, the heroes equal the gods. After all, it must be allowed that most things throughout the whole *Pharsalia* are greatly and justly said, with regard even to the language and expression. But the sentiments are everywhere so beautiful and elevated that they appear, as he describes Caesar in Amyclas' cottage in the fifth book, noble and magnificent in any dress. It's in this elevation of thought that Lucan justly excels; this is his fort,* and what raises him up to an equality with the greatest of the ancient poets.

I cannot omit here the delicate character of Lucan's genius, as mentioned by Strada* in the emblematic way. It's commonly known that Pope Leo the Tenth* was not only learned himself, but a great patron of learning, and used to be present at the conversations and performances of all the polite writers of his time. The wits of Rome entertained him one day at his villa on the banks of the Tiber, with an interlude in the nature of a poetical masquerade. They had their Parnassus, their Pegasus, their Helicon, and everyone of the ancient poets in their several characters, where each acted the part that was suitable to his manner of writing, and among the rest one that acted Lucan. 'There was none', says he 'that was placed in a higher station or had a greater prospect under him than Lucan. He vaulted upon Pegasus with all the heat and intrepidity of youth, and seemed desirous of mounting into the clouds upon the back of him. But as the hinder feet of the horse stuck to the mountain, while the body reared up in the air, the poet with great difficulty kept himself from sliding off, in so much that the spectators often gave him for gone, and cried out now and then he was tumbling.' Thus Strada.

I shall sum up all I have time to say of Lucan with another character, as it is given by one of the most polite men of the age he lived in, and who under the protection of the same Pope Leo X was one of the first restorers of learning in the latter end of the fifteenth and the beginning of the sixteenth century. I mean Johannes Sulpitius Verulanus, who with the assistance of Beroaldus, Badius, and some others of the first form in the republic of letters, published Lucan with notes at Rome in the year 1514,* being the first impression, if I mistake not, that ever was made of him. Poetry and painting, with the knowledge of the Greek and Latin tongues, rose about that time to a prodigious height in a small compass of years, and, whatever we may think to the contrary, they have declined ever since. Verulanus in his dedication to Cardinal Palavicini, prefixed to that edition, has not only given us a delicate sententious criticism on his *Pharsalia*, but a beautiful judicious comparison between him* and Virgil, and that in a style which in my opinion comes but little short of Sallust, or the writers of the Augustan age. It is to the following purpose in English, and it may not be unacceptable to the reader that I have put the Latin* in the margin.

'I come now to the author I have commented upon', says Sulpitius Verulanus, 'and shall endeavour to describe him, as well as observe in what he differs from that great poet Virgil. Lucan, in the opinion of Fabius,* is no less a pattern for orators than for poets, and, always adhering strictly to truth, he seems to have as fair a pretence to the character of an historian, for he equally performs each of these offices. His expression is bold and lively, his sentiments are clear, his fictions within compass of probability, and his digressions proper; his orations artful, correct, manly and full of matter. In the other parts of his work he is grave, fluent, copious and elegant, abounding with great variety and wonderful erudition. And in unriddling the intricacy of contrivances, designs and actions, his style is so masterly that you rather seem to see than read of those transactions. But as for enterprises and battles, you imagine them not related but acted – towns alarmed, armies engaged, the eagerness and terror of the several soldiers, seem present to your view. As our author is frequent and fertile in descriptions, and none more skilful in discovering the secret springs of action and their rise in human passions, as he is an acute searcher into the manners of men, and most dextrous in applying all sorts of learning to his subject; what other cosmographer, astrologer, philosopher or mathematician do we stand in need of, while we read him? Who has more judiciously handled, or treated with more delicacy, whatever topics his fancy has led him to, or have casually fallen in his way? Maro* is, without doubt, a great poet; so is Lucan. In so apparent an equality, 'tis hard to decide which excels. For both have justly obtained the highest commendations. Maro is rich and magnificent, Lucan sumptuous and splendid; the first is discreet, inventive and sublime, the latter free, harmonious and full of spirit. Virgil seems to move with the devout solemnity of a reverend prelate, Lucan to march with the noble haughtiness of a victorious general. One owes most to labour and application, the other to nature and practice. One lulls the soul with the sweetness and music of his verse, the other raises it by his fire and rapture. Virgil is sedate, happy in his conceptions, free from faults; Lucan quick, various and florid. He seems to fight with stronger weapons, this with more. The first surpasses all in solid strength, the latter excels in vigour and poignancy. You would think that the one sounds rather a larger and deeper toned trumpet, the other a less indeed, but clearer. In short, so great is the affinity and the struggle for precedence between them that, though nobody be allowed to come up to that divinity in Maro, yet, had he not been possessed of the chief seat on Parnassus, our author's claim to it had been indisputable.'

Thus much for Lucan. And it may be expected I should give some account of Mr Rowe, who has obliged the world with the following translation of him in English verse. Never man had it more in his nature than he to love and oblige his friends living, or celebrate their memory when dead. What pity is it then that, for want of information, there cannot be paid to his name that just encomium he every way deserved!

He was born at Little Berkford in Bedfordshire, at the house of Jasper Edwards Esq, his mother's father, in the year 1673,* of an ancient family in Devonshire that for many ages had made a handsome figure in their country, and was known by the name of Rowes of Lambertoun. He could trace his ancestors, in a direct line, up to the times of the Holy War, where one of them so distinguished himself in the Holy Land that at his return he had the coat of arms given him which they bore ever since, that being in those days all the reward of military virtue or of blood spilt in those expeditions. From that time downward to Mr Rowe's father, the family kept themselves to the frugal management of a private fortune and the innocent pleasures of a country life. Having a handsome seat and a competent estate, they lived beyond the fear of want, or reach of envy. In all the changes of governments, they are said to have ever leaned towards the side of public liberty, and in that retired situation of life to have beheld with grief and concern the many encroachments that have been made upon it from time to time.

His father was John Rowe, and the first of the family, as his son has told me, that changed a country life for a liberal profession. After he had past the schools at home he was brought up to London, and entered a student of the law in the Middle Temple, where some time after he was called to the bar, and at length made a sergeant at law. He was a gentleman in great esteem for many engaging qualities, of very considerable practice at the bar, and stood fair for the first vacancy on the bench, when he died the 30th day of April, 1692, and was buried in the Temple Church the 7th of May following. Let it be mentioned to the honour of this gentleman that, when he published Sergeant Benloe and Judge Dalison's reports, he had the honesty and boldness to observe in the preface how moderate these two great lawyers had been in their opinions concerning the extent of the royal prerogative, and that he durst do this in the late King James' reign, at a time when a dispensing power was set up, as inherent in the crown. From such worthy ancestors Nicholas Rowe was descended, who, together with the ancient paternal seat of the family, inherited their probity and good nature, contentment of mind and an unbiased love to their country.

His father took all the care possible of his education, and, when he was fit for it, sent him to Westminster School, under the famous Dr Busby.* He made an extraordinary progress in all the parts of learning taught in that school, and about the age of twelve years was chosen one of the King's Scholars. He became in a little time master to a great perfection of all the classical authors, both Greek and Latin, and made a tolerable proficiency in the Hebrew, but poetry was his early bent, and his darling study. He composed at that time several copies of verses upon different subjects both in Greek and Latin, and some in English, which were much admired, and the more that they cost him very little pains and seemed to flow from his imagination almost as fast as his pen.

His father, designing him for his own profession, took him from that school when he was about sixteen years of age, and entered him a student in the Middle Temple, whereof he himself was a member, that he might have him under his immediate care and instruction. Being capable of any part of knowledge he applied his mind to, he made very remarkable advances in the study of the law, and was not content, as he told me, to know it as a collection of statutes or customs only, but as a system founded upon right reason and calculated for the good of mankind. Being afterwards called to the bar, he appeared in as promising a way to make a figure in that profession as any of his contemporaries, if the love of the *belleslettres*, and that of poetry in particular, had not stopped him in his career. He had the advantage of the friendship and protection of one of the finest gentlemen, as well as one of the greatest lawyers of that time, Sir George Treby, Lord Chief Justice of the Common Pleas, who was fond of him to a great degree, and had it both in his power and inclination to promote his interest.

But the muses had stolen away his heart from his infancy, and

his passion for them rendered the study of the law dry and tasteless
to his palate. He struggled for some time against the natural bent
of his mind, but in vain, for Homer and Virgil, Sophocles and
Euripides, had infinitely more charms with him than the best
authors that had writ of the law of England. He now and then
could not refrain from making some copies of verses on subjects
that fell in his way, which being approved of by his intimate friends,
to whom only he showed them, that approbation proved his snare,
so that from that time he began to give way to the natural bias of
his mind, and would needs try what he could do in tragedy.

The first he wrote was *The Ambitious Step-Mother*, which meeting with universal applause, as it well deserved, he laid aside all
thoughts of rising in the law, and turned them ever after in their
main channel, towards poetry. This his first tragedy he writ when
twenty-five years of age, and as a trial only of his genius that way.
The purity of the English* language, the justness of his characters,
the noble elevation of the sentiments were all of them admirably
adapted to the plan of the play. His talent lay in heroic poetry, and
consequently in tragedy; for comedy, he once tried it, but found his
genius did not lean that way. He writ several tragedies afterwards,
which are in everybody's hands, and all of them highly approved
by men of taste upon the account of the loftiness of thought and
the delicate propriety of the language, in which last I may venture
to say no one has ever outdone him, few equalled him.

The tragedy he valued himself most upon, and which was most
valued, was his *Tamerlane*; and never author, in my opinion, did
more justice to his hero than he to that excellent prince, for
Tamerlane was the very man that Mr Rowe has painted him. In
that play he aimed at a parallel between the late King William of
immortal memory and Tamerlane, as also between Bajazet and a
monarch* who is since dead. That glorious ambition and noble
ardour in Tamerlane, to break the chains of enslaved nations and
set mankind free from the encroachments of lawless power, are
painted in the most lively as well as the most amiable colours. On
the other side, his manner of introducing on the stage a prince that
thinks mankind is made but for him, and whose chief aim is to
perpetuate his name to posterity by that havoc and ruin he scatters
through the world, are all drawn with that pomp of horror and
detestation which such monstrous actions do deserve. And since
nothing could be more calculated for raising in the minds of the
audience a true passion for liberty and a just abhorrence for slavery,

how this play came to be discouraged, next to a prohibition, in the latter end of a late reign, I leave it to others to give a reason.

I shall say nothing of any of the rest of Mr Rowe's plays, in particular, but it may be justly said of them all that never poet painted virtue or religion in a more charming dress on the stage, nor were ever vice and impiety better exposed to contempt and hatred. There runs through every one of them an air of religion and virtue, attended with all the social duties of life and a constant untainted love to his country. The same principles of liberty he had early imbibed himself, and seemed a part of his constitution, appeared in everything he wrote, and he took all occasions that fell in his way to make the stage subservient to them. His muse was so religiously chaste that I do not remember one word in any of his plays or writings that might admit but of a *double entendre* in point of decency or morals. There is nothing to be found in them to humour the depraved taste of the age, by nibbling at scripture, or depreciating things in themselves sacred, and it was the less wonder that he observed this rule in his dramatic performances, since in his ordinary conversation, and when his mirth and humour enlivened the whole company, he used to express his dissatisfaction, in the severest manner, with anything that looked that way. Being much conversant in the holy scriptures, it's observable that, to raise the highest ideas of virtue, he has with great art in several of his tragedies made use of those expressions and metaphors in them that taste most of the sublime.

Besides his plays, Mr Rowe wrote a great many copies of verses on different subjects, which it's hoped his friends may some time or other publish together, and whereof many have already printed apart. Being a great admirer of Shakespeare, he obliged the public with a new edition of his works, and prefixed to it a short account of his life. In that account he lay under the same misfortune that I have done in this acount of Mr Rowe; he wanted information to do justice to Shakespeare. He took all occasions to express the vast esteem he had for that wonderful man, and endeavoured in some of his pieces to imitate his manner of writing, particularly in the tragedy of *Jane Shore*. He has given him the character he well deserved in the prologue to that play in the following verses, which I am the more willing to insert here because I believe there is no man of taste but pays to Shakespeare's memory the homage that's due to one of the greatest geniuses that ever appeared in dramatic poetry. The lines are these:

> In such an age immortal Shakespeare wrote,
> By no quaint rules nor hampering critics taught,
> With rough, majestic force he moved the heart,
> And strength and nature made amends for art.
> Our humble author does his steps pursue,
> He owns he had the mighty bard in view,
> And in these scenes has made it more his care
> To rouse the passions than to charm the ear.

But Mr Rowe's last and perhaps his best poem is this his translation of Lucan, which he just lived to finish. He had entertained an early inclination for that author, and I believe it was the darling passion he had for the liberty and constitution of his country that first inclined him to think of translating him. He thought it was a pity that a work in which the cause of liberty was set in such a shining light should be preserved only in the dead language wherein it was written, and therefore thought it well worth his pains to put it in an English dress for the benefit of his countrymen. As this is the happiest nation of the world in its constitution, and happy even in spite of ourselves, he judged that all who are in love with it must needs be fond of an author who not only wrote for the ancient constitution of his own country, but fell a sacrifice for endeavouring to support it.

As to the translation itself, I persuade myself it will meet with a kind reception in the world. I dare be bold to say the language is pure, and the versification both musical and adapted to the subject. I have no reason to doubt but the true meaning of the original is faithfully preserved through the whole work, and, if I may venture to judge, the translation comes up to the spirit of the original, as far as the difference between the Roman and English languages will allow of.

I am afraid I have gone out of my depth in giving my opinion of a piece of this kind, being no poet myself, so I leave this translation of Lucan to make its way by its own merit. I know May has translated it near an age ago, and I confess it is many years since I read it. But it must be owned that it's but a lame performance, and does not reach the spirit or sense of Lucan. The language and versification are yet worse, and fall infinitely short of the lofty numbers and propriety of expression in which Mr Rowe excels. I know of no other translation of Lucan in any of the living languages in verse, except that of Brebeuf* in French. I have a very great value for it, and the author, if it were for no other reason but that he had the honest boldness to publish such a work in his native language that was diametrically opposite to the maxims of government pursued by the prince then reigning. His courage in this matter deserves yet the more to be applauded, that, when all the other classics were published for the use of the Dauphin, Lucan alone was prohibited. It's observable he has carried in some places in the French language the heat of Lucan farther than Lucan himself in the Latin, and that, by attempting the fire of his author, he has, if I may be allowed the expression, fired himself much more. This is what happens to him frequently; but again at other times he flags, and, when Lucan happily hits on the true beauty of a thought, Brebeuf falls infinitely below him, through an affectation of appearing easy and natural, when he ought to exert all his force. I might give a great many instances of this last, but shall confine myself to one which will set in a true light the difference between the two translations of Lucan by Brebeuf and Mr Rowe. That strong, celebrated line in Lucan:

victrix causa diis* placuit, sed victa Catoni

is with the whole period thus done by Mr Rowe, though none of the brightest lines in his translation:

Justly to name the better cause were hard,
While greatest names for either side declared –
Victorious Caesar by the gods was crowned,
The vanquished party was by Cato owned.

When Brebeuf comes to translate this passage, he does it after this manner:

De si hauts partisans s'arment pour chacun d'eux,
Qu'on ne scait qui défendre, ou qui blamer des* deux,
Qui des deux a tiré plus justement l'epée,
Les dieux servent César, & Caton suit Pompée.

What can be poorer than this last? It does not answer the nobleness of the Latin, and besides it maims the sense of the author. For Lucan, who had his imagination full of the virtue of Cato, intended to raise him above, or at least equal him to, the gods, as to the merit of the cause that occasioned the opposition. But Brebeuf, instead of raising him to a competition with the gods, makes him only a retainer of Pompey's. This puts me in mind of an observation I have frequently made upon most of our English translations.

Whenever there happens an expression or period of a distinguished beauty, it's there they fall often not only short of the original, but mistake entirely the sense. I shall give but one instance in Dryden's Virgil. There is not in all the inimitable *Aeneid* a more beautiful period than that in the sixth book concerning Marcellus, which Virgil sums up in this hemisticon:*

Tu Marcellus eris

Dryden turns it thus:

> O! could'st thou break through fate's severe decree,
> A new Marcellus shall arise in thee.

which is altogether wide from the meaning of Virgil, and sinks infinitely below the dignity of his verse.

I might take notice here of several passages of Lucan left out in Brebeuf, which well deserved a place in his translation. I shall only mention one in the sixth book concerning the witch Erictho, which in my opinion is a very beautiful picture of horror. Brebeuf cuts it short, and in its place gives us a love story of his own invention between Burrhus and Octavia, which is nothing to the purpose, and falls infinitely short of the spirit of Lucan. Yet after all it cannot be denied but Brebeuf's performance is in the main admirably well done, and in many places he appears animated with the same fire we find in Lucan. I cannot omit one instance of this in that passage of the third book concerning the origin of letters, which is one of the finest in Lucan, and excellently done into French by Brebeuf. Lucan has it thus:

> Phoenices primi, famae si creditur, ausi
> Mansuram rudibus vocem signare figuris.

Brebeuf turns it after this manner:

> C'est de luy que nous vient cet art ingénieux,
> De peindre la parole & de parler aux yeux,
> Et par les traits divers des figures tracées,
> Donner de la couleur, & du corps aux pensées.

The translation of this passage by Brebeuf is excellently imitated in English by a young lady[1] that I had the honour to be acquainted

---

[1] A daughter of the Viscount Molesworth (original note). This was Mary Monck (d.1715). She wrote poetry under the name Marinda, and knew Italian, Latin and Spanish.

with, which, if I mistake not, transcends Brebeuf or even Lucan himself. It's thus:

> The noble art from Cadmus took its rise
> Of painting words, and speaking to the eyes.
> He first in wondrous magic fetters bound
> The airy voice, and stopped the flying sound.
> The various figures by his pencil wrought
> Gave colour, and a body to the thought.

To return to Mr Rowe. He just lived to put an end to this translation of Lucan's *Pharsalia*, and, if he had but lived a little longer, it's probable he had prefixed to it another kind of preface than this, with a thorough criticism on the whole work. I shall say nothing further of him in the quality of a poet, since this translation and his other works will sufficiently justify his title to it. As to his person, it was graceful and well made, his face regular and of a manly beauty. As his soul was well lodged, so its rational and animal faculties excelled in a high degree. He had a quick and fruitful invention, a deep penetration, and a large compass of thought, with a singular dexterity and easiness in making his thoughts to be understood. He was master of most parts of polite learning, especially the classical authors both Greek and Latin, understood the French, Italian and Spanish languages, and spoke the first fluently, and the other two tolerably well.

He had likewise read most of the Greek and Roman histories in their original languages, and most that are writ in English, French, Italian and Spanish. He had a good taste in philosophy, and, having a firm impression of religion upon his mind, he took great delight in divinity and ecclesiastical history, in both which he made great advances in the times he retired into the country, which were frequent. He expressed on all occasions his full persuasion of the truth of revealed religion, and, being a sincere member of the established church himself, he pitied, but condemned not, those that dissented from it. He abhorred the principle of persecuting men upon the account of their opinions in religion, and, being strict in his own, he took it not upon him to censure those of another persuasion. His conversation was pleasant, witty and learned, without the least tincture of affectation or pedantry, and his inimitable manner of diverting and enlivening the company made it impossible for anyone to be out of humour when he was in it. Envy and detraction seemed to be entirely foreign to his constitution, and

whatever provocations he met with at any time, he past them over
without the least thought of resentment or revenge. As Homer had
a Zoilus,* so Mr Rowe had sometimes his, for there were not
wanting malevolent people, and pretenders to poetry too, that
would now and then bark at his best performances, but he was so
much conscious of his own genius, and had so much good nature
as to forgive them, nor could he ever be tempted to return them an
answer.*

The love of learning and poetry made him not the less fit for
business, and nobody applied himself closer to it when it required
his attendance. The late Duke of Queensbury, when he was Secretary of State, made him his Secretary for Public Affairs, and when
that truly great man came to know him well, he was never so
pleased as when Mr Rowe was in his company. After the duke's
death all avenues were stopped to his preferment, and during the
rest of that reign he passed his time with the muses and his books,
and sometimes the conversation of his friends.

Upon the King's* accession to the throne his merit was taken
notice of. The King gave him a lucrative place in the customs, and
made him Poet Laureate; the Prince of Wales conferred on him the
place of Clerk of his Council, and the Lord Parker, Lord Chancel-
lor, made him his Secretary for the Presentations the very day he
received the seals, and without his asking it. He was much loved
and cherished by the latter, and it was no wonder that one of his
endowments was in favour with that noble person, who, together
with a profound knowledge in the law worthy of his high station,
has adorned his mind with all the other more polite parts of
learning. When he had just got to be easy in his fortune, and was
in a fair way to make it better, death swept him away, and in him
deprived the world of one of the best men, as well as one of the
best geniuses of the age. He died like a Christian and a philosopher,
in charity with all mankind, and with an absolute resignation to
the will of God. He kept up his good humour to the last, and took
leave of his wife and friends immediately before his last agony, with
the same tranquillity of mind and the same indifference for life as
though he had been upon taking but a short journey. He was twice
married, first to a daughter of the deceased Mr Persons, one of the
auditors of the revenue, and afterwards to a daughter of Mr
Devenish of a good family in Dorsetshire. By the first he had a son,
and by the second a daughter, both yet living. He died the sixth of
December 1718, in the 45th year of his age, and was buried the

nineteenth of the same month in Westminster Abbey, in the aisle where many of our English poets are interred, over against Chaucer, his body being attended by a select number of his friends, and the Dean and choir officiating at the funeral.

Feb. 26, 1719.

PHARSALIA

LUCAN's

PHARSALIA.

Translated into *English* Verse

By *NICHOLAS ROWE*, Esq;

Servant to His MAJESTY.

—Ne tanta animis assuescite Bella,
Neu Patriæ validas in viscera vertite Vires.   Virg.

LONDON:

Printed for JACOB TONSON at *Shakespear's-Head* over-
against *Katharine-Street* in the *Strand*. MDCCXVIII.

BOOK ONE

Emathian* plains with slaughter covered o'er,*
And rage unknown to civil wars before,
Established violence and lawless might,
Avowed and hallowed by the name of right,
5   A race renowned, the world's victorious lords,
Turned on themselves with their own hostile swords,
Piles* against piles opposed in impious fight,*
And eagles against eagles* bending flight,
Of blood by friends, by kindred, parents, spilt,
10 One common horror and promiscuous guilt,
A shattered world in wild disorder tossed,*
Leagues, laws, and empire in confusion lost,
Of all the woes which civil discords bring,
And Rome o'ercome by Roman arms, I sing.   Accord
15   What blind, detested madness could afford
Such horrid licence to the murdering sword?
Say, Romans, whence so dire a fury rose,
To glut with Latian blood your barbarous foes?
Could you in wars like these provoke your fate,
20 Wars where no triumphs on the victor wait,*
While Babylon's* proud spires yet rise so high,
And rich in Roman spoils invade the sky,
While yet no vengeance is to Crassus paid,*
But unatoned repines the wandering shade?
25 What tracts of land, what realms unknown before,
What seas wide-stretching to the distant shore,
What crowns, what empires might that blood have
        gained,
With which Emathia's fatal fields were stained!
Where Seres* in their silken woods* reside,
30 Where swift Araxes rolls his rapid tide,
Where-e'er, if such a nation can be found,
Nile's secret fountain* springing cleaves the ground,*
Where southern suns with double ardour rise,
Flame o'er the land, and scorch the mid-day skies,
35 Where winter's hand the Scythian seas* constrains,

And binds the frozen floods in crystal chains,*
Where-e'er the shady night and day-spring come,
All had submitted to the yoke of Rome.
   O Rome! if slaughter be thy only care,
40   If such thy fond desire of impious war,
Turn from thyself, at least, the destined wound,
Till thou art mistress of the world around,
And none to conquer but thyself be found.
Thy foes as yet a juster war afford,
45   And barbarous blood remains to glut thy sword.
But see! her hands on her own vitals seize,
And no destruction but her own can please.
Behold her fields unknowing of the plough!*
Behold her palaces and towers laid low!
50   See where o'erthrown the massy column lies,
While weeds obscene* above the cornice rise.
Here, gaping wide, half-ruined walls remain,
There mouldering pillars nodding roofs sustain.
The landscape, once in various beauty spread
55   With yellow harvests and the flowery mead,
Displays a wild uncultivated face,
Which bushy brakes and brambles vile disgrace;
No human footstep prints th'untrodden green,
No cheerful maid nor villager is seen.
60   Ev'n in her cities famous once and great,
Where thousands crowded in the noisy street,
No sound is heard of human voices now,
But whistling winds through empty dwellings blow,
While passing strangers wonder if they spy
65   One single melancholy face go by.
Nor Pyrrhus'* sword nor Cannae's fatal field
Such universal desolation yield:
Her impious sons have her worst foes surpassed,
And Roman hands have laid Hesperia* waste.
70   But if our fates severely have decreed*
No way but this for Nero to succeed,
If only thus our heroes can be gods,
And earth must pay for their divine abodes,
If heav'n could not the Thunderer* obtain
75   Till giants' wars made room for Jove to reign,
'Tis just, ye gods, nor ought we to complain.

Oppressed with death though dire Pharsalia groan,
Though Latian blood the Punic ghosts* atone,*
Though Pompey's hapless sons renew the war,
80 And Munda view the slaughtered heaps from far,
Though meagre famine in Perusia reign,
Though Mutina with battles fill the plain,
Though Leuca's isle and wide Ambracia's bay
Record the rage of Actium's fatal day,
85 Though servile hands are armed to man the fleet
And on Sicilian seas the navies meet,
All crimes, all horrors, we with joy regard,
Since thou, O Caesar,* art the great reward.
    Vast are the thanks thy grateful Rome should pay
90 To wars which usher in thy sacred sway.*
When, the great business of the world achieved,
Late by the willing stars thou art received,
Through all the blissful seats the news shall roll,
And heaven resound with joy from pole to pole.
95 Whether great Jove resign supreme command
And trust his sceptre to thy abler hand,
Or if thou choose the empire of the day*
And make the sun's unwilling steeds obey,
Auspicious if thou drive the flaming team
100 While earth rejoices in thy gentler beam,
Where-e'er thou reign, with one consenting voice,
The gods and nature shall approve thy choice.
But oh! whatever be thy godhead great,
Fix not in regions too remote thy seat,
105 Nor deign thou near the frozen Bear* to shine,
Nor where the sultry southern stars decline;
Less kindly thence thy influence shall come,
And thy blessed rays obliquely visit Rome.
Press not too much on any part the sphere,
110 Hard were the task thy weight divine to bear;
Soon would the axis feel th'unusual load,
And groaning bend beneath th'incumbent god.*
O'er the mid orb more equal shalt thou rise,
And with a juster balance fix the skies.
115 Serene for ever be that azure space,
No blackening clouds the purer heaven disgrace,
Nor hide from Rome her Caesar's radiant face.

Then shall mankind consent in sweet accord,
And warring nations sheathe the wrathful sword,
120   Peace shall the world in friendly leagues compose,
And Janus' dreadful gates for ever close.*
To me thy present godhead stands confessed,*
Oh, let thy sacred fury fire my breast;
So thou vouchsafe to hear, let Phoebus dwell
125   Still uninvoked in Cirrha's mystic cell,*
By me uncalled, let sprightly Bacchus reign,
And lead the dance on Indian Nysa's plain;
To thee, O Caesar, all my vows belong,
Do thou alone inspire the Roman song.
130   And now the mighty task demands our care*
The fatal source of discord to declare:
What cause accursed produced the dire event,)
Why rage so dire the madding nations rent,)
And peace was driv'n away by one consent.)
135   But thus the malice of our fate commands,
And nothing great to long duration stands:
Aspiring Rome had risen too much in height,
And sunk beneath her own unwieldy weight.
So shall one hour, at last, this globe control,)
140   Break up the vast machine, dissolve the whole,)
And time no more through measured ages roll;)
Then Chaos hoar shall seize his former right,*
And reign with Anarchy and eldest Night;
The starry lamps shall combat in the sky,
145   And lost and blended in each other die;
Quenched in the deep the heavenly fires shall fall,
And ocean, cast abroad, o'erspread the ball;
The moon no more her well-known course shall run,
But rise from western waves, and meet the sun,
150   Ungoverned shall she quit her ancient way,
Herself ambitious to supply the day;
Confusion wild shall all around be hurled,
And discord and disorder tear the world.
Thus power and greatness to destruction haste,)
155   Thus bounds to human happiness are placed,)
And Jove forbids prosperity to last.)
Yet Fortune, when she meant to wreak her hate,
From foreign foes preserved the Roman state,

Nor suffered barbarous hands to give the blow
160   That laid the queen of earth and ocean low;
To Rome herself for enemies she sought,
And Rome herself her own destruction wrought –
Rome, that ne'er knew three lordly heads* before,
First fell by fatal partnership of power.
165   What blind ambition bids your force combine?
What means this frantic league in which you join?
Mistaken men, who hope to share the spoil,
And hold the world within one common toil!
While earth the seas shall in her bosom bear,
170   While earth herself shall hang in ambient air,*
While Phoebus shall his constant task renew,
While through the zodiac night shall day pursue,
No faith, no trust, no friendship shall be known
Among the jealous partners of a throne,
175   But he who reigns shall strive to reign alone.
Nor seek for foreign tales to make this good –
Were not our walls first built in brother's blood?*
Nor did the feud for wide dominion rise,
Nor was the world their impious fury's* prize:
180   Divided power contention still* affords,
And for a village strove the petty lords.*
    The fierce Triumvirate, combined in peace,
Preserved the bond but for a little space,
Still with an awkward, disagreeing grace.
185   'Twas not a league by inclination made,
But bare agreement such as friends persuade.
Desire of war in either chief was seen,
Though interposing Crassus stood between.
Such in the midst the parting Isthmus* lies,
190   While swelling seas on either side arise;
The solid boundaries of earth restrain
The fierce Ionian and Aegean main;
But, if the mound gives way, straight roaring loud
In at the breach the rushing torrents crowd,
195   Raging they meet, the dashing waves run high,
And work their foamy waters to the sky.
So when unhappy Crassus, sadly slain,
Dyed with his blood Assyrian Carrhae's plain,
Sudden the seeming friends in arms engage,*

200   The Parthian sword let loose the Latian rage.
        Ye fierce Arsacidae,* ye foes of Rome,
        Now triumph, you have more than overcome!
        The vanquished felt your victory from far,
        And from that field received their civil war.

205   The sword is now the umpire to decide,
        And part what friendship knew not to divide.
        'Twas hard an empire of so vast a size
        Could not for two ambitious minds suffice;
        The peopled earth and wide extended main

210   Could furnish room for only one to reign.
        When dying Julia* first forsook the light,
        And Hymen's* tapers sunk in endless night,
        The tender ties of kindred-love were torn,
        Forgotten all, and buried in her urn.

215   Oh, if her death had haply been delayed,
        How might the daughter and the wife persuade!
        Like the famed Sabine dames she had been seen*
        To stay the meeting war and stand between,
        On either hand had wooed them to accord,

220   Soothed her fierce father and her furious lord
        To join in peace and sheathe the ruthless sword.
        But this the fatal sisters' doom denied – *
        The friends were severed when the matron died.
        The rival leaders mortal war proclaim,

225   Rage fires their souls with jealousy of fame,
        And emulation fans the rising flame.
       Thee, Pompey, thy past deeds by turns infest,*
        And jealous glory burns within thy breast;
        Thy famed piratic laurel* seems to fade

230   Beneath successful Caesar's rising shade;
        His Gallic wreaths thou viewst with anxious eyes*
        Above thy naval crowns triumphant rise.
        Thee, Caesar, thy long labours past incite,
        Thy use of war, and custom of the fight,

235   While bold ambition prompts thee in the race,
        And bids thy courage scorn a second place.
        Superior power, fierce faction's dearest care,
        One could not brook, and one disdained to share.
        Justly to name the better cause were hard,

240   While greatest names for either side declared –

Victorious Caesar by the gods was crowned,*
The vanquished party was by Cato owned.
Nor came the rivals equal to the field;
One to increasing years began to yield,*
245 Old age came creeping in the peaceful gown,*
And civil functions weighed the soldier down;
Disused to arms, he turned him to the laws,
And pleased himself with popular applause,
With gifts and liberal bounty sought for fame,
250 And loved to hear the vulgar shout his name,
In his own theatre* rejoiced to sit,
Amidst the noisy praises of the pit.
Careless of future ills that might betide, ⎫
No aid he sought to prop his failing side, ⎬
255 But on his former fortune much relied. ⎭
Still seemed he to possess and fill his place,
But stood the shadow of what once he was.
So in the field, with Ceres' bounty spread,
Uprears some ancient oak his reverend head,
260 Chaplets and sacred gifts his boughs adorn,
And spoils of war by mighty heroes worn;
But the first vigour of his root now gone,
He stands dependent on his weight alone,
All bare his naked branches are displayed,
265 And with his leafless trunk he forms a shade;
Yet though the winds his ruin daily threat,
As every blast would heave him from his seat,
Though thousand fairer trees the field supplies
That rich in youthful verdure round him rise,
270 Fixed in his ancient state he yields to none,
And wears the honours of the grove alone.
But Caesar's greatness and his strength was more
Than past renown and antiquated power;
'Twas not the fame of what he once had been,
275 Or tales in old records* and annals seen,
But 'twas a valour, restless, unconfined,
Which no success could sate nor limits bind;
'Twas shame, a soldier's shame, untaught to yield,
That blushed for nothing but an ill-fought field;
280 Fierce in his hopes he was, nor knew to stay,
Where vengeance or ambition led the way,

Still prodigal of war whene'er withstood,
Nor spared to stain the guilty sword with blood;
Urging advantage he improved all odds,
285   And made the most of fortune and the gods,
Pleased to o'erturn whate'er withheld his prize,
And saw the ruin with rejoicing eyes.
Such, while earth trembles and heaven thunders
              loud,*
Darts the swift lightning from the rending cloud,
290   Fierce through the day it breaks and in its flight
The dreadful blast confounds the gazer's sight;
Resistless in its course delights to rove,
And cleaves the temples of its master Jove;
Alike where-e'er it passes or returns,
295   With equal rage the fell destroyer burns;
Then with a whirl full in its strength retires,
And recollects the force of all its scattered fires.
        Motives like these the leading chiefs inspired,
But other thoughts the meaner vulgar fired.
300   Those fatal seeds luxurious vices sow,*
Which ever lay a mighty people low.
To Rome the vanquished earth her tribute paid,
And deadly treasures to her view displayed;
Then truth and simple manners left the place,
305   While riot reared her lewd, dishonest face;
Virtue to full prosperity gave way,
And fled from rapine and the lust of prey.
On every side proud palaces arise,
And lavish gold each common use supplies;
310   Their fathers' frugal tables stand abhorred,   ⎫
And Asia now and Afric* are explored   ⎬
For high-priced dainties and the citron board.*   ⎭
In silken robes the minion* men appear,
Which maids and youthful brides should blush to
              wear.
315   That age, by honest poverty adorned,*
Which brought the manly Romans forth, is scorned;
Wherever aught pernicious does abound,   ⎫
For luxury all lands are ransacked round,   ⎬
And dear-bought deaths the sinking state confound.   ⎭
320   The Curii's and Camilli's little field*

To vast extended territories yield,
And foreign tenants reap the harvest now,
Where once the great dictator held the plough.*
    Rome, ever fond of war, was tired with ease,
325 Ev'n liberty had lost the power to please;
Hence rage and wrath their ready minds invade,
And want could every wickedness persuade;
Hence impious power was first esteemed a good,
Worth being fought with arms and bought with
        blood,
330 With glory tyrants did their country awe,
And violence prescribed the rule to law;
Hence pliant servile voices were constrained,
And force in popular assemblies reigned,
Consuls and tribunes, with opposing might,
335 Joined to confound and overturn the right;
Hence shameful magistrates were made for gold,
And a base people by themselves were sold;
Hence slaughter in the venal field* returns,
And Rome her yearly competitions mourns;
340 Hence debt unthrifty, careless to repay,
And usury still watching for its day;
Hence perjuries in every wrangling court,
And war, the needy bankrupt's last resort.
    Now Caesar, marching swift with wingèd haste,*
345 The summits of the frozen Alps had past,
With vast events and enterprises fraught,
And future wars revolving in his thought.*
Now near the banks of Rubicon he stood,   border to Italy.
When lo, as he surveyed the narrow flood,
350 Amidst the dusky horrors of the night,
A wondrous vision stood confessed to sight.
Her awful head Rome's reverend image reared,
Trembling and sad the matron form appeared,
A towery crown her hoary temples bound,
355 And her torn tresses rudely hung around;
Her naked arms uplifted e'er she spoke,
Then, groaning, thus the mournful silence broke:
'Presumptuous men! oh, whither do you run?
Oh, whither bear you these my ensigns on?
360 If friends to right, if citizens of Rome,

Here to your utmost barrier are you come.'
She said, and sunk within the closing shade;
Astonishment and dread the chief invade,
<u>Stiff rose his starting hair, he stood dismayed,</u>
And on the bank his slackening steps were stayed.
365 'O thou', at length he cried, 'whose hand controls
The forky fire and rattling thunder rolls,
Who from thy Capitol's* exalted height
Dost o'er the wide-spread city cast thy sight,
370 Ye Phrygian gods who guard the Julian line,*
Ye mysteries of Romulus* divine,
Thou Jove, to whom from young Ascanius came ⎫
Thy Alban temple,* and thy Latial name,   ⎬
And thou immortal, sacred vestal flame,   ⎭
375 But chief, oh chiefly, thou majestic Rome,* ⎫
My first, my great divinity, to whom,   ⎬
Thy still successful Caesar, am I come;   ⎭
Nor do thou fear the sword's destructive rage –
With thee my arms no impious war shall wage.
380 On him thy hate, on him thy curse bestow,
Who would persuade thee Caesar is thy foe.
And since to thee I consecrate my toil,
Oh, favour thou my cause, <u>and on thy soldier</u> smile!'
He said, and straight, impatient of delay,
385 Across the swelling flood pursued his way.
So when on sultry Libya's desert sand*
The lion spies the hunter hard at hand,
Couched on the earth the doubtful savage lies,
And waits awhile till all his fury rise,
390 His lashing tail provokes his swelling sides,
And high upon his neck his mane with horror rides;
Then if at length the flying dart infest,
Or the broad spear invade his ample breast,
Scorning the wound he yawns a dreadful roar,
395 And flies like lightning on the hostile Moor.
While with hot skies the fervent summer glows,
The Rubicon an humble river flows;
Through lowly vales he cuts his winding way,
And rolls his ruddy* waters to the sea.
400 His bank on either side a limit stands
Between the Gallic and Ausonian lands.

But stronger now the wintry torrent grows,
The wetting winds had thawed the Alpine snows,
And Cynthia* rising with a blunted beam
405   In the third circle drove her watery team,
A signal sure to raise the swelling stream.
For this, to stem the rapid water's course,
First plunged amidst the flood the bolder horse;
With strength opposed against the stream they lead,
410   While to the smoother ford the foot with ease
            succeed.
        The leader now had passed the torrent o'er,
And reached fair Italy's forbidden shore;
Then rearing on the hostile bank his head,
'Here farewell peace and injured laws,' he said;
415   'Since faith is broke, and leagues are set aside,
Henceforth thou, goddess Fortune, art my guide;
Let fate and war the great event decide.'
He spoke, and, on the dreadful task intent,
Speedy to near Ariminum he bent;
420   To him the Balearic* sling is slow,
And the shaft loiters from the Parthian bow.*
With eager marches swift he reached the town;
As the shades fled the sinking stars were gone,
And Lucifer* the last was left alone.
425   At length the morn, the dreadful morn arose,
Whose beams the first tumultuous rage disclose;
Whether the stormy South prolonged the night,
Or the good gods abhorred the impious sight,
The clouds awhile withheld the mournful light.
430   To the mid forum on the soldier passed,
There halted, and his victor ensigns placed;
With dire alarms from band to band around
The fife, hoarse horn, and rattling trumpets sound.
The starting citizens uprear their heads,*
435   The lustier youth at once forsake their beds;
Hasty they snatch the weapons, which among
Their household-gods in peace had rested long;
Old bucklers of the covering hides bereft,
The mouldering frames disjoined and barely left,
440   Swords with foul rust indented deep they take,
And useless spears with points inverted shake.

*useless tools
as they are
shaking the
bells.*

Soon as their crests the Roman eagles reared,
And Caesar high above the rest appeared,
Each trembling heart with secret horror shook,
445   And silent thus within themselves they spoke:
'O hapless city, O ill-fated walls,
Reared for a curse so near the neighbouring Gauls!
By us destruction ever takes its way,
We first become each bold invader's prey!
450   O that by fate we rather had been placed
Upon the confines of the utmost east!
The frozen north much better might we know,
Mountains of ice and everlasting snow.
Better with wandering Scythians choose to roam,
455   Than fix in fruitful Italy our home,
And guard these dreadful passages to Rome.
Through these the Cimbrians* laid Hesperia waste,
Through these the swarthy Carthaginian passed;*
Whenever fortune threats the Latian states,
460   War, death, and ruin enter at these gates.'
    In secret murmurs thus they sought relief,
While no bold voice proclaimed aloud their grief.
O'er all, one deep, one horrid silence reigns;
As when the rigour of the winter's chains
465   All nature, heav'n and earth at once constrains;
The tuneful, feathered kind forget their lays,
And shivering tremble on the naked sprays;
Ev'n the rude seas composed forget to roar,
And freezing billows stiffen on the shore.
470   The colder shades of night forsook the sky,
When lo, Bellona* lifts her torch on high,
And if the chief, by doubt or shame detained,
Awhile from battle and from blood abstained,
Fortune and fate, impatient of delay,
475   Force every soft, relenting thought away.
A lucky chance a fair pretence supplies,
And justice in his favour seems to rise.
New accidents new stings to rage suggest,
And fiercer fires inflame the warrior's breast.
480   The Senate threatening high, and haughty grown,*
Had driven the wrangling tribunes* from the town,
In scorn of law had chased them through the gate,

And urged them with the factious Gracchi's fate.*
With these, as for redress their course they sped
485   To Caesar's camp, the busy Curio* fled,
Curio, a speaker turbulent and bold,
Of venal eloquence that served for gold,
And principles that might be bought and sold.
A tribune once himself, in loud debate,
490   He strove for public freedom and the state,
Essayed to make the warring nobles bow,
And bring the potent party-leaders low.
To Caesar thus, while thousand cares infest,
Revolving round, the warrior's anxious breast,
495   His speech the ready orator addressed:
    'While yet my voice was useful to my friend,
While 'twas allowed me, Caesar, to defend,
While yet the pleading bar was left me free,
While I could draw uncertain Rome to thee,
500   In vain their force the moody fathers* joined,
In vain to rob thee of thy power combined;
I lengthened out the date of thy command,*
And fixed thy conquering sword within thy hand.
But since the vanquished laws in war are dumb,
505   To thee, behold, an exiled band we come,
For thee with joy our banishment we take,
For thee our household hearths and gods forsake;
Nor hope to see our native city more,
Till victory and thou the loss restore.
510   Th'unready faction, yet confused with fear,
Defenceless, weak, and unresolved appear;
Haste then thy towering eagles on their way;
When fair occasion calls, 'tis fatal to delay.
If twice five years the stubborn Gaul withheld,
515   And set thee hard in many a well-fought field,*
A nobler labour now before thee lies,
The hazard less, yet greater far the prize:
A province that, and portion of the whole,
This the vast head that does mankind control.*
520   Success shall sure attend thee, boldly go,
And win the world at one successful blow.
No triumph now attends thee at the gate,
No temples for thy sacred laurel wait,

But blasting envy hangs upon thy name,
525   Denies thee right and robs thee of thy fame,
Imputes as crimes the nations overcome,
And makes it treason to have fought for Rome;
Ev'n he who took thy Julia's plighted hand,
Waits to deprive thee of thy just command.
530   Since Pompey then, and those upon his side,
Forbid thee the world's empire to divide,
Assume that sway which best mankind may bear,
And rule alone what they disdain to share.'
      He said; his words the listening chief engage,
535   And fire his breast already prone to rage.
Not peals of loud applause with greater force,
At Grecian Elis,* rouse the fiery horse,
When eager for the course each nerve he strains,
Hangs on the bit and tugs the stubborn reins,
540   At every shout erects his quivering ears,
And his broad breast upon the barrier bears.
Sudden he bids the troops draw out, and straight
The thronging legions round their ensigns wait;
Then thus, the crowd composing with a look,
545   And with his hand commanding silence, spoke:
      'Fellows in arms, who chose with me to bear ⎫
The toils and dangers of a tedious war,   ⎬
And conquer to this tenth revolving year,   ⎭
See what reward the grateful Senate yields,*
550   For the lost blood which stains yon northern fields,
For wounds, for winter camps, for Alpine snow,
And all the deaths the brave can undergo.
See! the tumultuous city is alarmed,
As if another Hannibal were armed;
555   The lusty youth are culled to fill the bands,
And each tall grove falls by the shipwright's hands;
Fleets are equipped, the field with armies spread,
And all demand devoted* Caesar's head.
If thus, while fortune yields us her applause,
560   While the gods call us on and own our cause,
If thus returning conquerors they treat,
How had they used us flying from defeat,
If fickle chance of war had proved unkind,
And the fierce Gauls pursued us from behind?

565 But let their boasted hero* leave his home, }
　　 Let him, dissolved with lazy leisure, come, }
　　 With every noisy, talking tongue in Rome; }
　　 Let loud Marcellus* troops of gown-men head,
　　 And their great Cato peaceful burghers lead.
570 Shall his base followers, a venal train,
　　 For ages bid their idol Pompey reign?
　　 Shall his ambition still be thought no crime,
　　 His breach of laws and triumph e'er the time?
　　 Still shall he gather honours and command,
575 And grasp all rule in his rapacious hand?
　　 What need I name the violated laws,*
　　 And famine made the servant of his cause?*
　　 Who knows not how the trembling judge beheld
　　 The peaceful court with armèd legions filled?
580 When the bold soldier, justice to defy,
　　 In the mid forum reared his ensigns high,
　　 When glittering swords the pale assembly scared, }
　　 When all for death and slaughter stood prepared, }
　　 And Pompey's arms were guilty Milo's guard?* }
585 And now, disdaining peace and needful ease,
　　 Nothing but rule and government can please.
　　 Aspiring still, as ever, to be great,
　　 He robs his age of rest to vex the state;
　　 On war intent, to that he bends his cares,
590 And for the field, for battle now prepares.
　　 He copies from his master Sulla* well,
　　 And would the dire example far excel.
　　 Hyrcanian* tigers fierceness thus retain, }
　　 Whom in the woods their horrid mothers train, }
595 To chase the herds, and surfeit on the slain. }
　　 Such, Pompey, still has been thy greedy thirst,
　　 In early love of impious slaughter nursed,
　　 Since first thy infant cruelty essayed
　　 To lick the cursed dictator's* reeking blade.
600 None ever give the savage nature o'er,
　　 Whose jaws have once been drenched in floods of
　　　　 gore.
　　　 But whither would a power so wide extend?
　　 Where will thy long ambition find an end?

Remember him who taught thee to be great; ⎫
605 Let him who chose to quit the sovereign seat, ⎬
Let thy own Sulla warn thee to retreat.* ⎭
Perhaps for that too boldly I withstand,
Nor yield my conquering eagles on command,
Since the Cilician pirate strikes his sail,*
610 Since o'er the Pontic king* thy arms prevail,
Since the poor prince, a weary life o'er-past,
By thee and poison is subdued at last,
Perhaps one latest province* yet remains,
And vanquished Caesar* must receive thy chains.
615 But though my labours lose their just reward,
Yet let the Senate these my friends regard;
Whate'er my lot, my brave victorious bands
Deserve to triumph, whosoe'er commands.
Where shall my weary veteran rest? Oh, where
620 Shall virtue worn with years and arms repair?
What town is for his late repose assigned?
Where are the promised lands he hoped to find,
Fields for his plough, a country village seat,
Some little, comfortable,* safe retreat,
625 Where failing age at length from toil may cease,
And waste the poor remains of life in peace?
But march! Your long victorious ensigns rear,
Let valour in its own just cause appear.
When for redress entreating armies call,
630 They who deny just things permit them all.
The righteous gods shall surely own the cause
Which seeks not spoil nor empire but the laws.
Proud lords and tyrants to depose we come,
And save from slavery submissive Rome.'
635   He said; a doubtful, sullen, murmuring sound
Ran through the unresolving vulgar* round;
The seeds of piety their rage restrained,
And somewhat* of their country's love remained;
These the rude passions of their souls withstood,
640 Elate with conquest and inured to blood;
But soon the momentary virtue failed,
And war and dread of Caesar's frown prevailed.
Straight Laelius* from amidst the rest stood forth;
An old centurion of distinguished worth;

645 The oaken wreath* his hardy temples wore,
  Mark of a citizen preserved he bore.
   'If against thee', he cried, 'I may exclaim,
  Thou greatest leader of the Roman name,
  If truth for injured honour may be bold,
650 What lingering patience does thy arms withhold?
  Canst thou distrust our faith so often tried,
  In thy long wars not shrinking from thy side?
  While in my veins this vital torrent flows,
  This heaving breath within my bosom blows,
655 While yet these arms sufficient vigour yield
  To dart the javelin and to lift the shield,
  While these remain, my general, would thou own
  The vile dominion of the lazy gown?
  Would thou the lordly Senate choose to bear
660 Rather than conquer in a civil war?
  With thee the Scythian wilds we'll wander o'er,
  With thee the burning Libyan sands explore,
  And tread the Syrt's* inhospitable shore.
  Behold! this hand, to nobler labours trained,
665 For thee the servile oar has not disdained,
  For thee the swelling seas was taught to plough,
  Through the Rhine's whirling stream to force thy prow,
  That all the vanquished world to thee might bow.
  Each faculty, each power thy will obey,
670 And inclination ever leads the way.
  No friend, no fellow-citizen I know,
  Whom Caesar's trumpet once proclaims a foe.
  By the long labours of thy sword I swear,
  By all thy fame acquired in ten years war,
675 By thy past triumphs and by those to come,
  No matter where the vanquished be, nor whom,
  Bid me to strike my dearest brother dead,
  To bring my aged father's hoary head,
  Or stab the pregnant partner of my bed,
680 Though nature plead, and stop my trembling hand,
  I swear to execute thy dread command.
  Dost thou delight to spoil the wealthy gods,
  And scatter flames through all their proud abodes?
  See through thy camp our ready torches burn,
  Moneta* soon her sinking fane* shall mourn.

Would thou yon haughty factious Senate brave,
And awe the Tuscan river's yellow wave?
On Tiber's bank thy ensigns shall be placed,
And thy bold soldier lay Hesperia waste.
690　Dost thou devote some hostile city's walls?
Beneath our thundering rams the ruin falls –
She falls, ev'n though thy wrathful sentence doom
The world's imperial mistress, mighty Rome.'
　　　He said; the ready legions vow to join
695　Their chief beloved in every bold design;
All lift their well-approving hands on high,
And rend with peals of loud applause the sky.
Such is the sound when Thracian Boreas* spreads
His weighty wing o'er Ossa's piney heads –
700　At once the noisy groves are all inclined,*
And, bending, roar beneath the sweeping wind,
At once their rattling branches all they rear,
And drive the leafy clamour through the air.
　　　Caesar with joy the ready bands beheld,
705　Urged on by fate and eager for the field;
Swift orders straight the scattered warriors call
From every part of wide-extended Gaul;
And lest his fortune languish by delay,
To Rome the moving ensigns speed their way.*
710　　Some, at the bidding of the chief, forsake
Their fixed encampment near the Leman lake;*
Some from Vogesus'* lofty rocks withdraw,
Placed on those heights the Lingones to awe –
The Lingones still frequent in alarms,
715　And rich in many-coloured painted arms.
Others from Isara's low torrent came,
Who winding keeps through many a mead his name,
But seeks the sea with waters not his own,
Lost and confounded in the nobler Rhone.
720　Their garrison the Ruthen city send,
Whose youth's long locks in yellow rings depend.*
No more the Varus and the Atax feel
The lordly burden of the Latian keel.
Alcides' fane* the troops commanded leave,
725　Where winding rocks the peaceful flood receive;
Nor Corus there, nor Zephyrus resort,*

Nor roll rude surges in the sacred port;
Circius' loud blast alone is heard to roar,
And vex the safety of Monoechus' shore.
730   The legions move from Gallia's farthest side,
Washed by the restless ocean's various tide;
Now o'er the land flows in the pouring main, ⎱
Now rears the land its rising head again, ⎱
And seas and earth alternate rule maintain. ⎭
735   If, driv'n by winds from the far distant pole,
This way and that the floods revolving roll,
Or if, compelled by Cynthia's silver beam,
Obedient Tethys* heaves the swelling stream,
Or if, by heat attracted to the sky, ⎱
740   Old Ocean lifts his heapy waves on high, ⎱
And briny deeps the wasting sun supply, ⎭
What cause so e'er the wondrous motion guide,*
And press the ebb or raise the flowing tide,
Be that your task, ye sages, to explore,
745   Who search the secret springs of nature's power;
To me, for so the wiser gods ordain,
Untraced the mystery shall still remain.
From fair Nemossus moves a warlike band,
From Atur's banks and the Tarbellian strand,
750   Where winding round the coast pursues its way,
And folds the sea within a gentle bay.
The Santones are now with joy released
From hostile inmates and their Roman guest;
Now the Bituriges forget their fears,
755   And Suessons nimble with unwieldy spears,
Exult the Leuci and the Remi now,
Expert in javelins and the bending bow;
The Belgae taught on covered wains to ride,
The Sequani the wheeling horse to guide;
760   The bold Averni* who from Ilium come,
And boast an ancient brotherhood with Rome;
The Nervii, oft rebelling, oft subdued,
Whose hands in Cotta's slaughter were imbrued;*
Vangiones like loose Sarmatians dressed,
765   Who with rough hides their brawny thighs invest;
Batavians fierce, whom brazen trumps delight,
And with hoarse rattlings animate to fight;

The nations where the Cinga's waters flow,
And Pyrenean mountains stand in snow;
770 Those where slow Arar meets the rapid Rhone,
And with his stronger stream is hurried down;
Those o'er the mountains' lofty summit spread,
Where high Gebenna lifts her hoary head;
With these the Trevir, and Ligurian shorn,
775 Whose brow no more long falling locks adorn,
Though chief amongst the Gauls he wont to deck,
With ringlets comely spread, his graceful neck;
And you, where Hesus' horrid altar stands,*
Where dire Teutates human blood demands,
780 Where Taranis by wretches is obeyed,
And vies in slaughter with the Scythian maid – *
All see with joy the war's departing rage
Seek distant lands and other foes engage.
You too, ye bards,* whom sacred raptures fire
785 To chant your heroes to your country's lyre,
Who consecrate in your immortal strain
Brave patriot souls in righteous battle slain,
Securely now the tuneful task renew,
And noblest themes in deathless songs pursue.
790 The druids now, while arms are heard no more,
Old mysteries and barbarous rites restore,
A tribe who singular religion love,
And haunt the lonely coverts of the grove.
To these, and these of all mankind alone,*
795 The gods are sure revealed or sure unknown;
If dying mortals' dooms they sing aright,
No ghosts descend to dwell in dreadful night,
No parting souls to grisly Pluto go,
Nor seek the dreary, silent shades below,
800 But forth they fly immortal in their kind,
And other bodies in new worlds they find;
Thus life for ever runs its endless race,
And, like a line, death but divides the space,
A stop which can but for a moment last,
805 A point between the future and the past.
Thrice happy they beneath their northern skies,
Who that worst fear, the fear of death, despise;
Hence they no cares for this frail being feel,

But rush undaunted on the pointed steel,
810   Provoke approaching fate, and bravely scorn
To spare that life which must so soon return.
You too towards Rome advance, ye warlike band,
That wont the shaggy Cauci to withstand,
Whom once a better order did assign
815   To guard the passes of the German Rhine;
Now from the fenceless banks you march away,
And leave the world the fierce barbarians' prey.
    While thus the numerous troops, from every part
Assembling, raise their daring leader's heart,
820   O'er Italy he takes his warlike way;
  The neighbouring towns his summons straight obey,
And on their walls his ensigns high display.
Meanwhile the busy messenger of ill,
Officious fame, supplies new terror still;
825   A thousand slaughters and ten thousand fears
She whispers in the trembling vulgar's ears.
Now comes a frighted messenger to tell
Of ruins which the country round befell;
The foe to fair Mevania's walls is passed,
830   And lays Clitumnus' fruitful pastures waste;
Where Nar's white waves* with Tiber mingling fall,
Range the rough German and the rapid Gaul.
But when himself, when Caesar they would paint,
The stronger image makes description faint;
835   No tongue can speak with what amazing dread
Wild thought presents him at his army's head;
Unlike the man familiar to their eyes,
Horrid he seems and of gigantic size;
Unnumbered eagles rise amidst his train,
840   And millions seem to hide the crowded plain.
Around him all the various nations join,
Between the snowy Alps and distant Rhine.
He draws the fierce barbarians from their home,
With rage surpassing theirs he seems to come,
845   And urge them on to spoil devoted Rome.
Thus fear does half the work of lying fame,
And cowards thus their own misfortunes frame,
By their own feigning fancies are betrayed,
And groan beneath those ills themselves have made.

850   Nor these alarms the crowd alone infest,
        But ran alike through every beating breast;
        With equal dread the grave patricians shook,
        Their seats abandoned, and the court forsook.
        The scattering fathers quit the public care,
855   And bid the consuls for the war prepare.
        Resolved on flight, yet still unknowing where
        To fly from danger or for aid repair,
        Hasty and headlong differing paths they tread,
        As blind impulse* and wild distraction lead;
860   The crowd, a hurrying, heartless* train, succeed.
        Who that the lamentable sight beheld,
        The wretched fugitives that hid the field,
        Would not have thought the flames with rapid haste
        Destroying wide had laid their city waste,
865   Or groaning earth had shook beneath their feet,
        While threatening fabrics nodded o'er the street.
        By such unthinking rashness were they led,
        Such was the madness which their fears had bred,
        As if, of every other hope bereft,
870   To fly from Rome were all the safety left.
        So when the stormy South* is heard to roar,
        And rolls huge billows from the Libyan shore,
        When rending sails flit* with the driving blast,
        And with a crash down comes the lofty mast,
875   Some coward master leaps from off the deck,
        And hasty to despair prevents the wreck,
        And, though the bark unbroken hold her way,
        His trembling crew all plunge into the sea.
        From doubtful thus they run to certain harms,
880   And flying from the city rush to arms.
        Then sons forsook their sires unnerved* and old,
        Nor weeping wives their husbands could withhold,
        Each left his guardian Lares* unadored,
        Nor with one parting prayer their aid implored;
885   None stopped, or sighing turned for one last view,
        Or bid the city of his birth adieu.
        The headlong crowd regardless urge their way,
        Though ev'n their gods and country ask their stay,
        And pleading nature beg them to delay.
890   What means, ye gods, this changing in your doom?

Freely you grant, but quickly you resume.
Vain is the short-lived sovereignty you lend,
The pile you raise you deign not to defend.
See where, forsaken by her native bands,
895   All desolate the once great city stands!
She whom her swarming citizens made proud,
Where once the vanquished nations wont to crowd,
Within the circuit of whose ample space
Mankind might meet at once,* and find a place;
900   A wide defenceless desert now she lies,
And yields herself the victor's easy prize.
The camp entrenched securest slumbers yields,
Though hostile arms beset the neighbouring fields;
Rude banks of earth the hasty soldier rears,
905   And in the turfy wall forgets his fears,
While, Rome, thy sons all tremble from afar,
And scatter at the very name of war,
Nor on thy towers depend nor rampart's height,
Nor trust their safety with thee for a night.
910   Yet one excuse absolved the panic dread –
The vulgar justly feared when Pompey fled.
And lest sweet hope might mitigate their woes,
And expectation better times disclose,
On every breast presaging terror sate,
915   And threatened plain some yet more dismal fate.
The gods declare their menaces around,*
Earth, air, and seas in prodigies abound;
Then stars, unknown before, appeared to burn,
And foreign flames about the pole to turn;
920   Unusual fires by night were seen to fly,
And dart obliquely through the gloomy sky.
Then horrid comets shook their fatal hair,*
And bade proud royalty for change prepare;
Now dart swift lightnings through the azure clear,
925   And meteors now in various forms appear;
Some like the javelin shoot extended long,
While some like spreading lamps in heaven are hung.
And though no gathering clouds the day control,
Through skies serene portentous thunders roll,
930   Fierce blasting bolts from northern regions come,
And aim their vengeance at imperial Rome.

The stars that twinkled in the lonely night
Now lift their bolder head in day's broad light;
The moon, in all her brother's beams arrayed,
935   Was blotted by the earth's approaching shade;
The sun himself, in his meridian race,
In sable darkness veiled his brighter face;
The trembling world beheld his fading ray,
And mourned despairing for the loss of day.
940   Such was he seen, when backward to the east   *not good.*
He fled, abhorring dire Thyestes' feast.*
Sicilian Etna then was heard to roar,
While Mulciber* let loose his fiery store;
Nor rose the flames, but with a downward tide
945   Tow'rds Italy their burning torrent guide.
Charybdis' dogs howl doleful o'er the flood,*
And all her whirling waves run red with blood;
The vestal fire upon the altar died,*
And o'er the sacrifice the flames divide;
950   The parting points with double streams ascend,*
To show the Latian festivals must end.
Such from the Theban brethren's pile arose,*
Signal of impious and immortal foes.
With openings vast the gaping earth gave way,*
955   And in her inmost womb received the day;
The swelling seas o'er lofty mountains flow,
And nodding Alps shook off their ancient snow.
Then wept the demigods of mortal birth,
And sweating Lares trembled on the hearth.
960   In temples then, recording stories tell,
Untouched the sacred gifts and garlands fell;
Then birds obscene, with inauspicious flight
And screamings dire, profaned the hallowed light;
The savage kind forsook the desert wood,
965   And in the streets disclosed their horrid brood;
Then speaking beasts with human sounds were heard,
And monstrous births the teeming mothers scared.
Among the crowd religious fears disperse
The saws of Sibyls and foreboding verse.
970   Bellona's priests, a barbarous frantic train,*
Whose mangled arms a thousand wounds distain,*
Toss their wild locks, and with a dismal yell

The wrathful gods and coming woes foretell.
Lamenting ghosts amidst their ashes mourn,
975 And groanings echo from the marble urn;
The rattling clank of arms is heard around,
And voices loud in lonely woods resound;
Grim spectres everywhere affright the eye,
Approaching glare, and pass with horror by.
980 A Fury fierce about the city walks,
Hell-born and horrible of size she stalks;
A flaming pine she brandishes in air,
And hissing loud uprise her snaky hair;
Where-e'er her round accursed the monster takes,
985 The pale inhabitant his house forsakes.
Such to Lycurgus was the phantom seen,*
Such the dire visions of the Theban queen;*
Such, at his cruel stepmother's command,*
Before Alcides did Megaera stand;
990 With dread till then unknown the hero shook,
Though he had dared on Hell's grim king to look.*
Amid the deepest silence of the night
Shrill-sounding clarions animate the fight,
The shouts of meeting armies seem to rise,
995 And the loud battle shakes the gloomy skies.
Dead Sulla in the Martian Field* ascends,
And mischiefs mighty as his own portends;
Near Anio's stream old Marius* rears his head,
The hinds* beheld his grisly form, and fled.
1000   The state thus threatened, by old custom taught,
For counsel to the Tuscan prophets sought;*
Of these the chief, for learning famed and age,
Arruns by name, a venerable sage,
At Luna* lived; none better could descry
1005 What bodes the lightning's journey through the sky;
Presaging* veins and fibres well he knew,
And omens read aright from every wing that flew.
First he commands to burn the monstrous breed,
Sprung from mixed species and discordant seed,
1010 Forbidden and accursèd births, which come
Where nature's laws designed a barren womb.
Next the remaining trembling tribes he calls,
To pass with solemn rites about their walls,

In holy march to visit all around,
1015   And with lustrations purge the utmost bound.
The sovereign priests the long procession lead, ⎫
Inferior orders in the train succeed,   ⎬
Arrayed all duly in the Gabine weed.*   ⎭
There the chaste head of Vesta's choir appears,
1020   A sacred fillet binds her reverend hairs;
To her in sole preeminence is due
Phrygian Minerva's* awful shrine to view.
Next the Fifteen* in order pass along,
Who guard the fatal Sibyls' secret song;
1025   To Almon's stream Cybele's form they bear,*
And wash the goddess each returning year.
The Titian brotherhood,* the augur's band,
Observing flights on the left lucky hand,
The Seven ordained Jove's holy feast to deck,
1030   The Salii* blithe with bucklers* on the neck,
All marching in their order just appear,
And last the generous Flamens* close the rear.
While these through ways uncouth and tiresome
              ground
Patient perform their long, laborious round,
1035   Arruns collects the marks of heaven's dread flame,* ⎫
In earth he hides them with religious hand,   ⎬
Murmurs a prayer, then gives the place a name,   ⎬
And bids the fixed bidental* hallowed stand.   ⎭
Next from the herd a chosen male is sought,
1040   And soon before the ready altar brought.
And now the seer the sacrifice began,
The pouring wine upon the victim ran,
The mingled meal upon his brow was placed,
The crooked knife the destined line had traced,
1045   When with reluctant rage th'impatient beast
The rites unpleasing to the god confessed.
At length compelled his stubborn head to bow,
Vanquished he yields him to the fatal blow;
The gushing veins no cheerful crimson pour,
1050   But stain with poisonous black the sacred floor.
The paler prophet stood with horror struck,
Then with a hasty hand the entrails took,
And sought the angry gods again, but there

Prognostics worse and sadder signs appear:
1055 The pallid guts with spots were marbled o'er,
With thin, cold serum stained and livid gore;
The liver wet with putrid streams he spied,
And veins that threatened on the hostile side;*
Part of the heaving lungs is nowhere found,
1060 And thinner films the severed entrails bound;
No usual motion stirs the panting heart,
The chinky vessels ooze on every part;
The caul,* where wrapped the close intestines lie,
Betrays its dark recesses to the eye.
1065 One prodigy superior threatened still,
The never-failing harbinger of.ill:
Lo, by the fibrous liver's rising head,
A second rival prominence is spread;
All sunk and poor the friendly part appears,
1070 And a pale, sickly, withering visage wears,
While high and full the adverse vessels ride,*
And drive impetuous on their purple tide.
Amazed the sage foresaw th'impending fate, ⎫
'Ye gods!', he cried, 'forbid me to relate ⎬
1075 What woes on this devoted people wait. ⎭
Nor dost thou, Jove, in these our rites partake,
Nor smile propitious on the prayer we make;
The dreadful Stygian gods this victim claim,
And to our sacrifice the Furies came.
1080 The ills we fear command us to be dumb,
Yet somewhat worse than what we fear shall come.
But may the gods be gracious from on high, ⎫
Some better prosperous event supply; ⎬
Fibres may err and augury may lie; ⎭
1085 Arts may be false by which our sires divined,
And Tages* taught them to abuse mankind.'
Thus darkly he the prophecy expressed,
And riddling sung the double-dealing* priest.
    But Figulus* exclaims (to science bred,
1090 And in the gods' mysterious secrets read,
Whom nor Egyptian Memphis' sons excelled,
Nor with more skill the rolling orbs beheld –
Well could he judge the labours of the sphere,
And calculate the just revolving year);

1095   'The stars', he cries, 'are in confusion hurled,
        And wandering error quite misguides the world,
        Or, if the laws of nature yet remain,
        Some swift destruction now the fates ordain.
        Shall earth's wide opening jaws for ruin call,
1100   And sinking cities to the centre fall?
        Shall raging drought infest the sultry sky?
        Shall faithless earth the promised crop deny?
        Shall poisonous vapours o'er the waters brood,
        And taint the limpid spring and silver flood?
1105   Ye gods! what ruin does your wrath prepare?
        Comes it from heav'n, from earth, from seas, or air?
        The lives of many to a period* haste,
        And thousands shall together breathe their last.
        If Saturn's sullen beams were lifted high,
1110   And baleful reigned ascendant o'er the sky,
        Then moist Aquarius deluges might rain,
        And earth once more lie sunk beneath the main;
        Or did thy glowing beams, O Phoebus, shine
        Malignant in the Lion's scorching sign,
1115   Wide o'er the world consuming fires might roll,
        And heaven be seen to flame from pole to pole.
        Through peaceful orbits these unangry glide – ⎞
        But, god of battles, what dost thou provide,   ⎟
        Who in the threatening Scorpion dost preside? ⎠
1120   With potent wrath around thy influence streams,
        And the whole monster kindles at thy beams,
        While Jupiter's more gentle rays decline,
        And Mercury with Venus faintly shine;
        The wandering lights are darkened all and gone,
1125   And Mars now lords it o'er the heavens alone.
        Orion's starry falchion* blazing wide*
        Refulgent glitters by his dreadful side.
        War comes, and savage slaughter must abound,
        The sword of violence shall right confound;
1130   The blackest crimes fair virtue's name shall wear,
        And impious fury rage for many a year.
        Yet ask not thou an end of arms, O Rome,
        Thy peace must with a lordly master come.

Protract destruction and defer thy chain, }
1135 The sword alone prevents the tyrant's reign, }
And civil wars thy liberty maintain.' }
  The heartless vulgar to the sage give heed,
New rising fears his words foreboding breed,
When lo, more dreadful wonders strike their eyes:
1140 Forth through the streets a Roman matron flies,
Mad as the Thracian dames that bound along,
And chant Lyaeus* in their frantic song;
Enthusiastic heavings swelled her breast,
And thus her voice the Delphic god confessed:
1145   'Where dost thou snatch me, Paean,* wherefore
          bear
Through cloudy heights and tracts of pathless air?
I see Pangaean mountains white with snow,*
Haemus, and wide Philippi's fields below.
Say, Phoebus, wherefore does this fury rise?
1150 What mean these spears and shields before my eyes?
I see the Roman battles crowd the plain,
I see the war, but seek the foe in vain.
Again I fly, I seek the rising day,
Where Nile's Egyptian waters take their way;
1155 I see, I know upon the guilty shore
The hero's* headless trunk besmeared with gore.
The Syrts and Libyan sands beneath me lie,
Thither Emathia's scattered relics* fly.
Now o'er the cloudy Alps I stretch my flight,
1160 And soar above Pyrene's* airy height;
To Rome, my native Rome, I turn again,
And see the Senate reeking with the slain.*
Again the moving chiefs their arms prepare,
Again I follow through the world the war.
1165 O give me, Phoebus, give me to explore }
Some region new, some undiscovered shore – }
I saw Philippi's fatal fields before.' }
  She said; the weary rage began to cease,
And left the fainting prophetess in peace.

BOOK TWO

Now manifest the wrath divine appeared,
And nature through the world the war declared;
Teeming with monsters, sacred law she broke,
And dire events in all her works bespoke.
5   Thou Jove, who dost in heaven supremely reign, ⎫
Why does thy providence these signs ordain, ⎬
And give us prescience to increase our pain? ⎭
Doubly we bear thy dread inflicting doom,
And feel our miseries before they come.
10 Whether the great, creating parent soul,*
When first from chaos rude he formed the whole,
Disposed futurity with certain hand,
And bade the necessary causes stand,
Made one decree for ever to remain,
15 And bound himself in fate's eternal chain,
Or whether fickle fortune leads the dance,
Nothing is fixed, but all things come by chance,
Whate'er thou shalt ordain, thou ruling power,
Unknown and sudden be the dreadful hour;
20 Let mortals to their future fate be blind,
And hope relieve the miserable mind.
      While thus the wretched citizens behold
What certain ills the faithful gods foretold,*
Justice suspends her course in mournful Rome,
25 And all the noisy courts at once are dumb;*
No honours shine in the distinguished weed,
Nor rods* the purple magistrate precede;
A dismal, silent sorrow spreads around,
No groan is heard, nor one complaining sound.
30 So when some generous youth resigns his breath,
And parting sinks in the last pangs of death,
With ghastly eyes, and many a lift-up hand,
Around his bed the still attendants stand,
No tongue as yet presumes his fate to tell,
35 Nor speaks aloud the solemn last farewell;
As yet the mother by her darling lies,

Nor breaks lamenting into frantic cries,
And, though he stiffens in her fond embrace
His eyes are set and livid pale his face;

40 Horror a while prevents the swelling tear,
Nor is her passion grief as yet but fear;
In one fixed posture motionless she keeps,
And wonders at her woe before she weeps.
The matrons sad their rich attire lay by,

45 And to the temples madly crowding fly;
Some on the shrines their gushing sorrows pour,
Some dash their breasts against the marble floor,
Some on the sacred thresholds rend their hair,
And howling seek the gods with horrid prayer.

50 Nor Jove received the wailing suppliants all,
In various fanes* on various powers they call.
No altar then, no god was left alone,
Unvexed by some impatient parent's moan.
Of these one wretch her grief above the rest,

55 With visage torn and mangled arms, confessed.
'Ye mothers, beat', she cried, 'your bosoms now,
Now tear the curling honours* from your brow.
The present hour ev'n all your tears demands,*
While doubtful fortune yet suspended stands.

60 When one shall conquer, then for joy prepare,
The victor chief, at least, shall end the war.'
Thus from renewed complaints they seek relief,
And only find fresh causes out for grief.
    The men too, as to different camps they go,

65 Join their sad voices to the public woe;
Impatient to the gods they raise their cry,
And thus expostulate with those on high:
    'O hapless times! Oh, that we had been born,
When Carthage made our vanquished country
            mourn!

70 Well had we then been numbered with the slain
On Trebia's banks, or Cannae's fatal plain.*
Nor ask we peace, ye powers, nor soft repose –
Give us new wars and multitudes of foes;
Let every potent city arm for fight,

75 And all the neighbour nations round unite;
From Median Susa let the Parthians come,

And Massagetes* beyond their Ister roam;
Let Elbe and Rhine's unconquered springs send forth
The yellow* Suevi* from the farthest north;
80   Let the conspiring world in arms engage,
And save us only from domestic rage.
Here let the hostile Dacian inroads make,*
And there his way the Gete invader take;
Let Caesar in Iberia* tame the foe,   ⎫
85   Let Pompey break the deadly eastern bow,*   ⎬
And Rome no hand unarmed for battle know.   ⎭
But if Hesperia stand condemned by fate,
And ruin on our name and nation wait,
Now dart thy thunder, dread almighty sire,
90   Let all thy flaming heavens descend in fire,
On chiefs and parties hurl thy bolts alike,
And, e'er their crimes have made them guilty, strike.
Is it a cause so worthy of our care
That power may fall to this or that man's share?
95   Do we for this the gods and conscience brave,
That one may rule and make the rest a slave?
When thus, ev'n liberty we scarce should buy,
But think a civil war a price too high.'
     Thus groan they at approaching dire events,
100   And thus expiring piety laments.
Meanwhile the hoary sire* his years deplores,
And age that former miseries restores;
He hates his weary life prolonged for woe,
Worse days to see, more impious rage to know.
105   Then fetching old examples from afar,
''Twas thus', he cries, 'fate ushered in the war,*
When Cimbrians fierce, and Libya's swarthy lord,*
Had fall'n before triumphant Marius' sword;
Yet to Minturnae's marsh the victor fled,*
110   And hid in oozy flags* his exiled head.
The faithless soil the hunted chief relieved,
And sedgy waters fortune's pledge received.
Deep in a dungeon plunged at length he lay,*   ⎫
Where gyves* and rankling* fetters eat their way,   ⎬
115   And noisome vapours on his vitals prey.   ⎭
Ordained at ease to die in wretched Rome,
He suffered then for wickedness to come.

In vain his foes had armed the Cimbrian's hand –
Death will not always wait upon command;
120 About to strike, the slave with horror shook,
The useless steel his loosening gripe* forsook;
Thick flashing flames a light unusual gave,
And sudden shone around the gloomy cave;
Dreadful the gods of guilt before him stood,
125 And Marius terrible in future blood,
When thus a voice began: "Rash man forbear,
Nor touch that head which fate resolves to spare;
Thousands are doomed beneath his arm to bleed,
And countless deaths before his own decreed;
130 Thy wrath and purpose to destroy is vain –
Would'st thou avenge thee for thy nation slain?*
Preserve this man, and in some coming day
The Cimbrian slaughter well he shall repay."
No pitying god, no power to mortals good,
135 Could save a savage wretch who joyed in blood,
But fate reserved him to perform its doom,
And be the minister of wrath to Rome.
By swelling seas too favourably tossed,
Safely he reached Numidia's hostile coast;
140 There, driv'n from man, to wilds he took his way,
And on the earth, where once he conquered, lay;
There in the lone, unpeopled desert field
Proud Carthage in her ruins he beheld,
Amidst her ashes pleased he sat him down,
145 And joyed in the destruction of the town.
The genius of the place, with mutual hate,
Reared its sad head and smiled at Marius' fate;
Each with delight surveyed their fallen foe,
And each forgave the gods that laid the other low.
150 There with new fury was his soul possessed,
And Libyan rage* collected in his breast.
Soon as returning fortune owned his cause,*
Troops of revolting bond-men forth he draws,
Cut-throats and slaves resort to his command,
155 And arms were giv'n to every baser hand.
None worthily the leader's standard bore,
Unstained with blood or blackest crimes before;
Villains of fame to fill his bands were sought,

And to his camp increase of crimes they brought.
160   Who can relate the horrors of that day,
When first these walls became the victor's prey?
With what a stride devouring slaughter passed,
And swept promiscuous orders in her haste!*
O'er noble and plebeian ranged the sword,
165   Nor pity or remorse one pause afford.
The sliding streets with blood were clotted o'er,
And sacred temples stood in pools of gore.
The ruthless steel, impatient of delay,
Forbade the sire to linger out his day;
170   It struck the bending father to the earth,
And cropped the wailing infant at his birth.
(Can innocents the rage of parties know,
And they who ne'er offended find a foe?)
Age is no plea, and childhood no defence,
175   To kill is all the murderer's pretence.
Rage stays not to enquire who ought to die,
Numbers must fall, no matter which or why;
Each in his hand a grisly visage bears,
And as the trophy of his virtue wears.
180   Who wants a prize straight rushes through the streets,
And undistinguished mows the first he meets;
The trembling crowd with fear officious strive,
And those who kiss the tyrant's* hand survive.*
Oh, could you fall so low, degenerate race,
185   And purchase safety at a price so base?
What though the sword was master of your doom,
Though Marius could have giv'n you years to come,
Can Romans live by infamy so mean?
But soon your changing fortune shifts the scene;
190   Short is your date, you only live to mourn
Your hopes deceived, and Sulla's swift return.
The vulgar falls and none laments his fate –
Sorrow has hardly leisure for the great.
What tears could Baebius'* hasty death deplore?
195   A thousand hands his mangled carcass tore,
His scattered entrails round the streets were tossed,
And in a moment all the man was lost.
Who wept Antonius'* murder to behold,
Whose moving tongue the mischief oft foretold?

200 Spite of his age and eloquence he bled,
The barbarous soldier snatched his hoary head,
Dropping* he bore it to his joyful lord,
And, while he feasted, placed it on the board.
The Crassi* both by Fimbria's* hand were slain,
205 And bleeding magistrates the pulpit* stain.
Then did the doom of that neglecting hand,*
Thy fate, O holy Scaevola, command;
In vain for succour to the gods he flies,
The priest before the vestal altar dies;
210 A feeble stream poured forth th'exhausted sire,
And spared to quench the ever-living fire.
The seventh returning fasces now appear,*
And bring stern Marius' latest destined year;
Thus the long toils of changing life o'erpast,
215 Hoary and full of days he breathed his last.
While fortune frowned, her fiercest wrath he bore,
And, while she smiled, enjoyed her amplest power;
All various turns of good and bad he knew,
And proved the most that chance or fate could do.
220   What heaps of slain the Colline gate* did yield,
What bodies strewed the Sacriportan field,*
When empire was ordained to change her seat,*
To leave her Rome and make Praeneste great,
When the proud Samnites'* troops the state defied,
225 In terms beyond their Caudine treaty's pride!*
Nor Sulla with less cruelty returns,
With equal rage the fierce avenger burns;
What blood the feeble city yet retained,
With too severe a healing hand he drained;
230 Too deeply was the searching steel employed:
What maladies had hurt, the leech* destroyed.
The guilty only were of life bereft,
Alas, the guilty only then were left!
Dissembled hate and rancour ranged at will,
235 All as they pleased took liberty to kill,
And, while revenge no longer feared the laws,
Each private murder was the public cause.
The leader bade destroy, and at the word
The master fell beneath the servant's sword.
240 Brothers on brothers were for gifts bestowed,

And sons contended for their fathers' blood.*
For refuge some to caves and forests fled,
Some to the lonely mansions of the dead,
Some, to prevent the cruel victor, die,
245   These strangled hang from fatal beams on high,
While those, from tops of lofty turrets thrown,
Came headlong on the dashing pavement down.
Some for their funerals the wood prepare,*
And build the sacred pile with hasty care,
250   Then bleeding to the kindling flames they press,
And Roman rites, while yet they may, possess.
Pale heads of Marian chiefs are borne on high,
And heaped together in the forum lie;
There join the meeting slaughters of the town,
255   There each performing villain's deeds are known.
No sight like this the Thracian stables knew,*
Antaeus'* Libyan spoils to these were few.
Nor Greece beheld so many suitors fall*
To grace the Pisan tyrant's horrid hall.
260   At length, when putrid gore with foul disgrace
Hid the distinguished features of the face,
By night the miserable parents came,
And bore their sons to some forbidden flame.*
Well I remember in that woeful reign,
265   How I my brother sought amongst the slain,
Hopeful by stealth his poor remains to burn,
And close his ashes in a peaceful urn;
His visage in my trembling hand I bore,
And turned pacific Sulla's* trophies o'er;
270   Full many a mangled trunk I tried, to see
Which carcass with the head would best agree.
Why should my grief to Catulus* return,
And tell the victim offered at his urn,
When, struck with horror, the relenting shade
275   Beheld his wrongs too cruelly repaid?
I saw where Marius' hapless brother stood,*
With limbs all torn and covered o'er with blood –
A thousand gaping wounds increased his pain,
While weary life a passage sought in vain;
280   That mercy still his ruthless foes deny,
And whom they mean to kill, forbid to die.

This from the wrist the suppliant hands divides,
That hews his arms from off his naked sides,
One crops his breathing nostrils, one his ears,
285 While from the roots his tongue another tears – *
Panting awhile upon the earth it lies,
And with mute motion trembles e'er it dies;
Last, from the sacred caverns where they lay,
The bleeding orbs of sight are rent away.

290 Can late posterity believe, whene'er
This tale of Marius and his foes they hear,
They could inflict so much, or he could bear?
Such is the broken carcass seen to lie,
Crushed by some tumbling turret from on high,
295 Such to the shore the shipwrecked corse* is borne,
By rending rocks and greedy monsters torn.
Mistaken rage, thus mangling to disgrace
And blot the lines of Marius' hated face!
What joy can Sulla take, unless he know
300 And mark the features of his dying foe?
Fortune beheld, from her Praenestine fane,*
Her helpless worshippers around her slain;
One hour of fate was common to them all,
And like one man she saw a people fall.

305 Then died the lusty youth in manly bloom,
Hesperia's flower and hope for times to come;
Their blood, Rome's only strength, disdains the fold*
Ordained th'assembling centuries to hold.
Numbers have oft been known on sea and land
310 To sink of old by death's destructive hand,
Battles with multitudes have strewn the plain,
And many perish on the stormy main,
Earthquakes destroy, malignant vapours blast,
And plagues and famines lay whole nations waste,
315 But justice, sure, was never seen till now
To massacre her thousands at a blow.
Satiety of death the victors prove,
And slowly through th'encumbering ruin move:
So many fall, there scarce is room for more,
320 The dying nod on those who fell before,
Crowding in heaps their murderers they aid,
And by the dead the living are o'erlaid.

Meanwhile the stern dictator, from on high,*
Beholds the slaughter with a fearless eye,
325   Nor sighs to think his dread commands ordain
So many thousand wretches to be slain.
Amidst the Tiber's waves the load is thrown,
The torrent rolls the guilty burden down,
Till rising mounds obstruct his watery way,
330   And carcasses the gliding vessels stay.
But soon another stream to aid him rose –
Swift o'er the fields a crimson deluge flows;
The Tuscan river swells above his shores,
And floating bodies to the land restores;
335   Struggling at length he drives his rushing flood,
And dyes the Tyrrhene ocean round with blood.
Could deeds like these the glorious style demand*
Of "prosperous", and "saviour of the land"?
Could this renown, could these achievements build
340   A tomb for Sulla in the Martian Field?
Again behold the circling woes return,
Again the curse of civil wars we mourn;
Battles and blood and vengeance shall succeed,
And Rome once more by Roman hands shall bleed.
345   Or if, for hourly thus our fears presage,*
With wrath more fierce the present chiefs shall rage,
Mankind shall some unheard-of plagues deplore,
And groan for miseries unknown before.
Marius an end of exile only sought,
350   Sulla to crush a hated faction fought –
A larger recompense these leaders* claim,
And higher is their vast ambition's aim;
Could these be satisfied with Sulla's power,
Nor, all he had possessing, ask for more,
355   Neither had force and impious arms employed,
Or fought for that which guiltless each enjoyed.'
     Thus wept lamenting age o'er hapless Rome,
Remembering evils past, and dreading those to come.
    But Brutus'* temper failed not with the rest,
360   Nor with the common weakness was oppressed;
Safe and in peace he kept his manly breast.

'Twas when the solemn dead of night came on, ⎤
When bright Callisto with her shining son* ⎟
Now half their circle round the pole had run, ⎦
365   When Brutus, on the busy times intent,
To virtuous Cato's humble dwelling went.
Waking he found him, careful for the state,
Grieving and fearing for his country's fate –
For Rome, and wretched Rome alone, he feared,
370   Secure within himself, and for the worst prepared.
    To him thus Brutus spoke: 'O thou, to whom*
Forsaken virtue flies as to her home,
Driv'n out, and by an impious age oppressed,
She finds no room on earth but Cato's breast;
375   There in her one good man she reigns secure,
Fearless of vice or fortune's hostile power:
Then teach my soul, to doubt and error prone,
Teach me a resolution like thy own.
Let partial favour, hopes or interest guide, ⎤
380   By various motives, all the world beside ⎟
To Pompey's or ambitious Caesar's side: ⎦
Thou Cato art my leader – whether peace
And calm repose amidst these storms shall please,
Or whether war thy ardour shall engage, ⎤
385   To gratify the madness of this age, ⎟
Herd with the factious chiefs and urge the people's ⎟
    rage. ⎦
  The ruffian, bankrupt, loose adulterer, ⎤
All who the power of laws and justice fear, ⎟
From guilt learn specious reason for the war. ⎦
390   By starving want and wickedness prepared,
Wisely they arm for safety and reward.
But oh, what cause, what reason canst thou find?
Art thou to arms, for love of arms, inclined?
Hast thou the manners of this age withstood, ⎤
395   And for so many years been singly good, ⎟
To be repaid with civil wars and blood? ⎦
Let those to vice inured for arms prepare, ⎤
In thee 'twill be impiety to dare – ⎟
Preserve at least, ye gods, these hands from war. ⎦
400   Nor do thou meanly with the rabble join,
Nor grace their cause with such an arm as thine.

To thee, the fortune of the fatal field*
Inclining, unauspicious fame shall yield;
Each to thy sword shall press, and wish to be
405   Imputed as thy crime, and charged on thee.
Happy thou wert, if with retirement blessed,
Which noise and faction never should molest,
Nor break the sacred quiet of thy breast,
Where harmony and order ne'er should cease,
410   But every day should take its turn in peace.
So, in eternal steady motion, roll
The radiant spheres around the starry pole;
Fierce lightnings, meteors, and the winter's storm,
Earth and the face of lower heaven deform,
415   Whilst all by nature's laws is calm above –
No tempest rages in the court of Jove.
Light particles and idle atoms fly,
Tossed by the winds and scattered round the sky,
While the more solid parts the force resist,
420   And fixed and stable on the centre rest.
Caesar shall hear with joy that thou art joined
With fighting factions to disturb mankind;
Though sworn his foe, he shall applaud thy choice,*
And think his wicked war approved by Cato's voice.
425   See, how to swell their mighty leader's state,
The consuls and the servile Senate wait!
Ev'n Cato's self to Pompey's yoke must bow,
And all mankind are slaves but Caesar now.
If war, however, be at last our doom,
430   If we must arm for liberty and Rome,
While undecided yet their fate depends,
Caesar and Pompey are alike my friends;
Which party I shall choose is yet to know –
That let the war decide: who conquers is my foe.'
435   Thus spoke the youth, when Cato thus expressed
The sacred counsels of his inmost breast:*
    'Brutus, with thee I own the crime is great,
With thee, this impious civil war I hate,
But virtue blindly follows, led by fate.
440   Answer yourselves, ye gods, and set me free:
If I am guilty, 'tis by your decree.
If yon fair lamps above should lose their light,

And leave the wretched world in endless night,
If chaos should in heaven and earth prevail,
445   And universal nature's frame should fail,
What Stoic would not the misfortune share,
And think that desolation worth his care?
Princes and nations, whom wide seas divide,
Where other stars far distant heavens do guide,
450   Have brought their ensigns to the Roman side.
Forbid it gods! when barbarous Scythians come
From their cold north, to prop declining Rome,
That I should see her fall, and sit secure at home.
As some unhappy sire by death undone,
455   Robbed of his age's joy, his only son,
Attends the funeral with pious care,
To pay his last paternal office there,
Takes a sad pleasure in the crowd to go,
And be himself part of the pompous woe,
460   Then waits till, every ceremony past,
His own fond hand may light the pile at last:
So fixed, so faithful to thy cause, O Rome,
With such a constancy and love I come,
Resolved for thee and liberty to mourn,
465   And never, never from your sides be torn!
Resolved to follow still your common fate,
And on your very names, and last remains to wait.
Thus let it be, since thus the gods ordain,
Since hecatombs of Romans must be slain,
470   Assist the sacrifice with every hand,
And give them all the slaughter they demand.
O were the gods contented with my fall,
If Cato's life could answer for you all,
Like the devoted Decius* would I go,
475   To force from either side the mortal blow,
And for my country's sake wish to be thought her
      foe.
To me, ye Romans, all your rage confine,
To me, ye nations from the barbarous Rhine,
Let all the wounds this war shall make be mine.
480   Open my vital streams and let them run,
O let the purple sacrifice atone
For all the ills offending Rome has done.

If slavery be all the faction's end,
If chains the prize for which the fools contend,
485 To me convert the war, let me be slain,
Me, only me, who fondly strive in vain*
Their useless laws and freedom to maintain;
So may the tyrant safely mount his throne,
And rule his slaves in peace, when I am gone.
490 How-e'er, since free as yet from his command,
For Pompey and the commonwealth* we stand.
Nor he, if fortune should attend his arms,
Is proof against ambition's fatal charms,
But, urged with greatness and desire of sway,
495 May dare to make the vanquished world his prey.
Then, lest the hopes of empire swell his pride,
Let him remember I was on his side,
Nor think he conquered for himself alone,
To make the harvest of the war his own,
500 Where half the toil was ours.' So spoke the sage.
His words the listening eager youth engage*
Too much to love of arms, and heat of civil rage.
     Now 'gan the sun to lift his dawning light,
Before him fled the colder shades of night,
505 When lo, the sounding doors are heard to turn –
Chaste Marcia* comes from dead Hortensius' urn
Once to a better husband's happier bed
With bridal rites a virgin was she led.
When every debt of love and duty paid,
510 And thrice a parent by Lucina* made,
The teeming matron, at her lord's command,
To glad Hortensius gave her plighted hand,
With a fair stock his barren house to grace,
And mingle by the mother's side the race.*
515 At length this husband in his ashes laid,
And every rite of due religion paid,
Forth from his monument the mournful dame,
With beaten breasts and locks dishevelled, came;
Then with a pale, dejected, rueful look,
520 Thus pleasing,* to her former lord she spoke:
     'While nature yet with vigour fed my veins,
And made me equal to a mother's pains,
To thee obedient, I thy house forsook,

And to my arms another husband took;
525   My powers at length with genial labours worn,
      Weary to thee and wasted I return.
      At length a barren wedlock let me prove –
      Give me the name without the joys of love;
      No more to be abandoned, let me come,
530   That "Cato's wife" may live upon my tomb.
      So shall my truth to latest times be read,   }
      And none shall ask if guiltily I fled,   }
      Or thy command estranged me from thy bed. }
      Nor ask I now thy happiness to share –
535   I seek thy days of toil, thy nights of care;
      Give me with thee to meet my country's foe,
      Thy weary marches and thy camps to know;
      Nor let posterity with shame record
      Cornelia* followed, Marcia left her lord.'
540   She said. The hero's manly heart was moved,
      And the chaste matron's virtuous suit approved.
      And though the times far differing thoughts demand,
      Though war dissents from Hymen's holy band,
      In plain unsolemn wise his faith he plights,
545   And calls the gods to view the lonely rites.
      No garlands gay the cheerful portal crowned,*
      Nor woolly fillets* wove the posts around;
      No genial* bed, with rich embroidery graced,
      On ivory steps in lofty state was placed;
550   No hymeneal torch preceding shone,   }
      No matron put the towery frontlet* on,   }
      Nor bade her feet the sacred threshold shun.* }
      No yellow veil was loosely thrown, to hide
      The rising blushes of the trembling bride;
555   No glittering zone* her flowing garments bound,
      Nor sparkling gems her neck encompassed round;
      No silken scarf, nor decent winding lawn,*
      Was o'er her naked arms and shoulders drawn,
      But, as she was, in funeral attire,
560   With all the sadness sorrow could inspire,
      With eyes dejected, with a joyless face,
      She met her husband's, like a son's, embrace.
      No Sabine mirth* provokes the bridegroom's ears,
      Nor sprightly wit the glad assembly cheers.

565 No friends, nor ev'n their children grace the feast –
Brutus attends, their only nuptial guest;
He stands a witness of the silent rite,
And sees the melancholy pair unite.
Nor he, the chief, his sacred visage cheered,
570 Nor smoothed his matted locks or horrid beard,
Nor deigns his heart one thought of joy to know,
But met his Marcia with the same stern brow.
(For when he saw the fatal factions arm,
The coming war, and Rome's impending harm,
575 Regardless quite of every other care,
Unshorn he left his loose neglected hair,
Rude hung the hoary honours of his head,
And a foul growth his mournful cheeks o'erspread.
No stings of private hate his peace infest,*
580 Nor partial favour grew upon his breast,
But safe from prejudice, he kept his mind
Free, and at leisure to lament mankind.)
Nor could his former love's returning fire ⎫
The warmth of one connubial wish inspire, ⎬
585 But strongly he withstood the just desire. ⎭
These were the stricter manners of the man,
And this the stubborn course in which they ran:
The golden mean unchanging to pursue,
Constant to keep the purposed end in view;
590 Religiously to follow nature's laws,
And die with pleasure in his country's cause;
To think he was not for himself designed,
But born to be of use to all mankind.
To him 'twas feasting hunger to repress,
595 And home-spun garments were his costly dress;
No marble pillars reared his roof on high –
'Twas warm, and kept him from the winter sky;
He sought no end of marriage but increase,
Nor wished a pleasure but his country's peace;
600 That took up all the tenderest parts of life –
His country was his children and his wife.
From justice' righteous lore he never swerved,
But rigidly his honesty preserved.
On universal good his thoughts were bent,
605 Nor knew what gain or self-affection meant,

And, while his benefits the public share,
Cato was always last in Cato's care.
　　Meantime the trembling troops, by Pompey led,
Hasty to Phrygian Capua* were fled.
610　Resolving here to fix the moving war,
He calls his scattered legions from afar;
Here he decrees the daring foe to wait,
And prove at once the great event of fate,
Where Appenine's delightful shades arise,
615　And lift Hesperia lofty to the skies.
Between the higher and inferior sea
The long extended mountain takes his way;
Pisa and Ancon bound his sloping sides,
Washed by the Tyrrhene and Dalmatic tides.
620　Rich in the treasure of his watery stores,
A thousand living springs and streams he pours,
And seeks the different seas by different shores.
From his left falls Crustumium's rapid flood,
And swift Metaurus red with Punic blood,*
625　There gentle Sapis with Isaurus joins,
And Sena there the Senones confines;
Rough Aufidus the meeting ocean braves,
And lashes on the lazy Adria's* waves;
Hence vast Eridanus* with matchless force,
630　Prince of the streams, directs his regal course;
Proud with the spoils of fields and woods he flows,
And drains Hesperia's rivers as he goes.
His sacred banks, in ancient tales renowned,*
First by the spreading poplar's shade were crowned,
635　When the sun's fiery steeds forsook their way,
And downward drew to earth the burning day,
When every flood and ample lake was dry,
The Po alone his channel could supply;
Hither rash Phaëthon was headlong driven,
640　And in these waters quenched the flames of heaven.
Nor wealthy Nile a fuller stream contains,
Though wide he spreads o'er Egypt's flatter plains,
Nor Ister rolls a larger torrent down,
Sought he the sea with waters all his own;
645　But meeting floods to him their homage pay,
And heave the blended river on his way.

These from the left, while from the right there come
The Rutuba and Tiber dear to Rome;
Thence slides Vulturnus' swift descending flood,
650   And Sarnus hid beneath his misty cloud;
Thence Lyris, whom the Vestin fountains aid,
Winds to the sea through close Marica's* shade;
Thence Siler through Salernian pastures falls,
And shallow Macra creeps by Luna's walls.
655   Bordering on Gaul the loftiest ridges rise,
And the low Alps from cloudy heights despise;
Thence his long back the fruitful mountain bows,
Beneath the Umbrian and the Sabine ploughs;
The race primeval, natives all of old,
660   His woody rocks within their circuit hold;
Far as Hesperia's utmost limits pass,
The hilly father runs his mighty mass,
Where Juno rears her high Lacinian fane,
And Scylla's raging dogs molest the main.
665   Once farther yet, 'tis said, his way he took,
Till through his side the seas conspiring broke,
And still we see on fair Sicilia's sands
Where, part of Appenine, Pelorus stands.
     But Caesar for destruction eager burns,
670   Free passages and bloodless ways he scorns;
In fierce conflicting fields his arms delight,
He joys to be opposed, to prove his might,
Resistless through the widening breach to go,
To burst the gate, to lay the bulwark low,
675   To burn the villages, to waste the plains,
And massacre the poor, laborious swains.
Abhorring law, he chooses to offend,
And blushes to be thought his country's friend.
The Latian cities now with busy care,
680   As various they inclined, for arms prepare.
Though doomed before the war's first rage to yield,
Trenches they dig and ruined walls rebuild,
Huge stones and darts their lofty towers supply,
And guarded bulwarks menace from on high.
685   To Pompey's part the proner people lean,*
Though Caesar's stronger terrors stand between.
So when the blasts of sounding Auster* blow,

The waves obedient to his empire flow,
And, though the stormy god* fierce Eurus* frees
690 And sends him rushing cross the swelling seas,
Spite of his force, the billows yet retain
Their former course, and that way roll the main,
The lighter clouds with Eurus driving sweep,
While Auster still commands the watery deep.
695 Still fear too sure o'er vulgar minds prevails,
And faith before successful fortune fails.
Etruria vainly trusts in Libo's* aid,
And Umbria by Thermus* is betrayed;
Sulla,* unmindful of his father's fame,
700 Fled at the dreadful sound of Caesar's name.
Soon as the horse near Auximon appear, ⎫
Retreating Varus* owns his abject fear, ⎬
And with a coward's haste neglects his rear; ⎭
On flight alone intent without delay,
705 Through rocks and devious woods he wings his way.
Th'Esculean fortress Lentulus* forsakes;
A swift pursuit the speedy victor makes;
All arts of threats and promises applied,
He wins the faithless cohorts to his side.*
710 The leader with his ensigns fled alone,
To Caesar fell the soldier and the town.
Thou, Scipio,* too dost for retreat prepare,
Thou leav'st Luceria trusted to thy care;
Though troops well tried attend on thy command*
715 (The Roman power can boast no braver band),
By wily arts of old from Caesar rent,
Against the hardy Parthians were they sent;
But their first chief the legion now obeys,
And Pompey thus the Gallic loss repays.
720 Aid to his foe too freely he affords,
And lends his hostile father Roman swords.
    But in Corfinium bold Domitius lies,*
And from his walls th'advancing power defies;
Secure of heart, for all events prepared,
725 He heads the troops,* once bloody Milo's guard.
Soon as he sees the cloudy dust arise,
And glittering arms reflect the sunny skies,
'Away, companions of my arms!', he cried,

'And haste to guard the river's sedgy side;
730 Break down the bridge, and thou that dwellst below,
Thou watery god, let all thy fountains go,
And rushing bid thy foamy torrent flow,
Swell to the utmost brink thy rapid stream,
Bear down the planks and every floating beam,
735 Upon thy banks the lingering war delay;
Here let the headlong chief be taught to stay –
'Tis victory to stop the victor's way.'
   He ceased, and shooting swiftly cross the plain
Drew down the soldier to the flood in vain.
740 For Caesar early from the neighbouring field
The purpose to obstruct his march beheld;
Kindling to wrath, 'O basest fear!', he cries,
'To whom nor towers nor sheltering walls suffice.
Are these your coward stratagems of war?
745 Hope you with brooks my conquering arms to bar?
Though Nile and Ister* should my way control,
Though swelling Ganges should to guard you roll,
What streams, what floods so e'er athwart me fall,
Who passed the Rubicon shall pass them all.
750 Haste to the passage then, my friends.' He said;
Swift as a storm the nimble horse obeyed,
Across the stream their deadly darts they throw,
And from their station drive the yielding foe.
The victors at their ease the ford explore,
755 And pass the undefended river o'er.
The vanquished to Corfinium's strength retreat,
Where warlike engines round the ramparts threat.
Close to the wall the creeping vinea* lies,
And mighty towers in dread approaches rise.
760   But see the stain of war, the soldier's shame,
And vile dishonour of the Latian name!
The faithless garrison betray the town,
And captive drag their valiant leader down.
The noble Roman, fearless, though in bands,
765 Before his haughty fellow-subject stands;
With looks erect and with a daring brow,
Death he provokes and courts the fatal blow.
But Caesar's arts his inmost thoughts descry,
His fear of pardon and desire to die.

770 'From me thy forfeit life', he said, 'receive,
And, though repining, by my bounty live,
That all by thy example taught may know
How Caesar's mercy treats a vanquished foe;
Still arm against me, keep thy hatred still,
775 And if thou conqu'rest, use thy conquest, kill.
Returns of love or favour seek I none,
Nor give thy life to bargain for my own.'
So saying, on the instant he commands
To loose the galling fetters from his hands.
780 O fortune! Better were it he had died,
And spared the Roman shame and Caesar's pride.
What greater grief can on a Roman seize
Than to be forced to live on terms like these,
To be forgiven fighting for the laws,
785 And need a pardon in his country's cause!
Struggling with rage, undaunted he repressed
The swelling passions in his labouring breast,
Thus murmuring to himself, 'Would thou to Rome,
Base as thou art, and seek thy lazy home?
790 To war, to battle, to destruction fly,
And haste, as it becomes thee well, to die;
Provoke the worst effects of deadly strife,
And rid thee of this Caesar's gift, this life.'
    Meanwhile, unknowing of the captived chief,
795 Pompey prepares to march to his relief.
He means the scattering forces to unite,
And with increase of strength expect the fight.
Resolving with the following sun to move,
First he decrees the soldier's heart to prove;
800 Then into words like these revered he broke,
The silent legions listening while he spoke:
    'Ye brave avengers of your country's wrong,
You who to Rome and liberty belong,
Whose breasts our fathers' virtue truly warms,
805 Whose hands the Senate's sacred order arms,
With cheerful ardour meet the coming fight,
And pray the gods to smile upon the right.
Behold the mournful view Hesperia yields,
Her flaming villages and wasted fields!
810 See where the Gauls a dreadful deluge flow

And scorn the boundaries of Alpine snow.
Already Caesar's sword is stained in blood –
Be that, ye gods, to us an omen good,
That glory still be his peculiar care:
815   Let him begin, while we sustain the war.
Yet call it not a war to which we go –
We seek a malefactor, not a foe;
Rome's awful injured majesty demands
The punishment of traitors at our hands.
820   If this be war, then war was waged of old
By curst Cethegus,* Catiline the bold,
By every villain's hand who durst conspire
In murder, robbery or midnight fire.
O wretched rage! Thee, Caesar, fate designed
825   To rank amongst the patrons of mankind,
With brave Camillus* to enrol thy fame,
And mix thee with the great Metelli's* name,
While to the Cinnas thy fierce soul inclines,*
And with the slaughter-loving Marii joins.
830   Since then thy crimes like theirs for justice call,
Beneath our axe's vengeance shalt thou fall;
Thee rebel Carbo's* sentence, thee the fate
Of Lepidus* and bold Sertorius* wait.
Believe me yet, if yet I am believed,
835   My heart is at the task unpleasing grieved;
I mourn to think that Pompey's hand was chose
His Julia's hostile father to oppose,
And mark thee down amongst the Roman foes.
O that, returned in safety from the East,
840   This province* victor Crassus had possessed,
New honours to his name thou* mightst afford
And die like Spartacus* beneath his sword,
Like him have fall'n a victim to the laws,
The same th'avenger, and the same the cause.
845   But since the gods do otherwise decree,
And give thee as my latest palm to me,
Again my veins confess the fervent juice,*
Nor has my hand forgot the javelin's use;
And thou shalt learn that those who humbly know
850   To peace and just authority to bow
Can, when their country's cause demands their care,

Resume their ardour and return to war.
But let him think my fonder vigour fled,
Distrust not you your general's hoary head;
855 The marks of age and long declining years,
Which I your leader, his whole army wears;
Age still is fit to counsel or command,
But falters in an unperforming hand.
Whate'er superior power a people free*
860 Could to their fellow citizen decree,
All lawful glories have my fortunes known,
And reached all heights of greatness but a crown.
Who to be more than Pompey was desires,
To kingly rule and tyranny aspires.
865 Amidst my ranks, a venerable band,
The conscript fathers and the consuls stand.
And shall the Senate and the vanquished state
Upon victorious Caesar's triumph wait?
Forbid it gods in honour of mankind!
870 Fortune is not so shameless, nor so blind.
What fame achieved, what unexampled praise,*
To these high hopes the daring hero raise?
Is it his age of war* for trophies calls,
His two whole years spent on the rebel Gauls?
875 Is it the hostile Rhine forsook with haste?
Is it the shoaly channel which he passed,
That ocean huge he talks of? Does he boast
His flight on Britain's new discovered coast?
Perhaps abandoned Rome new pride supplies, ⎫
880 He views the naked town with joyful eyes, ⎬
While from his rage an armèd people flies. ⎭
But know, vain man, no Roman fled from thee –
They left their walls, 'tis true, but 'twas to follow me;
Me, who e'er twice the moon her orb renewed,
885 The pirates' formidable fleet subdued;
Soon as the sea my shining ensigns bore,
Vanquished they fled, and sought the safer shore,
Humbly content their forfeit lives to save,
And take the narrow lot my bounty gave.
890 By me the mighty Mithridates* chased
Through all the windings of his Pontus passed.
He who the fate of Rome delayed so long,

While in suspense uncertain empire hung,
He who to Sulla's fortune scorned to yield,
895   To my prevailing arms resigned the field;
Driv'n out at length and pressed where-e'er he fled,
He sought a grave to hide his vanquished head.
O'er the wide world my various trophies rise,
Beneath the vast extent of distant skies;
900   Me the cold Bear, me northern climates know,
And Phasis' waters through my conquests flow,
My deeds in Egypt and Syene live,*
Where high meridian suns no shadow give.
Hesperian Baetis* my commands obeys,
905   Who rolls remote to seek the western seas.
By me the captive Arabs' hands were bound,
And Colchians for their ravished fleece renowned;
O'er Asia wide my conquering ensigns spread,
Armenia me, and lofty Taurus dread;
910   To me submit Cilicia's warlike powers,
And proud Sophene veils her wealthy towers;
The Jews I tamed, who with religion bow
To some mysterious name which none beside them
          know.
Is there a land, to sum up all at last,*
915   Through which my arms with conquest have not
          past?
The world by me, the world is overcome,
And Caesar finds no enemy but Rome.'
    He said. The crowd in dull suspension* hung,
Nor with applauding acclamations rung;
920   No cheerful ardour waves the lifted hand,
Nor military cries the fight demand.
The chief perceived the soldiers' fire to fail,
And Caesar's fame fore-running to prevail;
His eagles he withdraws with timely care,
925   Nor trusts Rome's fate to such uncertain war.
As when with fury stung and jealous rage*
Two mighty bulls for sovereignty engage,
The vanquished far to banishment removes,
To lonely fields and unfrequented groves;
930   There for a while with conscious shame he burns,
And tries on every tree his angry horns,

But when his former vigour stands confessed
And larger muscles shake his ample breast,
With better chance he seeks the fight again,
935   And drives his rival bellowing o'er the plain;
Then uncontrolled the subject herd he leads,
And reigns the master of the fruitful meads.
Unequal thus to Caesar, Pompey yields
The fair dominion of Hesperia's fields;
940   Swift through Apulia march his flying powers,
And seek the safety of Brundisium's towers.
     This city a Dictaean* people hold,
Here placed by tall Athenian barks of old,
When with false omens from the Cretan shore*
945   Their sable sails victorious Theseus bore.
Here Italy a narrow length extends,
And in a scanty slip* projected ends.
A crooked mole around the waves she winds,
And in her folds the Adriatic binds;
950   Nor yet the bending shores could form a bay, ⎫
Did not a barrier isle the winds delay,   ⎬
And break the seas tempestuous in their way. ⎭
Huge mounds of rocks are placed by nature's hand
To guard around the hospitable* strand,
955   To turn the storm, repulse the rushing tide,
And bid the anchoring bark securely ride.
Hence Nereus* wide the liquid main displays,
And spreads to various ports his watery ways,
Whether the pilot for Corcyra stand,
960   Or for Illyrian Epidamnus' strand;
Hither when all the Adriatic roars,
And thundering billows vex the double shores,
When sable clouds around the welkin* spread,
And frowning storms involve* Ceraunia's head,
965   When white with froth Calabrian Sason lies,
Hither the tempest-beaten vessel flies.
     Now Pompey, on Hesperia's utmost coast,
Sadly surveyed how all behind was lost;
Nor to Iberia could he force his way,
970   Long interposing Alps his passage stay;
At length amongst the pledges of his bed
He chose his eldest born,* and thus he said:

'Haste thee, my son! to every distant land,
And bid the nations rouse at my command,
975 Where famed Euphrates flows, or where the Nile
With muddy waves improves the fattening soil,
Where-e'er diffused by victory and fame
Thy father's arms have borne the Roman name;
Bid the Cilician quit the shore again,
980 And stretch his swelling canvas on the main;
Bid Ptolemy with my Tigranes* come,
And bold Pharnaces* lend his aid to Rome.
Through each Armenia* spread the loud alarm,
And bid the cold Riphaean* mountains arm,
985 Pontus and Scythia's wandering tribes explore,
The Euxine, and Maeotis'* icy shore,
Where heavy loaden wains slow journeys take,
And print with groaning wheels the frozen lake.
But wherefore should my words delay thy haste?
990 Scatter my wars around through all the East,
Summon the vanquished world to share my fate,
And let my triumphs on my ensigns wait.
But you whose names the Roman annals bear,
You who distinguish the revolving year,*
995 Ye consuls, to Epirus straight repair,
With the first northern winds that wing the air;
From thence the powers of Greece united raise,
While yet the wintry year the war delays.'
So spoke the chief; his bidding all obey,
1000 Their ships forsake the port without delay,
And speed their passage o'er the yielding way.

But Caesar, never patient long in peace,
Nor trusting in his fortune's present face,
Closely pursues his flying son* behind,
1005 While yet his fate continued to be kind:
Such towns, such fortresses, such hostile force,
Swept* in the torrent of one rapid course,
Such trains of long success attending still,
And Rome herself abandoned to his will;
1010 Rome, the contending party's noblest prize,
To every wish but Caesar's might suffice.
But he, with empire fired and vast desires,
To all and nothing less than all aspires;

He reckons not the past while aught remained
1015 Great to be done, or mighty to be gained.
Though Italy obey his wide command,
Though Pompey linger on her farthest strand,
He grieves to think they tread one common land;
His heart disdains to brook a rival power,
1020 Ev'n on that utmost margin of the shore,
Nor would he leave or earth or ocean free –
The foe he drives from land, he bars from sea.
With moles the opening flood he would restrain,*
Would block the port and intercept the main;
1025 But deep devouring seas his toil deride,
The plunging quarries sink beneath the tide,
And yielding sands the rocky fragments hide.
Thus if huge Gaurus headlong should be thrown
In fathomless Avernus deep to drown,
1030 Or if from fair Sicilia's distant strand
Eryx uprooted by some giant hand,
If ponderous with his rocks the mountain vast
Amidst the wide Aegean should be cast,
The rolling waves o'er either mass would flow,
1035 And each be lost within the depths below.
When no firm basis for his work he found,
But still it failed in ocean's faithless ground,
Huge trees and barks in massy chains he bound.
For planks and beams he ravages the wood,
1040 And the tough boom extends across the flood;
Such was the road by haughty Xerxes made,*
When o'er the Hellespont his bridge he laid;
Vast was the task, and daring the design,
Europe and Asia's distant shores to join,
1045 And make the world's divided parts combine;
Proudly he passed the flood tumultuous o'er,
Fearless of waves that beat and winds that roar,
Then spread his sails, and bid the land obey,
And through mid Athos find his fleet a way.
1050 Like him bold Caesar yoked the swelling tide,
Like him the boisterous elements defied;
This floating bank the straitening entrance bound,
And rising turrets trembled on the mound.
    But anxious cares revolve in Pompey's breast,

1055 The new surrounding shores his thoughts molest;
      Secret he meditates the means to free
      And spread the war wide-ranging o'er the sea.
      Oft driving on the work with well-filled sails,
      The cordage stretching with the freshening gales,
1060 Ships with a thundering shock the mole divide,
      And through the watery breach securely glide.
      Huge engines oft by night their vengeance pour,
      And dreadful shoot from far a fiery shower;
      Through the black shade the darting flame descends,
1065 And, kindling, o'er the wooden wall extends.
      At length arrived, with the revolving night,*
      The chosen hour appointed for his flight;
      He bids his friends prevent the seaman's roar,
      And still the deafening clamours on the shore;
1070 No trumpets may the watch by hours renew,
      Nor sounding signals call aboard the crew.
      The heavenly maid* her course had almost run,
      And Libra waited on the rising sun,
      When hushed in silence deep they leave the land;
1075 No loud-mouthed voices call with hoarse command
      To heave the flooky* anchors from the sand.
      Lowly the careful master's order's past,
      To brace the yards and rear the lofty mast;
      Silent they spread the sails, the cables haul,
1080 Nor to their mates for aid tumultuous call.
      The chief himself to fortune breathed a prayer
      At length to take him to her kinder care,
      That swiftly he might pass the liquid deep,
      And lose the land which she forbade to keep.
1085 Hardly the boon his niggard fate allowed,
      Unwillingly the murmuring seas were ploughed,
      The foamy furrows roared beneath his prow,
      And sounding to the shore alarmed the foe.
      Straight through the town their swift pursuit they
          sped
1090 (For wide her gates the faithless city spread),*
      Along the winding port they took their way,
      But grieved to find the fleet had gained the sea.
      Caesar with rage the lessening sails descries,
      And thinks the conquest mean, though Pompey flies.

1095 A narrow pass the hornèd mole divides,
Narrow as that where Eurypus' strong tides
Beat on Eubaean Chalcis' rocky sides;*
Here two tall ships become the victor's prey,
Just in the strait they stuck, the foes belay,*
1100 The crooked grappling's steely hold they cast,
Then drag them to the hostile shore with haste.
Here civil slaughter first the sea profanes,
And purple Nereus blushed in guilty stains;
The rest pursue their course before the wind,
1105 These of the rearmost only left behind.
So when the Pagasaean Argo* bore
The Grecian heroes to the Colchian shore,
Earth her Cyanean islands* floating sent,
The bold adventurers' passage to prevent,
1110 But the famed bark a fragment only lost,
While swiftly o'er the dangerous gulf she crossed;
Thundering the mountains met and shook the main,
But move no more, since that attempt was vain.*
Now through night's shade the early dawning broke,
1115 And changing skies the coming sun bespoke;
As yet the morn was dressed in dusky white,*
Nor purpled o'er the east with ruddy light;
At length the Pleiads' fading beams gave way,
And dull Boötes* languished into day,
1120 Each larger star withdrew his fainting head,
And Lucifer from stronger Phoebus fled,
When Pompey, from Hesperia's hostile shore
Escaping, for the azure offing* bore.
O hero, happy once, once styled 'the Great',*
1125 What turns* prevail in thy uncertain fate!
How art thou changed, since sovereign of the main,
Thy navies covered o'er the liquid plain!*
When the fierce pirates fled before thy prow,
Wherever waves could waft or winds could blow!
1130 But fortune is grown weary of thee now.*
With thee thy sons and tender wife prepare
The toils of war and banishment to bear,
And holy household gods thy sorrows share.
And yet a mighty exile shalt thou go,
1135 While nations follow to partake thy woe;

Far lies the land in which thou art decreed
Unjustly, by a villain's hand, to bleed;
Nor think the gods a death so distant doom,*
To rob thy ashes of an urn in Rome;
1140 But fortune favourably removed the crime,
And forced the guilt on Egypt's cursèd clime,
The pitying powers to Italy were good,
And saved her from the stain of Pompey's blood.

BOOK THREE

Through the mid ocean now the navy sails,
Their yielding canvas stretched by southern gales.
Each to the vast Ionian turns his eye,
Where seas and skies the prospect wide supply;
5   But Pompey backward ever bent his look,
Nor to the last his native coast forsook.
His watery eyes the lessening objects mourn,
And parting shores that never shall return;
Still the loved land attentive they pursue,
10   Till the tall hills are veiled in cloudy blue,
Till all is lost in air and vanished from his view. ⎫
At length the weary chieftain sunk to rest,*
And creeping slumbers soothed his anxious breast,
When lo, in that short moment of repose,
15   His Julia's shade a dreadful vision rose;*
Through gaping earth her ghastly head she reared,
And by the light of livid flames appeared.
'Thy impious arms', she cried, 'my peace infest,*
And drive me from the mansions of the blessed;
20   No more Elysium's happy fields I know,
Dragged to the guilty Stygian shades below.
I saw the fury's horrid hands prepare
New rage, new flames to kindle up thy war.
The sire no longer trusts his single boat,*
25   But navies on the joyless river float.
Capacious hell complains for want of room,
And seeks new plagues for multitudes to come.
Her nimble hands each fatal sister* plies –
The sisters scarcely to the task suffice.
30   When thou wert mine, what laurels crowned thy
        head!
Now thou hast changed thy fortune with thy bed.
In an ill hour thy second choice was made –
To slaughter thou, like Crassus,* art betrayed.
Death is the dower Cornelia's love affords,
35   Ruin still waits upon her potent lords;

While yet my ashes glowed, she took my place,
And came a harlot to thy loose embrace.
But let her partner of thy warfare go,
Let her by land and sea thy labours know;
40   In all thy broken sleeps I will be near,
In all thy dreams sad Julia shall appear.
Your loves shall find no moment for delight,
The day shall all be Caesar's, mine the night.
Not the dull stream* where long oblivions roll
45   Shall blot thee out, my husband, from my soul.
The powers beneath my constancy approve,
And bid me follow wheresoe'er you rove.
Amidst the joining battles will I stand,
And still remind thee of thy plighted hand;
50   Nor think those sacred ties no more remain – ⎫
The sword of war divides the knot in vain,   ⎬
That very war shall make thee mine again.'*   ⎭
        The phantom spoke, and gliding from the place*
Deluded her astonished lord's embrace;
55   But he, though gods forewarn him of his fate,
And furies with destruction threatening wait,
With new resolves his constant bosom warms,
And sure of ruin rushes on to arms.
'What mean these terrors of the night?' he cries,
60   'Why dance these visions vain before our eyes?
Or endless apathy succeeds to death*
And sense is lost with our expiring breath,
Or, if the soul some future life shall know,
To better worlds immortal shall she go;
65   Whate'er event the doubtful question clears,*
Death must be still unworthy of our fears.'
        Now headlong to the west the sun was fled,   ॑ʳ·ᵖᵖʳ·
And half in seas obscured his beamy head,
Such seems the moon while growing yet she shines,
70   Or waning from her fuller orb declines,
When hospitable shores appear at hand,
Where fair Dyrrachium* spreads her friendly strand.
The seamen furl the canvas, strike the mast,
Then dip their nimble oars and landward haste.
75   Thus while they fled and, lessening by degrees,
The navy seemed to hide beneath the seas,

Caesar, though left the master of the field,
With eyes unpleased the foes escape beheld,
With fierce impatience victory he scorns,
80 And viewing Pompey's flight his safety mourns.
To vanquish seems unworthy of his care
Unless the blow decides the lingering war;
No bounds his headlong vast ambition knows,
Nor joys in aught, though fortune all bestows.
85 At length his thoughts from arms and vengeance
          cease,
And for a while revolve the arts of peace,
Careful to purchase popular applause,
And gain the lazy vulgar to his cause;
He knew the constant practice of the great
90 That those who court the vulgar bid them eat;
When pinched with want all reverence they
          withdraw,
For hungry multitudes obey no law;
Thus therefore factions make their parties good,
And buy authority and power with food.
95 The murmurs of the many to prevent,
Curio to fruitful Sicily is sent.*
Of old the swelling sea's impetuous tide
Tore the fair island from Hesperia's* side;
Still foamy wars the jealous waves maintain,
100 For fear the neighbouring lands should join again.
Sardinia too renowned for yellow fields
With Sicily her bounteous tribute yields;
No lands a glebe of richer tillage boast,
Nor waft more plenty to the Roman coast,
105 Not Libya more abounds in wealthy grain,
Nor with a fuller harvest spreads the plain,
Though northern winds their cloudy treasures bear ⎤
To temper well the soil and sultry air, ⎟
And fattening rains increase the prosperous year. ⎦
110 This done, to Rome his way the leader took,
His train* the rougher shows of war forsook;
No force, no fears their hands unarmèd bear,
But looks of peace and gentleness they wear.
Oh, had he now his country's friend returned,
115 Had none but barbarous foes his conquest mourned,

What swarming crowds had issued at the gate,
On the glad triumph's lengthening train to wait!
How might his wars in various glories shine,
The ocean vanquished, and in bonds the Rhine!*
120   How would his lofty chariot roll along
Through loud applauses of the joyful throng!
How might he view from high his captive thralls,
The beauteous Britons,* and the noble Gauls!
But oh, what fatal honours has he won,
125   How is his fame by victory undone!
No cheerful citizens the victor meet,
But hushed with awful dread his passage greet.
He too the horrors of the crowd approved,
Joyed in their fears, and wished not to be loved.
130   Now steepy Anxur passed, and the moist way*
Which o'er the faithless Pomptine marshes lay,
Through Scythian Dian's Aricinian grove,*
Caesar approached the fane* of Alban Jove.*
Thither with yearly rites the consuls come,*
135   And thence the chief surveyed his native Rome;
Wondering awhile he viewed her from afar,
Long from his eyes withheld by distant war.
'Fled they from thee, thou seat of gods!', he cried,
'E'er yet the fortune of the fight was tried?
140   If thou art left, what prize can earth afford
Worth the contention of the warrior's sword?
Well for thy safety now the gods provide,
Since Parthian inroads spare thy naked side,
Since yet no Scythians and Pannonians join,
145   Nor warlike Daci with the Getes combine,
No foreign armies are against thee led,
While thou art cursed with such a coward head.
A gentler fate the heavenly powers bestow –
A civil war, and Caesar for thy foe.'
150   He said, and straight the frighted city sought;
The city with confusion wild was fraught,
And labouring shook with every dreadful thought.
They think he comes to ravage, sack and burn,
Religion, gods and temples to o'erturn;
155   Their fears suggest him willing to pursue
Whatever ills unbounded power can do.

Their hearts by one low passion only move,
Nor dare show hate nor can dissemble love.
The lurking Fathers, a disheartened band,
160 Drawn from their houses forth by proud command,
In Palatine Apollo's temple meet,*
And sadly view the consuls' empty seat;
No rods, no chairs curule* adorn the place,
Nor purple magistrates th'assembly grace.
165 Caesar is all things in himself alone,
The silent court is but a looker on;
With humble votes obedient they agree
To what their mighty subject* shall decree,
Whether as king or god he will be feared,
170 If royal thrones or altars shall be reared.
Ready for death or banishment they stand,
And wait their doom from his disposing hand.
But he, by secret shame's reproaches stayed,
Blushed to command what Rome would have obeyed.
175 Yet liberty thus slighted and betrayed
One last effort* with indignation made,
One man she chose to try th'unequal fight,
And prove the power of justice against might.
While with rude uproar armèd hands essay
180 To make old Saturn's treasuring fane* their prey,
The bold Metellus, careless of his fate,*
Rushed through, and stood to guard the holy gate.
So daring is the sordid love of gold!
So fearless death and dangers can behold!
185 Without a blow defenceless fell the laws,
While wealth, the basest, most inglorious cause
Against oppressing tyranny makes head,
Finds hands to fight, and eloquence to plead.
The bustling tribune, struggling in the crowd,
190 Thus warns the victor of the wrong aloud:
    'Through me, thou robber, force thy horrid way,
My sacred blood* shall stain thy impious prey.
But there are gods to urge thy guilty fate –
Sure vengeance on thy sacrilege shall wait.
195 Remember, by the tribune's curse pursued,
Crassus, too late, the violation rued.*
Pierce then my breast, nor shall the crime displease –

This crowd is used to spectacles like these.
In a forsaken city are we left,
200 Of virtue with her noblest sons bereft.
Why seeks't thou ours? Is there not foreign gold?
Towns to be sacked and people to be sold?
With those reward the ruffian soldier's toil,
Nor pay him with thy ruined country's spoil.
205 Hast thou not war? Let war thy wants provide.'
    He spoke; the victor high in wrath replied:*
'Soothe not thy soul with hopes of death so vain –
No blood of thine my conquering sword shall stain;
Thy titles and thy popular command
210 Can never make thee worthy Caesar's hand.
Art thou thy country's sole defender? Thou!
Can liberty and Rome be fall'n so low?
Nor time nor chance breed such confusions yet,
Nor are the mean so raised, nor sunk the great,
215 But laws themselves would rather choose to be
Suppressed by Caesar than preserved by thee.'
    He said; the stubborn tribune kept his place,
While anger reddened on the warrior's face;
His wrathful hand descending grasped his blade,
220 And half forgot the peaceful part he played;
When Cotta,* to prevent the kindling fire,
Thus soothed the rash Metellus to retire:
    'Where kings prevail, all liberty is lost,
And none but he who reigns can freedom boast;
225 Some shadow of the bliss thou shalt retain,
Choosing to do what sovereign powers ordain;
Vanquished and long accustomed to submit,
With patience underneath our loads we sit,
Our chains alone our slavish fears excuse –
230 While we bear ill, we know not to refuse.
Far hence the fatal treasures let him bear,
The seeds of mischief and the cause of war.
Free states might well a loss like this deplore;
In servitude none miss the public store,
235 And 'tis the curse of kings for subjects to be poor.'
    The tribune with unwilling steps withdrew,
While impious hands the rude assault renew;
The brazen gates with thundering strokes resound,

And the Tarpeian mountain* rings around.
240 At length the sacred store-house open laid
The hoarded wealth of ages past displayed:
There might be seen the sums proud Carthage sent,*
Her long impending ruin to prevent;
There heaped the Macedonian treasures shone, ⎫
245 What great Flaminius and Aemilius* won ⎬
From vanquished Philip and his hapless son,* ⎭
There lay what flying Pyrrhus lost, the gold*
Scorned by the patriot's honesty of old,
Whate'er our parsimonious sires could save,
250 What tributary gifts rich Syria gave,*
The hundred Cretan cities' ample spoil,*
What Cato gathered from the Cyprian isle,*
Riches of captive kings by Pompey borne,* ⎫
In happier days his triumph to adorn, ⎬
255 From utmost India and the rising morn. ⎭
Wealth infinite, in one rapacious day,
Became the needy soldiers' lawless prey,
And wretched Rome, by robbery laid low,
Was poorer than the bankrupt Caesar now.

260   Meanwhile the world, by Pompey's fate alarmed,*
Nations ordained to share his fall had armed.
Greece first with troops the neighbouring war
      supplied,
And sent the youth of Phocis to his side;
From Cyrrha and Amphissa's towers they moved,
265 And high Parnassus by the Muse beloved;
Cephissus' sacred flood assistance lends,
And Dirce's spring her Theban leaders sends.
Alpheus too affords his Pisa's aid* ⎫
(By Pisa's walls the stream is first conveyed, ⎬
270 Then seeks through seas the loved Sicilian maid); ⎭
From Maenalus Arcadian shepherds swarm,
And warriors in Herculean Trachyn* arm;
The Dryopes Chaonia's hills forsook;
And Selloi left Dodona's silent oak.*
275 Though Athens now had drained her naval store,
And the Phoebaean* arsenal was poor,

Three ships of Salamis to Pompey came,* ⎫
To vindicate their isle's contested name, ⎬
And justify the ancient Attic claim. ⎭

280 Jove's Cretan people* hastening to the war
The Gnossian* quiver and the shaft prepare,
The bending bow they draw with deadly art,
And rival ev'n the flying Parthian's dart.
Wild Athamans, who in the woods delight,

285 With Dardan Oriconians unite;*
With these th'Encheliae who the name partake*
Since Theban Cadmus first became a snake,
The Colchians planted on Illyrian shores
Where rushing down Absyrtos foamy roars;*

290 With those where Peneus runs, and hardy swains,
Whose ploughs divide Iolcos' fruitful plains
(From thence, e'er yet the seaman's art was taught,
Rude Argo* through the deep a passage sought;
She first explored the distant foreign land,

295 And showed her strangers to the wondering strand;
Then nations nations knew, in leagues were joined,
And universal commerce mixed mankind;
By her made bold, the daring race defied
The winds tempestuous and the swelling tide;

300 Much she enlarged destruction's ample power,
And opened ways to death unknown before);
Then Pholoe's heights, that fabled centaurs boast,
And Thracian Haemus then his warriors lost;
Then Strymon was forsook, whose wintry flood

305 Commits to warmer Nile his feathered brood,*
Then bands from Cone and from Peuce came,
Where Ister loses his divided stream,
From Idalis* where cold Caïcus flows,
And where Arisbe thin her sandy surface strows.*

310 From Pitane, and sad Celenae's walls,*
Where now in streams the vanquished Marsyas falls
(Still his lamenting progeny deplore
Minerva's tuneful gift and Phoebus' power,
While through steep banks his torrent swift he leads,

315 And with Maeander winds among the meads);
Proud Lydia's plains send forth her wealthy sons,
Pactolus there, and golden Hermus runs – *

From earth's dark womb hid treasures they convey,
And rich in yellow waters rise to day.
320 From Ilium too ill-omened ensigns move,*
Again ordained their former fate to prove;
Their arms they ranged on Pompey's hapless side,*
Nor sought a chief to Dardan kings allied,
Though tales of Troy proud Caesar's lineage grace
325 With great Aeneas and the Julian race.
The Syrians swift Orontes' banks forsake,
And from Idume's palms their journey take;
Damascus, obvious to* the driving wind,
With Ninos' and with Gaza's force is joined.
330 Unstable Tyre now knit to firmer ground,
With Sidon for her purple shells renowned,
Safe in the Cynosure,* their glittering guide,
With well directed navies stem the tide
(Phoenicians first, if ancient fame be true,
335 The sacred mystery of letters knew;
They first by sound in various lines designed,
Expressed the meaning of the thinking mind,
The power of words by figures rude conveyed,
And useful science everlasting made;
340 Then Memphis, e'er the reedy leaf was known,
Engraved her precepts and her arts in stone,
While animals in various order placed
The learned hieroglyphic column graced);
Then left they lofty Taurus' spreading grove,
345 And Tarsos, built by Perseus born of Jove,
Then Mallian and Corycian towers they leave,
Where mouldering rocks disclose a gaping cave.
The bold Cilicians, pirates now no more,
Unfurl a juster sail and ply the oar;
350 To Aegae's port they gather all around,
The shores with shouting mariners resound.
Far in the east war spreads the loud alarm,
Where worshippers of distant Ganges arm;
Right to the breaking day his waters run,
355 The only stream that braves the rising sun
(By this strong flood, and by the ocean bound,
Proud Alexander's arms a limit found;
Vain in his hopes the youth had grasped at all,

And his vast thought took in the vanquished ball,*
360   But owned, when forced from Ganges to retreat,
        The world too mighty and the task too great);
        Then on the banks of Indus nations rose,
        Where unperceived the mixed Hydaspes flows;
        In numbers vast they coast the rapid flood,
365   Strange in their habit, manners and their food;
        With saffron dyes their dangling locks they stain, ⎫
        With glittering gems their flowing robes constrain, ⎬
        And quaff rich juices from the luscious cane;   ⎭
        On their own funerals and death they smile,
370   And living leap amidst the burning pile –
        Heroic minds, that can ev'n fate command,
        And bid it wait upon a mortal hand,
        Who full of life forsake it as a feast,
        Take what they like, and give the gods the rest.
375   Descending then fierce Cappadocian swains
        From rude Amanus' mountains sought the plains,
        Armenians from Niphates' rolling stream,
        And from their lofty woods Coastrians came.
        Then, wondering, Arabs from the sultry line*
380   For ever northward saw the shade incline.
        Then did the madness of the Roman rage
        Carmanian and Olostrian* chiefs engage;
        Beneath far distant southern heavens they lie,* ⎫
        Where half the setting Bear forsakes the sky,   ⎬
385   And swift our slow Boötes seems to fly.   ⎭
        These furies* to the sunburned Ethiops* spread,
        And reach the great Euphrates' rising head
        (One spring the Tigris and Euphrates know,
        And joined awhile the kindred rivers flow,
390   Scarce could we judge between the doubtful claim,
        If Tigris or Euphrates give the name,
        But soon Euphrates' parting waves divide,
        Covering like fruitful Nile the country wide,
        While Tigris, sinking from the sight of day,
395   Through subterranean channels cuts his way,
        Then from a second fountain springs again,
        Shoots swiftly on, and rushing seeks the main);
        The Parthian power, to neither chief a friend,
        The doubtful issue in suspense attend,

400 With neutral ease they view the strife from far,
 And only lend occasion to the war.*
 Not so the Scythians where cold Bactros flows,
 Or where Hyrcania's wilder forest grows,
 Their baneful shafts they dip, and string their deadly
  bows.
405 Th'Heniochi of Sparta's valiant breed,
 Skilful to press and rein the fiery steed,
 Sarmatians with the fiercer Moschi joined,
 And Colchians rich where Phasis' waters wind,
 To Pompey's side their aid assembling bring,
410 With Halys, fatal to the Lydian king,*
 With Tanais falling from Riphaean snows,
 Who forms the world's division as he goes
 (With noblest names his rising banks are crowned,
 This stands for Europe's, that for Asia's bound,
415 While, as they wind, his waves with full command,
 Diminish or enlarge th'adjacent land);
 Then armed the nations on Cimmerian shores,
 Where through the Bosporus Maeotis roars,
 And her full lake amidst the Euxine pours.
420 This strait, like that of Hercules, supplies
 The midland seas, and bids th' Aegean rise.
 Sithonians* fierce and Arimaspians bold,
 Who bind their plaited hair in shining gold,
 The Gelon nimble, and Areian strong,
425 March with the hardy Massagete along,
 The Massagete, who at his savage feast
 Feeds on the generous steed which once he pressed.
  Not Cyrus, when he spread his Eastern reign*
 And hid with multitudes the Lydian plain,
430 Not haughty Xerxes, when, his power to boast,*
 By shafts he counted all his mighty host,
 Not he who drew the Grecian chiefs along,*
 Bent to revenge his injured brother's wrong,
 Or with such navies ploughed the foamy main,
435 Or led so many kings amongst their warlike train.
 Sure in one cause such numbers never yet,
 Various in countries, speech and manners, met;
 But fortune gathered, o'er the spacious ball,
 These spoils to grace her once loved favourite's fall.

440 Nor then the Libyan Moor withheld his aid,
Where sacred Ammon lifts his hornèd head;*
All Afric,* from the western ocean's bound
To eastern Nile, the cause of Pompey owned.
Mankind assembled for Pharsalia's day,
445 To make the world at once the victor's prey.
   Now, trembling Rome forsook, with swiftest
      haste*
Caesar the cloudy Alpine hills had past.*
But while the nations, with subjection tame,
Yield to the terrors of his mighty name,
450 With faith uncommon to the changing Greeks,*
What duty bids, Massilia bravely seeks;
And true to oaths, their liberty and laws,
To stronger fate prefer the juster cause.
But first to move his haughty soul they try,
455 Entreaties and persuasion soft apply,
Their brows Minerva's peaceful branches wear,*
And thus in gentlest terms they greet his ear:
   'When foreign wars molest the Roman state,*
With ready arms our glad Massilians wait
460 To share your dangers and partake your fate.
This our unshaken friendship vouches well,
And your recording annals best can tell.
Ev'n now we yield our still devoted hands
On foreign foes to wreak your dread commands.
465 Would you to worlds unknown your triumphs
      spread?
Behold! we follow wheresoe'er you lead.
But if you rouse at discord's baleful call,
If Romans fatally on Romans fall,
All we can offer is a pitying tear,
470 And constant refuge for the wretched here.
Sacred to us you are – oh, may no stain
Of Latian blood our innocence profane!
Should heaven itself be rent with civil rage,
Should giants once more with the gods engage,
475 Officious piety would hardly dare
To proffer Jove assistance in the war;

Man unconcerned and humble should remain,
Nor seek to know whose arms the conquest gain –
Jove's thunder will convince them of his reign.

480 Nor can your horrid discords want our swords –
The wicked world its multitudes affords,
Too many nations at the call will come,
And gladly join to urge the fate of Rome;
Oh, had the rest like us their aid denied,*

485 Yourselves must then the guilty strife decide;
Then who but should withhold his lifted hand,
When for his foe he saw his father stand?
Brothers their rage had mutually repressed,
Nor driv'n their javelins on a brother's breast.

490 Your war had ended soon, had you not chose
Hands for the work which nature meant for foes,
Who,* strangers to your blood, in arms delight,
And rush remorseless to the cruel fight.
Briefly, the sum of all that we request

495 Is to receive thee as our honoured guest;
Let those thy dreadful ensigns shine afar –
Let Caesar come, but come without the war.
Let this one place from impious rage be free,*
That, if the gods the peace of Rome decree,

500 If your relenting angers yield to treat,
Pompey and thou in safety here may meet.
Then wherefore dost thou quit thy purposed way?
Why thus Iberia's nobler wars delay?
Mean and of little consequence we are,

505 A conquest much unworthy of thy care.
When Phocis'* towers were laid in ashes low,
Hither we fled for refuge from the foe,
Here, for our plain integrity renowned,
A little town in narrow walls we bound;

510 No name in arms nor victories we boast,
But live poor exiles on a foreign coast.
If thou art bent on violence at last,
To burst our gates, and lay our bulwarks waste,
Know we are equally resolved whate'er

515 The victor's fury can inflict to bear.
Shall death destroy, shall flames the town o'erturn?
Why, let our people bleed, our buildings burn.

Would thou forbid the living stream to flow?
We'll dig, and search the watery stores below.
520 Hunger and thirst with patience will we meet,
And what offended nature nauseates eat.
Like brave Saguntum* daring to be free,
Whate'er they suffered we'll expect from thee.
Babes, ravished from the fainting mother's breast,
525 Shall headlong in the burning pile be cast;
Matrons shall bare their bosoms to their lords,
And beg destruction from their pitying swords;
The brother's hand the brother's heart shall wound,
And universal slaughter rage around.
530 If civil wars must waste this hapless town,
No hands shall bring that ruin but our own.'
    Thus said the Grecian messengers, when lo,
A gathering cloud involved* the Roman's brow;
Much grief, much wrath his troubled visage spoke,
535 Then into these disdainful words he broke:
    'This trusting in our speedy march to Spain,
These hopes, this Grecian confidence is vain;
Whate'er we purpose, leisure will be found
To lay Massilia level with the ground;
540 This bears, my valiant friends, a sound of joy –
Our useless arms at length shall find employ.
Winds lose their force that unresisted fly,
And flames unfed by fuel sink and die.
Our courage thus would soften in repose,
545 But fortune and rebellion yield us foes.
Yet mark what love their friendly speech expressed!
Unarmed and single Caesar is their guest.
Thus first they dare to stop me on my way,
Then seek with fawning treason to betray.
550 Anon, they pray that civil rage may cease –
But war shall scourge them for those hopes of peace,
And make them know the present times afford,
At least while Caesar lives, no safety like the sword.'
    He said, and to the city bent his way;
555 The city, fearless all, before him lay,
With armèd hands her battlements were crowned,
And lusty youth the bulwarks manned around.
    Near to the walls, a rising mountain's head

Flat with a little level plain is spread;
560 Upon this height the wary chief designs
His camp to strengthen with surrounding lines.
Lofty alike, and with a warlike mien,   ⎫
Massilia's neighbouring citadel is seen;   ⎬
An humble valley fills the space between.   ⎭
565 Straight he decrees the middle vale to fill,
And run a mole athwart from hill to hill.
But first a lengthening work extends its way,   ⎫
Where open to the land the city lay,   ⎬
And from the camp projecting joins the sea.   ⎭
570 Low sinks the ditch, the turfy breastworks* rise,
And cut the captive town from all supplies.
While gazing from their towers the Greeks bemoan
The meads, the fields and fountains, once their own.
    Well have they thus acquired the noblest name,
575 And consecrated these their walls to fame.
Fearless of Caesar and his arms they stood,
Nor drove before the headlong, rushing flood;
And while he swept whole nations in a day,   ⎫
Massilia bade th'impatient victor stay,   ⎬
580 And clogged his rapid conquest with delay.   ⎭
Fortune a master for the world prepared,
And these th'approaching slavery retard.
Ye times to come, record the warriors' praise,
Who lengthened out expiring freedom's days.
585 Now while with toil unwearied rose the mound,
The sounding axe invades the groves around;
Light earth and shrubs the middle bank supplied,
But firmer beams must fortify the side,
Lest, when the towers advance their ponderous
        height,
590 The mouldering mass should yield beneath the
        weight.
        Not far away for ages past had stood*
An old, unviolated, sacred wood,
Whose gloomy boughs, thick interwoven, made
A chilly, cheerless, everlasting shade;
595 There nor the rustic gods nor satyrs sport*
Nor fauns and sylvans with the nymphs resort,
But barbarous priests* some dreadful power adore,

And lustrate* every tree with human gore.
If mysteries in times of old received,
600   And pious ancientry be yet believed,
There nor the feathered songster builds her nest,
Nor lonely dens conceal the savage beast;
There no tempestuous winds presume to fly,
Ev'n lightnings glance aloof, and shoot obliquely by.
605   No wanton breezes toss the dancing leaves,
But shivering horror in the branches heaves.
Black springs with pitchy streams divide the ground,
And bubbling tumble with a sullen sound.
Old images of forms misshapen stand,
610   Rude and unknowing of the artist's hand;
With hoary filth begrimed, each ghastly head
Strikes the astonished gazer's soul with dread.
No gods, who long in common shapes appeared,
Were e'er with such religious awe revered,
615   But zealous crowds in ignorance adore,
And still* the less they know, they fear the more.
Oft, as fame tells, the earth in sounds of woe
Is heard to groan from hollow depths below,
The baleful yew,* though dead, has oft been seen
620   To rise from earth, and spring with dusky green;
With sparkling flames the trees unburning shine,
And round their boles prodigious serpents twine.
The pious worshippers approach not near,
But shun their gods and kneel with distant fear;
625   The priest himself, when or the day or night
Rolling have reached their full meridian height,
Refrains* the gloomy paths with wary feet,
Dreading the demon* of the grove to meet,
Who, terrible to sight, at that fixed hour
630   Still treads the round about his dreary bower.
      This wood near neighbouring to th'encompassed
            town
Untouched by former wars remained alone,
And, since the country round it naked stands,
From hence the Latian chief supplies demands.
635   But lo! the bolder hands that should have struck
With some unusual horror trembling shook;
With silent dread and reverence they surveyed

The gloom majestic of the sacred shade;
None dares with impious steel the bark to rend,
640   Lest on himself the destined stroke descend.
Caesar perceived the spreading fear to grow,
Then eager caught an axe and aimed a blow;
Deep sunk within a violated oak*
The wounding edge, and thus the warrior spoke:
645   'Now, let no doubting hand the task decline;
Cut you the wood and let the guilt be mine.'
The trembling bands unwillingly obeyed;
Two various ills were in the balance laid,
And Caesar's wrath against the gods' was weighed.
650   Then Jove's Dodonian tree* was forced to bow,
The lofty ash and knotty holm* lay low;
The floating alder by the current borne,
The cypress by the noble mourner worn,
Veil their aërial summits and display
655   Their dark recesses to the golden day;
Crowding they fall, each o'er the other lies,
And heaped on high the leafy piles arise.
With grief and fear the groaning Gauls beheld
Their holy grove by impious soldiers felled,
660   While the Massilians, from th'encompassed wall,
Rejoiced to see the sylvan honours* fall;
They hope such power can never prosper long,
Nor think the patient gods will bear the wrong.
But ah, too oft success to guilt is given,
665   And wretches only stand the mark of heaven.*
With timber largely from the wood supplied,
For wains* the legions search the country wide,
Then from the crooked plough unyoke the steer,
And leave the swain to mourn the fruitless year.
670   Meanwhile, impatient of the lingering war,*
The chieftain to Iberia bends afar,
And gives the leaguer* to Trebonius' care.
With diligence the destined task he plies,
Huge works of earth with strengthening beams arise,
675   High tottering towers, by no fixed basis bound,*
Roll nodding on along the stable mound.
The Greeks with wonder on the movement look,
And fancy earth's foundations deep are shook;

Fierce winds they think the beldame's* entrails tear,
680   And anxious for their walls and city fear.
The Roman from the lofty top looks down,
And rains a wingèd war upon the town.
      Nor with less active rage the Grecians burn,
But larger ruin on their foes return;
685   Nor hands alone the missile* deaths supply –
From nervous crossbows whistling arrows fly;
The steely corslet and the bone they break,
Through multitudes their fatal journeys take;
Nor wait the lingering Parcae's* slow delay,
690   But wound, and to new slaughter wing their way.
Now by some vast machine a ponderous stone,
Pernicious,* from the hostile wall is thrown;
At once, on many, swift the shock descends,
And the crushed carcasses confounding blends.
695   So rolls some falling rock by age long worn,   ⎫
Loose from its root by raging whirlwinds torn,   ⎬
And thundering down the precipice is borne;   ⎭
O'er crashing woods the mass is seen to ride,
To grind its way and plane* the mountain side.
700   Galled with the shot from far, the legions join,*
Their bucklers in the warlike shell combine;
Compact and close the brazen roof they bear,
And in just order to the town draw near;
Safe they advance, while with unwearied pain
705   The wrathful engines waste their stores in vain;
High o'er their heads the destined deaths are tossed,
And far behind in vacant earth are lost,
Nor sudden could they change their erring aim,
Slow and unwieldy moves the cumbrous frame.
710   This seen, the Greeks their brawny arms employ,
And hurl a stony tempest from on high;
The clattering shower the sounding fence assails, ⎫
But vain as when the stormy winter hails,   ⎬
Nor on the solid marble roof prevails,   ⎭
715   Till tired at length the warriors fall* their shields,
And, spent with toil, the broken phalanx yields.
Now other stratagems the war supplies,
Beneath the vinea* close th'assailant lies;
The strong machine, with planks and turf bespread,

720 Moves to the walls its well defended head;
    Within the covert safe the miners lurk,
    And to the deep foundation urge their work.
    Now justly poised the thundering ram they fling,
    And drive him forceful with a launching spring,
725 Haply* to loose some yielding part at length,
    And shake the firm cemented bulwark's strength.
    But from the town the Grecian youth prepare
    With hardy vigour to repel the war,
    Crowding they gather on the rampart's height,
730 And with tough staves and spears maintain the fight;
    Darts, fragments of the rock and flames they throw,
    And tear the planky shelter fixed below;
    Around by all the warring tempest beat,*
    The baffled Romans sullenly retreat.
735   Now by success the brave Massilians fired
    To fame of higher enterprise aspired;
    Nor longer with their walls' defence content,
    In daring sallies they the foe prevent.*
    Nor armed with swords nor pointed spears they go,
740 Nor aim the shaft, nor bend the deadly bow:
    Fierce Mulciber* supplies the bold design,
    And for their weapons kindling torches shine.
    Silent they issue through the gloomy night,
    And with broad shields restrain the beamy light;*
745 Sudden the blaze on every side began,
    And o'er the Latian works resistless ran;
    Catching and driving with the wind it grows,
    Fierce through the shade the burning deluge glows,
    Nor earth nor greener planks* its force delay,
750 Swift o'er the hissing beams it rolls away;
    Embrowned with smoke the wavy flames ascend,
    Shivered with heat the crackling quarries* rend,
    Till with a roar at last the mighty mound,
    Towers, engines, all, come thundering to the ground.
755 Widespread the discontinuous* ruins lie,
    And vast confusion fills the gazer's eye.
        Vanquished by land, the Romans seek the main,
    And prove the fortune of the watery plain;
    Their navy rudely built and rigged in haste
760 Down through the rapid Rhone descending passed.

No golden gods protect the shining prow,
Nor silken streamers lightly dancing flow,
But rough in stable floorings* lies the wood,
As in the native forest once it stood.

765   Rearing above the rest her towery head,
Brutus'* tall ship the floating squadron led.
To sea soon wafted by the hasty tide,
Right to the Stoechades their course they guide.
Resolved to urge their fate, with equal cares,

770   Massilia for the naval war prepares;
All hands the city for the task requires,
And arms her striplings young and hoary sires.
Vessels of every sort and size she fits,
And speedy to the briny deep commits.

775   The crazy hulk,* that, worn with winds and tides,)
Safe in the dock and long neglected rides,
She planks anew and caulks* her leaky sides.)

      Now rose the morning, and the golden sun
With beams refracted on the ocean shone,

780   Clear was the sky, the waves from murmur cease,
And every ruder wind was hushed in peace,
Smooth lay the glassy surface of the main,
And offered to the war its ample plain,
When to the destined stations all repair,

785   Here Caesar's powers, the youth of Phocis there.
Their brawny arms are bared, their oars they dip,
Swift o'er the water glides the nimble ship;
Feels the strong blow the well compacted oak,*
And trembling springs at each repeated stroke.

790   Crooked in front the Latian navy stood,*
And wound a bending crescent o'er the flood.
With four full banks of oars advancing high,)
On either wing the larger vessels ply,
While in the centre safe the lesser galiots* lie.)

795   Brutus the first, with eminent command,
In the tall admiral* is seen to stand;
Six rows of lengthening pines* the billows sweep,
And heave the burden o'er the groaning deep.

      Now prow to prow advance each hostile fleet,
800   And want but one concurring stroke to meet,*
When peals of shouts and mingling clamours roar,

And drown the brazen trump and plunging oar.
The brushing pine* the frothy surface plies,
While on their banks the lusty rowers rise;
805   Each brings the stroke back on his ample chest,
Then firm upon his seat he lights repressed.*
With clashing beaks the launching vessels meet,
And from the mutual shock alike retreat.
Thick clouds of flying shafts the welkin* hide,
810   Then fall, and floating strew the ocean wide.
At length the stretching wings their order leave,
And in the line the mingling foe receive.
Then might be seen how, dashed from side to side,
Before the stemming* vessels drove the tide;
815   Still as each keel her foamy furrow ploughs,
Now back, now forth, the surge obedient flows.
Thus warring winds alternate rule maintain,
And this and that way roll the yielding main.
Massilia's navy, nimble, clean and light,
820   With best advantage seek or shun the fight,
With ready ease all answer to command,
Obey the helm and feel the pilot's hand.
Not so the Romans – cumbrous hulks they lay,
And slow and heavy hung upon the sea,
825   Yet strong, and for the closer combat good,
They yield firm footing on th'unstable flood.
This Brutus saw, and to the master cries
(The master in the lofty poop he spies,
Where streaming the pretorian* ensign flies):
830   'Still would thou bear away, still shift thy place,
And turn the battle to a wanton chase?
Is this a time to play so mean a part,
To tack, to veer, and boast thy trifling art?
Bring to. The war shall hand to hand be tried;
835   Oppose thou to the foe our ample side,
And let us meet like men.' The chieftain said;
The ready master the command obeyed,
And sidelong to the foe the ship was laid.
Upon his waist* fierce fall the thundering Greeks,
840   Fast in his timbers stick their brazen beaks;
Some lie by chains and grapplings* strong compelled,
While others by the tangling oars are held.*

The seas are hid beneath the closing war,
Nor need they cast the javelin now from far;
845   With hardy strokes the combatants engage,
And with keen falchions* deal their deadly rage,
Man against man, and board by board they lie,
And on those decks their arms defended die.
The rolling surge is stained around with blood,
850   And foamy purple swells the rising flood;
The floating carcasses the ships delay,
Hang on each keel, and intercept her way;
Helpless beneath the deep the dying sink,
And gore with briny ocean mingling drink.
855   Some, while amidst the tumbling waves they strive
And struggling with destruction float alive,
Or by some ponderous beam are beaten down,
Or sink transfixed by darts at random thrown.
That fatal day no javelin flies in vain –
860   Missing their mark they wound upon the main.
It chanced a warrior ship on Caesar's side
By two Massilian foes was warmly plied,
But with divided force she meets th'attack,
And bravely drives the bold assailants back,
865   When from the lofty poop where fierce he fought
Tagus* to seize the Grecian ancient* sought.
But double death his daring hand repressed – ⎤
One spear transfixed his back, and one his breast, ⎟
And deadly met within his heaving chest. ⎦
870   Doubtful awhile the flood was seen to stay,
At length the steely shafts at once gave way –
Then fleeting life a twofold passage found,
And ran divided from each streaming wound.
Hither his fate unhappy Telon* led,
875   To naval arts from early childhood bred;
No hand the helm more skilfully could guide,*
Or stem the fury of the boisterous tide;
He knew what winds should on the morrow blow,
And how the sails for safety to bestow;
880   Celestial signals well he could descry, ⎤
Could judge the radiant lights that shine on high, ⎟
And read the coming tempest of the sky. ⎦
Full on a Latian bark his beak he drives,

The brazen beak the shivering alder rives,*
885   When from some hostile hand a Roman dart,
Deep piercing, trembled in his panting heart.
Yet still his careful hand its task supplies,
And turns the guiding rudder as he dies.
To fill his place bold Gyareus essayed,
890   But passing from a neighbouring ship was stayed;
Swift through his loins a flying javelin struck,
And nailed him to the vessel he forsook.

    Friendlike, and side by side, two brethren fought,*
Whom at a birth their fruitful mother brought;*
895   So like the lines of each resembling face,
The same the features and the same the grace,
That fondly erring oft their parents look,
And each for each alternately mistook;
But death too soon a dire distinction makes,
900   While one, untimely snatched, the light forsakes.
His brother's form the sad survivor wears,
And still renews his hapless parents' tears;
Too sure they see their single hope remain,
And, while they bless the living, mourn the slain.
905   He, the bold youth, as board and board* they stand,
Fixed on a Roman ship his daring hand;
Full on his arm a mighty blow descends,
And the torn limb from off the shoulder rends;
The rigid nerves are cramped with stiffening cold,
910   Convulsive grasp, and still retain their hold.
Nor sunk his valour by the pain depressed,
But nobler rage inflamed his mangled breast:
His left remaining hand the combat tries,
And fiercely forth to catch the right he flies;
915   The same hard destiny the left demands,
And now a naked, helpless trunk he stands.
Nor deigns he, though defenceless to the foe,
To seek the safety of the hold below;
For every coming javelin's point prepared,
920   He steps between and stands his brother's guard,
Till, fixed and horrid with a wood of spears,
A thousand deaths at others aimed he wears.

Resolved at length his utmost force t'exert, |
His spirits gathered to his fainting heart, |
925   And the last vigour roused in every part; |
Then nimble from the Grecian deck he rose,
And with a leap sprung fierce amidst his foes;
And when his hands no more could wreak his hate, |
His sword no more could minister to fate, |
930   Dying he pressed them with his hostile weight. |
O'ercharged the ship with carcasses and blood
Drunk fast at many a leak the briny flood;
Yielding at length the waters wide give way,
And fold her in the bosom of the sea,
935   Then o'er her head returning rolls the tide,
And covering waves the sinking hatches hide.
    That fatal day was slaughter seen to reign
In wonders various on the liquid plain.
    On Lycidas* a steely grappling struck;
940   Struggling he drags with the tenacious hook,
And deep had drowned beneath the greedy wave,
But that his fellows strove their mate to save;
Clung to his legs, they clasp him all they can –
The grappling tugs, asunder flies the man.
945   No single wound the gaping rupture seems,
Where trickling crimson wells in slender streams,
But from an opening horrible and wide
A thousand vessels pour the bursting tide;
At once the winding channel's course was broke,
950   Where wandering life her mazy journey took;
At once the currents all forgot their way,
And lost their purple in the azure sea.
Soon from the lower parts the spirits fled,
And motionless th'exhausted limbs lay dead;
955   Not so the nobler regions, where the heart
And heaving lungs their vital powers exert;
There lingering late, and long conflicting, life
Rose against fate, and still maintained the strife;
Driv'n out at length, unwillingly and slow,
960   She left her mortal house and sought the shades
      below.
    While eager for the fight, an hardy crew
To one sole side their force united drew,

The bark, unapt th'unequal poise to bear,
Turned o'er and reared her lowest keel in air;
965 In vain his active arms the swimmer tries,
No aid the swimmer's useless art supplies,
The covering vast o'erwhelming shuts them down,
And helpless in the hollow hold they drown.
    One slaughter terrible above the rest
970 The fatal horror of the fight expressed.
As o'er the crowded surface of the flood
A youthful swimmer swift his way pursued,
Two meeting ships, by equal fury pressed,
With hostile prows transfixed his ample breast;
975 Suspended by the dreadful shock he hung,
The brazen beaks within his bosom rung;
Blood, bones, and entrails, mashing with the blow,
From his pale lips a hideous mixture flow.
At length the backing oars the fight restrain,
980 The lifeless body drops amidst the main,
Soon enter at the breach the rushing waves,
And the salt stream the mangled carcass laves.
    Around the watery champaign* wide dispread
The living shipwrecks float amidst the dead,
985 With active arms the liquid deep they ply,
And panting to their mates for succour cry;
Now to some social* vessel press they near,
Their fellows pale the crowding numbers fear,
With ruthless hearts their well-known friends
      withstand,
990 And with keen falchions lop each grasping hand.
The dying fingers cling and clench the wood,
The heavy trunk sinks helpless in the flood.
    Now spent was all the warriors' steely store, ⎤
New darts they seek, and other arms explore, ⎬
995 This wields a flagstaff, that a ponderous oar. ⎦
Wrath's ready hands are never at a loss –
The fragments of the shattered ship they toss.
The useless rower from his seat is cast,
Then fly the benches, and the broken mast.
1000 Some seizing, as it sinks, the breathless corse,*
From the cold grasp the bloodstained weapon force.
Some from their own fresh bleeding bosoms take,

And at the foe the dropping javelin shake;
The left hand stays the blood and soothes the pain,
1005   The right sends back the reeking* spear again.
        Now gods of various elements conspire –
To Nereus, Vulcan joins his hostile fire;*
With oils and living sulphur darts they frame,
Prepared to spread afar the kindling flame;
1010   Around, the catching mischiefs swift succeed,
The floating hulks their own destruction feed,
The smeary wax the brightening blaze supplies,
And wavy fires from pitchy planks arise;
Amidst the flood the ruddy torrent strays,
1015   And fierce upon the scattering shipwrecks preys.
Here one with haste a flaming vessel leaves,)
Another, spent and beaten by the waves,   }
As eager to the burning ruin cleaves.   )
Amidst the various ways of death to kill,
1020   Whether by seas, by fires, or wounding steel,
The dreadfullest is that whose present force we feel.)
        Nor valour less her fatal rage maintains
In daring breasts that swim the liquid plains;
Some gather up the darts that floating lie,
1025   And to the combatants new deaths supply;
Some struggling in the deep the war provoke,
Rise o'er the surge and aim a languid stroke;
Some with strong grasp the foe conflicting* join,
Mix limbs with limbs, and hostile wreathings twine,
1030   Till plunging, pressing to the bottom down,
Vanquished and vanquishers, alike they drown.
        One, chief above the rest, is marked by fame
For watery fight, and Phoceus* was his name;
The heaving breath of life he knew to keep,
1035   While long he dwelt within the lowest deep;
Full many a fathom down he had explored
For treasures lost, old ocean's oozy hoard;
Oft when the flooky* anchor stuck below,
He sunk, and bade the captive vessel go.
1040   A foe he seized close cleaving to his breast,
And underneath the tumbling billows pressed;
But when the skilful victor would repair
To upper seas, and sought the freer air,

Hapless beneath the crowding keels he rose –
1045 The crowding keels his wonted way oppose;
Back beaten and astonished with the blow,
He sinks, to bide for ever now below.
　　Some hang upon the oars with weighty force
To intercept the hostile vessel's course,
1050 Some to the last the cause they love defend,
And valiant lives by useful deaths would end;
With breasts opposed the thundering beaks they
　　　　brave,
And what they fought for living, dying save.
　　As Tyrrhen,* from a Roman poop on high,
1055 Ran o'er the various combat with his eye,
Sure aiming, from his Balearic* thong,
Bold Lygdamus a ponderous bullet slung,
Through liquid air the ball shrill whistling flies,
And cuts its way through hapless Tyrrhen's eyes.
1060 Th'astonished youth stands struck with sudden night,
While bursting start the bleeding orbs of sight.
At first he took the darkness to be death,
And thought himself amidst the shades beneath,
But soon, recovering from the stunning stound,*
1065 He lived, unhappily he lived he found.
Vigour at length and wonted force returns,
And with new rage his valiant bosom burns:
'To me, my friends', he cried, 'your aid supply,
Nor useless let your fellow soldier die;
1070 Give me, opposed against the foe, to stand,
While like some engine you direct my hand.
And thou, my poor remaining life, prepare
To meet each hazard of the various war;
At least my mangled carcass shall pretend
1075 To interpose and shield some valiant friend;
Placed like a mark their darts I may sustain,
And, to preserve some better man, be slain.'
　　Thus said, unaiming he a javelin threw –
The javelin winged with sure destruction flew;
1080 In Argus the descending steel takes place,
Argus, a Grecian of illustrious race.
Deep sinks the piercing point, where to the loins
Above the navel high the belly joins;

The staggering youth falls forward on his fate,
1085 And helps the goring weapon with his weight.
     It chanced, so ruthless destiny designed,
To the same ship his agèd sire was joined;
While young for high achievements was he known,
The first in fair Massilia for renown;
1090 Now an example merely, and a name,   ⎤
Willing to rouse the younger sort he came,   ⎬
And fire their souls to emulate his fame.   ⎦
When from the prow, where distant far he stood,
He saw his son lie weltering in his blood,
1095 Soon to the poop, oft stumbling in his haste,
With faltering steps the feeble father passed.
No falling tears his wrinkled cheeks bedew,
But stiffening, cold and motionless he grew;
Deep night and deadly shades of darkness rise,
1100 And hide his much loved Argus from his eyes.
As to the dizzy youth the sire appears,
His dying, weak, unwieldy head he rears,
With lifted eyes he cast a mournful look,
His pale lips moved, and fain he would have spoke,
1105 But unexpressed th'imperfect accent hung,
Lost in his falling jaws and murmuring tongue;
Yet in his speechless visage seems expressed
What, had he words, would be his last request –
That agèd hand to seal his closing eye,
1110 And in his father's fond embrace to die.
But he, when grief with keenest sense revives,
With nature's strongest pangs conflicting strives;
'Let me not lose this hour of death', he cries,
'Which my indulgent destiny supplies;
1115 And thou forgive, forgive me, O my son,
If thy dear lips and last embrace I shun.
Warm from thy wound the purple current flows,
And vital breath yet heaving comes and goes;
Yet my sad eyes behold thee, yet alive,
1120 And thou shalt yet thy wretched sire survive.'*
He said, and fierce, by frantic sorrow pressed,
Plunged his sharp sword amidst his agèd breast,
And, though life's gushing streams the weapon stain,
Headlong he leaps amidst the greedy main,

1125   While this last wish ran ever in his mind –
       To die, and leave his darling son behind;
       Eager to part, his soul disdained to wait,
       And trust uncertain to a single fate.
          And now Massilia's vanquished force gives way,
1130   And Caesar's fortune claims the doubtful day.
       The Grecian fleet is all dispersed around;
       Some in the bottom of the deep lie drowned,
       Some, captives made, their haughty victors bore,
       While some, but those a few, fled timely to the shore.
1135   But oh, what verse, what numbers* can express,
       The mournful city, and her sore distress?
       Upon the beach lamenting matrons stand,
       And wailings echo o'er the lengthening strand;
       Their eyes are fixed upon the waters wide,
1140   And watch the bodies driving with the tide.
       Here a fond wife with pious error pressed
       Some hostile Roman to her throbbing breast,
       There to a mangled trunk two mothers* run –
       Each grasps, and each would claim it for her son,
1145   Each, what her boding heart persuades, believes,
       And for the last sad office fondly strives.
         But Brutus,* now victorious on the main,
       To Caesar vindicates the watery plain;
       First to his brow he binds the naval crown,
1150   And bids the spacious deep the mighty master own.

BOOK FOUR

But Caesar in Iberian fields afar
Ev'n to the western ocean spreads the war;
And though no hills of slaughter heap the plain, ⎫
No purple deluge leaves a guilty stain,   ⎬
5   Vast is the prize, and great the victor's gain. ⎭
For Pompey, with alternative* command,
The brave Petreius and Afranius* stand;
The chiefs in friendship's just conditions join,
And cordial to the common cause combine;
10 By turns they quit, by turns resume the sway,
The camp to guard, or battle to array;
To these their aid the nimble Vectons* yield,
With those who till Asturia's hilly field;
Nor wanted then the Celtiberians bold
15 Who draw their long descent from Celtic Gauls of
      old.
   Where rising grounds the fruitful champaign*
      end,*
And unperceived by soft degrees ascend,
An ancient race their city chose to found,
And with Ilerda's walls the summit crowned.
20 The Sicoris, of no ignoble name,
Fast by the mountain pours his gentle stream.
A stable bridge runs cross from side to side,   ⎫
Whose spacious arch transmits the passing tide, ⎬
And jutting piers the wintry floods abide.   ⎭
25 Two neighbouring hills their heads distinguished
      raise;
The first great Pompey's ensigns high displays;
Proud Caesar's camp upon the next is seen,
The river interposing glides between.
Wide-spread beyond an ample plain extends,
30 Far as the piercing eye its prospect sends;
Upon the spacious level's utmost bound
The Cinga rolls his rapid waves around;
But soon in full Iberus' channel lost,

His blended waters seek Iberia's coast;
35   He yields to the superior torrent's fame,
     And with the country takes his nobler name.
        Now 'gan the lamp of heaven the plains to gild,
     When moving legions hide th'embattled field,
     When front to front opposed in just array
40   The chieftains each their hostile powers display;
     But whether conscious shame their wrath repressed
     And soft reluctance rose in every breast,
     Or virtue did a short-lived rule resume
     And gained one day for liberty and Rome,
45   Suspended rage yet lingered for a space,
     And to the west declined the sun in peace;
     Night rose, and blackening shades involved the sky,
     When Caesar bent war's wily arts to try,
     Through his extended battle gives command
50   The foremost lines in order fixed shall stand;
     Meanwhile the last,* low lurking from the foe,
     With secret labour sink a trench below;
     Successful they the destined task pursue,
     While closing files prevent the hostile view.
55   Soon as the morn renewed the dawning grey,* ⎫
     He bids the soldier urge his speedy way   ⎬
     To seize a vacant height that near Ilerda lay. ⎭
     This saw the foe, and, winged with fear and shame,
     Through secret paths with swift prevention came.
60   Now various motives various hopes afford,
     To these the place, to those the conquering sword;
     Oppressed beneath their armour's cumbrous weight,
     Th'assailants labouring tempt the steepy height;
     Half bending back they mount with panting pain –
65   The following crowd their foremost mates sustain;
     Against the shelving precipice they toil,
     And prop their hands upon the steely pile;*
     On cliffs and shrubs their steps some climbing stay,
     With cutting swords some clear the woody way;
70   Nor death nor wounds their enemies annoy,
     While other uses now their arms employ.
     Their chief the danger from afar surveyed,
     And bade the horse fly timely to their aid.

In order just the ready squadrons ride,)
75   Then, wheeling, to the right and left divide,)
To flank the foot, and guard each naked side.)
Safe in the middle space retire the foot,
Make good the rear and scorn the foe's pursuit;
Each side retreat, though each disdain to yield,
80   And claim the glory of the doubtful field.
     Thus far the cause of Rome by arms was tried,*
And human rage alone the war supplied;
But now the elements new wrath prepare,
And gathering tempests vex the troubled air.
85   Long had the earth by wintry frost been bound,
And the dry North* had numbed the lazy ground.
No furrowed fields were drenched with drisly rain –
Snow hid the hills, and hoary ice the plain.
All desolate the western climes were seen,)
90   Keen were the blasts, and sharp the blue serene,)
To parch* the fading herb, and nip the springing)
          green.
At length the genial heat* began to shine*
With stronger beams in Aries' vernal* sign;
Again the golden day resumed its right,
95   And ruled in just equation with the night.
The moon her monthly course had now begun,
And with increasing horns forsook the sun,
When Boreas,* by night's silver empress driven,
To softer airs resigned the western heaven.
100   Then with warm breezes gentler Eurus* came,
Glowing with India's and Arabia's flame.
The sweeping wind the gathering vapours pressed
From every region of the farthest east,
Nor hang they heavy in the midway sky,
105   But speedy to Hesperia driving fly;
To Calpe's hills the sluicy* rains repair,)
From north and south the clouds assemble there,)
And darkening storms lour in the sluggish air.)
Where western skies the utmost ocean bound,
110   The watery treasures heap the welkin* round,
Thither they crowd and scanted* in the space,
Scarce between heaven and earth can find a place.
Condensed at length the spouting torrents pour,

Earth smokes and rattles with the gushing shower;
115 Jove's forky fires are rarely seen to fly –
Extinguished in the deluge soon they die;
Nor e'er before did dewy Iris* show
Such fady* colours or so maimed a bow:
Unvaried by the light's refracting beam,
120 She stooped to drink* from ocean's briny stream,
Then to the dropping sky restored the rain –
Again the falling waters sought the main.
Then first the covering snows began to flow
From off the Pyrenean's hoary brow;*
125 Huge hills of frost a thousand ages old,
O'er which the summer suns had vainly rolled,
Now melting rush from every side amain,
Swell every brook and deluge all the plain.
And now o'er Caesar's camp the torrents sweep,
130 Bear down the works, and fill the trenches deep.
Here men and arms in mixed confusion swim,
And hollow tents drive with th'impetuous stream;
Lost in the spreading flood the landmarks lie,
Nor can the forager his way descry.
135 No beasts for food the floating pastures yield,
Nor herbage rises in the watery field.
And now, to fill the measure of their fears,
Her baleful visage meagre famine rears;
Seldom alone, she troops among the fiends,*
140 And still on war and pestilence attends.
Unpressed, unstraitened by besieging foes,
All miseries of want the soldier knows.
Gladly he gives his little wealth to eat,
And buys a morsel with his whole estate.
145 Cursed merchandise, where life itself is sold,
And avarice consents to starve for gold!
No rock, no rising mountain rears his head, ⎫
No single river winds along the mead, ⎬
But one vast lake o'er all the land is spread. ⎭
150 No lofty grove, no forest haunt is found,
But in his den deep lies the savage* drowned;
With headlong rage resistless in its course
The rapid torrent whirls the snorting horse.
High o'er the sea the foamy freshes* ride,

155 While backward Tethys* turns her yielding tide.
     Meantime continued darkness veils the skies,
     And suns with unavailing ardour rise,
     Nature no more her various face can boast,
     But form is huddled up in night, and lost.
160 Such are the climes beneath the frozen zone*
     Where cheerless winter plants her dreary throne;
     No golden stars their gloomy heavens adorn,
     Nor genial seasons to their earth return,
     But everlasting ice and snows appear,
165 Bind up the summer signs,* and curse the barren
         year.
       Almighty sire,* who dost supremely reign,
     And thou, great ruler* of the raging main,
     Ye gracious gods! in mercy give command
     This desolation may for ever stand.
170 Thou Jove! for ever cloud thy stormy sky;
     Thou Neptune! bid thy angry waves run high;
     Heave thy huge trident for a mighty blow,
     Strike the strong earth, and bid her fountains flow;
     Bid every river god exhaust his urn,
175 Nor let thy own alternate tides return;
     Wide let their blended waters waste around,
     These regions Rhine, and those the Rhone confound.
     Melt, ye hoar mountains of Riphaean snow,
     Brooks, streams and lakes, let all your sources go;
180 Your spreading floods the guilt of Rome shall spare,
     And save the wretched world from civil war.
       But fortune stayed her short displeasure here,*
     Nor urged her minion* with too long a fear;
     With large increase her favours full returned,
185 As if the gods themselves his* anger mourned,
     As if his name were terrible to heaven,
     And providence could sue to be forgiven.
       Now 'gan the welkin clear to shine serene,
     And Phoebus potent in his rays was seen.
190 The scattering clouds disclosed the piercing light,
     And hung the firmament with fleecy white;
     The troublous storm had spent his wrathful store,
     And clattering rains were heard to rush no more.
     Again the woods their leafy honours raise,

195 And herds upon the rising mountains graze.
    Day's genial heat upon the damps prevails,
    And ripens into earth the slimy vales.
    Bright glittering stars adorn night's spangled air,
    And ruddy evening skies foretell the morning fair.
200   Soon as the falling Sicoris begun
    A peaceful stream within his banks to run,
    The bending willow into barks they twine,
    Then line the work with spoils of slaughtered kine –
    Such are the floats Venetian fishers know,
205 Where in dull marshes stands the settling Po;
    On such to neighbouring Gaul, allured by gain,
    The bolder Britons cross the swelling main;
    Like these, when fruitful Egypt lies afloat,
    The Memphian artist builds his reedy boat.
210 On these embarking, bold with eager haste,
    Across the stream his legions Caesar passed;
    Straight the tall woods with sounding strokes are
            felled,
    And with strong piles a beamy bridge they build,
    Then, mindful of the flood so lately spread,
215 They stretch the lengthening arches o'er the mead.
    And lest his bolder waters rise again,
    With numerous dykes they canton out* the plain,
    And by a thousand streams the suffering river drain.
        Petreius now a fate superior* saw,
220 While elements obey proud Caesar's law,
    Then straight Ilerda's lofty walls forsook,
    And to the farthest west his arms betook;
    The nearer regions faithless all around
    And basely to the victor bent he found,
225 When with just rage and indignation fired
    He to the Celtiberians fierce retired,
    There sought, amidst the world's extremest parts,
    Still daring hands and still unconquered hearts.
        Soon as he viewed the neighbouring mountain's
            head
230 No longer by the hostile camp o'erspread,
    Caesar commands to arm. Without delay
    The soldier to the river bends his way;
    None then with cautious care the bridge explored,

Or sought the shallows of the safer ford,
235 Armed at all points they plunge amidst the flood,
And with strong sinews make the passage good;
Dangers they scorn that might the bold affright,
And stop ev'n panting cowards in their flight.
At length the farther bank attaining safe,
240 Chilled by the stream, their dropping limbs they
        chafe,
Then with fresh vigour urge the foe's pursuit,
And in the sprightly chase the powers of life recruit.
Thus they, till half the course of light was run,
And lessening shadows owned the noonday sun;
245 The fliers now a doubtful fight maintain,
While the fleet horse in squadrons scour the plain;
The stragglers scattering round they force to yield,
And gather up the gleanings of the field.
    Midst a wide plain two lofty rocks arise,*
250 Between the cliffs an humble valley lies;
Long rows of ridgy mountains run behind,
Where ways obscure and secret passes wind.
But Caesar, deep within his thought, foresees
The foe's attempt the covert strong to seize:
255 So may their troops at leisure range afar,
And to the Celtiberians lead the war.
'Be quick!', he cries, 'nor minding just array
Swift to the combat wing your speedy way.
See where yon cowards to the fastness haste,
260 But let your terrors in their way be placed;
Pierce not the fearful backs of those that fly,
But on your meeting javelins let them die.'
He said; the ready legions took the word,
And hastily obey their eager lord,
265 With diligence the coming foe prevent,
And stay their marches, to the mountains bent.
Near neighbouring now the camps entrenched are
        seen,
With scarce a narrow interval between.
    Soon as their eyes o'ershoot the middle space,*
270 From either host sires, sons and brothers trace
The well-known features of some kindred face.
Then first their hearts with tenderness were struck,

First with remorse for civil rage they shook;
Stiffening with horror cold and dire amaze,*
275   Awhile in silent interviews they gaze;
Anon with speechless signs their swords salute,
While thoughts conflicting keep their masters mute.
At length, disdaining still to be repressed,
Prevailing passion rose in every breast,
280   And the vain rules of guilty war transgressed.
As at a signal both their trenches quit,
And spreading arms in close embraces knit;
Now friendship runs o'er all her ancient claims –
Guest and companion are their only names;
285   Old neighbourhood they fondly call to mind,
And how their boyish years in leagues were joined.
With grief each other mutually they know,
And find a friend in every Roman foe.
Their falling tears their steely arms bedew,
290   While interrupting sighs each kiss pursue,
And though their hands are yet unstained by guilt,
They tremble for the blood they might have spilt.
But speak, unhappy Roman, speak thy pain,
Say for what woes thy streaming eyes complain.
295   Why dost thou groan? Why beat thy sounding
          breast?
Why is this wild fantastic grief expressed?
Is it that yet thy country claims thy care?
Dost thou the crimes of war unwilling share?
Ah! whither art thou by thy fears betrayed?
300   How canst thou dread that power thyself hast made?
Do Caesar's trumpets call thee? Scorn the sound.
Does he bid march? Dare thou to keep thy ground.
So rage and slaughter shall to justice yield,
And fierce Erinyes* quit the fatal field,
305   Caesar in peace a private state shall know,
And Pompey be no longer called his foe.
   Appear, thou heavenly concord, blessed appear!
And shed thy better influences here.
Thou who the warring elements dost bind,
310   Life of the world, and safety of mankind,
Infuse thy sovereign balm, and heal the wrathful
          mind.

But if the same dire fury rages yet,
Too well they know what foes their swords shall
          meet;
No blind pretence of ignorance remains –
315   The blood they shed must flow from Roman veins.
O fatal truce! the brand of guilty Rome!
From thee worse wars and redder slaughters come.
See with what free and unsuspecting love
From camp to camp the jocund warriors rove;
320   Each to his turfy table bids his guest,
And Bacchus crowns the hospitable feast.
The grassy fires refulgent lend their light,
While conversation sleepless wastes the night;
Of early feats of arms by turns they tell,
325   Of fortunes that in various fields befell,
With well-becoming pride their deeds relate,
And now agree, and friendly now debate.
At length their unauspicious hands are joined,
And sacred leagues with faith renewed they bind.
330   But oh, what worse could cruel fate afford!
The furies smiled upon the cursed accord,
And dyed with deeper stains the Roman sword.
      By busy fame Petreius soon is told*
His camp, himself, to Caesar all are sold,
335   When straight the chief indignant calls to arm,
And bids the trumpet spread the loud alarm.
With war encompassed round he takes his way,
And breaks the short-lived truce with fierce affray;
He drives th'unarmed and unsuspecting guest
340   Amazed and wounded from th'unfinished feast;
With horrid steel he cuts each fond embrace,
And violates with blood the new-made peace.
And lest the fainting flames of wrath expire,
With words like these he fans the deadly fire:
345   'Ye herd, unknowing of the Roman worth,
And lost to that great cause which led you forth,
Though victory and captive Caesar were
Honours too glorious for your swords to share,
Yet something, abject as you are, from you,
350   Something to virtue and the laws is due;
A second praise ev'n yet you may partake –

Fight and be vanquished for your country's sake.
Can you, while fate as yet suspends our doom,
While you have blood and lives to lose for Rome,
355   Can you with tame submission seek a lord,
And own a cause by men and gods abhorred?
Will you in lowly wise his mercy crave?
Can soldiers beg to wear the name of slave?
Would you for us your suit to Caesar move?
360   Know we disdain his pardoning power to prove;
No private bargain shall redeem this head –
For Rome and not for us the war was made.
Though peace a specious poor pretence afford,
Baseness and bondage lurk beneath the word.
365   In vain the workmen search the steely mine
To arm the field and bid the battle shine,
In vain the fortress lifts her towery height,
In vain the warlike steed provokes the fight,
In vain our oars the foamy ocean sweep,
370   In vain our floating castles* hide the deep,
In vain by land, in vain by sea we fought,
If peace shall e'er with liberty be bought.
See with what constancy, what gallant pride,
Our steadfast foes defend an impious side!
375   Bound by their oaths, though enemies to good,
They scorn to change from what they once have
     vowed.
While each vain breath your slackening faith
     withdraws,
Yours, who pretend to arm for Rome and laws,
Who find no fault, but justice in your cause.
380   And yet methinks I would not give you o'er –
A brave repentance still is in your power.
While Pompey calls the utmost east from far,
And leads the Indian monarchs on to war,
Shall we, O shame, prevent his great success,
385   And bind his hands by our inglorious peace?'
    He spoke, and civil rage at once returns;
Each breast the fonder thought of pity scorns,
And ruthless with redoubled fury burns.
So when the tiger or the spotted pard,*
390   Long from the woods and savage haunts debarred,

From their first fierceness for a while are won,
And seem to put a gentler nature on,
Patient their prison and mankind they bear,
Fawn on their lords, and looks less horrid wear;
395   But let the taste of slaughter be renewed,
And their fell jaws again with gore imbrued,
Then dreadfully their wakening furies rise,
And glaring fires rekindle in their eyes,
With wrathful roar their echoing dens they tear,
400   And hardly ev'n the well-known keeper spare –
The shuddering keeper shakes and stands aloof for
      fear.
From friendship freed, and conscious nature's tie,
To undistinguished* slaughters loose they fly,
With guilt avowed their daring crimes advance,
405   And scorn th'excuse of ignorance and chance.
Those whom so late their fond embraces pressed,
The bosom's partner and the welcome guest,
Now at the board* unhospitable* bleed,
While streams of blood the flowing bowl succeed.*
410   With groans at first each draws the glittering brand,*
And lingering death stops in th'unwilling hand,*
Till urged at length returning force they feel,
And catch new courage from the murdering steel;
Vengeance and hatred rise with every blow,
415   And blood paints every visage like a foe.
Uproar and horror through the camp abound,
While impious sons their mangled fathers wound,
And lest the merit of the crime be lost,
With dreadful joy the parricide they boast;
420   Proud to their chiefs the cold, pale heads they bear,
The gore yet dropping from the silver hair.
    But thou, O Caesar, to the gods be dear!
Thy pious mercy well becomes their care;
And though thy soldier falls by treacherous peace,
425   Be proud, and reckon this thy great success.
Not all thou ow'st to bounteous fortune's smile,
Not proud Massilia nor the Pharian Nile,
Not the full conquest of Pharsalia's field,
Could greater fame or nobler trophies yield;
430   Thine and the cause of justice now are one,

Since guilty slaughter brands thy foes alone.
    Nor dare the conscious* leaders longer wait,*
Or trust to such unhallowed hands their fate,
Astonished and dismayed they shun the fight,
435 And to Ilerda turn their hasty flight.
But e'er their march achieves its destined course,
Preventing Caesar sends the wingèd horse;
The speedy squadrons seize th'appointed ground,
And hold their foes on hills encompassed round.
440 Pent up in barren heights, they strive in vain
Refreshing springs and flowing streams to gain,
Strong hostile works their camp's extension stay,
And deep-sunk trenches intercept their way.
    Now deaths in unexpected forms arise:
445 Thirst and pale famine stalk before their eyes.
Shut up and close besieged, no more they need ⎫
The strength or swiftness of the warlike steed, ⎬
But doom the generous coursers all to bleed.* ⎭
Hopeless at length, and barred around from flight,
450 Headlong they rush to arms and urge the fight;
But Caesar, who with wary eyes beheld*
With what determined rage they sought the field,
Restrained his eager troops. 'Forbear', he cried,
'Nor let your swords in madmen's blood be dyed.
455 But since they come devoted* by despair, ⎫
Since life is grown unworthy of their care, ⎬
Since 'tis their time to die, 'tis ours to spare. ⎭
Those naked bosoms that provoke the foe
With greedy hopes of deadly vengeance glow;
460 With pleasure shall they meet the pointed steel,
Nor smarting wounds nor dying anguish feel,
If, while they bleed, your Caesar shares the pain,
And mourns his gallant friends among the slain.
But wait awhile, this rage shall soon be passed,
465 This blaze of courage is too fierce to last,
This ardour for the fight shall faint away,
And all this fond desire of death decay.'
    He spoke, and at the word the war was stayed,
Till Phoebus fled from night's ascending shade.
470 Ev'n all the day, embattled on the plain,
The rash Petreians urge to arms in vain;

At length the weary fire began to cease,
And wasting fury languished into peace;
Th'impatient arrogance of wrath declined,
475 And slackening passions cooled upon the mind.
So when, the battle roaring loud around,
Some warrior warm receives a fatal wound,
While yet the griding* sword has newly passed,
And the first pungent pains and anguish last,
480 While full with life the turgid vessels rise,*
And the warm juice the sprightly nerve supplies,
Each sinewy* limb with fiercer force is pressed,
And rage redoubles in the burning breast;
But if, as conscious of th'advantage gained,
485 The cooler victor stays his wrathful hand,
Then sinks his thrall* with ebbing spirits low,
The black blood stiffens and forgets to flow,
Cold damps and numbness close the deadly stound,*
And stretch him pale and fainting on the ground.
490   For water now on every side they try,
Alike the sword and delving spade employ,
Earth's bosom dark laborious they explore,
And search the sources of her liquid store;
Deep in the hollow hill the well descends,
495 Till level with the moister plain it ends.
Not lower down from cheerful day decline
The pale Assyrians* in the golden mine.
In vain they toil, no secret streams are found
To roll their murmuring tides beneath the ground,
500 No bursting springs repay the workman's stroke,
Nor glittering gush from out the wounded rock,
No sweating caves in dewy droppings stand,
Nor smallest rills run gurgling o'er the sand.
Spent and exhausted with the fruitless pain,
505 The fainting youth ascend to light again.
And now less patient of the drought they grow
Than in those cooler depths of earth below;
No savoury viands crown the cheerful board,
Ev'n food for want of water stands abhorred;
510 To hunger's meagre refuge they retreat,
And, since they cannot drink, refuse to eat.
Where yielding clods a moister clay confess,

With griping* hands the clammy glebe* they press;
Where-e'er the standing puddle loathsome lies,
515 Thither in crowds the thirsty soldier flies;
Horrid to sight, the miry filth they quaff,
And drain with dying jaws the deadly draff.*
Some seek the bestial mothers for supply,
And draw the herd's extended udders dry,
520 Till thirst, unsated with the milky store,
With labouring lips drinks in the putrid gore;
Some strip the leaves and suck the morning dews, ⎫
Some grind the bark, the woody branches bruise, ⎬
And squeeze the sapling's unconcocted juice. ⎭

525 O happy those, to whom the barbarous kings*
Left their envenomed floods and tainted springs!
Caesar be kind, and every bane prepare,
Which Cretan rocks* or Libyan serpents bear;
The Romans to thy poisonous stream shall fly,
530 And, conscious of the danger, drink and die.
With secret flames their withering entrails burn,
And fiery breathings from their lungs return;
The shrinking veins contract their purple flood,
And urge, laborious, on the beating blood;
535 The heaving sighs through straiter passes blow,
And scorch the painful palate as they go;
The parched, rough tongue night's humid vapour
   draws,
And restless rolls within the clammy jaws;
With gaping mouths they wait the falling rain,
540 And want those floods that lately spread the plain.
Vainly to heaven they turn their longing eyes,
And fix them on the dry, relentless skies.
Nor here by sandy Afric* are they cursed,
Nor Cancer's sultry line inflames their thirst,
545 But, to enhance their pain, they view below
Where lakes stand full and plenteous rivers flow;
Between two streams expires the panting host,
And in a land of waters are they lost.

  Now pressed by pinching want's unequal weight,*
550 The vanquished leaders yield to adverse fate;
Rejecting arms, Afranius seeks relief,
And sues submissive to the hostile chief.

Foremost himself, to Caesar's camp he leads
His famished troops; a fainting band succeeds.
555　At length, in presence of the victor placed,
A fitting dignity his gesture graced
That spoke his present fortunes, and his past.
With decent mixture in his manly mien
The captive and the general were seen;
560　Then with a free, secure, undaunted breast
For mercy thus his pious suit he pressed:
　　'Had fate and my ill fortune laid me low
Beneath the power of some ungenerous foe,
My sword hung ready to protect my fame,
565　And this right hand had saved my soul from shame;
But now with joy I bend my suppliant knee:
Life is worth asking since 'tis given by thee.
No party zeal our factious arms inclines,
No hate of thee or of thy bold designs.
570　War with its own occasions came unsought,
And found us on the side for which we fought;
True to our cause, as best becomes the brave,
Long as we could, we kept that faith we gave.
Nor shall our arms thy stronger fate delay –
575　Behold! our yielding paves thy conquering way;
The western nations all at once we give,
Securely these behind thee shalt thou leave;
Here while thy full dominion stands confessed,
Receive it as an earnest of the east.
580　Nor this thy easy victory disdain,
Bought with no seas of blood nor hills of slain;
Forgive the foes that spare thy sword a pain.
Nor is the boon for which we sue too great –
The weary soldier begs a last retreat;
585　In some poor village, peaceful at the plough,
Let them enjoy the life thou dost bestow.
Think, in some field, among the slain we lie,
And lost to thy remembrance cast us by.
Mix not our arms in thy successful war,
590　Nor let thy captives in thy triumph share.
These unprevailing bands their fate have tried,
And proved that fortune fights not on their side.
Guiltless to cease from slaughter we implore,

Let us not conquer with thee, and we ask no more.'
595   He said. The victor, with a gentler grace
And mercy softening his severer face,
Bade his attending foes their fears dismiss,
Go free from punishment, and live in peace.
The truce on equal terms at length agreed,
600 The waters from the watchful guard are freed;
Eager to drink, down rush the thirsty crowd,
Hang o'er the banks, and trouble all the flood.
Some, while too fierce the fatal draughts they drain,
Forget the gasping lungs that heave in vain;
605 No breathing airs the choking channels fill,
But every spring of life at once stands still.
Some drink, nor yet the fervent pest* assuage,
With wonted fires their bloated entrails rage,
With bursting sides each bulk enormous heaves,
610 While still for drink th'insatiate fever craves.
At length returning health dispersed the pain.
And lusty vigour strung the nerves again.*
    Behold, ye sons of luxury, behold,
Who scatter in excess your lavish gold,
615 You who the wealth of frugal ages waste
T'indulge a wanton, supercilious taste,
For whom all earth, all ocean are explored
To spread the various, proud, voluptuous board,
Behold how little thrifty nature craves,
620 And what a cheap relief the lives of thousands saves!
No costly wines these fainting legions know,
Marked by old consuls many a year ago,
No waiting slaves the precious juices pour
From myrrhine* goblets, or the golden ore,
625 But with pure draughts they cool the boiling blood,
And seek their succour from the crystal flood.
Who but a wretch would think it worth his care
The toils and wickedness of war to share,
When all we want thus easily we find –
630 The field and river can supply mankind.
Dismissed, and safe from danger and alarms,
The vanquished to the victor quits his arms,
Guiltless from camps to cities he repairs,
And in his native land forgets his cares.

635   There in his mind he runs repenting o'er
       The tedious toils and perils once he bore;
       His spear and sword of battle stand accursed,
       He hates the weary march and parching thirst,
       And wonders much that e'er with pious pain
640   He prayed so oft for victory in vain –
       For victory, the curse of those that win,
       The fatal end where still new woes begin.
       Let the proud masters of the horrid field
       Count all the gains their dire successes yield;
645   Then let them think what wounds they yet must feel
       E'er they can fix revolving fortune's wheel;
       As yet th'imperfect task by halves is done:
       Blood, blood remains, more battles must be won,
       And many a heavy labour undergone.
650   Still conquering, to new guilt they shall succeed,
       Wherever restless fate and Caesar lead.
       How happier lives the man to peace assigned
       Amidst this general storm that wrecks mankind!
       In his own quiet house ordained to die,
655   He knows the place in which his bones shall lie.
       No trumpet warns him put his harness on,
       Though faint and all with weariness foredone;
       But when night falls he lies securely down,
       And calls the creeping slumber all his own.
660   His kinder fates the warrior's hopes prevent,*
       And e'er the time the wished dismission* sent;
       A lowly cottage and a tender wife
       Receive him in his early days of life,
       His boys, a rustic tribe, around him play,
665   And homely pleasures wear the vacant day.
       No factious parties here the mind engage,
       Nor work th'embittered passions up to rage;
       With equal eyes the hostile chiefs they view –
       To this their faith, to that their lives are due;*
670   To both obliged alike, no part they take,
       Nor vows for conquest, nor against it, make.
       Mankind's misfortunes they behold from far,
       Pleased to stand neuter,* while the world's at war.*
          But fortune, bent to check the victor's pride,
675   In other lands forsook her Caesar's side,

With changing cheer the fickle goddess frowned,
And for a while her favourite cause disowned.
Where Adria's swelling surge Salonae laves,
And warm Iader* rolls his gentle waves,
680 Bold in the brave Curictan's warlike band,
Antonius* camps upon the utmost strand;
Begirt around by Pompey's floating power,
He braves the navy from his well fenced shore.
But while the distant war no more he fears,*
685 Famine, a worse resistless foe, appears;
No more the meads their grassy pasture yield,
Nor waving harvests crown the yellow field.
On every verdant leaf the hungry feed,
And snatch the forage from the fainting steed,
690 Then ravenous on their camp's defence they fall,
And grind with greedy jaws the turfy wall.
Near on the neighbouring coast at length they spy
Where Basilus* with social sails* draws nigh,
While led by Dolabella's* bold command
695 Their Caesar's legions spread the Illyrian strand;
Straight with new hopes their hearts recovering beat,
Aim to elude the foe, and meditate retreat.
    Of wondrous form a vast machine they build,
New and unknown upon the floating field.
700 Here nor the keel its crooked length extends,
Nor o'er the waves the rising deck ascends:
By beams and grappling chains compacted strong,
Light skiffs and casks two equal rows prolong;
O'er these, of solid oak securely made,
705 Stable and tight a flooring firm is laid;
Sublime* from hence two planky towers run high,
And nodding battlements the foe defy.
Securely placed, each rising range between,
The lusty rower plies his task unseen.
710 Meanwhile nor oars upon the sides appear,
Nor swelling sails receive the driving air,
But living seems the mighty mass to sweep,
And glide self-moved athwart the yielding deep.
Three wondrous floats of this enormous size
715 Soon by the skilful builder's craft arise,
The ready warriors all aboard them ride,

And wait the turn of the retiring tide.
Backward at length revolving Tethys* flows,
And ebbing waves the naked sands disclose;
720 Straight by the stream the launching piles are borne,
Shields, spears and helms their nodding towers adorn,
Threatening they move in terrible array,
And to the deeper ocean bend their way.
      Octavius* now, whose naval powers command
725 Adria's rude seas and wide Illyria's strand,
Full in their course his fleet advancing stays,
And each impatient combatant delays;
To the blue offing* wide he seems to bear,
Hopeful to draw th'unwary vessels near,
730 Aloof* he rounds them, eager on his prey,
And tempts them with an open, roomy sea.
Thus when the wily huntsman spreads his nets,
And with his ambient toil* the wood besets,
While yet his busy hands, with skilful care,
735 The meshy hays* and forky props prepare,*
E'er yet the deer the painted plumage spy,*
Snuff the strong odour* from afar, and fly,
His mates the Cretan hound and Spartan bind
And muzzle all the loud Molossian* kind;
740 The quester* only to the wood they loose,
Who silently the tainted* track pursues;
Mute signs alone the conscious* haunt betray,
While fixed he points, and trembles to the prey.*
      'Twas at the season when the fainting light
745 Just in the evening's close brought on the night,
When the tall, towery floats their isle forsook,
And to the seas their course adventurous took.
But now the famed Cilician pirates,* skilled*
In arts and warfare of the liquid field,
750 Their wonted wiles and stratagems provide,
To aid their great acknowledged victor's* side.
Beneath the glassy surface of the main
From rock to rock they stretch a ponderous chain;
Loosely the slacker links suspended flow,
755 T'enwrap the driving fabrics* as they go.
Urged from within and wafted by the tide,
Smooth o'er the boom the first and second glide;

The third the guileful, latent* chain enfolds,
And in his steely grasp entwining holds;
760 From the tall rocks the shouting victors roar,
And drag the resty* captive to the shore.
For ages past an ancient cliff there stood,
Whose bending brow hung threatening o'er the
flood;*
A verdant grove was on the summit placed,
765 And o'er the waves a gloomy shadow cast,
While near the base wide hollows sink below,
There roll huge seas and bellowing tempests blow;
Thither what-e'er the greedy waters drown,
The shipwreck and the driving corpse, are thrown;
770 Anon the gaping gulf the spoil restores,
And from his lowest depths loud spouting pours.
Not rude Charybdis* roars in sounds like these,
When thundering with a burst she spews the foamy
seas.
Hither, with warlike Opitergians fraught,
775 The third ill-fated prisoner float was brought;
The foe, as at a signal, speed their way,
And haste to compass in the destined prey;
The crowding sails from every station press,
While armèd bands the rocks and shores possess.
780 Too late the chief, Vulteius,* found the snare,
And strove to burst the toil with fruitless care;
Driv'n by despair at length, nor thinking yet
Which way to fight, or whither to retreat,
He turns upon the foe, and though distressed,
785 By wiles entangled and by crowds oppressed,
With scarce a single cohort to his aid,
Against the gathering host a stand he made.
Fierce was the combat fought, with slaughter great,
Though thus on odds unequally they meet –
790 One with a thousand matched, a ship against a fleet.
But soon on dusky wings arose the night,
And with her friendly shade restrains the fight;
The combatants from war consenting cease,
And pass the hours of darkness o'er in peace.
795   When to the soldier, anxious for his fate,
And doubtful what success the dawn might wait,

The brave Vulteius thus his speech addressed,
And thus composed the cares of every beating breast:
   'My gallant friends! whom our hard fates decree,
800   This night, this short night only, to be free,
Think what remains to do, but think with haste,
E'er the brief hour of liberty be past.
Perhaps, reduced to this so hard extreme,
Too short to some the date of life may seem;
805   Yet know, brave youths, that none untimely fall,
Whom death obeys, and comes but when they call.
'Tis true the neighbouring danger waits us nigh, |
We meet but that from which we cannot fly – * }
Yet think not but with equal praise we die. |
810   Dark and uncertain is man's future doom,
If years, or only moments are to come;
All is but dying,* he who gives an hour,
Or he who gives an age, gives all that's in his power.
Sooner or late, all mortals know the grave,
815   But to choose death distinguishes the brave.
Behold where, waiting round, yon hostile band,
Our fellow citizens, our lives demand.
Prevent we then their cruel hands, and bleed – |
'Tis but to do what is too sure decreed, }
820   And, where our fate would drag us on, to lead. |
A great, conspicuous slaughter shall we yield,
Nor lie the carnage of a common field,
Where one ignoble heap confounds the slain,
And men and beasts promiscuous strew the plain.
825   Placed on this float by some diviner hand,
As on a stage for public view, we stand.*
Illyria's neighbouring shores, her isles around,
And every cliff with gazers shall be crowned;
The seas and earth our virtue shall proclaim,
830   And stand eternal vouchers for our fame,
Alike the foes and fellows of our cause*
Shall mark the deed, and join in vast applause.
Blessed be thou, fortune, that hast marked us forth,
A monument of unexampled* worth;
835   To latest times our story shall be told,
Ev'n raised beyond the noblest names of old;
Distinguished praise shall crown our daring youth,

Our pious honour and unshaken truth.
Mean is our offering, Caesar, we confess:
840   For such a chief what soldier can do less?
Yet oh, this faithful pledge of love receive!
Take it, 'tis all that captives have to give.
Oh, that to make the victim yet more dear,
Our aged sires, our children had been here;
845   Then with full horror should the slaughter rise,
And blast our paler foes' astonished eyes,
Till, awed beneath that scorn of death we wear,
They bless the time our fellows 'scaped their snare,
Till with mean tears our fate the cowards mourn,
850   And tremble at the rage with which we burn.
Perhaps they mean our constant souls to try,
Whether for life and peace we may comply.
Oh, grant, ye gods, their offers may be great,
That we may gloriously disdain to treat,
855   That this last proof of virtue we may give,
And show we die not now because we could not live.
That valour to no common heights must rise,
Which he our godlike chief himself shall prize.
Immortal shall our truth for ever stand, ⎫
860   If Caesar thinks this little faithful band ⎬
A loss, amidst the host of his command. ⎭
For me, my friends, my fixed resolve is ta'en,*
And fate or chance may proffer life in vain;
I scorn whatever safety they provide,
865   And cast the worthless trifling thought aside.
The sacred rage of death devours me whole,
Reigns in my heart, and triumphs in my soul;
I see, I reach the period* of my woe,
And taste those joys the dying only know.
870   Wisely the gods conceal the wondrous good,
Lest man no longer should endure his load,
Lest every wretch like me from life should fly,
Seize his own happiness himself, and die.'
      He spoke; the band his potent tongue confessed,
875   And generous ardour burned in every breast.
No longer now they view with watery eyes
The swift revolving circle of the skies,
No longer think the setting stars in haste,

Nor wonder slow Boötes moves so fast,
880   But with high hearts exulting all, and gay,
They wish for light and call the tardy day.
Yet nor the heavenly axis long delays
To roll the radiant signs beneath the seas,
In Leda's twins* now rose the warmer sun,
885   And near the lofty Crab exalted shone,
Swiftly night's shorter shades began to move,
And to the west Thessalian Chiron* drove.
At length the morning's purple beams disclose
The wide horizon covered round with foes,
890   Each rock and shore the crowding Istrians keep,
While Greeks and fierce Liburnians spread the deep,
When yet, e'er fury lets the battle loose,
Octavius woos them with the terms of truce,
If haply Pompey's chains they choose to wear,
895   And captive life to instant death prefer.
But the brave youth, regardless of his might,
Fierce in the scorn of life, and hating light,
Fearless, and careless of whate'er may come,
Resolved and self-determined to their doom,
900   Alike disdain the threatening of the war,
And all the flattering wiles their foes prepare.
Calmly the numerous legions round they view,
At once by land and sea the fight renew;
Relief, or friends, or aid expect they none,
905   But fix one certain trust in death alone.
In opposition firm awhile they stood,
But soon were satisfied with hostile blood.
Then turning from the foe, with gallant pride,
'Is there a generous youth', Vulteius cried,
910   'Whose worthy sword may pierce your leader's
          side?'
He said, and at the word, from every part,
A hundred pointed weapons reached his heart;
Dying he praised them all, but him the chief
Whose eager duty brought the first relief:
915   Deep in his breast he plunged his deadly blade,
And with a grateful stroke the friendly gift repaid.
    At once all rush, at once to death they fly,
And on each other's swords alternate die,

Greedy to make the mischief all their own,
920 And arrogate the guilt of war alone.
A fate like this did Cadmus' harvest prove,*
When mortally the earth-born brethren strove,
When, by each other's hands of life bereft,
An omen dire to future Thebes they left;
925 Such was the rage inspired the Colchian foes,*
When from the dragon's wondrous teeth they rose,
When, urged by charms and magic's mystic power,
They dyed their native field with streaming gore,
Till ev'n the fell enchantress stood dismayed,
930 And wondered at the mischiefs which she made.
Furies* more fierce the dying Romans feel,
And with bare breasts provoke the lingering steel,
With fond embraces catch the deadly darts,
And press them plunging to their panting hearts.
935 No wound imperfect for a second calls,
With certain aim the sure destruction falls.
This last best gift,* this one unerring blow,
Sires, sons and brothers mutually bestow;
Nor piety nor fond remorse prevail,
940 And if they fear, they only fear to fail.
Here with red streams the blushing waves they stain,
Here dash their mangled entrails in the main,
Here with a last disdain they view the skies,
Shut out heaven's hated light with scornful eyes,
945 And with insulting joy the victor foe despise.
At length the heapy slaughter rose on high,
The hostile chiefs the purple pile* descry,
And while the last accustomed rites they give,
Scarcely the unexampled deed believe;
950 Much they admire a faith by death approved,
And wonder lawless power could e'er be thus
    beloved.
   Wide through mankind eternal fame displays
This hardy crew, this single vessel's praise.
But oh, the story of the godlike rage
955 Is lost upon a vile, degenerate age;
The base, the slavish world will not be taught
With how much ease their freedom may be bought.

Still arbitrary power on thrones commands, }
Still liberty is galled by tyrants' bands, }
960   And swords in vain are trusted to our hands. }
O death! thou pleasing end of human woe,
Thou cure for life, thou greatest good below,
Still may'st thou fly the coward and the slave,
And thy soft slumbers only bless the brave.

965   Nor war's pernicious* god less havoc yields
Where swarthy Libya spreads her sunburned fields.
For Curio now the stretching canvas spread,
And from Sicilian shores his navy led;
To Afric's coast he cuts the foamy way
970   Where low the once victorious Carthage lay.
There landing, to the well-known camp he hies,
Where from afar the distant seas he spies,
Where Bagrada's dull waves the sands divide,
And slowly downward roll their sluggish tide.
975   From thence he seeks the heights renowned by fame,
And hallowed by the great Cornelian* name;
The rocks and hills which, long traditions say,
Were held by huge Antaeus' horrid sway.*
Here, as by chance, he lights upon the place,
980   Curious he tries the reverend tale to trace,
When thus in short the ruder Libyans tell
What from their sires they heard and how the case
          befell:
      'The teeming earth, for ever fresh and young,*
Yet,* after many a giant son, was strong,
985   When labouring here with the prodigious birth
She brought her youngest-born Antaeus forth.
Of all the dreadful brood which erst she bore,
In none the fruitful beldame* gloried more;
Happy for those above she brought him not
990   Till after Phlegra's* doubtful field was fought.
That this, her darling, might in force excel,
A gift she gave whene'er to earth he fell,
Recruited strength he from his parent drew,
And every slackening nerve was strung anew.
995   Yon cave his den he made, where oft for food
He snatched the mother lion's horrid brood.
Nor leaves nor shaggy hides his couch prepared,

Torn from the tiger or the spotted pard,
But stretched along the naked earth he lies –
1000　New vigour still the native earth supplies.
Whate'er he meets his ruthless hands invade,
Strong in himself without his mother's aid.
The strangers that unknowing seek the shore
Soon a worse shipwreck on the land deplore.
1005　Dreadful to all, with matchless might he reigns, ⎫
Robs, spoils and massacres the simple swains, ⎬
And all unpeopled lie the Libyan plains. ⎭
At length, around the trembling nations spread,
Fame of the tyrant to Alcides* fled.
1010　The godlike hero, born by Jove's decree
To set the seas and earth from monsters free,
Hither in generous pity bent his course,
And set himself to prove the giant's force.
　　'Now met, the combatants for fight provide,*
1015　And either doffs the lion's yellow hide.
Bright in Olympic oil Alcides shone, ⎫
Antaeus with his mother's dust is strown,* ⎬
And seeks her friendly force to aid his own. ⎭
Now seizing fierce their grasping hands they mix,
1020　And labour on the swelling throat to fix,
Their sinewy arms are writhed in many a fold,
And front to front they threaten stern and bold.
Unmatched before, each bends a sullen frown
To find a force thus equal to his own.
1025　At length the godlike victor Greek prevailed,
Nor yet the foe with all his force assailed.
Faint dropping sweats bedew the monster's brows,
And panting thick with heaving sides he blows,
His trembling head the slackening nerves confessed,
1030　And from the hero shrunk his yielding breast.
The conqueror pursues, his arms entwine, ⎫
Enfolding gripe, and strain his crashing chine,* ⎬
While his broad knee bears forceful on his groin. ⎭
At once his faltering feet from earth he rends,
1035　And on the sands the mighty length extends.
The parent earth her vanquished son deplores,
And with a touch his vigour lost restores,
From his faint limbs the clammy dews she drains,

And with fresh streams recruits his ebbing veins;
1040   The muscles swell, the hardening sinews rise,
And bursting from th'Herculean* grasp he flies.
Astonished at the sight Alcides stood,
Nor more he wondered when in Lerna's flood
The dreadful snake her falling heads renewed.*
1045   Of all his varied labours none was seen
With equal joy by heaven's unrighteous queen;*
Pleased she beheld what toil, what pains he proved,
He who had borne the weight of heaven unmoved.
Sudden again upon the foe he flew –
1050   The falling foe to earth for aid withdrew;
The earth again her fainting son supplies,
And with redoubled forces bids him rise;
Her vital powers to succour him she sends,
And earth herself with Hercules contends.
1055   Conscious at length of such unequal fight,
And that the parent touch renewed his might,
"No longer shalt thou fall", Alcides cried,
"Henceforth the combat standing shall be tried;
If thou would lean, to me alone incline,
1060   And rest upon no other breast but mine."
He said, and as he saw the monster stoop,
With mighty arms aloft he rears him up.
No more the distant earth her son supplies,
Locked in the hero's strong embrace he lies,
1065   Nor thence dismissed, nor trusted to the ground,
Till death in every frozen limb was found.
      'Thus, fond of tales, our ancestors of old
The story to their children's children told;
From thence a title to the land they gave,
1070   And called this hollow rock Antaeus' cave.
But greater deeds this rising mountain grace,
And Scipio's* name ennobles much the place,
While, fixing here his famous camp, he calls
Fierce Hannibal from Rome's devoted walls.*
1075   As yet the mouldering works remain in view,
Where dreadful once the Latian eagles flew.'
      Fond of the prosperous, victorious name,
And trusting fortune would be still the same,
Hither his hapless ensigns Curio leads,

1080 And here his unauspicious camp he spreads.
A fierce superior foe his arms provoke,
And rob the hills of all their ancient luck.
O'er all the Roman powers in Libya's land
Then Atius Varus* bore supreme command;
1085 Nor trusting in the Latian strength alone,
With foreign force he fortified his own,
Summoned the swarthy monarchs all from far,
And called remotest Juba* forth to war.
O'er many a country runs his wide command
1090 To Atlas huge, and Gades' western strand;
From thence to hornèd Ammon's fane renowned,
And the waste Syrts'* unhospitable bound;
Southward as far he reigns, and rules alone
The sultry regions of the burning zone.
1095 With him unnumbered nations march along:
Th'Autololes with wild Numidians throng,
The rough Getulian with his ruder steed,
The Moor, resembling India's swarthy breed;
Poor Nasamons and Garamantines joined
1100 With swift Marmaridans that match the wind;
The Mazax, bred the trembling dart to throw,
Sure as the shaft that leaves the Parthian bow;
With these Massylia's nimble horsemen ride –
They nor the bit nor curbing rein provide,
1105 But with light rods the well-taught courser guide;
From lonely cots the Libyan hunters came,
Who still unarmed invade the savage game,
And with spread mantles tawny lions tame.
   But not Rome's fate nor civil rage alone*
1110 Incite the monarch* Pompey's cause to own;
Stung by resenting wrath the war he sought,
And deep displeasures past by Curio wrought.
He, when the tribune's sacred power he gained,
When justice, laws and gods were all profaned,
1115 At Juba's ancient sceptre aimed his hate,
And strove to rob him of his royal seat,
From a just prince would tear his native right,
While Rome was made a slave to lawless might.
The king, revolving causes from afar,
1120 Looks on himself as party to the war.

That grudge, too well remembering, Curio knew;
To this he joins his troops, to Caesar new – *
None of those old experienced, faithful bands,
Nursed in his fear and bred to his commands,
1125 But a loose, neutral, light, uncertain train,
Late with Corfinium's captive fortress ta'en,
That wavering pause and doubt for whom to strike,
Sworn to both sides, and true to both alike.
The careful chief beheld with anxious heart
1130 The faithless sentinels each night desert;
Then thus resolving to himself he cried:
'By daring shows* our greatest fears we hide;
Then let me haste to bid the battle join, ⎫
And lead my army while it yet is mine – ⎟
1135 Leisure and thinking still to change incline. ⎭
Let war and action busy thought control,
And find a full employment for the soul.
When with drawn swords determined soldiers stand,
When shame is lost and fury prompts the hand,
1140 What reason then can find a time to pause,
To weigh the differing chiefs and juster cause?
That cause seems only just for which they fight:
Each likes his own and all are in the right.
On terms like these, within th'appointed space,*
1145 Bold gladiators gladiators face,
Unknowing why, like fiercest foes they greet,
And only hate and kill because they meet.'
   He said, and ranged his troops upon the plain, ⎫
While fortune met him with a semblance vain, ⎟
1150 Covering her malice keen and all his future pain. ⎭
Before him Varus' vanquished legions yield,
And with dishonest flight forsake the field;
Exposed to shameful wounds their backs he views,
And to their camp the fearful rout pursues.
1155   Juba with joy the mournful news receives,*
And haughty in his own success believes.
Careful his foes in error to maintain
And still preserve them confident and vain,
Silent he marches on in secret sort,
1160 And keeps his numbers close from loud report.
Sabbura, great in the Numidian race,

And second to their swarthy king in place,
First with a chosen slender band precedes,
And seemingly the force of Juba leads,
1165   While hidden he, the prince himself, remains,
And in a secret vale his host constrains.
Thus oft th'ichneumon,* on the banks of Nile,
Invades the deadly aspic by a wile:
While artfully his slender tail is played,*
1170   The serpent darts upon the dancing shade,
Then turning on the foe with swift surprise,
Full at his throat the nimble seizer flies;
The gasping snake expires beneath the wound,
His gushing jaws with poisonous floods abound,
1175   And shed the fruitless mischief on the ground.
Nor fortune failed to favour his intent,
But crowned the fraud with prosperous event.
Curio, unknowing of the hostile power,
Commands his horse the doubtful plain to scour,
1180   And ev'n by night the regions round explore.
Himself, though oft forewarned by friendly care
Of Punic* arts and danger to beware,
Soon as the dawn of early day was broke,
His camp, with all the moving foot, forsook.
1185   It seemed necessity inspired the deed,
And fate required the daring youth should bleed.
War, that cursed war which he himself begun,
To death and ruin drove him headlong on.
O'er devious rocks long time his way he takes,
1190   Through rugged paths and rude, encumbering brakes,
Till from afar at length the hills disclose
Assembling on their heights his distant foes.
Oft hasty flight with swift retreat they feign,
To draw th'unwary leader to the plain.
1195   He, rash and ignorant of Libyan wiles,
Wide o'er the naked champaign spreads his files,
When sudden all the circling mountains round
With numberless Numidians thick are crowned;
At once the rising ambush stands confessed,
1200   And dread strikes cold on every Roman breast.
Helpless they view th'impending danger nigh,
Nor can the valiant fight, nor coward fly.

The weary horse neglects the trumpet's sound,
Nor with impatient ardour paws the ground,
1205 No more he champs the bit nor tugs the rein,
Nor pricks his ears, nor shakes his flowing mane;
With foamy sweat his smoking limbs are spread,
And all o'er-laboured hangs his heavy head,
Hoarse and with pantings thick his breath he draws,
1210 While ropy* filth begrimes his clammy jaws;
Careless the rider's heartening voice he hears,
And motionless the wounding spur he bears.
At length by swords and goading darts compelled,
Dronish* he drags his load across the field,
1215 Nor once attempts to charge, but drooping goes
To bear his dying lord amidst his foes.
      Not so the Libyans fierce their onset make,
With thundering hooves the sandy soil they shake;
Thick o'er the battle wavy clouds arise,
1220 As when through Thrace Bistonian Boreas flies,
Involves* the day in dust, and darkens all the skies.
And now the Latian foot, encompassed round,
Are massacred, and trodden to the ground;
None in resistance vainly prove their might,
1225 But death is all the business of the fight.
Thicker than hail the steely showers descend,
Beneath the weight the falling Romans bend.
On every side the shrinking front grows less,
And to the centre madly all they press;
1230 Fear, uproar and dismay increase the cry –
Crushing and crushed, an armèd crowd they die;
Ev'n thronging on their fellows' swords they run,
And the foes' business by themselves is done.
But the fierce Moors disdain a crowd should share*
1235 The praise of conquest or the task of war;
Rivers of blood they wish, and hills of slain,
With mangled carcasses to strew the plain.
      Genius of Carthage, rear thy drooping head,*
And view thy fields with Roman slaughter spread!
1240 Behold, O Hannibal, thou hostile shade,
A large amends by fortune's hand is made,
And the lost Punic blood is well repaid.
Thus do the gods the cause of Pompey bless?*

Thus, is it thus, they give our arms success?
1245 Take, Afric, rather take the horrid good,
And make thy own advantage of our blood.
    The dust at length in crimson floods was laid,
And Curio now the dreadful field surveyed.
He saw 'twas lost, and knew it vain to strive,
1250 Yet bravely scorned to fly, or to survive;
And though thus driv'n to death, he met it well,
And in a crowd of dying Romans fell.
    Now what avail thy pop'lar* arts and fame,
Thy restless mind that shook thy country's frame,
1255 Thy moving tongue that knew so well to charm
And urge the madding multitude to arm?
What boots it to have sold the Senate's right,
And driv'n the furious leaders on to fight?
Thou the first victim of thy war art slain,
1260 Nor shalt thou see Pharsalia's fatal plain.
Behold, ye potent troublers of the state,
What wretched ends on cursed ambition wait!
See where a prey unburied Curio lies
To every fowl that wings the Libyan skies.
1265 Oh, were the gods as gracious as severe,
Were liberty, like vengeance, still their care,
Then, Rome, what days, what people might'st thou
        see,
If providence would equally decree
To punish tyrants and preserve thee free!
1270   Nor yet, O generous Curio,* shall my verse
Forget thy praise, thy virtues, to rehearse –
Thy virtues which with envious time shall strive,
And to succeeding ages long survive.
In all our pregnant mother's tribes before
1275 A son of nobler hope she never bore,
A soul more bright, more great she never knew,
While to thy country's interest thou wert true.
But thy bad fate o'er-ruled thy native worth,
And in an age abandoned brought thee forth,
1280 When vice in triumph through the city passed,
And dreadful wealth and power laid all things waste.
The sweeping stream thy better purpose crossed,
And in the headlong torrent wert thou lost.

Much to the ruin of the state was done,
1285 When Curio by the Gallic spoils was won,
Curio, the hope of Rome, and her most worthy son.
Tyrants of old, whom former times record,
Who ruled and ravaged with the murdering sword,
Sulla, whom such unbounded power made proud,
1290 Marius and Cinna, red with Roman blood,
Ev'n Caesar's mighty race who lord it now,
Before whose throne the subject nations bow,
All bought that power which lavish Curio sold –
Curio, who bartered liberty for gold.

BOOK FIVE

Thus equal, fortune holds awhile the scale,*
And bids the leading chiefs by turns prevail;
In doubt the goddess yet their fate detains,
And keeps them for Emathia's fatal plains.
5   And now the setting Pleiades grew low,
The hills stood hoary in December's snow,
The solemn season* was approaching near ⎫
When other names renewed the fasti* wear, ⎬
And double Janus* leads the coming year. ⎭
10   The consuls,* while their rods they yet maintained,
While yet some show of liberty remained,
With missives round the scattered Fathers greet,
And in Epirus bid the Senate meet.
There the great rulers of the Roman state,
15   In foreign seats, consulting, meanly sate.*
No face of war the grave assembly wears,
But civil power in peaceful pomp appears;
The purple order* to their place resort,
While waiting lictors* guard the crowded court.
20   No faction these nor party seem to be,*
But a full Senate, legal, just and free.
Great as he is, here Pompey stands confessed
A private man, and one among the rest.
    Their mutual groans, at length, and murmurs
      cease,
25   And every mournful sound is hushed in peace,
When from the consular distinguished throne,
Sublimely raised, thus Lentulus* begun:
    'If yet our Roman virtue is the same, ⎫
Yet worthy of the race from which we came, ⎬
30   And emulates our great forefathers' name, ⎭
Let not our thoughts, by sad remembrance led,
Bewail those captive walls from whence we fled.
This time demands that to ourselves we turn,
Nor, Fathers, have we leisure now to mourn;
35   But let each early care, each honest heart,

Our Senate's sacred dignity assert.
To all around proclaim it, wide and near,
That power which kings obey and nations fear,
That only legal power of Rome, is here.
40 For whether to the northern Bear* we go
Where pale she glitters o'er eternal snow,
Or whether in those sultry climes we burn
Where night and day with equal hours return,
The world shall still acknowledge us its head,
45 And empire follow wheresoe'er we lead.
When Gallic flames the burning city felt,*
At Veii Rome with her Camillus dwelt.
Beneath forsaken roofs proud Caesar reigns,
Our vacant courts and silent laws constrains,
50 While slaves obedient to his tyrant will,
Outlaws and profligates, his Senate fill;
With him a banished, guilty crowd appear,*
All that are just and innocent are here.
Dispersed by war, though guiltless of its crimes,
55 Our order yielded to these impious times;
At length returning each from his retreat,
In happy hour the scattered members meet.*
The gods and fortune greet us on the way,
And with the world lost Italy repay.
60 Upon Illyria's favourable coast
Vulteius with his furious band are lost,
While in bold Curio, on the Libyan plain,
One half of Caesar's senators lie slain.
March then, ye warriors! second fate's design,
65 And to the leading gods your ardour join.
With equal constancy to battle come,
As when you shunned the foe, and left your native
          Rome.
The period of the consuls' power is near,
Who yield our fasces with the ending year;
70 But you, ye Fathers, whom we still obey,
Who rule mankind with undetermined* sway,
Attend the public weal with faithful care,
And bid our greatest Pompey lead the war.'
          In loud applause the pleased assembly join,*
75 And to the glorious task the chief assign;

His country's fate they trust to him alone,
And bid him fight Rome's battles, and his own.
Next to their friends their thanks are dealt around,
And some with gifts, and some with praise are
    crowned:
80   Of these the chief are Rhodes, by Phoebus loved,*
And Sparta rough, in virtue's lore approved;
Of Athens much they speak; Massilia's aid
Is with her parent Phocis'* freedom paid;
Deiotarus* his* truth they much commend,
85   Their still unshaken, faithful Asian friend;
Brave Cotys and his valiant son* they grace,
With bold Rhasipolis* from stormy Thrace;
While gallant Juba justly is decreed
To his paternal sceptre to succeed.
90   And thou too, Ptolemy, (unrighteous fate!)
Wert raised unworthy to the regal state,
The crown upon thy perjured temples shone,
That once was borne by Philip's godlike son;*
O'er Egypt shakes the boy his cruel sword –
95   Oh, that he had been only Egypt's lord!
But the dire gift more dreadful mischiefs wait,
While Lagus'* sceptre gives him Pompey's fate –
Preventing Caesar's, and his sister's hand,*
He seized his parricide and her command.
100   Th'assembly rose, and all on war intent
Bustle to arms, and blindly wait th'event.
Appius* alone, impatient to be taught
With what the threatening future times were fraught,
With busy curiosity explores
105   The dreadful purpose of the heavenly powers.
To Delphos straight he flies, where long the god
In silence had possessed his close abode;
His oracles had long been known to cease,
And the prophetic virgin lived in peace.*
110   Between the ruddy west and eastern skies,
In the mid earth, Parnassus' tops arise;
To Phoebus and the cheerful god of wine*
Sacred in common stands the hill divine.

Still as the third revolving year comes round,*⎤
115 The Maenades,* with leafy chaplets crowned,   ⎥
The double deity* in solemn songs resound.   ⎦
When o'er the world the deluge wide was spread,
This only mountain reared his lofty head;
One rising rock preserved, a bound was given,*
120 Between the vasty deep and ambient heaven.
Here, to revenge long vexed Latona's pain,*   ⎤
Python by infant Paean's darts was slain,   ⎥
While yet the realm was held by Themis' righteous ⎥
        reign.*   ⎦
But when the god perceived how from below
125 The conscious caves diviner breathings blow,
How vapours could unfold th'enquirer's doom,
And talking winds could speak of things to come,
Deep in the hollows plunging he retired,   ⎤
There with foretelling fury first inspired,   ⎥
130 From thence the prophet's art and honours he   ⎦
        acquired.
    So runs the tale. And oh, what god indeed
Within this gloomy cavern's depth is hid?
What power divine forsakes the heaven's fair light
To dwell with earth and everlasting night?
135 What is this spirit, potent, wise and great,
Who deigns to make a mortal frame his seat,
Who the long chain of secret causes knows,
Whose oracles the years to come disclose,
Who through eternity at once foresees,
140 And tells that fate which he himself decrees?*
Part of that soul, perhaps, which moves in all,*
Whose energy informs the pendant ball,
Through this dark passage seeks the realms above,
And strives to reunite itself to Jove.
145 Whate'er the demon,* when he stands confessed
Within his raging priestess' panting breast,
Dreadful his godhead from the virgin* breaks,
And thundering from her foamy mouth he speaks.
Such is the burst of bellowing Etna's sound,
150 When fair Sicilia's pastures shake around;
Such from Inarime Typhoeus* roars,
While rattling rocks bestrew Campania's shores.

      The listening god, still ready with replies,
To none his aid or oracle denies,
155 Yet, wise and righteous ever, scorns to hear
The fool's fond wishes, or the guilty's prayer;
Though vainly in repeated vows they trust,
None e'er find grace before him but the just.
Oft to a banished, wandering, houseless race*
160 The sacred dictates have assigned a place.
Oft from the strong he saves the weak in war –⎤
This truth, ye Salaminian seas, declare! –⎟
And heals the barren land, and pestilential air.⎦
Of all the wants with which this age is cursed,
165 The Delphic silence surely is the worst.
But tyrants, justly fearful of their doom,*
Forbid the gods to tell us what's to come.
Meanwhile the prophetess may well rejoice,
And bless the ceasing of the sacred voice,
170 Since death too oft her holy task attends,
And immature her dreadful labour ends.
Torn by the fierce distracting rage she springs,*
And dies beneath the god for whom she sings.
      These silent caves, these tripods* long unmoved,*
175 Anxious for Rome, inquiring Appius proved;
He bids the guardian of the dread abode
Send in the trembling priestess to the god.
The reverend sire the Latian chief obeyed,⎤
And sudden seized the unsuspecting maid,⎟
180 Where careless in the peaceful grove she strayed.⎦
Dismayed, aghast, and pale he drags her on;
She stops, and strives the fatal task to shun;
Subdued by force, to fraud and art she flies,
And thus to turn the Roman's purpose tries:
185 'What curious hopes thy wandering fancy move
The silent Delphic oracle to prove?
In vain, Ausonian* Appius, art thou come –
Long has our Phoebus and his cave been dumb.
Whether, disdaining us, the sacred voice*
190 Has made some other distant land its choice,
Or whether, when the fierce barbarians' fires*
Low in the dust had laid our lofty spires,
In heaps the smouldering ashes heavy rod*

And choked the channels of the breathing god,
195 Or whether heav'n no longer gives replies,
     But bids the Sybil's mystic verse suffice,*
     Or if he deigns not this bad age to bear
     And holds the world unworthy of his care –
     Whate'er the cause, our god has long been mute,
200 And answers not to any suppliant's suit.'
         But ah! too well her artifice is known –
     Her fears confess the god whom they disown.
     Howe'er each rite she seemingly prepares,
     A fillet gathers up her foremost hairs,
205 While the white wreath* and bays her temples bind,
     And knit the looser locks which flow behind.
     Sudden the stronger priest, though yet she strives,*
     The lingering maid within the temple drives;
     But still she fears, still shuns the dreadful shrine,
210 Lags in the outer space, and feigns the rage divine.
     But far unlike the god, her calmer breast
     No strong enthusiastic throes confessed,
     No terrors in her starting hairs were seen
     To cast from off her brow the wreathing green,
215 No broken accents half obstructed hung,
     Nor swelling murmurs roll her labouring tongue,
     From her fierce jaws no sounding horrors come,
     No thunders bellow through the working foam*
     To rend the spacious cave, and shake the vaulted
         dome.
220 Too plain the peaceful groves and fane betrayed
     The wily, fearful, god-dissembling maid.
     The furious Roman soon the fraud espied,
     And 'Hope not thou to 'scape my rage,' he cried;
     'Sore shalt thou rue thy fond deceit, profane,*
225 (The gods and Appius are not mocked in vain)
     Unless thou cease thy mortal sounds* to tell,
     Unless thou plunge thee in the mystic cell,
     Unless the gods themselves reveal the doom
     Which shall befall the warring world, and Rome.'
230   He spoke, and, awed by the superior dread,
     The trembling priestess to the tripod fled,
     Close to the holy breathing vent she cleaves,
     And largely the unwonted god receives.

Nor age the potent spirit had decayed,
235　But with full force he fills the heaving maid;
Nor e'er so strong inspiring Paean* came,
Nor stretched as now her agonizing frame;
The mortal mind driv'n out forsook her breast,
And the sole godhead every part possessed.
240　Now swell her veins, her turgid* sinews rise,
And bounding frantic through the cave she flies;
Her bristling locks the wreathy fillet scorn,
And her fierce feet the tumbling tripods spurn.
Now wild she dances o'er the vacant fane,
245　And whirls her giddy head, and bellows with the
　　　pain.
Nor yet the less th'avenging, wrathful god
Pours in his fires and shakes his sounding rod;
He lashes now and goads her on amain,
And now he checks her stubborn to the rein,
250　Curbs in her tongue, just labouring to disclose
And speak that fate which in her bosom glows.
Ages on ages throng, a painful load,
Myriads of images, and myriads crowd –
Men, times and things, or present or to come,*
255　Work labouring up and down, and rage for room.
Whatever is, shall be, or e'er has been,
Rolls in her thought and to her sight is seen.
The ocean's utmost bounds her eyes explore,
And number every sand on every shore;
260　Nature and all her works at once they see,
Know when she first begun, and when her end shall
　　　be.
　　　And as the Sybil once in Cumae's cell,*
When vulgar fates she proudly ceased to tell,
The Roman destiny distinguished took,
265　And kept it careful in her sacred book,
So now Phemonoë,* in crowds of thought,
The single doom of Latian Appius sought.
Nor in that mass, where multitudes abound,
A private fortune can with ease be found.
270　At length her foamy mouth begins to flow,
Groans more distinct, and plainer murmurs go,
A doleful howl the roomy cavern shook,

And thus the calmer maid in fainting accents spoke:
   'While guilty rage the world tumultuous rends,*
275   In peace for thee Euboea's vale attends;
   Thither as to thy refuge shalt thou fly,
   There find repose, and unmolested lie.'
   She said; the god her labouring tongue suppressed,
   And in eternal darkness veiled the rest.
280   Ye sacred tripods, on whose doom we wait,
   Ye guardians of the future laws of fate,
   And thou, O Phoebus, whose prophetic skill
   Reads the dark counsels of the heavenly will,
   Why did your wary oracles refrain
285   To tell what kings, what heroes must be slain,
   And how much blood the blushing earth should
        stain?
   Was it that yet the guilt was undecreed?
   That yet our Pompey was not doomed to bleed?
   Or chose you wisely rather to afford*
290   A just occasion to the patriot's sword,
   As if you feared t'avert the tyrant's doom,
   And hinder Brutus from avenging Rome?
     Through the wide gates at length by force
           displayed,
   Impetuous sallies the prophetic maid;
295   Nor yet the holy rage was all suppressed,
   Part of the god still heaving in her breast;
   Urged by the demon, yet she rolls her eyes,
   And wildly wanders o'er the spacious skies.
   Now horrid purple flushes in her face,
300   And now a livid pale supplies the place;
   A double madness paints her cheeks by turns –
   With fear she freezes, and with fury burns;*
   Sad breathing sighs with heavy accent go,
   And doleful from her fainting bosom blow.
305   So when no more the storm sonorous* sings,*
   But noisy Boreas hangs his weary wings,
   In hollow groans the falling winds complain,
   And murmur o'er the hoarse-resounding main.
     Now by degrees the fire ethereal failed,
310   And the dull human sense again prevailed,
   While Phoebus, sudden in a murky shade,

Hid the past vision from the mortal maid.
Thick clouds of dark oblivion rise between,
And snatch away at once the wondrous scene;
315   Stretched on the ground the fainting priestess lies,
While to the tripod back th'informing spirit flies.
    Meanwhile fond Appius, erring in his fate,
Dreamed of long safety and a neutral state, -
And e'er the great event of war was known,
320   Fixed on Euboean Chalcis for his own.
Fool, to believe that power could ward the blow,
Or snatch thee from amidst the general woe!
In times like these, what god but death can save? –
The world can yield no refuge but the grave.
325   Where struggling seas Carystos rude constrains,*
And, dreadful to the proud, Rhamnusia* reigns,
Where by the whirling current barks are tossed
From Chalcis to unlucky Aulis'* coast,
There shalt thou meet the gods' appointed doom:
330   A private death and long-remembered tomb.
    To other wars the victor now succeeds,*
And his proud eagles from Iberia leads,
When the changed gods his ruin seem to threat,
And cross the long successful course of fate.
335   Amidst his camp, and fearless of his foes,
Sudden he saw where inborn dangers rose;
He saw those troops that long had faithful stood, ⎫
Friends to his cause, and enemies to good, ⎬
Grown weary of their chief, and satiated* with ⎭
     blood –
340   Whether the trumpet's sound too long had ceased,
And slaughter slept in unaccustomed rest,
Or whether, arrogant by mischief made,
The soldier held his guilt but half repaid,
Whilst avarice and hope of bribes prevail, ⎫
345   Turn against Caesar and his cause the scale, ⎬
And set the mercenary sword to sale. ⎭
Nor e'er before so truly could he read
What dangers strew those paths the mighty tread.
Then first he found on what a faithless base
350   Their nodding towers ambition's builders place;
He who so late, a potent faction's head,

Drew in the nations, and the legions led,
Now stripped of all, beheld in every hand
The warriors' weapons at their own command;
355   Nor service now nor safety they afford,
But leave him single to his guardian sword.
Nor is this rage the grumbling of a crowd
That shun to tell their discontents aloud,
Where all with gloomy looks suspicious go,
360   And dread of an informer chokes their woe,
But bold in numbers proudly they appear,
And scorn the bashful, mean restraints of fear.
For laws in great rebellions lose their end,
And all go free, when multitudes offend.
365   Among the rest, one thus: 'At length 'tis time
To quit thy cause, O Caesar, and our crime;
The world around for foes thou hast explored,
And lavishly exposed us to the sword;
To make thee great, a worthless crowd we fall,
370   Scattered o'er Spain, o'er Italy and Gaul;
In every clime beneath the spacious sky,
Our leader conquers, and his soldiers die.
What boots our march beneath the frozen zone,
Or that lost blood which stains the Rhine and
            Rhone?
375   When, scarred with wounds and worn with labours
            hard,
We come with hopes of recompense prepared,
Thou giv'st us war, more war, for our reward.
Though purple rivers in thy cause we spilt,
And stained our horrid hands in every guilt,
380   With unavailing wickedness we toiled,
In vain the gods, in vain the Senate spoiled;
Of virtue and reward alike bereft,
Our pious poverty is all we've left.
Say to what height thy daring arms would rise –
385   If Rome's too little, what can e'er suffice?
Oh, see at length, with pity, Caesar, see
These withering arms, these hairs grown white for
            thee!
In painful wars our joyless days have past,
Let weary age lie down in peace at last;

390   Give us on beds our dying limbs to lay,
       And sigh, at home, our parting souls away.
       Nor think it much we make the bold demand,
       And ask this wondrous favour at thy hand;
       Let our poor babes and weeping wives be by
395   To close our drooping eyelids when we die.
       Be merciful, and let disease afford
       Some other way to die beside the sword;
       Let us no more a common carnage burn,
       But each be laid in his own decent urn.
400   Still would thou urge us, ignorant and blind,
       To some more monstrous mischief yet behind?
       Are we the only fools, forbid to know*
       How much we may deserve by one sure blow?
       Thy head, thy head is ours, whene'er we please –
405   Well has thy war inspired such thoughts as these;
       What laws, what oaths can urge their feeble bands
       To hinder these determined, daring hands?
       That Caesar, who was once ordained our head,
       When to the Rhine our lawful arms he led,
410   Is now no more our chieftain, but our mate –
       Guilt equal gives equality of state.
       Nor shall his foul ingratitude prevail,
       Nor weigh our merits in his partial scale;
       He views our labours with a scornful glance,
415   And calls our victories the works of chance;
       But his proud heart henceforth shall learn to own
       His power, his fate, depends on us alone.
       Yes, Caesar, spite of all those rods* that wait,
       With mean obsequious service, on thy state,
420   Spite of thy gods and thee, the war shall cease,
       And we thy soldiers will command a peace.'
           He spoke, and fierce, tumultuous rage inspired, ⎤
       The kindling legions round the camp were fired,   ⎬
       And with loud cries their absent chief required.   ⎦
425   Permit it thus, ye righteous gods, to be,
       Let wicked hands fulfil your great decree,
       And since lost faith and virtue are no more,
       Let Caesar's bands the public peace restore.
       What leader had not now been chilled with fear,
430   And heard this tumult with the last despair?

But Caesar, formed for perils hard and great,
Headlong to drive, and brave opposing fate,
While yet with fiercest fires their furies flame,
Secure and scornful of the danger came.

435 Nor was he wroth to see the madness rise,
And mark the vengeance threatening in their eyes;
With pleasure could he crown their cursed designs,
With rapes of matrons and the spoils of shrines;
Had they but asked it, well he could approve

440 The waste and plunder of Tarpeian Jove;*
No mischief he, no sacrilege denies,
But would himself bestow the horrid prize.
With joy he sees their souls by rage possessed,*
Soothes and indulges every frantic breast,

445 And only fears what reason may suggest.
Still, Caesar, would thou tread the paths of blood,
Would thou, thou singly, hate thy country's good?
Shall the rude soldier first of war complain,
And teach thee to be pitiful in vain?

450 Give o'er at length, and let thy labours cease,
Nor vex the world, but learn to suffer peace.
Why shouldst thou force each now unwilling hand,
And drive them on to guilt by thy command,
When ev'n relenting rage itself gives place,

455 And fierce Enyo* seems to shun thy face?
    High on a turfy bank the chief was reared,
Fearless, and therefore worthy to be feared;
Around the crowd he cast an angry look,
And, dreadful, thus with indignation spoke:

460 'Ye noisy herd, who in so fierce a strain
Against your absent leader dare complain,
Behold where naked and unarmed he stands,
And braves the malice of your threatening hands.
Here find your end of war, your long-sought rest,

465 And leave your useless swords in Caesar's breast.
But wherefore urge I the bold deed to you?
To rail is all your feeble rage can do.
In grumbling factions are you bold and loud,
Can sow sedition, and increase a crowd –

470 You, who can loathe the glories of the great,
And poorly meditate a base retreat.

But, hence, begone from victory and me!
Leave me to what my better fates decree;
New friends, new troops, my fortune shall afford,
475   And find a hand for every vacant sword.
Behold, what crowds on flying Pompey wait,
What multitudes attend his abject state!
And shall success, and Caesar, droop the while? }
Shall I want numbers to divide the spoil, }
480   And reap the fruits of your forgotten toil? }
Legions shall come to end the bloodless war,
And shouting follow my triumphal car,
While you, a vulgar, mean, abandoned race, }
Shall view our honours with a downward face, }
485   And curse yourselves in secret as we pass. }
Can your vain aid, can your departing force,
Withhold my conquest, or delay my course?
So trickling brooks their waters may deny, }
And hope to leave the mighty ocean dry – }
490   The deep shall still be full, and scorn the poor }
       supply. }
Nor think such vulgar souls as yours were given
To be the task of fate and care of heaven;
Few are the lordly, the distinguished great,
On whom the watchful gods, like guardians, wait;
495   The rest for common use were all designed,
An unregarded rabble of mankind.
By my auspicious name and fortune led, }
Wide o'er the world your conquering arms were }
       spread – }
But say, what had you done with Pompey at your }
       head? }
500   Vast was the fame by Labienus* won,
When ranked amidst my warlike friends he shone:
Now mark what follows on his faithless change,
And see him with his chief new chosen range;
By land and sea, where-e'er my arms he spies,
505   An ignominious runagate* he flies.
Such shall you prove. Nor is it worth my care
Whether to Pompey's aid your arms you bear;
Who quits his leader, wheresoe'er he go,*
Flies like a traitor, and becomes my foe.

510 Yes, ye great gods! your kinder care I own,
     You made the faith of these false legions known;
     You warn me well to change these coward bands,
     Nor trust my fate to such betraying hands.
     And thou too, fortune, point'st me out the way
515 A mighty debt thus cheaply to repay;
     Henceforth my care regards myself alone,
     War's glorious gain shall now be all my own.
     For you, ye vulgar herd,* in peace return –
     My ensigns shall by manly hands be borne.
520 Some few of you my sentence here shall wait,
     And warn succeeding factions by your fate.
     Down, grovelling down to earth, ye traitors, bend,
     And with your prostrate necks my doom attend.*
     And you, ye younger striplings of the war,
525 You, whom I mean to make my future care,
     Strike home! to blood, to death, inure your hands,
     And learn to execute my dread commands.'
         He spoke, and at th'imperious sound dismayed
     The trembling, unresisting crowd obeyed;
530 No more their late equality they boast,
     But bend beneath his frown, a suppliant host.
     Singly secure, he stands confessed their lord,*
     And rules, in spite of him, the soldier's sword.
     Doubtful at first their patience he surveys,
535 And wonders why each haughty heart obeys;
     Beyond his hopes he sees the stubborn bow,
     And bare their breasts obedient to the blow,
     Till ev'n his cooler thoughts the deed disclaim,
     And would not find their fiercer souls so tame.*
540 A few, at length, selected from the rest,
     Bled for example, and the tumult ceased,
     While the consenting host the victims viewed,
     And in that blood their broken faith renewed.
         Now to Brundisium's walls he bids them tend,
545 Where ten long days their weary marches end;
     There he commands assembling barks to meet,
     And furnish from the neighbouring shores his fleet.
     Thither the crooked keels from Leuca glide,
     From Taras old, and Hydrus' winding tide;
550 Thither with swelling sails their way they take

From lowly Sipus, and Salapia's lake,
From where Apulia's fruitful mountains rise, ⎫
Where high along the coast Garganus lies ⎬
And beating seas and fighting winds defies. ⎭

555   Meanwhile the chief to Rome directs his way,
Now fearful, awed and fashioned to his sway.
There, with mock prayers, the suppliant vulgar wait,
And urge on him the great dictator's state.*
Obedient he, since thus their wills ordain,
560 A gracious tyrant condescends to reign.*
His mighty name the joyful fasti wear,
Worthy to usher in the cursed Pharsalian year.
Then was the time when sycophants began*
To heap all titles on one lordly man,
565 Then learned our sires that fawning, lying strain,*
Which we, their slavish sons, so well retain;
Then first were seen to join, an ill-matched pair,
The axe of justice with the sword of war;
Fasces* and eagles, mingling, march along,
570 And in proud Caesar's train promiscuous throng.
And while all powers in him alone unite,*
He mocks the people with the shows of right.
The Martian Field th'assembling tribes receives,
And each his unregarded suffrage gives;
575 Still with the same solemnity of face,*
The reverend augur seems to fill his place,*
Though now he hears not when the thunders rowl,*
Nor sees the flight of the ill-boding owl.*
Then sunk the state and dignity of Rome,
580 Thence monthly consuls nominally come;*
Just as the sovereign bids, their names appear
To head the calendar and mark the year.
Then too, to finish out the pageant show,
With formal rites to Alban Jove they go;*
585 By night the festival was huddled o'er,
Nor could the god, unworthy, ask for more –
He who looked on, and saw such foul disgrace,
Such slavery befall his Trojan race.
    Now Caesar, like the flame that cuts the skies, ⎫
590 And swifter than the vengeful tigress, flies ⎬
Where waste and overgrown Apulia lies; ⎭

O'er-passing soon the rude, abandoned plains,
Brundisium's crooked shores* and Cretan walls he
    gains.
Loud Boreas there his navy close confines,
595   While wary seamen dread the wintry signs.
But he, th'impatient chief, disdains to spare
Those hours that better may be spent in war;
He grieves to see his ready fleet withheld,
While others boldly plough the watery field.
600   Eager to rouse their sloth, 'Behold', he cries,
'The constant wind that rules the wintry skies,
With what a settled certainty it flies,
Unlike the wanton, fickle gales that bring
The cloudy changes of the faithless spring!
605   Nor need we now to shift, to tack and veer,
Steady the friendly North commands to steer.
Oh, that the fury of the driving blast
May swell the sail and bend the lofty mast!
So shall our navy soon be wafted o'er,
610   E'er yon Phaeacian* gallies dip the oar,
And intercept the wished-for Grecian shore.
Cut every cable then, and haste away;
The waiting winds and seas upbraid our long delay.'
    Low in the west the setting sun was laid,
615   Up rose the night in glittering stars arrayed,
And silver Cynthia* cast a lengthening shade,
When, loosing from the shore the moving fleet,
All hands at once unfurl the spreading sheet;*
The slacker tacklings let the canvas flow,
620   To gather all the breath the winds can blow.
Swift for a while they scud before the wind,
And leave Hesperia's* lessening shores behind;
When lo, the dying breeze begins to fail,
And flutters on the mast the flagging sail,
625   The duller waves with slower heavings creep,
And a dead calm benumbs the lazy deep.
As when the winter's potent breath constrains
The Scythian Euxine in her icy chains,
No more the Bospori* their streams maintain,
630   Nor rushing Ister heaves the languid main;
Each keel enclosed at once forgets its course,

While o'er the new made champaign* bounds the
    horse,
Bold on the crystal plains the Thracians ride,
And print with sounding heels the stable tide;
635   So still a form th'Ionian waters take,
Dull as the muddy marsh and standing lake;
No breezes o'er the curling* surface pass,
Nor sunbeams tremble in the liquid glass,
No usual turns revolving Tethys* knows,
640   Nor with alternate rollings ebbs and flows,
But sluggish ocean sleeps in stupid* peace,
And weary nature's motion seems to cease.
With differing eyes the hostile fleets beheld
The falling winds and useless watery field.
645   There Pompey's daring prows attempt in vain
To plough their passage through th'unyielding main,
While, pinched by want, proud Caesar's legions here
The dire distress of meagre famine fear.
With vows unknown before they reach the skies*
650   That waves may dash and mounting billows rise,
That storms may with returning fury reign,
And the rude ocean be itself again.
At length the still, the sluggish, darkness fled,
And cloudy morning reared its louring head.
655   The rolling flood the gliding navy bore,
And hills appeared to pass upon the shore.
Attending breezes waft them to the land,
And Caesar's anchors bite Palaeste's strand.
   In neighbouring camps the hostile chiefs sit down,
660   Where Genusus the swift and Apsus run;*
Among th'ignobler crowd of rivers these
Soon lose their waters in the mingling seas;
No mighty streams nor distant springs they know,
But rise from muddy lakes and melting snow.
665   Here meet the rivals who the world divide,
Once by the tend'rest bands of kindred tied.
The world with joy their interview beheld,
Now only parted by a single field.
Fond of the hopes of peace, mankind believe,
670   Whene'er they come thus near, they must forgive.
Vain hopes! for soon they part to meet no more,

Till both shall reach the cursed Egyptian shore,
Till the proud father* shall in arms succeed,
And see his vanquished son* untimely bleed,
675   Till he beholds his ashes on the strand,
Views his pale head within a villain's hand,
Till Pompey's fate shall Caesar's tears demand.
    The latter yet his eager rage restrains,
While Antony the lingering troops detains.*
680   Repining much, and grieved at war's delay,
Impatient Caesar often chides his stay,
Oft he is heard to threat, and humbly oft to pray.
    'Still shall the world', he cries, 'thus anxious wait?
Still would thou* stop the gods and hinder fate?
685   What could be done before was done by me –
Now ready fortune only stays for thee.
What holds thee then? Do rocks thy course
      withstand?
Or Libyan Syrts oppose their faithless strand?
Or dost thou fear new dangers to explore?
690   I call thee not, but where I passed before.
For all those hours thou losest, I complain,
And sue to heaven for prosperous winds in vain.
My soldiers (often has their faith been tried),
If not withheld, had hastened to my side.
695   What toil, what hazards will they not partake?
What seas and shipwrecks scorn, for Caesar's sake?
Nor will I think the gods so partial are
To give thee fair Ausonia for thy share,
While Caesar and the Senate are forgot,
700   And in Epirus bound their barren lot.'
    In words like these he calls him oft in vain,*
And thus the hasty missives oft complain.
At length the lucky chief, who oft had found
What vast success his rasher darings crowned,
705   Who saw how much the favouring gods had done,
Nor would be wanting when they urged him on,
Fierce and impatient of the tedious stay,
Resolves by night to prove the doubtful way;
Bold in a single skiff he means to go,
710   And tempt those seas that navies dare not plough.
    'Twas now the time when cares and labour cease,*

And ev'n the rage of arms was hushed to peace;
Snatched from their guilt and toil the wretched lay,
And slept the sounder for the painful day;
715   Through the still camp the night's third hour
              resounds,
And warns the second watches to their rounds,
When through the horrors of the murky shade
Secret the careful warrior's footsteps tread.
His train, unknowing, slept within his tent,
720   And fortune only followed where he went.
With silent anger he perceived around
The sleepy sentinels bestrew the ground,
Yet unreproving now he passed them o'er,
And sought with eager haste the winding shore.
725   There, through the gloom, his searching eyes explored
Where to the mouldering* rock a bark was moored.
The mighty master of this little boat
Securely slept within a neighbouring cot;*
No massy beams support his humble hall,*
730   But reeds and marshy rushes wove the wall,
Old shattered planking for a roof was spread*
And covered in from rain the needy shed.
Thrice on the feeble door the warrior strook,*
Beneath the blow the trembling dwelling shook.
735   'What wretch forlorn', the poor Amyclas cries,
'Driven by the raging seas and stormy skies,
To my poor, lowly roof for shelter flies?'
He spoke, and hasty left his homely bed,
With oozy flags* and withering seaweed spread.
740   Then from the hearth the smoking match* he takes,
And in the tow* the drowsy fire awakes;
Dry leaves and chips for fuel he supplies,
Till kindling sparks and glittering flames arise.
O happy poverty, thou greatest good
745   Bestowed by heaven, but seldom understood!
Here nor the cruel spoiler seeks his prey,
Nor ruthless armies take their dreadful way;
Security thy narrow limits keeps,
Safe are thy cottages and sound thy sleeps.
750   Behold, ye dangerous dwellings of the great,
Where gods and godlike princes choose their seat,

See in what peace the poor Amyclas lies,
Nor starts, though Caesar's call commands to rise.
What terrors had you felt that call to hear?
755   How had your towers and ramparts shook with
                fear,
And trembled as the mighty man drew near!
The door unbarred, 'Expect', the leader said,
'Beyond thy hopes or wishes to be paid,
If on this instant hour thou waft me o'er
760   With speedy haste to yon Hesperian shore.
No more shall want thy weary hand constrain
To work thy bark upon the boisterous main;
Henceforth good days and plenty shall betide –
The gods and I will for thy age provide.
765   A glorious change attends thy low estate,
Sudden and mighty riches round thee wait –
Be wise, and use the lucky hour of fate.'
        Thus he, and, though in humble vestments
                dressed,
Spite of himself, his words his power expressed,
770   And Caesar in his bounty stood confessed.
        To him the wary pilot thus replies:
'A thousand omens threaten from the skies,
A thousand boding signs* my soul affright,
And warn me not to tempt the seas by night.
775   In clouds the setting sun obscured his head,
Nor painted o'er the ruddy west with red;
Now north, now south, he shot his parted beams,
And tipped the sullen black with golden gleams;
Pale shone his middle orb with faintish rays,
780   And suffered mortal eyes at ease to gaze.
Nor rose the silver queen of night serene –
Supine and dull her blunted horns were seen,
With foggy stains and cloudy blots between;
Dreadful awhile she shone all fiery red,*
785   Then sickened into pale, and hid her drooping head.
Nor less I fear from that hoarse, hollow roar
In leafy groves and on the sounding shore.
In various turns the doubtful dolphins play,
And thwart,* and run across, and mix their way.
790   The cormorants the watery deep forsake,

And soaring herns* avoid the plashy* lake;
While, waddling on the margin of the main,*
The crow bewets her, and prevents* the rain.
Howe'er, if some great enterprise demand,
795   Behold, I proffer thee my willing hand;
My vent'rous bark the troubled deep shall try,
To thy wished port her plunging prows shall ply,
Unless the seas resolve to beat us by.'
      He spoke, and spread his canvas to the wind,*
800   Unmoored his boat, and left the shore behind.
Swift flew the nimble keel, and, as they passed,
Long trails of light the shooting meteors cast;
Ev'n the fixed fires above in motion seem,
Shake through the blast, and dart a quivering beam;
805   Black horrors* on the gloomy ocean brood,
And in long ridges rolls the threatening flood,
While loud and louder murmuring winds arise,
And growl from every quarter of the skies;
When thus the trembling master, pale with fear:
810   'Behold what wrath the dreadful gods prepare.
My art is at a loss – the various tide
Beats my unstable bark on every side;
From the nor-west the setting current swells,
While southern storms the driving rack* foretells.
815   Howe'er it be, our purposed way is lost,
Nor can one relic of our wreck be tossed,
By winds like these, on fair Hesperia's coast.
Our only means of safety is to yield,
And measure back with haste the foamy field,
820   To give our unsuccessful labour o'er,
And reach, while yet we may, the neighbouring
          shore.'
      But Caesar, still superior to distress,
Fearless and confident of sure success,
Thus to the pilot loud: 'The seas despise,
825   And the vain threatening of the noisy skies;
Though gods deny thee yon Ausonian strand,
Yet go, I charge thee, go at my command.
Thy ignorance alone can cause thy fears –
Thou know'st not what a freight thy vessel bears,
830   Thou know'st not I am he, to whom 'tis given

Never to want the care of watchful heaven.
Obedient fortune waits my humble thrall,
And always ready comes before I call.
Let winds and seas loud wars at freedom wage,
835   And waste upon themselves their empty rage;
A stronger, mightier demon is thy friend –
Thou and thy bark on Caesar's fate depend.
Thou standst amazed to view this dreadful scene,
And wonder'st what the gods and fortune mean.
840   But artfully their bounties thus they raise,
And from my dangers arrogate new praise,
Amidst the fears of death they bid me live,
And still enhance what they are sure to give.
Then leave yon shore behind with all thy haste,
845   Nor shall this idle fury longer last.
Thy keel auspicious shall the storm appease, ⎫
Shall glide triumphant o'er the calmer seas, ⎬
And reach Brundisium's safer port with ease. ⎭
Nor can the gods ordain another* now –
850   'Tis what I want, and what they must bestow.'
    Thus while in vaunting words the leader spoke,
Full on his bark the thundering tempest strook;*
Off rips the rending canvas from the mast,
And whirling flits before the driving blast;
855   In every joint the groaning alder* sounds,
And gapes wide-opening with a thousand wounds.
Now rising all at once and unconfined
From every quarter roars the rushing wind.
First, from the wide Atlantic ocean's bed,
860   Tempestuous Corus* rears his dreadful head,
Th'obedient deep his potent breath controls,
And mountain-high the foamy flood he rolls.
Him the North-east, encountering fierce, defied,
And back rebuffeted the yielding tide.
865   The curling surges loud conflicting meet,
Dash their proud heads, and bellow as they beat,
While piercing Boreas, from the Scythian strand,
Ploughs up the waves and scoops the lowest sand.
Nor Eurus then, I ween, was left to dwell,
870   Nor showery Notus* in th'Aeolian cell,
But each from every side, his power to boast,

Ranged his proud forces to defend his coast.
Equal in might, alike they strive in vain,*
While in the midst the seas unmoved remain;
875 In lesser wars they yield to stormy heaven,
And captive waves to other deeps are driven,
The Tyrrhene billows dash Aegean shores,*
And Adria in the mixed Ionian roars.
How then must earth the swelling ocean dread,
880 When floods ran higher than each mountain's head!
Subject* and low the trembling beldame* lay,
And gave herself for lost, the conquering water's
     prey.
What other worlds, what seas unknown before,
Then drove their billows on our beaten shore!
885 What distant deeps, their prodigies to boast,
Heaved their huge monsters on th'Ausonian coast!
So when avenging Jove long time had hurled*
And tired* his thunders on a hardened world,
New wrath, the god, new punishment, displayed,
890 And called his watery brother to his aid;
Offending earth to Neptune's lot he joined,
And bade his floods no longer stand confined;
At once the surges o'er the nations rise,
And seas are only bounded by the skies.
895 Such now the spreading deluge had been seen,
Had not th'almighty ruler stood between;
Proud waves the cloud-compelling sire obeyed,
Confessed his hand suppressing, and were stayed.
     Nor was that gloom the common shade of night,
900 The friendly darkness that relieves the light,
But fearful, black, and horrible to tell,
A murky vapour breathed from yawning hell;*
So thick the mingling seas and clouds were hung,
Scarce could the struggling lightning gleam along.
905 Through nature's frame the dire convulsion strook,
Heav'n groaned, the labouring poles and axis shook;
Uproar and chaos old prevailed again,
And broke the sacred elemental chain;
Black fiends, unhallowed, sought the blessed abodes,
910 Profaned the day, and mingled with the gods.
One only hope, when every other failed,

With Caesar, and with nature's self, prevailed:
The storm that sought their ruin proved them strong,
Nor could they fall who stood that shock so long.
915 High as Leucadia's lessening cliffs arise,
On the tall billow's top the vessel flies,
While the pale master, from the surge's brow,
With giddy eyes surveys the depth below;
When straight the gaping main at once divides,
920 On naked sands the rushing bark subsides,
And the low liquid vale the topmast hides.
The trembling shipman, all distraught with fear,
Forgets his course, and knows not how to steer;
No more the useless rudder guides the prow,
925 To meet the rolling swell, or shun the blow.
But lo, the storm itself assistance lends –
While one assaults, another wave defends:
This lays the sidelong alder on the main,
And that restores the leaning bark again.
930 Obedient to the mighty winds she plies,
Now seeks the depths and now invades the skies;
There borne aloft, she apprehends no more*
Or shoaly Sason or Thessalia's shore:
High hills she dreads, and promontories now,
935 And fears to touch Ceraunia's airy brow.
   At length the universal wreck* appeared
To Caesar's self ev'n worthy to be feared.
'Why all these pains, this toil of fate', he cries,
'This labour of the seas and earth and skies?
940 All nature and the gods at once alarmed
Against my little boat and me are armed.
If, O ye powers divine, your will decrees
The glory of my death to these rude seas,
If warm,* and in the fighting field to die,
945 If that, my first of wishes, you deny,
My soul no longer at her lot repines,
But yields to what your providence assigns.
Though immature I end my glorious days,
Cut short my conquest, and prevent new praise,
950 My life already stands the noblest theme
To fill long annals of recording fame.
Far northern nations own me for their lord,

And envious factions crouch beneath my sword;
Inferior Pompey yields to me at home,
955 And only fills a second place in Rome.
My country has my high behests obeyed,
And at my feet her laws obedient laid;
All sovereignty, all honours are my own:
Consul, dictator, I am all alone.
960 But thou, my only goddess, and my friend,
Thou, on whom all my secret prayers attend,
Conceal, O fortune, this inglorious end!*
Let none on earth, let none beside thee, know
I sunk thus poorly to the shades below.
965 Dispose, ye gods, my carcase as you please,
Deep let it drown beneath these raging seas;
I ask no urn my ashes to enfold,
Nor marble monuments, nor shrines of gold;
Let but the world, unknowing of my doom,
970 Expect me still, and think I am to come;
So shall my name with terror still be heard,
And my return in every nation feared.'
   He spoke, and sudden, wondrous to behold,
High on a tenth huge wave* his bark was rolled;
975 Nor sunk again, alternate, as before,
But rushing, lodged, and fixed upon the shore.*
Rome and his fortune were at once restored,
And earth again received him for her lord.
   Now through the camp his late arrival told,
980 The warriors crowd their leader to behold;
In tears around the murmuring legions stand,
And welcome him with fond complaints to land.
   'What means too daring Caesar', thus they cry,
'To tempt the ruthless seas and stormy sky?
985 What a vile helpless herd had we been left,
Of every hope at once in thee bereft?
While on thy life so many thousands wait,
While nations live dependent on thy fate,
While the whole world on thee, their head, rely,
990 'Tis cruel in thee to consent to die.
And couldst thou not one faithful soldier find,
One equal to his mighty master's mind,
One that deserved not to be left behind?

While tumbling billows tossed thee on the main,
995 We slept at ease, unknowing of thy pain.
Were we the cause, O shame, unworthy we,
That urged thee on to brave the raging sea?
Is there a slave whose head thou hold'st so light
To give him up to this tempestuous night,
1000 While Caesar, whom the subject earth obeys,
To seasons such as these his sacred self betrays?
Still would thou weary out indulgent heaven,
And scatter all the lavish gods have given?
Dost thou the care of providence employ,
1005 Only to save thee when the seas run high?
Auspicious Jove thy wishes would promote –
Thou ask'st the safety of a leaky boat;
He proffers thee the world's supreme command –
Thy hopes aspire no farther than to land,
1010 And cast thy shipwreck on th'Hesperian strand.'
    In kind reproaches thus they waste the night,
Till the grey east disclosed the breaking light;
Serene the sun his beamy face displayed,
While the tired storm and weary waves were laid.
1015 Speedy the Latian chiefs unfurl their sails,
And catch the gently rising northern gales;
In fair appearance the tall vessels glide,
The pilots and the wind conspire to guide,
And waft them fitly o'er the smoother tide;
1020 Decent* they move, like some well-ordered band,
In ranged battalions marching o'er the land;
Night fell at length, the winds the sails forsook,
And a dead calm the beauteous order broke.
So when, from Strymon's wintry banks, the cranes*
1025 In feathered legions cut th'ethereal plains,
To warmer Nile they bend their airy way,
Formed in long lines and ranked in just array;
But if some rushing storm the journey cross,
The wingy leaders all are at a loss,
1030 Now close, now loose, the breaking squadrons fly,
And scatter in confusion o'er the sky.
The day returned, with Phoebus Auster* rose
And hard upon the straining canvas blows.

Scudding afore him swift the fleet he bore,
1035 O'erpassing Lissus to Nymphaeum's shore;
There safe from northern winds, within the port
    they moor.

While thus united Caesar's arms appear,*
And fortune draws the great decision near,
Sad Pompey's soul uneasy thoughts infest,*
1040 And his Cornelia pains his anxious breast.
To distant Lesbos fain he would remove,
Far from the war, the partner of his love.
Oh, who can speak, what numbers* can reveal,
The tenderness which pious lovers feel?
1045 Who can their secret pangs and sorrows tell,
With all the crowd of cares that in their bosoms
    dwell?
See what new passions now the hero knows:*
Now first he doubts success, and fears his foes,
Rome and the world he hazards in the strife,
1050 And gives up all to fortune, but his wife.
Oft he prepares to speak, but knows not how,
Knows they must part, but cannot bid her go,
Defers the killing news with fond delay,
And, ling'ring, puts off fate from day to day.
1055 The fleeting shades began to leave the sky,
And slumber soft forsook the drooping eye,
When, with fond arms, the fair Cornelia pressed
Her lord, reluctant, to her snowy breast;
Wondering, she found he shunned her just embrace,
1060 And felt warm tears upon his manly face.
Heartwounded with the sudden woe, she grieved,
And scarce the weeping warrior yet believed,
When, with a groan, thus he: 'My truest wife,
To say how much I love thee more than life
1065 Poorly expresses what my heart would show,
Since life, alas, is grown my burden now.
That long, too long delayed, that dreadful doom,
That cruel parting hour, at length is come.
Fierce, haughty and collected in his might,*
1070 Advancing Caesar calls me to the fight.
Haste then, my gentle love, from war retreat,
The Lesbian isle attends thy peaceful seat;

Nor seek, oh seek not to increase my cares!
Seek not to change my purpose with thy prayers;
1075   Myself in vain the fruitless suit have tried,
And my own pleading heart has been denied.
Think not thy distance will increase thy fear: ⎱
Ruin, if ruin comes, will soon be near,   ⎬
Too soon the fatal news shall reach thy ear. ⎭
1080   Nor burns thy heart with just and equal fires
Nor dost thou love as virtue's law requires,*
If those soft eyes can ev'n thy husband bear
Red with the stains of blood and guilty war.
When horrid trumpets sound their dire alarms, ⎱
1085   Shall I indulge my sorrows with thy charms,   ⎬
And rise to battle from these tender arms?   ⎭
Thus mournful, from thee rather let me go,
And join thy absence to the public woe.
But thou be hid, be safe from every fear,
1090   While kings and nations in destruction share;
Shun thou the crush of my impending fate,
Nor let it fall on thee with all its weight.
Then if the gods my overthrow ordain,
And the fierce victor chase me o'er the plain,
1095   Thou shalt be left me still, my better part,
To soothe my cares, and heal my broken heart;
Thy open arms I shall be sure to meet,
And fly with pleasure to the dear retreat.'
        Stunned and astonished at the deadly stroke,
1100   All sense at first the matron sad forsook.
Motion and life and speech at length returns,
And thus in words of heaviest woe she mourns:
'No Pompey! 'Tis not that my lord is dead,
'Tis not the hand of fate has robbed my bed,
1105   But like some base plebeian I am cursed,
And by my cruel husband stand divorced.*
But Caesar bids us part! Thy father comes!
And we must yield to what that tyrant dooms!
Is thy Cornelia's faith so poorly known ⎞
1110   That thou should'st think her safer whilst alone? ⎟
Are not our loves, our lives, our fortunes one? ⎠
Canst thou, inhuman, drive me from thy side,
And bid my single head the coming storm abide?

Do I not read thy purpose in thy eye?
1115 Dost thou not hope and wish ev'n now to die?
And can I then be safe? Yet death is free,
That last relief is not denied to me;
Though banished by thy harsh command I go,
Yet I will join thee in the realms below.
1120 Thou bidst me with the pangs of absence strive,
And, till I hear thy certain loss, survive.
My vowed obedience, what it can, shall bear,
But oh, my heart's a woman, and I fear!
If the good gods, indulgent to my prayer,
1125 Should make the laws of Rome, and thee, their care,
In distant climes I may prolong my woe,
And be the last thy victory to know.
On some bleak rock, that frowns upon the deep,
A constant watch thy weeping wife shall keep,
1130 There from each sail misfortune shall I guess,
And dread the bark that brings me thy success.
Nor shall those happier tidings end my fear –
The vanquished foe may bring new danger near;
Defenceless I may still be made a prize,
1135 And Caesar snatch me with him as he flies,
With ease my known retreat he shall explore,
While thy great name distinguishes the shore.
Soon shall the Lesbian exile stand revealed –
The wife of Pompey cannot live concealed.
1140 But if th'o'er-ruling powers thy cause forsake,
Grant me this only last request I make:
When thou shalt be of troops and friends bereft,
And wretched flight is all thy safety left,
Oh, follow not the dictates of thy heart,
1145 But choose a refuge in some distant part.
Where-e'er thy unauspicious bark shall steer,
Thy sad Cornelia's fatal shore forbear,
Since Caesar will be sure to seek thee there.'
    So saying, with a groan the matron fled,
1150 And, wild with sorrow, left her holy bed;
She sees all lingering, all delays are vain,
And rushes headlong to possess the pain;
Nor will the hurry of her griefs afford
One last embrace from her forsaken lord.

Caesar in Amyclas' boat

1155   Uncommon cruel was the fate, for two ⎫
      Whose loves had lasted long and been so true, ⎬
      To lose the pleasure of one last adieu. ⎭
      In all the woeful days that crossed their bliss,
      Sure never hour was known so sad as this;
1160   By what they suffered now, inured to pain, ⎫
      They met all after-sorrows with disdain, ⎬
      And fortune shot her envious shafts in vain. ⎭
        Low on the ground the fainting dame is laid;*
      Her train officious hasten to her aid,
1165   Then gently rearing, with a careful hand,
      Support her slow descending o'er the strand.
      There, while with eager arms she grasped the shore,
      Scarcely the mourner to the bark they bore.
      Not half this grief of heart, these pangs, she knew,
1170   When from her native Italy she flew;
      Lonely and comfortless she takes her flight,
      Sad seems the day, and long the sleepless night.
      In vain her maids the downy couch provide –
      She wants the tender partner of her side;
1175   When weary oft in heaviness she lies,
      And dozy slumber steals upon her eyes,
      Fain with fond arms her lord she would have pressed,
      But weeps to find the pillow at her breast.
      Though raging in her veins a fever burns,

1180 Painful she lies, and restless oft she turns,
  She shuns his sacred side with awful fear,
  And would not be convinced he is not there.
  But oh, too soon the want shall be supplied!
  The gods too cruelly for that provide:
1185 Again the circling hours bring back her lord,
  And Pompey shall be fatally restored.

BOOK SIX

Now, near encamped, each on a neighbouring
    height,*
The Latian chiefs prepare for sudden fight.
The rival pair seem hither brought by fate, ⎫
As if the gods would end the dire debate, ⎬
5   And here determine of the Roman state. ⎭
Caesar, intent upon his hostile son,*
Demands a conquest here, and here alone,
Neglects what laurels captive towns might yield,
And scorns the harvest of the Grecian field.
10   Impatient he provokes the fatal day, ⎫
Ordained to give Rome's liberties away, ⎬
And leave the world the greedy victor's prey. ⎭
Eager that last great chance of war he waits,
Where either's fall determines both their fates.
15   Thrice on the hills, all drawn in dread array,
His threatening eagles wide their wings display;
Thrice, but in vain, his hostile arms he showed,
His ready rage and thirst of Latian blood.
But when he saw how cautious Pompey's care,
20   Safe in his camp, declined the proffered war,
Through woody paths he bent his secret way,
And meant to make Dyrrachium's towers his prey.
This Pompey saw, and swiftly shot before,
With speedy marches on the sandy shore,
25   Till on Taulantian Petra's top he stayed,
Sheltering the city with his timely aid.
This place nor walls nor trenches deep can boast,*
The works of labour and expensive cost.
Vain prodigality and labour vain,
30   Lost is the lavished wealth, and lost the fruitless pain!
What walls, what towers soe'er they rear sublime,
Must yield to wars, or more destructive time,
While fences like Dyrrachium's fortress, made ⎫
Where nature's hand the sure foundation laid, ⎬
35   And with her strength the naked town arrayed, ⎭

Shall stand secure against the warrior's rage,
Nor fear the ruinous decays of age;
Guarded around by steepy* rocks it lies,
And all access from land, but one, denies.
40 No venturous vessel there in safety rides, }
But foaming surges break, and swelling tides }
Roll roaring on, and wash the craggy sides; }
Or when contentious winds more rudely blow, }
Then mounting o'er the topmost cliff they flow, }
45 Burst on the lofty domes, and dash the town below. }
    Here Caesar's daring heart vast hopes conceives,*
And high with war's vindictive pleasures heaves;
Much he revolves within his thoughtful mind }
How in this camp the foe may be confined, }
50 With ample lines from hill to hill designed. }
Secret and swift he means the task to try,
And runs each distance over with his eye.
Vast heaps of sod and verdant turf are brought,
And stones in deep, laborious quarries wrought;
55 Each Grecian dwelling round the work supplies,
And sudden ramparts from their ruins rise.
With wondrous strength the stable mound they rear, }
Such as th'impetuous ram can never fear,* }
Nor hostile might o'erturn, nor forceful engine tear. }
60 Through hills, resistless, Caesar plains* his way,
And makes the rough, unequal rocks obey.
Here, deep beneath, the gaping trenches lie,
There forts advance their airy turrets high.
Around vast tracts of land the labours* wind, }
65 Wide fields and forests in the circle bind, }
And hold as in a toil the savage kind. }
Nor ev'n the foe too strictly pent remains:
At large he forages upon the plains;
The vast enclosure gives free leave around,
70 Oft to decamp and shift the various ground.
Here, from far fountains, streams their channels
        trace, }
And, while they wander through the tedious space, }
Run many a mile their long extended race, }
While some, quite worn and weary of the way,
75 Sink and are lost before they reach the sea;

Ev'n Caesar's self, when through the works he goes,
Tires in the midst, and stops to take repose.
Let fame no more record the walls of Troy,*
Which gods alone could build, and gods destroy,
80 Nor let the Parthian wonder to have seen
The labours of the Babylonian queen.*
Behold this large, this spacious tract of ground*
Like that which Tigris or Orontes bound!
Behold this land, that majesty might bring,
85 And form a kingdom for an Eastern king!
Behold a Latian chief this land enclose
Amidst the tumult of impending foes! –
He bade the walls arise, and as he bade they rose.
But ah, vain pride of power, ah, fruitless boast!
90 Ev'n these, these mighty labours are all lost!
A force like this what barriers could withstand?
Seas must have fled, and yielded to the land;
The lovers' shores united might have stood*
Spite of the Hellespont's opposing flood,
95 While the Aegean and Ionian tide,
Might meeting o'er the vanquished Isthmus ride,
And Argive realms from Corinth's walls divide.*
This power might change unwilling nature's face,
Unfix each order, and remove each place.
100 Here, as if closed within a list,* the war
Does all its valiant combatants prepare;
Here ardent glows the blood which fate ordains
To dye the Libyan and Emathian plains;
Here the whole rage of civil discord joined
105 Struggles for room, and scorns to be confined.
Nor yet, while Caesar his first labours tried,
The warlike toil by Pompey was descried.
So, in mid Sicily's delightful plain,
Safe from the horrid sound, the happy swain
110 Dreads not loud Scylla* barking o'er the main;
So northern Britons never hear the roar*
Of seas that break on the far Cantian shore.
Soon as the rising rampart's hostile height
And towers advancing struck his anxious sight,
115 Sudden from Petra's safer camp he led,
And wide his legions on the hills dispread,*

So Caesar, forced his numbers to extend,
More feebly might each various strength defend.
His camp far o'er the large enclosure reached,
120   And guarded lines along the front were stretched,
Far as Rome's distance from Aricia's groves*
(Aricia which the chaste Diana loves),
Far as from Rome old Tiber seeks the sea,
Did he not wander in his winding way.*
125   While yet no signals for the fight prepare, ⎫
Unbidden some the javelin dart from far, ⎬
And skirmishing provoke the lingering war. ⎭
But deeper cares the thoughtful chiefs distress,*
And move the soldiers' ardour to repress.
130   Pompey with secret, anxious thought beheld*
How trampling hooves the rising grass repelled;
Waste lie the russet fields, the generous steed
Seeks on the naked soil, in vain, to feed;
Loathing, from racks* of husky straw he turns,
135   And pining for the verdant pasture mourns.
No more his limbs their dying load sustain, ⎫
Aiming a stride he falters in the strain, ⎬
And sinks a ruin on the withering plain; ⎭
Dire maladies upon his vitals prey,
140   Dissolve his frame, and melt the mass away.
Thence deadly plagues invade the lazy air,
Reek to the clouds, and hang malignant there.
From Nesis* such the Stygian vapours rise,
And with contagion taint the purer skies;
145   Such do Typhoeus'* steamy caves convey,
And breathe blue poisons* on the golden day.
Thence liquid streams the mingling plague receive,
And deadly potions to the thirsty give;
To man the mischief spreads, the fell disease
150   In fatal draughts does on his entrails seize;
A rugged scurf, all loathsome to be seen,*
Spreads like a bark upon his silken skin;
Malignant flames his swelling eyeballs dart,
And seem with anguish from their seats to start;
155   Fires o'er his glowing cheeks and visage stray,
And mark, in crimson streaks, their burning way;
Low droops his head, declining from its height,

And nods and totters with the fatal weight.*
With wingèd haste the swift destruction flies
160   And scarce the soldier sickens e'er he dies;
Now falling crowds at once resign their breath,
And doubly taint the noxious air with death.
Careless their putrid carcasses are spread,
And on the earth, their dank unwholesome bed,
165   The living rest in common with the dead.
Here none the last funereal rites receive –
To be cast forth the camp is all their friends can give.
At length kind heav'n their sorrows bade to cease,
And stayed the pestilential foe's increase;
170   Fresh breezes from the sea begin to rise,
While Boreas through the lazy vapour flies,
And sweeps, with healthy wings, the rank, polluted
      skies.
Arriving vessels now their freight unload,
And furnish plenteous harvests from abroad;
175   Now spritely strength, now cheerful health returns,
And life's fair lamp rekindled brightly burns.
      But Caesar, unconfined and camped on high,*
Feels not the mischief of the sluggish sky;
On hills sublime he breathes the purer air,
180   And drinks no damps* nor poisonous vapours there.
Yet hunger keen an equal plague is found,
Famine and meagre want besiege him round;*
The fields as yet no hopes of harvest wear,
Nor yellow stems disclose the bearded ear.
The scattered vulgar search around the fields,
185   And pluck whate'er the doubtful herbage yields;
Some strip the trees in every neighbouring wood,
And with the cattle share their grassy food.
Whate'er the softening flame can pliant make,
190   Whate'er the teeth or labouring jaws can break,
What flesh, what roots, what herbs soe'er they get,
Though new and strange to human taste as yet,
At once the greedy soldiers seize and eat.
What want, what pain soe'er they undergo,
195   Still they persist in arms, and close beset the foe.
      At length, impatient longer to be held*
Within the bounds of one appointed field,

O'er every bar which might his passage stay
Pompey resolves to force his warlike way,
200   Wide o'er the world the ranging war to lead,
And give his loosened legions room to spread.
Nor takes he mean advantage from the night,
Nor steals a passage, nor declines the fight,
But bravely dares, disdainful of the foe,
205   Through the proud towers and ramparts' breach to
          go.
Where shining spears and crested helms are seen,
Embattled thick to guard the walls within,
Where all things death, where ruin all afford,
There Pompey marks a passage for his sword.
210   Near to the camp a woody thicket lay –
Close was the shade, nor did the greensward way,*
With smoky clouds of dust, the march betray.
Hence sudden they appear in dread array,
Sudden their wide extended ranks display;
215   At once the foe beholds with wondering eyes
Where on broad wings Pompeian eagles rise,
At once the warriors' shouts and trumpet-sounds
          surprise.
Scarce was the sword's destruction needful here,
So swiftly ran before preventing fear;
220   Some fled amazed, while vainly valiant some
Stood but to meet in arms a nobler doom.
Where-e'er they stood, now scattered lie the slain,
Scarce yet a few for coming deaths remain,
And clouds of flying javelins fall in vain.
225   Here swift consuming flames the victors throw,
And here the ram impetuous aims a blow,
Aloft the nodding turrets feel the stroke,
And the vast rampart groans beneath the shock.
And now propitious fortune seemed to doom
230   Freedom and peace to Pompey and to Rome;
High o'er the vanquished works his eagles tower,
And vindicate the world from Caesar's power.
      But what nor Caesar nor his fortune could,
What not ten thousand warlike hands withstood,
235   Scaeva* resists alone, repels the force,
And stops the rapid victor in his course –

Scaeva, a name e'erwhile to fame unknown,
And first distinguished on the Gallic Rhone;
There seen in hardy deeds of arms to shine,
240   He reached the honours of the Latian vine.*
Daring and bold, and ever prone to ill, ⎫
Inured to blood, and active to fulfil   ⎬
The dictates of a lawless tyrant's will, ⎭
Nor virtue's love nor reason's laws he knew,
245   But, careless of the right, for hire his sword he drew.
Thus courage by an impious cause is cursed,
And he that is the bravest is the worst.
Soon as he saw his fellows shun the fight,
And seek their safety in ignoble flight:*
250   'Whence does', he said, 'this coward's terror grow,
This shame unknown to Caesar's arms till now?
Can you, ye slavish herd, thus tamely yield,
Thus fly unwounded from this bloody field?
Behold where piled in slaughtered heaps on high,
255   Firm to the last, your brave companions lie;
Then blush to think what wretched lives you save,
From what renown you fly, from what a glorious
          grave.
Though sacred fame, though virtue yield to fear,
Let rage, let indignation keep you here.
260   We, we the weakest, from the rest are chose*
To yield a passage to our scornful foes!
Yet, Pompey, yet, thou shalt be yet withstood,
And stain thy victor's laurel deep in blood.
With pride, 'tis true, with joy I should have died, ⎫
265   If haply I had fall'n by Caesar's side,   ⎬
But fortune has the noble death denied.   ⎭
Then Pompey, thou, thou on my fame shalt wait,
Do thou be witness and applaud my fate.
Now push we on, disdain we now to fear,   ⎫
270   A thousand wounds let every bosom bear,   ⎬
Till the keen sword be blunt, be broke the pointed ⎪
          spear.   ⎭
And see, the clouds of dusty battle rise!
Hark how the shout runs rattling through the skies!
The distant legions catch the sounds from far,
275   And Caesar listens to the thundering war.

He comes, he comes, yet e'er his soldier dies,
Like lightning swift the wingèd warrior flies;
Haste then to death, to conquest, haste away!
Well do we fall, for Caesar wins the day.'

280   He spoke, and straight, as at the trumpet's sound,
Rekindled warmth in every breast was found;
Recalled from flight, the youth admiring wait
To mark their daring fellow-soldier's fate,
To see if haply virtue might prevail,
285   And ev'n, beyond their hopes, do more than greatly
       fail.

     High on the tottering wall he rears his head,
With slaughtered carcasses around him spread;
With nervous arms uplifting, these he throws,
These rolls oppressive, on ascending foes.
290   Each where* materials for his fury lie,
And all the ready ruins arms supply;
Ev'n his fierce self he seems to aim below,
Headlong to shoot, and dying dart a blow.
Now his tough staff repels the fierce attack,
295   And tumbling drives the bold assailants back;
Now heads, now hands he lops – the carcass falls,
While the clenched fingers gripe* the topmost walls;
Here stones he heaves; the mass descending full
Crushes the brain, and shivers the frail skull.
300   Here burning, pitchy brands he whirls around; ⎫
Infixed, the flames hiss in the liquid wound,   ⎬
Deep drenched in death, in flowing crimson   ⎭
       drowned.
     And now the swelling heaps of slaughtered foes
Sublime* and equal to the fortress rose;
305   Whence forward, with a leap, at once he sprung,
And shot himself amidst the hostile throng.
So daring, fierce with rage, so void of fear,
Bounds forth the spotted pard,* and scorns the
       hunter's spear.
The closing ranks the warrior strait enfold,
310   And compassed in their steely circle hold.
Undaunted still, around the ring he roams,
Fights here and there, and everywhere o'ercomes,
Till clogged with blood his sword obeys but ill

The dictates of its vengeful master's will;
315   Edgeless it falls, and, though it pierce no more,
Still breaks the battered bones, and bruises sore.
Meantime on him the crowding war is bent,
And darts from every hand to him are sent;
It looked as fortune did in odds delight,
320   And had in cruel sport ordained the fight:
A wondrous match of war she seemed to make –
Her thousands here, and there her one to stake,
As if on knightly terms in lists they ran,
And armies were but equal to the man.
325   A thousand darts upon his buckler* ring,
A thousand javelins round his temples sing;
Hard bearing on his head, with many a blow,
His steely helm is inward taught to bow.
The missive* arms fixed all around he wears, ⎫
330   And ev'n his safety in his wounds he bears,* ⎬
Fenced with a fatal wood, a deadly grove of ⎭
          spears.
     Cease, ye Pompeian warriors, cease the strife,*
Nor vainly thus attempt this single life;
Your darts, your idle javelins cast aside,
335   And other arms for Scaeva's death provide;
The forceful ram's resistless horns* prepare,
With all the ponderous vast machines of war;
Let dreadful flames, let massy rocks be thrown, ⎫
With engines thunder on, and break him down, ⎬
340   And win this Caesar's soldier, like a town. ⎭
At length, his fate disdaining to delay,
He hurls his shield's neglected aid away,
Resolves no part whate'er from death to hide,
But stands unguarded now on every side.
345   Encumbered sore with many a painful wound,
Tardy and stiff he treads the hostile round;
Gloomy and fierce his eyes the crowd survey,
Mark where to fix, and single out the prey.*
Such, by Gaetulian hunters compassed in,
350   The vast, unwieldy elephant is seen;
All covered with a steely shower* from far,
Rousing he shakes, and sheds the scattered war;*
In vain the distant troop the fight renew,

And with fresh rage the stubborn foe pursue;
355 Unconquered still the mighty savage stands,
And scorns the malice of a thousand hands;
Not all the wounds a thousand darts can make,
Though all find place, a single life can take.*
When lo, addressed with some successful vow,
360 A shaft sure flying from a Cretan bow
Beneath the warrior's brow was seen to light,
And sunk, deep piercing the left orb of sight.
But he (so rage inspired and mad disdain)
Remorseless fell, and, senseless of the pain,
365 Tore forth the bearded arrow from the wound, ⎫
With stringy nerves* besmeared and wrapped   ⎬
            around,   ⎭
And stamped the gory jelly on the ground.
So in Pannonian woods the growling bear,
Transfixed, grows fiercer for the hunter's spear,
370 Turns on her wound, runs madding round with pain,
And catches at the flying shaft in vain.
Down from his eyeless hollow ran the blood,
And hideous o'er his mangled visage flowed.
Deformed each awful, each severer grace,
375 And veiled the manly terrors of his face.
The victors raise their joyful voices high,
And with loud triumph strike the vaulted sky;
Not Caesar thus a general joy had spread,
Though Caesar's self like Scaeva thus had bled.
380 Anxious, the wounded soldier in his breast ⎫
The rising indignation deep repressed,   ⎬
And thus, in humble vein, his haughty foes   ⎪
            addressed: ⎭
'Here let your rage, ye Romans, cease', he said,
'And lend your fellow-citizen your aid;
385 No more your darts nor useless javelins try, ⎫
These which I bear will deaths enow* supply – ⎬
Draw forth your weapons,* and behold I die.   ⎭
Or rather bear me hence, and let me meet
My doom beneath the mighty Pompey's feet;
390 'Twere great, 'twere brave, to fall in arms, 'tis true,
But I renounce that glorious fate for you.
Fain would I yet prolong this vital breath,

And quit ev'n Caesar, so I fly from death.'
The wretched Aulus listened to the wile,
395   Intent and greedy of the future spoil;
Advancing fondly on, with heedless ease,
He thought the captive and his arms to seize,
When, e'er he was aware, his thundering sword*
Deep in his throat the ready Scaeva gored.
400   Warmed with the slaughter, with fresh rage he burns,
And vigour with the new success returns.
'So may they fall', he said, 'by just deceit,
Such be their fate, such as this fool has met,
Who dares believe that I am vanquished yet.
405   If you would stop the vengeance of my sword,
From Caesar's mercy be your peace implored,
There let your leader kneel, and humbly own his
         lord.
Me! could you meanly dare to fancy me
Base, like yourselves, and fond of life to be?
410   But know, not all the names which grace your cause,
Your reverend Senate, and your boasted laws,
Not Pompey's self, not all for which you fear,
Were e'er to you, like death to Scaeva, dear.'
Thus while he spoke, a rising dust betrayed
415   Caesarean legions marching to his aid.
Now Pompey's troops with prudence seem to yield,
And to increasing numbers quit the field;
Dissembling shame, they hide their foul defeat,
Nor vanquished by a single arm retreat.
420   Then fell the warrior, for till then he stood –
His manly mind supplied the want of blood.
It seemed as rage had kindled life anew,
And courage to oppose from opposition grew.
But now, when none were left him to repel,
425   Fainting for want of foes, the victor fell.
Straight with officious haste his friends draw near,
And, raising, joy the noble load to bear;
To reverence and religious awe inclined,
Admiring, they adore his mighty mind,
430   That god within his mangled breast enshrined.
The wounding weapons, stained with Scaeva's blood,
Like sacred relics to the gods are vowed;

Forth are they drawn from every part with care,
And kept to dress the naked god of war.*
435 O happy soldier, had thy worth been tried,
In pious daring, on thy country's side!
Oh, had thy sword Iberian battles known, ⎤
Or purple with Cantabrian slaughter grown, ⎟
How had thy name in deathless annals shone! ⎦
440 But now no Roman paeans* shalt thou sing,
Nor peaceful triumphs to thy country bring,
Nor loudly blessed in solemn pomp shalt move ⎤
Through crowding streets to Capitolian Jove,* ⎟
The laws' defender, and the people's love: ⎦
445 O hapless victor thou, oh, vainly brave,
How hast thou fought to make thyself a slave!
      Nor Pompey, thus repulsed, the fight declines,*
Nor rests encompassed round by Caesar's lines;
Once more he means to force his warlike way,
450 And yet retrieve the fortune of the day.
So when fierce winds with angry ocean strive,
Full on the beach the beating billows drive,
Stable awhile the lofty mounds abide,
Check the proud surge, and stay the swelling tide;
455 Yet restless still the waves unwearied roll,
Work underneath at length, and sap the sinking
      mole.
With force renewed the baffled warrior bends,
Where to the shore the jutting wall extends,
There proves by land and sea his various might,
460 And wins his passage by the double fight.
Wide o'er the plains diffused his legions range,
And their close camp for freer fields exchange.
So, raised by melting streams of Alpine snow, ⎤
Beyond his utmost margin swells the Po, ⎟
465 And loosely lets the spreading deluge flow; ⎦
Where-e'er the weaker banks oppressed retreat,
And sink beneath the heapy waters' weight,
Forth gushing at the breach they burst their way,
And wasteful o'er the drownded* country stray;
470 Far distant fields and meads they wander o'er,
And visit lands they never knew before;
Here from its seat the mouldering earth is torn,

And by the flood to other masters borne,
While gathering there it heaps the growing soil,
475   And loads the peasant with his neighbour's spoil.
      Soon as, ascending high, a rising flame
To Caesar's sight, the combat's signal, came,
Swift to the place approaching near he found ⎫
The ruin scattered by the victor round,   ⎬
480   And his proud labours humbled to the ground. ⎭
Thence to the hostile camp his eyes he turns,   ⎫
Where for their peace and sleep secure he mourns, ⎬
With rancorous despite and envious anguish   ⎪
      burns.   ⎭
At length resolved (so rage inspired his breast)
485   He means to break the happy victor's rest,
Once more to kindle up the fatal strife,
And dash their joys, with hazard of his life.
Straight to Torquatus* fierce he bends his way
(Torquatus near a neighbouring castle lay),
490   But he, by prudent caution taught to yield,
Trusts to his walls, and quits the open field;
There safe within himself he stands his ground,
And lines the guarded rampart strongly round.
So when the seamen from afar descry   ⎫
495   The clouds grow black upon the louring sky, ⎬
Hear the winds roar, and mark the seas run high, ⎭
They furl the fluttering sheet* with timely care,
And wisely for the coming storm prepare.
But now the victor, with resistless haste,
500   Proud o'er the ramparts of the fort had passed,
When swift descending from the rising grounds
Pompey with lengthening files the foe surrounds.
As when in Etna's hollow caves below
Round the vast furnace kindling whirlwinds blow,
505   Roused in his baleful bower the giant roars,*
And with a burst the burning deluge pours;
Then pale with horror shrieks the shuddering swain
To see the fiery ruin spread the plain;
Nor with less horror Caesar's bands behold
510   Huge, hostile, dusty clouds their rear enfold;
Unknowing whom to meet or whom to shun,
Blind with their fear, full on their fates they run.

Well, on that day, the world repose had gained,
And bold rebellion's blood had all been drained,
515   Had not the pious chief the rage of war restrained.
O Rome, how free, how happy hadst thou been,
Thy own great mistress, and the nation's queen,
Had Sulla* then thy great avenger stood,
And dyed his thirsty sword in traitors' blood!
520   But oh, for ever shalt thou now bemoan
The two extremes by which thou wert undone,
The ruthless father, and too tender son.*
With fatal pity, Pompey, hast thou spared,
And giv'n the blackest crime the best reward;
525   How had that one, one happy day withheld
The blood of Utica, and Munda's field!*
The Pharian Nile had known no crime more great
Than some vile Ptolemy's untimely fate,*
Nor Afric, then, her Juba had bemoaned,*
530   Nor Scipio's blood the Punic ghosts atoned,
Cato* had for his country's good survived,
And long in peace a hoary patriot lived,
Rome had not worn a tyrant's hated chain,
And fate had undecreed Pharsalia's plain.
535   But Caesar, weary of th'unlucky land,
Swift to Emathia leads his shattered band,
While Pompey's wary friends, with caution wise,*
To quit the baffled foe's pursuit advise.
To Italy they point his open way,
540   And bid him make the willing land his prey.
'Oh, never', he replies, 'shall Pompey come,
Like Caesar, armed and terrible, to Rome;
Nor need I from those sacred walls have fled,
Could I have borne our streets with slaughter red,
545   And seen the forum piled with heaps of dead.
Much rather let me pine in Scythia's frost,
Or burn on swarthy Libya's sultry coast –
No clime, no distant region is too far,
Where I can banish with me fatal war.
550   I fled to bid my country's sorrows cease,
And shall my victories invade her peace?
Let her but safe and free from arms remain,
And Caesar still shall think she wears his chain.'

He spoke, and eastward sought the forest wide
555   That rising clothes Candavia's shady side,
Thence to Emathia took his destined way,
Reserved by fate for the deciding day.
      Where Eurus* blows, and wintry suns arise,*
Thessalia's boundary* proud Ossa lies,*
560   But when the god protracts the longer day,
Pelion's broad back receives the dawning ray;
Where through the Lion's* fiery sign he* flies,
Othrys his leafy groves for shade supplies;
On Pindus strikes the fady western light,
565   When glittering Vesper* leads the starry night;
Northward, Olympus hides the lamps that roll
Their paler fires around the frozen pole.
The middle space, a valley* low depressed,
Once a wide, lazy, standing lake possessed,
570   While growing still the heapy waters stood,
Nor down through Tempe ran the rushing flood;
But when Alcides* to the task applied,*
And cleft a passage through the mountains wide,
Gushing at once the thundering torrent flowed,
575   While Nereus* groaned beneath th'increasing load;
Then rose (oh, that it still a lake had lain!) ⎫
Above the waves Pharsalia's fatal plain,   ⎬
Once subject to the great Achilles' reign.* ⎭
Then Phylace was built, whose warriors boast
580   Their chief* first landed on the Trojan coast;
Then Pteleos* ran her circling wall around,
And Dorion,* for the Muses' wrath renowned;
Then Trachin* high, and Meliboea stood,*
Where Hercules his fatal shafts bestowed;
585   Larisa strong arose, and Argos,* now
A plain, submitted to the labouring plough;
Here stood the town, if there be truth in fame,*
That from Boeotian Thebes received its name –
Here sad Agave's wandering sense returned,
590   Here for her murdered son the mother mourned,
With streaming tears she washed his ghastly head,*
And on the funeral pile the precious relic laid.
      The gushing waters various soon divide,
And every river rules a separate tide:

595 The narrow Aeas runs a limpid flood,
     Evenos blushes with the centaur's blood – *
     That gently mingles with th'Ionian sea,
     While this through Calydonia cuts his way;
     Slowly fair Io's aged father falls,*
600 And in hoarse murmurs his lost daughter calls;
     Thick Achelous* rolls his troubled waves,
     And heavily the neighbour isles* he laves,
     While pure Amphrysus winds along the mead*
     Where Phoebus once was wont his flocks to feed
605 (Oft on the banks he sat a shepherd swain,
     And watched his charge upon the grassy plain);
     Swift to the main his course Spercheos bends,
     And sounding to the Malian gulf descends;
     No breezy air near calm Anauros* flies,
610 No dewy mists, nor fleecy clouds arise;
     Here Phoenix, Melas, and Asopas run,
     And strong Apidanus* drives slow Enipeus* on;
     A thousand little brooks unknown to fame
     Are mixed and lost in Peneus' nobler name,
615 Bold Titaresus scorns his rule alone,
     And, joined to Peneus, still himself is known,
     As o'er the land his haughty waters glide,
     And roll unmingling, a superior tide
     ('Tis said, through secret channels winding forth,
620 Deep as from Styx he takes his hallowed birth;*
     Thence, proud to be revered by gods on high,
     He scorns to mingle with a mean ally).
         When rising grounds upreared at length their
             heads,
     And rivers shrunk within their oozy beds,
625 Bebrycians first are said, with early care,
     In furrows deep to sink the shining share.
     The Lelegians* next, with equal toil,
     And Dolopes invade the mellow soil.
     To these the bold Aeolidae succeed,   ⎫
630 Magnetes, taught to rein the fiery steed,   ⎬
     And Minyae, to explore the deep decreed.   ⎭
     Here, pregnant by Ixion's bold embrace,*
     The mother cloud disclosed the centaurs' race,
     In Pelethronian caves* she brought them forth,

635 And filled the land with many a monstrous birth:
Here dreadful Monychus first saw the light,*
And proved on Pholoe's rending rocks his might;
Here tallest trees uprooting Rhoecus bore,
Which baffled storms had tried in vain before;
640 Here Pholus, of a gentler human breast,
Received the great Alcides for his guest;
Here, with brute fury, lustful Nessus tried }
To violate the hero's beauteous bride, }
Till justly by the fatal shaft he died;* }
645 This parent land the pious leach* confessed,
Chiron, of all the double race the best –
Midst golden stars he stands refulgent now,*
And threats the Scorpion with his bended bow.
       Here love of arms and battle reigned of old,
650 And formed the first Thessalians fierce and bold;
Here, from rude rocks, at Neptune's potent stroke,*
Omen of war, the neighing courser* broke;
Here taught by skilful riders to submit,
He champed indignant on the foamy bit.
655 From fair Thessalia's Pagasaean shore* }
The first bold pine the daring warriors bore, }
And taught the sons of earth wide oceans to }
       explore. }
Here, when Itonus* held the regal seat, }
The stubborn steel he first subdued with heat, }
660 And the tough bars on sounding anvils beat; }
In furnaces he ran the liquid brass,
And cast in curious works the molten mass;
He taught the ruder artist to refine, }
Explored the silver and the golden mine, }
665 And stamped the costly metal into coin: – }
From that old era avarice was known,
Then all the deadly seeds of war were sown;
Wide o'er the world, by tale, the mischief ran,
And those cursed pieces were the bane of man.
670 Huge Python here, in many a scaly fold,*
To Cirrha's cave a length enormous rolled;
Hence Pythian games the hardy Greeks renown,*
And laurel wreaths the joyful victor crown.
Here proud Aloeus durst the gods defy,*

675   And taught his impious brood to scale the sky,
       While mountains piled on mountains interfere
       With heav'n's bright orbs, and stop the circling
          sphere.
         To this cursed land, by fate's appointed doom,*
       With one consent the warring leaders come;
680   Their camps are fixed, and now the vulgar fear
       To see the terrible event so near.
       A few, and but a few, with souls serene,
       Wait the disclosing of the dubious scene.
       But Sextus,* mixed among the vulgar herd,
685   Like them was anxious, and unmanly feared,
       A youth unworthy of the hero's race,
       And born to be his nobler sire's disgrace.
        A day shall come when this inglorious son*
       Shall stain the trophies all by Pompey won,
690   A thief and spoiler shall he live confessed,
       And act those wrongs his father's arms redressed.
       Vexed with a coward's fond impatience now,
       He pries into that fate he fears to know;
       Nor seeks he with religious vows to move
695   The Delphic* tripod, or Dodonian Jove;*
       No priestly augur's art employs his cares,
       Nor Babylonian seers who read the stars,*
       He nor by fibres, birds or lightning's fires,
       Nor any just, though secret rites enquires,
700   But horrid altars and infernal powers,   ⎫
       Dire mysteries of magic he explores,   ⎬
       Such as high heaven and gracious Jove abhors. ⎭
       He thinks 'tis little those above can know,
       And seeks accursed assistance from below.
705   The place itself the impious means supplies,
       While near Haemonian* hags encamped he lies;
       All dreadful deeds, all monstrous forms of old,
       By fear invented and by falsehood told,
       Whate'er transcends belief and reason's view,
710   Their art can furnish, and their power makes true.
        The pregnant fields a horrid crop produce,
       Noxious, and fit for witchcraft's deadly use;
       With baleful weeds each mountain's brow is hung,
       And listening rocks attend the charmer's song.

715   There potent and mysterious plants arise,
        Plants that compel the gods and awe the skies;
        There leaves unfolded to Medea's view*
        Such as her native Colchis never knew.
        Soon as the dread Haemonian voice ascends
720   Through the whole vast expanse, each power
                attends –
        Ev'n all those sullen deities, who know
        No care of heaven above or earth below,
        Hear and obey. Th'Assyrian then, in vain,
        And Memphian priests their local gods detain;
725   From every altar loose at once they fly,
        And with the stronger foreign call comply.
            The coldest hearts Thessalian numbers* warm,
        And ruthless bosoms own* the potent charm;
        With monstrous power they rouse perverse desire,
730   And kindle into lust the wintry sire;
        Where noxious cups and poisonous philtres fail,
        More potent spells and mystic verse prevail.
        No draughts so strong the knots of love prepare,
        Cropped from her younglings by the parent mare.*
735   Oft sullen bridegrooms, who unkindly fled
        From blooming beauty and the genial bed,
        Melt as the thread runs on, and, sighing, feel*
        The giddy whirling of the magic wheel.
        Whene'er the proud enchantress gives command,*
740   Eternal motion stops her active hand.*
        No more heav'n's rapid circles journey on,
        But universal nature stands foredone,
        The lazy god of day forgets to rise,
        And everlasting night pollutes the skies.
745   Jove wonders to behold her shake the pole,
        And, unconsenting, hears his thunders roll.
        Now, with a word, she hides the sun's bright face,
        And blots the wide, ethereal, azure space,
        Loosely, anon, she shakes her flowing hair,
750   And straight the stormy, louring heavens are fair;
        At once she calls the golden light again –
        The clouds fly swift away, and stops the drizzly rain.
        In stillest calms she bids the waves run high,

And smooths the deep, though Boreas* shakes the
    sky;
755 When winds are hushed her potent breath prevails,
    Wafts on the bark, and fills the flagging sails.
    Streams have run back at murmurs of her tongue,
    And torrents from the rock suspended hung.
    No more the Nile his wonted seasons knows,
760 And in a line the straight Maeander* flows.
    Arar has rushed with headlong waters down,*
    And driv'n unwillingly the sluggish Rhone.
    Huge mountains have been levelled with the plain,
    And far from heaven has tall Olympus lain.
765 Riphaean crystal* has been known to melt,
    And Scythian snows a sudden summer felt.
    No longer pressed by Cynthia's* moister beam,
    Alternate Tethys* heaves her swelling stream;
    By charms forbid, her tides revolve no more,
770 But shun the margin of the guarded shore.
    The ponderous earth, by magic numbers strook,*
    Down to her inmost centre deep has shook,
    Then, rending with a yawn, at once made way
    To join the upper and the nether day,
775 While wondering eyes, the dreadful cleft between,*
    Another starry firmament have seen.
    Each deadly kind, by nature formed to kill,
    Fear the dire hags, and execute their will.
    Lions to them their nobler rage submit,
780 And fawning tigers couch beneath their feet;
    For them the snake foregoes her wintry hold,
    And on the hoary frost untwines her fold;
    The poisonous race they strike with stronger death,
    And blasted vipers die by human breath.
785   What law the heavenly natures thus constrains,
    And binds ev'n godheads in resistless chains?
    What wondrous power do charms and herbs imply,*
    And force them thus to follow and to fly?
    What is it can command them to obey?
790 Does choice incline, or awful terror sway?
    Do secret rites their deities atone,*
    Or mystic piety to man unknown?
    Do strong enchantments all immortals brave,*

Or is there one determined god their slave,*

795 One whose command obedient nature awes, ⎫
Who, subject still himself to magic laws, ⎬
Acts only as a servile second cause? ⎭

Magic the starry lamps from heaven can tear,
And shoot them gleaming through the dusky air,

800 Can blot fair Cynthia's countenance serene,
And poison with foul spells the silver queen;
Now pale the ghastly goddess shrinks with dread,
And now black smoky fires involve* her head,
As when earth's envious interposing shade*

805 Cuts off her beamy brother from her aid;
Held by the charming* song, she strives in vain,
And labours with the long pursuing pain,
Till down, and downward still, compelled to come,
On hallowed herbs she sheds her fatal foam.*

810   But these, as arts too gentle and too good, ⎫
Nor yet with death or guilt enough imbrued, ⎬
With haughty scorn the fierce Erictho viewed. ⎭
New mischief she, new monsters* durst explore,
And dealt in horrors never known before.

815 From towns and hospitable roofs she flies,
And every dwelling of mankind defies,
Through unfrequented deserts lonely roams,
Drives out the dead, and dwells within their tombs.
Spite of all laws which heaven or nature know,

820 The rule of gods above and man below,*
Grateful to hell the living hag descends,
And sits in black assemblies of the fiends.
Dark matted elf-locks* dangling on her brow,
Filthy and foul, a loathsome burden grow;

825 Ghastly and frightful-pale her face is seen,
Unknown to cheerful day and skies serene;
But when the stars are veiled, when storms arise,
And the blue, forky flame at midnight flies,
Then forth from graves she takes her wicked way,

830 And thwarts* the glancing lightnings as they play.
Where-e'er she breathes, blue poisons round her ⎫
     spread, ⎮
The withering grass avows her fatal tread, ⎬
And drooping Ceres* hangs her blasted head. ⎭

Nor holy rites nor suppliant prayer she knows,
835   Nor seeks the gods with sacrifice or vows;
Whate'er she offers is the spoil of urns,
And funeral fire upon her altars burns;
Nor need she send a second voice on high:
Scared at the first, the trembling gods comply.
840   Oft in the grave the living has she laid,
And bid reviving bodies leave the dead;
Oft at the funeral pile she seeks her prey,
And bears the smoking ashes warm away,
Snatches some burning bone, or flaming brand,
845   And tears the torch from the sad father's hand,*
Seizes the shroud's loose fragments as they fly,
And picks the coal where clammy juices fry.*
But when the dead in marble tombs are placed,
Where the moist carcase by degrees shall waste,
850   There greedily on every part she flies,
Strips the dry nails, and digs the gory eyes.
Her teeth from gibbets gnaw the strangling noose,
And from the cross dead murderers unloose;
Her charms the use of sun-dried marrow find,
855   And husky* entrails withered in the wind;
Oft drops the ropy* gore upon her tongue,
With cordy sinews oft her jaws are strung,
And thus suspended oft the filthy hag has hung.
Where-e'er the battle bleeds and slaughter lies,
860   Thither, preventing birds and beasts, she hies;*
Nor then content to seize the ready prey,
From their fell jaws she tears their food away;
She marks the hungry wolf's pernicious tooth,
And joys to rend the morsel from his mouth.
865   Nor ever yet remorse could stop her hand,
When human gore her cursèd rites demand.
Whether some tender infant, yet unborn,
From the lamenting mother's side is torn,
Whether her purpose asks some bolder shade*
870   And by her knife the ghost she wants is made,
Or whether, curious in the choice of blood,
She catches the first gushing of the flood,*
All mischief is of use, and every murder good.
When blooming youths in early manhood die,

875 She stands a terrible attendant by,
       The downy growth from off their cheeks she tears,
       Or cuts, left-handed,* some selected hairs.
       Oft when in death her gasping kindred lay,
       Some pious office would she feign to pay,*
880 And, while close hovering o'er the bed she hung,
       Bit the pale lips, and cropped the quivering tongue;
       Then in hoarse murmurs, ere the ghost could go,
       Muttered some message to the shades below.
           A fame like this, around the region spread,
885 To prove her power the younger Pompey led.
       Now half her sable course the night had run,
       And low beneath us rolled the beamy sun,
       When the vile youth in silence crossed the plain,
       Attended by his wonted, worthless train.
890 Through ruins waste and old, long wandering round,
       Lonely upon a rock the hag they found.
       There, as it chanced, in sullen mood she sate,*
       Pondering upon the war's approaching fate;
       At that same hour she ran new numbers o'er,
895 And spells unheard by hell itself before;
       Fearful lest wavering destiny might change,*
       And bid the war in distant regions range,
       She charmed Pharsalia's field with early care
       To keep the warriors and the slaughter there;
900 So may her impious arts in triumph reign,
       And riot in the plenty of the slain;
       So many a royal ghost she may command,
       Mangle dead heroes with a ruthless hand,
       And rob of many an urn Hesperia's* mourning
           land.
905 Already she enjoys the dreadful field,
       And thinks what spoils the rival chiefs shall yield,
       With what fell rage each corse* she shall invade,*
       And fly rapacious on the prostrate dead.
           To her, a lowly suppliant, thus begun
910 The noble Pompey's much unworthy son:
           'Hail, mighty mistress of Haemonian arts,
       To whom stern fate her dark decrees imparts,
       At thy approving bids her purpose stand,
       Or alters it at thy revered command.

915 From thee, my humbler, awful hopes presume
    To learn my father's and my country's doom.
    Nor think this grace to one unworthy done,
    When thou shalt know me for great Pompey's son;
    With him all fortunes am I born to share,
920 His ruin's partner, or his empire's heir.
    Let not blind chance for ever wavering stand,
    And awe us with her unresolving hand;
    I own my mind unequal to the weight,
    Nor can I bear the pangs of doubtful fate:
925 Let it be certain what we have to fear,
    And then – no matter – let the time draw near.
    Oh, let thy charms this truth from heaven compel,
    Or force the dreadful Stygian gods to tell.
    Call death, all pale and meagre, from below,
930 And from herself her fatal purpose know;
    Constrained by thee, the phantom shall declare
    Whom she decrees to strike, and whom to spare.
    Nor ever can thy skill divine foresee,
    Through the blind maze of long futurity,
935 Events more worthy of thy arts, and thee.'
        Pleased that her magic fame diffusely flies,*
    Thus, with a horrid smile, the hag replies:
        'Hadst thou, O noble youth, my aid implored
    For any less decision of the sword,
940 The gods, unwilling, should my power confess,
    And crown thy wishes with a full success.
    Hadst thou desired some single friend to save,
    Long had my charms withheld him from the grave;
    Or would thy hate some foe this instant doom,
945 He dies, though heaven decrees him years to come.
    But when effects are to their causes chained,
    From everlasting mightily ordained,*
    When all things labour for one certain end
    And on one action centre and depend,
950 Then far behind, we own, our arts are cast,
    And magic is by fortune's power surpassed.
    Howe'er, if yet thy soul can be content
    Only to know that undisclosed event,
    My potent charms o'er nature shall prevail,
955 And from a thousand mouths extort the tale.

This truth the fields, the floods, the rocks shall tell,
The thunder of high heav'n, or groans of hell;
Though still more kindly oracles remain
Among the recent deaths of yonder plain –
960 Of these a corse our mystic rites shall raise
As yet unshrunk by Titan's* parching blaze;
So shall no maim* the vocal pipes confound,
But the sad shade shall breathe, distinct in human
       sound.'
     While yet she spoke, a double darkness spread,
965 Black clouds and murky fogs involve her head,
While o'er th'unburied heaps her footsteps tread.*
Wolves howled and fled where-e'er she took her way,
And hungry vultures left the mangled prey,
The savage race, abashed, before her yield,
970 And, while she culls her prophet, quit the field.
To various carcasses by turns she flies,*
And, griping with her gory fingers, tries
Till one of perfect organs can be found,
And fibrous lungs uninjured by a wound.*
975 Of all the flitting shadows of the slain,
Fate doubts which ghost shall turn to life again.
At her strong bidding – such is her command –
Armies at once had left the Stygian strand,
Hell's multitudes had waited on her charms,
980 And legions of the dead had risen to arms.
Among the dreadful carnage strewed around,
One, for her purpose fit, at length she found;
In his pale jaws a rusty hook she hung,
And dragged the wretched, lifeless load along;
985 Anon beneath a craggy cliff she stayed,
And in a dreary delve* her burden laid;
There evermore the wicked witch delights
To do her deeds accursed, and practise hellish rites.
     Low as the realms where Stygian Jove is crowned
990 Subsides the gloomy vale within the ground;
A downward grove, that never knew to rise
Or shoot its leafy honours to the skies,
From hanging rocks declines its drooping head,
And covers in the cave with dreadful shade;
995 Within dismay and fear and darkness dwell,

And filth obscene besmears the baleful cell.
There lasting night no beamy dawning knows,
No light but such as magic flames disclose;
Heavy, as in Taenarian caverns,* there
1000 In dull stagnation sleeps the lazy air.
There meet the boundaries of life and death,
The borders of our world, and that beneath;
Thither the rulers of th'infernal court
Permit their airy vassals* to resort;
1005 Thence with like ease the sorceress could tell,
As if descending down, the deeds of hell.
And now she for the solemn task prepares,   )
A mantle patched with various shreds she wears,   )
And binds with twining snakes her wilder hairs.   )
1010 All pale for dread the dastard youth she spied,
Heartless* his mates stood quivering by his side.
'Be bold!', she cries, 'dismiss this abject fear;   )
Living and human shall the form appear,   )
And breathe no sounds but what ev'n you may   )
      hear.   )
1015 How had your vile, your coward souls been quelled,
Had you the livid Stygian lakes beheld,
Heard the loud floods of rolling sulphur roar,
And burst in thunder on the burning shore!
Had you surveyed yon prison-house of woe,
1020 And giants bound in adamant below,
Seen the vast dog with curling vipers swell,   )
Heard screaming furies at my coming yell,   )
Double their rage, and add new pains to hell!'   )
    This said, she runs the mangled carcass o'er,
1025 And wipes from every wound the crusty gore,
Now with hot blood the frozen breast she warms,
And with strong lunar dews* confirms her charms.
Anon she mingles every monstrous birth,
Which nature, wayward and perverse, brings forth:
1030 Nor entrails of the spotted lynx she lacks,*
Nor bony joints from fell hyenas' backs,
Nor deer's hot marrow rich with snaky food,*
Nor foam of raging dogs that fly the flood;*
Her store the tardy remora supplies,*
1035 With stones from eagles warm,* and dragons' eyes;

Snakes that on pinions cut their airy way,
And nimbly o'er Arabian deserts prey;
The viper bred in Erythraean streams*
To guard in costly shells the growing gems;
1040 The slough by Libya's hornèd serpent cast, ⎫
With ashes by the dying phoenix placed* ⎬
On odorous altars in the fragrant east. ⎭
To these she joins dire drugs without a name,
A thousand poisons never known to fame,
1045 Herbs o'er whose leaves the hag her spells had sung,
And wet with cursèd spittle as they sprung,
With every other mischief most abhorred
Which hell, or worse Erictho, could afford.
    At length, in murmurs hoarse, her voice was ⎫
        heard – ⎬
1050 Her voice, beyond all plants, all magic, feared, ⎪
And by the lowest Stygian gods revered.* ⎭
Her gabbling tongue a muttering tone confounds,
Discordant, and unlike to human sounds:
It seemed of dogs the bark, of wolves the howl,
1055 The doleful screeching of the midnight owl,
The hiss of snakes, the hungry lion's roar,
The bound of billows beating on the shore,
The groan of winds amongst the leafy wood,
And burst of thunder from the rending cloud –
1060 'Twas these, all these in one. At length she breaks
Thus into magic verse, and thus the gods bespeaks:
    'Ye furies, and thou black accursèd hell,
Ye woes in which the damned forever dwell,
Chaos, the world's* and form's eternal foe,
1065 And thou sole arbiter of all below,
Pluto, whom ruthless fates a god ordain
And doom to immortality of pain,
Ye fair Elysian mansions of the blessed,
Where no Thessalian charmer hopes to rest,
1070 Styx, and Persephone, compelled to fly
Thy fruitful mother and the cheerful sky,
Third Hecate,* by whom my whispers breathe
My secret purpose to the shades beneath,
Thou greedy dog,* who at th'infernal gate
1075 In everlasting hunger still dost wait,

And thou old Charon,* horrible and hoar,
For ever labouring back from shore to shore,
Who murmuring dost in weariness complain
That I so oft demand thy dead again:
1080 Hear, all ye powers! If e'er your hell rejoice
In the loved horrors of this impious voice,
If still with human flesh I have been fed,
If pregnant mothers have, to please you, bled,
If from the womb these ruthless hands have torn
1085 Infants mature and struggling to be born,
Hear and obey! Nor do I ask a ghost,
Long since received upon your Stygian coast,
But one that, new to death, for entrance waits,
And loiters yet before your gloomy gates.
1090 Let the pale shade these herbs, these numbers, hear,
And in his well-known, warlike form appear.
Here let him stand before his leader's son, ⎤
And say what dire events are drawing on – ⎬
If blood be your delight, let this be done.' ⎦
1095   Foaming she spoke, then reared her hateful head,
And hard at hand beheld th'attending shade.
Too well the trembling sprite the carcass knew,*
And feared to enter into life anew;
Fain from those mangled limbs it would have run,
1100 And, loathing, strove that house of pain to shun.
Ah wretch, to whom the cruel fates deny
That privilege of humankind – to die!
Wroth was the hag at lingering death's delay,
And wondered hell could dare to disobey;
1105 With curling snakes the senseless trunk she beats,
And curses dire at every lash repeats,
With magic numbers cleaves the groaning ground,
And thus barks downwards to th'abyss profound:
    'Ye fiends hell-born, ye sisters of despair,*
1110 Thus, is it thus my will becomes your care?
Still sleep those whips within your idle hands,
Nor drive the loitering ghost this voice demands?
But mark me well! my charms, in fate's despite,
Shall drag you forth, ye Stygian dogs, to light;
1115 Through vaults and tombs where now secure you
      roam

My vengeance shall pursue, and chase you home.
And thou, O Hecate, that dar'st to rise
Various and altered to immortal eyes,
No more shalt veil thy horrors in disguise;
1120   Still in thy form accursèd shalt thou dwell,
Nor change the face that nature made for hell.
Each mystery beneath I will display,
And Stygian loves shall stand confessed to day.
Thee, Proserpine, thy fatal feast I'll show,*
1125   What leagues* detain thee in the realms below,
And why thy once fond mother loathes thee now.
At my command earth's barrier shall remove,
And piercing Titan vex infernal Jove,*
Full on his throne the blazing beams shall beat,
1130   And light abhorred afflict the gloomy seat.
Yet, am I yet, ye sullen fiends, obeyed,
Or must I call your master* to my aid,
At whose dread name the trembling furies quake,
Hell stands abashed, and earth's foundations shake,
1135   Who views the Gorgons with intrepid eyes,
And your unviolable flood defies?'*
     She said, and at the word the frozen blood
Slowly began to roll its creeping flood,
Through the known channels stole the purple tide,
1140   And warmth and motion through the members glide;
The nerves are stretched, the turgid muscles swell,
And the heart moves within its secret cell;
The haggard eyes their stupid lights disclose,
And heavy by degrees the corpse arose.*
1145   Doubtful and faint th'uncertain life appears,
And death all o'er the livid visage wears;
Pale, stiff and mute, the ghastly figure stands,
Nor knows to speak, but at her dread commands;
When thus the hag: 'Speak what I wish to know,
1150   And endless rest attends thy shade below,
Reveal the truth, and, to reward thy pain,
No charms shall drag thee back to life again;
Such hallowed wood shall feed thy funeral fire,
Such numbers to thy last repose conspire,
1155   No sister of our art thy ghost shall wrong,
Or force thee listen to her potent song.

Since the dark gods in mystic tripods dwell,
Since doubtful truths ambiguous prophets tell,
While each event aright and plain is read
1160 To every bold enquirer of the dead,
Do thou unfold what end these wars shall wait, ⎫
Persons and things and time and place relate, ⎬
And be the just interpreter of fate.'   ⎭
    She spoke, and, as she spoke, a spell she made
1165 That gave new prescience to th'unknowing shade.
    When thus the spectre, weeping all for woe:
'Seek not from me the Parcae's* will to know.
I saw not what their dreadful looms ordain,*
Too soon recalled to hated life again,
1170 Recalled e'er yet my waiting ghost had passed
The silent stream that wafts us all to rest.
All I could learn was from the loose report
Of wandering shades that to the banks resort.
Uproar and discord, never known till now,
1175 Distract the peaceful realms of death below;
From blissful plains of sweet Elysium some,
Others from doleful dens and torments come,
While in the face of every various shade
The woes of Rome too plainly might be read.
1180 In tears lamenting, ghosts of patriots stood,
And mourned their country in a falling flood:
Sad were the Decii and the Curii* seen,
And heavy was the great Camillus' mien;
On fortune loud indignant Sulla railed,
1185 And Scipio* his unhappy race bewailed,
The Censor sad foresaw his Cato's doom,*
Resolved to die for liberty, and Rome.
Of all the shades that haunt the happy field,
Thee only, Brutus, smiling I beheld,*
1190 Thee, thou first consul, haughty Tarquin's dread, ⎫
From whose just wrath the conscious* tyrant fled, ⎬
When freedom first upreared her infant head.   ⎭
Meanwhile the damned exult amidst their pains,*
And Catiline* audacious breaks his chains.
1195 There the Cethegan naked race* I viewed,
The Marii* fierce, with human gore imbrued,

The Gracchi,* fond of mischief-making laws, ⎫
And Drusi,* popular in faction's cause –   ⎬
All clapped their hands in horrible applause. ⎭

1200 The crash of brazen fetters rung around,
And hell's wide caverns trembled with the sound.
No more the bounds of fate their guilt constrain,*
But proudly they demand th'Elysian plain.
Thus they, while dreadful Dis, with busy cares,

1205 New torments for the conquerors prepares,
New chains of adamant he forms below,
And opens all his deep reserves of woe;
Sharp are the pains for tyrants kept in store,
And flames yet ten times hotter than before.

1210 But thou, O noble youth, in peace depart,
And soothe with better hopes thy doubtful heart;
Sweet is the rest, and blissful is the place,*
That wait thy sire, and his illustrious race.
Nor fondly seek to lengthen out thy date,

1215 Nor envy the surviving victor's fate;
The hour draws near when all alike must yield,
And death shall mix the fame of every field.
Haste then with glory to your destined end,
And proudly from your humbler urns descend;

1220 Bold in superior virtue shall you come,
And trample on the demigods of Rome.*
Ah, what shall it import the mighty dead, ⎫
Or by the Nile or Tiber to be laid? –   ⎬
'Tis only for a grave your wars are made. ⎭

1225 Seek not to know what for thyself remains – *
That shall be told in fair Sicilia's plains;
Prophetic there, thy father's shade shall rise
In awful vision to thy wondering eyes,
He shall thy fate reveal, though doubting yet

1230 Where he may best advise thee to retreat.
In vain to various climates shall you run,* ⎫
In vain pursuing fortune strive to shun,   ⎬
In Europe, Afric, Asia, still undone. ⎭
Wide as your triumphs shall your ruins lie,

1235 And all in distant regions shall you die.
Ah wretched race, to whom the world can yield
No safer refuge than Emathia's field.'

He said, and with a silent, mournful look,
A last dismission* from the hag bespoke.
1240 Nor can the sprite, discharged by death's cold hand,
Again be subject to the same command;
But charms and magic herbs must lend their aid,
And render back to rest the troubled shade.
1245 A pile of hallowed wood Erictho builds,
The soul with joy its mangled carcass yields;
She bids the kindling flames ascend on high,
And leaves the weary wretch at length to die.
Then, while the secret dark their footsteps hides,
Homeward the youth, all pale for fear, she guides,
1250 And (for the light began to streak the east)
With potent spells the dawning she repressed,
Commanded night's obedient queen to stay,
And, till they reached the camp, withheld the rising
        day.

L. Cheron del.   E. Kirkall.

Erictho and the Corpse

BOOK SEVEN

Late and unwilling from his watery bed,*
Upreared the mournful sun his cloudy head;
He sickened to behold Emathia's plain,*
And would have sought the backward east again;
5   Full oft he turned him from the destined race,
And wished some dark eclipse might veil his radiant
        face.
    Pompey, meanwhile, in pleasing visions passed
The night, of all his happy nights the last.
It seemed as if, in all his former state,
10   In his own theatre* secure he sate;*
About his side unnumbered Romans crowd,
And joyful shout his much-loved name aloud;
The echoing benches seem to ring around,
And his charmed ears devour the pleasing sound.
15   Such both himself and such the people seem,
In the false prospect of the feigning dream,
As when, in early manhood's beardless bloom,
He stood the darling hope and joy of Rome;
When fierce Sertorius, by his arms suppressed,*
20   And Spain subdued the conqueror confessed;
When, raised with honours never known before,
The consul's purple,* yet a youth, he wore;
When the pleased Senate sat with new delight,
To view the triumph of a Roman knight.
25   Perhaps, when our good days no longer last,
The mind runs backward, and enjoys the past,
Perhaps the riddling visions of the night
With contrarieties delude our sight,
And when fair scenes of pleasure they disclose,
30   Pain they foretell, and sure ensuing woes.
Or was it not that since the fates ordain
Pompey should never see his Rome again,
One last good office yet they meant to do,
And gave him in a dream this parting view?
35   Oh may no trumpet bid the leader wake!

Long, let him long the blissful slumber take!
Too soon the morrow's sleepless night will come
Full fraught with slaughter, misery and Rome;
With horror and dismay those shades shall rise,
40   And the lost battle live before his eyes.
        How blessed his fellow citizens had been,
Though but in dreams, their Pompey to have seen;
Oh, that the gods in pity would allow
Such long tried friends their destiny to know;
45   So each to each might their sad thoughts convey,
And make the most of their last mournful day.
But now, unconscious of the ruin nigh,
Within his native land he thinks to die,
While her* fond hopes with confidence presume ⎫
50   Nothing so terrible from fate can come   ⎬
As to be robbed of her loved Pompey's tomb.   ⎭
Had the sad city fate's decree foreknown,
What floods* fast falling should her loss bemoan;
Then should the lusty youth and fathers hoar,
55   With mingling tears, their chief renowned deplore;*
Maids, matrons, wives and babes, a helpless train,
As once for godlike Brutus, should complain,*
Their tresses should they tear, their bosoms beat,
And cry loud-wailing in the doleful street.
60   Nor shalt thou, Rome, thy gushing sorrows keep,
Though awed by Caesar, and forbid* to weep,
Though, while he tells thee of thy Pompey dead,
He shakes his threatening falchion* o'er thy head.
Lamenting crowds the conqueror shall meet,
65   And with a peal of groans his triumph greet,
In sad procession sighing shall they go,
And stain his laurels with the streams of woe.
        But now the fainting stars at length gave way,
And hid their vanquished fires in beamy day,
70   When round the leader's tent the legions crowd,
And, urged by fate, demand the fight aloud.
Wretches, that long their little life to waste,
And hurry on those hours that fly too fast!
Too soon for thousands shall the day be done,
75   Whose eyes no more shall see the setting sun.
Tumultuous speech th'impulsive rage confessed,

And Rome's bad genius rose in every breast.*
With vile disgrace they blot their leader's name, }
Pronounce ev'n Pompey fearful, slow and tame, }
80   And cry: 'He sinks beneath his father's* fame.' }
Some charge him with ambition's guilty views,
And think 'tis power and empire he pursues,
That, fearing peace, he practises delay,
And would for ever make the world obey,
85   While eastern kings of lingering wars complain,
And wish to view their native realms again.
Thus when the gods are pleased to plague mankind,
Our own rash hands are to the task assigned;
By them ordained the tools of fate to be,
90   We blindly act the mischiefs they decree;
We call the battle, we the sword prepare,
And Rome's destruction is the Roman prayer.
    The general voice, united, Tully* takes,
And for the rest the sweet persuader speaks,
95   Tully, for happy eloquence renowned,
With every Roman grace of language crowned,
Beneath whose rule and government revered
Fierce Catiline* the peaceful axes feared;*
But now, detained amidst an armèd throng, }
100 Where lost his arts and useless was his tongue, }
The orator had borne the camp too long. }
He to the vulgar side his pleading draws,*
And thus enforces much their feeble cause:
    'For all that fortune for thy arms has done,
105 For all thy fame acquired, thy battles won,
This only boon her* suppliant vows implore,
That thou wouldst deign to use her aid once more;
In this, O Pompey, kings and chiefs unite,
And, to chastise proud Caesar, ask the fight.
110 Shall he, one man against the world combined,
Protract destruction, and embroil mankind?
What will the vanquished nations murmuring say,
Where once thy conquests cut their wingèd way,
When they behold thy virtue lazy now,
115 And see thee move thus languishing and slow?
Where are those fires that warmed thee to be great,
That stable soul, and confidence in fate?

Canst thou the gods ungratefully mistrust,
Or think the Senate's sacred cause unjust?
120 Scarce are th'impatient ensigns yet withheld –
Why art thou thus to victory compelled?
Dost thou Rome's chief, and in her cause, appear?
'Tis hers to choose the field, and she appoints it here.
Why is this ardour of the world withstood,
125 The injured world that thirsts for Caesar's blood?
See where the troops with indignation stand,
Each javelin trembling in an eager hand,
And wait, unwillingly, the last command.
Resolve the Senate then, and let them know,
130 Are they thy servants, or their servant thou?'
    Sore sighed the listening chief, who well could read
Some dire delusion by the gods decreed;
He saw the fates malignantly inclined,
To thwart his purpose, and perplex his mind.
135 'Since thus', he cried, 'it is by all decreed,*
Since my impatient friends and country need
My hand to fight, and not my head to lead,
Pompey no longer shall your fate delay,
But let pernicious fortune take her way,
140 And waste the world on one devoted* day.
But oh, be witness thou, my native Rome,
With what a sad foreboding heart I come;
To thy hard fate unwillingly I yield,
While thy rash sons compel me to the field.
145 How easily had Caesar been subdued,*
And the blessed victory been free from blood!
But the fond* Romans cheap renown disdain,
They wish for deaths to purple o'er the plain,
And reeking gore their guilty swords to stain.
150 Driv'n by my fleets, behold the flying foe
At once the empire of the deep forego;
Here by necessity they seem to stand,
Cooped up within a corner of the land.
By famine to the last extremes compelled,
155 They snatch green harvests from th'unripened field,
And wish we may this only grace afford –
To let them die like soldiers, by the sword.
'Tis true it seems an earnest of success

That thus our bolder youth for action press,
160   But let them try their inmost hearts with care,
And judge betwixt true valour and rash fear:
Let them be sure this eagerness is right,
And certain fortitude demands the fight.
In war, in dangers, oft it has been known
165   That fear has driv'n the headlong coward on.
Give me the man whose cooler soul can wait,
With patience, for the proper hour of fate.
See what a prosperous face our fortunes bear!
Why should we trust them to the chance of war?
170   Why must we risk the world's uncertain doom,
And rather choose to fight than overcome?
Thou goddess Chance, who to my careful hand
Hast giv'n this wearisome supreme command,
If I have, to the task of empire just,
175   Enlarged the bounds committed to my trust,
Be kind, and to thyself the rule resume,
And in the fight defend the cause of Rome;
To thy own crowns the wreath of conquest join,
Nor let the glory nor the crime be mine.
180   But see, thy hopes, unhappy Pompey, fail;
We fight, and Caesar's stronger vows prevail.
Oh what a scene of guilt this day shall show,
What crowds shall fall, what nations be laid low!
Red shall Enipeus run with Roman blood,
185   And to the margin swell his foamy flood.
Oh, if our cause my aid no longer need,
Oh, may my bosom be the first to bleed!
Me let the thrilling* javelin foremost strike,
Since death and victory are now alike!
190   Today with ruin shall my name be joined,*
Or stand the common curse of all mankind;
By every woe the vanquished shall be known,
And every infamy the victor crown.'
        He spoke, and, yielding to th'impetuous crowd,
195   The battle to his frantic bands allowed.
So, when long vexed by stormy Corus'* blast,
The weary pilot quits the helm at last,
He leaves his vessel to the winds to guide,
And drive unsteady with the tumbling tide.

200   Loud through the camp the rising murmurs sound,
       And one tumultuous hurry runs around;
       Sudden their busy hearts began to beat,*
       And each pale visage wore the marks of fate.
       Anxious, they see the dreadful day is come
205   That must decide the destiny of Rome.
       This single, vast concern employs the host,
       And private fears are in the public lost.
       Should earth be rent, should darkness quench the
              sun,
       Should swelling seas above the mountains run,
210   Should universal nature's* end draw near,
       Who could have leisure for himself to fear?
       With such consent his safety each forgot,
       And Rome and Pompey took up every thought.
          And now the warriors all, with busy care,
215   Whet the dull sword, and point the blunted spear;
       With tougher nerves* they string the bended bow,
       And in full quivers steely shafts bestow;
       The horseman sees his furniture made fit,
       Sharpens the spur, and burnishes the bit,
220   Fixes the rein to check or urge his speed,
       And animates to fight the snorting steed.
       Such once the busy gods' employments were,* ⎫
       If mortal men to gods we may compare,   ⎬
       When earth's bold sons began their impious war: ⎭
225   The Lemnian* power with many a stroke restored
       Blue Neptune's trident, and stern Mars's sword;
       In terrible array, the blue-eyed maid*
       The horrors of her Gorgon-shield displayed;
       Phoebus his once victorious shafts renewed,
230   Disused and rusty with the Python's* blood,
       While, with unwearied toil, the Cyclops* strove
       To forge new thunders for imperial Jove.
          Nor wanted then dire omens to declare*
       What cursed events Thessalia's plains prepare.*
235   Black storms opposed against the warriors lay,
       And lightnings thwarted* their forbidden way –
       Full in their eyes the dazzling flashes broke,
       And with amaze their troubled senses stroke;*
       Tall, fiery columns in the skies were seen,

240   With watery typhons* interwove* between.
       Glancing along the bands swift meteors shoot,
       And from the helm the plumy honours cut;
       Sudden the flame dissolves the javelin's head,
       And liquid runs the shining, steely blade;
245   Strange to behold, their weapons disappear,
       While sulphurous odour taints the smoking air.
       The standard, as unwilling to be borne,*
       With pain from the tenacious earth is torn;
       Anon black swarms hang clustering on its height,
250   And press the bearer with unwonted weight.
       Big drops of grief each sweating marble wears,
       And Parian gods and heroes stand in tears.*
       No more th'auspicious victim tamely dies,*
       But furious from the hallowed fane he flies,
255   Breaks off the rites with prodigies profane,
       And bellowing seeks Emathia's fatal plain.
           But who, O Caesar, who were then thy gods,
       Whom didst thou summon from their dark abodes?
       The furies listened to thy grateful vows,
260   And dreadful to the day the powers of hell arose.
           Did then the monsters fame records appear,
       Or were they only phantoms formed by fear? -
       Some saw the moving mountains meet like foes,
       And rending earth new-gaping caves disclose;
265   Others beheld a sanguine torrent take
       Its purple course through fair Boebeis' lake,
       Heard each returning night, portentous, yield
       Loud shouts of battle on Pharsalia's field,
       While others thought they saw the light decay,
270   And sudden shades oppress the fainting day,
       Fancied wild horrors in each other's face,
       And saw the ghosts of all their buried race,
       Beheld them rise and glare with pale affright,
       And stalk around them in the new-made night.
275   Whate'er the cause, the crowd, by fate decreed* ⎫
       To make their brothers, sons and fathers bleed, ⎬
       Consenting, to the prodigies agreed,   ⎭
       And, while they thirst impatient for that blood,
       Bless these nefarious omens all as good.
280   But wherefore should we wonder to behold

That death's approach by madness was foretold?
Wild are the wandering thoughts which last survive,
And these had not another day to live.
These* shook for what they saw, while distant
          climes,
285   Unknowing, trembled for Emathia's crimes.
Where Tyrian Gades sees the setting sun,
And where Araxes' rapid waters run,
From the bright orient to the glowing west,)
In every nation every Roman breast   )
290   The terrors of that dreadful day confessed.)
Where Aponus first springs in smoky steam,
And full Timavus rolls his nobler stream,
Upon a hill that day, if fame be true,
A learned augur* sat the skies to view:
295   ' 'Tis come, the great event is come,'* he cried;
'Our impious chiefs their wicked war decide.'
Whether the seer observed Jove's forky flame
And marked the firmament's discordant frame,
Or whether, in that gloom of sudden night,
300   The struggling sun declared the dreadful fight,
From the first birth of morning in the skies
Sure never day like this was known to rise;
In the blue vault, as in a volume spread,
Plain might the Latian destiny be read.
305   O Rome! O people by the gods assigned
To be the worthy masters of mankind!
On thee the heavens with all their signals wait,
And suffering nature labours with thy fate.
When thy great names, to latest times conveyed,
310   By fame or by my verse immortal made,
In freeborn nations justly shall prevail,
And rouse their passions with this noblest tale,
How shall they fear for thy approaching doom,
As if each past event were yet to come!
315   How shall their bosoms swell with vast concern,*
And long the doubtful chance of war to learn!
Ev'n then the favouring world with thee* shall join,
And every honest heart to Pompey's cause incline.
      Descending now, the bands in just array
320   From burnished arms reflect the beamy day;

In an ill hour they spread the fatal field,
And with portentous blaze the neighbouring
        mountains gild.
On the left wing bold Lentulus,* their head,*
The first and fourth selected legions led;
325   Luckless Domitius,* vainly brave in war,
Drew forth the right with unauspicious care;
In the mid battle daring Scipio* fought,
With eight full legions* from Cilicia brought;
Submissive here to Pompey's high command,
330   The warrior undistinguished* took his stand,
Reserved to be the chief on Libya's burning sand.
Near the low marshes and Enipeus' flood,
The Pontic horse and Cappadocian stood,
While kings and tetrarchs* proud, a purple train,
335   Liegemen and vassals to the Latian reign,
Possessed the rising grounds and drier plain.
Here troops of black Numidians scour the field,
And bold Iberians narrow bucklers wield,
Here twang the Syrian and the Cretan bow,
340   And the fierce Gauls* provoke their well-known foe.
        Go, Pompey, lead to death th'unnumbered host;
Let the whole human race at once be lost,
Let nations upon nations heap the plain,
And tyranny want subjects for its reign.
345   Caesar, as chance ordained, that morn decreed
The spoiling bands of foragers to lead,
When, with a sudden but a glad surprise,
The foe descending struck his wondering eyes.
Eager and burning for unbounded sway,
350   Long had he borne the tedious war's delay,
Long had he struggled with protracting time,
That saved his country, and deferred his crime;
At length he sees the wished-for day is come,
To end the strife for liberty, and Rome,
355   Fate's dark, mysterious threatenings to explain,
And ease th'impatience of ambition's pain.
But when he saw the vast event so nigh,
Unusual horror damped his impious joy,
For one cold moment sunk his heart suppressed,
360   And doubt hung heavy on his anxious breast.

Though his past fortunes promise now success,
Yet Pompey from his own expects no less.
His changing thoughts revolve with various cheer,
While these forbid to hope, and those to fear.
365 At length his wonted confidence returns,
With his first fires his daring bosom burns,
As if secure of victory he stands,
And fearless thus bespeaks the listening bands:
    'Ye warriors, who have made your Caesar great,*
370 On whom the world, on whom my fortunes wait,
Today the gods whate'er you wish afford,
And fate attends on the deciding sword.
By your firm aid alone your leader stands,
And trusts his all to your long-faithful hands.
375 This day shall make our promised glories good,
The hopes* of Rubicon's distinguished flood;
For this blessed morn we trusted long to fate,
Deferred our fame, and bade the triumph wait;
This day, my gallant friends, this happy day,
380 Shall the long labours of your arms repay,
Shall give you back to every joy of life,
To the loved offspring and the tender wife,*
Shall find my veteran out a safe retreat,
And lodge his age within a peaceful seat.
385 The long dispute of guilt shall now be cleared,
And conquest shall the juster cause reward.
Have you, for me, with sword and fire laid waste
Your country's bleeding bosom as you passed?
Let the same swords as boldly strike today,
390 And the last wounds shall wipe the first away.
Whatever faction's partial notions are,
No hand is wholly innocent in war.
Yours is the cause to which my vows are joined,
I seek to make you free, and masters of mankind.
395 I have no hopes, no wishes of my own,
But well could hide me in a private gown;*
At my expense of fame* exalt your powers –
Let me be nothing, so the world be yours.
Nor think the task too bloody shall be found –
400 With easy glory shall our arms be crowned;
Yon host come learn'd in academic rules,*

A band of disputants from Grecian schools.
To these, luxurious eastern crowds are joined,
Of many a tongue and many a differing kind;
405 Their own first shouts shall fill each soul with fears,
And their own trumpets shock their tender ears.
Unjustly this a civil war we call,
Where none but foes of Rome, barbarians, fall.
On then, my friends, and end it at a blow;
410 Lay these soft, lazy, worthless nations low.
Show Pompey, that subdued them, with what ease
Your valour gains such victories as these;
Show him, if justice still the palm confers,
One triumph was too much for all his wars.
415 From distant Tigris shall Armenians come
To judge between the citizens of Rome?
Will fierce, barbarian aliens waste their blood
To make the cause of Latian Pompey good?
Believe me, no. To them we're all the same,
420 They hate alike the whole Ausonian* name,
But most those haughty masters whom they know,
Who taught their servile, vanquished necks to bow.
Meanwhile, as round my joyful eyes are rolled,
None but my tried companions I behold;
425 For years in Gaul we made our hard abode,
And many a march in partnership have trod.
Is there a soldier to your chief unknown,
A sword to whom I trust not like my own?
Could I not mark each javelin in the sky,
430 And say from whom the fatal weapons fly?
Ev'n now I view auspicious furies rise,
And rage redoubled flashes in your eyes.
With joy those omens of success I read,
And see the certain victory decreed;
435 I see the purple deluge float the plain,
Huge piles of carnage, nations of the slain;
Dead chiefs, with mangled monarchs, I survey,
And the pale Senate crowns the glorious day.
But oh, forgive my tedious, lavish tongue –
440 Your eager virtue I withhold too long;
My soul exults with hopes too fierce to bear,
I feel good fortune and the gods draw near.

All we can ask, with full consent they yield
And nothing bars us but this narrow field.
445   The battle o'er, what boon can I deny? –
The treasures of the world before you lie.
O Thessaly, what stars, what powers divine,
To thy distinguished land this great event assign?
Between extremes today our fortune lies,
450   The vilest punishment, and noblest prize;
Consider well the captive's lost estate,
Chains, racks and crosses for the vanquished wait.
My limbs are each allotted to its place,
And my pale head the rostrum's* height shall grace;
455   But that's a thought unworthy Caesar's care –
More for my friends than for myself I fear.
On my good sword securely I rely,*
And, if I conquer not, am sure to die.
But oh, for you, my anxious soul foresees
460   Pompey shall copy Sulla's cursed decrees,
The Martian Field shall blush with gore again,
And massacres once more the peaceful Saepta stain.*
Hear, O ye gods, who in Rome's strugglings share,
Who leave your heav'n to make our earth your care,
465   Hear, and let him, the happy victor, live,
Who shall with mercy use the power you give,
Whose rage for slaughter with the war shall cease,
And spare his vanquished enemies in peace.
Nor is Dyrrachium's fatal field forgot,
470   Nor what was then our brave companions' lot,
When, by advantage of the straiter ground,
Successful Pompey compassed us around,
When quite disarmed your useless valour stood,
Till his fell sword was satiated* with blood.
475   But gentler hands, but nobler hearts you bear,
And oh, remember 'tis your leader's prayer,
Whatever Roman flies before you, spare.
But while opposed and menacing they stand,
Let no regard withhold the lifted hand,
480   Let friendship, kindred, all remorse give place,
And mangling wounds deform the reverend face;
Still let resistance be repaid with blood,
And hostile force by hostile force subdued;

Stranger or friend, whatever be the name,
485 Your merit still to Caesar is the same.
Fill then the trenches, break the ramparts round,
And let our works lie level with the ground;
So shall no obstacles our march delay,
Nor stop one moment our victorious way.
490 Nor spare your camp; this night we mean to lie
In that from whence the vanquished foe shall fly.'
    Scarce had he spoke, when sudden at the word
They seize the lance, and draw the shining sword;
At once the turfy fences* all lie waste,
495 And through the breach the crowding legions haste;
Regardless all of order and array
They stand, and trust to fate alone the day.
Had each proposed an empire to be won,
Had each once known a Pompey for his son,
500 Had Caesar's soul informed each private breast,
A fiercer fury could not be expressed.
    With sad presages* Pompey now beheld
His foes advancing o'er the neighbouring field;
He saw the gods had fixed the day of fate,
505 And felt his heart hang heavy with new weight.
Dire is the omen when the valiant fear,
Which yet he strove to hide with well dissembled
            cheer.
High on his warrior steed the chief o'er-ran
The wide array, and thus at length began:
510   'The time to ease your groaning country's pain,
Which long your eager valour sought in vain,
The great deciding hour at length is come,
To end the strivings of distracted Rome;
For this one last effort* exert your power:
515 Strike home today, and all your toils are o'er.
If the dear pledges of connubial love,
Your household gods and Rome your souls can
            move,
Hither by fate they seem together brought,
And for that prize today the battle shall be fought.
520 Let none the favouring gods' assistance fear –
They always make the juster cause their care.*
The flying dart to Caesar shall they guide,

And point the sword at his devoted side,
Our injured laws shall be on him made good,
525 And liberty established in his blood.
Could heaven, in violence of wrath, ordain
The world to groan beneath a tyrant's reign,
It had not spared your Pompey's head so long,
Nor lengthened out my age to see the wrong.
530 All we can wish for, to secure success,
With large advantage here our arms possess;
See, in the ranks of every common band,
Where Rome's illustrious names for soldiers stand.
Could the great dead revisit life again,
535 For us, once more, the Decii* would be slain,
The Curii and Camilli might we boast,*
Proud to be mingled in this noblest host.
If men, if multitudes, can make us strong,
Behold what tribes unnumbered march along!
540 Where-e'er the zodiac turns its radiant round,
Wherever earth or people can be found,
To us the nations issue forth in swarms,
And in Rome's cause all human nature arms.
What then remains, but that our wings enclose,
545 Within their ample fold, our shrinking foes?
Thousands and thousands useless may we spare –
Yon handful will not half employ our war.*
Think, from the summit of the Roman wall,
You hear our loud-lamenting matrons call,
550 Think with what tears, what lifted hands they sue,
And place their last, their only hopes in you;
Imagine kneeling age before you spread,
Each hoary, reverend, majestic head;
Imagine Rome herself your aid implored,
555 To save her from a proud, imperious lord;
Think how the present age, how that to come,
What multitudes from you expect their doom;
On your success dependent all rely,
These to be born in freedom, those to die.
560 Think – if there be a thought can move you more,
A pledge more dear than those I named before –
Think you behold, were such a posture meet,
Ev'n me, your Pompey, prostrate at your feet.

Myself, my wife, my sons, a suppliant band,
565   From you our lives and liberties demand;
Or conquer you, or I, to exile borne,*
My last dishonourable years shall mourn,
Your long reproach, and my proud father's scorn;
From bonds, from infamy, your general save,
570   Nor let this hoary head descend to earth a slave.'
    Thus while he spoke, the faithful legions round
With indignation caught the mournful sound;
Falsely, they think, his fears those dangers view,
But vow to die e'er Caesar proves them true.
575   What differing thoughts the various hosts incite,
And urge their deadly ardour for the fight!
Those bold ambition kindles into rage,
And these their fears for liberty engage.
How shall this day the peopled earth deface,
580   Prevent* mankind, and rob the growing race!*
Though all the years to come should roll in peace,
And future ages bring their whole increase,
Though nature all her genial powers employ,
All shall not yield what these cursed hands destroy.
585   Soon shall the greatness of the Roman name
To unbelieving ears be told by fame;
Low shall the mighty Latian towers be laid,
And ruins crown our Alban mountain's head,
While yearly magistrates, in turns compelled*
590   To lodge by night upon th'uncovered field,
Shall at old doting Numa's laws repine,
Who could to such bleak wilds his Latin rites assign.
Ev'n now behold where waste Hesperia lies,
Where empty cities shock our mournful eyes;
595   Untouched by time, our infamy they stand,
The marks of civil discord's murderous hand.
How is the stock of humankind brought low! –
Walls want inhabitants, and hands the plough.
Our fathers' fertile fields by slaves are tilled,
600   And Rome with dregs of foreign lands is filled;
Such were the heaps, the millions of the slain,
As 'twere the purpose of Emathia's plain
That none for future mischiefs should remain.
Well may our annals less misfortunes yield,

605 Mark Allia's* flood, and Cannae's* fatal field;
    But let Pharsalia's day be still forgot,
    Be razed at once from every Roman thought.
    'Twas there that fortune in her pride displayed
    The greatness her own mighty hands had made;
610 Forth in array the powers of Rome she drew,
    And set her subject nations all to view,
    As if she meant to show the haughty queen,*
    Ev'n by her ruins, what her height had been.
    Oh countless loss, that well might have supplied*
615 The desolation of all deaths beside.
    Though famine with blue pestilence conspire,
    And dreadful earthquakes with destroying fire,
    Pharsalia's blood the gaping wounds had joined,
    And built again the ruins of mankind.
620 Immortal gods, with what resistless force
    Our growing empire ran its rapid course,
    Still every year with new success was crowned,
    And conquering chiefs enlarged the Latian bound,
    Till Rome stood mistress of the world confessed,
625 From the grey orient to the ruddy west;
    From pole to pole her wide dominions run,   ⎫
    Where-e'er the stars or brighter Phoebus shone,   ⎬
    As* heaven and earth were made for her alone –   ⎭
    But now behold how fortune tears away
630 The gift of ages in one fatal day!
    One day shakes off the vanquished Indians' chain,
    And turns the wandering Dahae loose again,
    No longer shall the victor consul now*
    Trace out Sarmatian cities with the plough,
635 Exulting Parthia shall her slaughters boast,
    Nor feel the vengeance due to Crassus' ghost,*
    While liberty, long wearied by our crimes,
    Forsakes us for some better, barbarous climes;
    Beyond the Rhine and Tanais* she flies,
640 To snowy mountains and to frozen skies,
    While Rome, who long pursued that chiefest good
    O'er fields of slaughter and through seas of blood,
    In slavery her abject state shall mourn,
    Nor dare to hope the goddess will return.
645 Why were we ever free? Oh why has heaven

A shortlived, transitory blessing given?
Of thee, first Brutus,* justly we complain –
Why didst thou break thy groaning country's chain,
And end the proud, lascivious tyrant's reign?
650   Why did thy patriot hand on Rome bestow
Laws and her consuls' righteous rule to know?
In servitude more happy had we been,
Since Romulus first walled his refuge in,*
Ev'n since the twice six vultures bade him build,*
655   To this cursed period of Pharsalia's field.
Medes and Arabians of the slavish east
Beneath eternal bondage may be blessed,
While, of a differing mould and nature, we,
From sire to son accustomed to be free,
660   Feel indignation rising in our blood,
And blush to wear the chains that make them proud.
Can there be gods who rule yon azure sky?
Can they behold Emathia from on high,
And yet forbear to bid their lightnings fly?
665   Is it the business of a thundering Jove*
To rive the rocks and blast the guiltless grove,
While Cassius holds the balance in his* stead,
And wreaks due vengeance on the tyrant's head?
The sun ran back from Atreus' monstrous feast,*
670   And his fair beams in murky clouds suppressed –
Why shines he now, why lends his golden light,
To these worse parricides, this more accursèd sight?
But chance guides all, the gods their task forego,
And providence no longer reigns below.
675   Yet are they just, and some revenge afford,*
While their own heavens are humbled by the sword,
And the proud victors, like themselves, adored;
With rays adorned, with thunders armed they stand,*
And incense, prayers and sacrifice demand,
680   While trembling, slavish, superstitious Rome
Swears by a mortal wretch that moulders in a tomb.
      Now either host the middle plain had passed,
And front to front in threatening ranks were placed;
Then every well-known feature stood to view:
685   Brothers their brothers, sons their fathers knew.

Then first they feel the curse of civil hate,
Mark where their mischiefs are assigned by fate,
And see from whom themselves* destruction wait.
Stupid* awhile and at a gaze* they stood,
690 While creeping horror froze the lazy blood,
Some small remains of piety withstand,
And stop the javelin in the lifted hand;
Remorse for one short moment stepped between,
And motionless as statues all were seen.
695 And oh, what savage fury could engage,*
While lingering Caesar yet suspends his rage?
For him, ye gods, for Crastinus,* whose spear,
With impious eagerness, began the war,
Some more than common punishment prepare,
700 Beyond the grave long-lasting plagues ordain,
Surviving sense, and never-ceasing pain.
Straight, at the fatal signal, all around
A thousand fifes, a thousand clarions sound;
Beyond where clouds or glancing lightnings fly,
705 The piercing clangours strike the vaulted sky.
The joining battles* shout, and the loud peal
Bounds from the hill, and thunders down the vale;
Old Pelion's caves the doubling roar return,
And Oeta's rocks and groaning Pindus mourn;
710 From pole to pole the tumult spreads afar,
And the world trembles at the distant war.
    Now flit the thrilling darts through liquid air,
And various vows from various masters bear;
Some seek the noblest Roman hearts to wound,
715 And some to err upon the guiltless ground,
While chance decrees the blood that shall be spilt,
And blindly scatters innocence and guilt.
But random shafts too scanty death afford –
A civil war is business for the sword,
720 Where face to face the parricides may meet,
Know whom they kill, and make the crime complete.
    Firm in the front, with joining bucklers closed,
Stood the Pompeian infantry disposed;
So crowded was the space, it scarce affords
725 The power to toss their piles,* or wield their swords.
Forward, thus thick embattled though they stand,

With headlong wrath rush furious Caesar's band;
In vain the lifted shield their rage retards,
Or plated mail devoted bosoms guards;
730   Through shields, through mail, the wounding
                weapons go,
And to the heart drive home each deadly blow;
O rage ill matched, O much unequal war,
Which those wage proudly, and these tamely bear!
These, by cold, stupid piety disarmed,*
735   Those, by hot blood and smoking slaughter warmed.
Nor in suspense uncertain fortune hung,⎫
But yields, o'er-mastered by a power too strong, ⎬
And borne by fate's impetuous stream along. ⎭
    From Pompey's ample wings, at length, the horse*
740   Wide o'er the plain extending take their course;
Wheeling around the hostile line they wind,
While lightly armed the foot* succeed behind.
In various ways the various bands engage,
And hurl upon the foe the missile rage;*
745   There fiery darts and rocky fragments fly,
And heating bullets* whistle through the sky;
Of feathered shafts a cloud thick-shading goes,
From Arab, Mede and Ituraean bows,*
But driv'n by random aim they seldom wound –
750   At first they hide the heaven, then strew the ground,
While Roman hands unerring mischief send,
And certain deaths on every pile attend.
    But Caesar, timely careful to support
His wavering front against the first effort,*
755   Had placed his bodies of reserve behind,
And the strong rear with chosen cohorts lined.
There, as the careless foe the fight pursue,
A sudden band and stable forth he drew,
When soon, oh shame, the loose barbarians yield,
760   Scattering their broken squadrons o'er the field,
And show too late that slaves attempt in vain
The sacred cause of freedom to maintain.
The fiery steeds, impatient of a wound,
Hurl their neglected riders to the ground,
765   Or on their friends with rage ungoverned turn,
And trampling o'er the helpless foot are borne.

Hence foul confusion and dismay succeed,
The victors murder, and the vanquished bleed;
Their weary hands the tired destroyers ply:
770   Scarce can these kill so fast as those can die.
Oh that Emathia's ruthless, guilty plain
Had been contented with this only stain,
With these rude bones had strewn her verdure o'er,
And dyed her springs with none but Asian gore!
775   But if so keen her thirst for Roman blood,
Let none but Romans make the slaughter good!
Let not a Mede nor Cappadocian fall,
No bold Iberian, nor rebellious Gaul;
Let these alone survive for times to come,
780   And be the future citizens of Rome.
But fear on all alike her powers employed,
Did Caesar's business, and like fate destroyed.
      Prevailing still, the victors held their course,
Till Pompey's main reserve opposed their force;
785   There in his strength the chief unshaken stood,
Repelled the foe, and made the combat good;
There in suspense th'uncertain battle hung,
And Caesar's favouring goddess doubted long;
There no proud monarchs led their vassals on,
790   Nor eastern bands in gorgeous purple shone;
There the last force of laws and freedom lay,
And Roman patriots struggled for the day.
What parricides the guilty scene affords –
Sires, sons and brothers rush on mutual swords!
795   There every sacred bond of nature bleeds,
There met the war's worst rage, and Caesar's
            blackest deeds.
      But oh, my Muse, the mournful theme forebear,*
And stay thy lamentable numbers here;
Let not my verse to future times convey
800   What Rome committed on this dreadful day;
In shades and silence hide her crimes from fame,
And spare thy miserable country's shame.
      But Caesar's rage shall with oblivion strive,
And for eternal infamy survive.
805   From rank to rank, unwearied, still he flies,
And with new fires their fainting wrath supplies;

His greedy eyes each sign of guilt explore,
And mark whose sword is deepest dyed in gore,
Observe where pity and remorse prevail,
810 What arm strikes faintly, and what cheek turns pale;
Or, while he rides the slaughtered heaps around,
And views some foe expiring on the ground,
His cruel hands the gushing blood restrain,
And strive to keep the parting soul in pain.
815 As when Bellona drives the world to war,
Or Mars comes thundering in his Thracian car;*
Rage horrible darts from his Gorgon shield,
And gloomy terror broods upon the field;
Hate, fell and fierce, the dreadful gods impart,
820 And urge the vengeful warrior's heaving heart;
The many shout, arms clash, the wounded cry,
And one promiscuous peal groans upwards to the
        sky;
Nor furious Caesar, on Emathia's plains,
Less terribly the mortal strife sustains;
825 Each hand unarmed he fills with means of death,
And cooling wrath rekindles at his breath;
Now with his voice, his gesture now, he strives,
Now with his lance the lagging soldier drives,
The weak he strengthens, and confirms the strong,
830 And hurries war's impetuous stream along.
'Strike home', he cries, 'and let your swords erase*
Each well-known feature of the kindred face;
Nor waste your fury on the vulgar band –
See where the hoary, doting Senate stand;
835 There laws and right at once you may confound,
And liberty shall bleed at every wound.'
    The cursed destroyer spoke, and at the word
The purple nobles sunk beneath the sword,
The dying patriots groan upon the ground,
840 Illustrious names, for love of laws renowned.
The great Metelli and Torquati bleed,*
Chiefs worthy, if the state had so decreed,
And Pompey were not there, mankind to lead.
    Say thou, thy sinking country's only prop,
845 Glory of Rome, and liberty's last hope,
What helm, O Brutus, could, amidst the crowd,

Thy sacred, undistinguished* visage shroud?
Where fought thy arm that day? But ah, forbear,
Nor rush unwary on the pointed spear;
850   Seek not to hasten on untimely fate,
But patient for thy own Emathia wait;*
Nor hunt fierce Caesar on this bloody plain –
Today thy steel pursues his life in vain.
Somewhat is wanting to the tyrant yet
855   To make the measure of his crimes complete;
As yet he has not every law defied,
Nor reached the utmost heights of daring pride;
E'er long thou shalt behold him Rome's proud lord,
And ripened by ambition for thy sword;
860   Then thy grieved country vengeance shall demand,
And ask the victim at thy righteous hand.
    Among huge heaps of the patrician slain
And Latian chiefs, who strewed that purple plain,
Recording story has distinguished well*
865   How brave, unfortunate Domitius fell.*
In every loss of Pompey still he shared,
And died in liberty, the best reward;
Though vanquished oft by Caesar, ne'er enslaved,
Ev'n to the last the tyrant's power he braved;
870   Marked o'er with many a glorious, streaming wound,
In pleasure sunk the warrior to the ground,
No longer forced on vilest terms to live,
For chance to doom, and Caesar to forgive.
Him, as he passed insulting o'er the field,
875   Rolled in his blood, the victor proud beheld:
'And can', he cried, 'the fierce Domitius fall,
Forsake his Pompey, and expecting Gaul?*
Must the war lose that still successful sword,
And my neglected province want a lord?'
880   He spoke, when, lifting slow his closing eyes,
Fearless the dying Roman thus replies:
'Since wickedness stands unrewarded yet,
Nor Caesar's arms their wished success have met,
Free and rejoicing to the shades I go,
885   And leave my chief* still equal to his foe;
And if my hopes divine thy doom aright,
Yet shalt thou bow thy vanquished head e'er night.

Dire punishments the righteous gods decree,*
For* injured Rome, for Pompey, and for me;
890 In hell's dark realms thy tortures I shall know,
And hear thy ghost lamenting loud below.'
　　He said, and soon the leaden sleep prevailed,
And everlasting night his eyelids sealed.
　　But oh, what grief the ruin can deplore,*
895 What verse can run the various slaughter o'er!
For lesser woes our sorrows may we keep –
No tears suffice a dying world to weep.
In differing groups ten thousand deaths arise,
And horrors manifold the soul surprise.
900 Here the whole man is opened at a wound,
And gushing bowels pour upon the ground;
Another through the gaping jaws is gored,
And in his inmost throat receives the sword;
At once a single blow a third extends,
905 The fourth a living trunk dismembered stands;
Some in their breasts erect the javelin bear,
Some cling to earth with the transfixing spear;
Here, like a fountain, springs a purple flood,
Spouts on the foe, and stains his arms with blood;
910 There horrid brethren on their brethren prey,
One starts and hurls a well-known head away,
While some detested son, with impious ire,
Lops by the shoulders close his hoary sire;
Ev'n his rude fellows damn the cursèd deed,
915 And bastard-born* the murderer aread.*
　　No private house its loss lamented then,
But count the slain by nations, not by men.
Here Grecian streams and Asiatic run,
And Roman torrents drive the deluge on.
920 More than the world at once was given away,
And late posterity was lost that day,
A race of future slaves received their doom,
And children yet unborn were overcome.
How shall our miserable sons complain
925 That they are born beneath a tyrant's reign?
Did our base hands, with justice shall they say,
The sacred cause of liberty betray?
Why have our fathers giv'n us up a prey?

Their age to ours the curse of bondage leaves;
930   Themselves were cowards and begot us slaves.
       'Tis just, and fortune, that imposed a lord,*
       One struggle for their freedom might afford,
       Might leave their hands their proper cause to fight,
       And let them keep, or lose themselves, their right.
935   But Pompey now the fate of Rome descried,
       And saw the changing gods forsake her side.
       Hard to believe, though from a rising ground
       He viewed the universal ruin round,
       In crimson streams he saw destruction run,
940   And in the fall of thousands felt his own.
       Nor wished he, like most wretches in despair,
       The world one common misery might share,
       But with a generous, great, exalted mind
       Besought the gods to pity poor mankind,
945   To let him die, and leave the rest behind.
       This hope came smiling to his anxious breast,
       For this his earnest vows were thus addressed:
       'Spare man, ye gods, oh let the nations live!
       Let me be wretched, but let Rome survive;
950   Or if this head suffices not alone,
       My wife, my sons, your anger shall atone;
       If blood the yet unsated war demand,
       Behold my pledges left in fortune's hand!
       Ye cruel powers, who urge me with your hate,
955   At length behold me crushed beneath the weight;
       Give then your long, pursuing vengeance o'er,
       And spare the world, since I can lose no more.'
           So saying, the tumultuous field he crossed,*
       And warned from battle his despairing host.
960   Gladly the pains of death he had explored,
       And fall'n undaunted on his pointed sword,
       Had he not feared th'example might succeed,
       And faithful nations by his side would bleed.
       Or did his swelling soul disdain to die,
965   While his insulting father stood so nigh?
       Fly where he will, the gods shall still pursue,
       Nor his pale head shall 'scape the victor's view.
       Or else perhaps – and fate the thought approved –
       For her dear sake he fled whom best he loved;

970   Malicious fortune to his wish agreed,
     And gave him in Cornelia's sight to bleed.
     Borne by his wingèd steed at length away,
     He quits the purple plain and yields the day;
     Fearless of danger, still secure and great,
975   His daring soul supports his lost estate;
     Nor groans his breast, nor swell his eyes with tears,
     But still the same majestic form he wears;
     An awful grief sat decent in his face,
     Such as became his loss, and Rome's disgrace;
980   His mind, unbroken, keeps her constant frame,
     In greatness and misfortune still the same,
     While fortune, who his triumphs once beheld,
     Unchanging sees him leave Pharsalia's field.
     Now disentangled from unwieldy power,
985   O Pompey, run thy former honours o'er!
     At leisure now review the glorious scene,
     And call to mind how mighty thou hast been.
     From anxious toils of empire turn thy care,
     And from thy thoughts exclude the murderous war;
990   Let the just gods bear witness on thy side
     Thy cause no more shall by the sword be tried.
     Whether sad Afric* shall her loss bemoan,
     Or Munda's* plains beneath their burden groan,
     The guilty bloodshed shall be all their own.
995   No more the much-loved Pompey's name shall charm
     The peaceful world with one consent to arm;
     Nor for thy sake, nor awed by thy command,
     But for themselves the fighting Senate stand;
     The war but one distinction shall afford,
1000 And liberty, or Caesar, be the word.
       Nor, oh, do thou thy vanquished lot deplore,
     But fly with pleasure from those seas of gore!
     Look back upon the horror, guiltless thou,
     And pity Caesar for whose sake they flow.
1005 With what a heart, what triumph shall he come,
     A victor red with Roman blood, to Rome?
     Though misery thy banishment attends,
     Though thou shalt die by thy false Pharian* friends,
     Yet trust securely to the choice of heaven,
1010 And know thy loss was for a blessing given;

Though flight may seem the warrior's shame and
　　curse,
To conquer, in a cause like this, is worse.
And, oh, let every mark of grief be spared –
May no tear fall, no groan, no sigh be heard,
1015　Still let mankind their Pompey's fate adore,
And reverence thy fall, ev'n as thy height of power.
Meanwhile survey th'attending world around,
Cities* by thee possessed and monarchs crowned,*
On Afric, or on Asia cast thy eye,
1020　And mark the land where thou shalt choose to die.
　　Larisa first the constant chief beheld,
Still great, though flying from the fatal field;
With loud acclaim her crowds his coming greet,
And sighing pour their presents at his feet.
1025　She crowns her altars, and proclaims a feast,⎫
Would put on joy to cheer her noble guest,　⎬
But weeps, and begs to share his woes at least.⎭
So was he loved e'en in his lost estate,
Such faith, such friendship on his ruins wait;
1030　With ease Pharsalia's loss might be supplied,
While eager nations hasten to his side,
As if misfortune meant to bless him more
Than all his long prosperity before.
'In vain', he cries, 'you bring the vanquished aid;⎫
1035　Henceforth to Caesar be your homage paid,　　⎬
Caesar, who triumphs o'er yon heaps of dead.'⎭
With that, his courser* urging on to flight,
He vanished from the mournful city's sight.
With cries and loud laments they fill the air,
1040　And curse the cruel gods in fierceness of despair.
　　Now in huge lakes Hesperian crimson stood,
And Caesar's self grew satiated with blood.
The great patricians fall'n, his pity spared
The worthless, unresisting, vulgar herd.
1045　Then, while his glowing fortune yet was warm,*
And scattering terror spread the wild alarm,
Straight to the hostile camp his way he bent,⎫
Careful to seize the hasty flyer's tent,*　　⎬
The leisure of a night and thinking to prevent.⎭
1050　Nor recked he much the weary soldiers' toil,

But led them prone and greedy to the spoil.
'Behold', he cries, 'our victory complete,
The glorious recompense attends ye yet;
Much have you done today for Caesar's sake,
1055 'Tis mine to show the prey, 'tis yours to take,
'Tis yours, whate'er the vanquished foe has left,
'Tis what your valour gained, and not my gift.
Treasures immense yon wealthy tents enfold,
The gems of Asia, and Hesperian gold;
1060 For you the once great Pompey's store attends,
With regal spoils of his barbarian friends;
Haste then, prevent the foe, and seize that good,
For which you paid so well with Roman blood.'
He said, and, with the rage of rapine stung,
1065 The multitude tumultuous rush along,
On swords and spears, on sires and sons they tread,
And all remorseless spurn* the gory dead.
What trench can intercept, what fort withstand
The brutal soldier's rude, rapacious hand,
1070 When eager to his crime's reward he flies,
And, bathed in blood, demands the horrid prize?
There wealth collected from the world around,
The destined recompense of war, they found.
But oh, not golden Arimaspus'* store,
1075 Nor all that Tagus or rich Iber* pour,
Can fill the greedy victors' griping* hands –
Rome and the Capitol their pride demands;
All other spoils they scorn as worthless prey,
And count their wicked labours robbed of pay.
1080 Here in patrician tents plebeians rest,
And regal couches are by ruffians pressed,
There impious parricides the bed invade,
And sleep where late their slaughtered sires were laid.
Meanwhile the battle stands in dreams renewed,*
1085 And Stygian horrors o'er their slumbers brood.
Astonishment and dread their souls infest,
And guilt sits painful on each heaving breast;
Arms, blood, and death work in the labouring
        brain –
They sigh, they start, they strive, and fight it o'er
        again.

1090 Ascending fiends infect the air around,
   And hell breathes baleful through the groaning
     ground;
   Hence dire affright* distracts the warriors' souls, ⎫
   Vengeance divine their daring hearts controls, ⎬
   Snakes hiss, and livid flame tormenting rolls. ⎭
1095 Each, as his hands in guilt have been imbrued,
   By some pale spectre flies all night pursued.
   In various forms the ghosts unnumbered groan –
   The brother, friend, the father and the son;
   To every wretch his proper phantom fell,
1100 While Caesar sleeps the general care of hell.
   Such were his pangs as mad Orestes felt,*
   E'er yet the Scythian altar purged his guilt;
   Such horrors Pentheus, such Agave knew,*
   He when his rage first came, and she when hers
     withdrew.
1105 Present and future swords his bosom bears,
   And feels the blow that Brutus now defers.
   Vengeance in all her pomp of pain attends, ⎫
   To wheels she binds him, and with vultures rends,* ⎬
   With racks of conscience and with whips of fiends. ⎭
1110 But soon the visionary horrors pass,
   And his first rage with day resumes its place;
   Again his eyes rejoice to view the slain,
   And run unwearied o'er the dreadful plain.
   He bids his train prepare his impious board,
1115 And feasts amidst the heaps of death abhorred.
   There each pale face at leisure he may know,
   And still behold the purple current flow;
   He views the woeful wide horizon round, ⎫
   Then joys that earth is nowhere to be found, ⎬
1120 And owns those gods he serves his utmost wish ⎭
     have crowned.
   Still greedy to possess the cursed delight,
   To glut his soul and gratify his sight,
   The last funereal honours he denies,
   And poisons with the stench Emathia's skies.
1125 Not thus the sworn inveterate foe of Rome*
   Refused the vanquished consul's bones a tomb;
   His piety the country round beheld,

And bright with fires shone Cannae's fatal field.
But Caesar's rage from fiercer motives rose:
1130 These were his countrymen, his worst of foes.
But oh, relent, forget thy hatred past,
And give the wandering shades to rest at last!
Nor seek we single honours for the dead,
At once let nations on the pile be laid;
1135 To feed the flame let heapy forests rise,   ⎫
Far be it seen to fret* the ruddy skies,   ⎬
And grieve despairing Pompey where he flies.   ⎭
    Know too, proud conqueror, thy wrath in vain
Strews with unburied carcasses the plain.
1140 What is it to thy malice if they burn,
Rot in the field, or moulder in the urn?
The forms of matter all dissolving die,
And lost in nature's blending bosom lie.
Though now thy cruelty denies a grave,*
1145 These and the world one common lot shall have;
One last appointed flame, by fates's decree,
Shall waste yon azure heavens, this earth and sea,
Shall knead the dead up* in one mingled mass,
Where stars and they shall undistinguish'd pass;
1150 And though thou scorn their fellowship, yet know,   ⎫
High as thy own can soar, these souls shall go,   ⎬
Or find, perhaps, a better place below.   ⎭
Death is beyond thy goddess fortune's power,
And parent earth receives whate'er she bore.
1155 Nor will we mourn those Romans' fate who lie
Beneath the glorious covering of the sky;
That starry arch for ever round them turns,
A nobler shelter far than tombs or urns.
    But wherefore parts the loathing victor hence?
1160 Does slaughter strike too strongly on thy sense?
Yet stay, yet breathe the thick, infectious steam,
Yet quaff with joy the blood-polluted stream.
But see, they fly, the daring warriors yield,
And the dead heaps drive Caesar from the field!
1165   Now to the prey gaunt wolves, a howling train,
Speed hungry from the far Bistonian plain,
From Pholoë the tawny lion comes,
And growling bears forsake their darksome homes;

With these lean dogs in herds obscene repair,
1170 And every kind that snuffs the tainted air.
For food the cranes their wonted flight delay,
That erst to warmer Nile had winged their way;
With them the feathered race convene from far,
Who gather to the prey, and wait on war.
1175 Ne'er were such flocks of vultures seen to fly,
And hide with spreading plumes the crowded sky;
Gorging on limbs in every tree they sat,
And dropped raw morsels down and gory fat;
Oft their tired talons, loosening as they fled,
1180 Rained horrid offals on the victor's head;
But while the slain supplied too full a feast,
The plenty bred satiety at last,
The ravenous feeders riot at their ease,
And single out what dainties best may please.
1185 Part borne away, the rest neglected lie,
For noonday suns and parching winds to dry,
Till length of time shall wear them quite away,
And mix them with Emathia's common clay.
     O fatal Thessaly, O land abhorred!
1190 How have thy fields the hate of heaven incurred
That thus the gods to thee destruction doom,
And load thee with the curse of falling Rome!
Still to new crimes, new horrors, dost thou haste,*
When yet thy former mischiefs scarce were past.
1195 What rolling years, what ages, can repay
The multitudes thy wars have swept away!
Though tombs and urns their numerous store should
          spread,
And long antiquity yield all her dead,
Thy guilty plains more slaughtered Romans hold
1200 Than all those tombs and all those urns enfold.
Hence bloody spots shall stain thy grassy green,
And crimson drops on bladed corn be seen,
Each ploughshare some dead patriot shall molest,
Disturb his bones and rob his ghost of rest.
1205 Oh, had the guilt of war been all thy own,
Were civil rage confined to thee alone,
No mariner his labouring bark should moor,
In hopes of safety, on thy dreadful shore,

No swain thy spectre-haunted plain should know,
1210 Nor turn thy blood-stained fallow with his plough,
No shepherd e'er should drive his flock to feed,
Where Romans slain enrich the verdant mead;
All desolate should lie thy land, and waste,
As in some scorched or frozen region placed.
1215 But the great gods forbid our partial hate
On Thessaly's distinguished land to wait;
New blood and other slaughters they decree,
And others shall be guilty too, like thee.
Munda and Mutina shall boast their slain,* ⎱
1220 Pachynus' waters share the purple stain, ⎰
And Actium* justify* Pharsalia's plain. ⎰

BOOK EIGHT

Now, through the vale by great Alcides* made
And the sweet maze of Tempe's pleasing shade,
Cheerless the flying chief renewed his speed,
And urged with gory spurs his fainting steed;
5   Fall'n from the former greatness of his mind,*
He turns where doubtful paths obscurely wind.
The fellows of his flight increase his dread,
While hard behind the trampling horsemen tread;
He starts at every rustling of the trees,
10 And fears the whispers of each murmuring breeze.
He feels not yet, alas, his lost estate,
And, though he flies, believes himself still great,*
Imagines millions for his life are bid,
And rates his own as he would Caesar's head.
15 Where-e'er his fear explores untrodden ways,
His well-known visage still his flight betrays.
Many he meets unknowing of his chance,
Whose gathering forces to his aid advance;
With gaze astonished these their chief behold,
20 And scarce believe what by himself is told.
In vain, to covert,* from the world he flies;
Fortune still grieves him with pursuing eyes,
Still aggravates, still urges his disgrace,
And galls him with the thoughts of what he was.
25 His youthful triumph sadly now returns,
His Pontic and piratic* wars he mourns,
While stung with secret shame and anxious care he
        burns.
Thus age to sorrows oft the great betrays,
When loss of empire comes with length of days;
30 Life and enjoyment still one end should have,
Lest early misery prevent the grave;
The good that lasts not was in vain bestowed,
And ease, once past, becomes the present load;
Then let the wise, in fortune's kindest hour,*
35 Still keep one safe retreat within his power –

Let death be near, to guard him from surprise,
And free him when the fickle goddess flies.
   Now to those shores the hapless Pompey came
Where hoary Peneus rolls his ancient stream;
40   Red with Emathian slaughter ran his flood,
And dyed the ocean deep in Roman blood.
There a poor bark, whose keel perhaps might glide
Safe down some river's smooth descending tide,
Received the mighty master of the main,
45   Whose spreading navies hide the liquid plain.
In this he braves the winds and stormy sea,
And to the Lesbian isle directs his way.
There the kind partner of his every care,
His faithful, loved Cornelia, languished there,
50   At that sad distance more unhappy far
Than in the midst of danger, death and war.
There on her heart, ev'n all the livelong day,
Foreboding thought a weary burden lay,
Sad visions haunt her slumbers with affright,
55   And Thessaly returns with every night.
Soon as the ruddy morning paints the skies,*
Swift to the shore the pensive mourner flies;
There, lonely sitting on the cliff's bleak brow,
Her sight she fixes on the seas below,
60   Attentive marks the wide horizon's bound,
And kens each sail that rises in the round;*
Thick beats her heart as every prow draws near,
And dreads the fortunes of her lord to hear.
   At length, behold, the fatal bark is come –
65   See the swoll'n canvas labouring with her doom!
Preventing* fame, misfortune lends him wings,
And Pompey's self his own sad story brings.
Now bid thy eyes, thou lost Cornelia, flow,
And change thy fears to certain sorrows now.
70   Swift glides the woeful vessel on to land,
Forth flies the headlong matron to the strand;
There soon she found what worst the gods could
      do,
There soon her dear much altered lord she knew,
Though fearful all, and ghastly was his hue;
75   Rude o'er his face his hoary locks were grown,

And dust was cast upon his Roman gown.
She saw, and fainting sunk in sudden night,
Grief stopped her breath and shut out loathsome
        light,
The loosening nerves no more their force exert,
80   And motion ceased within the freezing heart;
Death kindly seemed her wishes to obey,
And, stretched upon the beach, a corse* she lay.
    But now the mariners the vessel moor,
And Pompey, landing, views the lonely shore.
85   The faithful maids their loud lamentings ceased,
And reverently their ruder grief suppressed;
Straight, while with duteous care they kneel around
And raise their wretched mistress from the ground,
Her lord enfolds her with a strict* embrace,
90   And joins his cheek close to her lifeless face;
At the known touch her failing sense returns,
And vital warmth in kindling blushes burns.
At length from virtue thus he seeks relief,
And kindly chides her violence of grief:
95   'Canst thou then sink, thou daughter of the
        great,
Sprung from the noblest guardians of our state?*
Canst thou thus yield to the first shock of fate?
Whatever deathless monuments of praise
Thy sex can merit, 'tis in thee to raise.
100   On man alone life's ruder trials wait,
The fields of battle and the cares of state,
While the wife's virtue then is only tried
When faithless fortune quits her husband's side.
Arm then thy soul the glorious task to prove,
105   And learn thy miserable lord to love.
Behold me of my power and pomp bereft,
By all my kings and by Rome's Fathers* left;
Oh make that loss thy glory, and be thou
The only follower of Pompey now.
110   This grief becomes thee not, while I survive –
War wounds not thee, since I am still alive;
These tears a dying husband should deplore,*
And only fall when Pompey is no more.

'Tis true my former greatness all is lost;
115   Who* weep for that, no love for me can boast,
But mourn the loss of what they valued most.'
    Moved at her lord's reproof, the matron rose,
Yet, still complaining, thus avowed her woes:
    'Ah, wherefore was I not much rather led,*
120   A fatal bride, to Caesar's hated bed?
To thee unlucky and a curse I came,
Unblessed by yellow Hymen's holy flame;*
My bleeding Crassus and his sire stood by,*
And fell Erynis* shook her torch on high;
125   My fate on thee the Parthian vengeance draws,
And urges heaven to hate the juster cause.
Ah, my once greatest lord, ah cruel hour,
Is thy victorious head in fortune's power?
Since miseries my baneful love pursue,
130   Why did I wed thee only to undo?
But see, to death my willing neck I bow,
Atone the angry gods by one kind blow.
Long since for thee my life I would have given,
Yet, let me yet prevent the wrath of Heaven.
135   Kill me and scatter me upon the sea –
So shall propitious tides thy fleets convey,
Thy kings be faithful, and the world obey;
And thou, where-e'er thy sullen phantom flies,*
O Julia, let thy rival's blood suffice!
140   Let me the rage of jealous vengeance bear,
But him, thy lord, thy once loved Pompey, spare.'
    She said, and sunk within his arms again.
In streams of sorrow melt the mournful train;
Ev'n his, the warrior's eyes, were forced to yield,
145   That saw without a tear Pharsalia's field.
    Now to the strand the Mitylenians pressed,
And humbly thus bespoke their noble guest:
    'If to succeeding times our isle shall boast
The pledge* of Pompey left upon her coast,
150   Disdain not, if thy presence now we claim,
And fain would consecrate our walls to fame.
Make thou this place in future story great,
Where pious Romans may direct their feet
To view with adoration thy retreat.

155 This may we plead, in favour of the town,
That, while mankind the prosperous victor own,
Already Caesar's foes avowed are we,*
Nor add new guilt by duty paid to thee.
Some safety too our ambient seas secure –
160 Caesar wants ships and we defy his power.
Here may Rome's scattered Fathers well unite,
And arm against a second happier fight;
Our Lesbian youth with ready courage stands.
To man thy navies or recruit thy bands.
165 For gold, whate'er to sacred use is lent,
Take it, and the rapacious foe prevent.
This only mark of friendship we entreat:
Seek not to shun us in thy low estate,
But let our Lesbos in thy ruin prove,
170 As in thy greatness, worthy of thy love.'
      Much was the leader moved, and joyed to find
Faith had not quite abandoned humankind.
'To me', he cried, 'forever were you dear –
Witness the pledge committed to your care;
175 Here in security I placed my home,
My household gods, my heart, my wife, my Rome.
I know what ransom might your pardon buy,*
And yet I trust you, yet to you I fly.
But oh, too long my woes you singly bear;
180 I leave you, not for lands which I prefer,
But that the world the common load may share.
Lesbos, for ever sacred be thy name,
May late posterity thy truth proclaim,
Whether thy fair example spread around,
185 Or whether, singly, faithful thou art found!
For 'tis resolved, 'tis fixed within my mind,
To try the doubtful world, and prove mankind.
Oh grant good heaven, if there be one alone,
One gracious power so lost a cause to own,
190 Grant, like the Lesbians, I my friends may find,
Such who, though Caesar threaten, dare be kind,
Who, with the same just, hospitable* heart,
May leave me free to enter or depart.'
      He ceased, and to the ship his partner bore,
195 While loud complainings fill the sounding shore;

It seemed as if the nation with her passed,
And banishment had laid their island waste.
Their second sorrows they to Pompey give:
For her, as for their citizen, they grieve.
200 Ev'n though glad victory had called her thence,
And her lord's bidding been the just pretence,
The Lesbian matrons had in tears been drowned,
And brought her weeping to their watery bound.
So was she loved, so winning was her grace,
205 Such lowly sweetness dwelt upon her face,
In such humility her life she led,
Ev'n while her lord was Rome's commanding head,
As if his fortune were already fled.
    Half hid in seas descending Phoebus lay,
210 And upwards half, half downwards shot the day,
When wakeful cares revolve in Pompey's soul,
And run the wide world o'er, from pole to pole.
Each realm, each city in his mind are weighed,
Where he may fly, from whence depend on aid.
215 Wearied at length beneath that load of woes,
And those sad scenes his future views disclose,
In conversation for relief he sought,
And exercised on various themes his thought.
Now sits he by the careful pilot's side,
220 And asks what rules their watery journey guide,
What lights of heaven his art attends to most,
Bound for the Libyan or the Syrian coast.
    To him, intent upon the rolling skies,
The heaven-instructed shipman thus replies:
225 'Of all yon multitude of golden stars,
Which the wide, rounding sphere incessant bears,
The cautious mariner relies on none,
But keeps him to the constant Pole alone.
When o'er the yard the lesser Bear aspires,
230 And from the topmast gleam its paly fires,
Then Bosporus near neighbouring we explore,
And hear loud billows beat the Scythian shore;
But when Callisto's shining son descends,*
And the low Cynosure* tow'rds ocean bends,
235 For Syria straight we know the vessel bears,
Where first Canopus'* southern sign appears.

If still upon the left those stars thou keep,
And, passing Pharos,* plough the foamy deep,
Then right ahead thy luckless bark shall reach
240 The Libyan shoals and Syrts' unfaithful beach.
But say, for lo on thee attends my hand,
What course dost thou assign, what seas, what
    land?
Speak, and the helm shall turn at thy command.'
    To him the chief, by doubts uncertain tossed:
245 'Oh fly the Latian and Thessalian coast.
Those only lands avoid. For all beside,
Yield to the driving winds and rolling tide;
Let fortune where she please a port provide.
Till Lesbos did my dearest pledge restore,
250 That thought determined me to seek that shore;
All ports, all regions, but those fatal two,
Are equal to unhappy Pompey now.'
    Scarce had he spoke, when straight the master
        veered,
And right for Chios and for Asia* steered;
255 The working waves the course inverted feel,
And dash and foam beneath the winding keel.
With art like this, on rapid chariots borne,*
Around the column skilful racers turn;
The nether wheels bear nicely on the goal,
260 The farther, wide, in distant circles roll.
    Now day's bright beams the various earth disclose,
And o'er the fading stars the sun arose,
When Pompey gathering to his side beheld
The scattered relics of Pharsalia's field.
265 First from the Lesbian isle his son* drew near,
And soon a troop of faithful chiefs appear.
Nor purple princes yet disdain to wait
On vanquished Pompey's humbler low estate;
Proud monarchs, who in eastern kingdoms reign,
270 Mix in the great, illustrious exile's train.
From these, apart, Deiotarus* he draws,
The long-approved companion of his cause.
'Thou best', he cries, 'of all my royal friends,
Since with our loss Rome's power and empire ends,
275 What yet remains but that we call from far

The eastern nations to support the war?
Euphrates has not owned proud Caesar's side,
And Tigris rolls a yet unconquered tide.
Let it not grieve thee then to seek for aid
280 From the wild Scythian and remotest Mede;
To Parthia's monarch my distress declare,*
And at his throne speak this my humble prayer.
If faith in ancient leagues is to be found,
Leagues by our altars and your magi* bound,
285 Now string the Getic and Armenian bow,
And in full quivers feathered shafts bestow.
If when o'er Caspian hills my troops I led
'Gainst Alans, in eternal warfare bred,
I sought not once to make your Parthians yield,
290 But left them free to range the Persian field.
Beyond th'Assyrian bounds my eagles* flew,
And conquered realms that Cyrus* never knew;
Ev'n to the utmost east I urged my way,
And, ere* the Persian, saw the rising day;
295 Yet while beneath my yoke the nations bend,
I sought the Parthian only as my friend.
Yet more; when Carrhae blushed with Crassus'
        blood,
And Latium her severest vengeance vowed,
When war with Parthia was the common cry,*
300 Who stopped the fury of that rage but I?
If this be true, through Zeugma* take your way,
Nor let Euphrates' stream the march delay,
In gratitude to my assistance come,
Fight Pompey's cause and conquer willing Rome.'
305   He said; the monarch* cheerfully obeyed,
And straight aside his royal robes he laid,
Then bid his slaves their humbler vestments bring,
And in that servile veil conceals the king.
Thus majesty gives its proud trappings o'er,
310 And humbly seeks for safety from the poor –
The poor, who no disguises need, nor wear,
Unblessed with greatness and unvexed with fear!
His princely friend now safe conveyed to land,
The chief* o'erpassed the famed Ephesian strand,
315 Icaria's rocks with Colophon's smooth deep,

And foamy cliffs which rugged Samos keep.
From Coan* shores soft breathes the western wind,
And Rhodes and Cnidos soon are left behind;
Then, crossing o'er Telmessus' ample bay,
320 Right to Pamphilia's coast he cuts his way;
Suspicious of the land he keeps the main,
Till poor Phaselis first receives his wandering train.
There, free from fears, with ease he may command
Her citizens, scarce equal to his band.
325 Nor lingering there, his swelling sails are spread,
Till he discerns proud Taurus' rising head;
A mighty mass he stands, while down his side
Descending Dipsas* rolls his headlong tide.
In a slight bark he runs securely o'er
330 The pirates' once-infested dreadful shore.
Ah, when he set the watery empire free,
And swept the fierce Cilician* from the sea,
Could the successful warrior have forethought
'Twas for his future safety then he fought!
335 At length the gathering Fathers of the state*
In full assembly on their leader wait;
Within Syhedra's walls their Senate meets,
Whom, sighing, thus th'illustrious exile greets:
   'My friends, who with me fought, who with me
       fled,
340 And now are to me in my country's stead,
Though quite defenceless and unarmed we stand,
On this Cilician, naked, foreign strand,
Though every mark of fortune's wrath we bear,
And seem to seek for counsel in despair,
345 Preserve your souls undaunted, free and great,
And know I am not fall'n entirely yet.
Spite of the ruins of Emathia's plain,
Yet can I rear my drooping head again.
From Afric's dust abandoned Marius rose*
350 To seize the fasces, and insult his foes;
My loss is lighter, less is my disgrace –
Shall I despair to reach my former place?
Still on the Grecian seas my navies ride,
And many a valiant leader owns my side;
355 All that Pharsalia's luckless field could do

Was to disperse my forces, not subdue.
Still safe beneath my former fame I stand,
Dear to the world and loved in every land.
'Tis yours to counsel and determine whom
360 We shall apply to, in the cause of Rome,
What faithful friend may best assistance bring:
The Libyan, Parthian or Egyptian king.
For me, what course my thoughts incline to take,
Here freely and at large I mean to speak.
365 What most dislike me* in the Pharian prince*
Are his raw years and yet unpractised sense;
Virtue in youth no stable footing finds,
And constancy is built on manly minds.
Nor with less danger may our trust explore
370 The faith uncertain of the crafty Moor;*
From Carthaginian blood he draws his race,*
Still mindful of the vanquished town's disgrace;
From thence Numidian mischiefs he derives,
And Hannibal in his false heart survives;
375 With pride he saw submissive Varus* bow,
And joys to hear the Roman power lies low.
To warlike Parthia therefore let us turn,
Where stars unknown in distant azure burn,
Where Caspian hills to part the world arise,
380 And night and day succeed in other skies,
Where rich Assyrian plains Euphrates laves,*
And seas discoloured roll their ruddy waves.*
Ambition there delights in arms to reign,
There rushing squadrons thunder o'er the plain,
385 There young and old the bow promiscuous* bend,
And fatal shafts with aim unerring send.
They first the Macedonian phalanx broke,
And hand to hand repelled the Grecian stroke;
They drove the Mede and Bactrian from the field,
390 And taught aspiring Babylon to yield;
Fearless against the Roman pile* they stood,
And triumphed in our vanquished Crassus' blood.
Nor trust they to the points of piercing darts,
But furnish death with new improving arts;
395 In mortal juices dipped their arrows fly,
And, if they taste the blood, the wounded die.

Too well their powers and favouring gods we
    know,*
And wish our fate much rather would allow
Some other aid, against the common foe.
400   With unauspicious succour shall they come,
Nursed in the hate and rivalship of Rome.
With these the neighbouring nations round shall arm,
And the whole east rouse at the dire alarm.
Should the barbarian race their aid deny,
405   Yet would I choose in that strange land to die;
There let our shipwrecked, poor remains be thrown,
Our loss forgotten and our names unknown;
Securely there ill fortune would I brave,
Nor meanly sue to kings whose crowns I gave,
410   From Caesar free enjoy my latest hour,
And scorn his anger's and his mercy's power.
Still when my thoughts my former days restore,
With joy methinks I run those regions o'er;
There much the better parts of life I proved,
415   Revered by all, applauded and beloved;
Wide o'er Maeotis spread my happy name,
And Tanais ran conscious of my fame;
My vanquished enemies my conquests mourned,
And covered still* with laurels I returned.
420   Approve then, Rome, my present cares for thee;
Thine is the gain whate'er th'event shall be.
What greater boon canst thou from heaven demand
Than in thy cause to arm the Parthian's hand?
Barbarians thus shall wage thy civil war,
425   And those that hate thee in thy ruin share.
When Caesar and Phraates* battle join,
They must revenge or Crassus' wrongs or mine.'
    The leader ceased, and straight a murmuring
        sound*
Ran through the disapproving Fathers round.
430   With these in high preeminence there sate*
Distinguished Lentulus,* the consul late;
None with more generous indignation stung,
Or nobler grief, beheld his country's wrong.
Sudden he rose, revered, and thus began,
435   In words that well became the subject and the man:

'Can then Pharsalia's ruins thus control
The former greatness of thy Roman soul?
Must the whole world, our laws and country yield
To one unlucky day, one ill-fought field?
440   Hast thou no hopes of succour, no retreat,
But mean prostration at the Parthian's feet?
Art thou grown weary of our earth and sky
That thus thou seek'st a fugitive to fly,
New stars to view, new regions to explore,
445   To learn new manners, and new gods adore?
Would thou before Chaldaean altars bend,
Worship their fires, and on their kings depend?*
Why didst thou draw the world to arms around,
Why cheat mankind with liberty's sweet sound,
450   Why on Emathia's plain fierce Caesar brave,*
When thou canst yield thyself a tyrant's slave?
Shall Parthia, who with terror shook from far
To hear thee named to head the Roman war,
Who saw thee lead proud monarchs in thy chain
455   From wild Hyrcania and the Indian main,
Shall she, that very Parthia, see thee now,
A poor, dejected, humble suppliant bow,
Then haughtily with Rome her greatness mate,
And scorn thy country for thy grovelling fate?
460   Thy tongue, in eastern languages untaught,
Shall want the words that should explain thy
               thought;
Tears, then, unmanly, must thy suit declare,
And suppliant hands uplifted speak thy prayer.
Shall Parthia – shall it to our shame be known –
465   Revenge Rome's wrongs e'er Rome revenge her own?
Our war no interfering kings demands,
Nor shall be trusted to barbarian hands;
Among ourselves our bonds we will deplore,
And Rome shall serve the rebel son* she bore.
470   Why wouldst thou bid our foes transgress their
               bound,
And teach their feet to tread Hesperian ground?
With ensigns torn from Crassus shall they come,
And with his ravished honours threaten Rome;
His fate those bloodstained eagles shall recall,

475   And hover dreadful o'er their native wall.
      Canst thou believe the monarch who withheld
      His only forces from Emathia's field
      Will bring his succours to thy waning state,)
      And bravely now defy the victor's hate? –   )
480   No eastern courage forms a thought so great.   )
      In cold, laborious climes the wintry north
      Brings her undaunted, hardy warriors forth,
      In body and in mind untaught to yield,
      Stubborn of soul and steady in the field,
485   While Asia's softer climate, formed to please,
      Dissolves her sons in indolence and ease.
      Here silken robes invest unmanly limbs,
      And in long trains the flowing purple streams.
      Where no rude hills Sarmatia's wilds restrain,
490   Or rushing Tigris cuts the level plain,
      Swifter than winds along the champaign* borne,)
      At liberty they fly, or fight, or turn,   )
      And, distant still, the vain pursuer scorn.   )
      Not with like ease they force their warlike way,
495   Where rough, unequal grounds their speed delay;
      Whene'er the thicker shades of night arise,*
      Unaimed the shaft, and unavailing, flies.
      Nor are they formed with constancy to meet
      Those toils that make the panting soldier sweat:
500   To climb the heights, to stem the rapid flood,   )
      To make the dusty, noonday battle good,   )
      Horrid with wounds, and crusted o'er in blood.   )
      Nor war's machines they know, nor have the skill
      To shake the rampire,* or the trench to fill;
505   Each fence that can their wingèd shafts endure
      Stands like a fort impregnable, secure.
      Light are their skirmishes, their war is flight,
      And still to wheel their wavering troops' delight;*
      To taint their coward darts is all their care,
510   And then to trust them to the flitting* air;
      Whene'er their bows have spent the feathered
          store,*
      The mighty business of their war is o'er;
      No manly strokes they try, nor hand to hand
      With cleaving swords in sturdy combat stand.

515   With swords the valiant still their foes invade –
       These call in drugs and poison to their aid.
       Are these the powers to whom thou bidst us fly?
       Is this the land in which thy bones would lie?
       Shall these barbarian hands for thee provide
520   The grave to thy unhappy friend* denied?
       But be it so – that death shall bring thee peace,
       That here thy sorrows and thy toils shall cease!
       Death is what man should wish. But oh, what fate
       Shall on thy wife, thy sad survivor, wait!
525   For her, where lust with lawless empire reigns,
       Somewhat* more terrible than death* remains.
       Have we not heard with what abhorred desires
       The Parthian Venus feeds her guilty fires,
       How their wild monarch, like the bestial race,*
530   Spreads the pollution of his lewd embrace?
       Unawed by reverence of connubial rites,
       In multitudes, luxurious, he delights;
       When gorged with feasting and inflamed with wine,
       No joys can sate him and no laws confine;
535   Forbidding nature then commands in vain
       From sisters and from mothers to abstain.
       The Greek and Roman with a trembling ear
       Th'unwilling crime of Oedipus* may hear,
       While Parthian kings like deeds with glory own,
540   And boast incestuous titles to the throne.
       If crimes like these they can securely brave,
       What laws, what power shall thy Cornelia save?
       Think how the helpless matron may be led,
       The thousandth harlot, to the royal bed.
545   Though when the tyrant clasps his noble slave,
       And hears to whom her plighted hand she gave,*
       Her beauties oft in scorn he shall prefer,
       And choose t'insult the Roman name in her.
       These are the powers to whom thou wouldst submit,
550   And Rome's revenge and Crassus' quite forget.
       Thy cause, preferred to his, becomes thy shame,
       And blots in common thine and Caesar's name.
       With how much greater glory might you join*
       To drive the Daci or to free the Rhine;
555   How well your conquering legions might you lead

'Gainst the fierce Bactrian and the haughty Mede,
Level proud Babylon's aspiring domes,
And with their spoils enrich our slaughtered leaders'
    tombs.*
No longer, fortune, let our friendship last,
560   Our peace, ill-omened, with the barbarous east;
If civil strife with Caesar's conquest end,
To Asia let his prosperous arms extend,
Eternal wars there let the victor wage,
And on proud Parthia pour the Roman rage.
565   There I, there all, his victories may bless,
And Rome herself make vows for his success.
When-e'er thou pass the cold Araxes o'er,
An agèd shade* shall greet thee on the shore,
Transfixed with arrows, mournful, pale and hoar.
570   "And art thou", shall he cry, complaining, "come
In peace and friendship to these foes of Rome?
Thou, from whose hand we hoped revenge in vain,
Poor naked ghosts, a thin unburied train,
That flit lamenting o'er this dreary plain?"
575   On every side new objects shall disclose
Some mournful monument of Roman woes,
On every wall fresh marks thou shalt descry
Where pale Hesperian heads were fixed on high;
Each river, as he rolls his purple tide,
580   Shall own his waves in Latian slaughter dyed.
If sights like these thou canst with patience bear,
What are the horrors which thy soul would fear?
Ev'n Caesar's self with joy may be beheld,
Enthroned on slaughter in Emathia's field.
585   Say then, we grant, thy cautions were not vain*
Of Punic frauds and Juba's faithless reign,
Abounding Egypt shall receive thee yet,
And yield, unquestioned, a secure retreat.
By nature strengthened with a dangerous strand,
590   Her Syrts and untried channels guard the land.
Rich in the fatness of her plenteous soil
She plants her only confidence in Nile.
Her monarch, bred beneath thy guardian cares,
His crown the largesse of thy bounty* wears;
595   Nor let unjust suspicions brand his truth –

Candour and innocence still dwell with youth.
Trust not a power accustomed to be great,
And versed in wicked policies of state;
Old kings, long hardened in the regal trade, ⎫
600   By interest and by craft alone are swayed, ⎬
And violate with ease the leagues they made, ⎭
While new ones still make conscience of the trust,
True to their friends and to their subjects just.'
　　He spoke; the listening Fathers all were moved,
605   And with concurring votes the thought approved.
So much ev'n dying liberty prevailed,
When Pompey's suffrage and his counsel failed.
　　And now Cilicia's coast the fleet forsake,*
And o'er the watery plain for Cyprus make,
610   Cyprus to love's ambrosial goddess* dear –
For ever grateful smoke the altars there;
Indulgent still she hears the Paphian vows,
And loves the favourite seas from when she rose;*
So fame reports, if we may credit fame, ⎫
615   When her fond tales the birth of gods proclaim, ⎬
Unborn,* and from eternity the same. ⎭
The craggy cliffs of Cyprus quickly past,
The chief runs southward o'er the ocean vast;
Nor views he, through the murky veil of night, ⎫
620   The Casian mountain's far distinguished height, ⎬
The high-hung lantern or the beamy light.* ⎭
Haply at length the labouring canvas bore
Full on the farthest bounds of Egypt's shore,
Where near Pelusium parting Nile descends,
625   And in her utmost eastern channel ends.
'Twas now the time when equal Jove on high*
Had hung the golden Balance* of the sky
(But ah, not long such just proportions last –
The righteous season soon was changed and passed,
630   And spring's encroachment on the shortening shade
Was fully to the wintry nights repaid),
When to the chief from shore they made report
That near high Casium lay the Pharian court.
This known, he thither turns his ready sail,
635   The light yet lasting with the favouring gale.
The fleet arrived,* the news flies swiftly round,

And their new guests the troubled court confound.
The time was short; howe'er the council met,*
Vile ministers, a monstrous motley set.
640 Of these the chief in honour and the best
Was old Acoreus, the Memphian priest;
In Isis* and Osiris* he believed,
And reverend tales from sire to son received,
Could mark the swell of Nile's increasing tide,
645 And many an Apis* in his time had died;
Yet was his age with gentlest manners fraught,
Humbly he spoke and modestly he taught.
With good intent the pious seer arose,
And told how much their state to Pompey owes,
650 What large amends their monarch ought to make,
Both for his own and for his father's sake.
But fate had placed a subtler speaker there,
A tongue more fitted for a tyrant's ear –
Pothinus, deep in arts of mischief read,
655 Who thus, with false persuasion, blindly led
The easy king to doom his guardian dead:
    'To strictest justice many ills belong,*
And honesty is often in the wrong,
Chiefly when stubborn rules her* zealots push
660 To favour those whom fortune means to crush.
But thou, O royal Ptolemy, be wise:
Change with the gods, and fly whom fortune flies.
Not earth from yon high heavens which we admire,
Not from the watery element the fire,
665 Are severed by distinctions half so wide
As interest and integrity divide.
The mighty power of kings no more prevails,
When justice comes with her deciding scales.
Freedom for all things and a lawless sword
670 Alone support an arbitrary lord.
He that is cruel must be bold in ills,
And find his safety from the blood he spills.
For piety and virtue's starving rules,
To mean retirements let them lead their fools,
675 There may they still ingloriously be good –
None can be safe in courts who blush at blood.
Nor let this fugitive despise thy years,

Or think a name like his can cause thy fears;
Exert thyself, and let him feel thy power,
680   And know that we dare drive him from our shore.
But if thou wish to lay thy greatness down,
To some more just succession yield thy crown –
Thy rival sister* willingly shall reign,
And save our Egypt from a foreign chain.
685   As now, at first, in neutral peace we lay,
Nor would be Pompey's friends nor Caesar's prey.
Vanquished, where-e'er his fortune has been tried,
And driv'n with scorn from all the world beside,
By Caesar chased, and left by his allies,*
690   To us a baffled vagabond he flies.
The poor remaining Senate loathe his sight,
And ruined monarchs curse his fatal flight,
While thousand phantoms from th'unburied slain,
Who feed the vultures of Emathia's plain,
695   Disastrous still pursue him in the rear,
And urge his soul with horror and despair.
To us for refuge now he seeks to run,
And would once more with Egypt be undone.
Rouse then, O Ptolemy, repress the wrong,*
700   He thinks we have enjoyed our peace too long,
And therefore kindly comes, that we may share
The crimes of slaughter and the woes of war.
His friendship shown to thee suspicions draws,*
And makes us seem too guilty of his cause;
705   Thy crown bestowed, the victor may impute
The Senate gave it but at Pompey's suit.
Nor, Pompey, thou thyself shall think it hard
If from thy aid by fate we are debarred.
We follow where the gods, constraining, lead:
710   We strike at thine, but wish 'twas Caesar's head.
Our weakness this, this fate's compulsion call – *
We only yield to him who conquers all.
Then doubt not, if thy blood we mean to spill:
Power awes us – if we can, we must and will.
715   What hopes thy* fond mistaking soul betrayed
To put thy trust in Egypt's feeble aid?
Our slothful nation, long disused to toil,
With pain suffice to till their slimy soil.

Our idle force due modesty should teach,
720 Nor dare to aim beyond its humble reach.
Shall we resist where Rome was forced to yield,
And make us parties to Pharsalia's field?
We mixed not in the fatal strife before –
And shall we when the world has given it o'er,
725 Now, when we know th'avenging victor's power?
Nor do we turn unpitying* from distress –
We fly not Pompey's woes, but seek success.
The prudent on the prosperous still attends,
And none but fools choose wretches for their
          friends.'
730   He said; the vile assembly all assent,
And the boy king his glad concurrence lent,
Fond of the royalty his slaves bestowed,*
And by new power of wickedness made proud.
        Where Casium high o'erlooks the shoaly strand,
735 A bark with armèd ruffians straight is manned,
And the task trusted to Achillas'* hand.
        Can then Egyptian souls thus proudly dare?
Is Rome, ye gods, thus fall'n by civil war?
Can you to Nile transfer the Roman guilt,
740 And let such blood by cowards' hands be spilt?
Some kindred murderer at least afford,
And let him fall by Caesar's worthy sword.
And thou, inglorious, feeble, beardless boy,
Dar'st thou thy hand in such a deed employ?
745 Does not thy trembling heart, with horror, dread
Jove's thunder grumbling o'er thy guilty head?
Had not his arms with triumphs oft been crowned,
And ev'n the vanquished world his conquest owned,
Had not the reverend Senate called him head,
750 And Caesar given fair Julia to his bed,
He was a Roman still – a name* should be
For ever sacred to a king like thee.
Ah fool! thus blindly by thyself undone,
Thou seek'st his ruin who upheld thy throne;
755 He only could thy feeble power maintain,
Who gave thee first o'er Egypt's realm to reign.
        The seamen now, advancing near to shore,
Strike the wide sail, and ply the plunging oar,

When the false miscreants the navy meet,
760   And with dissembled cheer the Roman greet.
They feign their hospitable land addressed*
With ready friendship to receive her guest,
Excusing much an inconvenient shore,
Where shoals lie thick and meeting currents roar;
765   From his tall ship, unequal to the place,
They beg him to their lighter bark to pass.

　　　Had not the gods unchangeably decreed
Devoted* Pompey in that hour to bleed,
A thousand signs the danger near foretell,
770   Seen by his sad, presaging friends too well.
Had their low fawning justly been designed,
If truth could lodge in an Egyptian mind,
Their king himself with all his fleet had come
To lead, in pomp, his benefactor home.
775   But thus fate willed, and Pompey chose to bear
A certain death before uncertain fear.

　　　While now aboard the hostile boat he goes, ⎤
To follow him the frantic matron vows,   ⎟
And claims her partnership in all his woes.   ⎦
780   'But oh, forbear', he cries, 'my love, forbear;
Thou and my son remain in safety here.
Let this old head the danger first explore,
And prove the faith of yon suspected shore.'
He spoke, but she, unmoved at his commands,
785   Thus loud exclaiming, stretched her eager hands:
'Whither, inhuman, whither art thou gone?
Still must I weep our common griefs alone?
Joy still, with thee, forsakes my boding heart,
And fatal is the hour whene'er we part.
790   Why did thy vessel to my Lesbos turn?
Why was I from the faithful island borne?
Must I all lands, all shores, alike forbear,
And only on the seas thy sorrows share?'
Thus to the winds loud plained* her fruitless tòngue,
795   While eager from the deck on high she hung; ⎤
Trembling with wild astonishment and fear,   ⎟
She dares not, while her parting lord they bear, ⎟
Turn her eyes from him once, or fix them there. ⎦
On him his anxious navy all are bent,

800 And wait solicitous the dire event;
    No danger aimed against his life they doubt –
    Care for his glory only fills their thought;
    They wish he may not stain his name renowned
    By mean submission to the boy he crowned.

805 Just as he entered o'er the vessel's side,
    'Hail General!', the cursed Septimius cried,*
    A Roman once in generous warfare bred,
    And oft in arms by mighty Pompey led,
    But now – what vile dishonour must it bring! –

810 The ruffian slave of an Egyptian king.
    Fierce was he, horrible, inured to blood,
    And ruthless as the savage of the wood.
    O fortune, who but would have called thee kind,
    And thought thee mercifully now inclined,

815 When thy o'er-ruling providence withheld
    This hand of mischief from Pharsalia's field?
    But thus thou scatterest thy destroying swords,
    And every land thy victims thus affords.
    Shall Pompey at a tyrant's bidding bleed?

820 Can Roman hands be to the task decreed?
    Ev'n Caesar and his gods abhor the deed.
    Say you, who with the stain of murder brand*
    Immortal Brutus's avenging hand,
    What monstrous title, yet to speech unknown,

825 To latest times shall mark Septimius down!
        Now in the boat defenceless Pompey sate,
    Surrounded and abandoned to his fate.
    Nor long they hold him in their power aboard,
    Ere every villain drew his ruthless sword;

830 The chief perceived their purpose soon, and spread
    His Roman gown with patience o'er his head,
    And, when the cursed Achillas pierced his breast,
    His rising indignation close repressed.
    No sighs, no groans, his dignity profaned,

835 Nor tears his still unsullied glory stained;
    Unmoved and firm he fixed him on his seat,
    And died, as when he lived and conquered, great.*
    Meanwhile, within his equal* parting soul,
    These latest pleasing thoughts revolving roll:

840 'In this my strongest trial, and my last,

As in some theatre I here am placed;
The faith of Egypt and my fate shall be
A theme for present times and late posterity.
Much of my former life was crowned with praise,

845   And honours waited on my early days;
Then fearless let me this dread period* meet,
And force the world to own the scene complete.
Nor grieve, my heart, by such base hands to bleed –
Whoever strikes the blow, 'tis Caesar's deed.

850   What though this mangled carcass shall be torn,
These limbs be tossed about for public scorn,
My long prosperity has found its end,
And death comes opportunely, like a friend;
It comes to set me free from fortune's power,

855   And gives what she can rob me of no more.
My wife and son behold me now, 'tis true –
Oh, may no tears, no groans, my fate pursue!
My virtue rather let their praise approve,
Let them admire my death, and my remembrance
          love.'

860   Such constancy in that dread hour remained,
And, to the last, the struggling soul sustained.
      Not so the matron's feebler powers repressed
The wild impatience of her frantic breast;
With every stab her bleeding heart was torn,

865   With wounds much harder to be seen than borne.
''Tis I, 'tis I have murdered him!', she cries;
'My love the sword and ruthless hand supplies.
'Twas I allured him to my fatal isle,
That cruel Caesar first might reach the Nile;

870   For Caesar sure is there – no hand but his
Has right to such a parricide as this.
But whether Caesar or whoe'er thou art,
Thou has mistook the way to Pompey's heart;
That sacred pledge in my sad bosom lies –

875   There plunge thy dagger, and he more than dies.
Me too most worthy of thy fury know,
The partner of his arms and sworn your foe.
Of all our Roman wives I singly bore
The camp's fatigue, the sea's tempestuous roar;

880   No dangers, not the victor's wrath, I feared,

What mighty monarchs durst not do I dared.
These guilty arms did their glad refuge yield,
And clasped him flying from Pharsalia's field.
Ah Pompey! Dost thou thus my faith reward?
885   Shalt thou be doomed to die, and I be spared?
But fate shall many means of death afford,
Nor want th'assistance of a tyrant's sword.
And you, my friends, in pity let me leap
Hence headlong, down amidst the tumbling deep,
890   Or to my neck the strangling cordage tie;
If there be any friend of Pompey nigh,
Transfix me, stab me, do but let me die.
My lord, my husband – yet thou art not dead,
And see, Cornelia is a captive led!
895   From thee their cruel hands thy wife detain,
Reserved to wear th'insulting victor's chain.'
     She spoke, and stiffening sunk in cold despair;
Her weeping maids the lifeless burden bear,
While the pale mariners the bark unmoor,
900   Spread every sail, and fly the faithless shore.
     Nor agonies nor livid death disgrace
The sacred features of the hero's face;
In the cold visage, mournfully serene,
The same indignant majesty was seen;
905   There virtue still unchangeable abode,
And scorned the spite of every partial god.
     The bloody business now complete and done,
New furies urge the fierce Septimius on;
He rends the robe that veiled the hero's head,
910   And to full view exposed the recent dead;
Hard in his horrid gripe the face he pressed,
While yet the quivering muscles life confessed;
He drew the dragging body down with haste,
Then cross a rower's seat the neck he placed,
915   There awkward, haggling,* he divides the bone
(The headsman's art was then but rudely known);
Straight on the spoil his Pharian partner flies,
And robs the heartless villain of his prize.
The head, his trophy, proud Achillas bears;
920   Septimius an inferior drudge appears,
And in the meaner mischief poorly shares.

Caught by the venerable locks which grow
In hoary ringlets on his generous brow,
To Egypt's impious king that head they bear
925   That laurels used to bind and monarchs fear.
Those sacred lips and that commanding tongue,
On which the listening forum oft has hung,
That tongue which could the world with ease
          restrain,
And ne'er commanded war or peace in vain,
930   That face in which success came smiling home
And doubled every joy it brought to Rome,
Now pale and wan, is fixed upon a spear,
And borne for public view aloft in air.
The tyrant, pleased, beheld it and decreed
935   To keep this pledge of his detested deed.
His slaves straight drain the serous* parts away,*
And arm the wasting flesh against decay;
Then drugs and gums through the void vessels pass,
And for duration fix the stiffening mass.
940   Inglorious boy, degenerate and base,
Thou last and worst of the Lagaean* race!
Whose feeble throne ere long shall be compelled
To thy lascivious sister's* reign to yield,
Canst thou with altars and with rites divine
945   The rash, vain youth of Macedon* enshrine,
Can Egypt such stupendous fabrics build,
Can her wide plains with pyramids be filled,
Canst thou beneath such monumental pride
Thy worthless Ptolemean fathers hide,
950   While the great Pompey's headless trunk is tossed,
In scorn, unburied, on thy barbarous coast?
Was it so much? Could not thy care suffice
To keep him whole and glut his father's eyes?
In this his fortune ever held the same –
955   Still wholly kind or wholly cross she came.
Patient his long prosperity she bore,
But kept this death and this sad day in store.
No meddling god did e'er his power employ
To ease his sorrows or to damp his joy;
960   Unmingled came the bitter and the sweet,
And all his good and evil was complete.

No sooner was he struck by fortune's hand,
But, see, he lies unburied on the sand;
Rocks tear him, billows toss him up and down,
965   And Pompey by a headless trunk is known.
        Yet, e'er proud Caesar touched the Pharian Nile,*
Chance found his mangled foe a funeral pile;
In pity half, and half in scorn, she gave
A wretched, to prevent a nobler, grave.
970   Cordus, a follower* long of Pompey's fate,
His quaestor* in Idalian* Cyprus late,
From a close cave in covert where he lay
Swift to the neighbouring shore betook his way;
Safe in the shelter of the gloomy shade,
975   And by strong ties of pious duty swayed,
The fearless youth the watery strand surveyed.
'Twas now the thickest darkness of the night
And waning Phoebe* lent a feeble light,
Yet soon the glimmering goddess plainly showed
980   The paler corse amidst the dusky flood.
The plunging Roman flies to its relief,
And with strong arms enfolds the floating chief.
Long strove his labour with the tumbling main,
And dragged the sacred burden on with pain.
985   Nigh weary now, the waves instruct him well
To seize th'advantage of th'alternate swell;
Borne on the mounting surge, to shore he flies,
And on the beach in safety lands his prize.
There o'er the dead he hangs with tender care,
990   And drops in every gaping wound a tear;
Then, lifting to the gloomy skies his head,
Thus to the stars and cruel gods he prayed:
        'See, fortune, where thy Pompey lies, and oh,
In pity one last, little boon bestow.
995   He asks no heaps of frankincense to rise,*
No eastern odours to perfume the skies,
No Roman necks his patriot corse to bear,*
No reverend train of statues to appear,*
No pageant shows his glories to record,
1000 And tell the triumphs of his conquering sword,
No instruments in plaintive notes to sound,
No legions sad to march in solemn round –

A bier, no better than the vulgar need,
A little wood the kindling flame to feed,
1005 With some poor hand to tend the homely fire,
Is all these wretched relics now require.
Your wrath, ye powers, Cornelia's hand denies;*
Let that for every other loss suffice.
She takes not her last leave, she weeps not here,
1010 And yet she is, ye gods, she is too near!'*
    Thus while he spoke he saw where through the
        shade
A slender flame its gleamy light displayed;
There as it chanced, abandoned and unmourned,
A poor, neglected body lonely burned.
1015 He seized the kindled brands, 'and oh!', he said,
'Whoe'er thou art, forgive me, friendless shade,
And, though unpitied and forlorn thou lie,
Thyself a better office shalt supply.
If there be sense in souls departed, thine
1020 To my great leader shall her rites resign,
With humble joy shall quit her meaner claim,
And blush to burn, when Pompey wants the flame.'
    He said, and, gathering in his garment, bore
The glowing fragments to the neighbouring shore.
1025 There soon arrived the noble trunk he found,
Half washed into the flood, half resting on the
        ground.
With diligence his hands a trench prepare,
Fit it around, and place the body there.
No cloven oaks in lofty order lie
1030 To lift the great patrician to the sky;
By chance a few poor planks were hard at hand,
By some late shipwreck cast upon the strand;
These pious Cordus gathers where they lay,
And plants about the chief as best he may.
1035   Now while the blaze began to rise around,
The youth sat mournful by upon the ground;
'And oh', he cried, 'if this unworthy flame
Disgrace thy great, majestic, Roman name,
If the rude outrage of the stormy seas
1040 Seem better to thy ghost than rites like these,
Yet let thy injured shade the wrong forget,

Which duty and officious zeal commit.
Fate seems itself in my excuse to plead,
And thy hard fortune justifies my deed.
1045　I only wished – nor is that wish in vain –
To save thee from the monsters of the main,
From vultures' claws, from lions that devour,
From mortal malice, and from Caesar's power.
No longer then this humbler flame withstand –
1050　'Tis lighted to thee by a Roman hand.
If e'er the gods permit unhappy me
Once more thy loved Hesperian land to see,
With me thy exiled ashes shall return,
And chaste Cornelia give thee to thy urn.
1055　Meanwhile a signal shall my care provide,
Some future Roman votary to guide,
When with due rites thy fate he would deplore,
And thy pale head to these thy limbs restore,
Then shall he mark the witness of my stone,
1060　And, taught by me, thy sacred ghost atone.'
　　He spoke, and straight with busy, pious hands
Heaped on the smoking corse the scattered brands.
Slow sunk amidst the fire the wasting dead,
And the faint flame with dropping marrow fed.
1065　Now 'gan the glittering stars to fade away
Before the rosy promise of the day,
When the pale youth th'unfinished rites forsook,
And to the covert* of his cave betook.
　　Ah, why thus rashly would thy fears disclaim*
1070　That only deed which must record thy name?
Ev'n Caesar's self shall just applause bestow,*
And praise the Roman that inters his foe;
Securely tell him where his son is laid,
And he shall give thee back his mangled head.
1075　　But soon, behold, the bolder youth returns,
While, half-consumed, the smouldering carcass
　　　　burns,
Ere yet the cleansing fire had melted down
The fleshy muscles from the firmer bone.
He quenched the relics in the briny wave,
1080　And hid them hasty in a narrow grave;
Then with a stone the sacred dust he binds,

To guard it from the breath of scattering winds,
And, lest some heedless mariner should come
And violate the warrior's humble tomb,
1085 Thus with a line the monument he keeps:
Beneath this stone the once great Pompey sleeps.
O fortune! Can thy malice swell so high?
Canst thou with Caesar's every wish comply?
Must he, thy Pompey once, thus meanly lie?
1090 But oh, forbear, mistaken man, forbear!
Nor dare to fix the mighty Pompey there;
Where there are seas, or air, or earth, or skies,
Where-e'er Rome's empire stretches, Pompey lies.
Far be the vile memorial then conveyed,
1095 Nor let this stone the partial gods upbraid!*
Shall Hercules all Oeta's heights demand,*
And Nysa's hill for Bacchus only stand,
While one poor pebble is the warrior's doom
That fought the cause of liberty and Rome?
1100 If fate decrees he must in Egypt lie,
Let the whole fertile realm his grave supply,
Yield the wide country to his awful shade;
Nor let us dare on any part to tread,
Fearful to violate the mighty dead.
1105 But if one stone must bear the sacred name,
Let it be filled with long records* of fame;
There let the passenger,* with wonder, read,
The pirates vanquished and the ocean freed,
Sertorius taught to yield, the Alpine war,*
1110 And the young Roman knight's triumphal car;
With these the mighty Pontic king* be placed,
And every nation of the vanquished east;
Tell with what loud applause of Rome he drove
Thrice his glad wheels to Capitolian Jove,
1115 Tell too the patriot's greatest, best renown,
Tell how the victor laid his empire down,
And changed his armour for the peaceful gown.
But ah, what marbles to the task suffice?
Instead of these, turn, Roman,* turn thy eyes,
1120 Seek the known name our fasti used to wear,
The noble mark of many a glorious year,
The name that wont the trophied arch* to grace,

And ev'n in temples of the gods found place;
Decline thee lowly, bending to the ground,
1125 And there that name, that Pompey may be found.
      O fatal land! What curse can I bestow
Equal to those we to thy mischiefs owe?
Well did the wise Cumaean maid* of yore*
Warn our Hesperian chiefs to shun thy shore.
1130 Forbid, just heavens, your dews to bless the soil,
And thou withhold thy waters, fruitful Nile!
Let Egypt like the land of Ethiops* burn,
And her fat earth to sandy deserts turn.
Have we with honours dead Osiris crowned,
1135 And mourned him to the tinkling timbrel's* sound,
Received her Isis to divine abodes,
And ranked her dogs deformed with Roman gods,*
While in despite to Pompey's injured shade
Low in her dust his sacred bones are laid?*
1140 And thou, O Rome, by whose forgetful hand*
Altars and temples reared to tyrants stand,
Canst thou neglect to call thy hero home,
And leave his ghost in banishment to roam?
What though the victor's frown and thy base fear
1145 Bade thee at first the pious task forbear,
Yet now, at least, oh let him now return,
And rest with honour in a Roman urn.
Nor let mistaken superstition dread
On such occasions to disturb the dead;
1150 Oh, would commanding Rome my hand employ,*
The impious task should be performed with joy;*
How would I fly to tear him from that tomb,
And bear his ashes in my bosom home!
Perhaps, when flames their dreadful ravage make,
1155 Or groaning earth shall from the centre shake,
When blasting dews the rising harvest seize,
Or nations sicken with some dire disease,
The gods in mercy to us shall command
To fetch our Pompey from th'accursèd land.
1160 Then, when his venerable bones draw near,
In long procession shall the priests appear,
And their great chief* the sacred relics bear.
Or if thou still possess the Pharian shore,

L. Cheron Inv.   *G. V.d Gucht Sculp.*

Cordus with the headless body of Pompey

What traveller but shall thy grave explore,
1165 Whether he tread Syene's burning soil,
Or visit sultry Thebe* or fruitful Nile,
Or if the merchant, drawn by hopes of gain,
Seek rich Arabia and the ruddy main,
With holy rites thy shade he shall atone,
1170 And bow before thy venerable stone.
For who but shall prefer thy tomb above
The meaner fane* of an Egyptian Jove?*
Nor envy thou if abject Romans raise
Statues and temples to their tyrant's praise;
1175 Though his proud name on altars may preside,
And thine be washed by every rolling tide,
Thy grave shall the vain pageantry despise,
Thy grave, where that great god, thy fortune, lies.
Ev'n those who kneel not to the gods above,
1180 Nor offer sacrifice or prayer to Jove,
To the bidental* bend their humble eyes,
And worship where the buried thunder lies.
    Perhaps fate wills, in honour to thy fame,
No marble shall record thy mighty name;

1185   So may thy dust, e'er long, be worn away,
       And all remembrance of thy wrongs decay;
       Perhaps a better age shall come, when none
       Shall think thee ever laid beneath this stone,
       When Egypt's boast of Pompey's tomb shall prove
1190   As unbelieved a tale as Crete relates of Jove.*

BOOK NINE

Nor in the dying embers of its pile*
Slept the great soul upon the banks of Nile,
Nor longer, by the earthly parts restrained,
Amidst its wretched relics was detained,
5   But active and impatient of delay*
Shot from the mouldering heap and upwards urged
        its way.
Far in those azure regions of the air
Which border on the rolling starry sphere,
Beyond our orb and nearer to that height
10 Where Cynthia* drives around her silver light,
Their happy seats the demigods possess,*
Refined by virtue and prepared for bliss,
Of life unblamed, a pure and pious race,   ⎤
Worthy that lower heav'n and stars to grace,   ⎬
15 Divine and equal to the glorious place.   ⎦
There Pompey's soul, adorned with heavenly light,
Soon shone among the rest, and as the rest was
        bright.
New to the blessed abode, with wonder filled,
The stars and moving planets he beheld;
20 Then looking down on the sun's feeble ray   ⎤
Surveyed our dusky, faint, imperfect day,   ⎬
And under what a cloud of night we lay.   ⎦
But when he saw how on the shore forlorn
His headless trunk was cast for public scorn,
25 When he beheld how envious fortune still
Took pains to use a senseless carcass ill,
He smiled at the vain malice of his foe,
And pitied impotent mankind below.
Then lightly passing o'er Emathia's plain,
30 His flying navy scattered on the main,*
And cruel Caesar's tents, he fixed at last
His residence in Brutus' sacred breast;
There brooding o'er his country's wrongs he sate,*
The state's avenger and the tyrant's fate;

35   There mournful Rome might still her Pompey find –
      There and in Cato's free, unconquered mind.
          He,* while in deep suspense the world yet lay,
      Anxious and doubtful whom it should obey,
      Hatred avowed to Pompey's self did bear,
40   Though his companion in the common war,
      Though by the Senate's just command they stood
      Engaged together for the public good;
      But dread Pharsalia did all doubts decide,
      And firmly fixed him to the vanquished side.
45   His helpless country, like an orphan left,
      Friendless and poor, of all support bereft,
      He took and cherished with a father's care,
      He comforted, he bade her not to fear,
      And taught her feeble hands once more the trade
          of war.
50   Nor lust of empire did his courage sway,
      Nor hate, nor proud repugnance to obey;
      Passions and private interest he forgot –
      Not for himself but liberty he fought.
      Straight to Corcyra's port his way he bent,*
55   The swift advancing victor to prevent,
      Who marching sudden on, to new success,
      The scattered legions might with ease oppress;
      There with the ruins of Emathia's field,
      The flying host, a thousand ships he filled.
60   Who that* from land with wonder had descried*
      The passing fleet, in all its naval pride,
      Stretched wide and o'er the distant ocean spread,
      Could have believed those mighty numbers fled?
      Malea o'erpast, and the Taenarian shore,
65   With swelling sails he for Cythera* bore;
      Then Crete he saw, and with a northern wind
      Soon left the famed Dictaean isle behind.*
      Urged by the bold Phycuntine's churlish pride,
      (Their shores, their haven, to his fleet denied)
70   The chief revenged the wrong, and, as he passed,
      Laid their unhospitable city waste.
      Thence wafted forward, to the coast he came
      Which took of old from Palinure its name.*

(Nor Italy this monument alone*

75   Can boast, since Libya's Palinure has shown
     Her peaceful shores were to the Trojan known.)
     From hence they soon descry, with doubtful pain,
     Another navy on the distant main.
     Anxious they stand, and now expect the foe,

80   Now their companions in the public woe;
     The victor's haste inclines them most to fear;
     Each vessel seems a hostile face to wear,
     And, every sail they spy, they fancy Caesar there.
     But oh, those ships a different burden bore,

85   A mournful freight they wafted to the shore,
     Sorrows that might tears ev'n from Cato gain,
     And teach the rigid Stoic to complain.
          When long the sad Cornelia's prayers in vain
     Had tried the flying navy to detain,

90   With Sextus long had strove, and long implored,
     To wait the relics of her murdered lord –
     The waves perchance might the dear pledge restore,
     And waft him bleeding from the faithless shore –
     Still grief and love their various hopes inspire,

95   Till she beholds her Pompey's funeral fire,
     Till on the land she sees th'ignoble flame
     Ascend unequal to the hero's name;
     Then into just complaints at length she broke,
     And thus with pious indignation spoke:

100 'O fortune, dost thou then disdain t'afford
     My love's last office to my dearest lord?
     Am I one chaste, one last embrace denied?
     Shall I not lay me by his clay-cold side,
     Nor tears to bathe his gaping wounds provide?

105 Am I unworthy the sad torch to bear,
     To light the flame and burn my flowing hair,
     To gather from the shore the noble spoil,
     And place it decent* on the fatal pile?
     Shall not his bones and sacred dust be borne,

110 In this sad bosom, to their peaceful urn?
     Whate'er the last consuming flame shall leave
     Shall not this widowed hand by right receive,
     And to the gods the precious relics give?

Perhaps this last respect which I should show ⎫
115 Some vile Egyptian hand does now bestow,   ⎬
Injurious to the Roman shade below.   ⎭
Happy, my Crassus, were thy bones which lay*
Exposed to Parthian birds and beasts of prey!
Here the last rites the cruel gods allow,
120 And for a curse my Pompey's pile bestow.
For ever will the same sad fate return?   ⎫
Still an unburied husband must I mourn,   ⎬
And weep my sorrows o'er an empty urn?   ⎭
But why should tombs be built or urns be made?
125 Does grief like mine require their feeble aid?
Is he not lodged, thou wretch,* within thy heart,
And fixed in every dearest vital part?
O'er monuments surviving wives may grieve –
She ne'er will need them who disdains to live.
130 But oh, behold where yon malignant flames
Cast feebly forth their mean, inglorious beams;
From my loved lord, his dear remains, they rise,
And bring my Pompey to my weeping eyes;
And now they sink, the languid lights decay,   ⎫
135 The cloudy smoke all eastward rolls away, ⎬
And wafts my hero to the rising day.   ⎭
Me too the winds demand, with freshening gales;
Envious they call, and stretch the swelling sails.
No land on earth seems dear as Egypt now,   ⎫
140 No land that crowns and triumphs did bestow, ⎬
And with new laurels bound my Pompey's brow.   ⎭
That happy Pompey to my thoughts is lost –
He that is left lies dead on yonder coast;
He, only he, is all I now demand,
145 For him I linger near this cursèd land;
Endeared by crimes, for horrors loved the more,
I cannot, will not, leave the Pharian shore.
Thou, Sextus, thou shalt prove the chance of war, ⎫
And through the world thy father's ensigns bear; ⎬
150 Then hear his last command entrusted to my care: ⎭
"Whene'er my last, my fatal hour shall come,*
Arm you, my sons, for liberty and Rome;
While one shall of our freeborn race remain,
Let him prevent the tyrant Caesar's reign.

155   From each free city round, from every land,
    Their warlike aid in Pompey's name demand.
    These are the parties, these the friends he leaves,
    This legacy your dying father gives.
    If for the sea's wide rule your arms you bear,
160   A Pompey ne'er can want a navy there;
    Heirs of my fame, my sons, shall wage my war.
    Only be bold, unconquered in the fight,
    And, like your father, still defend the right.
    To Cato, if for liberty he stand,
165   Submit, and yield you to his ruling hand,
    Brave, just, and only worthy to command."
    At length to thee, my Pompey, I am just –*
    I have survived and well discharged my trust;
    Through chaos now and the dark realms below,*
170   To follow thee, a willing shade I go;
    If longer with a lingering fate I strive,
    'Tis but to prove the pain of being* alive,
    'Tis to be cursed for daring to survive.
    She who could bear to see thy wounds and live
175   New proofs of love and fatal grief shall give.
    Nor need she fly for succour to the sword,*
    The steepy precipice, and deadly cord –
    She from herself shall find her own relief,
    And scorns to die of any death but grief.'
180   So said the matron, and about her head
    Her veil she draws, her mournful eyes to shade.
    Resolved to shroud in thickest shades her woe,
    She seeks the ship's deep, darksome hold below;
    There lonely left, at leisure to complain,
185   She hugs her sorrows and enjoys her pain;
    Still with fresh tears the living grief would feed,
    And fondly loves it in her husband's stead.
    In vain the beating surges rage aloud,
    And swelling Eurus* grumbles in the shroud;
190   Her nor the waves beneath nor winds above
    Nor all the noisy cries of fear can move;
    In sullen peace composed for death she lies,
    And, waiting, longs to hear the tempest rise,
    Then hopes the seamen's vows shall all be crossed,
195   Prays for the storm, and wishes to be lost.

Soon from the Pharian coast the navy bore,*
And sought through foamy seas the Cyprian shore;
Soft eastern gales prevailing thence alone
To Cato's camp and Libya waft them on.
200   With mournful looks from land (as oft we know,*
A sad, prophetic spirit waits on woe)
Pompey* his brother and the fleet beheld
Now near advancing o'er the watery field;
Straight to the beach with headlong haste he flies;
205   'Where is our father, Sextus, where?', he cries;
'Do we yet live? Stands yet the sovereign state?
Or does the world, with Pompey, yield to fate?
Sink we at length before the conquering foe?
And is the mighty head of Rome laid low?'
210   He said; the mournful brother thus replied:
'O happy thou, whom lands and seas divide
From woes which did to these sad eyes betide –
These eyes, which of their horror still complain,
Since they beheld our godlike father slain!
215   Nor did his fate an equal death afford,
Nor suffered him to fall by Caesar's sword.
Trusting in vain to hospitable gods,
He died, oppressed by vile Egyptian odds;*
By the cursed monarch of Nile's slimy wave
220   He fell, a victim to the crown he gave.
Yes, I beheld the dire, the bloody deed,
These eyes beheld our valiant father bleed;
Amazed I looked, and scarce believed my fear,
Nor thought th'Egyptian could so greatly dare,
225   But still I looked, and fancied Caesar there.
But oh, not all his wounds so much did move,
Pierced my sad soul, and struck my filial love,
As that his venerable head they bear,
Their wanton trophy, fixed upon a spear;
230   Through every town 'tis shown, the vulgar's sport,
And the lewd laughter of the tyrant's court.
'Tis said that Ptolemy preserves this prize,
Proof of the deed, to glut the victor's eyes.
The body, whether rent or borne away
235   By foul Egyptian dogs and birds of prey,
Whether within their greedy maws entombed,

Or by those wretched flames we saw consumed,
Its fate as yet we know not, but forgive;
That crime unpunished to the gods we leave –
240   'Tis for the part preserved alone we grieve.'
       Scarce had he ended thus when Pompey, warm
With noble fury, calls aloud to arm,
Nor seeks in sighs and helpless tears relief,
But thus in pious rage expressed his grief:
245   'Hence all aboard, and haste to put to sea,
Urge on against the winds our adverse way;
With me let every Roman leader go,
Since civil wars were ne'er so just as now.*
Pompey's unburied relics ask your aid,
250   Call for due rites and honours to be paid.
Let Egypt's tyrant pour a purple flood,
And soothe the ghost with his inglorious blood.
Not Alexander shall his priests defend,*
Forced from his golden shrine he shall descend –
255   In Mareotis* deep I'll plunge him down,
Deep in the sluggish waves the royal carcass drown.
From his proud pyramid Amasis torn,*
With his long dynasties, my rage shall mourn,
And floating down their muddy Nile be borne.
260   Each stately tomb and monumental stone
For thee, unburied Pompey, shall atone.
Isis no more shall draw the cheated crowd,
Nor god Osiris in his linen shroud;
Stripped of their shrines, with scorn they shall be
          cast,
265   To be by ignominious hands defaced;
Their holy Apis of diviner breed*
To Pompey's dust a sacrifice shall bleed,
While burning deities the flame shall feed.*
Waste shall the land be laid, and never know
270   The tiller's care, nor feel the crooked plough;
None shall be left for whom the Nile may flow,
Till, the gods banished and the people gone,
Egypt to Pompey shall be left alone.'
       He said; then hasty to revenge he flew,
275   And seaward out the ready navy drew.
But cooler Cato did the youth assuage,

And, praising much, compressed his filial rage.
　　Meantime the shores, the seas and skies around
With mournful cries for Pompey's death resound.
280　A rare example have their sorrows shown,
　　Yet* in no age beside nor people known,
　　How falling power did with compassion meet,
　　And crowds deplored* the ruins of the great.
　　But when the sad Cornelia first appeared,
285　When on the deck her mournful head she reared,
　　Her locks hung rudely o'er the matron's face,
　　With all the pomp of grief's disordered grace;
　　When they beheld her, wasted quite with woe,
　　And spent with tears that never ceased to flow,
290　Again they feel their loss, again complain,
　　And heaven and earth ring with their cries again.
　　Soon as she landed on the friendly strand,*
　　Her lord's last rites employ her pious hand,
　　To his dear shade she builds a funeral pile,
295　And decks it proud with many a noble spoil.
　　There shone his arms with antique gold inlaid,　⎤
　　There the rich robes which she herself had made,　⎬
　　Robes to imperial Jove in triumph erst*　　　　　 ⎟
　　　　displayed;*　　　　　　　　　　　　　　　　⎦
　　The relics of his past victorious days　　⎤
300　Now this his latest trophy serve to raise,　⎬
　　And in one common flame together blaze.　⎦
　　Such was the weeping matron's pious care;
　　The soldiers, taught by her, their fires prepare,
　　To every valiant friend a pile they build
305　That fell for Rome in cursed Pharsalia's field;
　　Stretched wide along the shores the flames extend,
　　And grateful to the wandering shades ascend.
　　So when Apulian hinds* with art renew
　　The wintry pastures to their verdant hue,
310　That flowers may rise and springing grass return,
　　With spreading flames the withered fields they burn;
　　Garganus then and lofty Vultur blaze,
　　And draw the distant wondering swains to gaze;
　　Far are the glittering fires descried by night,
315　And gild the dusky skies around with light.
　　　　But oh, not all the sorrows of the crowd

That spoke their free, impatient thoughts aloud,
That taxed the gods, as authors of their woe,
And charged them with neglect of things below,
320 Not all the marks of the wild people's love
The hero's* soul, like Cato's praise, could move;
Few were his words, but from an honest heart,*)
Where faction and where favour had no part,   }
But truth made up for passion and for art.)

325 'We've lost a Roman citizen', he said;*
'One of the noblest of that name is dead,
Who, though not equal to our fathers found,
Nor by their strictest rules of justice bound,
Yet from his faults this benefit we draw,   )
330 He, for his country's good, transgressed her law, }
To keep a bold, licentious age in awe.   )
Rome held her freedom still, though he was great;*
He swayed the Senate, but they ruled the state.
When crowds were willing to have worn his chain,)
335 He chose his private station to retain,   }
That all might free and equal all remain.   )
War's boundless power he never sought to use,
Nor asked but what the people might refuse;
Much he possessed, and wealthy was his store,)
340 Yet still he gathered but to give the more,   }
And Rome, while he was rich, could ne'er be poor.)
He drew the sword, but knew its rage to charm,
And loved peace best when he was forced to arm;
Unmoved with all the glittering pomp of power,
345 He took with joy, but laid it down with more;
His chaster household and his frugal board)
Nor lewdness did nor luxury afford,   }
Ev'n in the highest fortunes of their lord.)
His noble name, his country's honour grown,)
350 Was venerably round the nations known,   }
And as Rome's fairest light and brightest glory }
     shone.   )
When betwixt Marius and fierce Sulla tossed
The commonwealth her ancient freedom lost,
Some shadow yet was left, some show of power –
355 Now ev'n the name with Pompey is no more:
Senate and people* all at once are gone,

Nor need the tyrant blush to mount the throne.
O happy Pompey, happy in thy fate,
Happy by falling with the falling state,
360   Thy death a benefit the gods did grant –
Thou might'st have lived those Pharian swords to
            want.*
Freedom, at least, thou dost by dying gain,
Nor liv'st to see thy Julia's father reign;
Free death is man's first bliss, the next is to be
            slain.*
365   Such mercy only I from Juba* crave,
If fortune should ordain me Juba's slave:
To Caesar let him show, but show me dead,
And keep my carcass, so he takes my head.'
        He said, and pleased the noble shade below
370   More than a thousand orators could do,
Though Tully* too had lent his charming tongue,
And Rome's full forum with his praise had rung.
        But discord new infects the sullen crowd,*
And now they tell their discontents aloud,
375   When Tarchon* first his flying ensigns bore,
Called out to march, and hastened to the shore;
Him Cato thus, pursuing as he moved,
Sternly bespoke, and justly thus reproved:
        'O restless author of the roving war,
380   Dost thou again piratic arms prepare?
Pompey, thy terror and thy scourge, is gone,
And now thou hop'st to rule the seas alone.'
        He said, and bent his frown upon the rest,
Of whom one bolder thus the chief addressed,
385   And thus their weariness of war confessed:
        'For Pompey's sake – nor thou disdain to hear –
The civil war we wage, these arms we bear;
Him we preferred to peace, but, Cato, now,
That cause, that master of our arms lies low.
390   Let us no more our absent country mourn,
But to our homes and household gods return,
To the chaste arms from whose embrace we fled,
And the dear pledges of the nuptial bed.
For oh, what period can the war attend,*

395   Which nor Pharsalia's field nor Pompey's death can
           end?
       The better times of flying life are past –
       Let death come gently on in peace at last;
       Let age at length with providential care
       The necessary pile and urn prepare.
400   All rites the cruel civil war denies –
       Part ev'n of Pompey yet unburied lies.
       Though vanquished, yet by no barbarian hand,*
       We fear not exile in a foreign land,
       Nor are our necks by fortune now bespoke
405   To bear the Scythian or Armenian yoke;
       The victor still a citizen we own,
       And yield obedience to the Roman gown.
       While Pompey lived, he bore the sovereign sway –
       Caesar was next, and him we now obey;
410   With reverence be the sacred shade adored,
       But war has given us now another lord:
       To Caesar and superior chance we yield –
       All was determined in Emathia's field.
       Nor shall our arms on other leaders wait,
415   Nor for uncertain hopes molest the state –
       We followed Pompey once, but now we follow
           fate.
       What terms, what safety can we hope for now
       But what the victor's mercy shall allow?
       Once Pompey's presence justified the cause,
420   Then fought we for our liberties and laws;
       With him the honours of that cause lie dead,
       And all the sanctity of war is fled.
       If, Cato, thou for Rome these arms dost bear,
       If still thy country only be thy care,
425   Seek we the legions where Rome's ensigns fly,
       Where her proud eagles wave their wings on high;
       No matter who to Pompey's power succeeds,
       We follow where a Roman consul* leads.'
           This said, he leaped aboard; the youthful sort
430   Join in his flight, and haste to leave the port.
       The senseless crowd their liberty disdain,*
       And long to wear victorious Caesar's chain.

Tyrannic power now sudden seemed to threat ⎫
The ancient glories of Rome's freeborn state, ⎬
435   Till Cato spoke, and thus deferred her fate: ⎭
     'Did then your vows and servile prayers conspire
Nought but a haughty master to desire?
Did you, when eager for the battle, come*
The slaves of Pompey, not the friends of Rome?
440   Now weary of the toil from war you fly,
And idly lay your useless armour by,
Your hands neglect to wield the shining sword,
Nor can you fight but for a king and lord.
Some mighty chief you want, for whom to sweat; ⎫
445   Yourselves you know not, or at least forget, ⎬
And fondly* bleed that others may be great. ⎭
Meanly you toil to give yourselves away,
And die to leave the world a tyrant's prey.
The gods and fortune do at length afford
450   A cause most worthy of a Roman sword.
At length 'tis safe to conquer. Pompey now*
Cannot by your success too potent grow;
Yet now ignobly you withhold your hands,
When nearer liberty your aid demands.
455   Of three who durst the sovereign power invade,
Two by your fortune's kinder doom lie dead;*
And shall the Pharian sword and Parthian bow
Do more for liberty and Rome than you?
Base as ye are, in vile subjection go,
460   And scorn what Ptolemy did ill bestow.*
Ignobly innocent and meanly good
You durst not stain your hardy hands in blood;
Feebly awhile you fought, but soon did yield,
And fled the first from dire Pharsalia's field;
465   Go then secure, for Caesar will be good,
Will pardon those who are with ease subdued;
The pitying victor will in mercy spare
The wretch who never durst provoke his war.
Go, sordid slaves! One lordly master gone,
470   Like heirlooms go from father to the son.
Still to enhance your servile merit more,
Bear sad Cornelia weeping from the shore,
Meanly for hire expose the matron's life,

Metellus' daughter sell, and Pompey's wife;
475 Take too his sons – let Caesar find in you
Wretches that may ev'n Ptolemy outdo.
But let not my devoted* life be spared –
The tyrant greatly shall that deed reward.
Such is the price of Cato's hated head
480 That all your former wars shall well be paid;
Kill me, and in my blood do Caesar right –
'Tis mean to have no other guilt but flight.'
     He said, and stopped the flying naval power;
Back they returned, repenting, to the shore.
485 As when the bees their waxen town forsake,
Careless in air their wandering way they take;
No more in clustering swarms condensed they fly,
But fleet* uncertain through the various sky,
No more from flowers they suck the liquid sweet,
490 But all their care and industry forget;
Then, if at length the tinkling brass they hear,*
With swift amaze their flight they soon forbear,
Sudden their flowery labours they renew,
Hang on the thyme and sip the balmy dew;
495 Meantime, secure on Hybla's fragrant plain,
With joy exults the happy shepherd swain;
Proud that his art had thus preserved his store,
He scorns to think his homely cottage poor.
With such prevailing force did Cato's care* ⎫
500 The fierce, impatient soldiers' minds prepare, ⎬
To learn obedience and endure the war. ⎭
     And now their minds, unknowing of repose,
With busy toil to exercise he chose;
Still with successive labours are they plied,
505 And oft in long and weary marches tried.
Before Cyrene's walls they now sit down, ⎫
And here the victor's mercy well was shown – ⎬
He takes no vengeance of the captive town; ⎭
Patient he spares, and bids the vanquished live,
510 Since Cato, who could conquer, could forgive.
Hence Libyan Juba's realms they mean t'explore,
Juba, who borders on the swarthy Moor,
But nature's boundaries the journey stay –
The Syrts* are fixed athwart the middle way;

515   Yet led by daring virtue on they press,
       Scorn opposition, and still hope success.
           When nature's hand the first formation tried,
       When seas from lands she did at first divide,
       The Syrts, nor quite of sea nor land bereft,
520   A mingled mass uncertain still she left;
       For nor the land with seas is quite o'er-spread,
       Nor sink the waters deep their oozy bed,
       Nor earth defends its shore, nor lifts aloft its head.
       The site with neither and with each complies,
525   Doubtful and inaccessible it lies:
       Or 'tis a sea with shallows banked around,
       Or 'tis a broken land with waters drowned;
       Here shores advanced o'er Neptune's rule we find,
       And there an inland ocean lags behind.
530   Thus nature's purpose, by herself destroyed,
       Is useless to herself and unemployed,
       And part of her creation still is void.
       Perhaps, when first the world and time began,
       Here swelling tides and plenteous waters ran,
535   But, long confining on the burning zone,
       The sinking seas have felt the neighbouring sun;
       Still by degrees we see how they decay,
       And scarce resist the thirsty god of day.
       Perhaps, in distant ages, 'twill be found,
540   When future suns have run the burning round,
       These Syrts shall all be dry and solid ground;
       Small are the depths their scanty waves retain,
       And earth grows daily on the yielding main.
           And now the loaden* fleet with active oars*
545   Divide the liquid plain,* and leave the shores;
       When cloudy skies a gathering storm presage,*
       And Auster* from the south began to rage,
       Full from the land the sounding tempest roars,
       Repels the swelling surge and sweeps the shores;
550   The wind pursues, drives on the rolling sand,
       And gives new limits to the growing land.
       Spite of the seaman's toil the storm prevails:
       In vain with skilful strength he hands* the sails,
       In vain the cordy cables bind them fast,
555   At once it rips and rends them from the mast.

At once the winds the fluttering canvas tear,
Then whirl and whisk it through the sportive air.
Some timely for the rising rage prepared
Furl the loose sheet, and lash it to the yard;
560   In vain their care – sudden the furious blast
Snaps by the board, and bears away the mast;
Of tacklings, sails and mast at once bereft,
The ship a naked, helpless hull is left;
Forced round and round she quits her purposed way,
565   And bounds uncertain o'er the swelling sea.
But happier some a steady course maintain,
Who stand far out and keep the deeper main;
Their masts they cut, and, driving with the tide,
Safe o'er the surge beneath the tempest ride;
570   In vain did from the southern coast their foe,
All black with clouds, old stormy Auster blow;
Lowly secure amidst the waves they lay,
Old ocean heaved his back, and rolled them on their
          way.
Some on the shallows strike,* and doubtful stand,
575   Part beat* by waves, part fixed upon the sand.
Now pent amidst the shoals the billows roar,
Dash on the banks, and scorn the new-made shore;
Now by the wind driv'n on in heaps they swell –
The steadfast banks both winds and waves repel;
580   Still with united force they rage in vain,
The sandy piles their station fixed maintain,*
And lift their heads secure amidst the watery plain.
There 'scaped from seas, upon the faithless strand,
With weeping eyes the shipwrecked seamen stand,
585   And, cast ashore, look vainly out for land.
Thus some were lost, but far the greater part,
Preserved from danger by the pilot's art,
Keep on their course, a happier fate partake,
And reach in safety the Tritonian lake.
590   These waters to the tuneful god* are dear,
Whose vocal shell the sea-green Nereids hear;
These Pallas* loves, so tells reporting fame,
Here first from heaven to earth the goddess came
(Heaven's neighbourhood the warmer clime betrays,
595   And speaks the nearer sun's immediate rays),

Here her first footsteps on the brink she stayed,
Here in the watery glass her form surveyed,
And called herself from hence the chaste Tritonian
    maid.
Here Lethe's* streams from secret springs below
600 Rise to the light; here heavily and slow
The silent, dull, forgetful waters flow.
Here by the wakeful dragon kept of old
Hesperian plants grew rich with living gold;
Long since the fruit was from the branches torn,*
605 And now the gardens their lost honours* mourn.
Such was in ancient times the tale received,
Such by our good forefathers was believed,
Nor let enquirers the tradition wrong,*
Or dare to question now the poet's sacred song.
610 Then take it for a truth: the wealthy wood
Here under golden boughs low bending stood;
On some large tree his folds the serpent wound;
The fair Hesperian virgins watched around,
And joined to guard the rich, forbidden ground.
615 But great Alcides came to end their care,
Stripped the gay grove, and left the branches bare,
Then back returning sought the Argive* shore,
And the bright spoil to proud Eurystheus* bore.
    These famous regions and the Syrts o'erpast,
620 They reached the Garamantian coast at last;*
Here under Pompey's* care the navy lies
Beneath the gentlest clime of Libya's skies.
    But Cato's soul, by dangers unrestrained,*
Ease and a dull, unactive life disdained.
625 His daring virtue urges to go on
Through desert lands and nations yet unknown,
To march and prove th'unhospitable ground,
To shun the Syrts, and lead the soldier round,
Since now tempestuous seasons vex the sea,
630 And the declining year forbids the watery way;
He sees the cloudy, drizzling winter near,
And hopes kind rains may cool the sultry air –
So haply may they journey on secure,
Nor burning heats nor killing frosts endure;

635 But, while cool winds the winter's breath supplies, ⎫
With gentle warmth the Libyan sun may rise,   ⎬
And both may join and temper well the skies.   ⎭
  But e'er the toilsome march he undertook,
The hero thus the listening host bespoke:
640 'Fellows in arms, whose bliss, whose chiefest good,
Is Rome's defence and freedom bought with blood,
You, who, to die with liberty, from far
Have followed Cato in this fatal war,
Be now for virtue's noblest task prepared,
645 For labours many, perilous and hard.
Think through what burning climes, what wilds ⎫
  we go: ⎬
No leafy shades the naked deserts know,   ⎪
Nor silver streams through flowery meadows flow; ⎭
But horrors there and various deaths abound,
650 And serpents guard th'unhospitable ground.
Hard is the way, but thus our fate demands –
Rome and her laws we seek amidst these sands.
Let those who, glowing with their country's love,
Resolve with me these dreadful plains to prove,
655 Nor of return nor safety once debate,
But only dare to go, and leave the rest to fate.
Think not I mean the dangers to disguise,
Or hide them from the cheated vulgar's eyes;
Those, only those, shall in my fate partake,
660 Who love the daring for the danger's sake,
Those who can suffer all that worst can come,
And think it what they owe themselves and Rome.
If any yet shall doubt, or yet shall fear, *
If life be more than liberty his care,
665 Here, e'er we journey further, let him stay, ⎫
Inglorious let him like a slave obey,   ⎬
And seek a master in some safer way.   ⎭
Foremost, behold, I lead you to the toil,
My feet shall foremost print the dusty soil;
670 Strike me the first, thou flaming god of day,
First let me feel thy fierce, thy scorching ray;
Ye living poisons all, ye snaky train, *
Meet me the first upon the fatal plain.
In every pain which you my warriors fear

675 Let me be first and teach you how to bear.
 Who sees me pant for drought or fainting first,*
 Let him upbraid me and complain of thirst.
 If e'er for shelter to the shades I fly,
 Me let him curse, me, for the sultry sky.
680 If while the weary soldier marches on, ⎫
 Your leader by distinguished* ease be known, ⎬
 Forsake my cause, and leave me there alone. ⎭
 The sands, the serpents, thirst and burning heat
 Are dear to patience and to virtue sweet –
685 Virtue, that scorns on cowards' terms to please,
 Or cheaply to be bought, or won with ease;
 But then she joys, then smiles upon her state, ⎫
 Then fairest to herself, then most complete, ⎬
 When glorious danger makes her truly great. ⎭
690 So Libya's plains alone shall wipe away
 The foul dishonours of Pharsalia's day;
 So shall your courage now transcend that fear –
 You fled with glory there to conquer here.'
  He said, and hardy love of toil inspired,
695 And every breast with godlike ardour fired.
 Straight, careless of return, without delay,
 Through the wide waste he took his pathless way.
 Libya, ordained to be his last retreat,*
 Receives the hero, fearless of his fate;
700 Here the good gods his last of labours doom, ⎫
 Here shall his bones and sacred dust find room, ⎬
 And his great head be hid within an humble tomb. ⎭
  If this large globe be portioned right by fame,*
 Then one third part shall sandy Libya claim;*
705 But if we count as suns descend and rise,
 If we divide by east and west the skies,
 Then with fair Europe Libya shall combine,
 And both to make the western half shall join,
 Whilst wide-extended Asia fills the rest, ⎫
710 Of all from Tanais to Nile possessed, ⎬
 And reigns sole empress of the dawning east. ⎭
 Of all the Libyan soil the kindliest found*
 Far to the western seas extends its bound,
 Where cooling gales, where gentle zephyrs fly,
715 And setting suns adorn the gaudy sky;

And yet ev'n here no liquid fountain's vein
Wells through the soil and gurgles o'er the plain,
But from our northern clime, our gentler heaven,
Refreshing dews and fruitful rains are driven,
720   All bleak the god, cold Boreas, spreads his wing,
And with our winter gives the Libyan spring.
No wicked wealth infects the simple soil,
Nor golden ores disclose their shining spoil;*
Pure is the glebe, 'tis earth and earth alone,
725   To guilty pride and avarice unknown.
There citron groves,* the native riches, grow,
There cool retreats and fragrant shades bestow,
And hospitably screen their guests below.
Safe by their leafy office,* long they stood
730   A sacred, old, unviolated wood,
Till Roman luxury to Afric past,
And foreign axes laid their honours waste.
Thus utmost lands are ransacked to afford
The farfetched dainties and the costly board.
735   But rude and wasteful all those regions lie
That border on the Syrts, and feel too nigh
Their sultry summer sun and parching sky.
No harvest there the scattered grain repays,
But withering dies, and e'er it shoots decays;
740   There never loves to spring the mantling vine,*
Nor wanton ringlets round her elm to twine;
The thirsty dust prevents the swelling fruit,
Drinks up the generous juice, and kills the root;
Through secret veins no tempering moistures pass,
745   To bind with viscous force the mouldering mass,
But genial Jove, averse, disdains to smile,*
Forgets and curses the neglected soil.
Thence lazy nature droops her idle head,
As every vegetable* sense were dead;
750   Thence the wide, dreary plains one visage wear,
Alike in summer, winter, spring appear,
Nor feel the turns of the revolving year.
Thin herbage here – for some ev'n here is found –
The Nasamonian hinds collect around,
755   A naked race, and barbarous of mind,
That live upon the losses of mankind;

The Syrts supply their wants and barren soil,
And strew th'unhospitable shores with spoil.
Trade they have none, but ready still they stand,* ⎱
760 . Rapacious to invade the wealthy strand,   ⎰
And hold a commerce thus with every distant land. ⎰

    Through this dire country Cato's journey lay;
Here he pursued, while virtue led the way.
Here the bold youth,* led by his high command,
765 Fearless of storms and raging winds, by land
Repeat the dangers of the swelling main,
And strive with storms and raging winds again.
Here all at large, where nought restrains his force,
Impetuous Auster runs his rapid course;
770 Nor mountains here nor steadfast rocks resist,
But free he sweeps along the spacious list.*
No stable groves of ancient oaks arise
To tire his rage and catch him as he flies,
But wide around the naked plains appear,   ⎱
775 Here fierce he drives unbounded through the air, ⎰
Roars and exerts his dreadful empire here.   ⎰
The whirling dust, like waves in eddies wrought,
Rising aloft, to the mid heaven is caught,
There hangs a sullen cloud, nor falls again,
780 Nor breaks like gentle vapours into rain.
Gazing, the poor inhabitant descries
Where high above his land and cottage flies,
Bereft he sees his lost possessions there,
From earth transported and now fixed in air.
785 Not rising flames attempt a bolder flight;   ⎱
Like smoke by rising flames uplifted, light   ⎰
The sands ascend, and stain the heavens with night. ⎰

    But now, his utmost power and rage to boast,
The stormy god invades the Roman host;
790 The soldier yields, unequal to the shock,
And staggers at the wind's stupendous stroke.
Amazed he sees that earth which lowly lay
Forced from beneath his feet and torn away.
O Libya! Were thy pliant surface bound,
795 And formed a solid, close-compacted ground,
Or hadst thou rocks whose hollows deep below
Would draw those ranging winds that loosely blow,

Their fury, by thy firmer mass opposed
Or in those dark, infernal caves enclosed,
800   Thy certain ruin would at once complete,
Shake thy foundations, and unfix thy seat.
But well thy flitting plains have learned to yield; ⎱
Thus, not contending, thou thy place hast held, ⎰
Unfixed art fixed, and flying keep'st the field. ⎰
805   Helms, spears and shields, snatched from the warlike
           host,
Through heaven's wide regions far away were tossed,
While distant nations, with religious fear, ⎱
Beheld them as some prodigy in air, ⎰
And thought the gods by them denounced* a war. ⎰
810   Such haply was the chance which first did raise*
The pious tale in priestly Numa's days,
Such were those shields, and thus they came from
           heaven,
A sacred charge to young patricians given;
Perhaps, long since, to lawless winds a prey,
815   From far barbarians were they forced away,
Thence through long airy journies safe did come
To cheat the crowd with miracles at Rome.
Thus wide o'er Libya raged the stormy South,
Thus every way assailed the Latian youth;
820   Each several method for defence they try,
Now wrap their garments tight, now close they lie,
Now sinking to the earth with weight they press,
Now clasp it to them with a strong embrace,
Scarce in that posture safe – the driving blast*
825   Bears hard, and almost heaves them off at last.
Meantime a sandy flood comes rolling on,*
And swelling heaps the prostrate legions drown;
New to the sudden danger, and dismayed, ⎱
The frighted soldier hasty calls for aid, ⎰
830   Heaves at the hill, and struggling rears his head. ⎰
Soon shoots the growing pile, and, reared on high,
Lifts up its lofty summit to the sky;
High sandy walls, like forts, their passage stay,
And rising mountains intercept their way;

835   The certain bounds which should their journey
          guide
    The moving earth and dusty deluge hide –
    So landmarks sink beneath the flowing tide.
    As through mid seas uncertainly they move,
    Led only by Jove's sacred lights* above;
840   Part ev'n of them the Libyan clime denies,
    Forbids their native northern stars to rise,
    And shades the well-known lustre from their eyes.
      Now near approaching to the burning zone,
    To warmer, calmer skies they journeyed on.
845   The slackening storms the neighbouring sun confess,
    The heat strikes fiercer, and the winds grow less,
    Whilst parching thirst and fainting sweats increase.
    As forward on the weary way they went,*
    Panting with drought and all with labour spent,
850   Amidst the desert, desolate and dry,
    One chanced a little trickling spring to spy;
    Proud of the prize, he drained the scanty store,
    And in his helmet to the chieftain bore.
    Around in crowds the thirsty legions stood,
855   Their throats and clammy jaws with dust bestrewed,
    And all with wishful eyes the liquid treasure viewed.
    Around the leader cast his careful look,
    Sternly the tempting, envied gift he took,
    Held it, and thus the giver fierce bespoke:
860   'And thinks thou then that I want virtue* most?
    Am I the meanest of this Roman host?
    Am I the first soft coward that complains,
    That shrinks unequal to these glorious pains?
    Am I in ease and infamy the first?
865   Rather be thou, base as thou art, accursed,
    Thou that dar'st drink, when all beside thee thirst.'
    He said, and wrathful stretching forth his hand
    Poured out the precious draught upon the sand.*
    Well did the water thus for all provide,
870   Envied by none, while thus to all denied –
    A little thus the general want supplied.
      Now to the sacred temple they draw near,*
    Whose only altars Libyan lands revere;
    There, but unlike the Jove by Rome adored,

875   A form uncouth stands heaven's almighty lord.
       No regal ensigns grace his potent hand,
       Nor shakes he there the lightning's flaming brand,
       But, ruder to behold, a hornèd ram
       Belies the god, and Ammon is his name.
880   There though he reigns unrivalled and alone,
       O'er the rich neighbours of the torrid zone,
       Though swarthy Ethiops are to him confined,
       With Araby the blest and wealthy Ind,
       Yet no proud domes are raised, no gems are seen,
885   To blaze upon his shrines with costly sheen,
       But plain and poor and unprofaned he stood,
       Such as to whom our great forefathers bowed,
       A god of pious times and days of old
       That keeps his temple safe from Roman gold.
890   Here, and here only, through wide Libya's space,
       Tall trees, the land, and verdant herbage grace;*
       Here the loose sands by plenteous springs are bound,
       Knit to a mass and moulded into ground;
       Here smiling nature wears a fertile dress,
895   And all things here the present god confess.
       Yet here the sun to neither pole declines,*
       But from his zenith vertically shines,
       Hence ev'n the trees no friendly shelter yield –
       Scarce their own trunks the leafy branches shield;
900   The rays descend direct, all round embrace,
       And to a central point the shadow chase.
       Here equally the middle line is found,
       To cut the radiant zodiac in its round;
       Here unoblique the Bull and Scorpion rise,*
905   Nor mount too swift, nor leave too soon the skies;
       Nor Libra does too long the Ram attend,
       Nor bids the Maid the fishy sign* descend;
       The Boys and Centaur justly time divide,
       And equally their several seasons guide;
910   Alike the Crab and wintry Goat return,
       Alike the Lion and the flowing Urn.*
       If any farther nations yet are known
       Beyond the Libyan fires and scorching zone,
       Northward from them the sun's bright course is made,
915   And to the southward strikes the leaning shade;

There slow Boötes, with his lazy wain
Descending, seems to reach the watery main.
Of all the lights which high above they see,
No star whate'er from Neptune's waves is free –
920   The whirling axle drives them round, and plunges
        in the sea.
    Before the temple's entrance, at the gate,
Attending crowds of eastern pilgrims* wait;
These from the hornèd god expect relief,
But all give way before the Latian chief.
925   His host – as crowds are superstitious still –
Curious of fate, of future good and ill,
And fond to prove prophetic Ammon's skill,
Entreat their leader to the god would go,
And from his oracle Rome's fortunes know;
930   But Labienus* chief the thought approved,
And thus the common suit to Cato moved:*
    'Chance, and the fortune of the way', he said,
'Have brought Jove's sacred counsels to our aid;
This greatest of the gods, this mighty chief,
935   In each distress shall be a sure relief,
Shall point the distant dangers from afar,
And teach the future fortunes of the war.
To thee, O Cato, pious, wise and just,
Their dark decrees the cautious gods shall trust,*
940   To thee their foredetermined will shall tell –
Their will has been thy law, and thou hast kept it
        well.
Fate bids thee now the noble thought improve,
Fate brings thee here to meet and talk with Jove.
Enquire betimes what various chance shall come
945   To impious Caesar and thy native Rome;
Try to avert at least thy country's doom.
Ask if these arms our freedom shall restore,
Or else if laws and right shall be no more.
Be thy great breast with sacred knowledge fraught,
950   To lead us in the wandering maze of thought;
Thou, that to virtue ever wert inclined,
Learn what it is, how certainly defined,
And leave some perfect rule to guide mankind.'
    Full of the god that dwelt within his breast,

955   The hero thus his secret mind expressed,
And inborn truths revealed, truths which might well
Become ev'n oracles themselves to tell:
   'Where would thy fond, thy vain enquiry go?*
What mystic* fate, what secret would'st thou know?

960   Is it a doubt if death should be my doom
Rather than live till kings and bondage come,
Rather than see a tyrant crowned in Rome?
Or would'st thou know if what we value here,
Life, be a trifle hardly worth our care?

965   What by old age and length of days we gain
More than to lengthen out the sense of pain?
Or if this world, with all its forces joined,
The universal malice of mankind,
Can shake or hurt the brave and honest mind?

970   If stable virtue can her ground maintain,
While fortune feebly threats and frowns in vain?
If truth and justice with uprightness dwell,
And honesty consist in meaning well?
If right be independent of success,*

975   And conquest cannot make it more nor less?
Are these, my friend, the secrets thou would'st know,
Those doubts for which to oracles we go?
'Tis known, 'tis plain, 'tis all already told,
And hornèd Ammon can no more unfold.

980   From God* derived, to God by nature joined,
We act the dictates of his mighty mind,
And, though the priests are mute and temples still,
God never wants a voice to speak his will.
When first we from the teeming womb were
      brought,

985   With inborn precepts then our souls were fraught,
And then the maker his new creatures taught.
Then, when he formed and gave us to be men,
He gave us all our useful knowledge, then.
Canst thou believe the vast eternal mind*

990   Was e'er to Syrts and Libyan sands confined?
That he would choose this waste, this barren
      ground,
To teach the thin* inhabitants around,
And leave his truth in wilds and deserts drowned?

Is there a place that God would choose to love
995   Beyond this earth, the seas, yon heaven above,
And virtuous minds, the noblest throne for Jove?
Why seek we farther then? Behold around
How all thou see'st does with the god abound –
Jove is alike in all, and always to be found.
1000 Let those weak minds, who live in doubt and fear,
To juggling priests for oracles repair;
One certain hour of death to each decreed*
My fixed, my certain soul from doubt has freed.
The coward and the brave are doomed to fall,
1005 And when Jove told this truth, he told us all.'
So spoke the hero; and, to keep his word,
Nor Ammon nor his oracle explored,
But left the crowd at freedom to believe,
And take such answers as the priest should give.
1010   Foremost on foot he treads the burning sand,*
Bearing his arms in his own patient hand,
Scorning another's weary neck to press,
Or in a lazy chariot loll at ease;
The panting soldier to his toil succeeds,
1015 Where no command but great example leads;
Sparing of sleep, still for the rest he wakes,
And at the fountain last his thirst he slakes;
Whene'er by chance some living stream is found,
He stands, and sees the cooling draughts go round,
1020 Stays till the last and meanest drudge be past,
And, till his slaves have drunk, disdains to taste.
If true good men deserve immortal fame,
If virtue, though distressed, be still the same,
Whate'er our fathers greatly dared to do,
1025 Whate'er they bravely bore and wisely knew,
Their virtues all are his, and all their praise his
    due.
Whoe'er, with battles fortunately fought,
Whoe'er, with Roman blood, such honours bought?
This triumph, this, on Libya's utmost bound,
1030 With death and desolation compassed round,
To all thy glories, Pompey, I prefer,
Thy trophies and thy third triumphal car,
To Marius' mighty name and great Jugurthine war.

His country's father here, O Rome, behold,
1035 Worthy thy temples, priests and shrines of gold!
If e'er thou break thy lordly master's chain,
If liberty be e'er restored again,
Him shalt thou place in thy divine abodes,
Swear by his holy name, and rank him with thy gods.

1040 Now to those sultry regions were they past,* ⎫
Which Jove to stop enquiring mortals placed,   ⎬
And as their utmost, southern limits cast.   ⎭
Thirsty, for springs they search the desert round,
And only one amidst the sands they found.

1045 Well stored it was, but all access* was barred –
The stream ten thousand noxious serpents* guard:
Dry aspics* on the fatal margin stood,
And dipsas* thirsted in the middle flood.
Back from the stream the frighted soldier flies;
1050 Though parched and languishing for drink he dies.
The chief beheld and said, 'You fear in vain, ⎫
Vainly from safe and healthy draughts abstain; ⎬
My soldier, drink, and dread not death or pain. ⎭
When urged to rage, their teeth the serpents fix,
1055 And venom with our vital juices mix;
The pest* infused through every vein runs round,
Infects the mass, and death is in the wound.
Harmless and safe, no poison here they shed.'
He said, and first the doubtful draught essayed,
1060 He, who through all their march, their toil, their
            thirst,
Demanded, here alone, to drink the first.

   Why plagues like these infest the Libyan air,*
Why deaths unknown in various shapes appear,
Why, fruitful to destroy, the cursèd land
1065 Is tempered thus by nature's secret hand,
Dark and obscure the hidden cause remains,
And still deludes the vain enquirer's pains –
Unless a tale for truth may be believed,
And the good-natured world be willingly deceived.

1070 Where western waves on farthest Libya beat, ⎫
Warmed with the setting sun's descending heat, ⎬
Dreadful Medusa fixed her horrid seat.   ⎭
No leafy shade with kind protection shields

The rough, the squalid,* unfrequented fields,
1075 No mark of shepherds, or the ploughman's toil,
To tend the flocks or turn the mellow soil,
But rude with rocks, the region all around*
Its mistress and her potent visage owned.
'Twas from this monster to afflict mankind
1080 That nature first produced the snaky kind;
On her at first their forky tongues appeared,
From her their dreadful hissings first were heard.
Some wreathed in folds upon her temples hung,
Some backwards to her waist depended* long,
1085 Some with their rising crests her forehead deck,
Some wanton play, and lash her swelling neck;
And, while her hands the curling vipers comb,
Poisons distil around, and drops of livid foam.
       None who beheld the Fury could complain,
1090 So swift their fate, preventing death and pain;
E'er they had time to fear, the change came on,
And motion, sense and life were lost in stone.
The soul itself, from sudden flight debarred,
Congealing, in the body's fortune shared.
1095 The dire Eumenides could rage inspire,
But could no more;* the tuneful Thracian lyre*
Infernal Cerberus did soon assuage,
Lulled him to rest and soothed his triple rage;*
Hydra's sev'n heads the bold Alcides viewed –
1100 Safely he saw, and what he saw subdued;
Of these in various terrors each excelled,
But all to this superior Fury yield.
Phorcus* and Ceto,* next to Neptune he,*
Immortal both and rulers of the sea,
1105 This monster's parents, did their offspring dread,
And from her sight her sister Gorgons fled;
Old ocean's waters and the liquid air,
The universal world, her power might fear;
All nature's beauteous works she could invade, ⎫
1110 Through every part a lazy numbness shed,   ⎬
And over all a stony surface spread.   ⎭
Birds in their flight were stopped and ponderous
                grown,
Forgot their pinions, and fell senseless down.

Beasts to the rocks were fixed, and all around
1115 Were tribes of stone and marble nations found.
No living eyes so fell a sight could bear –
Her snakes themselves, all deadly though they were,
Shot backward from her face, and shrunk away for
        fear.
By her a rock Titanian Atlas grew,*
1120 And heav'n by her the giants did subdue –
Hard was the fight, and Jove was half dismayed,
Till Pallas brought the Gorgon to his aid;*
The heavenly nation laid aside their fear,
For soon she finished the prodigious war;
1125 To mountains turned, the monster race remains
The trophies of her power on the Phlegraean plains.
    To seek this monster, and her fate to prove,
The son of Danaë and golden Jove*
Attempts a flight through airy ways above.
1130 The youth Cyllenian* Hermes' aid implored;
The god assisted with his wings* and sword,
His sword, which late made watchful Argus bleed,*
And Io from her cruel keeper freed;
Unwedded Pallas lent a sister's aid,
1135 But asked for recompense Medusa's head.
Eastwards she warns her brother* bend his flight,
And from the Gorgon realms avert his sight;
Then arms his left with her refulgent* shield,
And shows how there the foe might be beheld.*
1140 Deep slumbers had the drowsy fiend possessed,
Such as drew on, and well might seem, her last,
And yet she slept not whole – one half her snakes
Watchful to guard their horrid mistress wakes;
The rest, dishevelled loosely, round her head
1145 And o'er her drowsy lids and face were spread.
Backward the youth draws near, nor dares to look,
But blindly, at a venture, aims a stroke;
His faltering hand the virgin goddess guides,
And from the monster's neck her snaky head divides.
1150 But oh, what art, what numbers can express
The terrors of the dying Gorgon's face!
What clouds of poison from her lips arise,

What death, what vast destruction threatened in her
    eyes!
'Twas somewhat* that immortal gods might fear,
1155 More than the warlike maid herself could bear.
The victor Perseus still had been subdued,
Though wary still with eyes averse he stood,
Had not his heavenly sister's timely care
Veiled the dread visage with the hissing hair.
1160 Seized of his prey, heavenwards uplifted light,
On Hermes' nimble wings he took his flight.
Now, thoughtful of his course, he hung in air,
And meant through Europe's happy clime to steer,
Till pitying Pallas warned him not to blast
1165 Her fruitful fields, nor lay her cities waste.
For who would not have upwards cast their sight,
Curious to gaze at such a wondrous flight?
Therefore by gales of gentle zephyrs borne
To Libya's coast the hero minds to turn.
1170 Beneath the sultry line exposed it lies
To deadly planets and malignant skies;
Still with his fiery steeds the god of day
Drives through that heaven and marks his burning
    way;
No land more high erects its lofty head,*
1175 The silver moon in dim eclipse to shade,
If through the summer signs direct she run, ⎤
Nor bends obliquely, north or south, to shun ⎟
The envious earth that hides her from the sun. ⎦
Yet could this soil accursed, this barren field,
1180 Increase of deaths and poisonous harvests yield.
Where-e'er sublime in air the victor flew, ⎤
The monster's head distilled a deadly dew; ⎟
The earth received the seed, and pregnant grew. ⎦
Still* as the putrid gore dropped on the sand,
1185 'Twas tempered up by nature's forming hand;
The glowing climate makes the work complete,
And broods upon the mass, and lends it genial heat.
    First of those plagues the drowsy asp appeared,*
Then first her crest and swelling neck she reared;
1190 A larger drop of black, congealing blood*
Distinguished her amidst the deadly brood;

Of all the serpent race are none so fell,
None with so many deaths, such plenteous venom
    swell;
Chill in themselves, our colder climes they shun,
1195 And choose to bask in Afric's warmer sun;
But Nile no more confines them now – what bound
Can for insatiate avarice be found?
Freighted with Libyan deaths our merchants come,
And poisonous asps are things of price at Rome.
1200   Her scaly folds th'haemorrhoïs* unbends,
And her vast length along the sands extends;
Where-e'er she wounds, from every part the blood
Gushes resistless in a crimson flood.
     Amphibious some do in the Syrts abound,
1205 And now on land, in waters now are found.
     Slimy chelyders* the parched earth distain,
And trace a reeking furrow on the plain.
     The spotted cenchris,* rich in various dyes,
Shoots in a line, and forth directly flies;
1210 Not Theban marbles are so gaily dressed,
Nor with such particoloured beauties graced.
     Safe in his earthy hue and dusky skin,
Th'ammodytes* lurks in the sands unseen;
The 'swimmer'* there the crystal stream pollutes,
1215 And swift through air the flying 'javelin'* shoots.
The scytale,* e'er yet the spring returns,
There casts her coat, and there the dipsas burns;
The amphisbaena* doubly armed appears –
At either end a threatening head she rears.
1220 Raised on his active tail the pareas* stands,
And as he passes furrows up the sands.
The prester* by his foaming jaws is known;   ⎫
The seps* invades the flesh and firmer bone,   ⎬
Dissolves the mass of man, and melts his fabric ⎭
    down.
1225 The basilisk,* with dreadful hissings heard,
And from afar by every serpent feared,
To distance drives the vulgar, and remains
The lonely monarch of the desert plains.
     And you, ye dragons of the scaly race,*
1230 Whom glittering gold and shining armours grace,

In other nations harmless are you found,
Their guardian genii and protectors owned;
In Afric only are you fatal – there
On wide expanded wings sublime you rear
1235 Your dreadful forms, and drive the yielding air.
The lowing kine in droves you chase, and cull
Some master of the herd, some mighty bull;
Around his stubborn sides your tails you twist,
By force compress and burst his brawny chest.
1240 Not elephants are by their larger size
Secure, but with the rest become your prize.
Resistless in your might you all invade,*
And for destruction need not poison's aid.
    Thus, through a thousand plagues around them
       spread,*
1245 A weary march the hardy soldiers tread,
Through thirst, through toil and death, by Cato led.
Their chief, with pious grief and deep regret,
Each moment mourns his friends' untimely fate;
Wondering, he sees some small, some trivial wound
1250 Extend a valiant Roman on the ground.
Aulus, a noble youth of Tyrrhene* blood,
Who bore the standard, on a dipsas trod;
Backward the wrathful serpent bent her head,
And, fell with rage, th'unheeded wrong repaid.
1255 Scarce did some little mark of hurt remain,
And scarce he found some little sense of pain;
Nor could he yet the danger doubt,* nor fear
That death with all its terrors threatened there –
When lo, unseen, the secret venom spreads,
1260 And every nobler part at once invades;
Swift flames consume the marrow and the brain,
And the scorched entrails rage with burning pain;
Upon his heart the thirsty poisons prey,
And drain the sacred juice of life away.
1265 No kindly floods of moisture bathe his tongue,
But cleaving to the parchèd roof it hung;
No trickling drops distil, no dewy sweat,
To ease his weary limbs, and cool the raging heat.

Nor could he weep; ev'n grief could not supply ⎫
1270   Streams for the mournful office of his eye – ⎬
The never-failing source of tears was dry. ⎭
Frantic he flies, and with a careless hand ⎫
Hurls the neglected eagle on the sand, ⎬
Nor hears nor minds his pitying chief's command; ⎭
1275   For springs he seeks, he digs, he proves the ground,
For springs in vain explores the desert round,
For cooling draughts which might their aid impart,
And quench the burning venom in his heart.
Plunged in the Tanaïs, the Rhone, or Po, ⎫
1280   Or Nile, whose wandering streams o'er Egypt ⎬
   flow, ⎥
Still would he rage, still with the fever glow; ⎭
The scorching climate to his fate conspires,
And Libya's sun assists the dipsas' fires;
Now everywhere for drink in vain he pries, ⎫
1285   Now to the Syrts and briny seas he flies – ⎬
The briny seas delight, but seem not to suffice. ⎭
Nor yet he knows what secret plague he nursed,
Nor found the poison but believed it thirst;
Of thirst, and thirst alone, he still complains,
1290   Raving for thirst he tears his swelling veins;
From every vessel drains a crimson flood,
And quaffs in greedy draughts his vital blood.
   This Cato saw, and straight, without delay,
Commands the legions on to urge their way,
1295   Nor give th'enquiring soldier time to know
What deadly deeds a fatal thirst could do.
   But soon a fate more sad, with new surprise,
From the first object turns their wondering eyes.
Wretched Sabellus by a seps was stung –
1300   Fixed to his leg with deadly teeth it hung;
Sudden the soldier shook it from the wound,
Transfixed and nailed it to the barren ground.
Of all the dire, destructive serpent race
None have so much of death, though none are less.*
1305   For straight around the part the skin withdrew, ⎫
The flesh and shrinking sinews backward flew, ⎬
And left the naked bones exposed to view. ⎭
The spreading poisons all the parts confound,

And the whole body sinks within the wound.
1310 The brawny thighs no more their muscles boast,
But, melting, all in liquid filth are lost;
The well-knit groin above and ham below,
Mixed in one putrid stream, together flow;
The firm peritoneum,* rent in twain,
1315 No more the pressing entrails could sustain –
It yields, and forth they fall, at once they gush
          amain.
Small relics of the mouldering mass were left,
At once of substance as of form bereft;
Dissolved the whole in liquid poison ran,
1320 And to a nauseous puddle shrunk the man.
Then burst the rigid nerves, the manly breast,
And all the texture of the heaving chest;
Resistless way the conquering venom made,
And secret nature was at once displayed;
1325 Her sacred privacies all open lie
To each profane, enquiring, vulgar eye.
Then the broad shoulders did the pest invade,
Then o'er the valiant arms and neck it spread;
Last sunk the mind's imperial seat, the head.
1330 So snows dissolved by southern breezes run,
So melts the wax before the noonday sun.
Nor ends the wonder here – though flames are
          known
To waste the flesh, yet still they spare the bone;
Here none were left, no least remains were seen,
1335 No marks to show that once the man had been.
Of all the plagues which curse the Libyan land,
If death and mischief may a crown demand,
Serpent, the palm is thine. Though others may
Boast of their power to force the soul* away,
1340 Yet soul and body both become thy prey.
     A fate of different kind Nasidius found –
A burning prester* gave the deadly wound,
And straight a sudden flame began to spread,
And paint his visage with a glowing red.
1345 With swift expansion swells the bloated skin;
Nought but an undistinguished mass is seen,
While the fair human form lies lost within.

The puffy poison spreads and heaves around,
Till all the man is in the monster drowned.
1350　No more the steely plate his breast can stay,
But yields, and gives the bursting poison way.
Not waters so, when fire the rage supplies,
Bubbling on heaps in boiling cauldrons rise;
Nor swells the stretching canvas half so fast,
1355　When the sails gather all the driving blast,
Strain the tough yards and bow the lofty mast.
The various parts no longer now are known –
One headless, formless heap remains alone;
The feathered kind avoid the fatal feast,
1360　And leave it deadly to some hungry beast;
With horror seized, his sad companions too
In haste from the unburied carcass flew,
Looked back, but fled again, for still the monster
　　　grew.
　　　But fertile Libya still new plagues supplies,
1365　And to more horrid monsters turns their eyes:
Deeply the fierce haemorrhoïs impressed
Her fatal teeth on Tullus' valiant breast.
The noble youth, with virtue's love inspired,
Her,* in her Cato, followed and admired,
1370　Moved by his great example, vowed to share
With him each chance of that disastrous war.
And as when mighty Rome's spectators meet*
In the full theatre's capacious seat,
At once, by secret pipes and channels fed,
1375　Rich tinctures gush from every antique head,
At once ten thousand saffron currents flow,
And rain their odours on the crowd below;
So the warm blood at once from every part
Ran purple poison down, and drained the fainting
　　　heart.
1380　Blood falls for tears, and o'er his mournful face
The ruddy drops their tainted passage trace;
Where-e'er the liquid juices find a way,
There streams of blood, there crimson rivers stray;
His mouth and gushing nostrils pour a flood,
1385　And ev'n the pores ooze out the trickling blood;
In the red deluge all the parts lie drowned,

And the whole body seems one bleeding wound.*
    Laevus* a colder aspic bit, and straight
His blood forgot to flow, his heart to beat;
1390 Thick shades upon his eyelids seemed to creep,
And lock him fast in everlasting sleep;
No sense of pain, no torment did he know,
But sunk in slumbers to the shades below.
    Not swifter deaths attend the noxious juice*
1395 Which dire Sabaean aconites produce.
Well may their crafty priests divine, and well
The fate, which they themselves can cause, foretell.
    Fierce from afar a darting 'javelin' shot –
For such the serpent's name has Afric taught –
1400 And through unhappy Paulus' temples flew;
Nor poison but a wound the soldier slew.
No flight so swift, so rapid none we know;
Stones from the sounding sling, compared,* are slow,
And the shaft loiters from the Scythian bow.
1405   A basilisk bold Murrus killed in vain,
And nailed it dying to the sandy plain;
Along the spear the sliding venom ran,
And sudden from the weapon seized the man;
His hand first touched, e'er it his arm invade,
1410 Soon he divides it with his shining blade;
The serpent's force by sad example taught,*
With his lost hand his ransomed life he bought.
    Who that the scorpion's insect form surveys
Would think that ready death his call obeys?
1415 Threatening he rears his knotty tail on high;
The vast Orion thus he doomed to die,*
And fixed him, his proud trophy, in the sky.
    Or could we the salpuga's* anger dread,
Or fear upon her little cell to tread?
1420 Yet she the fatal threads of life commands,
And quickens oft the Stygian sisters'* hands.
    Pursued by dangers, thus they passed away
The restless night, and thus the cheerless day;
Ev'n earth itself they feared, the common bed,
1425 Where each lay down to rest his weary head;
There no kind trees their leafy couches strow,*

The sands no turf nor mossy beds bestow,
But, tired and fainting with the tedious toil,
Exposed they sleep upon the fatal soil.
1430 With vital heat they brood upon the ground,
And breathe a kind, attractive vapour round,
While, chill with colder night's ungentle air, ⎞
To man's warm breast his snaky foes repair, ⎬
And find, ungrateful guests, a shelter there. ⎠
1435 Thence fresh supplies of poisonous rage return,
And fiercely with recruited deaths they burn.*
    'Restore', thus sadly oft the soldier said,
'Restore Emathia's plains from whence we fled;
This grace at least, ye cruel gods, afford,
1440 That we may fall beneath the hostile sword.
The dipsas here in Caesar's triumph share,
And fell cerastae* wage his civil war.
Or let us haste away, press farther on, ⎞
Urge our bold passage to the burning zone, ⎬
1445 And die by those ethereal flames alone. ⎠
Afric,* thy deserts we accuse no more,
Nor blame, O nature, thy creating power –
From man thou wisely didst these wilds divide, ⎞
And for thy monsters here alone provide, ⎬
1450 A region waste and void of all beside. ⎠
Thy prudent care forbade the barren field
The yellow harvest's ripe increase to yield;
Man and his labours well thou didst deny,
And bad'st him from the land of poisons fly.
1455 We, impious we, the bold irruption made,
We this the serpent's world did first invade;
Take then our lives a forfeit for the crime,
Whoe'er thou art that rul'st this cursèd clime,
What god soe'er that lonely lov'st to reign,
1460 And dost the commerce of mankind disdain,
Who, to secure thy horrid empire's bound,
Hast fixed the Syrts and torrid realms around,
Here the wild waves, there the flames' scorching
        breath,
And filled the dreadful middle space with death.
1465 Behold to thy retreats our arms we bear,
And with Rome's civil rage profane thee here,

Ev'n to thy inmost seats we strive to go,
And seek the limits of the world to know.
Perhaps more dire events attend us yet:
1470 New deaths, new monsters, still we go to meet.
Perhaps to those far seas our journey bends,
Where to the waves the burning sun descends,
Where, rushing headlong down heav'n's azure steep,
All red he plunges in the hissing deep.
1475 Low sinks the pole, declining from its height,
And seems to yield beneath the rapid weight.
    Nor farther lands from fame herself are known,
But Mauritanian Juba's realms alone.
Perhaps, while rashly daring on we pass,
1480 Fate may discover some more dreadful place,
Till, late repenting, we may wish in vain
To see these serpents and these sands again.
One joy at least do these sad regions give:
Ev'n here we know 'tis possible to live –
1485 That,* by the native plagues,* we may perceive.
Nor ask we now for Asia's gentler day,
Nor now for European suns we pray –
Thee, Afric, now thy absence we deplore,
And sadly think we ne'er shall see thee more.
1490 Say in what part, what climate art thou lost,
Where have we left Cyrene's happy frost?
Cold skies we felt, and frosty winter there,
While more than summer suns are raging here,
And break the laws of the well-ordered year.
1495 Southward, beyond earth's limits, are we passed,
And Rome at length beneath our feet is placed.
Grant us, ye gods, one pleasure e'er we die,
Add to our harder fate this only joy,
That Caesar may pursue, and follow where we fly.'
1500   Impatient thus the soldier oft complains,
And seems by telling to relieve his pains.
But most the virtues of their matchless chief
Inspire new strength to bear with* every grief;
All night, with careful thoughts and watchful eyes,
1505 On the bare sands exposed the hero lies,
In every place alike, in every hour,
Dares his ill fortune and defies her power.

Unwearied still, his common care attends
On every fate, and cheers his dying friends;
1510 With ready haste at each sad call he flies,
And more than health or life itself supplies,
With virtue's noblest precepts arms their souls,
And ev'n their sorrows, like his own, controls;
Where-e'er he comes, no signs of grief are shown, }
1515 Grief, an unmanly weakness, they disown,   }
And scorn to sigh, or breathe one parting groan. }
Still urging on his pious cares he strove
The sense of outward evils to remove,
And by his presence taught them to disdain
1520 The feeble rage and impotence of pain.
    But now, so many toils and dangers past,
Fortune grew kind and brought relief at last.
Of all who scorching Afric's sun endure
None like the swarthy Psyllians* are secure.
1525 Skilled in the lore of powerful herbs and charms,
Them nor the serpent's tooth nor poison harms,
Nor do they thus in arts alone excel,   }
But nature too their blood has tempered well, }
And taught, with vital force, the venom to repel. }
1530 With healing gifts and privileges graced,
Well in the land of serpents were they placed,
Truce with the dreadful tyrant death they have,
And border safely on his realm, the grave.
Such is their confidence in true-born blood
1535 That oft with asps they prove their doubtful brood;
When wanton wives their jealous rage inflame,
The new-born infant clears or damns the dame:
If subject to the wrathful serpent's wound,
The mother's shame is by the danger found,
1540 But, if unhurt the fearless infant laugh,
The wife is honest and the husband safe.
So when Jove's bird on some tall cedar's head
Has a new race of generous eaglets bred,
While yet unplumed within the nest they lie,
1545 Wary she turns them to the eastern sky,
Then, if unequal to the god of day   }
Abashed they shrink and shun the potent ray, }
She spurns them forth and casts them quite away; }

But if with daring eyes unmoved they gaze,
1550 Withstand the light, and bear the golden blaze,
Tender she broods* them with a parent's love,
The future servants of her master Jove.
Nor safe themselves alone the Psyllians are,
But to their guests extend their friendly care.
1555 First, where the Roman camp is marked, around ⎫
Circling they pass, then chanting charm the   ⎬
    ground,   ⎪
And chase the serpents with the mystic* sound. ⎭
Beyond the farthest tents rich fires they build,
That healthy, medicinal* odours yield;
1560 There foreign galbanum* dissolving fries,
And crackling flames from humble wallwort* rise;
There tamarisk, which no green leaf adorns,
And there the spicy Syrian costos* burns;
There centaury* supplies the wholesome flame,
1565 That from Thessalian Chiron takes its name;
The gummy larch tree and the thapsos* there,
Woundwort* and maidenweed* perfume the air;
There the large branches of the long-lived hart
With southernwood* their odours strong impart.
1570 The monsters of the land, the serpents fell,
Fly far away and shun the hostile smell.
Securely thus they pass the nights away,   ⎫
And, if they chance to meet a wound by day,   ⎬
The Psyllian artists straight their skill display. ⎭
1575 Then strives the leach* the power of charms to show,
And bravely combats with the deadly foe;
With spittle first he marks the part around,
And keeps the poison prisoner in the wound;
Then sudden he begins the magic song,
1580 And rolls the numbers hasty o'er his tongue;
Swift he runs on, nor pauses once for breath,
To stop the progress of approaching death;
He fears the cure might suffer by delay,
And life be lost, but for a moment's stay.
1585 Thus oft, though deep within the veins it lies,
By magic numbers chased the mischief flies,
But if it hear too slow, if still it stay,
And scorn the potent charmer to obey,

With forceful lips he fastens on the wound,
1590   Drains out and spits the venom to the ground.
Thus by long use and oft experience taught,
He knows from whence his hurt the patient got,
He proves the part through which the poison past,
And knows each various serpent by the taste.
1595   The warriors thus relieved amidst their pains
Held on their passage through the desert plains;
And now the silver empress of the night*
Had lost and twice regained her borrowed light,
While Cato, wandering o'er the wasteful field,
1600   Patient in all his labours, she beheld.
At length condensed in clods the sands appear,
And show a better soil and country near;
Now from afar thin tufts of trees arise,
And scattering cottages delight their eyes.
1605   But when the soldier once beheld again*
The raging lion shake his horrid mane,
What hopes of better lands his soul possessed,
What joys he felt to view the dreadful beast!
Leptis at last they reached, that nearest lay;
1610   There, free from storms and the sun's parching
     ray,
At ease they passed the wintry year away.
   When, sated with the joys which slaughters yield,*
Retiring Caesar left Emathia's field,
His other cares laid by, he sought alone
1615   To trace the footsteps of his flying son.*
Led by the guidance of reporting fame,
First to the Thracian Hellespont he came.
Here young Leander perished in the flood,*
And here the tower of mournful Hero stood;
1620   Here, with a narrow stream, the flowing tide
Europe from wealthy Asia does divide.
From hence the curious victor passing o'er,
Admiring, sought the famed Sigaean* shore;
There might he tombs of Grecian chiefs behold,
1625   Renowned in sacred verse by bards of old.
There the long ruins of the walls appeared
Once by great Neptune and Apollo reared;*
There stood old Troy, a venerable name,

Forever consecrate to deathless fame.
1630 Now blasted, mossy trunks with branches sear,*
Brambles and weeds a loathsome forest rear,
Where once in palaces of regal state,
Old Priam* and the Trojan princes sate.
Where temples once, on lofty columns borne,
1635 Majestic did the wealthy town adorn,
All rude, all waste and desolate is laid,
And ev'n the ruined ruins are decayed.
Here Caesar did each storied place survey, ⎫
Here saw the rock where, Neptune to obey,* ⎬
1640 Hesione was bound the monster's prey; ⎭
Here in the covert of a secret grove
The blessed Anchises clasped the Queen of Love;*
Here fair Oenone* played, here stood the cave
Where Paris once the fatal judgment gave;*
1645 Here lovely Ganymede* to heaven was borne –
Each rock and every tree recording tales adorn.
Here all that does of Xanthus' stream remain
Creeps a small brook along the dusty plain.
Whilst careless and securely on they pass,
1650 The Phrygian* guide forbids to press the grass;
'This place', he said, 'for ever sacred keep,
For here the sacred bones of Hector* sleep.'
Then warns him to observe where, rudely cast,
Disjointed stones lay broken and defaced;
1655 'Here his last fate', he cries, 'did Priam prove,
Here on this altar of Hercean Jove.'*
    O poesy divine, O sacred song!*
To thee bright fame and length of days belong;
Thou goddess, thou eternity canst give,
1660 And bid secure the mortal hero live.
Nor, Caesar, thou disdain that I rehearse
Thee and thy wars in no ignoble verse,
Since, if in aught the Latian Muse excel,
My name and thine immortal I foretell;
1665 Eternity our labours shall reward,
And Lucan* flourish like the Grecian bard;*
My numbers* shall to latest times convey
The tyrant Caesar, and Pharsalia's day.
    When long the chief his wondering eyes had cast

1670 On ancient monuments of ages past,
Of living turf an altar straight he made,
Then on the fire rich gums and incense laid,
And thus, successful in his vows, he prayed:
'Ye shades divine, who keep this sacred place,
1675 And thou, Aeneas, author of my race,*
Ye powers, whoe'er from burning Troy did come,
Domestic gods of Alba and of Rome,
Who still preserve your ruined country's name,
And on your altars guard the Phrygian flame,
1680 And thou, bright maid, who art to men denied,
Pallas, who dost thy sacred pledge confide*
To Rome, and in her inmost temple hide,
Hear, and auspicious to my vows incline,
To me the greatest of the Julian line;
1685 Prosper my future ways, and lo, I vow
Your ancient state and honours to bestow;
Ausonian* hands shall Phrygian walls restore,*
And Rome repay what Troy conferred before.'
He said, and hasted to his fleet away,*
1690 Swift to repair the loss of this delay.
Up sprung the wind, and with a freshening gale
The kind North-West filled every swelling sail;
Light o'er the foamy waves the navy flew,
Till Asia's shores and Rhodes no more they view.
1695 Six times the night her sable round had made;
The seventh now passing on, the chief surveyed
High Pharos shining through the gloomy shade;
The coast descried, he waits the rising day,
Then safely to the port directs his way.
1700 There wide with crowds o'erspread he sees the shore,
And echoing hears the loud, tumultuous roar.
Distrustful of his fate, he gives command
To stand aloof, nor trust the doubted land,
When lo, a messenger appears, to bring
1705 A fatal pledge of peace from Egypt's king;
Hid in a veil and closely covered o'er,
Pompey's pale visage in his hand he bore.
An impious orator the tyrant sends,
Who thus with fitting words the monstrous gift
     commends:

1710   'Hail, first and greatest of the Roman name,
            In power most mighty, most renowned in fame!
            Hail, rightly now the world's unrivalled lord! –
            That benefit thy Pharian friends afford.
            My king bestows the prize thy arms have sought,
1715   For which Pharsalia's field in vain was fought.
            No task remains for future labours now –
            Thy civil wars are finished at a blow.
            To heal Thessalia's ruins Pompey fled
            To us for succour, and by us lies dead.
1720   Thee, Caesar, with this costly pledge we buy,
            Thee to our friendship, with this victim, tie.
            Egypt's proud sceptre freely then receive,
            Whate'er the fertile, flowing Nile can give;
            Accept the treasures which this deed has spared,
1725   Accept the benefit, without reward.
            Deign, Caesar, deign to think my royal lord
            Worthy the aid of thy victorious sword;
            In the first rank of greatness shall he stand,
            He who could Pompey's destiny command.
1730   Nor frown disdainful on the proffered spoil,
            Because not dearly bought with blood and toil,
            But think, oh think, what sacred ties were broke,
            How friendship pleaded and how nature spoke,
            That Pompey, who restored Auletes'* crown,
1735   The father's ancient guest, was murdered by the son.
            Then judge thyself, or ask the world and fame,
            If services like these deserve a name.
            If gods and men the daring deed abhor,
            Think for that reason Caesar owes the more:
1740   This blood for thee, though not by thee, was spilt –
            Thou hast the benefit and we the guilt.'
                He said, and straight the horrid gift unveiled,
            And steadfast to the gazing victor held.
            Changed was the face, deformed with death all
                    o'er,
1745   Pale, ghastly, wan and stained with clotted gore,
            Unlike the Pompey Caesar knew before.
            He nor at first disdained the fatal boon,*
            Nor started from the dreadful sight too soon.
            Awhile his eyes the murderous scene endure –

1750 Doubting they view, but shun it when secure.
     At length he stood convinced the deed was done,
     He saw 'twas safe to mourn his lifeless son,
     And straight the ready tears that stayed till now
     Swift at command with pious semblance flow;
1755 As if detesting, from the sight he turns,
     And, groaning, with a heart triumphant mourns.
     He fears his impious thought should be descried,
     And seeks in tears the swelling joy to hide.
     Thus the cursed Pharian tyrant's hopes were crossed,
1760 Thus all the merit of his gift was lost,
     Thus for the murder Caesar's thanks were spared –
     He chose to mourn it rather than reward.
     He who relentless through Pharsalia rode,
     And on the Senate's mangled Fathers trode,*
1765 He who, without one pitying sigh beheld
     The blood and slaughter of that woeful field,
     Thee, murdered Pompey, could not ruthless see,
     But paid the tribute of his grief to thee.
     O mystery of fortune and of fate!*
1770 O ill consorted piety and hate!
     And canst thou, Caesar, then thy tears afford
     To the dire object of thy vengeful sword?
     Didst thou for this devote his hostile head,
     Pursue him living, to bewail him dead?
1775 Could not the gentle ties of kindred move?
     Wert thou not touched with thy sad Julia's love?
     And weep'st thou now? Dost thou these tears
          provide
     To win the friends of Pompey to thy side?
     Perhaps with secret rage thou dost repine*
1780 That he should die by any hand but thine;
     Thence fall thy tears, that Ptolemy has done
     A murder due to Caesar's hand alone.
     What secret springs soe'er these currents know,
     They ne'er by piety were taught to flow.
1785 Or didst thou kindly, like a careful friend,
     Pursue him flying, only to defend?
     Well was his fate denied to thy command!
     Well was he snatched by fortune from thy hand!
     Fortune withheld this glory from thy name,

1790   Forbade thy power to save, and spared the Roman
                shame.
            Still he goes on to vent his griefs aloud,
        And artful thus deceives the easy crowd:
            'Hence from my sight, nor let me see thee more;
        Haste, to thy king his fatal gift restore.
1795   At Caesar have you aimed the deadly blow,
        And wounded Caesar worse than Pompey now;
        The cruel hands by which this deed was done
        Have torn away the wreaths my sword had won,
        That noblest prize this civil war could give –*
1800   The victor's right to bid the vanquished live.
        Then tell your king his gift should be repaid –
        I would have sent him Cleopatra's head,
        But that he wishes to behold her dead.
        How has he dared, this Egypt's petty lord,
1805   To join his murders to the Roman sword?
        Did I for this in heat of war distain*
        With noblest blood Emathia's purple plain,
        To licence Ptolemy's pernicious reign?
        Did I with Pompey scorn the world to share,
1810   And can I an Egyptian partner bear?
        In vain the warlike trumpet's dreadful sound
        Has roused to war the universe around;
        Vain was the shock of nations if they own
        Now any power on earth but mine alone.
1815   If hither to your impious shores I came,
        'Twas to assert at once my power and fame,
        Lest the pale fury Envy should have said
        Your crimes I damned not, or your arms I fled.
        Nor think to fawn before me and deceive –
1820   I know the welcome you prepare to give.
        Thessalia's field preserves me from your hate,
        And guards the victor's head from Pompey's fate.
        What ruin, gods, attended on my arms,
        What dangers unforeseen, what waiting harms!
1825   Pompey and Rome and exile were my fear,
        See yet a fourth, see Ptolemy appear! –
        The boy-king's vengeance loiters in the rear.
        But we forgive his youth, and bid him know
        Pardon and life's the most we can bestow.

1830   For you, the meaner herd, with rites divine
        And pious cares, the warrior's head enshrine,
        Atone with penitence the injured shade,
        And let his ashes in their urn be laid;
        Pleased let his ghost lamenting Caesar know,
1835   And feel my presence here ev'n in the realms below.
        Oh, what a day of joy was lost to Rome,
        When hapless Pompey did to Egypt come,
        When, to a father and a friend unjust,
        He rather chose the Pharian boy to trust!
1840   The wretched world that loss of peace shall rue,
        Of peace which from our friendship might ensue;
        But thus the gods their hard decrees have made –
        In vain for peace and for repose I prayed,
        In vain implored that wars and rage might end, ⎤
1845   That suppliant-like I might to Pompey bend, |
        Beg him to live, and once more be my friend. ⎦
        Then had my labours met their just reward,
        And, Pompey, thou in all my glories shared,
        Then, jars and enmities all past and gone,
1850   In pleasure had the peaceful years rolled on;
        All should forgive to make the joy complete –
        Thou shouldst thy harder fate, and Rome my wars
            forget.'
            Fast falling still the tears, thus spoke the chief,
        But found no partner in the specious grief.
1855   O glorious liberty, when all shall dare*
        A face unlike their mighty lord to wear!
        Each in his breast the rising sorrow kept,
        And thought it safe to laugh, though Caesar wept.

BOOK TEN

Soon as the victor reached the guilty shore,
Yet red with stains of murdered Pompey's gore,
New toils his still prevailing fortune met,
By impious Egypt's genius hard beset.
5 The strife was now if this detested land
Should own imperial Rome's supreme command, ⎞
Or Caesar bleed beneath some Pharian* hand. ⎠
But thou, O Pompey, thy diviner shade
Came timely to this cruel father's aid;
10 Thy influence the deadly sword withstood,
Nor suffered Nile again to blush with Roman blood.
Safe in the pledge of Pompey, slain so late,
Proud Caesar enters Alexandria's gate;
Ensigns on high the long procession lead,
15 The warrior and his armèd train succeed.
Meanwhile, loud murmuring, the moody throng
Behold his fasces borne in state along;
Of innovations fiercely they complain,
And scornfully reject the Roman reign.
20 Soon saw the chief th'untoward bent they take,
And found that Pompey fell not for his sake.
Wisely, howe'er, he hid his secret fear,
And held his way with well dissembled cheer.
Careless, he runs their gods and temples o'er,*
25 The monuments of Macedonian power;
But neither god nor shrine nor mystic rite,
Their city nor her walls, his soul delight;
Their caves beneath his fancy chiefly led,*
To search the gloomy mansions of the dead;
30 Thither with secret pleasure he descends,*
And to the guide's recording tale attends.
   There the vain youth who made the world his prize,
That prosperous robber, Alexander, lies.
When pitying death at length had freed mankind,
35 To sacred rest his bones were here consigned –
His bones that better had been tossed and hurled

With just contempt around the injured world.
But fortune spared the dead, and partial fate,
For ages, fixed his Pharian empire's date.
40 If e'er our long-lost liberty return,
That carcass is reserved for public scorn;
Now it remains a monument confessed*
How one proud man could lord it o'er the rest.
To Macedon, a corner of the earth,
45 The vast, ambitious spoiler owed his birth;
There soon he scorned his father's humbler reign,
And viewed his vanquished Athens with disdain.*
Driv'n headlong on by fate's resistless force,
Through Asia's realms he took his dreadful course;
50 His ruthless sword laid human nature waste,
And desolation followed where he passed.
Red Ganges blushed, and famed Euphrates' flood,
With Persian this, and that with Indian blood.
Such is the bolt which angry Jove employs,
55 When, undistinguishing,* his wrath destroys;
Such, to mankind, portentous meteors rise,
Trouble the gazing earth, and blast the skies.
Nor flame nor flood his restless rage withstand,
Nor Syrts unfaithful nor the Libyan sand;
60 O'er waves unknown he meditates his way,
And seeks the boundless empire of the sea;*
Ev'n to the utmost west he would have gone,
Where Tethys' lap receives the setting sun,*
Around each pole his circuit would have made, ⎫
65 And drunk from secret Nile's remotest head,* ⎬
When nature's hand his wild ambition stayed. ⎭
With him that power his pride had loved so well,
His monstrous universal empire, fell;
No heir, no just successor left behind, ⎫
70 Eternal wars he to his friends assigned, ⎬
To tear the world and scramble for mankind. ⎭
Yet still he died the master of his fame,
And Parthia to the last revered his name;
The haughty east from Greece received her doom,*
75 With lower homage than she pays to Rome.
Though from the frozen pole our empire run,
Far as the journeys of the southern sun,

In triumph though our conquering eagles fly,
Where-e'er soft zephyrs fan the western sky,
80 Still to the haughty Parthian must we yield,
And mourn the loss of Carrhae's* dreadful field,
Still shall the race untamed their pride avow,
And lift those heads aloft which Pella taught to bow.*
    From Casium now the beardless monarch* came,
85 To quench the kindling Alexandrians' flame.
Th'unwarlike rabble soon the tumult cease,
And he, their king, remains the pledge of peace;*
When, veiled in secrecy and dark disguise,*
To mighty Caesar Cleopatra flies.
90 Won by persuasive gold and rich reward,   ⎫
Her keeper's hand her prison gates unbarred,   ⎬
And a light galley for her flight prepared.*   ⎭
O fatal form, thy native Egypt's shame,*
Thou lewd perdition of the Latian name!
95 How wert thou doomed our furies* to increase,
And be what Helen was to Troy and Greece!
When with an host, from vile Canopus led,
Thy vengeance aimed at great Augustus'* head,
When thy shrill timbrels'* sound was heard from far,
100 And Rome herself shook at the coming war,
When doubtful fortune near Leucadia's strand   ⎫
Suspended long the world's supreme command,   ⎬
And almost gave it to a woman's hand.*   ⎭
Such daring courage swells her wanton heart,
105 While Roman lovers Roman fires impart;
Glowing alike with greatness and delight,
She rose still bolder from each guilty night.
Then blame we hapless Antony no more,*
Lost and undone by fatal beauty's power,
110 If Caesar, long inured to rage and arms,
Submits his stubborn heart to those soft charms,
If reeking from Emathia's dreadful plain,
And horrid with the blood of thousands slain,
He sinks lascivious in a lewd embrace,
115 While Pompey's ghastly spectre haunts the place,
If Julia's chastest name he can forget,
And raise her brethren of a bastard set,*
If indolently he permits from far

Bold Cato to revive the fainting war,
120   If he can give away the fruits of blood,
And fight to make a strumpet's title good.
   To him, disdaining or* to feign a tear,*
Or spread her artfully dishevelled hair,
In comely sorrow's decent garb arrayed,
125   And trusting to her beauty's certain aid,
In words like these began the Pharian maid:
   'If royal birth and the Lagaean* name,
Thy favouring pity, greatest Caesar, claim,
Redress my wrongs, thus humbly I implore,
130   And to her state an injured queen restore.
Here shed thy juster influence, and rise
A star auspicious to Egyptian skies.
Nor is it strange for Pharos to behold
A woman's temples bound with regal gold;
135   No laws our softer sex's powers restrain,
But undistinguished* equally we reign.
Vouchsafe my royal father's will to read,
And learn what dying Ptolemy decreed;
My just pretensions stand recorded there,
140   My brother's empire and his bed to share.
Nor would the gentle boy his love refuse,
Did cursed Pothinus leave him free to choose,
But now in vassalage he holds his crown,
And acts by power and passions not his own.
145   Nor is my soul on empire fondly set,
But could with ease my royal rights forget,
So* thou the throne from vile dishonour save,
Restore the master, and depose the slave.*
What scorn, what pride his haughty bosom swell,
150   Since, at his bidding, Roman Pompey fell!
Ev'n now – which, O ye righteous gods, avert –
His sword is levelled at thy noble heart.
Thou and mankind are wronged when he shall dare
Or in thy prize or in thy crime to share.'
155   In vain her words the warrior's ears assailed,
Had not her face beyond her tongue prevailed;
From thence resistless eloquence she draws,
And with the sweet persuasion gains her cause.
His stubborn heart dissolves in loose delight,

160 And grants her suit for one lascivious night.
      Egypt and Caesar now in peace agreed,*
      Riot* and feasting to the war succeed;
      The wanton queen displays her wealthy store,
      Excess unknown to frugal Rome before.
165 Rich as some fane* by lavish zealots reared,
      For the proud banquet stood the hall prepared;
      Thick golden plates the latent* beams enfold,
      And the high roof was fretted o'er with gold;
      Of solid marble all, the walls were made,
170 And onyx ev'n the meaner floor inlaid,
      While porphyry and agate round the court
      In massy columns rose, a proud support.
      Of solid ebony* each post was wrought,
      From swarthy Meroë profusely brought;
175 With ivory was the entrance crusted o'er,
      And polished tortoise* hid each shining door,
      While on the cloudy spots* enchased was seen
      The lively emerald's never-fading green.
      Within, the royal beds and couches shone,
180 Beamy and bright with many a costly stone;
      In glowing purple rich the coverings lie –
      Twice had they drank the noblest Tyrian dye;*
      Others, as Pharian artists have the skill
      To mix the particoloured web at will,
185 With winding trails of various silks were made,
      Where branching gold set off the rich brocade.
      Around, of every age and choicer form,
      Huge crowds, whole nations of attendants swarm;
      Some wait in yellow rings of golden hair
190 (The vanquished Rhine showed Caesar none so fair),
      Others were seen with swarthy, woolly heads,
      Black as eternal night's unchanging shades.
      Here squealing eunuchs, a dismembered* train,
      Lament the loss of genial joys* in vain;
195 There nature's noblest work, a youthful band,
      In the full pride of blooming manhood stand.
      All duteous on the Pharian princes wait;
      The princes round the board recline in state,
      With mighty Caesar, more than princes great.
200 On ivory feet the citron board* was wrought,

Richer than those with captive Juba* brought.
With every wile ambitious beauty tries
To fix the daring Roman's heart her prize.
Her brother's meaner bed and crown she scorns,
205 And with fierce hopes for nobler empire burns,
Collects the mischiefs of her wanton eyes,
And her faint cheeks with deeper roses dyes;
Amidst the braidings of her flowing hair
The spoils of orient rocks and shells appear;
210 Like midnight stars ten thousand diamonds deck
The comely rising of her graceful neck;
Of wondrous work, a thin, transparent lawn
O'er each soft breast in decency was drawn,
Where still by turns the parting threads withdrew,
215 And all the panting bosom rose to view.
Her robe, her every part, her air, confess
The power of female skill exhausted in her dress.
Fantastic madness of unthinking pride
To boast that wealth which prudence strives to hide,
220 In civil wars such treasures to display,
And tempt a soldier with the hopes of prey!
Had Caesar not been Caesar, impious, bold,* ⎫
And ready to lay waste the world for gold,   ⎬
But just as all our frugal names of old,   ⎭
225 This wealth could Curius or Fabricius* know,
Or ruder Cincinnatus* from the plough –
As Caesar, they had seized the mighty spoil,
And to enrich their Tiber robbed the Nile.
Now by a train of slaves the various feast
230 In massy gold magnificent was placed;
Whatever earth, or air, or seas afford,
In vast profusion crowns the labouring board.
For dainties Egypt every land explores,
Nor spares those very gods her zeal adores.*
235 The Nile's sweet wave capacious crystals pour,
And gems of price* the grapes' delicious store,*
No growth of Mareotis' marshy fields,
But such as Meroë maturer yields,
Where the warm sun the racy* juice refines,
240 And mellows into age the infant wines.
With wreaths of nard* the guests their temples bind,

And blooming roses of immortal kind;*
Their dropping locks with oily odours flow,
Recent from near Arabia where they grow;
245 The vigorous spices breathe their strong perfume,*
And the rich vapour fills the spacious room.
  Here Caesar Pompey's poverty disdained,
And learned to waste that world his arms had gained.
He saw th'Egyptian wealth with greedy eyes,
250 And wished some fair pretence to seize the prize.
Sated at length with the prodigious feast,
Their weary appetites from riot ceased,
When Caesar, curious of some new delight,
In conversation sought to wear* the night,
255 Then gently thus addressed the good old priest,
Reclining decent in his linen vest:*
'O wise Acoreus,* venerable seer,
Whose age bespeaks thee heaven's peculiar care,
Say from what origin thy nation sprung,
260 What boundaries to Egypt's land belong,
What are thy people's customs and their modes,
What rites they teach, what forms they give their gods?
Each ancient, sacred mystery explain,
Which monumental sculptures yet retain.
265 Divinity disdains to be confined,
Fain would be known and reverenced by mankind.
'Tis said thy holy predecessors thought
Cecropian* Plato* worthy to be taught,
And sure the sages of your schools have known
270 No soul more formed for science than my own.
Fame of my potent rival's flight, 'tis true,   ⎤
To this your Pharian shore my journey drew –   ⎬
Yet know the love of learning led me too.   ⎦
In all the hurries of tumultuous war,
275 The stars, the gods and heavens were still my care.
Nor shall my skill to fix the rolling year*
Inferior to Eudoxus'* art appear.
Long has my curious soul, from early youth,
Toiled in the noble search of sacred truth,
280 Yet still no views have urged my ardour more
Than Nile's remotest fountain to explore.
Then say what source the famous stream supplies,

And bids it at revolving periods rise,
Show me that head from whence, since time begun,
285 The long succession of his waves has run;
This let me know, and all my toils shall cease,
The sword be sheathed, and earth be blessed with
     peace.'
  The warrior spoke, and thus the seer replied:*
'Nor shalt thou, mighty Caesar, be denied.
290 Our sires forbade all but themselves to know,
And kept with care profaner laymen low;*
My soul, I own, more generously inclined,
Would let in daylight to inform the blind.
Nor would I truth in mysteries restrain,
295 But make the gods, their power and precepts plain,
Would teach their miracles, would spread their praise,
And well-taught minds to just devotion raise.
Know, then, to all those stars by nature driven* ⎫
In opposition to revolving heaven,   ⎬
300 Some one peculiar influence was given.   ⎭
The sun the seasons of the year supplies,
And bids the evening and the morning rise,
Commands the planets with superior force,
And keeps each wandering light to his appointed course;
305 The silver moon o'er briny seas presides,
And heaves huge ocean with alternate tides;
Saturn's cold rays in icy climes prevail,
Mars rules the winds, the storm and rattling hail;
Where Jove ascends the skies are still serene,
310 And fruitful Venus is the genial queen,
While every limpid spring and falling stream
Submits to radiant Hermes' reigning beam;
When in the Crab the humid ruler shines,*
And to the sultry Lion near inclines,
315 There fixed immediate o'er Nile's latent source
He strikes the watery stores with ponderous force;
Nor can the flood bright Maia's son* withstand,
But heaves like ocean at the moon's command;
His waves ascend, obedient as the seas,
320 And reach their destined height by just degrees;
Nor to its bank returns th'enormous tide,
Till Libra's equal scales the days and nights divide.

Antiquity, unknowing and deceived,
In dreams of Ethiopian snows believed;
325 From hills they taught how melting currents ran,
When the first swelling of the flood began.
But ah how vain the thought! No Boreas there
In icy bonds constrains the wintry year,
But sultry southern winds eternal reign,
330 And scorching suns the swarthy natives stain.
Yet more, whatever flood the frost congeals,
Melts as the genial spring's return he feels,
While Nile's redundant waters never rise,
Till the hot Dog* inflames the summer skies,
335 Nor to his banks his shrinking stream confines,
Till high in heaven th'autumnal balance shines.
Unlike his watery brethren he presides,
And by new laws his liquid empire guides.
From dropping seasons no increase he knows,
340 Nor feels the fleecy showers of melting snows.
His river swells not idly e'er the land
The timely office of his waves demand,
But knows his lot, by providence assigned,
To cool the season and refresh mankind.
345 When-e'er the Lion sheds his fires around,
And Cancer burns Syene's parching ground,
Then at the prayer of nations comes the Nile,
And kindly tempers up the mouldering soil.
Nor from the plains the covering god retreats,
350 Till the rude fervour of the skies abates,
Till Phoebus into milder autumn fades,
And Meroë projects her lengthening shades.
Nor let enquiring sceptics ask the cause:
'Tis Jove's command, and these are nature's laws.
355 'Others of old, as vainly too, have thought
By western winds the spreading deluge brought,
While at fixed times for many a day they last,
Possess the skies and drive a constant blast;
Collected clouds united zephyrs bring,
360 And shed huge rains from many a dropping wing,
To heave the flood, and swell th'abounding spring.
Or when the airy brethren's* steadfast force
Resists the rushing current's downward course,

Backward he rolls indignant to his head,*
365　While o'er the plains his heapy waves are spread.
　　'Some have believed that spacious channels go
Through the dark entrails of the earth below;
Through these, by turns, revolving rivers pass,
And secretly pervade the mighty mass;
370　Through these the sun, when from the north he flies,
And cuts the glowing Ethiopic skies,
From distant streams attracts their liquid stores,
And through Nile's spring th'assembled waters pours,
Till Nile, o'er burdened, disembogues* the load,
375　And spews the foamy deluge all abroad.
　　'Sages there have been too who long maintained
· That ocean's waves through porous earth are drained;
'Tis thence their saltness they no longer keep,
By slow degrees still freshening as they creep,
380　Till at a period Nile receives them all,
And pours them loosely spreading as they fall.
　　'The stars, and sun himself, as some have said,
By exhalations from the deep are fed,
And when the golden ruler of the day
385　Through Cancer's fiery sign pursues his way,
His beams attract too largely from the sea;
The refuse of his draughts the nights return,
And more than fill the Nile's capacious urn.
　　'Were I the dictates of my soul to tell,
390　And speak the reasons of the watery swell,
To providence the task I should assign,
And find the cause in workmanship divine.
Less* streams we trace unerring to their birth,
And know the parent earth which brought them forth,
395　While this, as early as the world begun,
Ran thus, and must continue thus to run;
And still, unfathomed by our search, shall own
No cause but Jove's commanding will alone.
　　'Nor, Caesar, is thy search of knowledge strange –
400　Well may thy boundless soul desire to range,
Well may she strive Nile's fountain to explore,
Since mighty kings have sought the same before;
Each for the first discoverer would be known,
And hand to future times the secret down;

405 But still their powers were exercised in vain,
While latent nature mocked their fruitless pain.
Philip's great son,* whom Memphis still records*
The chief of her illustrious sceptred lords,
Sent of his own a chosen number forth,
410 To trace the wondrous stream's mysterious birth.
Through Ethiopia's plains they journeyed on,
Till the hot sun opposed the burning zone;
There, by the god's resistless beams repelled,
An unbeginning stream they still beheld.
415 Fierce came Sesostris from the eastern dawn,*
On his proud car by captive monarchs drawn:
His lawless will, impatient of a bound,
Commanded Nile's hid fountain to be found;
But sooner much the tyrant might have known*
420 Thy famed Hesperian Po, or Gallic Rhone.
Cambyses* too his daring Persians led
Where hoary age makes white the Ethiop's head,*
Till, sore distressed and destitute of food,
He stained his hungry jaws with human blood,
425 Till half his host the other half devoured,
And left the Nile behind them unexplored.
   'Of thy forbidden head, thou sacred stream,
Nor fiction dares to speak, nor poets dream.
Through various nations roll thy waters down, ⎫
430 By many seen, though still by all unknown; ⎬
No land presumes to claim thee for her own. ⎭
For me, my humble tale no more shall tell
Than what our just records demonstrate* well,
Than God, who bade thee thus mysterious flow,*
435 Permits the narrow mind of man to know.
   'Far in the south thy daring waters rise,
As in disdain of Cancer's burning skies;
Thence with a downward course they seek the main,
Direct against the lazy Northern Wain,*
440 Unless when, partially, thy winding tide
Turns to the Libyan or Arabian side.
The distant Seres* first behold thee flow,
Nor yet thy spring the distant Seres know.
Midst sooty Ethiops next thy current roams –
445 The sooty Ethiops wonder whence it comes;

Nature conceals thy infant stream with care,
Nor lets thee but in majesty appear.
Upon thy banks astonished nations stand,
Nor dare assign thy rise to one peculiar land.
450 Exempt from vulgar laws thy waters run,
Nor take their various seasons from the sun;
Though high in heaven the fiery solstice stand,
Obedient winter comes at thy command.
From pole to pole thy boundless waves extend;
455 One never knows thy rise, nor one thy end.
By Meroë thy stream divided roves,
And winds encircling round her ebon groves;
Of sable hue the costly timbers stand,
Dark as the swarthy natives of the land,
460 Yet, though tall woods in wide abundance spread,
Their leafy tops afford no friendly shade;
So vertically shine the solar rays,
And from the Lion dart the downward blaze.
From thence through deserts dry thou journey'st on, ⎫
465 Nor shrink'st diminished by the torrid zone,   ⎬
Strong in thyself, collected, full and one.   ⎭
Anon thy streams are parcelled o'er the plain,
Anon the scattered currents meet again;
Jointly they flow, where Philae's gates divide
470 Our fertile Egypt from Arabia's side;
Thence with a peaceful, soft descent they creep,
And seek insensibly the distant deep,
Till through seven mouths the famous flood is lost
On the last limits of our Pharian coast,
475 Where Gaza's isthmus rises to restrain
The Erythraean* from the midland main.
Who that beholds thee, Nile, thus gently flow,
With scarce a wrinkle on thy glassy brow,
Can guess thy rage when rocks resist thy force,
480 And hurl thee headlong in thy downward course,
When spouting cataracts thy torrent pour,
And nations tremble at the deafening roar,
When thy proud waves with indignation rise,
And dash their foamy fury to the skies?
485 These wonders reedy Abatos can tell,
And the tall cliffs that first declare thy swell,

The cliffs with ignorance of old believed
Thy parent veins and for thy spring received.
From thence huge mountains nature's hand provides,
490 To bank thy too luxurious river's sides;
As in a vale thy current she restrains,
Nor suffers thee to spread the Libyan plains;
At Memphis first free liberty she yields,
And lets thee loose to float the thirsty fields.'

495   In unsuspected peace securely laid*
Thus waste they silent night's declining shade.
    Meanwhile accustomed furies still infest,*
With usual rage, Pothinus' horrid breast,
Nor can the ruffian's hand from slaughter rest.
500 Well may the wretch, distained* with Pompey's blood,
Think every other dreadful action good.
Within him still the snaky sisters dwell,*
And urge his soul with all the powers of Hell.
Can fortune to such hands such mischief doom,
505 And let a slave revenge the wrongs of Rome,
Prevent* th'example preordained to stand
The great renown of Brutus' righteous hand!
Forbid it, gods, that Caesar's hallowed blood,
To liberty by fate a victim vowed,
510 Should on a less occasion e'er be spilt,
And prove a vile Egyptian eunuch's guilt.
Hardened by crimes, the bolder villain now
Avows his purpose with a daring brow,
Scorns the mean aids of falsehood and surprise,
515 And openly the victor chief defies.
Vain in his hopes, nor doubting to succeed,
He trusts that Caesar must like Pompey bleed.
    The feeble boy* to cursed Achillas' hand
Had, with his army, giv'n his crown's command;
520 To him, by wicked sympathy of mind,
By leagues and brotherhood of murder joined,
To him, the first and fittest of his friends,
Thus by a trusty slave Pothinus sends:
    'While stretched at ease the great Achillas lies,
525 And sleep sits heavy on his slothful eyes,
The bargain for our native land is made,
And the dishonest price already paid.

The former rule* no longer now we own,*
Usurping Cleopatra wears the crown.
530   Dost thou alone withdraw thee from her state,*
Nor on the bridals of thy mistress wait?
Tonight at large she lavishes her charms,
And riots in luxurious Caesar's arms.
E'er long her brother may the wanton wed,
535   And reap the refuse of the Roman's bed;
Doubly a bride, then doubly shall she reign,
While Rome and Egypt wear, by turns, her chain.
Nor trust thou to thy credit with the boy,
When arts and eyes like hers their powers employ.
540   Mark with what ease her fatal charms can mould
The heart of Caesar, ruthless, hard and old?
Were the soft king his thoughtless head to rest,
But for a night, on her incestuous breast,
His crown and friends he'd barter for the bliss,
545   And give thy head and mine for one lewd kiss;
On crosses, or in flames, we should deplore*
Her beauty's terrible, resistless power;
On both her sentence is already passed –
She dooms us dead because we kept her chaste.
550   What potent hand shall then assistance bring?
Caesar's her lover, and her husband king.
Haste, I adjure thee by our common guilt,
By that great blood which we in vain have spilt,*
Haste, and let war, let death with thee return,
555   And the funereal torch for* Hymen's* burn.
Whate'er embrace the hostile charmer hold,
Find and transfix her in the luscious fold.
Nor let the fortune of this Latian lord
Abash thy courage, or restrain thy sword;
560   In the same glorious, guilty paths we tread
That raised him up, the world's imperious head.
Like him, we seek dominion for our prize,
And hope, like him, by Pompey's fall to rise.
Witness the stains of yonder blushing wave,
565   Yon bloody shore and yon inglorious grave.
Why fear we then to bring our wish to pass? –
This Caesar is not more than Pompey was.
What though we boast nor birth nor noble name,

Nor kindred with some purple monarch claim?
570 Conscious of fate's decree, such aid we scorn,
And know we were for mighty mischief born.
See how kind fortune, by this offered prey,
Finds means to purge all past offence away;
With grateful thanks Rome shall the deed approve,
575 And this last merit the first crime* remove.
Stripped of his titles and the pomp of power,
Caesar's a single soldier, and no more.
Think then how easily the task were done,
How soon we may an injured world atone,
580 Finish all wars, appease each Roman shade,
By sacrificing one devoted* head.
Fearless, ye dread united legions, go,
Rush all, undaunted, on your common foe;
This right, ye Romans,* to your country do,
585 Ye Pharians, this your king expects from you!
But chief, Achillas, may the praise be thine, ⎫
Haste thou, and find him on his bed supine, ⎬
Weary with toiling lust and gorged with wine; ⎭
Then strike, and what their Cato's prayers demand
590 The gods shall give to thy more favoured hand.'
    Nor failed the message, fitted to persuade,*
But, prone to blood, the willing chief obeyed.
No noisy trumpets sound the loud alarm,
But silently the moving legions arm,
595 All unperceived for battle they prepare,
And bustle through the night with busy care.
The mingled bands who formed this mongrel host,
To the disgrace of Rome, were Romans most,
A herd who, had they not been lost to shame
600 And long forgetful of their country's name,
Had blushed to own ev'n Ptolemy their head,
Yet now were by his meaner vassal led.
Oh, mercenary war, thou slave of gold,
How is thy faithless courage bought and sold!
605 For base reward thy hireling hands obey,* ⎫
Unknowing right or wrong they fight for pay, ⎬
And give their country's great revenge away. ⎭
Ah wretched Rome, for whom thy fate prepares,
In every nation, new domestic wars;

610   The fury that from pale Thessalia fled
     Rears on the banks of Nile her baleful head.
     What could protecting Egypt more have done,
     Had she received the haughty victor's son?*
     But thus the gods our sinking state confound,
615   Thus tear our mangled empire all around,
     In every land fit instruments employ,
     And suffer ruthless slaughter to destroy.
     Thus ev'n Egyptian parricides presume
     To meddle in the sacred cause of Rome;
620   Thus, had not fate those hands of murder tied,
     Success had crowned the vile Achillas' side.
     Nor wanted fit occasion for the deed:
     Timely the traitors to the place succeed,
     While in security the careless guest,
625   Lingering as yet, his couch supinely pressed.
     No gates, no guards forbade their open way,
     But all dissolved in sleep and surfeits lay;
     With ease the victor at the board had bled,
     And lost in riot his defenceless head.
630   But pious caution now their rage withstands,*
     And care for Ptolemy withholds their hands;
     With reverence and remorse, unknown before,
     They dread to spill their royal master's gore,
     Lest in the tumult of the murderous night,
635   Some erring mischief on his youth may light.
     Swayed by this thought, nor doubting to succeed,
     They hold it fitting to defer the deed.
     Gods, that such wretches should so proudly dare!
     Can such a life* be theirs to take or spare?
640   Till dawn of day the warrior stood reprieved,
     And Caesar at Achillas' bidding lived.
       Now o'er aspiring Casium's eastern head
     The rosy light by Lucifer* was led,
     Swift through the land the piercing beams were borne,
645   And glowing Egypt felt the kindling morn,
     When from proud Alexandria's walls afar
     The citizens behold the coming war.
     The dreadful legions shine in just array,
     And firm as to the battle hold their way.
650   Conscious meanwhile of his unequal force,

Straight to the palace Caesar bends his course,
Nor in the lofty bulwarks dares confide,
Their ample circuit stretching far too wide;
To one fixed part his little band retreats,
655 There mans the walls and towers, and bars the gates.
There fear, there wrath by turns his bosom tears –
He fears, but still with indignation fears;
His daring soul, restrained, more fiercely burns
And proudly the ignoble refuge scorns.
660 The captive lion thus, with generous rage,
Reluctant foams and roars and bites his cage;
Thus, if some power could Mulciber enslave,
And bind him down in Etna's smoky cave,
With fires more fierce th'imprisoned god would glow,
665 And bellow in the dreadful deeps below.
He who so lately, with undaunted pride,
The power of mighty Pompey's arms defied,
With justice and the Senate on his side,
Who with a cause, which gods and men must hate,
670 Stood up and struggled for success with fate,
Now abject foes and slaves insulting fears,
And shrinks beneath a shower of Pharian spears.
The warrior, who disdained to be confined
By Tyrian Gades or the eastern Ind,*
675 Now in a narrow house conceals that head
From which the fiercest Scythians once had fled*
And horrid Moors beheld with awful dread.
From room to room irresolute he flies,
And on some guardian bar or door relies;
680 So boys and helpless maids, when towns are won,
To secret corners for protection run.
Still by his side the beardless king he bears,*
Ordained to share in every ill he fears;
If he must die he dooms the boy to go,
685 Alike devoted to the shades below,
Resolves his head a victim first shall fall,
Hurled at his slaves from off the lofty wall.
So from Aeëtes fierce Medea fled,*
Her sword still aimed at young Absyrtus' head;
690 When-e'er she sees her vengeful sire draw nigh,
Ruthless she dooms the wretched boy to die.

Yet e'er these cruel last extremes he proves,*
By gentler steps of peace the Roman moves:
He sends an envoy in the royal name,
695   To chide their fury and the war disclaim.
But impious they nor gods nor kings regard,
Nor universal laws by all revered,
No right of sacred characters they know,
But tear the olive from the hallowed brow,
700   To death the messenger of peace pursue,
And in his blood their horrid hands imbrue.
    Such are the palms which cursed Egyptians claim,
Such prodigies* exalt their nation's name.
Nor purple* Thessaly's destructive shore,
705   Nor dire Pharnaces* nor the Libyan Moor,*
Nor every barbarous land, in every age,
Equal a soft Egyptian eunuch's rage.
    Incessant still the roar of war prevails,
While the wild host the royal pile assails.
710   Void of device, no thundering rams they bring,
Nor kindling flames with spreading mischief fling;
Bellowing, around they run with fruitless pain,
Heave at the doors, and thrust and strive in vain;
More than* a wall great Caesar's fortune stands,
715   And mocks the madness of their feeble hands.
    On one proud side the lofty fabric stood,*
Projected bold into th'adjoining flood;
There, filled with armèd bands, their barks draw near,
But find the same defending Caesar there;
720   To every part the ready warrior flies,
And with new rage the fainting fight supplies;
Headlong he drives them with his deadly blade,
Nor seems to be invaded, but t'invade.
Against the ships phalaric darts* he aims –
725   Each dart with pitch and livid sulphur flames.
The spreading fire o'er-runs their unctuous sides,*
And, nimbly mounting, on the topmast rides;
Planks, yards and cordage feed the dreadful blaze,
The drowning vessel hisses in the seas,
730   While floating arms and men, promiscuous strowed,*
Hide the whole surface of the azure flood.
Nor dwells destruction on their fleet alone,

But, driv'n by winds, invades the neighbouring town;
On rapid wings the sheety flames they bear,
735 In wavy lengths along the reddening air;
Nor much unlike the shooting meteors fly,
In gleamy trails, athwart the midnight sky.
　　Soon as the crowd behold their city burn,*
Thither all headlong from the siege they turn;
740 But Caesar, prone to vigilance and haste,
To snatch the just occasion e'er it passed,
Hid in the friendly night's involving* shade,
A safe retreat to Pharos timely made.
In elder times of holy Proteus' reign*
745 An isle it stood encompassed by the main;
Now by a mighty mole the town it joins,
And from wide seas the safer port confines.
Of high importance to the chief it lies,
To him brings aid, and to the foe denies;
750 In close restraint the captive town is held,
While free behind he views the watery field.*
There safe, with cursed Pothinus in his power,
Caesar defers the villain's doom no more.
Yet ah, by means too gentle he expires:
755 No gashing knives he feels, no scorching fires,
Nor were his limbs by grinning tigers torn,
Nor pendant on the horrid cross are borne –
Beneath the sword the wretch resigns his breath,
And dies too gloriously by Pompey's death.*
760 　　Meanwhile, by wily Ganymede conveyed,*
Arsinoë, the younger royal maid,
Fled to the camp, and with a daring hand
Assumes the sceptre of supreme command;
And – for her feeble brother was not there –
765 She calls herself the sole Lagaean heir;
Then, since he dares dispute her right to reign,
She dooms the fierce Achillas to be slain.
With just remorse repenting fortune paid
This second victim to her Pompey's shade.
770 But oh, nor this, nor Ptolemy, nor all
The race of Lagus doomed at once to fall,
Not hecatombs of tyrants shall suffice,
Till Brutus strikes, and haughty Caesar dies.

Nor yet the rage of war was hushed in peace,
775   Nor would that storm with him* who raised it cease.
A second eunuch to the task succeeds,
And Ganymede the power of Egypt leads;
He cheers the drooping Pharians with success,
And urged the Roman chief with new distress.
780   Such dangers did one dreadful day afford,
As annals might to latest times record,
And consecrate to fame the warrior's sword.
While to their barks his faithful band descends,*
Caesar the mole's contracted space defends.
785   Part from the crowded quay aboard were passed,
The careful chief remained among the last,
When sudden Egypt's furious powers unite,
And fix on him alone th'unequal fight.
By land the numerous foot, by sea the fleet,
790   At once surround him, and prevent retreat.
No means for safety or escape remain –
To fight or fly were equally in vain;
A vulgar period* on his wars attends,
And his ambitious life obscurely ends.
795   No seas of gore, no mountains of the slain,
Renown* the fight on some distinguished plain,
But meanly in a tumult must he die,
And overborne by crowds inglorious lie;
No room was left to fall as Caesar should,
800   So little were the hopes his foes and fate allowed.
At once the place and danger he surveys,
The rising mound and the near neighbouring seas;
Some fainting, struggling doubts as yet remain:
Can he perhaps his navy still regain,
805   Or shall he die, and end th'uncertain pain?
At length, while madly thus perplexed he burns,*
His own brave Scaeva to his thoughts returns,
Scaeva, who in the breach undaunted stood,
And singly made the dreadful battle good,
810   Whose arm advancing Pompey's host repelled,
And cooped within a wall the captive leader held.*
Strong in his soul the glorious image rose,
And taught him sudden to disdain his foes,
The force opposed in equal scales to weigh,

815   (Himself was Caesar, and Egyptians they)
      To trust that fortune and those gods once more
      That never failed his daring hopes before.
      Threatening, aloft his flaming blade he shook,
      And through the throng his course resistless took;
820   Hands, arms and helmèd heads before him fly,
      While mingling screams and groans ascend the sky.
      So winds, imprisoned, force their furious way,
      Tear up the earth, and drive the foamy sea.
      Just on the margin of the mound he stayed,
825   And for a moment thence the flood surveyed.
      'Fortune divine, be present now!', he cried,
      And plunged undaunted in the foamy tide.
      Th'obedient deep, at fortune's high command,
      Received the mighty master of the land;
830   Her servile waves officious Tethys spread*
      To raise with proud support his awful head.
      And – for he scorned th'inglorious race of Nile
      Should pride themselves in aught of Caesar's spoil –
      In his left hand, above the water's power,
835   Papers and scrolls of high import he bore,
      Where his own labours faithfully record
      The battles of ambition's ruthless sword;
      Safe in his right the deadly steel he held,
      And ploughed with many a stroke the liquid field,
840   While his fixed teeth tenaciously retain
      His ample Tyrian robe's imperial train;
      Th'encumbered folds the curling surface sweep,
      Come slow behind and drag along the deep.
      From the high mole, from every Pharian prow,
845   A thousand hands a thousand javelins throw;
      The thrilling* points dip bloodless in the waves,
      While he their idle wrath securely braves.
      So when some mighty serpent of the main
      Rolls his huge length athwart the liquid plain,
850   Whether he range voracious for the prey,
      Or to the sunny shore directs his way,
      Him if by chance the fishers view from far,
      With flying darts they wage a distant war;
      But the fell monster, unappalled with dread,
855   Above the seas exerts his poisonous head;

He rears his livid crest and kindling eyes,
And terrible the feeble foe defies;
His swelling breast a foamy path divides,
And careless o'er the murmuring flood he glides.
860   Some looser Muse,* perhaps, who lightly treads
The devious* paths where wanton fancy leads,
In heaven's high court would feign the Queen of Love
Kneeling in tears before the throne of Jove,
Imploring sad th'almighty father's grace
865 For the dear offspring of her Julian race –
While, to the just recording Roman's eyes,
Far other forms and other gods arise;
The guardian furies round him rear their heads,
And Nemesis* the shield of safety spreads;
870 Justice and fate the floating chief convey,
And Rome's glad genius wafts him on his way;
Freedom and laws the Pharian darts withstand,
And save him for avenging Brutus' hand.
His friends, unknowing what the gods decree,
875 With joy receive him from the swelling sea;
In peals on peals their shouts triumphant rise,
Roll o'er the distant flood, and thunder to the skies.

NOTES

Our notes to accompany the text fulfil a number of different functions and are designed to make the poem as accessible as possible to a varied audience. The undergraduate or general reader will certainly require a good deal of guidance, and even the professional classicist or eighteenth-century scholar will probably need to consult the notes or the glossary on occasion.

Some of the notes are intended simply to help readers negotiate their way round the narrative of the poem, by summarizing the action of a particular passage. Much-discussed episodes, such as the account of Erictho in Book VI, or the panegyric to the Emperor Nero in Book I, require longer notes, giving some indication of the way readers have responded to them. But most of the annotation is of a simpler nature, explaining the historical background to a reference, or identifying the historical figures alluded to by Lucan. Although Rowe's language does not present many problems to modern readers, he does use a number of unfamiliar words, or words whose meaning has substantially changed, and these are glossed in the notes. One common example is the verb 'prevent' which is generally used by Rowe to mean 'to go before' or 'to anticipate' rather than 'to hinder'. Similarly 'tedious' implies exhaustion caused by contemplating the awful (Johnson cites Dryden: 'the tedious sight of woes') rather than, as generally now, 'wearisome by continuance or prolixity'.

In some ways, however, more problems are presented to the reader by words which have changed more subtly, where the difference is one of nuance. 'Generous' (IV.817) is closer to Samuel Johnson's definition – 'noble of mind; magnanimous; open of heart' than to its usual modern meaning, although the two are not entirely discrete. 'Rage' is another word whose connotations have narrowed since the eighteenth century, and it is sometimes used by Rowe to denote enthusiasm rather than fury (see, for example, IV.866). 'Obscene' lacks the sexual resonance which it almost always has in modern usage and is used of anything which is offensive or disgusting, as well as sometimes simply to mean 'inauspicious' or 'ill omened'.

Many words used by Rowe have diminished greatly in force since the eighteenth century. We need to remember that 'dreadful' and 'awful' really meant 'full of awe', 'full of dread' to Rowe and his contemporaries. 'Horrid' and 'ghastly' have perhaps been even further trivialized – the beginning of this process can be seen in Jane Austen's *Northanger Abbey* in the discussions of satisfyingly 'horrid' Gothic romances. 'Horrid' is also an example of a word which Rowe uses with an eye to its Latin etymology – the primary meaning of *horridus* is 'bristling; standing on end'. Similarly when Rowe talks of Cato's 'virtue' (IX.860), he is translating Lucan's *virtus*, which signifies manliness and courage as well as moral rectitude. As Cato does indeed possess virtue in its most common modern sense, this is a particularly telling example of the elusive difficulties of Rowe's language.

It is not always easy for a modern reader to tell whether a word is poetic or not. We could take the case of 'nerve' and 'nervous'. 'Nerve', Johnson observes, is a word 'used by the poets for sinew or tendon' (he cites Chapman and Pope's *Odyssey*). 'Nervous', on the other hand, was not, it seems, regarded as poetical but as derived simply from the Latin *nervus* and thus meaning 'well strung; strong; vigorous'.

James Welwood's Preface

p. xlix Lucan: There are various, often conflicting and not very reliable, sources and *testimonia* for Lucan's life, including two ancient *vitae* (Suetonian life, life of Vacca). Welwood has constructed his own account out of this material, one that is highly favourable to Lucan (e.g. over his betrayal of his mother). Few modern scholars would accept this particular reconstruction (Ahl 1976; Heitland 1887, xii–xxxii).

p. xlix Welwood: James Welwood (1652–1727) was educated at Glasgow University, and went to Holland in 1679, where he is thought to have graduated MD. He was physician to William III and Queen Mary, and he returned to England with William in 1690, after which he was elected a fellow of the College of Physicians. He was a staunch Whig, and his works include *Memoirs of the most Material Transactions in England for the last Hundred Years preceeding the Revolution in 1688* (1700).

p. li Quintilian: X.90.

p. liii **The verses ... emperor:** It is not known whether these lines are quoted from the works of others or (as is more probable) are parodies by Persius himself. Although there is a tradition of ascribing them to Nero the evidence for this is highly dubious.

p. liv **27th year:** In fact Lucan was aged twenty-five.

p. lv *Marco ... Servata*: 'To Marcus Annaeus Lucanus, a poet from Cordoba, through the favour of Nero, and for the preservation of his fame.'

p. lv **He wrote ... age:** Modern scholars would agree with Welwood's assessment of the authorship of the *laus Pisonis*.

p. lvi **The poetry ... respect:** Welwood has misunderstood Statius, who lists four epic writers who must yield to Lucan: Ennius, Lucretius, Varro of Atax (author of an *Argonautica*) and Ovid. The last two are not named but described periphrastically. Welwood supposes only two writers are referred to and mistakenly assumes that Ennius wrote an *Argonautica*.

p. lvi **His:** 'Yours' in Lucan. Caesar is addressed. 'Fought by you and told by me' is his meaning (this is the translation suggested by Housman). Welwood appears to have thought that Homer was addressed, as 'verses' is the only noun which could go with 'his and mine'.

p. lvii **Helicon:** a mountain in Boeotia in Greece, supposed haunt of the Muses.

p. lvii **Fearing:** omitted in the first edition.

p. lviii **That ... father:** The reference is to the story told by Clarendon in *History of the Rebellion* concerning the appearance of the ghost of the father of George Villiers, first Duke of Buckingham, prophesying the duke's death (*The History of the Rebellion and Civil Wars in England* (1992), ed. W. Dunn Macray, Oxford: Clarendon Press, Vol. I, pp. 51–3).

p. lviii **Late two wars:** Welwood may be thinking of the siege of Namur, which ended in 1695, the Battle of Blenheim (1704) or the Battle of Malplaquet (1709). The Treaty of Utrecht ending the War of Spanish Succession was signed on 11 April 1713.

p. lviii **When:** corrected to 'though' in later editions.

p. lviii **Secret history:** i.e. a history describing secret affairs of state, which spoke of persons in authority too freely to allow of their being made public.

p. lxii **Antiochus:** Cf. Livy, XXXXV.12.

p. lxiii **Saint-Evremond:** Charles de Marguetel de Saint-Denis Saint-Evremond (1610–1703). His best-known work is *Conversation du Maréchal d'Hocquincourt avec le Père Canaye.*

p. lxiv **Than:** 'Of' is inserted after than in later editions.

p. lxvi **I remember . . . force:** Montaigne makes no such statement in the *Essais*, and in II.10 he explicitly names Virgil, though not Lucan, as one of the four greatest Latin poets. It is possible that Welwood has confused Montaigne with Corneille, who admired Lucan greatly and is said to have preferred him to Virgil.

p. lxviii **Fort:** forte.

p. lxviii **Strada:** Famianus Strada (1572–1649), a Roman Jesuit, author of *Prolusiones Academicae.*

p. lxviii **Pope Leo the Tenth:** Leo X, Giovanni de'Medici, was pope from 1513 to 1521. He was a renowned patron of learning.

p. lxviii **1514:** In fact several editions of the *Pharsalia* appeared before this date. The earliest listed in the British Museum Catalogue was published in 1469 and was edited by J. Andreas, Bishop of Aleria.

p. lxix **Him:** replaced by 'Lucan' in later editions.

p. lxix **Latin:** not included here.

p. lxix **Fabius:** Quintilian.

p. lxix **Maro:** Virgil.

p. lxx **1673:** This is the date in the first edition. 1674 is the date given in modern accounts.

p. lxxi **Dr Busby:** Richard Busby (1606–95), headmaster of Westminster School, was famous for his severity. Dryden was another of his pupils.

p. lxxii **English:** deleted in later editions.

p. lxxii **Monarch:** Louis XIV of France.

p. lxxiv **Brebeuf:** Georges de Brebeuf (1617?–61) completed his translation of the *Pharsalia* in 1655.

p. lxxv **Diis:** printed deis in modern texts.

p. lxxv **Des:** printed 'de' in the first edition.

p. lxxvi **Hemisticon:** half-line.

p. lxxviii Zoilus: a fourth-century rhetorician and critic, famous for his criticism of Homer. The name is synonymous with a carping critic.

p. lxxviii As Homer ... answer: Dr John Arbuthnot, writing in 1718, referred to Rowe's translation as 'a damned jade of a Pegasus'. Rowe is satirized as Mr Bays, 'a pedantic, reciting poet, admired by the mob and himself, but justly contemned by men of sense and learning, and a despiser of rules and art', in Charles Gildon's *A New Rehearsal*, 1714.

p. lxxviii King: George I.

Book One

l. 1 Emathian: Thessalian.

ll. 1–14 Emathian plains ... I sing: 'This first period contains a proposition of the whole work, the civil war; and I would only observe once for all that as the readers, who compare it with the original, may see that I have transposed the order of it in the translation, and that on purpose I have taken the same liberty in many other places of this work; especially where I thought such transposition would give an emphasis and a strength to the latter end of the period' (Rowe).

Rowe delays his rendition of Lucan's main verb, *canimus*, which comes in the second line of the *Pharsalia*, until the very end of his long opening sentence. Cf. *Paradise Lost* I.1–6. The plural first-person form *canimus* used by Lucan is suggestive of a possible division within the poet's narrating voice, but this peculiarity is not retained in Rowe's translation.

l. 7 Piles: 'I have chosen to translate the Latin word *pilum* thus nearly, or indeed rather to keep it and make it English, because it was a weapon, as eagles were the ensigns, peculiar to the Romans, and made use of here by Lucan purposely to denote the war made amongst themselves. This *pilum* was a sort of javelin which they darted at the enemies; the description of it may be found in Polybius, Vegetius, or in our own Dr Kennet's *Roman Antiquities*' (Rowe).

ll. 7–8 Piles ... flight: Cf. Dryden's Lucanian lines from *The Hind and the Panther*, 'That was but civil war, an equal set, / Where piles with piles and eagles eagles met' (II.160–1).

l. 8 Eagles: the standards used by the Roman army.

ll. 11–12 A shattered ... lost: Here, and elsewhere in this book, the evocation of disorder and confusion may recall the opening of Dryden's

Translation of the Latter Part of the Third Book of Lucretius; Against the Fear of Death, especially 'When heaven and earth were in confusion hurled / For the debated empire of the world' (5–6).

l. 20 Wars . . . wait: Only victories over foreign foes could be awarded triumphs.

l. 21 Babylon: used here as a metonymy for Parthia. The reference is to the standards captured at Carrhae.

l. 23 While . . . paid: Pompey and Caesar and Crassus formed the First Triumvirate in 60 BC. Crassus was defeated and killed by the Parthians at Carrhae in 53 BC.

l. 29 Seres: the Chinese.

l. 29 Silken woods: This striking phrase has no equivalent in Lucan and refers to the cultivation of mulberry trees in China.

l. 32 Nile's secret fountain: The location of the source of the Nile was a mystery often referred to by Roman writers. Cf. X.281–494.

ll. 32–4 Nile's . . . skies: Rowe adds details, not present in Lucan, suggestive of division – 'cleaving', 'double' – thus demonstrating his awareness of the pervasive civil war imagery in the *Pharsalia*. The line 'flame o'er the land, and scorch the mid-day sky' is another small addition to the Latin text which looks forward to the destructive images associated with Caesar.

l. 35 Scythian seas: the Euxine.

l. 36 And . . . chains: Cf. Marlowe's rendition, 'Fetters the Euxine sea with chains of ice'.

ll. 48–65 Behold . . . go by: The evocation of the decaying Italian cities is considerably altered by Rowe who has created a far more wistful picture than Lucan who includes none of the details suggesting the country's former charm. The ghostly footsteps, whistling wind and single melancholy face are all embellishments.

l. 51 Obscene: loathsome.

l. 66 Pyrrhus: a cousin of Alexander the Great and king of Epirus in the third century who won several battles against Rome.

l. 69 Hesperia: land of the West, Italy.

ll. 70–129 But if . . . song: The address to Nero has always been a focus of controversy for critics of Lucan, who disagree as to whether the panegyric is intended to be ironic. The problem is made more difficult by the violent shift in the emperor's attitude towards the poet, a shift presumably reflected in Lucan's own opinion of Nero. Lucan links Nero with Julius Caesar through similar language and imagery, and this might incline readers towards an ironic, condemnatory reading of the address. The reception of this passage by modern readers is likely to be affected by a distaste and lack of comprehension for the panegyric mode in general, and by the modern consensus that Nero was evil and debauched. These factors, combined with a post-Romantic prejudice that poets should be on the right side, perhaps tend to make an ironic reading more palatable, although a certain type of reader will be attracted to the less Whiggish, and less agreeable, option. Virgil similarly eulogizes the Emperor Augustus in *Georgics* I and such panegyrics became an accepted feature among later poets, including Ovid and Statius. It should of course be remembered that Augustus and Claudius were deified after their death, so Lucan's evocation of Nero's reception in heaven is not intrinsically risible. The note to this passage in the Latin edition used by Rowe suggests awareness of the possibility of reading the praise of Nero ironically: *assentatio quam vix excusaverit ironia* ('a piece of flattery which irony can scarcely excuse').

l. 74 **Thunderer:** Jupiter.

ll. 77–88 **Oppressed . . . reward:** The references which follow are all to battles and disasters of the civil war; not only to the war between Caesar and Pompey, but also to subsequent periods of conflict, including the battle of Actium.

l. 78 **Ghosts atone:** The 'Punic ghosts' of Carthage seek vengeance for the losses inflicted on them by the Romans during the three Punic wars.

l. 88 **Caesar:** Nero.

l. 90 **Sacred sway:** Lucan anticipates Nero's deification.

ll. 97–100 **Or . . . beam:** The obvious invitation to remember the fate of the overreaching Phaethon when he attempted the same feat may suggest that the praise of Nero is not to be taken at face value.

l. 105 **Bear:** the Great Bear constellation.

l. 112 **And . . . god:** Although the emphasis on Nero's great weight may seem ridiculous, there are precedents for associating weight with divinity, e.g. *Iliad* V.837–9. Yet it is perhaps significant that sources state that Nero was inclined to corpulence and had a squint. Renaissance commentaries on the passage suggest that Rowe and his readers might have been receptive either to an ironic or to a literal interpretation of this panegyric.

l. 121 And . . . close: Janus was the Roman god of gates and doorways. The doors of his temple were closed only in time of peace.

ll. 122–9 To . . . song: Lucan's rejection of a conventional divine muse fits with the poem's lack of supernatural machinery. The tone of the substitution of Nero for such an inspiration is uncertain.

l. 125 Still . . . cell: a reference to the Delphic oracle.

ll. 130–323 And now . . . plough: Lucan gives six causes of the civil war: fate, the formation of the First Triumvirate, the death of Crassus, the death of Julia, the rivalry between Caesar and Pompey, and the corruption of the Romans.

ll. 142–3 Then . . . Night: These personifications seem to owe a debt to their counterparts in *Paradise Lost*. Cf.I.543, 'Frighted the reign of Chaos and old Night'; also II.970, III.18. Lucan talks of chaos but not of anarchy or night at this point.

l. 163 Three lordly heads: the First Triumvirate.

l. 170 Ambient air: Cf. *Paradise Lost* VII.89–90, 'the ambient air wide interfused / Embracing round this florid earth'; also II.1051–2, 'And fast by hanging in a golden chain / This pendant world, in bigness as a star'.

l. 177 Brother's blood: Remus was murdered by his brother Romulus.

l. 179 Fury's: or perhaps one should read 'furies''. In either case the reference is to the madness of fraternal strife.

l. 180 Still: always.

l. 181 And . . . lords: Rome was only a village at the time of Romulus.

l. 189 Isthmus: the Isthmus of Corinth, which separates the Corinthian gulf from the Saronic.

ll. 199–204 Sudden . . . war: The latent rivalry between Pompey and Caesar erupted after the death of Crassus. Thus the Parthians were indirectly responsible for the civil war.

l. 201 Arsacidae: the Parthian royal dynasty.

l. 211 Julia: the daughter of Julius Caesar and the wife of Pompey. She died in childbirth in 54 BC.

l. 212 **Hymen:** the god of marriage.

ll. 217–20 **Like ... lord:** Romulus is supposed to have carried off the Sabine women to secure wives for the Romans. The Sabine men retaliated by besieging the Capitol but the Sabine women eventually reconciled them to the Romans.

l. 222 **But ... denied:** a reference to the three Fates.

l. 227 **Infest:** attack, annoy, trouble.

l. 229 **Piratic laurel:** Pompey successfully expelled pirates from the Mediterranean.

ll. 231–2 **His ... rise:** a reference to Caesar's victories in Gaul.

ll. 241–2 **Victorious ... owned:** This couplet translates one of Lucan's most famous lines – *victrix causa deis placuit, sed victa Catoni* (I.128) – which may be seen as the ultimate expression of Lucan's lack of faith in the gods as arbiters of mankind's destiny.

l. 244 **One ... yield:** Pompey was in fact only six years older than Caesar.

l. 245 **Gown:** toga, the garb of peace.

l. 251 **Theatre:** has three syllables.

l. 275 **Records:** accented on the second syllable.

ll. 288–97 **Such ... fires:** Lucan's comparison between Caesar and lightning is echoed in Marvell's description of his Caesarian Cromwell in 'An Horatian Ode':

> So restless Cromwell could not cease
> In the inglorious arts of peace,
> But through adventurous war
> Urgèd his active star;
> And, like the three-forked lightning, first
> Breaking the clouds where it was nursed,
> Did thorough his own side
> His fiery way divide.
> For 'tis all one to courage high
> The emulous or enemy;
> And with such to enclose
> Is more then to oppose.
> Then burning through the air he went,
> And palaces and temples rent;

> And Caesar's head at last
> Did through his laurels blast.
> 'Tis madness to resist or blame
> The force of angry heaven's flame.(9–26)

ll. 300–1 Those ... low: for an account of the supposed luxury and immorality at this time see, e.g. Sallust, *Bellum Catilinae* 10–11.

l. 311 Afric: Africa.

l. 312 Citron board: Rowe provides a note for the phrase 'citron board' which is not a direct translation of any word used by Lucan, but was part of the stock language of moral decay: 'This is not here taken for the lemon-tree, but for a tree something resembling the wild-cypress, and growing chiefly in Afric. It is very famous among the Roman authors, and was used by their great people for beds and tables at entertainments. The spots and crispness of the wood were its great excellence. Hence they were called *mensae tygrinae & pantherinae*.'

The inclusion of this detail was probably caused by a note in the Latin text used by Rowe which offers a quotation from Juvenal: *nil rhombus, nil dama sapit, nisi sustinet orbes grande ebur e citro factos* (XI.122–3). The lines quoted appear in a rather different form in modern texts of Juvenal, and the key word *citro* is not present.

l. 313 Minion: dainty, effeminate.

ll. 315–16 That ... scorned: Such comparisons of Rome's simple beginnings and austere Republican days with the decadence of the Empire were frequent.

l. 320 Curii, Camilli: Two families associated with upright, Roman values. It is possible that Lucan is using the plural form to stand for the singular, and intends to evoke only the most famous Camillus and Curius.

l. 323 Where ... plough: a reference to the legendary Roman hero Cincinnatus, supposedly called from the plough to be dictator in 458 BC to defeat the Aequi, an Italian tribe. He resigned his dictatorship after sixteen days to retire to his farm, and was seen to exemplify Roman austerity and simplicity. The reference is an addition by Rowe.

l. 338 Venal field: the Campus Martius, where elections to the magistracies were held.

ll. 344–419 Now ... bent: By crossing the Rubicon without disbanding his army as the Senate had ordered, Caesar effectively declared war on

Pompey and the Senate. The vision of Rome recalls the description of Cybele, *Aeneid* VI.784–6. She is described as *turrita*. Personified cities are often depicted with towers on their heads.

l. 347 **Revolving in his thought:** Dryden's Aeneas is often similarly described. The phrase 'revolving in his mind' is used five times in Dryden's translation of the *Aeneid*.

l. 368 **Capitol:** The Capitol was the site of the temple to Jupiter Optimus Maximus, Juno and Minerva and was the most sacred part of Rome.

l. 370 **Ye ... line:** a reference to the Trojan household gods who care for the Julian line because of the line of descent from Aeneas.

l. 371 **Romulus:** the legendary founder of Rome, deified after his death.

l. 373 **Alban temple:** The ancient Latin city Alba Longa was supposed to have been founded by Ascanius in *c.*1152 BC. Juppiter Latiaris (Latialis) was the guardian deity of the Latin confederacy; hence Rowe's Latinism 'Latial'.

l. 375 **But ... Rome:** Cf. *Paradise Lost* I.17, 'But chiefly thou O Spirit, that dost prefer ...'

ll. 386–95 **So ... Moor:** The simile is interesting in that it implies a veiled hostility between Caesar and Rome, by suggesting that the relationship between them resembles that between a lion and a hunter. The comparison with lightning is not in Lucan, but recalls the earlier extended simile between Caesar and lightning.

l. 399 **Ruddy:** The Rubicon derives its name from the Latin *rubicundus*, red or ruddy, and was supposed to be reddish in colour.

l. 404 **Cynthia:** the moon.

l. 420 **Balearic:** The inhabitants of the Balearic islands (including Majorca and Minorca) were famed for their skill with the sling.

l. 421 **Parthian bow:** The Parthians were famous for shooting backwards as they were fleeing.

l. 424 **Lucifer:** the Morning Star.

ll. 434–41 **The starting ... shake:** Cf. Marvell's 'An Horatian Ode':

> The forward youth that would appear
> Must now forsake his muses dear,
>   Nor in the shadows sing

His numbers languishing.
'Tis time to leave the books in dust,
And oil the unusèd armour's rust:
    Removing from the wall
    The corslet of the hall. (1–8)

l. 457 **Cimbrians:** a German tribe who invaded Italy.

l. 458 **Through ... passed:** During the second Punic war Hasdrubal crossed into Italy through Cisalpine Gaul. Ariminum was in a strategic position on this route.

l. 471 **Bellona:** goddess of war.

l. 480 **The Senate ... grown:** 'Caesar had on this occasion very favourable appearances of reason and equity on his side. He proffered to lay down his command if Pompey would do the same, but the violence of the consuls and Pompey's party was so great against him that they would hear of no proposals for an accommodation, though never so reasonable, and forced the tribunes who appeared for him to fly out of the city disguised like slaves for the immediate safety of their lives, so that when these came for protection to Caesar's camp, it seemed as if he had marched towards Rome for no other reason than the preservation of the privileges of so sacred a magistracy as the tribunes were, and the support of the laws of his country' (Rowe).

l. 481 **Wrangling tribunes:** Antony and Q. Cassius Longinus.

l. 483 **And ... fate:** The brothers Tiberius Sempronius Gracchus (c.164–133 BC) and Gaius Sempronius Gracchus (c.153–21 BC) attempted to carry out land and other reforms. Both were killed after strong opposition from the senatorial traditionalists.

l. 485 **Curio:** former tribune who had been expelled from Rome by the Senate.

l. 500 **Moody fathers:** angry Senators.

l. 502 **I ... command:** Curio vetoed proposals to end Caesar's command in Gaul.

l. 515 **And ... field:** Cf. Pope, *Iliad* I.158, 'The due reward of many a well-fought field'.

l. 519 **This ... control:** The 'vast head' is Rome, bringing with it control of the whole Roman empire.

l. 537 **Elis:** a Greek state famed for horse-breeding where the Olympic games were held.

ll. 549–50 **Yields, fields:** The first edition prints 'yield' and 'field', an apparent mistake which is corrected in later editions.

l. 558 **Devoted:** doomed.

l. 565 **Hero:** Pompey.

l. 568 **Marcellus:** Three consuls of this name opposed Caesar during this period: Gaius Claudius Marcellus, consul in 50 BC; Gaius Claudius Marcellus, consul in 49 BC; Marcus Claudius Marcellus, consul in 51 BC. The 'gown-men' are wearing togas, garments of peace.

l. 576 **What . . . laws:** Pompey claimed a triumph for a victory in Numidia when he was only twenty-four. The laws are 'violated' because triumphs were not legally permitted to generals under thirty.

l. 577 **And . . . cause:** a reference to Pompey's five-year control over the corn supply. It was thought by some that he created a corn shortage for his own ends.

l. 584 **And . . . guard:** Caesar claims that Pompey used soldiers to intimidate the forum and prevent the fair trial of Titus Annius Milo, accused of murder in 52 BC.

l. 591 **Sulla:** Lucius Cornelius Sulla, c.138–78 BC, was a Roman general who eventually became dictator for a period. He fought a civil war with Marius and was famous for his cruelty.

l. 593 **Hyrcania:** an area near the Caucasus and Caspian sea. The ferocity of Hyrcanian tigers is adduced by Dido as a parallel to Aeneas' cruelty (*Aeneid* IV.365–7).

l. 599 **Dictator:** Sulla.

l. 606 **Let . . . retreat:** Sulla resigned the dictatorship voluntarily.

l. 609 **Since . . . sail:** Pompey had successfully expelled pirates from the Mediterranean.

l. 610 **Pontic king:** King Mithridates of Pontus, eventually defeated by Pompey after a forty-year struggle with Rome, committed suicide by taking poison.

l. 613 **Province:** A *provincia* could signify a special task assigned by the Senate, and that is the meaning lying behind Rowe's usage here.

l. 614 **And vanquished Caesar:** 'This is a strong irony, a figure which the satirical genius of this author makes frequent use of' (Rowe).

l. 624 **Comfortable:** this has four syllables, the first of which should be accented.

l. 636 **Unresolving vulgar:** the uncertain crowd.

l. 638 **Somewhat:** something.

l. 643 **Laelius:** a fictional centurion.

l. 645 **Oaken wreath:** a sign that he had saved the life of a fellow citizen in battle.

l. 663 **Syrt's:** The Syrtes are two gulfs on the north coast of Africa, supposed to be dangerous for navigation. Syrt's rather than Syrts' is printed in the first edition.

l. 685 **Moneta:** Juno. Rowe has misunderstood Lucan's reference to melting down the gods' statues in the military mint. The Latin word for mint – *moneta* – is also one of Juno's cult titles. This misunderstanding arises from an erroneous note in his Latin text.

l. 685 **Fane:** temple.

l. 698 **Boreas:** the north wind.

l. 700 **Inclined:** sloped, slanting.

ll. 709–817 **To Rome ... prey:** There now follows Lucan's version of the traditional epic catalogue, normally a list of leaders or armies, but here a list of peoples abandoned by the Romans.

l. 711 **Leman lake:** Lake Geneva.

l. 712 **Vogesus:** Modern texts have 'Vosegi'. Rowe is following the spelling of his Latin text.

l. 721 **Depend:** hang down.

l. 724 **Fane:** the Portus Herculis Monoeci (Monaco). Alcides is a name meaning 'descendent of Alceus' used to designate Hercules.

ll. 726–8 **Nor ... roar:** Corus and Circius are north-west winds and Zephyr is the west wind.

l. 738 **Tethys:** a Titaness of the ocean, whose name is used here as metonymy for ocean.

ll. 742–7 What . . . remain: Lucan is referring to the tides of the Atlantic ocean.

l. 760 Averni: The text Rowe was using has 'Arverni' here, as do modern texts.

l. 763 Whose . . . embrued: Cotta was an officer of Caesar's who was ambushed and killed in Gaul.

ll. 778–80 And . . . obeyed: Hesus, Teutates and Taranis are Celtic gods.

l. 781 And . . . maid: a reference to the worship of Diana in Scythia which allegedly involved human sacrifice.

l. 784 Bards: ancient Gallic poets.

ll. 794–805 To these . . . past: Caesar discusses the druids' belief in the transmigration of souls and the spur this belief gives their valour in *De Bello Gallico* 6.14.

l. 831 White waves: The waves are not described as white by Lucan. 'Virgil gives the reason for this epithet, when he calls it

> *Sulpureis Nar albus aquis.*
> Nar with sulphureous waters white' (Rowe).

l. 859 Impulse: accented on the second syllable.

l. 860 Heartless: fearful.

l. 871 South: south wind.

l. 873 Flit: The OED quotes a 1750 definition of the verb: 'altering or removing a dead eye in the low, or top-mast shrouds or backstays, either to lengthen or to shorten them, is called flitting.'

l. 881 Unnerved; weak.

l. 883 Lares: gods of the hearth.

l. 899 At once: all together.

ll. 916–99 The gods . . . fled: Comparable descriptions of prodigies can be found in Virgil, *Georgics* I.464–88 and Ovid, *Metamorphoses* XV.779–806.

ll. 922–3 Then . . . prepare: Comets were seen as harbingers of war and of the death or overthrow of kings.

l. 941 Thyestes' feast: Thyestes was unwittingly fed the bodies of his sons by his brother Atreus. This terrible act made the sun turn in horror and set in the east. The myth is the subject of Seneca's play *Thyestes*.

l. 943 Mulciber: Vulcan.

l. 946 Charybdis' ... flood: The dogs to which Lucan refers should in fact be understood to be Scylla's, not Charybdis' (a whirlpool) as Rowe suggests.

l. 948 The vestal ... died: The extinction of the Vestal flame symbolized the destruction of Rome.

ll. 950-1 The parting ... end: 'These *Feriae Latinae*, or Latin Festivals, were performed by night to Jupiter at Alba. As I shall be always very ready to acknowledge any mistake, so I believe in this place I ought rather to have translated these verses thus:

> The parting points with double streams ascend,
> And Alba's Latian rites portentous end.

But I was led into the error by not considering enough the true meaning of the Latin expression, *confectas Latinas*' (Rowe).

ll. 952-3 Such ... foes: The Theban brothers Eteocles and Polyneices were burned together but the flame from their pyre separated, demonstrating their continuing mutual hatred.

ll. 954-5 With ... day: Rowe's translation is influenced by a note in his text. The Loeb translates, 'The earth also stopped short upon its axis'.

l. 970 Bellona's ... train: The Italian goddess of war Bellona was the focus of an orgiastic cult.

l. 971 Distain: stain.

l. 986 Such ... seen: Lycurgus, a Thracian king, persecuted Bacchus and was driven mad as a punishment, making him kill his own son.

l. 987 Theban queen: a reference to Agave of Thebes who denied Dionysus' divinity and was driven mad, causing her to kill her son Pentheus.

ll. 988-9 Such ... stand: Juno sent the Fury Megaera to Hercules, under whose influence he killed his wife and children.

l. 991 Though ... look: Hercules had already visited the underworld in order to bring back Cerberus.

l. 996 Martian field: the Campus Martius in Rome.

l. 998 **Marius:** Gaius Marius (157–86 BC) was a consul and a rival of Sulla. Sulla had his corpse disinterred and thrown into the Anio.

l. 999 **Hinds:** translates Lucan's *agricolae* and thus signifies country people.

l. 1001 **For ... sought:** The Tuscans were credited with inventing the art of divination by examining entrails.

l. 1004 **Luna:** Modern texts have 'Luca', but the Latin text used by Rowe has 'Luna', with a note explaining that the name is derived from the crescent shape of the town.

l. 1006 **Presaging:** accented on the second syllable.

l. 1018 **Gabine weed:** a way of wearing the toga associated with the ancient Latin town of Gabii.

l. 1022 **Phrygian Minerva:** the Palladium, an image of Pallas Athene which Aeneas brought to Italy and which was kept in the temple of Vesta.

l. 1023 **Fifteen:** the Quindecemviri, who were the custodians of the Sibylline prophetic books.

ll. 1025–6 **To ... year:** A statue of Cybele was bathed in the river Almo each year.

l. 1027 **Titian brotherhood:** a college of priests associated with the Sabine king, Titus Tatius.

l. 1030 **Salii:** priests of Mars.

l. 1030 **Bucklers:** shields.

l. 1032 **Flamens:** fifteen priests dedicated to particular gods.

ll. 1035–8 **Arruns ... stand:** Note the variation in Rowe's rhyme scheme here, with an abab pattern substituted for the usual couplet.

l. 1038 **Bidental:** a place which had been made sacred by being struck by lightning.

l. 1058 **Hostile side:** In divination the liver was divided and one part labelled for friends, the other for enemies. The 'hostile side' is that associated with Caesar.

l. 1063 **Caul:** fatty membrane surrounding the intestines.

ll. 1071–2 **While ... tide:** The 'adverse vessels' are aligned with Caesar.

l. 1086 **Tages:** an Etruscan seer.

l. 1088 **Double-dealing:** ambiguous.

l. 1089 **Figulus:** A Pythagorean philosopher and astrologer.

l. 1107 **Period:** end.

l. 1126 **Falchion:** sword.

ll. 1126-7 **Orion's . . . side:** It was thought to be a portent of evil if Orion was clearly visible in the sky.

l. 1142 **Lyaeus:** Bacchus.

l. 1145 **Paean:** The prophetic matron is addressing Apollo. *Paean* means healer.

ll. 1147-67 **I . . . before:** She has a vision of the battles of Pharsalia, Thapsus and Munda.

l. 1156 **Hero:** Pompey.

l. 1158 **Relics:** the surviving Republicans.

l. 1160 **Pyrene:** the Pyrenees.

l. 1162 **And . . . slain:** She seems to foretell the assassination of Caesar in the Senate House.

Book Two

ll. 10-17 **Whether . . . chance:** 'That is, whether, according to the Stoics, all things were by necessity, or, according to the Epicureans, by chance' (Rowe).

l. 23 **What . . . foretold:** The gods are described as faithful because disasters do indeed follow the portents they send.

ll. 25-6 **And all . . . weed:** The courts were suspended in times of crisis and the magistrates therefore wear their ordinary clothes, rather than the purple, 'distinguished weed', associated with their office.

l. 27 **Rods:** the lictors' rods of office.

l. 51 **Fanes:** temples.

l. 57 **Honours:** i.e. hair.

ll. 58-61 **The present . . . war:** This statement is at odds with that made by Figulus at the end of Book I. Although paradoxical, the woman's assertion may be explained. The loss of freedom brings hypocrisy, for as soon as there is a victor and a ruler only feigned joy is possible.

l. 71 On . . . plain: Cannae and Trebia were battles in the Second Punic War in which Hannibal defeated the Romans.

l. 77 Massagetes: The Massagetae lived between the Caspian and Aral seas.

l. 79 Yellow: yellow-haired.

l. 79 Suevi: 'Suebi' in modern texts.

ll. 82–3 Here . . . take: The Dacians and the Getae were both peoples from the lower Danube.

l. 84 Iberia: Spain.

l. 85 Let . . . bow: The reference is probably to the Parthians.

l. 101 Hoary sire: an unidentified old man.

ll. 106–356 'Twas . . . enjoyed: In a long digression this speaker recalls the civil wars between Marius and Sulla. Cf.I.998.

ll. 107–8 When . . . sword: The reference is to Marius' victories over a German tribe, the Cimbri, in 101 BC and over the Numidian king Jugurtha in 104 BC.

ll. 109–12 Yet . . . received: Marius hid in the marshes of Minturnae in 88 BC.

l. 110 Flags: reeds, rushes.

ll. 113–37 Deep . . . Rome: 'Minturnae was a city of Latium, now in ruins, near the river Garillan, in or near the territory of Trajetta. Hither, when Marius was driven out of Rome by Sulla, and declared a public enemy by the Senate, he fled and hid himself among some reeds and sedges; but being found out, and committed to the public gaol, he was condemned to die. But the slave who was ordered to execute him (a Cimbrian, according to Lucan) being affrighted at somewhat terrible that he saw in him, and fancying he heard a voice saying, "Darest thou kill Caius Marius?" dropped his sword, ran out of the prison, and told the people the whole story; who being moved partly by this, and partly by compassion for a man who had once saved Italy, dismissed him. See all the particulars here mentioned by Lucan more at large in Plutarch's life of Marius' (Rowe).

l. 114 Gyves: shackles.

l. 114 **rankling**: festering.

l. 121 **Gripe**: grip.

l. 131 **Would'st . . . slain**: The lictor in the dungeon was a Cimbrian.

l. 151 **Libyan rage**: This should probably be glossed 'a rage like Hannibal's', although the furious strength of the Libyan giant Antaeus might also be recalled.

ll. 152–5 **Soon . . . hand**: Marius proclaimed freedom for slaves when he returned from Africa in 87 BC.

l. 163 **And . . . haste**: The slaughter destroys the different ranks – senators, equites, plebs – indifferently.

l. 183 **Tyrant**: Marius.

l. 183 **And . . . survive**: Romans considered it a disgrace to kiss anyone's hand.

l. 194 **Baebius**: Marcus Baebius was torn to pieces in 87 BC.

l. 198 **Antonius**: The ex-consul and leading orator Marcus Antonius, a supporter of Sulla, was killed in 87 BC.

l. 202 **Dropping**: Dripping.

l. 204 **Crassi**: The Crassi were a father and son, opponents of Marius.

l. 204 **Fimbria**: Gaius Flavius Fimbria was a follower of Marius.

l. 205 **Pulpit**: scaffold, stage.

ll. 206–11 **Then . . . fire**: Scaevola was the Pontifex Maximus. He was killed by Marius' son in 82 BC when seeking refuge in the temple of Vesta, whose eternal flame men were not supposed to see.

l. 212 **The . . . appear**: Marius' seventh consulship.

l. 220 **Colline gate**: one of the gates of Rome, and the site of a battle between Sulla and the followers of Marius.

l. 221 **What . . . field**: The Sacriportan field was the site of the defeat of the younger Marius at the hands of Sulla in 82 BC.

ll. 222–3 **When . . . great**: The Samnite general, Telesinus, had threatened to raze Rome to the ground, and make another city the capital of Italy. In Lucan's day there were rumours that Nero might move his capital to the East.

l. 224 **Samnites**: the inhabitants of Samnium, an ancient country of Italy in the neighbourhood of Latium, and followers of Marius.

l. 225 **In . . . pride**: The Roman army was ambushed by the Samnites in the pass of the Caudine Forks and made to go unarmed through the yoke of surrender in 321 BC.

l. 231 **Leech**: physician.

l. 241 **And . . . blood**: The general evocation of impiety is also a specific reference to the acquisition of his Marian brother's estates by the Sullan Lucius Domitius Ahenobarbus.

ll. 248–51 **Some . . . possess**: This evocation of dying men ascending their funeral pyre while still alive may recall the death of Hercules.

l. 256 **No . . . knew**: a reference to Diomedes, the mythical king killed by Hercules, who is supposed to have fed his mares on human flesh.

l. 257 **Antaeus**: This giant, whose fight with Hercules is described by Lucan in Book IV, killed everyone whom he beat at wrestling.

ll. 258–9 **Nor . . . hall**: a reference to Oenomaus who killed the suitors of his daughter Hippodamia.

l. 263 **Forbidden flame**: Those who were executed were forbidden funeral rites.

l. 269 **Pacific Sulla's**: Sulla is pacific because he had made peace with Mithridates. The adjective is of course, as Rowe states in his notes, 'a strong irony'.

l. 272 **Catulus**: Quintus Lutatius Catulus was first an ally and then an opponent of Marius and committed suicide in 87 BC.

ll. 276–89 **I saw . . . away**: This passage refers to an adopted member of the Marian family, Marius Gratidianus, killed to avenge the death of Catulus, whom he had supposedly driven to suicide by his persecution.

ll. 285–7 **While . . . dies**: The apparent continuing autonomy of the tongue may recall Ovid's similar account of the mutilation of Philomela (*Metamorphoses* VI.554–60).

l. 295 **Corse**: corpse.

ll. 301–4 **Fortune . . . fall**: There was a temple of Fortune in Praeneste (Palestrina). Sulla ordered the town to be besieged, and it was sacked in 82 BC.

l. 307 **Fold:** The 'fold' (*ovilia*) was an enclosed space in the Campus Martius where polling took place. Sulla massacred his Samnite captives there.

ll. 323–6 **Meanwhile . . . slain:** Sulla's indifference to the slaughter may be linked with Caesar's reaction to Pharsalia in Book VII.

ll. 337–8 **Could . . . land:** This is an allusion to Sulla's self-appointed title *felix*, which he assumed in 82 BC, and an expression of disbelief that he should be thus described.

l. 345 **Presage:** accented on the second syllable.

l. 351 **These leaders:** Caesar and Pompey.

l. 359 **Brutus:** Marcus Junius Brutus (*c*.85–42 BC) plays only a small part in the *Pharsalia*, even though his role as Caesar's principal assassin makes him one of the era's most famous Republicans. Rowe's initial translation of this conversation between Brutus and Cato (II.232–325) appeared in Tonson's *Poetical Miscellanies* in 1705. The fact that Rowe singled out this particular passage suggests that part of the poem's attraction for him was its supposed Republican sympathies.

l. 363 **When . . . son:** a reference to the Great and Little Bear.

ll. 371–502 **To him . . . rage:** The disputation between Cato and Brutus was a common theme for debate. There is a conflict between Cato's personal stoical serenity and his concern for the good of Rome.

ll. 402–5 **To . . . thee:** These lines might be paraphrased as follows. 'If you go into battle, and things go your way, it will be a most unwelcomed fame which will yield to you (i.e. the reputation you will gain by your triumph will be a most undesirable one), since all your foes will rush towards you in the hope that they can be killed by your sword, thus causing the entire responsibility for the resulting slaughter to be laid to your charge.'

ll. 423–4 **Though . . . voice:** Simply by preferring one side to another Cato would be approving the civil war and thus in a sense approving Caesar.

l. 436 **The . . . breast:** Cato's reply is made to sound as though it were oracular. Cf. Pope, *Iliad*, I.662–3, 'Thus Thetis spoke, but Jove in silence held / The sacred counsels of his breast concealed.'

l. 474 **Decius:** Decius was a Roman consul in 340 BC. He allegedly gained a victory for Rome by the process of *devotio*. This meant that a general could devote himself to the gods of the underworld and then seek death by the hands of the enemy. If his dedication were accceptable to the gods, they would also take the enemy army. Cato goes on to elaborate his own desire to be allowed to make a similar sacrifice.

l. 486 Me . . . vain: Cf. *Paradise Lost* III.326 and X.831-4, 'first and last / On me, me only, as the source and spring / Of all corruption, all the blame lights due; / So might the wrath.' The Miltonic echo reinforces the sense of Cato as a Christlike figure.

l. 491 Commonweath: Although commonwealth may be glossed as 'general good', it also has Republican overtones in an English context, and is the usual way of referring to the rule of Oliver Cromwell.

l. 501 Engage: persuade.

l. 506 Marcia: Marcia had formerly been the wife of Cato and subsequently was married to Hortensius. Although Lucan suggests that her request to remarry Cato comes straight after Hortensius' funeral has taken place, he had in fact died some months before the remarriage.

l. 510 Lucina: a name given to Juno as goddess of childbirth.

l. 514 And . . . race: Marcia is to ally the two houses by mothering children by both men.

l. 520 Thus pleasing: 'As her melancholy condition and habit was most agreeable to that time of public calamity. See this story in Plutarch' (Rowe).

l. 539 Cornelia: the wife of Pompey.

ll. 546-65 No . . . feast: 'The poet here enumerates most of the ceremonies usually observed at the Roman marriages, by saying what was wanting at this of Cato and Marcia; so in the eighth book he gives an account of the magnificence of Roman funerals by deploring the misery and wretchedness of Pompey's' (Rowe).

l. 547 Woolly fillets: These were hung on the doorposts of a bridegroom's house.

l. 548 Genial: nuptial.

l. 551 Towery frontlet: 'This passage is diversely interpreted. I have taken that which I thought most probable: the bride was always crowned with flowers, and admonished not to touch the threshold by the *pronuba* or matron that attended her in honour of Vesta the goddess of chastity, to whom the threshold was sacred. The crown mentioned here seems to be like that given to the goddess Cybele, and so it is interpreted by Sulpitius upon this place. Perhaps it was worn in honour of that goddess' (Rowe).

l. 552   Nor ... shun: A bride should be carried over the threshold.

l. 555   Zone: girdle.

l. 557   Lawn: fine linen.

l. 563   Sabine mirth: a reference to the custom of singing bawdy songs outside the marriage chamber, which was supposed to be of Sabine origin.

l. 579   Infest: attack, annoy, trouble.

l. 609   Phrygian Capua: Capua was supposed to have been founded by a Trojan called Capys.

l. 624   Red with Punic blood: This phrase is added by Rowe. It is a reference to the battle at the Metaurus against the Carthaginians.

l. 628   Adria: the Adriatic.

l. 629   Eridanus: the Po.

ll. 633–40   His ... heaven: The reference is to the legend of Phaethon, who begged his father Phoebus Apollo to let him drive the horses of the sun. The conflagration he caused, and his fall and death, are referred to in the following passage. His sisters metamorphosed into poplars as they mourned.

l. 652   Marica: a nymph associated with the Liris, mother of Latinus.

ll. 685–6   To ... between: Although they are frightened by Caesar's strength, the people are more inclined to favour Pompey.

l. 687   Auster: the south wind.

l. 689   Stormy god: Aeolus.

l. 689   Eurus: the east wind.

l. 697   Libo: Scribonius Libo was one of Pompey's generals in Tuscany who joined the consuls in Campania at Caesar's approach.

l. 698   Thermus: Quintus Minucius Thermus was the commander at Iguvium. He had to withdraw when its inhabitants went over to Caesar's side.

l. 699   Sulla: Sulla's son, Faustus Cornelius Sulla, who went to Greece at Caesar's approach.

l. 702 **Varus:** Attius Varus fled from Auximum.

l. 706 **Lentulus:** Publius Cornelius Lentulus Spinther fled from Asculum when Caesar advanced.

l. 709 **He . . . side:** The reference to winning the soldiers over to his side may derive from a note in the commentary used by Rowe, which is itself derived from Caesar, *Bellum Civile.* I.15.

l. 712 **Scipio:** Q. Caecilius Metellus Pius Scipio Nasica commanded under Pompey at Pharsalus.

ll. 714–21 **Though . . . swords:** 'Marcellus, to weaken Caesar, counselled the Senate to make a decree that Caesar should deliver one legion, and Pompey another to Bibulus, whom they pretended to send to the Parthian war. Caesar, according to the Senate's decree, delivered to him one legion for himself, and another, which he had borrowed of Pompey for a present supply, after the great loss he had received under his praetors, Teturius and Cotta. These legions were now both in Scipio's camp' (Rowe).

ll. 722–93 **But . . . life:** Pompey's general Domitius Ahenobarbus was stationed in Corfinium. He tried to prevent Caesar's progress by breaking the bridge. He failed and was surrendered to Caesar by the people, and was spared against his will. Caesar used such *clementia* as an instrument of policy. Domitius was the ancestor of Nero and many scholars believe this fact explains Lucan's generous treatment of him here and in Book VII where (contrary to historical record) he dies heroically.

l. 725 **Troops:** those who had been stationed in the forum at Milo's trial. Cf.I.584.

l. 746 **Nile and Ister:** Only the Ganges is mentioned here by Lucan.

l. 758 **Vinea:** a kind of pent-house which was used for sheltering besiegers.

l. 821 **Cethegus:** Gaius Cornelius Cethegus was one of Catiline's fellow conspirators in 63 BC.

l. 826 **Camillus:** Furius Camillus was supposed to have ousted the Gauls from Rome in 390 BC.

l. 827 **Metelli:** Members of this family included Lucius Caecilius Metellus who was successful against the Carthaginians in the First Punic War, and rescued the Palladium from fire when he was high priest, and also Quintus Caecilius Metellus Macedonicus who was an opponent of the Gracchi.

ll. 828–9 **While . . . joins:** 'Cinnas' and 'Marii' seem to be examples of the rhetorical plural, although Lucan may have the younger Marius also in his mind. Both Cinna and Marius marched on Rome as military commanders.

l. 832   Carbo: a leader of the Marian faction who was defeated during the wars with Sulla. He was put to death in Sicily by Pompey in 81 BC.

l. 833   Lepidus: a consul and a follower of Sulla. He was declared an enemy of Rome, and was defeated by Catulus and Pompey.

l. 833   Sertorius: a supporter of Marius who led the Lusitanians in a revolt against Rome. Although at one time he held most of Roman Spain, he was eventually murdered in 72 BC by his lieutenant.

l. 840   Province: Cf.I.613.

l. 841   Thou: Caesar.

l. 842   Spartacus: a Thracian captive who led an army of Roman slaves. He was defeated and killed by Crassus in 71 BC.

l. 847   Again ... juice: Pompey says that the blood about his heart is heated up once again.

ll. 859–64   Whate'er ... aspires: Pompey was as great as a Roman could be while still being true to the ideals of Rome. Any more power would have made him a tyrant.

ll. 871–8   What ... coast: Pompey expresses his scorn for Caesar's exploits in Gaul and Britain.

l. 873   Age of war: the time he has spent on war.

l. 890   Mithridates: Cf.I.610–12.

ll. 902–13   My ... know: Pompey recalls his campaigns in Syria and Palestine.

l. 904   Baetis: The reference to this Spanish river recalls Pompey's campaigns against Sertorius.

ll. 914–17   Is ... Rome: The last four lines of this speech translate only one of Lucan's – *Quod socero bellum praeter civile reliqui?*, 'What did I leave to my father-in-law except civil war?'

l. 918   Dull suspension: sluggish hesitation.

ll. 926–37   As ... meads: The source for this simile is Virgil, *Georgics* III.220–36. There is a curious disjunction between the suggestion that the bull who represents Pompey will eventually triumph over his rival, and Pompey's eventual defeat.

l. 942 **Dictaean:** Cretan.

ll. 944–5 **When . . . bore:** Theseus caused his father to drown himself when he used black sails, indicating failure, rather than white ones on his return from victory over the Cretan Minotaur. Brundisium was supposed to have been founded by Cretans who sailed with Theseus on this voyage.

l. 947 **Slip:** landing place.

l. 954 **Hospitable:** accented on the first syllable.

l. 957 **Nereus:** a sea god.

l. 963 **Welkin:** sky.

l. 964 **Involve:** envelop.

l. 972 **Eldest born:** Gnaeus Pompeius.

l. 981 **Tigranes:** Tigranes I, the king of Armenia who had been re-established on his throne by Pompey.

l. 982 **Pharnaces:** a son of Mithridates who had been given the Bosporan kingdom by Pompey.

l. 983 **Each Armenia:** Armenia Major and Armenia Minor.

l. 984 **Riphaean:** refers to a region on the boundary between Europe and Asia whence flows the Don.

l. 986 **Maeotis:** The sea of Azov, which Scythian nomads were thought to cross when frozen.

l. 994 **You . . . year:** The consuls whose names were used to identify the year in the annual records or *fasti*.

l. 1004 **Son:** Pompey.

l. 1007 **Swept:** a past participle rather than an active verb.

ll. 1023–53 **With . . . mound:** Caesar tries to cut off Pompey's access to the sea.

ll. 1041–9 **Such . . . way:** The Persian king Xerxes built a bridge of ships across the Hellespont between Sestos and Abydos during the course of his invasion of Europe.

ll. 1066–71 At . . . crew: a recollection of Aeneas' secret preparations to leave Dido.

l. 1072 Heavenly maid: Virgo.

l. 1076 Flooky: Flooks are the sharp extremities of an anchor.

l. 1090 For . . . spread: Brundisium welcomed Caesar.

l. 1097 Beat . . . sides: The reference is to the Straits of Euboea which separate Chalcis from Attica.

l. 1099 Belay: make fast.

l. 1106 Pegasaean Argo: The *Argo* was built in Pagasae in Thessaly, and was the ship used by Jason when he sailed to Colchis to win the Golden Fleece.

l. 1108 Cyanean islands: sometimes known as the Symplegades or Clashing Rocks.

l. 1113 But . . . vain: The rocks were fated to move no more if any ship passed through them safely.

ll. 1116–17 As . . . light: Rowe's rendering is erroneous here, perhaps under the influence of a note in his Latin text. What Lucan in fact says is that the sky is still ruddy and is not yet white.

l. 1119 Boötes: Arctophylax, a constellation near the Great Bear.

l. 1123 Offing: deep sea.

ll. 1124–7 O . . . plain: This is an echo of Beelzebub's words to Satan in *Paradise Lost* I.84, 'If thou beest he; but O how fallen! how changed', which is itself an echo of Aeneas' exclamation when he sees the ghost of Hector (*Aeneid* II.274).

l. 1125 Turns: alterations, reversals.

l. 1127 Liquid plain: a Miltonic phrase. Cf. *Paradise Lost* IV.455.

ll. 1130–7 But . . . bleed: Again an ironic parallel with Aeneas' situation is suggested. Pompey's flight recalls Aeneas' departure from Troy, but he is moving away from Italy in failure, rather than towards Italy in triumph.

ll. 1138–43 Nor . . . blood: The gods decree that Pompey shall fall in Egypt, not in order to punish him but so that Italy may be spared the guilt of such a crime.

Book Three

ll. 12–54 At . . . embrace: Pompey's first wife, Julia, appears to him in a dream. Her appearance might be said to parallel Caesar's vision at the Rubicon, and, in the light of the ironic parallels established between Pompey and Aeneas, recalls the appearance of Creusa to Aeneas after his departure from Troy. Whereas Creusa offers hope and comfort to Aeneas, Julia foretells only disaster.

l. 15 His . . . rose: Lucan describes Julia as *furialis* – like a fury (III.11).

l. 18 Infest: attack, annoy, trouble.

ll. 24–5 The sire . . . float: In a typical Lucanian hyperbole Charon, ferryman of the underworld, abandons his small barque for a fleet of ships, so numerous are the dead.

l. 28 Each fatal sister: the Fates.

l. 33 Crassus: Julia's first husband, Publius Licinius Crassus, who was killed at the battle of Carrhae in 53 BC.

l. 44 Dull stream: Lethe, the river of forgetfulness in the Underworld.

l. 52 That . . . again: Pompey will be hers again after he has died.

ll. 53–4 The phantom . . . embrace: Aeneas' (rather more understandable) attempt to embrace Creusa is perhaps recalled.

ll. 61–4 Or . . . or: either . . . or.

ll. 65–6 Whate'er . . . fears: Whichever theory future events prove to be correct, death should not be feared.

l. 72 Dyrrachium: not named in the Latin text; Rowe draws on the note in his commentary.

l. 96 Curio . . . sent: C. Scribonius Curio is sent to fetch corn. His death is described at the end of Book IV.

l. 98 Hesperia: land of the West, Italy.

l. 111 Train: retinue of followers and attendants.

l. 119 The ocean . . . Rhine: Figures of conquered towns and rivers were commonly carried in triumphal processions.

l. 123 The beauteous Britons: Rowe seems to have been moved by patriotism here – Lucan describes the Britons only as fair haired and does not mention their beauty.

l. 130 **Moist way:** The reference may be to a drain channel which ran along the Via Appia.

l. 132 **Through . . . grove:** There was a grove and temple of Diana near Aricia. Each priest had to kill his predecessor.

l. 133 **Fane:** temple.

l. 133 **Alban Jove:** Cf.I.373.

l. 134 **Thither . . . come:** The consuls celebrated the Latin Festival on the Alban Mount.

l. 161 **In . . . meet:** Caesar orders the Senate to meet in the Temple of Apollo on the Palatine hill rather than in the Senate House. The reference to this temple is an anachronism as it was dedicated not before 28 BC. Rowe's note on this line reflects his sense that Lucan has misrepresented Caesar:

> Several historians tell us that Caesar, coming to Rome after Pompey had left Italy, called the Senate together in the temple of Apollo on the Palatine hill. In a speech to them there he excused the war he had undertaken, as a thing he was compelled to for his own defence against the injuries and envy of a few; and at the same time desired they would send messengers to Pompey and the consuls to propose a treaty for accommodating the present differences. Lucan in this, as in many other places, put Caesar's actions in an invidious light, and the Senate, according to him, make but a very mean figure upon this occasion.

l. 163 **Chairs curule:** A curule chair is a chair of office. They are empty because the consuls and praetors supported Pompey. Curule is accented on the second syllable.

l. 168 **Mighty subject:** As a *privatus* Caesar should be subject to the power of the Senate.

l. 176 **Effort:** accented on the second syllable.

l. 180 **Saturn's treasuring fane:** The treasury was located in a temple of Saturn, at the foot of the Capitoline hill.

ll. 181–205 **The bold . . . provide:** The tribune Metellus attempts to prevent Caesar's soldiers from robbing the treasury, but is unsuccessful. Lucan's attitude towards him seems ambivalent. Whereas his impulse to resist Caesar is no doubt laudable, the fact that he is spurred by love of gold detracts from the potential heroism of his action.

l. 192 **Sacred blood:** Tribunes were sacrosanct.

l. 196 **Crassus . . . rued:** Crassus was cursed by a tribune who opposed his expedition against the Parthians. Crassus' defeat and death could be perceived as a fulfilment of the curse.

ll. 206–16 **He . . . thee:** Here, as elsewhere in the poem, Lucan acknowl-edges Caesar's celebrated *clementia*, but places this quality in the least attractive possible light.

l. 221 **Cotta:** This might be either Aurelius Cotta, a tribune in 49 BC, or Lucius Aurelius Cotta, a tribune in 65 BC. The story of his intervention seems to have been invented by Lucan.

l. 239 **Tarpeian mountain:** Traitors were thrown from the Tarpeian rock.

ll. 242–3 **There . . . prevent:** Carthage paid large sums of money to Rome after both the first and the second Punic Wars.

l. 245 **Flaminius and Aemilius:** These men are not mentioned by Lucan at this point. Rowe seems to have derived their names from a note in his commentary.

l. 246 **From . . . son:** Philip V of Macedon was conquered by Rome in 197 BC, and his son, Perseus, the last king of Macedon, was conquered in 168 BC.

ll. 247–8 **There . . . old:** Pyrrhus, king of Epirus, tried to bribe the Roman general Fabricius. The implication is that the gold which was offered was captured by Rome when Pyrrhus was defeated at Beneventum in 275 BC. Some modern texts have replaced 'Pyrrhus' with 'Gallus', following a conjecture of Housman.

l. 250 **What . . . gave:** Rome acquired treasure from Antiochus XIII of Syria in 64 BC.

l. 251 **The . . . spoil:** Crete was conquered in 67 BC by Quintus Caecilius Metellus Creticus.

l. 252 **What . . . isle:** Marcus Porcius Cato brought back treasure from Cyprus when it became a Roman province in 58 BC.

l. 253 **Riches . . . borne:** Cf.II.884–917.

ll. 260–445 Meanwhile . . . prey: Greece and Asia supply Pompey with troops: another epic catalogue.

ll. 268–70 Alpheus . . . maid: The river-god Alpheus fell in love with Arethusa when she bathed in his stream and was supposed to have followed her to Sicily. See Ovid, *Metamorphoses* V.572–641. The reference to Alpheus' love for Arethusa is absent in Lucan, although the notes to the Latin edition used by Rowe would have reminded him of the well-known story.

l. 272 Herculean Trachyn: This was where the dying Hercules climbed on to his own funeral pyre. Herculean is accented on the second not the third syllable.

l. 274 Dodona's silent oak: The oak-tree oracle of Jove in Dodona was destroyed in 219 BC.

l. 276 Phoebaean: The epithet Phoebaean probably refers to a town called Apollonia in Epirus, occupied by ships of Pompey.

ll. 277–9 Three . . . claim: This corresponds to line 183 in Lucan which may be translated 'and but three keels claim credence for the tale of Salamis'; hence the Athenian victor is discredited. Rowe was worried by the reference and his version is influenced by the commentary.

l. 280 Jove's Cretan people: Jupiter was born in Crete.

l. 281 Gnossian: from Cnossos.

l. 285 With . . . unite: The town of Oricos is described as Dardan because it was supposed to have been founded by King Priam's son Helenus.

ll. 286–7 With . . . snake: The name of this people, the Encheliae, is derived from the Greek word for eel, then considered a snake. For the account of Cadmus' transformation into a snake see *Metamorphoses* IV.563–603.

l. 289 Where . . . roars: Although Absyrtos is in fact an island, Lucan seems to have thought it was a river, although the Latin is not unambiguous.

l. 293 Argo: Cf.II.1106.

l. 305 Feathered brood: cranes.

l. 308 Idalis: The reference is to the region around Mount Ida in Mysia and the Troad.

l. 309 Strows: strews.

ll. 310-15 From ... meads: The reference is to the music contest between Marsyas of Celaenae and Apollo. Apollo won the contest and flayed Marsyas. Marsyas' instrument was the flute, an invention of Athene's.

l. 317 Pactolus, Hermus: These rivers were supposed to have golden sand.

l. 320 From ... move: The ensigns are ill-omened because Ilium – Troy – was so famously defeated in war.

ll. 322-5 Their ... race: Caesar claimed descent from Aeneas.

l. 328 Obvious to: in the way of, meeting.

l. 332 Cynosure: the Little Bear.

l. 359 Ball: the earth.

l. 379 Sultry line: the equator.

l. 382 Olostrian: Modern texts have Orestas, whereas the edition used by Rowe has Olostras. The Orestae are Illyrian, the Olostrians Indian.

ll. 383-4 Beneath ... sky: In the Mediterranean world the Great Bear never sets.

l. 386 Furies: The madness of civil war spreads through Africa.

l. 386 Ethiops: Ethiopians.

l. 401 And ... war: The death of Crassus is the 'occasion'.

l. 410 Lydian king: Croesus, who was told that if he crossed the river Halys he would destroy a great empire. However the oracle referred to his own empire rather than his enemy's.

l. 422 Sithonians: Modern texts have Essedonians.

ll. 428-9 Not ... plain: Cyrus the Great (559-529 BC) was the founder of the Persian empire. He conquered much territory, including Lydia.

ll. 430-1 Not ... host: Xerxes was supposed to have so many men in his army that he could count them only by getting them all to throw a weapon, and then counting those.

ll. 432-3 Not ... wrong: The reference is to Agamemnon, who wished to revenge the rape of Helen, his brother Menelaus' wife.

l. 441 Where ... head: Jupiter was worshipped in the form of a ram in Libya.

l. 442 Afric: Africa.

ll. 446–531 Now . . . own: Massilia (Marseilles), a Greek colony, refuses to admit Caesar's army.

l. 447 Caesar . . . past: Although Caesar is marching away from Rome, the reference to him crossing the Alps might be intended to recall one of Rome's most famous enemies, Hannibal.

l. 450 Changing Greeks: The Romans had a poor opinion of the Greeks.

l. 456 Their . . . wear: The reference is to olive branches. The tree was sacred to Minerva and a symbol of peace.

ll. 458–531 When . . . own: An indefinite collective voice rather than a named speaker lies behind this speech.

ll. 484–93 Oh . . . fight: If the fighting had been confined only to Roman citizens, they would surely have been unable to pursue the civil war.

l. 492 Who: in this context 'you who'.

l. 498 Let . . . free: Massilia did not allow anyone to enter the town if they were armed.

l. 506 Phocis: a mistake for Phocaea in Asia Minor, the origin of the colony of Massilia.

l. 522 Saguntum: A Spanish city which was besieged for eight months by Hannibal in 219 BC. The citizens of Saguntum ended by slaughtering themselves. The bravery and resilience of its inhabitants were proverbial. The allusion strengthens the idea of a possible connection between Caesar and Hannibal.

l. 533 Involved: enveloped.

l. 570 Breastwork: 'A fieldwork (usually rough and temporary) thrown up a few feet in height for defence against an enemy; a parapet.' (OED)

ll. 591–669 Not far . . . year: 'I cannot but think Tasso took the hint of his enchanted wood, in the thirteenth book of his *Gerusalemme Liberata*, from this of Lucan' (Rowe). A parallel for the tree-felling episode may be found in Ovid, *Metamorphoses* VIII.738–78. Erysichthon cuts down a sacred tree and is cursed with an appetite so insatiable that he finally eats himself. Lucan is thought to have invented this episode on the model of Ovid; however, Caesar is unpunished and goes from strength to strength.

ll. 595–6 There . . . resort: The description of Eve's bower (*Paradise Lost*

IV.703-8) is perhaps recalled. Milton may have invoked Lucan at this point in order to draw an ironic parallel between the sacred wood and Paradise; in Lucan the demigods' absence reflects the frightening aspect of the grove, whereas in Milton the same absence is a result of his poem's Christian context.

l. 597 Barbarous priests: The wood is a cult location for indigenous Gallic peoples rather than the Massilians.

l. 598 Lustrate: to purify by propitiatory offering.

l. 616 Still: always.

l. 619 Baleful yew: Yews were traditionally associated with poison, death and the underworld.

l. 627 Refrains: avoids.

l. 628 Demon: inferior divinity, spirit.

l. 643 Deep ... oak: The comparison between Pompey and an oak in Book I may be recalled.

l. 650 Dodonian tree: oak.

l. 651 Holm: ilex tree.

l. 661 Sylvan honours: leafy branches.

l. 665 And ... heaven: This line may be paraphrased 'only the unlucky suffer the wrath of the gods'.

l. 667 Wains: wagons.

ll. 670-2 Meanwhile ... care: The continuing siege of Massilia is entrusted to the leadership of Gaius Trebonius, Caesar's legate. The Massilians have some success in repelling the Romans at first, but when the Romans engage them in a sea battle, Massilia is defeated.

l. 672 Leaguer: siege.

ll. 675-6 High ... mound: The towers were moved on rollers.

l. 679 Beldame: i.e. mother earth.

l. 685 Missile: here used as an adjective, signifying death by throwing.

l. 689 Parcae: Cf.I.222.

l. 692 Pernicious: means swift as well as ruinous. Both meanings may be invoked here. The emphasis on a single word at the beginning of a line, combined with the double meaning, gives this line a Miltonic ring.

l. 699   **Plane:** level.

ll. 700–9   **Galled . . . frame:** The military formation known as the tortoise is being described. The soldiers advance, protecting their heads with a roof made with their overlapping shields. Rowe's notes show a scholarly interest in the details of seige warfare.

l. 715   **Fall:** let fall.

l. 718   **Vinea:** a kind of pent-house which was used for sheltering besiegers.

l. 725   **Haply:** by chance.

l. 733   **Beat:** beaten.

l. 738   **Prevent:** anticipate.

l. 741   **Mulciber:** a name sometimes given to the Roman god of fire, Vulcan.

l. 744   **And . . . light:** They conceal the fire behind their shields.

l. 749   **Greener planks:** green, unseasoned wood.

l. 752   **Quarries:** the siege tunnels dug by the Roman sappers under the Massilian walls. 'Rend' is here used intransitively to mean 'collapse'.

l. 755   **Discontinuous:** not continuous in space or time, having interstices or breaks.

l. 763   **Stable floorings:** indicates that the ship's planks formed a firm platform for the forthcoming sea battle.

l. 766   **Brutus:** Caesar's admiral, Decimus Brutus.

l. 775   **Crazy hulk:** broken, decrepit ship.

l. 777   **Caulk:** to stop up the seams of a ship to prevent leakage.

ll. 788–9   **Feels . . . stroke:** The hulls tremble to the beat of the oars.

ll. 790–4   **Crooked . . . lie:** The reference is to a well-known naval formation in the shape of a half-moon.

l. 794   **Galiot:** a small galley or boat.

l. 796   **Admiral:** the command ship.

l. 797   **Pines:** Rowe is picking up on Lucan's apparently unique use of the word *pinus* in the metonymical sense 'oar'. The reference is to the six banks of oars used.

l. 800 **And ... meet:** One more stroke of oars from each side would bring the ships together.

l. 803 **Brushing pine:** sweeping oar.

l. 806 **Repressed:** driven back.

l. 809 **Welkin:** the sky.

l. 814 **Stemming:** making headway against a tide, breasting the waves.

l. 829 **Pretorian:** Pertaining to the office of praetor, an annually elected curule magistrate: the common standard. The ensign identifies the command ship.

l. 839 **Waist:** the middle part of the upper deck of a ship between the quarter-deck and the forecastle.

l. 841 **Grapplings:** instruments with iron claws used for seizing and holding an enemy ship.

ll. 842–3 **While ... war:** The ships have become so enmeshed together that the sea is no longer visible.

l. 846 **Falchions:** swords.

l. 866 **Tagus:** Catus in modern editions, but Tagus in Rowe's Latin text.

l. 866 **Ancient:** ensign.

l. 874 **Telon:** Telo in modern editions.

l. 876 **No ... guide:** Telo is a steersman, perhaps recalling Virgil's Palinurus.

l. 884 **Rives:** cleaves, divides.

ll. 893–904 **Friendlike ... slain:** Rowe compares Virgil's account of the death of two identical twins (*Aeneid* X.390–2) which he gives in Dryden's version.

l. 894 **Brought:** brought forth.

l. 905 **Board and board:** The oars of his and the enemy ship are entangled and overlap one another. In this context a board is a ship's side.

l. 939 **Lycidas:** According to one tradition Lucan recited his account of the death of Lycidas as he died as a result of cutting his own veins at Nero's command. Although the name Lycidas is also found in the pastorals of Virgil and Theocritus, it may be from Lucan that Milton derived the name of his poem. Milton's 'Lycidas' was written to commemmorate the death of a friend by drowning (Haskins, 1887, xxx, note 34).

l. 983 **Champaign:** plain, level ground. This word is spelled 'champian' in Rowe.

l. 987 **Social:** allied to them, on their own side.

l. 1000 **Corse:** corpse.

l. 1005 **Reeking:** emitting vapour or steam.

l. 1007 **To . . . fire:** Nereus and Vulcan are metonymies for sea-water and fire.

l. 1028 **Conflicting:** To conflict can be used in the sense of to fight, to do battle.

l. 1033 **Phoceus:** There is perhaps an etymological connection between his name and the Latin word for seal, *phoca*.

l. 1038 **Flooky:** flooks are the sharp extremities of an anchor.

l. 1054 **Tyrrhen:** 'Tyrrhenus' (the Etruscan man) in the Latin.

l. 1056 **Balearic:** The inhabitants of the Balearic islands (including Majorca and Minorca) were famed for their skill with the sling.

l. 1064 **Stound:** a state of stupefaction or amazement.

l. 1120 **And . . . survive:** It was considered a grave misfortune for a Roman to survive his own child.

l. 1135 **Numbers:** poetry.

l. 1143 **Mothers:** In Lucan it is fathers rather than mothers who rush to the same trunk. The text Rowe used also correctly refers to father in the marginal glosses.

l. 1147 **Brutus:** Decimus Brutus, Caesar's admiral, rather than Marcus Junius Brutus. The capture of the town passes unmentioned.

Book Four

l. 6 **Alternative:** alternating

l. 7 **Petreius and Afranius:** Marcus Petreius and Lucius Afranius were Pompey's commanders in Spain.

l. 12 **Vectons:** the Vettones, a people of Lusitania.

l. 16 **Champaign:** plain, level ground.

ll. 16–36 **Where ... name:** The topography of Ilerda may reflect Lucan's preoccupation with the idea of civil war (Masters 1992, 45–53).

l. 51 **Last:** the rearmost.

ll. 55–80 **Soon ... field:** This episode is unusual because it describes a perpendicular battle. It echoes the battle in II.317–22, where the troops are also compressed into such a small place that they hardly have room to fall.

l. 55 **Dawning grey:** The sky lightens to grey at the approach of morning.

l. 67 **And ... pile:** The soldiers drive their javelins into the mountain to create footholds.

ll. 81–165 **Thus ... year:** Lucan's description of the flood owes a debt to Ovid's description of the deluge in *Metamorphoses* I.262–347.

l. 86 **North:** i.e. north wind.

l. 91 **Parch:** 'The Latin word here is *urebant*, and seems to me by no means unelegant, extreme cold and extreme heat appearing to have much the same effects upon grass or other herbs.' (Rowe).

l. 92 **Genial heat:** warmth that is conducive to growth.

ll. 92–3 **At length ... sign:** The weather becomes warmer after the vernal equinox.

l. 93 **Vernal:** occurring in spring.

l. 98 **Boreas:** the north wind.

l. 100 **Eurus:** the east or south-east wind.

l. 106 **Sluicy:** copious, drenching.

l. 110 **Welkin:** sky.

l. 111 **Scanted:** restricted.

l. 117 **Iris:** the goddess of the rainbow as well as the messenger of the gods.

l. 118 **Fady:** tending to fade, shading off by degrees into a paler hue.

l. 120 **She stopped to drink:** 'So Virgil in the first *Georgic*,

> Et bibit ingens
Arcus.

> At either horn the rainbow drinks the flood. Mr Dryden

As if they fancied the rainbow drew up water from the sea or rivers, and poured it down again in showers of rain' (Rowe).

l. 124 **Hoary brow:** The mountain is personified as an old man; there is a wordplay on 'brow'.

l. 139 **Seldom ... fiends:** Famine generally accompanies other disasters. The 'fiends' are presumably war and pestilence (140) personified.

l. 151 **Savage:** any wild animal.

l. 154 **Freshes:** A fresh is a rush of water.

l. 155 **Tethys:** a sea-goddess – the name is used metonymically to represent the ocean.

l. 160 **Frozen zone:** 'The poet means here the polar regions. The hyperbole, a figure in which he is given to offend, is somewhat overstrained' (Rowe).

l. 165 **Signs:** translates the Latin *signa*, constellations.

l. 166 **Sire:** Jupiter.

l. 167 **Ruler:** Neptune.

ll. 182–7 **But ... forgiven:** Caesar seems to have quasi-divine status and can coerce heaven.

l. 183 **Minion:** i.e. Caesar. Minion here means one who is favoured or beloved.

l. 185 **His:** Caesar's.

l. 217 **Canton:** to divide or quarter.

l. 219 **Fate superior:** that of Caesar, who seems to control the elements.

l. 249 **Midst ... arise:** The parity and proximity of the two rocks reflect the bond between the two armies.

ll. 269–332 Soon ... sword: The opposing sides are temporarily united by love. The implication is that the slaughter which follows appears even more terrible after the short-lived concord.

l. 274 Amaze: amazement.

l. 304 Erinyes: the Furies: Tisiphone, Megaera and Allecto.

ll. 333–421 By ... hair: When Petreius realizes what has happened, he slaughters those of Caesar's soldiers who are in the Pompeian camp. Rowe's note suggests both his own Republican sympathies and his assumption that they were shared by Lucan. 'This jealousy of Petreius was certainly unworthy of a man who had the best cause; and even the poet himself cannot forbear running out in praise of Caesar on this occasion; the baseness and cruelty of Petreius was inexcusable.'

l. 370 Floating castles: turreted warships.

l. 389 Pard: leopard.

l. 403 Undistinguished: indiscriminate.

l. 408 Board: table.

l. 408 Unhospitable: accented on the second syllable.

l. 409 While ... succeed: This contrast between blood and wine is an embellishment of Rowe's, though Lucanian enough in timbre.

ll. 410–21 With ... hair: This little scene seems to have been expanded by Rowe in order to parallel the horrors of Sulla more precisely.

l. 410 Brand: 'This word is used for a sword by some of the best of our English poets, Spenser and Fairfax especially' (Rowe). By contrast Lucan has a fondness for 'prosaic' words, e.g. *gladius*, a sword.

l. 411 And ... hand: Death remains potential within the sword until the reluctant soldier begins the attack.

l. 432 Conscious: thoughtful.

ll. 432–5 Nor ... flight: Petreius and Afranius attempt to flee to Ilerda.

ll. 451–67 But ... decay: Once again Lucan presents Caesar's *clementia* in a hostile light.

l. 455 Devoted: doomed.

l. 478 Griding: piercing, wounding.

l. 480 **While . . . rise:** The blood vessels are swollen with blood.

l. 482 **Sinewy:** has only two syllables here.

l. 486 **Thrall:** bondman, one who is reduced to subjection. In Lucan a gladiatorial scene is being described here.

l. 488 **Stound:** a shock or pang.

l. 497 **Assyrians:** Astyrici in modern editions, but Assyrii in the text used by Rowe.

l. 513 **Griping:** clutching.

l. 513 **Glebe:** earth.

l. 517 **Draff:** refuse, swill.

ll. 525–6 **O . . . springs:** Lucan says that it would be preferable to drink poisoned water than suffer this slow death. Among those enemies of Rome who are said to have poisoned the rivers and springs are Mithridates and Juba.

l. 528 **Cretan rocks:** These are deadly because of the aconite which grows on them.

l. 543 **Afric:** Africa.

ll. 549–94 **Now . . . more:** His submissive behaviour presents a clear contrast with Petreius' defiance.

l. 607 **Pest:** can mean anything which is noxious or troublesome.

l. 612 **And . . . again:** The soldiers' muscles recover their power.

l. 624 **Myrrhine:** *Murra* was a precious mineral, possibly agate, from which costly vessels were made.

l. 660 **Prevent:** anticipate (his hopes of retirement).

l. 661 **Dismission:** disbanding.

l. 669 **To . . . due:** The first half of the line refers to Pompey, the second to Caesar.

l. 673 **Neuter:** neutral.

l. 673 **Pleased . . . war:** Lucan's apparent sympathy with neutrality may be contrasted with Cato's stance in Book I.

l. 679 **Iader:** Lucan refers to the Iader as a river, but the only Iader recorded elsewhere is a town on the Illyrian coast.

l. 681 **Antonius:** Caius Antonius, Caesar's legate, is besieged in Illyria.

ll. 684–91 **But . . . wall:** The picture of the famine parallels the drought described above.

l. 693 **Basilus:** Lucius Minucius Basilus was the admiral of Caesar's fleet.

l. 693 **Social sails:** allied ships.

l. 694 **Dolabella:** a legate of Caesar. He is not mentioned by Lucan, but he is referred to, in association with Antonius, in a note to the edition used by Rowe.

l. 706 **Sublime:** upwards.

l. 718 **Tethys:** metonymy for ocean.

l. 724 **Octavius:** Marcus Octavius was one of Pompey's generals.

l. 728 **Offing:** deep sea.

l. 730 **Aloof:** here used in its specialized, nautical sense meaning 'away to the windward'. Octavius goes round the other vessels.

l. 733 **Toil:** encircling snare.

l. 735 **Hays:** nets.

l. 735 **The . . . prepare:** The nets are set up on a line of forked props.

l. 736 **E'er . . . spy:** 'The Roman hunters, when they set toils to enclose their game, placed upon the top of the nets feathers that were painted of several colours, and likewise burnt, that by their dancing as well as strong scent they might scare the deer from coming up to, or attempting to break through them. So Virgil,

> *puniceaeve agitam trepidos formidine pennae.*

Nor scare the trembling deer with purple plumes' (Rowe).

l. 737 **Odour:** This might have been caused by red dye, or by the burning feathers.

l. 739 **Molossian:** Molossian hounds came from Epirus and were noted for their size and strength.

l. 740 **Quester:** A quiet hunting dog, who pulls on the leash rather than barks when he has discovered his prey.

l. 741 **Tainted:** The track is imbued with the quarry's scent.

l. 742 **Conscious:** here used in a poetic sense to suggest that inanimate things are privy to human actions or secrets.

l. 743 **While . . . prey:** The verb 'point' here describes the action of a hound when he indicates the presence and position of game by standing rigidly and looking towards it. The phrase 'trembles to the prey' is suggested by Lucan's expression *tremulo loro*, 'with trembling leash'.

l. 748 **Cilician pirates:** They had formerly been defeated by Pompey, but are now his clients.

ll. 748–61 **But . . . shore:** The Pompeians set an underwater trap which catches one of the rafts.

l. 751 **Victor's:** Pompey's.

l. 755 **Driving fabrics:** the oncoming ships.

l. 758 **Latent:** hidden.

l. 761 **Resty:** restive.

l. 763 **Whose . . . flood:** Cf. Dryden, *Aeneis* VIII.311, 'The leaning head hung threatening o'er the flood'.

l. 772 **Charybdis:** A dangerous whirlpool between Italy and Sicily.

l. 780 **Vulteius:** apparently a tribune in Caesar's army.

ll. 808–9 **We . . . die:** 'We die with as much honour, though death comes to our doors to seek us, as if we had gone out to meet it' (Rowe).

l. 812 **All is but dying:** Rowe's translation of *omnibus incerto venturae tempore vitae* is effective and uncharacteristically compressed.

l. 826 **As . . . stand:** The invocation of a theatrical parallel is an interesting addition of Rowe's. Such imagery is common in Lucan.

ll. 831–2 **Alike . . . applause:** This couplet does not precisely correspond to anything in Lucan, but instead may be traced to a note in the Latin text Rowe was using.

l. 834 **Unexampled:** unprecedented, unparalleled.

l. 862 **Ta'en:** taken.

l. 868 **Period**: end.

l. 884 **Leda's twins**: Gemini.

l. 887 **Chiron**: Sagittarius.

ll. 921-4 **A fate . . . left**: Cadmus, the founder of Thebes, sowed the teeth of the dragon he killed. He threw a stone at the armed men who sprang up, causing them to fight and kill each other.

ll. 925-30 **Such . . . made**: Jason also sowed dragon's teeth from which armed men sprang. They are defeated by the power of Medea.

l. 931 **Furies**: madness.

l. 937 **Last best gift**: an ironic echo of Milton's Eve who is described as Heaven's last best gift (*Paradise Lost* V.190).

l. 947 **Purple pile**: heap of bloody corpses.

l. 965 **Pernicious**: may mean both swift and destructive.

l. 976 **Cornelian**: Lucan refers to a camp named after Publius Cornelius Scipio Africanus the Elder, who defeated the Carthaginian leaders Hasdrubal and Syphax.

l. 978 **Were . . . sway**: 'I wonder Lucan, who seems to avoid the fabulous in his poem, should go so far out of the way for this. The place of Antaeus's abode and burial is by no author placed in this part of Afric; some fix it in Mauretania Tingitana, others in Libya, and Cellarius between the Nile and the Red Sea' (Rowe).

ll. 983-1066 **The teeming . . . found**: The well-known tale of Hercules' fight with the giant Antaeus, whose energy is renewed by contact with his mother the earth, is now told at some length.

l. 984 **Yet**: still.

l. 988 **Beldame**: mother earth. The earth is personified in this section. As Rowe capitalizes earth throughout, in accordance with eighteenth-century practice, it is perhaps inappropriate to introduce a distinction which did not originally exist by capitalizing earth in this section alone.

l. 990 **Phlegra**: the Macedonian site of the defeat by the gods of the giants. It was fortunate for the gods that Antaeus was not born until after this battle.

l. 1009 **Alcides**: Hercules.

l. 1014 **Provide:** prepare.

l. 1017 **Strown:** strewn.

l. 1032 **Chine:** spinal column.

l. 1041 **Herculean:** Accented on the second syllable.

l. 1044 **The ... renewed:** a reference to the Lernean Hydra, killed by Hercules as one of his twelve labours. It had numerous heads, and each time one was cut off another grew in its place.

l. 1046 **Unrighteous queen:** Juno, who imposed the labours on Hercules in her jealous anger.

l. 1072 **Scipio:** See note to line 976 above.

l. 1074 **Fierce ... walls:** Hannibal had to be recalled from Italy to deal with Scipio.

l. 1084 **Varus:** the Pompeian commander in Africa.

l. 1088 **Juba:** Juba, king of Numidia, owed his throne to Pompey.

l. 1092 **Syrts:** The Syrtes are two gulfs of shallow water and sandbanks off north Africa, notoriously treacherous to ships.

ll. 1109-18 **But ... might:** Curio had suggested that Juba's kingdom be reduced to a province.

l. 1110 **Monarch:** Juba.

l. 1122 **To ... new:** The newness of the troops is an additional source of worry for Curio, along with his fear of Juba.

l. 1132 **Daring shows:** displays of military strength.

l. 1144 **On ... space:** The gladiatorial arena is one of Lucan's commonest metaphors for civil war.

l. 1155 **Juba ... receives:** He feels joy because the glory of victory will now be his.

l. 1167 **Ichneumon:** a type of Egyptian rat.

l. 1169 **Played:** moved briskly.

l. 1182 **Punic:** Carthaginians were thought to be untrustworthy.

l. 1210 **Ropy:** sticky, stringy.

l. 1214 **Dronish**: sluggish.

l. 1221 **Involves**: wraps.

ll. 1234–5 **But . . . war**: 'That their conquest should be owing to the tumult and disorder of the enemy, they would have rather gained it with more slaughter' (Rowe).

ll. 1238–42 **Genius . . . repaid**: Juba's defeat of Curio may be seen as vengeance for Rome's victory over Hannibal, the Carthaginian leader. In addressing the 'genius of Carthage' Lucan evokes a ghost or tutelary spirit of Carthage as a whole.

ll. 1243–6 **Thus . . . blood**: Rowe's note, based on a note in his Latin text, emphasizes the favour apparently shown to Pompey here: 'The poet would not have any advantage accrue to Pompey (whose person and cause he always favours) from the blood of his countrymen, but would rather transfer the benefit of such success, as well as the guilt of it, to Juba and his Africans.'

l. 1253 **Pop'lar**: Curio was a *popularis*, a member of the 'people's party'.

l. 1270 **Curio**: This theme of the perverted talent of many of the Caesarians is common in Lucan.

Book Five

ll. 1–13 **Thus . . . meet**: The Senate meets at Epirus.

l. 7 **Solemn season**: the Kalends of January, the day on which the new consuls would enter office.

l. 8 **Fasti**: The Latin word refers to the list of annual festivals, the calendar; also the list of consuls by which the years were named. The reference here is to the election of new consuls.

l. 9 **Janus**: Janus, traditionally represented with two heads, gave his name to January.

l. 10 **Consuls**: At this time the consuls were Lucius Cornelius Lentulus Crus and Gaius Claudius Marcellus.

l. 15 **Sate**: sat. The original spelling has been retained here to preserve the rhyme.

l. 18 **Purple order**: Curule magistrates wore purple-bordered togas.

l. 19 Lictors: A lictor was an officer who attended upon a magistrate, bearing the fasces before him.

ll. 20–1 No . . . free: This praise is stronger than in Lucan, reflecting Rowe's political views.

l. 27 Lentulus: Lucan has apparently created a single 'composite' figure out of two Pompeians, Lucius Cornelius Lentulus Crus, consul in 49 BC, and Publius Cornelius Lentulus Spinther, consul in 57 BC. Informed readers can supply the correct *cognomen* in each instance if they wish, but the point is of little significance.

l. 40 Bear: the Great Bear.

ll. 46–7 When . . . dwelt: Rome is an idea, not a location. Lentulus refers to the emergency relocation of the Senate at Veii in the fourth century after the Gauls had sacked Rome. Marcus Furius Camillus was recalled from exile to act as temporary dictator.

l. 52 With . . . appear: Lucan suggests that although Pompey's supporters are in exile, those senators who obey Caesar in Rome are more truly 'banished'.

l. 57 In . . . meet: 'Members', like the Latin *membra* of the original, has the dual sense of limbs and participants.

l. 71 Undetermined: not restrained within bounds.

ll. 74–5 In . . . assign: Pompey is elected leader.

l. 80 Of . . . loved: There were a temple and statue of Apollo on Rhodes.

l. 83 Phocis: An error of Lucan's – the mother state of Massilia was in fact Phocaea.

l. 84 Deiotarus: a king of Galatia and supporter of Pompey.

l. 84 Deiotarus his: Deiotarus'.

l. 86 Brave . . . son: Cotys was king of Thrace. He and his son Sadalas provided Pompey with military support.

l. 87 Rhasipolis: a Thracian chief (Rhascypolis in modern editions).

l. 93 Philip's godlike son: Alexander the Great. Dryden uses the same phrase to describe him in *Alexander's Feast* (line 2).

l. 97 Lagus: the father of Ptolemy I.

ll. 98–9 **Preventing ... command:** In other words, Ptolemy stops Caesar from committing the act of parricide – Pompey was related to him by marriage – and Cleopatra from gaining power.

l. 102 **Appius:** Appius Claudius Pulcher was a censor and had a particular interest in the supernatural.

l. 109 **And ... peace:** There is no reference to the Sibyl yet in Lucan.

l. 112 **God of wine:** Bacchus.

l. 114 **Still ... round:** A reference to the Trieterica, feasts in honour of Bacchus' return from his victories in India. As the counting was inclusive, the feasts were in fact held on alternate years.

l. 115 **Maenades:** female followers of Bacchus.

l. 116 **Double deity:** They worship Bacchus and Apollo at the same time.

l. 119 **One ... given:** As is made clear in the Latin text, only one of Parnassus' twin peaks remained above water.

ll. 121–2 **Here ... slain:** 'A monstrous serpent sent by Juno to persecute Latona. He was killed by Paean or Apollo' (Rowe). Latona, or Leto, was the mother of Apollo and Artemis.

l. 123 **While ... reign:** The oracle at Delphi had previously belonged to Themis, goddess of justice.

l. 140 **And ... decrees:** Rowe obscures Lucan's expressed doubt as to whether the god merely predicts the future or whether he determines it. The note in the edition used by Rowe states: *ita fatum dici volunt quod deus fatus est, id est decrevit, constituit* ('Thus they suppose that what the god has spoken – i.e. what he has decided, determined – is fate').

l. 141 **Part ... all:** a reference to the Stoic doctrine of the *anima mundi*, the vital principle that permeates all things.

l. 145 **Demon:** inferior divinity, spirit.

l. 147 **Virgin:** the prophetess at Delphi, the Pythia.

l. 151 **Typhoeus:** a monster with a hundred serpent heads whom Zeus imprisoned under Mount Inarime.

ll. 159–63 **Oft ... air:** 'There are frequent instances in story of these useful oracles. The Phoenicians, driven by earthquakes from their first habitations, were taught to fix first at Sidon, and after at Tyre. When Greece was invaded by Xerxes, the Athenians were advised to trust in their wooden walls (their ships), and beat the Persians at sea at the battle of Salamis. A famine in Egypt, and the plague at Thebes for the murder of Laius, were both removed by consulting this oracle' (Rowe).

ll. 166–7 But . . . come: The oracles of Delphi, Dodona and Ammon had fallen into disuse by the time of Augustus. It has been suggested that Lucan refers here to a supposed suppression of the oracle by Nero.

l. 172 Springs: probably used here in its less common sense of cracks or breaks.

l. 174 Tripods: The tripod was a three-legged stand on which offerings were placed and from which the Sibyls delivered their prophecies.

l. 174 Long unmoved: The encounter between Appius and Phemonoë continually recalls Aeneas' meeting with Deiphobe in Book VI of the *Aeneid*.

l. 187 Ausonian: Italian.

ll. 189–200 Whether . . . suit: Phemonoë suggests four possible reasons to explain the oracle's silence.

ll. 191–4 Or . . . god: 'When Delphos was taken and sacked, and the temple burnt by Brennus and the Gauls' (Rowe).

l. 193 Rod: rode, were carried.

l. 196 But . . . suffice: 'That volume which was kept at Rome, and consulted upon the most important public occasions' (Rowe).

l. 205 White wreath: A white woollen band was worn by priests and priestesses.

l. 207 Strives: struggles, resists.

l. 218 No . . . foam: The foam froths from her mouth in her frenzy.

l. 224 Profane: translates Lucan's vocative *impia*; Appius is addressing Phemonoë.

l. 226 Mortal sounds: her own words, rather than those inspired by Apollo.

l. 236 Paean: an appellation of Apollo as the healing deity.

l. 240 Turgid: swollen.

l. 254 Or . . . or: either . . . or.

ll. 262–7 And as . . . sought: The Sybil was supposed to have honoured Rome by writing down only prophecies which pertained to her. Perhaps the apparent insigificance of Appius' fate throws a less flattering light on the Sybil's exclusivity. Alternatively the comparison might be a comment on Appius' self-importance.

l. 266 Phemonoë: The first Pythian priestess was thought to have been called Phemonoë. The name means 'speaker of thoughts' and is accented on the second syllable.

ll. 274–7 While . . . lie: Phemonoë obliquely refers to the death of Appius and his burial at Euboea.

ll. 289–92 Or . . . Rome: If Caesar's assassination had been foretold, it might have been frustrated.

l. 302 With . . . burns: Cf. the changing colour of Deiphobe in *Aeneid* VI.47. The admired blend of red and white in a blushing woman may be parodically invoked. Cf. Dryden, *Aeneis* XII.102.

l. 305 Sonorous: accented on the second syllable.

ll. 305–8 So . . . main: There may be a parallel between this simile and the actual storm at the end of the book.

l. 325 Where . . . constrains: The vocabulary of the Latin original serves to align the constraint of the sea with the way Apollo restrains Phemonoë.

l. 326 Rhamnusia: Rhamnus was a town in Attica, famed for a statue of Nemesis, referred to here as Rhamnusia.

l. 328 Aulis: unlucky because Iphigenia was sacrificed there.

ll. 331–543 To other . . . renewed: A mutiny among Caesar's troops now takes place.

l. 339 Satiated: accented on the first syllable.

ll. 402–3 Are . . . blow: 'Do you think we only are ignorant how greatly we may deserve of the commonwealth by killing you?' (Rowe).

l. 410 Is . . . mate: Compare the description of Pompey at line 23.

l. 418 Rods: fasces.

l. 440 Tarpeian Jove: This is a poetic expression for the Capitol.

ll. 443–5 With . . . suggest: In other words, he fears rational, humane objections to the way the war is conducted, but has no fear of objections based on greed and fury.

l. 455 **Enyo:** the goddess of war.

l. 500 **Labienus:** Titus Labienus was Caesar's second-in-command in the Gallic wars, but later went over to Pompey's side.

l. 505 **Runagate:** fugitive.

ll. 508-9 **Who ... foe:** 'It is very indifferent to me whether you only forsake me, and remain neuters, or go over to Pompey and assist him' (Rowe).

l. 518 **Vulgar herd:** In the Latin Caesar refers to the soldiers as *Quirites*. As the word is used only in civilian contexts, this is the equivalent to disbanding them.

l. 523 **And ... attend:** He is said to have put twelve soldiers to death (Appian, *The Civil Wars* II.47).

ll. 532-3 **Singly ... sword:** He seems able to make the men's swords obey him even when the men themselves are disobedient.

l. 539 **And ... tame:** 'As thinking such a disposition of mind too tame for the execution of designs like his' (Rowe).

l. 558 **And ... state:** Dictator was the appellation of a chief magistrate invested with absolute authority, elected in times of emergency by the Romans.

l. 560 **A gracious ... reign:** Caesar becomes dictator. He resigned after eleven days.

ll. 563-6 **Then ... retain:** 'Then began those names of flattery which were afterwards used to their emperors of *Divus, Semper Augustus, Pater Patriae* &c' (Rowe).

ll. 565-6 **Then ... retain:** These lines are an improvization of Rowe's and another indication of his Republican tastes. Caesar, though a successful general, had not been properly elected to any office, but Rowe's stress on the separation of military and political powers is even more revelant to England than to Rome where magistrates regularly commanded armies.

l. 569 **Fasces:** used as metonymy for the consulship.

ll. 571-88 **And while ... race:** A sham election takes place in the Campus Martius.

l. 575 Face: appearance.

l. 576 The ... place: As bad omens could stop elections, the various methods of augury are not used.

l. 577 Rowl: roll.

l. 578 Owl: considered a bird of particularly ill omen.

l. 580 Thence ... come: Lucan states that the choosing of consuls became a mere matter of form; during the Empire consuls sometimes held office for less than a year. They come 'nominally' because their names are needed in order to give a name to the year.

l. 584 With ... go: The reference is to the Latin festival held in honour of Jupiter Latiaris. As he has not averted Caesar's tyranny he does not deserve such worship. 'Lucan says, with little reverence for Jupiter, that the god deserved they should be thus disrespectfully huddled over by Caesar, for suffering the Romans, who were the race of Aeneas and Ascanius (the latter of whom instituted these rites) to be brought into slavery' (Rowe).

l. 593 Crooked shores: Cf.II.942–9.

l. 610 Phaeacian: Phaeacia stands for Corcyra.

l. 616 Cynthia: the moon.

l. 618 Sheet: sail.

l. 622 Hesperia: land of the West, Italy.

l. 629 Bospori: 'Two straits, the one called the Thracian, the other the Cimmerian Bosphorus, lie at each end of the Euxine Sea. The former is now the channel of Constantinople, and the latter the straits of Caffa' (Rowe).

l. 632 Champaign: plain, level ground.

l. 637 curling: undulating.

l. 639 Tethys: a sea-goddess, the ocean.

l. 641 Stupid: stupefied, dulled.

ll. 649–50 With ... rise: A storm would be preferable to being becalmed.

l. 660 Where ... run: The distinction between the swift Genusus and the more sluggish Hapsus is much stronger in Lucan, and there is a suggested affinity between the rivers and the two leaders.

l. 673 **Father:** Caesar.

l. 674 **Son:** Pompey.

l. 679 **While . . . detains:** Caesar is held up by Antony's delay in bringing the troops from Brundisium.

l. 684 **Thou:** Antony.

ll. 701–978 **In words . . . lord:** Caesar persuades Amyclas to ferry him to Italy, despite the storm, but the attempt is unsuccessful.

ll. 711–24 **'Twas . . . shore:** A parallel with Virgil's description of the departure from the camp of Nisus and Euryalus may be intended (*Aeneid* IX.314–15).

l. 726 **Mouldering:** crumbling.

l. 728 **Cot:** a humble cottage.

ll. 729–32 **No . . . shed:** A recollection of Ovid's description of the cottage of Baucis and Philemon may be intended, and the pattern and tone of the episode recall visitations of gods to mortals more generally. Throughout this episode Caesar operates as a kind of divinity more powerful than the elements or the gods of myth.

ll. 731–41 **Old . . . awakes:** Rowe adds characteristic descriptive embellishments to Lucan's account of Amyclas' hut: the oozy flags and the dry leaves and chips have no Latin equivalents.

l. 733 **Strook:** struck.

l. 739 **Flags:** reeds, rushes.

l. 740 **Match:** a slowly smouldering wick, here made of tow.

l. 741 **Tow:** rope.

l. 773 **Boding signs:** 'These prognostics of the weather are much the same with those in Virgil's first *Georgic*, and many of them are to be found in Aratus' (Rowe).

l. 784 **Fiery red:** Virgil associates the moon's reddening with winds in *Georgics* I.430–1.

l. 789 **Thwart:** pass, cross.

l. 791 **Hern:** a dialect or literary variant of heron.

l. 791 **Plashy:** marshy.

ll. 792–3 While . . . rain: A raven stalking the sand is associated with rain by Virgil in *Georgics* I.388–9.

l. 793 Prevents: anticipates.

ll. 799–808 He spoke . . . skies: One of the most common set pieces in Latin epic poetry was the description of a terrible storm. Obvious sources and analogues for Lucan are *Aeneid* I.81ff. *Aeneid* III.192ff. and *Metamorphoses* XI.47ff., but Lucan overgoes all his predecessors (Morford 1967, chapters 3 and 4).

l. 805 Horrors: Rowe lifts Lucan's own word *horror*, with its connotations of bristling, directly from the Latin.

l. 814 Rack: cloud.

l. 849 Another: another land or port.

l. 852 Strook: struck.

l. 855 Alder: Ships were frequently made of alder wood, and Rowe here and elsewhere uses alder as a poetic synonym for ship.

l. 860 Corus: the north-west wind.

l. 870 Notus: the south wind.

l. 873 Equal . . . vain: The winds in their battle cancel each other out.

ll. 877–8 The . . . roars: In a characteristic hyperbole the waters of four seas change places.

l. 881 Subject: subdued, submissive.

l. 881 Beldame: earth.

ll. 887–90 So . . . aid: The flood is compared to that survived by Pyrrha and Deucalion (Ovid, *Metamorphoses* I.262–347). It is also by implication linked with the cataclysmic flood which in Stoic theory caused periodic destructions of the world.

l. 888 Tired: Jove tires his thunderbolts by using them for so long. There is perhaps a pun on an obsolete meaning of tire: shot, volley.

ll. 902–10 A murky . . . gods: Although Rowe does not depart from the general meaning of Lucan here, the vocabulary is heavily Chritianized. Cf. *Paradise Lost*, VI.867–77; IX.1000–1.

ll. 932–5 **There ... brow:** The severity of the storm is indicated by the fact that the summits of high mountains now threaten shipwreck.

l. 936 **Wreck:** ruin.

l. 944 **Warm:** vigorous in battle.

ll. 962–4 **Conceal ... below:** Rowe may have misunderstood Lucan here. In the original Caesar wants Fortune to conceal the fact that he died disappointed at being uncrowned, rather than the fact that he was drowned.

l. 974 **Tenth wave:** Each tenth wave was believed to be particularly large.

l. 976 **But ... shore:** Caesar does not reach Italy – he is driven back to where he set out from.

l. 1020 **Decent:** in a seemly fashion.

ll. 1024–7 **So ... array:** In the original Lucan refers to the well-known resemblance between the cranes' ordered formation and certain letters of the Greek alphabet.

l. 1032 **Auster:** south wind.

ll. 1037–1186 **While ... restored:** Pompey sends his wife Cornelia to Lesbos for safekeeping. Their parting is described with particular pathos by Lucan.

l. 1039 **Infest:** attack, annoy, trouble.

l. 1043 **Numbers:** poetry.

ll. 1047–54 **See ... day:** This passage has been compared with Virgil's account of Aeneas' hesitation and unwillingness to break the news to Dido that he has been commanded to proceed on his travels by Mercury.

l. 1069 **Collected ... might:** Cf. the description of Agenor (Pope, *Iliad* XXI.675), 'He said, and stood, collected in his might.'

ll. 1081–3 **Nor ... war:** 'As if Cornelia could not come up to the virtue of the Roman matrons, if she did not look with detestation even upon her husband, when he was engaged in a civil war' (Rowe).

l. 1106 **Divorced:** 'Divorces were very frequent among the Romans, though Cornelia, who was a lady of singular virtue, complains here that she should be parted from her husband upon any other occasion than death' (Rowe).

ll. 1163–86 **Low ... restored:** The leavetaking of Ceyx and Alcyone, described by Ovid (*Metamorphoses* XI.466–73) is recalled.

Book Six

ll. 1–45 Now ... below: Caesar intends to capture Dyrrachium, but is prevented by Pompey.

l. 6 Son: Pompey.

ll. 27–39 This ... denies: Natural defences are more enduring than man-made ones.

l. 38 Steepy: precipitous.

ll. 46–9 Here ... confined: Caesar decides to besiege Dyrrachium and Pompey's troops.

l. 58 Such ... fear: So strong that it does not need to fear attack from a battering-ram.

l. 60 Plains: Caesar turns the hills into plains. There is also a wordplay on the action of planing (sometimes spelt plaining at this time) or smoothing.

l. 64 Labours: field-works.

ll. 78–9 Let ... destroy: Troy was supposed to have been built by Apollo and Neptune.

l. 81 The ... queen: Babylon, built by Queen Semiramis.

ll. 82–3 Behold ... bound: In other words, the space enclosed by Caesar is as large as Mesopotamia or Syria.

ll. 93–4 The lovers' ... flood: Caesar could have filled in the Hellespont, which divided the shores of Sestos and Abydos, and thus separated the lovers Hero and Leander.

l. 97 And ... divide: With this effort Caesar could have built a canal through the Isthmus of Corinth.

l. 100 List: arena. This is another example of Lucan's use of gladiatorial imagery.

l. 110 Scylla: a many-headed sea-monster girt with dogs in the straits of Messina.

ll. 111–12 So ... shore: Inhabitants of Scotland do not notice when the sea is disturbed off the coast of Kent.

l. 116 Dispread: extended.

l. 121 **Far . . . groves:** The distance between Rome and Aricia is about 16 miles (26 kilometres).

l. 124 **Did . . . way:** In other words, the distance as the crow flies, rather than the actual length of the river.

ll. 128–9 **But . . . repress:** The cares move the chiefs to repress the soldiers' ardour.

ll. 130–67 **Pompey . . . give:** Pompey's camp is afflicted by plague.

l. 134 **Rack:** a frame made with bars of wood or metal to hold fodder for horses and cattle.

l. 143 **Nesis:** a small island in the Bay of Naples which was once volcanic.

l. 145 **Typhoeus:** Cf.V.151.

l. 146 **Blue poisons:** Blue may refer simply to the colour of the vapours, although blue is often the colour of plagues and things hurtful. Cf.831.

ll. 151–2 **A rugged . . . skin:** Lucan refers to erysipelas, a febrile disease accompanied by inflammation of the skin.

l. 158 **And . . . weight:** Rowe's translation of *fessumque caput se ferre recusat* seems to respond to Lucan's tendency to use the language of weight and destruction in other parts of the poem.

ll. 177–95 **But . . . foe:** Caesar and his troops suffer from famine.

l. 180 **Damps:** noxious vapours.

l. 182 **Famine . . . round:** Lucan states that the besiegers are in turn besieged.

ll. 196–331 **At length . . . spears:** Pompey tries to break the siege but is defeated by the efforts of Scaeva.

l. 211 **Greensward way:** grassy path.

l. 235 **Scaeva:** Scaeva was made a centurion during the Gallic Wars. See Caesar, *Bellum Civile* III.53; Valerius Maximus 3.2.23. He is another example of perverted *virtus* and the theme of one against the many.

l. 240 **Vine:** 'The *vitis*, or rod made of a vine, was the badge of the centurion's office, which they bore in their hands, and with which the soldiers used to be corrected for lesser offences' (Rowe).

l. 249 **Safety . . . flight:** Cf. the accusation that Turnus 'sought his safety in ignoble flight' (Dryden, *Aeneis* XI.534).

l. 260 **Chose:** chosen.

l. 290 **Each where:** everywhere.

l. 297 **Gripe:** clutch.

l. 304 **Sublime:** lofty.

l. 308 **Pard:** leopard.

l. 325 **Buckler:** shield.

l. 329 **Missive:** capable of being thrown.

ll. 330–1 **And . . . spears:** With typical hyperbole, Lucan claims that the weapons sticking in Scaeva's wounds offer protection from further injury.

ll. 332–40 **Cease . . . town:** Lucan claims that Scaeva needs to be attacked with siege weapons as though he were a town.

l. 336 **Horns:** The battering-ram had a mass of iron at the end, sometimes in the form of a ram's head.

l. 348 **Prey:** Scaeva's prey will be Aulus, the soldier he deceives in his mock surrender.

l. 351 **Steely shower:** shower of weapons.

l. 352 **Rousing . . . war:** He dislodges the arrows stuck in his body.

l. 358 **Take:** The simile ends here.

l. 366 **Nerves:** sinews.

l. 386 **Enow:** enough.

l. 387 **Draw forth your weapons:** He invites them to pull out the weapons stuck in his body.

ll. 398–9 **When . . . gored:** Sword is the object of gored.

l. 430 **That . . . enshrined:** In Lucan this deity is identified as Virtus – a goddess. But the Stoics believed that the divine was immanent in men.

l. 434 **And . . . war:** Mars was often represented with no armour, only a spear and a shield.

l. 440 **Paean:** victory song.

l. 443 **Capitolian Jove:** Spoils were brought to the temple of Jupiter Capitolinus at the end of a triumph.

ll. 447–62 **Nor ... exchange:** Pompey again tries to break the siege and this time he is successful.

l. 469 **Drownded:** drowned.

l. 488 **Torquatus:** Lucius Manlius Torquatus was a follower of Pompey.

l. 497 **Sheet:** sail.

l. 505 **Roused ... roars:** A reference to the giant Enceladus, who was buried under Mount Etna.

l. 518 **Sulla:** Sulla would have been more ruthless and blood-thirsty than Pompey.

l. 522 **Father, son:** Caesar and Pompey.

l. 526 **The ... field:** The battles of Utica and Munda, in which the Republicans were defeated, took place in 46 and 45 BC.

l. 528 **Than ... fate:** The death of Pompey is referred to.

ll. 529–32 **Nor ... lived:** Juba, Scipio and Cato all died as a result of the war.

l. 531 **Cato:** 'Cato's story is made common, as well as immortal, by Mr Addison' (Rowe).

ll. 537–40 **While ... prey:** Pompey rejects the suggestion that he should march on Italy.

l. 558 **Eurus:** the east wind.

ll. 558–677 **Where ... sphere:** The extended chorographia marks the importance of the site. For a detailed interpretation of the description of Thessaly, its mountains, rivers, history and cultural inventions, see Masters 1992, 150–78. His main contention is that Lucan deliberately distorts the geography of Thessaly in order artificially to inflate its importance within legend and history.

l. 559 **Boundary:** This should be pronounced with three full syllables.

ll. 559–64 **Thessalia's ... light:** Ossa, Pelion, Othrys and Pindus are all mountains in Thessaly. Commentators have observed that Lucan appears to confuse the positions of Ossa and Pelion. Masters suggests that this is a deliberate error, designed to adumbrate gigantomachic disorder (Masters 1992, 154).

l. 562 **Lion:** Leo, the constellation.

l. 562 **He:** the sun.

l. 565 **Vesper:** the evening star.

l. 568 **Valley:** Tempe.

l. 572 **Alcides:** Hercules.

ll. 572–5 **But . . . load:** Hercules was supposed to have formed the valley of Tempe.

l. 575 **Nereus:** a sea-god, father of the Nereides, here signifying the sea.

l. 578 **Once . . . reign:** Achilles' kingdom was in Thessaly.

l. 580 **Chief:** Protesilaus, the first Greek to land – and die – at Troy.

l. 581 **Pteleos:** a port in Thessaly.

l. 582 **Dorion:** the site of a musical contest between the Muses and Thamyras. Dorion is accented on the first syllable.

l. 583 **Trachin:** Trachis.

ll. 583–4 **Then . . . bestowed:** Hercules gave his arrows to Philoctetes who came from Meliboea. They are described as fatal because they killed Paris.

l. 585 **Argos:** The Argos referred to is a town in Thessaly rather than the Argos in the Peloponnese.

ll. 587–92 **Here . . . laid:** 'The ancient geographers place a city called Thebes in Pthiotis. When Agave, queen of Thebes in Boeotia, had in her madness killed her son Pentheus, and cut off his head, at length recovering her senses, she fled into this country, and buried her son's head here, and probably gave the name of Thebes to the place where she settled' (Rowe).

ll. 591–2 **With . . . laid:** This description perhaps looks forward to the decapitation of Pompey.

l. 596 **Evenos . . . blood:** The centaur Nessus wished to marry Deianira but he was killed by Hercules while trying to kidnap her. He gave his blood-soaked tunic to Deianira, saying it was a love potion. She later sent it to Hercules and he was killed by the poison in the blood, which had come from the Lernean Hydra. (See Ovid, *Metamorphoses* IX.101–33.)

ll. 599–600 **Slowly . . . calls:** The river-god Inachus was the father of Io, who was transformed into a heifer by Jove to protect her from Juno's jealousy. (See Ovid, *Metamorphoses* I.568–746.)

l. 601 **Achelous:** The river-god Achelous and Hercules both wished to marry Oeneus' daughter Deianira. Hercules defeated his rival. (See Ovid, *Metamorphoses* IX.1–97.)

l. 602 **Neighbour isles:** The Echinades, islands in the Ionian sea, which according to legend had originally been nymphs until they were hurled into the sea by Achelous. (See Ovid, *Metamorphoses* VIII.573–89.)

ll. 603–4 **While . . . feed:** Apollo fed the flocks of King Admetus near this river.

l. 609 **Anauros:** The name signifies 'without air' in Greek.

l. 612 **Apidanus:** accented on the second syllable.

l. 612 **Enipeus:** has three syllables and is accented on the second.

ll. 620–2 **Deep . . . ally:** He is revered by the gods because they held an oath sworn on the waters of the Styx to be sacred. His waters remain separate from those of Peneus when they combine.

l. 627 **Lelegians:** accented on the third syllable.

ll. 632–3 **Here . . . race:** Ixion attempted to seduce Juno, but Jove formed a cloud in her likeness (Nephele) to trick him. By this cloud he became father of the centaurs, and was punished in the underworld by being bound to a fiery wheel.

l. 634 **Caves:** these were part of Mount Pelion.

ll. 636–8 **Here . . . bore:** Monychus, Pholus, Chiron and Rhoecus are all centaurs, the 'double race'.

l. 644 **Till . . . died:** Cf.596.

l. 645 **Leach:** doctor; Chiron was skilled in medicine and became a constellation. He acknowledges this land as his place of birth.

ll. 647–8 **Midst . . . bow:** The reference is to the constellation Sagittarius.

ll. 651–4 **Here . . . bit:** Neptune created the first horse.

l. 652 **Courser:** horse.

ll. 655–7 **From . . . explore:** The voyage of the Argonauts.

l. 658 Itonus: Ionus in modern texts, the first metal worker.

l. 670 In . . . fold: Cf. Milton's Sin, 'But ended foul in many a scaly fold', *Paradise Lost* II.651.

l. 672 Hence . . . renown: These games were held in honour of Apollo who had slain the Python.

ll. 674-7 Here . . . sphere: Aloeus encouraged his giant sons to rebel against Jove and they piled mountains up to reach heaven. The chorographia ends, as it begun, with Pelion and Ossa, linked with the gigantomachia.

ll. 678-1253 To this . . . day: Sextus Pompey consults the witch Erictho about the outcome of the contest. Erictho is the most full-blooded representation of a witch in ancient poetry and the whole episode has been frequently condemned for tasteless excess and grotesquerie. In recent criticism, however, Erictho is seen as one of Lucan's finest creations and even as the perhaps blackly humorous dark heart of the poem (Johnson 1987, 1-33): as a *vates* (the word signifies both seer and inspired poet) and composer of *carmina* (both spells and poems) she can indeed be seen as a perverse double of Lucan himself. She has long fascinated poets: in Dante's *Commedia (Inferno* 9.18-27) she sends Virgil to the depths of Hell to fetch up a dead soul, and she presides over an episode in Goethe's *Faust*. Welwood praises the description of Erictho as 'a beautiful picture of horror', and Rowe is at his best in rendering its 'Gothic' quality, which anticipates that taste of some later eighteenth-century readers who included an element of the eerie in their sense of the 'sublime'.

l. 684 Sextus: Pompey's younger son.

ll. 688-91 A day . . . redressed: Whereas Pompey gained victories against pirates, Sextus, after his exile in 43 BC, was guilty of piratical acts according to his opponents.

l. 695 Delphic: Although Rowe's text clearly differentiates between the tripods, from Delos, and the Pythia, at Delphi, Rowe has conflated the two.

l. 695 Dodonian Jove: the oracle of Jove in Epirus.

ll. 697-704 Nor . . . below: Lucan contrasts Thessalian witchcraft with more legitimate modes of enquiry into the future. The 'Babylonian seers' are Chaldaean astrologers.

l. 706 Haemonian: Thessalian.

ll. 717–18 There ... knew: Medea, the Colchian princess who helped Jason and the Argonauts secure the golden fleece against the wishes of her father, was the archetypal witch.

l. 727 Numbers: poetry. A connection may be perceived between the witches' spells and Lucan's own poetry, a connection which is emphasized by the fact Rowe translates *carmina* (spells, songs) as 'numbers'.

l. 728 Own: acknowledge.

l. 734 Cropped ... mare: A growth, 'hippomanes', supposedly found on the foreheads of all newborn foals, was used in love potions.

ll. 737–8 Melt ... wheel: The reference is to the use of the *rhombus*, a lozenge-shaped instrument whirled on a string to produce a whirring noise, used in magic rites. Cf. Virgil, *Eclogues* VIII.73–9.

ll. 739–84 Whene'er ... breath: An analogue for the account of feats performed by witchcraft is Medea's invocation in *Metamorphoses* VII.192–214.

l. 740 Eternal ... hand: Hand is the subject in this line.

l. 754 Boreas: the north wind.

l. 760 Maeander: a wandering river.

ll. 761–2 Arar ... Rhone: The characteristics of the two rivers are reversed.

l. 765 Crystal: ice.

l. 767 Cynthia: the moon.

l. 768 Alternate Tethys: the ebb and flow of the sea.

l. 771 Strook: struck.

ll. 771–6 The ponderous ... seen: A tunnel running through the earth is created by witchcraft.

l. 775 Dreadful cleft between: an absolute phrase with 'being' understood.

l. 787 Imply: involve, contain.

l. 791 Atone: propitiate.

l. 793 Brave: challenge.

l. 794 Or ... slave: 'The poet seems to allude here to that god whom they called Demogorgon, who was the father and creator of all the other gods;

who, though himself was bound in chains in the lowest hell, was yet so terrible to all the others that they could not bear the very mention of his name, as appears towards the end of this book. Him Lucan supposes to be subject to the power of magic, as all the other deities of what kind soever were to him' (Rowe). Demogorgon, the supposed name of the witch-deity (found in a scholium on Statius), is almost certainly simply a corruption of demiourgos, the creator-god. In the magic papyri (collections of ancient spells, etc.) mightier powers are regularly used to compel others less powerful, and the idea of a supreme god is often encountered. Throughout the episode Lucan displays considerable expertise about the details of magical practices (Gordon 1987).

l. 803 **Involve:** envelop.

ll. 804–5 **As . . . aid:** An eclipse is meant.

l. 806 **Charming:** exercizing magic powers.

l. 809 **On . . . foam:** Witches were supposed to be able to draw down the moon from the sky which would then shed a poisonous foam on plants.

l. 813 **Monster:** something extraordinary or unnatural.

l. 820 **Gods above and man below:** This pairing is common in Pope's Homer. Cf., for example, *Iliad* I.709, 'The first of gods above and men below'.

l. 823 **Elf-locks:** tangled, matted hair.

l. 830 **Thwarts:** obstructs.

l. 833 **Ceres:** metonymy for corn.

l. 845 **And . . . hand:** 'The nearest of kin to the deceased always set fire to the funeral pile' (Rowe).

l. 847 **Fry:** to undergo the action of fire.

l. 855 **Husky:** dried up.

l. 856 **Ropy:** sticky, stringy.

l. 860 **Thither . . . hies:** Erictho gets to the corpses before birds and beasts of prey.

ll. 869–70 **Whether . . . made:** Erictho sometimes kills her victims herself to get the ghost she wants.

l. 872 **Flood:** flowing blood.

l. 877 **Left-handed:** She cuts with her left hand, the hand proper for magic performances.

l. 879 **Some . . . pay:** 'As receiving the last breath of the dying person' (Rowe).

l. 892 **Sate:** sat.

ll. 896–7 **Fearful . . . range:** Erictho is anxious that the war should take place at Pharsalia so that she may use the corpses.

l. 904 **Hesperia:** land of the West, Italy.

l. 907 **Corse:** corpse.

l. 907 **Invade:** attack.

l. 936 **Pleased . . . flies:** She is pleased that she is widely famed for her magic skills.

l. 947 **From . . . ordained:** 'I have observed in the life of Lucan that he was a disciple of Cornutus the Stoic philosopher, of which this, and many other passages in this poem, are proofs. It is true he talks in many places of the wanton and unaccountable disposal of things below by fortune and the gods; yet that does not hinder us from supposing all those disposals necessarily preordained. Nay, I have heard it affirmed by a critic, who I think understands this author very well, that wherever he names fortune he means fate. How far that may be made good I don't know' (Rowe).

l. 961 **Titan:** the sun.

l. 962 **Maim:** injury.

l. 966 **While . . . tread:** As no fighting has yet taken place it is not clear why there are so many available corpses.

ll. 971–1237 **To . . . field:** The necromancy can be read as an inversion of *Aeneid* VI. 'Lucan has inverted a number of the features of Virgil's account, thus conveying his horror of civil war, e.g. hero Aeneas is replaced by worthless Sextus and dignified Sibyl by foul Erictho; instead of the living visiting the Underworld, a dead man is brought back to life to prophesy; the optimistic prophecy of the future is replaced by a pessimistic view of Rome's past' (Braund 1992, 282–3).

l. 974 **And . . . wound:** Erictho is careful to select a corpse still capable of speech.

l. 986 **Delve:** pit, den.

l. 999 Taenarian caverns: The fabled entrance to the infernal regions was in a cavern in Taenarus.

l. 1004 Airy vassals: ghostly inhabitants of Pluto's realm.

l. 1011 Heartless: afraid.

l. 1027 Lunar dews: Cf.809.

l. 1030 Nor . . . lacks: Lynxes' urine was supposed to change to stone.

l. 1032 Nor . . . food: 'It was an ancient tradition that deer, when they were grown old, had a power of drawing serpents out of their holes with their breath; which they afterwards killed and eat, and thereby renewed their youth' (Rowe).

l. 1033 Nor . . . flood: The reference is to rabid dogs suffering from hydrophobia.

l. 1034 Her . . . supplies: The remora (accented on the first syllable) was a fish which supposedly delayed ships.

l. 1035 Stones from eagles warm: 'What we call eagle-stones, said to be found in the nests of eagles. The eyes of dragons, pulverized and mixed with honey, were said to be used for anointing the eyes, in order to fortify them for beholding spectres or ghosts' (Rowe).

ll. 1038–9 The viper . . . gems: 'It was reported among the ancients that in the Red or Erythrean Sea a viper breeds in the same shell where the pearls grow; but I don't remember to have met any modern confirmation of this piece of natural history' (Rowe).

ll. 1041–2 With . . . east: The phoenix was reborn from its own ashes.

l. 1064 World's: printed 'world' in first edition.

l. 1072 Third Hecate: Hecate had three aspects: Luna the moon, Diana and Hecate herself, who was associated with witches and the underworld.

l. 1074 Greedy dog: In Lucan Erictho invokes here, not Cerberus, but a mysterious unnamed custodian of hell who feeds Cerberus on the flesh of men.

l. 1076 Charon: Charon ferried the dead across the river Styx.

ll. 1097–8 Too . . . anew: Masters suggests that the unwillingness of the spirit to enter the corpse is a reverse parallel of Phemonoë's unwillingness to be entered by Apollo (Masters 1992, 193).

l. 1109 Ye . . . despair: She is addressing the Erinyes, or Eumenides.

ll. 1124–6 Thee . . . now: 'Ascensius, in his notes upon this place, will have it to mean her immodest and incestuous commerce with her uncle Pluto. He says, the word *mala* apples, has often an obscene sense, and to prove it quotes that verse in Virgil's *Eclogues*:

ipse ego cana legam tenera lanugine mala' (Rowe).

Erictho threatens certain revelations about Proserpina (there are parallels in the magic papyri). She is not, however, referring to the pomegranate seeds eaten by Proserpina or her rape by Pluto, since these stories were well-known. As Housman notes, Erictho must boast some arcane knowledge, disreputable to the goddess.

l. 1125 League: compact.

l. 1128 Infernal Jove: Pluto.

l. 1132 Master: The identity of this master is uncertain. The note in Rowe's Latin text suggests that it is Demiurgus. See note to 794.

l. 1136 And . . . defies: The 'master' may swear falsely on the Styx with impunity, unlike all other gods.

l. 1144 And . . . arose: 'In the translation of this passage I have taken the liberty to vary so far from my author's sense as to make the English quite contrary to the Latin. Lucan says the corpse did not rise leisurely, but started up at once. I must own I could not but think the slow heavy manner of rising by degrees, as in the translation, much more solemn and proper for the occasion. I have taken so few liberties of this kind, in comparison of what Mons. Brebeuf the French translator has done, that I hope my readers, if they don't approve of it, will however be the more inclinable to pardon what I have altered from the original here' (Rowe).

l. 1167 Parcae: the Fates.

l. 1168 I . . . ordain: 'Looms' refers to the Parcae's weaving and translates Lucan's equally concrete *stamina*, threads.

l. 1182 Curii: The plural is probably being used for the singular here.

l. 1185 Scipio: Scipio Africanus, victor of Zama.

ll. 1186–7 The . . . Rome: Cato the Censor was the great-grandfather of the Cato who appears in the poem.

ll. 1189–92 Thee . . . head: Brutus, the first consul, drove out the kings from Rome, and is thus the traditional founder of the Roman Republic. He rejoices because his descendant will assassinate the tyrant Caesar.

l. 1191 Conscious: guilty.

ll. 1193–99 Meanwhile ... applause: Lucan contrasts evil ghosts, originally subverters of the *status quo* who welcome the present conflict, with worthy senatorial traditionalists. Sulla, despite his cruelty, supported the constitution and is thus on the right side here. Lucan is a supporter of the old Roman Republic rather than a democrat.

l. 1194 Catiline: Lucius Sergius Catilina rebelled against the state in 63 BC after being defeated in the consulship elections. He was defeated and killed in 62 BC.

l. 1195 Cethegan naked race: Gaius Cornelius Cethegus was a fellow conspirator with Catiline. The phrase 'naked race' refers to a family custom of keeping the arms bare.

l. 1196 Marii: Cf.I.998.

l. 1197 Gracchi: Cf.I.483.

l. 1198 Drusi: Marcus Livius Drusus, tribune in 122 BC, and his son of the same name, took up some of the measures of the Gracchi.

ll. 1202–3 No ... plain: They translate the insurrection on earth to their own situation and demand to be given a place in Elysium. Rowe says of the Drusi and the Gracchi that they were 'somewhat like the Levellers in Oliver Cromwell's time, and were the authors of very dangerous seditions and confusions in the state'.

ll. 1212–13 Sweet ... race: a covert allusion to their imminent death. 'The place' presumably is Elysium.

l. 1221 Demigods of Rome: a reference to deified emperors.

ll. 1225–30 Seek ... retreat: This reference to a future prophecy has suggested to some that Lucan projected its inclusion in a 'completed' *Pharsalia*. 'This passage is a plain proof that Lucan intended to carry on his poem much farther than the period at which he left it, since he alludes here to an appearance of Pompey's ghost to his son, which was undoubtedly to be introduced in the subsequent part of his story' (Rowe). The issue of the scope of the poem is much contested.

ll. 1231–5 In ... die: Pompey and his sons will all die in lands where Pompey experienced military success.

l. 1239 Dismission: release.

Book Seven

ll. 1–24 Late ... knight: Pompey has a misleading dream on the night before Pharsalia, a passage of rich pathos. 'Plutarch says that the night before the battle Pompey dreamed that as he went into the theatre the people received him with great applause, and that he himself adorned the temple of Venus the Victorious with many spoils. This vision partly encouraged and partly disheartened him, fearing lest that adorning a place consecrated to Venus should be performed with spoils taken from himself by Caesar, who derived his family from that goddess' (Rowe).

ll. 3–4 He ... again: The sun was thought to travel from west to east – the movement of the sky making the opposite appear to be the case. Lucan describes the sun trying to travel eastwards faster than usual to avoid rising. Rowe simplifies the sense.

l. 10 Theatre: has three full syllables.

l. 10 Sate: sat. The *theatrum Pompei* was the first stone theatre in Rome. It was completed in 55 BC and could seat 40,000 spectators.

l. 19 When ... suppressed: Sertorius, a supporter of Marius, was appointed governor of nearer Spain in 83–82 BC, and later accepted an invitation from the Lusitani to become their chief. Lucan falsely claims that Pompey defeated Sertorius; in fact he was murdered by his lieutenant.

l. 22 Purple: The *toga picta* was worn by triumphing generals. Rowe simplifies the Latin where there is a contrast between two differently coloured togas: as *triumphator* Pompey wore the *toga picta*, on other occasions he wore the white *toga pura* since as yet he held no office in the Senate.

l. 49 Her: Rome's.

l. 53 Floods: i.e. of tears.

l. 55 Deplore: mourn for.

l. 57 As ... complain: L. Junius Brutus was killed fighting the Etruscans who were trying to reinstate the Tarquin dynasty. The *matronae* of Rome mourned him for a year (Livy, II.7).

l. 61 **Forbid:** forbidden.

l. 63 **Falchion:** sword.

l. 77 **And ... breast:** Rome is imagined as having two opposed tutelary spirits, a good and bad genius.

l. 80 **His father:** Caesar.

l. 93 **Tully:** Cicero (Marcus Tullius Cicero), who was in fact lying ill at Dyrrachium at this time.

l. 98 **Catiline:** Cicero was consul at the time of Catiline's conspiracy.

l. 98 **Fierce ... feared:** The lictors' fasces (ceremonial bundles of rods) represented the renewal of peace by consular authority.

l. 102 **He ... draws:** Cicero uses his oratory on this occasion in support of the prevalent, popular ('vulgar') opinion.

l. 106 **Her:** fortune's.

ll. 135–40 **Since ... day:** Pompey's decision to give the signal for battle can be seen as a sign of his weakness and craving for popularity.

l. 140 **Devoted:** doomed, fatal.

ll. 145–6 **How ... blood:** Different tactics, such as a war of attrition, might have gained Pompey a bloodless victory.

l. 147 **Fond:** foolish.

l. 188 **Thrilling:** piercing.

ll. 190–1 **Today ... mankind:** 'If I conquer, it must be by the slaughter of my fellow-citizens, and consequently become the object of their hate: if I am conquered, I must be ruined myself' (Rowe).

l. 196 **Corus:** north-west wind.

l. 202 **Sudden ... beat:** 'It is by no means an improper thought that though the soldiers were very eager for the battle they might yet be in some consternation when they perceived it was resolved upon in earnest, especially when so much was to depend upon it' (Rowe).

l. 210 **Universal nature:** Perhaps an echo of Milton's *Lycidas* (60).

l. 216 **Nerves:** bowstrings.

ll. 222–4 **Such ... war:** the conflict between the giants and the gods.

l. 225 **Lemnian:** Vulcan was associated with Lemnos.

l. 227 **Blue-eyed maid:** Minerva.

l. 230 **Python's:** The Python had guarded the shrine of Delphi before it was slain by Apollo.

l. 231 **Cyclops:** The Cyclopes were sometimes said to have worked as smiths for Vulcan.

ll. 233–56 **Nor ... plain:** 'Most of these portents are related by Valerius Maximus to have happened to Pompey in his march from Dyrrachium into Thessaly, and according to him they were so many warnings to avoid a battle with Caesar' (Rowe).

l. 236 **Thwarted:** crossed athwart.

l. 238 **Stroke:** struck.

l. 240 **Typhons:** waterspouts.

l. 240 **Interwove:** interwoven.

ll. 247–50 **The standard ... weight:** 'The standards sticking too fast in the ground, or having bees swarm upon them, were omens always reckoned of the worst kind, of which Livy gives several instances, particularly before the battle of Trasimene in the second Punic War' (Rowe).

l. 252 **And ... tears:** The statues are made of Parian marble.

ll. 253–4 **No ... flies:** It was considered unlucky if the victim were unwilling to be sacrificed.

ll. 275–9 **Whate'er ... good:** 'These prodigies (the poet says) were agreeable to that horrid disposition of mind which at that time had possessed both parties, and prepared them for embruing their hands in the blood of their nearest relations and fellow-citizens' (Rowe).

l. 284 **These:** those who fought at Pharsalia.

l. 294 **Augur:** Gaius Cornelius, who fell into a trance and described the details of the war. This incident is described in Plutarch, *Caesar* 47.

l. 295 **'Tis ... come:** This is is an echo of Virgil's famous lines on the fall of Troy, beginning *venit summa dies et ineluctabile tempus / Dardaniae*, 'It has come – the last day and inevitable hour for Troy' (*Aeneid* II.324–5).

ll. 315–18 **How ... incline:** Lucan believes that future generations will support Pompey's cause.

l. 317 **Thee:** It is unclear whether Pompey or Rome is addressed here.

l. 323 **Lentulus:** P. Cornelius Lentulus Spinther had been consul in 49 BC. Appian states that Lentulus was in charge of the right wing.

ll. 323-40 **On . . . foe:** Pompey's battle formation is described. Compare Caesar, *Bellum Civile* III.88; Plutarch, *Pompey* 69; Appian, *Bellum Civile* II.76.

l. 325 **Domitius:** Lucius Domitius Ahenobarbus. Cf.II.722-93.

l. 327 **Scipio:** Q. Caecilius Metellus Pius Scipio was married to Pompey's daughter Cornelia.

l. 328 **Eight full legions:** As Lucan does not specify that there were eight legions Rowe probably derived the detail from his Latin text.

l. 330 **Undistinguished:** not marked by any distinction.

l. 334 **Tetrarchs:** A tetrarch was a ruler of one quarter of a country, and by extension any minor ruler.

l. 340 **Fierce Gauls:** Two chieftains of Gaul, Roucillus and Egus, had been made senators by Caesar during his dictatorship but afterwards deserted to Pompey.

ll. 369-491 **Ye . . . fly:** Caesar's forthright speech provides a contrast with Pompey's and appeals to his troops' worse instincts.

l. 376 **Hopes:** The hopes created by the crossing of the Rubicon and the consequent outbreak of war.

ll. 382-4 **To . . . seat:** Rowe includes in his translation two lines deleted from modern editions: *haec eadem est hodie quae pignora quaeque penates / reddat et emerito faciat vos Marte colonos.*

l. 396 **Private gown:** the toga of the private citizen.

l. 397 **At my expense of fame:** at the expense of my reputation.

ll. 401-6 **Yon . . . ears:** The Romans considered the Greeks impractical and the Eastern nations unmanly.

l. 420 **Ausonian:** Italian.

l. 454 **Rostrum:** the platform for public speakers in the Forum.

l. 457 **On . . . rely:** In case of defeat, Caesar intends to commit suicide.

l. 462 **And ... stain:** The Saepta were enclosures in the Campus Martius. Cf.II.307–8.

l. 474 **Satiated:** has three syllables and is accented on the first.

l. 494 **Fences:** fortifications.

l. 502 **Presages:** accented on the second syllable.

l. 514 **Effort:** accented on the second syllable.

l. 521 **They ... care:** This is in ironical contradiction to one of the poem's most famous lines. Cf.I.241–2.

l. 535 **Decii:** Cf.II.474.

l. 536 **The ... boast:** Cf.I.320.

l. 547 **Yon ... war:** Pompey's troops far outnumbered Caesar's.

l. 566 **Or ... borne:** Either you conquer or I shall be exiled.

l. 580 **Prevent:** Destroy in advance.

l. 580 **Prevent ... race:** Lucan is thinking of the unborn descendants of the men killed in battle, who will be deprived of liberty.

ll. 589–92 **While ... assign:** A yearly, movable festival which Roman magistrates had to attend. Offerings were made to Jupiter Latiaris on the summit of the Alban Mount.

l. 605 **Allia:** a tributary of the Tiber and the site of a Roman defeat at the hands of the Gauls in 390 BC.

l. 605 **Cannae:** Hannibal defeated the Romans at the Battle of Cannae in 216 BC.

l. 612 **Haughty queen:** Rome.

ll. 614–19 **Oh ... mankind:** Those killed at Pharsalia might have made up any loss of human life caused by the worst plague or earthquake.

l. 628 **As:** as if.

ll. 633–4 **No ... plough:** The consul would mark the founding of any new colony by driving a plough to mark the circuit of the walls.

l. 636 **nor ... ghost:** Cf.I.23. Augustus made a treaty with the Parthians, but they were not decisively defeated.

l. 639 **Tanais:** Tigris in modern texts.

l. 647 **Brutus**: L. Junius Brutus. See note to line 57.

l. 653 **Since ... in**: The refuge was a grove in Rome which Romulus declared an asylum for all refugees.

l. 654 **Ev'n ... build**: There was a dispute between Romulus who wanted to build Rome on the Palatine, and Remus, who favoured the Aventine. Augurs determined in Romulus' favour after the appearance of twelve vultures.

ll. 665–8 **Is ... head**: Lucan complains that Jove wastes his powers on inoffensive objects, while the task of punishing Caesar rests with Gaius Cassius Longinus, one of Caesar's assassins.

l. 667 **His**: Jove's.

l. 669 **The ... feast**: When Atreus fed his brother Thyestes with the flesh of his own sons, the sun withdrew his light in horror.

ll. 675–6 **Yet ... sword**: The justice of the gods is shown by the self-punishing act of adding the Caesars to their numbers.

l. 678 **With ... stand**: This line reflects the way Augustus and Claudius were represented on works of art after their deification.

l. 688 **Themselves**: they themselves.

l. 689 **Stupid**: stupefied.

l. 689 **At a gaze**: gazing.

l. 695 **Engage**: start the fight.

l. 697 **Crastinus**: The battle is started by Crastinus (accented on the first syllable by Rowe), an old soldier of Caesar's, serving as a volunteer.

l. 706 **Battles**: battle-lines.

l. 725 **Piles**: javelins.

ll. 735–6 **These, those**: the Pompeians, the Caesarians.

ll. 739–70 **From ... die**: Pompey's cavalry divides but is turned back by Caesar's cohorts.

l. 742 **Foot**: 'Shot' is printed in the first edition. This is apparently an error, and is replaced by 'foot' in later editions.

l. 744 **Missile rage**: weapons thrown in anger.

l. 746 **Bullets:** A bullet can refer to a missile from a sling.

ll. 748–52 **From . . . attend:** In Grotius the ordering of the lines differs from that in modern texts, where the lines which correspond to lines 748–52 in Rowe's translation follow the passage which Rowe ends at line 717.

l. 754 **Effort:** accented on the second syllable.

ll. 797–802 **But . . . shame:** Lucan now goes on to disobey his own plea that the violent deeds should not be recorded. There is a tension between the desire for silence and the need to tell the story. Cf. the figure of *praeteritio.*

l. 816 **Or . . . car:** Mars was particularly associated with Thrace.

ll. 831–6 **Strike . . . wound:** The purport of this speech is given as narrative by Lucan.

l. 841 **The . . . bleed:** Metellus Scipio was not killed at Pharsalia, but survived until Thapsus. L. Manlius Torquatus was a follower of Pompey and survived for two years after Pharsalia. Lucan is giving the impression that the flower of Rome's aristocracy fell that day. Thus these operate as both 'real' and 'rhetorical' plurals.

l. 847 **Undistinguished:** not clearly perceived. The adjective is hypothetical – Brutus would be undistinguished were he effectively shrouded with a helmet.

l. 851 **But . . . wait:** Brutus, Caesar's assassin, was to commit suicide after the battle of Philippi in 42 BC. 'The fields of Philippi, which, as I have observed before, not only Lucan, but even Virgil and Ovid, confound with Pharsalia' (Rowe). Virgil had established the trope of their identity.

l. 864 **Recording . . . well:** Lucan states that no plebeians lay among the patricians. Perhaps Rowe's political sensibilities made him omit this detail.

l. 865 **How . . . fell:** 'This whole passage seems to be the pure effect of Lucan's partiality against Caesar, and is of a piece with the cruelty he makes him guilty of both in the battle and after it' (Rowe). According to Caesar (*Bellum Civile* II.99.5) Domitius was killed as he fled from the battle. Lucan's adjustment might have been prompted by a desire to flatter Nero, who was descended from Domitius, although it is also possible to read this as a critique of Nero, unworthy of his ancestor who died defying a tyrant. He was spared by Caesar in Book II.

l. 877 **Expecting Gaul:** Domitius had been appointed to supersede Caesar in Gaul in 49 BC.

l. 885 **Chief:** Pompey. 'The fate of the battle not being then determined' (Rowe).

ll. 888–91 **Dire . . . below:** 'I don't know whether this passage is not a little too obscure in the English. The meaning is that Domitius did not doubt but the gods would punish Caesar severely for the injuries he had done to Rome, to Pompey, and even to himself (Domitius)' (Rowe).

l. 889 **For:** in punishment on behalf of.

ll. 894–7 **But . . . weep:** Lucan's point that it is impossible to focus on individuals when so many have died is rather lost in Rowe's translation, although it is very clearly glossed in his Latin text.

l. 915 **Bastard-born:** 'Concluding from so unnatural an action that the person killed could not be the real and true son of the man who killed him' (Rowe).

l. 915 **Aread:** adjudge.

ll. 931–4 **'Tis . . . right:** 'This complaint of our posterity is just' (Rowe). The meaning is that they should be allowed to keep their right to liberty: those born after its loss should have been given civil war as a chance to regain it. As often Rowe is not at his best when translating Lucan's more compressed and paradoxical thoughts.

ll. 958–71 **So . . . bleed:** Lucan ascribes honourable motives to Pompey's decision to quit the field.

l. 992 **Afric:** Further fighting took place in Africa after Pompey's death.

l. 993 **Munda:** the site of the final Pompeian defeat in Spain in 45 BC.

l. 1008 **Pharian:** Egyptian.

l. 1018 **Cities:** Rowe supposes that these are the cities in which the Cilician pirates were settled by Pompey.

l. 1018 **Monarchs crowned:** Lucan alludes to the fact that Pompey had helped instate Ptolemy and Juba on their thrones.

l. 1037 **Courser:** horse.

ll. 1045–83 **Then . . . laid:** Caesar captures Pompey's camp.

ll. 1048–9 **Careful . . . prevent:** 'Though Caesar, a few verses farther, tells his soldiers their victory was complete, 'tis plain he did not think it so till he was master of Pompey's camp; apprehending that the enemy might recollect themselves during the night, and perhaps make a new stand in their camp next morning' (Rowe).

l. 1067 **Spurn:** tread on, kick.

l. 1074 **Golden Arimaspus:** The Arimaspi were a Scythian tribe who were traditionally thought to possess much gold.

l. 1075 **Tagus, Iber:** These rivers ran through areas rich in gold.

l. 1076 **Griping:** clutching.

ll. 1084–1109 **Meanwhile . . . fiends:** Caesar and his troops are disturbed by nightmares.

l. 1092 **Affright:** fear.

ll. 1101–2 **Such . . . guilt:** Orestes was pursued by the Erinyes after killing his mother Clytemnestra.

l. 1103 **Such . . . knew:** Cf.VI.587.

ll. 1108–9 **To . . . fiends:** Details of the punishment are not included by Lucan, and Rowe would seem to have been influenced by a note in his Latin text.

ll. 1125–8 **Not . . . field:** Hannibal gave the consul L. Aemilius Paullus an honourable burial after the battle of Cannae.

l. 1136 **Fret:** chequer.

ll. 1144–9 **Though . . . pass:** The future destruction of the world by fire was a Stoic belief.

l. 1148 **Knead . . . up:** roll into a mass.

ll. 1193–4 **Still . . . past:** This seems to be a reference to Philippi.

ll. 1219–20 **Munda . . . stain:** Mutina was a town in Cisalpine Gaul, famous for its successful resistance to Pompey in 78 BC and to Antony in 43 BC. Antony was defeated at Mutina in 43 BC. The reference to Pachynus invokes the wars with Sextus Pompey, ended by the battle of Naulochus and Mylae off the coast of Sicily. Pachynus is accented on the second syllable.

l. 1221 **Actium:** a disyllable.

l. 1221 **Justify:** absolve from guilt.

Book Eight

l. 1 **Alcides:** Hercules. Cf.VI.572–5.

ll. 5–20 **Fall'n . . . told:** 'This is one of the passages which, if Lucan had lived to give the last hand to this work, I cannot but think he would have altered. The fear that he gives to Pompey on occasion of his flight is very unlike the character he himself, or indeed any other writer, has given him. It is something the more remarkable from a passage in the latter end of the foregoing book, where he is said to leave the field of battle with great bravery and constancy of mind. Though it is very judiciously observed, on comparing that passage and this together, by Martin Laso de Oropesa, the Spanish translator, that the desire of seeing his wife, which was the occasion of his resolution to leave the field, and survive such a loss as that battle was, in the seventh book, might in this place likewise be the reason for the fear and anxiety which he showed in his flight' (Rowe). Martin Laso de Oropesa was an early sixteenth-century Spanish humanist whose transla-tion of Lucan into Spanish was published in 1541.

l. 12 **Great:** another pun on his name, Pompey the Great.

l. 21 **Covert:** hiding.

l. 26 **Pontic and piratic:** A reference to Pompey's victory over King Mithri-dates of Pontus. Cf.I.610–12. Pompey defeated the Cilician pirates in 67 BC.

ll. 34–7 **Then . . . flies:** One should always be prepared to commit suicide.

ll. 56–63 **Soon . . . hear:** This evocation of Cornelia scanning the sea has a number of literary analogues, including the tale of Ceyx and Alcyone (Ovid, *Metamorphoses* XI.463–73).

l. 61 **In the round:** in every direction from where she's standing.

l. 66 **Preventing:** anticipating.

l. 82 **Corse:** corpse.

l. 89 **Strict:** close.

l. 96 **Sprung . . . state:** a reference to her descent from the Scipios.

l. 107 **Fathers:** senators.

l. 112 **Deplore:** lament.

l. 115 **Who:** those who.

ll. 119–20 **Ah . . . bed:** She wishes she had married Caesar because she believes she would have brought him ill luck.

l. 122 **Unblessed . . . flame:** Hymen is described as yellow by association with the orange-yellow veil worn by Roman brides.

ll. 123–5 **My . . . draws:** Cornelia's first husband, Publius Crassus, died at the battle of Carrhae in 53 BC. She believes that, as Crassus' widow, she brings with her the ill omen of the disaster at Carrhae.

l. 124 **Erinys:** Fury.

ll. 138–9 **And . . . suffice:** Julia was Pompey's first wife. Her ghost appeared to him at the beginning of Book III.

l. 149 **Pledge:** Cornelia.

l. 157 **Already . . . we:** They are already guilty because they sheltered Cornelia.

l. 177 **I . . . buy:** The Lesbians could gain pardon from Caesar by handing over Pompey to him.

l. 192 **Hospitable:** accented on the first syllable.

l. 233 **But . . . descends:** Callisto was transformed into a bear and both she and her son Arcas were changed into stars when he inadvertently tried to kill her.

l. 234 **Cynosure:** the Little Bear.

l. 236 **Canopus:** a star in the constellation Argo which is invisible in Italy.

l. 238 **Pharos:** Although sometimes used to indicate the whole of Egypt, here only the island of Pharos itself, on which there was a famous lighthouse, seems intended.

l. 254 **Asia:** *Asinae* in modern texts; *Asiae* in Grotius.

ll. 257–60 **With . . . roll:** 'This was a pillar of marble placed at the end of the course appointed for the chariot races among the ancients, and to turn nicely and closely round this without touching was reckoned a piece of great skill and dexterity in the driver' (Rowe).

l. 265 **Son:** Sextus.

l. 271 **Deiotarus:** accented on the second syllable; a Galatian king and a loyal supporter of Pompey.

ll. 281-2 **To ... prayer:** Deiotarus' mission to the Parthians is mentioned in no other source and may be Lucan's invention. It is striking because the Parthians were the traditional enemies of Rome.

l. 284 **Magi:** wise men.

l. 291 **Eagles:** standards.

l. 292 **Cyrus:** Cyrus founded the Persian monarchy.

l. 294 **Ere:** in advance of.

ll. 299-300 **When ... I:** Pompey dissuaded the Senate from continuing the Parthian war after the battle of Carrhae.

l. 301 **Zeugma:** This town was on the boundary between the Roman and Parthian empires.

l. 305 **Monarch:** Deiotarus.

l. 314 **Chief:** Pompey.

l. 317 **Coan:** Belonging to the island of Cos.

l. 328 **Dipsas:** a waterfall, possibly to be identified with the river Catarrhactes.

l. 332 **Cilician:** i.e. Pirates.

ll. 335-427 **At ... mine:** There is a meeting of Pompey and the senators at Syhedra. Pompey considers the advantages of Libya, Egypt and Parthia as destinations and urges them to take refuge with the king of Parthia.

l. 349 **From ... rose:** Marius returned from Carthage to take power in Rome again. Cf.II.591.

l. 365 **Dislike me:** I dislike.

l. 365 **Pharian prince:** the Egyptian boy pharaoh, Ptolemy.

l. 370 **Moor:** Juba.

l. 371 **From ... race:** Juba's ancestor, Masinissa, married the Carthaginian Sophonisba, who may have been related to Hannibal. However, they had no children.

l. 375 **Varus:** Publius Attius Varus was the leader of the Pompeian forces in Africa.

l. 381 **Laves:** washes along.

l. 382 **Ruddy waves:** Lucan seems to have confused the Persian Gulf with the Red Sea.

l. 385 **Promiscuous:** without distinction.

l. 391 **Pile:** javelin.

ll. 397–9 **Too ... foe:** Even when trying to present Parthia in a positive light, Pompey cannot prevent himself from revealing their unsuitability as allies.

l. 419 **Still:** ever.

l. 426 **Phraates:** This was the name of several kings of Parthia.

ll. 428–607 **The leader ... failed:** Lentulus disagrees with Pompey, favouring Egypt rather than Parthia. His arguments are successful.

l. 430 **Sate:** sat.

l. 431 **Lentulus:** See V.27.

l. 447 **Worship ... depend:** 'The worship of fire, or rather of the supreme being and principle of all things under that symbol, was first taught among the eastern nations by Zoroaster and his disciples the magi' (Rowe).

l. 450 **Brave:** challenge, defy.

l. 469 **Son:** Caesar.

l. 491 **Champaign:** plain, level ground.

l. 496 **Whene'er ... arise:** Rowe may have misunderstood the text here. Lucan's reference to darkness at this point could be meant to denote the darkness of woods, for fighting would not take place at night.

l. 504 **Rampire:** ramparts.

l. 508 **And ... delight:** The structure of the sentence suggests that delight is a noun rather than a verb. The fact that there is no apostrophe after troops in the first edition might seem to contradict this interpretation, but apostrophes are frequently omitted in this text.

l. 510 **Flitting:** here seems to be used to convey Lucan's idea that the winds carry the arrows whither they will.

l. 511 **Feathered store:** store of arrows.

l. 520 **Friend:** Crassus. 'Friend' may suggest *amicus* in the political sense and thus be a reference to the First Triumvirate.

l. 526 **Somewhat:** something.

l. 526 **Somewhat more terrible than death:** i.e. rape.

l. 529 **Bestial race:** beasts.

l. 538 **Oedipus:** unwittingly married his mother Jocasta.

l. 546 **And . . . gave:** In Lucan it is clear that Crassus rather than Pompey is indicated here.

ll. 553–4 **With . . . Rhine:** Lucan seems to be saying instead that the northern borders should be left unguarded so as to fight the east. In Rowe the point is that Caesar and Pompey combined could win major victories at various edges of the empire. The meaning in Lucan is different, but Rowe is rhetorically as effective.

l. 558 **And . . . tombs:** In Rowe the reference is unambiguously to the tomb of Crassus, but Lucan's phrase *in tumulos ducum* may refer to the tombs of the Parthian monarchs.

l. 568 **Shade:** Crassus.

ll. 585–6 **Say . . . reign:** Lentulus agrees with Pompey that Juba is untrustworthy.

l. 594 **The largesse of thy bounty:** i.e. as your generous gift.

ll. 608–25 **And now . . . ends:** Pompey sails for Egypt via Cyprus.

l. 610 **Goddess:** Venus.

l. 613 **And . . . rose:** Aphrodite sprang from the foam of the sea that gathered about the severed genitals of the god Uranus when he was castrated by his son Cronus.

l. 616 **Unborn:** The gods are not born because they are eternal and unchanging.

l. 621 **Beamy light:** the lighthouse at Pharos.

ll. 626–7 **'Twas . . . sky:** the autumnal equinox in September.

l. 627 **Balance:** Libra.

l. 636 **The fleet arrived**: an absolute phrase.

ll. 638–733 **The time . . . proud**: The Egyptian court meets to consider how to respond to Pompey's arrival. Acoreus (four syllables) reminds Ptolemy how much he owes to Pompey. However, a eunuch, Pothinus, argues that he should be murdered and his advice is followed.

l. 642 **Isis**: Egyptian goddess of nature, associated with both Demeter and Aphrodite.

l. 642 **Osiris**: brother and husband of Isis, god of male fertility in nature, associated with Dionysus. Rowe refers the reader to Selden's *Syntagma de Diis Syriis*.

l. 645 **Apis**: 'Apis was a living ox, worshipped likewise by the Egyptians. He was only suffered to live such a certain time, and then his own priests put him into the fountain of the sun, and killed him. Upon the death of one, they immediately, with great marks of grief, looked out for another, who was to be of the same race, and marked after the same manner, especially he was to have a white half-moon on the right side' (Rowe).

l. 657 **To . . . belong**: 'Many inconveniences and ill consequences, as to what regards the success of things in this world' (Rowe).

l. 659 **Her**: honesty's.

l. 683 **Sister**: Cleopatra.

l. 689 **Allies**: accented on the second syllable.

l. 699 **Wrong**: 'The destruction and ruin that Pompey would involve us in' (Rowe).

ll. 703–8 **His . . . debarred**: Pothinus warns Ptolemy not to become associated with Pompey and thus incur Caesar's enmity.

l. 711 **Call**: an imperative.

l. 715 **Thy**: Pompey's.

l. 726 **Unpitying**: has only three syllables.

l. 732 **Fond . . . bestowed**: 'As if he was pleased that his ministers, who governed and controlled him on all other occasions, would give him leave to exercise his royal power for the commission of so base a murder' (Rowe).

l. 736 **Achillas**: one of Ptolemy's generals.

l. 751 **Name:** Roman.

l. 761 **Addressed:** prepared.

l. 768 **Devoted:** doomed.

l. 794 **Plained:** lamented.

ll. 806–8 **Hail . . . led:** The information that Septimius had once served under Pompey is not in Lucan, although the Latin text used by Rowe includes a note to this effect.

ll. 822–5 **Say . . . down:** If Brutus' assassination of Caesar is called murder, what name is bad enough to describe Septimius' crime?

l. 837 **Great:** He lives up to his name, Pompeius Magnus. Lucan constantly plays on this word.

l. 838 **Equal:** even, undisturbed.

l. 846 **Period:** end.

l. 915 **Haggling:** mangling, hacking.

l. 936 **Serous:** of or like serum, watery.

ll. 936–9 **His . . . mass:** The head is embalmed.

l. 941 **Lagaean:** The Ptolemies were descended from the Macedonian Lagus.

l. 943 **Sister:** Cleopatra.

l. 945 **Youth of Macedon:** Alexander the Great was buried at Alexandria.

ll. 966–1086 **Yet . . . sleeps:** Cordus, a follower of Pompey invented by Lucan, gives Pompey a makeshift burial.

l. 970 **Follower:** a disyllable.

l. 971 **Quaestor:** a class of Roman magistrate concerned with public revenue and expenditure.

l. 971 **Idalian:** Icarian in modern texts; Mayer calls it a baffling allusion, but cautions against emendation. However Rowe's note on Idalian, which is derived from Farnaby's commentary, seems convincing: 'Cyprus is called Idalian from a town, grove, or mountain (perhaps there were all these) called Idalium, or Idalia, in that island sacred to Venus.'

l. 978 **Phoebe:** the moon.

ll. 995–1002 He . . . round: 'In ennumerating what was wanting to Pompey's funeral, the poet takes notice of the chief pieces of magnificence which were usual at the funerals of great men among the Romans. See the learned Dr Kennet upon this subject, in his Roman Antiquities, in his chapter of the Roman funerals' (Rowe).

l. 997 No . . . bear: a reference to carrying a funeral bier.

l. 998 No . . . appear: These 'statues' may be waxen images of a dead man's ancestors which were borne in state at funerals. This detail is not present in Lucan and was probably derived from Kennet's *Of the Antiquities of Rome*. Alternatively they may be triumphal insignia.

l. 1007 Your . . . denies: She cannot light the funeral pyre.

l. 1010 And . . . near: 'As having seen his murder, and now probably being in sight of his mean funeral' (Rowe).

l. 1068 Covert: hiding.

ll. 1069–70 Ah . . . name: Cordus, fearing that Pompey might not wish to be buried in this way, hides from the fame that should follow such a generous act. 'The piety of the person who took so much care to perform these rites of funeral, though but mean ones, to Pompey is the more insisted on by the poet, because the ancients had nothing in greater horror than to want them' (Rowe).

l. 1071 Ev'n . . . bestow: 'Insinuating that Caesar would willing reward the man who should tell him he had buried Pompey, since he might from thence certainly conclude he was dead' (Rowe).

l. 1095 Nor . . . upbraid: The stone stands as a mute rebuke to the gods for allowing Pompey to meet such an end.

ll. 1096–7 Shall . . . stand: The fact that both Bacchus and Hercules were deified mortals looks forward to Pompey's apotheosis in Book IX.

l. 1106 Records: accented on the second syllable.

l. 1107 Passenger: wayfarer.

l. 1109 Alpine war: Pompey was involved in wars against the Alpine tribes when he was marching through the Alps on Sertorius. Cf.II.833.

l. 1111 Pontic king: Mithridates.

l. 1119 Roman: The Roman reader is addressed.

l. 1122 Trophied arch: 'The triumphal arches were erected in honour of successful generals and emperors, and were properly adorned with military trophies. It may likewise be meant by the original that such arches were built by the spoils gained from the enemies, but the former sense seems the more obvious' (Rowe).

l. 1128 Cumaean maid: the Sybil.

ll. 1128–9 Well . . . shore: 'Cicero mentions a prophecy among the Sibyl's verses that forbade Roman soldiers, or rather the Roman soldiery in general, to go to Egypt' (Rowe).

l. 1132 Ethiops: Ethiopia.

l. 1135 Timbrel: 'The *sistrum*, which I have here translated timbrel, was an odd sort of a brazen instrument of music, with loose pieces of the same metal that ran along upon little bars or wires. It was peculiarly dedicated to the worship of Isis and Osiris' (Rowe).

l. 1137 And . . . gods: A reference to Anubis, traditionally depicted with a dog's head. This passage alludes to the practice of Egyptian religious rites in Rome.

l. 1139 Low . . . laid: Lucan's attitude towards the burial of Pompey is vacillating and contradictory. Mayer suggests that the incoherence may be intended to give an effect of spontaneity and convey the emotion of the poet (Mayer 1981, 185).

ll. 1140–1 And . . . stand: Julius Caesar was deified soon after his death. The reference extends to the emperors up to and including Nero. Cf. 1173–4.

ll. 1150–3 Oh . . . home: Lucan imagines retrieving Pompey's remains himself.

l. 1151 The . . . joy: Lucan asserts paradoxically that the impious desecration of Pompey's grave might be effected for pious ends.

l. 1162 Great chief: Pontifex Maximus.

l. 1166 Thebes: The Thebes in Upper Egypt is indicated.

l. 1172 Fane: temple.

l. 1172 The . . . Jove: Jupiter was worshipped on Mount Casius.

l. 1181 Bidental: This was a place where anyone who had been struck by lightning was buried. Its worship is invoked here as an example of an old-fashioned rite. There is a possible hint that Pompey's grave is a kind of bidental because Caesar is so often compared to lightning.

l. 1190 As ... Jove: The Cretans, traditionally thought of as great liars, boasted that Jupiter's tomb was located on Crete.

Book Nine

ll. 1–28 Nor ... below: Pompey's soul rises to the orbit of the moon, inhabited, according to some ancient philosophers, by the souls of the wise. An important literary predecessor is Cicero's *Somnium Scipionis*, from Book 6 of *De Re Publica*, itself partly derived from the end of Plato's *Republic*, and cf. Virgil, *Aeneid* VI.887 with Servius' note. The description of Pompey's apotheosis is one of the sources lying behind the similar description of Troilus' soul at the end of Chaucer's *Troilus and Criseyde* (V.1807–27).

l. 5 But ... delay: The phrase 'active and impatient of delay', which has no real counterpart in Lucan although the verb *prosilio*, meaning to leap or spring forth, is used, makes Pompey seem more like Caesar. His eagerness to leave earthly cares behind may be perceived as noble.

l. 10 Cynthia: the moon.

ll. 11–14 Their ... grace: The translation here is subtly Christianized by Rowe.

ll. 30–5 His ... find: The Republicans' struggle against Caesar continues, culminating in his assassination by Brutus.

l. 33 Sate: sat.

l. 37 He: Cato, who now goes on to continue the campaign in Africa.

ll. 54–63 Straight ... fled: Cato gathers up Pompey's forces and takes them to Africa via the port of Corcyra.

l. 60 Who that: anyone who.

ll. 60–3 Who ... fled: The fleet looks too splendid to belong to the vanquished side.

l. 65 Cythera: accented on the second syllable.

l. 67 Soon ... behind: Dictaean refers to a mountain in the east of Crete, and by extension is used simply as a synonym for Cretan.

l. 73 **Which . . . name:** The town is Paliurus, on the coast of Africa. Lucan seems to have thought the name was derived from Aeneas' drowned helsman, Palinurus.

ll. 74–5 **Nor . . . shown:** A reference to Cape Palinurus in southern Italy.

l. 108 **Decent:** fittingly.

ll. 117–20 **Happy . . . bestow:** She believes mangled rites are worse than none at all. In view of the importance of burial the sentiments are highly paradoxical.

l. 126 **Wretch:** Cornelia is addressing herself here.

ll. 151–4 **Whene'er . . . reign:** Pompey had wished his sons, Gnaeus and Sextus, to continue the struggle against Caesar.

ll. 167–70 **At . . . go:** Lucan implies that Pompey gave Cornelia this commission in order to prevent her from committing suicide.

ll. 169–70 **Through . . . go:** Cornelia's conception of the afterlife seems to differ from that presented at the opening of the book.

l. 172 **Being:** scans as a single syllable.

ll. 176–7 **Nor . . . cord:** Cf.VIII.134–5. These are the three traditional ways of committing suicide.

l. 189 **Eurus:** the east wind.

l. 196 **Bore:** sailed.

ll. 200–77 **With . . . rage:** After a digression, we are now returned to the point at which Lucan left Cato's camp at line 87, looking anxiously at the approaching ship. Gnaeus, who has been with Cato, now learns of his father's death from Sextus. He wishes to go to Egypt to avenge him but is restrained by Cato.

l. 202 **Pompey:** Gnaeus.

l. 218 **Odds:** superiority, balance of advantage.

l. 248 **Since . . . now:** This translates *nusquam civilibus armis / tanta fuit merces* (150–1) which is translated as 'nowhere was so great a prize offered to the fighters in civil war' in the Loeb edition.

l. 253 **Not . . . defend:** Alexander was buried at Alexandria.

l. 255 **Mareotis:** a lake and city of Lower Eygpt, not far from Alexandria.

l. 257 From . . . torn: 'Amasis was a famous king of Egypt who succeeded Apriez after having dethroned him. His story may be seen at large in the second book of Herodotus' (Rowe).

ll. 266–7 Their . . . bleed: Cf.VIII.645. This translates a line which is deleted by modern editors, *et sacer in Magni cineres mactabitur Apis.*

l. 268 While . . . feed: Gnaeus intends to use wooden effigies of the gods as fuel.

l. 281 Yet: thus far.

l. 283 Deplore: lament.

ll. 292–302 Soon . . . care: As she cannot bury his body, Cornelia performs the funeral rites over Pompey's robes and weapons.

l. 298 Erst: previously.

l. 298 Robes . . . displayed: A reference to Jupiter Capitolinus, whose temple was the final point of the triumphal procession.

l. 308 Hinds: agricultural labourers.

l. 321 Hero's: Pompey's.

ll. 322–4 Few . . . art: Cato supposedly speaks sincerely in a plain, unadorned and unwordy style. The elder Cato's stylistic credo was *rem tene, verba sequentur*, itself of course a rhetorical trope; in Cato's speech, designed to convey judicious and measured restraint, the principal figure is in fact antithesis.

ll. 325–68 We've . . . head: Cato delivers the funeral oration.

l. 332 Great: a pun on Pompey's name.

ll. 332–5 Rome . . . retain: Rowe exaggerates Lucan's emphasis on Pompey as a champion of democracy.

l. 356 Senate and people: 'All those laws that served for the preservation of the Senate's just authority and the people's liberty' (Rowe).

l. 361 Thou . . . want: If Pompey had survived to witness Caesar's triumph, he might have wished to be slain by the Egyptians.

l. 364 Free . . . slain: 'I don't think this is so clearly expressed as it ought to be. The author's meaning is that next to dying when and how one pleases is the happiness of being compelled to die by another' (Rowe).

l. 365 **Juba:** 'To whom Cato then resolved to join himself' (Rowe).

l. 371 **Tully:** Cicero, whom Lucan does not mention here.

ll. 373–6 **But . . . shore:** The troops, weary with war, desert.

l. 375 **Tarchon:** 'This Tarchon was a prince of the Cilicians, or perhaps rather a leader of some of the Cilician pirates, who had been formerly vanquished and pardoned by Pompey, and in this civil war came to his assistance. I have followed the common reading of Tarchon, though (according to the opinion of Grotius) this prince or general's name was Tarchondimotus' (Rowe).

l. 394 **For . . . attend:** How can this war have an end?

ll. 402–7 **Though . . . gown:** They are not afraid as they would have been if they had been vanquished by a foreign enemy.

l. 428 **Roman consul:** Caesar.

ll. 431–4 **The . . . state:** These lines are amplified and strengthened by Rowe.

ll. 438–9 **Did . . . Rome:** Cato distinguishes servile obedience to a specific strong leader from the pursuit of liberty.

l. 446 **Fondly:** foolishly.

ll. 451–2 **At . . . grow:** With the death of Pompey, the fight for liberty is untained by any personality – Cato saw Pompey as a potential tyrant.

l. 456 **Two . . . dead:** Only Caesar survives from the first Triumvirate. Crassus and Pompey are dead.

l. 460 **And . . . bestow:** Although Ptolemy's action was evil, the outcome, in that it frees Rome from a potential tyrant, could be seen as a gift.

l. 477 **Devoted:** doomed.

l. 488 **Fleet:** fly, flit.

l. 491 **Then . . . hear:** Bees were thought to congregate if they heard cymbals. Cf. *Georgics* IV.64.

ll. 499–501 **With . . . war:** The restoration of discipline in an army by an outstanding general is a standard trope of historical narrative.

l. 514 **Syrts:** The Syrtes are two rocky gulfs, now called Sidra and Gabès, on the north coast of Africa, between Cyrene and Carthage. They are described in a lengthy set piece which can be seen as a contribution to the poem's involvement with boundaries, most obviously found in the subject of civil war itself.

l. 544 **Loaden:** laden.

ll. 544–85 **And now … land:** Some of the ships are destroyed in a storm.

l. 545 **Liquid plain:** This common phrase acquires a new resonance in the context of the Syrtes.

l. 546 **Presage:** accented on the second syllable.

l. 547 **Auster:** south wind.

l. 553 **Hands:** takes in, furls.

l. 574 **Strike:** run aground.

l. 575 **Beat:** beaten.

ll. 581–5 **The sandy … land:** They are stranded upon a sandbank: shipwrecked on 'land' as it were.

l. 590 **Tuneful god:** Triton.

l. 592 **Pallas:** Minerva.

l. 599 **Lethe:** 'This is, according to Cellarius, a mistake in geography. He places both this river and the Hesperian gardens in the region of Cyrene, on the eastern side of the Syrtis Major. This river's taking its rise from Hell is a known fable' (Rowe). Christoph Cellarius (1638–1707) wrote numerous works on grammar and style, as well as on ancient history and geography.

l. 604 **Long … torn:** One of Hercules' labours was to steal the golden apples from the garden of the Hesperides which was sometimes located in Cyrene.

l. 605 **Honours:** ornaments.

ll. 608–9 **Nor … song:** Lucan's attitude towards fable here seems different from elsewhere, and his words may be intended ironically.

l. 617 **Argive:** the adjective relating to Argos.

l. 618 **Eurystheus:** the king of Argos who had imposed the labours on Hercules.

l. 620 **They … last:** 'This is another gross fault in geography, for the

Garamantes were an inland people of Libya, that joined on the south to Ethiopia. This tract of land is now called by the Arabians Zaara, or the desert' (Rowe).

l. 621 Pompey: Gnaeus.

ll. 623–93 But . . . here: Cato rallies his men with a speech before leading them across land.

ll. 663–7 If . . . way: He suggest that anyone who is too frightened to continue should join Caesar.

l. 672 Train: company.

ll. 676–82 Who . . . alone: He says that the men may complain freely if he shirks hardship himself.

l. 681 Distinguished: differentiated, singular.

ll. 698–702 Libya . . . tomb: Cato committed suicide at Utica in 46 BC following Caesar's victory at Thapsus. These events are the subject of Addison's play *Cato*.

l. 703 Fame: Fame here corresponds to the Latin *fama*, and refers here to what is commonly said.

l. 704 Then . . . claim: 'The ancients divided the world into three parts, Europe, Asia, and Africa or Libya; for that whole part is frequently called Libya; the other division, which was sometimes used, and is here mentioned by Lucan, was into the eastern and western parts' (Rowe).

ll. 712–52 Of . . . year: The description which follows recalls accounts of the golden age, e.g. Ovid *Metamorphoses*, I.89–112 and is appropriate for the pure and ascetic Cato. Africa represents the Other in ways that are both positive and negative.

l. 723 Nor . . . spoil: 'That which we call the Gold Coast and Guinea were very little if at all known to the ancients' (Rowe).

l. 726 Citron groves: Rowe suggests an implied comparison with the luxurious 'citron board'. Cf.I.312.

l. 729 Leafy office: Their capacity to provide shade prevents them from being cut down.

ll. 740–1 There . . . twine: a Miltonic echo. Cf. *Paradise Lost*. IV.304–7, V.215–18.

l. 746 **But . . . smile:** Jupiter was *inter alia* the god of rain and water.

l. 749 **Vegetable:** has four syllables, and is accented on the first.

ll. 759–61 **Trade . . . land:** The Nasamonians plunder wrecked vessels.

l. 764 **Bold youth:** i.e. the army.

l. 771 **List:** a place where a tournament is held. The word is well chosen, since Cato's journey is a sort of gladiatorial contest.

l. 809 **Denounced:** proclaimed.

ll. 810–17 **Such . . . Rome:** 'In the time of Numa Pompilius there was a buckler found in Rome, such as the Romans called *ancile*, which was supposed to be dropped down from heaven. The augurs, who were consulted upon the occasion, pronounced that wherever that shield should remain the chief command and empire of the world should be fixed. Upon this Numa gave orders to a workman called Mamurra that he should make eleven others exactly like that which came from heaven, to prevent the true one from being stolen. These *ancilia sacra*, or holy bucklers, were committed to the care of the Salii, who were priests of Mars, and always chosen out of the patricians, or Roman nobility' (Rowe).

ll. 824–42 **Scarce . . . eyes:** The sandstorm is a paradoxical variant of a seastorm.

ll. 826–34 **Meantime . . . way:** The description which follows is typical of Lucan's preoccupation with vast blockading masses.

l. 839 **Lights:** i.e. stars.

ll. 848–71 **As . . . supplied:** The men are now afflicted by thirst and Cato demonstrates his fortitude by refusing and spilling a gift of precious water. A similar story was told of Alexander the Great, whom Cato parallels but surpasses.

l. 860 **Virtue:** fortitude.

l. 868 **Poured . . . sand:** 'This action of Cato's is not much unlike that of David, when he refused to drink of the water of the well of Bethlehem, which three men had ventured their lives to fetch. See I *Chron*: xi.15' (Rowe). Christian readers of ancient texts were ever on the lookout for such analogies.

l. 872 **Now . . . near:** 'Lucan has made no scruple of committing here another great fault in geography, for the sake of bringing his great Cato to the temple of Jupiter Ammon. This famous oracle was certainly situated between the less and greater Catabathmus, to the west of Egypt, in what is now called the desert of Barca, a great way distant from the march Cato was then taking in the kingdom of Tunis' (Rowe). They reach the temple of Jupiter Ammon. Cato's response to the god provides a striking contrast to the superstitious behaviour of Appius and Sextus.

l. 891 **Tall . . . grace:** Land is the object of the verb grace here.

ll. 896–911 **Yet . . . Urn:** Lucan describes the equator.

ll. 904–11 **Here . . . Urn:** At the equator all twelve signs of the zodiac rise at the same height and take the same time to rise and set.

l. 907 **Fishy sign:** Pisces.

l. 911 **Urn:** Aquarius.

l. 922 **Pilgrims:** Rowe's translation of *populi* as 'pilgrims' reflects his anti-Catholic stance.

l. 930 **Labienus:** Cf.V.500.

l. 931 **And . . . moved:** Labienus advocates that Cato follow the wishes of the people.

l. 939 **Their . . . trust:** Cf. Dryden's translation of Horace III.29, 'But God has wisely hid from human sight / The dark decrees of future fate' (45–6).

ll. 958–77 **Where . . . go:** Cato's response to Labienus consists of a series of questions which are in fact statements of his Stoic belief. The correct answers are already known.

l. 959 **Mystic:** secret.

ll. 974–5 **If . . . less:** These lines echo the famous line *victrix causa deis placuit, sed victa Catoni* (I.128).

l. 980 **God:** God is capitalized here to reflect the overt Christianizing of this famous passage. As all nouns are routinely capitalized in eighteenth-century poetry this distinction is not present in Rowe.

ll. 989–1005 **Canst . . . all:** 'I cannot but observe here how finely our author, in this passage, reprehends the folly of those who are fond of and believe in a local sanctity, as if one part of the world were holier than another, and the ubiquity of the divine nature were confined to a particular place. But, thank God, the foppery of pilgrimages is out of fashion in England, or at least those who are weak enough to travel from one country to another in search of holiness are wise enough not to own it amongst us' (Rowe). Milton has a version of part of the speech in *Paradise Lost* XI.335–8.

l. 992 **Thin**: few.

ll. 1002–3 **One ... freed**: The inevitability of death makes Cato cease to fear it.

ll. 1010–39 **Foremost ... gods**: Lucan offers further testimony to the noble fortitude of Cato's character.

ll. 1040–61 **Now ... first**: The soldiers are frightened to drink from a spring which is surrounded by snakes until Cato demonstrates that it is safe.

l. 1045 **Access**: accented on the second syllable.

l. 1046 **Serpents**: Lucan's description of snakes in Book IX influenced Book X of *Paradise Lost*, where the transformation of Satan and the fallen angels into serpents is described (X.521–72).

l. 1047 **Aspics**: asps.

l. 1048 **Dipsas**: The bite of the dipsas caused thirst. Dipsas is a plural here.

l. 1056 **Pest**: i.e. poison.

ll. 1062–1187 **Why ... heat**: Lucan now relates the legend (*fabula* – a key word for Lucan here) of Medusa and Perseus, which explains why there are so many snakes in Libya. The mannered and frivolous preciosities of the writing, in strong contrast to the style of the preceding passages about Cato, may suggest that the story is a parody of an aetiological fiction.

l. 1074 **Squalid**: waste, barren.

ll. 1077–8 **But ... owned**: a reference to the petrifying power of Medusa's face.

l. 1084 **Depended**: hung.

l. 1096 **But could no more**: All the Eumenides could do was inspire rage.

l. 1096 **Thracian lyre**: This belonged to Orpheus.

l. 1098 **Triple rage**: a reference to Cerberus' three heads.

l. 1103 **Phorcus**: a sea-god, the father of the Gorgons.

l. 1103 **Ceto**: mother of the Gorgons.

l. 1103 **He**: Phorcus.

l. 1119 **By . . . grew**: Perseus used Medusa's head to turn Atlas into stone.

l. 1122 **Till . . . aid**: There was a picture of the Gorgon on Pallas' shield.

l. 1128 **The . . . Jove**: The nymph Danaë, mother of Perseus, was imprisoned in a tower, but was seduced by Jove in a shower of golden rain.

l. 1130 **Cyllenian**: Cyllene is a high mountain in Arcadia on which Mercury was supposed to have been born and brought up.

l. 1131 **Wings**: Perseus borrowed Mercury's winged sandals.

ll. 1132-3 **His . . . freed**: Argus was a many-eyed monster, killed by Mercury while he guarded the nymph Io in the form of a heifer. See Ovid, *Metamorphoses*, II.568–746.

l. 1136 **Brother**: Jupiter was the father of both Perseus and Pallas.

l. 1138 **Refulgent**: shining.

l. 1139 **And . . . beheld**: It is safe for Perseus to look at Medusa's reflection in his shining shield and thus defeat her without being turned to stone.

l. 1154 **Somewhat**: something.

ll. 1174-8 **No . . . sun**: 'Lucan erroneously supposes this part of the earth to rise higher under the equator than in any other part, and to project its shade farthest in eclipses of the moon' (Rowe).

l. 1184 **Still**: ever.

ll. 1188-1243 **First . . . aid**: One source for Lucan's catalogue of snakes is Nicander's *Theriaca*, written in the second century BC.

l. 1190 **Blood**: The reference is to Medusa's blood.

l. 1200 **Haemorrhoïs**: the snake's Greek name, 'flowing blood', expresses its nature. It is accented on the second syllable.

l. 1206 **Chelyders**: water snakes.

l. 1208 **Cenchris**: a serpent marked with small specks.

l. 1213 **Ammodytes**: a species of serpent which is said to bury itself in the sand: sand-burrower. It has four syllables and is accented on the second.

l. 1214 **Swimmer**: a literal translation of Lucan's *natrix*.

l. 1215 **Javelin**: a literal translation of Lucan's *iaculus*.

l. 1216 **Scytale:** The name of this snake is derived from the Greek for club.

l. 1218 **Amphisbaena:** The name means 'going both ways', because the snake's motion begins at either head or its tail.

l. 1220 **Pareas:** a red-brown snake.

l. 1222 **Prester:** a snake whose bite causes burning.

l. 1223 **Seps:** a venomous snake whose bite caused putrefaction.

l. 1225 **Basilisk:** a snake with crown-like markings, from the Greek for king.

ll. 1229–32 **And . . . owned:** Snakes were worshipped in the east. Cf. Pliny, *Natural History*, VIII.32–7.

l. 1242 **Invade:** attack.

ll. 1244–1421 **Thus . . . hands:** Cato is forced to witness the snakes destroying many of his men. The deaths by snake-bite pursue the etymological implications of the snakes' names: for example, seps means dissolver, and dipsas is from the Greek word for thirst.

l. 1251 **Tyrrhene:** Etruscan.

l. 1257 **Nor . . . doubt:** He did not realize the danger, the wound being so small.

l. 1304 **Less:** smaller.

l. 1314 **Peritoneum:** the membrane which lines the cavity of the abdomen. Rowe's use of a scientific technical term is in Lucan's manner.

l. 1339 **Soul:** life.

l. 1342 **Prester:** A double etymology from the Greek here creates the combination of burning and swelling.

l. 1369 **Her:** virtue, as embodied in Cato.

ll. 1372–7 **And as . . . below:** 'The public shows at Rome were all exhibited at the expense of the public, or some of the great men. This was done with great magnificence, of which this way of perfuming the whole place, and the spectators, is a pretty remarkable instance. I know this passage is rendered after a different manner, but I take this sense of it to be most easy and most probable' (Rowe).

l. 1387 **And . . . wound:** Cf. the description of the flayed Marsyas in Ovid, *Metamorphoses* VI.388.

l. 1388 **Laevus:** *Laevus* means on the left side, and by extension unlucky, in Latin.

ll. 1394–7 **Not . . . foretell:** 'The literal translation runs thus: Nor are those poisons more swift to destroy, which the prophetic Sabaeans compose of the tree resembling birch, of which last the Sabine (and Roman) magistrates' rods were made. I have taken very few liberties of adding or leaving out anything in this translation; the last circumstance, indeed, of this passage I did not think material enough to be insisted on' (Rowe). In modern texts the priests are *Saitae* (from Sais) rather than *Sabaeae*. Also modern texts read *Sabaeas* in 820: Rowe's had *Sabinas*.

l. 1403 **Compared:** in comparison.

ll. 1411–12 **The . . . bought:** With this punctuation taught is a past participle; alternatively taught could be a main verb with force as subject, in which case a semicolon would be needed.

l. 1416 **The . . . die:** A scorpion, later transformed into the constellation Scorpio, stung Orion to death.

l. 1418 **Salpuga:** a poisonous ant. Cf. Pliny, *Natural History* XXIX.92.

l. 1421 **Stygian sisters:** the Fates.

l. 1426 **Strow:** strew.

l. 1436 **And . . . burn:** The snakes' capacity to produce poison is restored by the warmth of the soldiers' bodies.

l. 1442 **Cerastae:** horned serpents.

l. 1446 **Afric:** Africa.

l. 1485 **That:** i.e. the possibility of life in the desert.

l. 1485 **Plagues:** serpents.

l. 1503 **Bear with:** endure.

l. 1524 **Psyllians:** This African people lived south-west of the Syrtis Major. They were celebrated as snake-charmers as well as resistant to their venom.

l. 1551 **Broods:** cherishes.

l. 1557 **Mystic:** magic.

l. 1559 **Medicinal:** accented on the third syllable.

l. 1560 **Galbanum:** gum resin from kinds of ferula, a genus which includes the giant fennel.

l. 1561 **Wallwort:** This word translates Lucan's *ebulum*, dwarf elder.

l. 1563 **Costos:** an Oriental aromatic plant.

l. 1564 **Centaury:** plant of the genus *Centaurium*, said to have been discovered by the centaur Chiron.

l. 1566 **Thapsos:** a poisonous shrub.

l. 1567 **Woundwort:** translates Lucan's *panacea*.

l. 1567 **Maidenweed:** translates Lucan's *peucedanum*, hog's-fennel or sulphurwort.

l. 1569 **Southernwood:** an aromatic plant.

l. 1575 **Leach:** healer.

l. 1597 **Silver empress of the night:** the moon. There is no equivalent phrase in the Latin. Lucan generally avoids such flowery 'poetic' periphrases.

ll. 1605–6 **But . . . mane:** 'Some of the commentators upon this verse,

qui primum saevos contra videre leones,

fancy that it refers to a custom which the natives of this country had to hang up the lions, which they had caught or killed, upon crosses, and that they were these crucified lions which Cato's soldiers were so glad to meet with. But I can see no reason for such a far-fetched interpretation; the meaning seems to me to be that by meeting with those beasts, who usually prey upon tame cattle, they found they were come into or near an inhabited country' (Rowe). After the snakes lions are a relief.

ll. 1612–88 **When . . . before:** The action now turns to Caesar, who visits the site of Troy. The episode parodies Aeneas' visit to Pallenteum in *Aeneid* VIII.

l. 1615 **Son:** Pompey.

ll. 1618–19 **Here . . . stood:** Leander of Abydos had to swim the Hellespont in order to see his love, Hero of Sestos. One night he was drowned during a storm.

l. **1623 Sigaean:** Sigeum, a promontory in the Troad, and a town of the same name, where Achilles was buried.

l. **1627 Once . . . reared:** Neptune and Apollo were said to have built the walls of Troy for King Laomedon.

l. **1630 Sear:** blighted, withered.

l. **1633 Priam:** king of Troy during the Trojan war.

ll. **1639–40 Here . . . prey:** Hesione, Laomedon's daughter, was rescued from a sea-monster by Hercules. The sea-monster had been sent by Neptune, angry because he and Apollo had not been paid to build the walls of Troy.

l. **1642 The . . . love:** Anchises and Venus were the parents of Aeneas.

l. **1643 Oenone:** the nymph whom Paris deserted for Helen.

l. **1644 Where . . . gave:** Paris awarded the apple to Venus, rather than to Juno or Minerva, and was given Helen as his reward, thus instigating the Trojan war.

l. **1645 Ganymede:** Jove's cupbearer.

l. **1650 Phrygian:** Trojan.

l. **1652 Hector:** The most famous Trojan warrior, killed by Achilles.

l. **1656 Hercean Jove:** Herceus is an epithet of Jove as the protector of the house.

ll. **1657–68 O . . . day:** Lucan now apostrophizes Caesar, promising him immortality through his poem. The passage can be read ironically.

l. **1666 Lucan:** Lucan does not name himself at this point.

l. **1666 Grecian bard:** Homer.

l. **1667 Numbers:** poetry.

l. **1675 And . . . race:** Caesar claimed descent from Aeneas.

ll. **1681–2 Pallas . . . hide:** The Palladium, an image of Pallas which had ensured the safety of Troy until it was stolen by Diomedes and Ulysses, was kept in the temple of Vesta.

l. **1687 Ausonian:** Italian.

l. **1687 Ausonian . . . restore:** 'I don't know whether Lucan does not hint in this passage at the design which Augustus Caesar had to translate the seat of empire from Rome to Troy, and which Mons. Dacier has observed, from Mr Le Fevre, gave occasion for one of the most beautiful odes in Horace' [3.3] (Rowe).

ll. 1689–99 He . . . way: Caesar now sails to Egypt.

l. 1734 Auletes: the surname of the exiled Egyptian king, young Ptolemy's father.

ll. 1747–56 He . . . mourns: Caesar waits until he is sure the head is Pompey's before feigning grief and displeasure.

l. 1764 Trode: trod.

ll. 1769–90 O . . . shame: an apostrophe to Caesar, attacking his hypocrisy.

ll. 1779–80 Perhaps . . . thine: Lucan muses that Caesar's tears may be genuine, but emerging from rage at being robbed of the chance to murder Pompey himself, rather than pity.

ll. 1799–1800 That . . . live: Caesar was famed for his *clementia*.

l. 1806 Distain: stain.

ll. 1855–6 O . . . wear: 'This is a very satirical irony. He means that the standers by durst not show any sign but that of joy, since Caesar, though outwardly he seemed to grieve, was in his heart pleased with that execrable action. But this is an instance of Lucan's prejudice against Caesar, a fault of which I am sorry an author, who seems to have been a lover of his country, should be so often guilty' (Rowe).

Book Ten

l. 7 Pharian: Egyptian.

ll. 24–83 Careless . . . bow: Caesar visits the tomb of Alexander the Great, to whom he is implicitly compared – both are associated with lightning. He scans the gods and temples rapidly before descending to the caves.

ll. 28–9 Their . . . dead: 'The Egyptians embalming their dead and burying them in these large caves in great numbers together is very well known. They are what are now called the catacombs, and are so frequently visited by travellers' (Rowe).

ll. 30–1 Thither . . . attends: These lines do not correspond to Lucan's text, and the guide is thus Rowe's invention. The trope of epic tourism, however, is very much in Lucan's manner.

l. 39 **For ... date:** 'From the first Ptolemy who succeeded Alexander, to this worthless prince, who murdered Pompey, about 280 years' (Rowe).

l. 42 **Confessed:** acknowledged.

l. 47 **And ... disdain:** Philip II, Alexander's father, conquered Athens in 338 BC.

l. 55 **Undistinguishing:** not discriminating.

l. 61 **And ... sea:** 'In this he hints at Alexander's design of discovering the Indian ocean mentioned by Q. Curtius' (Rowe).

l. 63 **Where ... sun:** The sun appears to sink into the ocean (Tethys) when it sets.

l. 65 **And ... head:** Cf.I.32.

ll. 74–5 **The ... Rome:** Rome's achievements in the east were less impressive than Alexander's.

l. 81 **Carrhae:** Scene of Crassus' defeat by the Parthians in 53 BC.

l. 83 **And ... bow:** Pella was the capital city of Macedonia. Alexander subdued the Parthians, Rome failed to do so.

l. 84 **Monarch:** Ptolemy.

l. 87 **Pledge of peace:** Caesar kept Ptolemy within his power, to secure his own safety.

ll. 88–160 **When ... night:** 'Cleopatra, having bribed those guards who had the custody of her person, was brought by Apollodorus, her tutor, wrapped up in a kind of quilt or flock-bed by night to Caesar' (Rowe). Cleopatra approaches Caesar and succeeds in winning him over to her cause.

ll. 93–103 **O ... hand:** Lucan looks forward to the battle of Actium.

l. 95 **Furies:** madness, including mad lust.

l. 98 **Great Augustus:** Lucan does not so describe him. (Rowe's politics are milder than his).

l. 99 **Timbrel:** Cf.VIII.1135.

l. 108 **Then ... more:** The reference is to Cleopatra's celebrated liaison with Mark Antony.

l. 117 **And ... set:** Caesar had a son, Caesarion, by Cleopatra.

l. 122 **Or:** either.

ll. 122-3 **To ... hair:** 'Cleopatra was so secure of the power of her beauty that she took no pains to set off her affliction, or appear more sorrowful than she really was' (Rowe).

l. 127 **Lagaean:** The Ptolemies were descended from the Macedonian Lagus.

l. 136 **Undistinguished:** No distinction is made between women and men.

l. 147 **So:** so long as.

l. 148 **Slave:** Pothinus.

ll. 161-246 **Egypt ... room:** The opulent luxury of Egypt is described. The scene contains echoes of Dido's feast in *Aeneid* I. Such excesses among the Romans were criticized by Lucan in Book I.

l. 162 **Riot:** debauchery.

l. 165 **Fane:** temple.

l. 167 **Latent:** hidden.

l. 173 **Solid ebony:** 'The wood-work used only to be covered over with thin pieces of ebony; here it was entirely made of that costly tree' (Rowe).

l. 176 **Tortoise:** tortoiseshell.

l. 177 **Spots:** the variation of colour naturally found on tortoiseshell.

l. 182 **Tyrian dye:** This was purple.

l. 193 **Dismembered:** castrated.

l. 194 **Genial joys:** nuptial or generative pleasures.

l. 200 **Citron board:** Cf.I.312.

l. 201 **With captive Juba:** 'It should rather be *from vanquished* Juba. The original is

> qualis ad Caesaris ora,
> Nec capto venere Juba.

Though it is certain that after Juba was vanquished he killed himself, and so was never Caesar's prisoner' (Rowe).

ll. 222-8 Had . . . Nile: In other words, even frugal Romans, if exposed to these luxuries, would have been tempted.

l. 225 Curius, Fabricius: Both were third-century Roman generals, bywords for severe simplicity.

l. 226 Cincinnatus: A legendary Roman hero, supposedly called from the plough to be dictator in 458 BC to defeat the Aequi, an Italian tribe. He resigned his dictatorship after sixteen days to retire to his farm and was seen to exemplify Roman austerity and simplicity.

l. 234 Nor . . . adores: 'The Egyptians worshipped not only several sorts of beasts and birds, but even plants, as leeks and onions' (Rowe).

l. 236 Gems of price: 'Drinking vessels made of precious stones. The Spanish translator renders *gemmae capaces* in this place *perlas*, pearls; but that is stretching the Egyptian magnificence a little too far' (Rowe).

l. 236 Store: this may either be a noun or a verb, meaning hold. There is no apostrophe in the first edition, but this evidence is not conclusive as punctuation is inconsistent.

l. 239 Racy: of excellent taste.

l. 241 Nard: a costly perfumed plant.

l. 242 Blooming . . . kind: 'Roses that were in bloom all the year' (Rowe).

l. 245 Perfume: accented on the second syllable.

l. 254 Wear: pass.

l. 256 Vest: robe.

l. 257 Acoreus: It was Acoreus who counselled Ptolemy to remain loyal to Pompey in Book VIII. Caesar now questions him about Egyptian beliefs and the source of the Nile.

l. 268 Cecropian: Athenian, from Cecrops, an ancient king of Athens.

l. 268 Plato: 'This philosopher was, according to Strabo, a considerable time in Egypt, where he was instructed by the priests in their most sacred mysteries' (Rowe).

ll. 276-7 Nor . . . appear: 'Caesar's regulation of the calendar, which we now call the Julian period, is well known' (Rowe).

l. 277 **Eudoxus:** Eudoxus of Cnidus, a fourth-century BC mathematician and astronomer, was the first to give a mathematical account of the movements of the heavenly bodies.

ll. 288–494 **The warrior . . . fields:** After alluding to various false theories about the Nile Acoreus offers his own views. Despite holding out a promise of revealing secret truths, the answers supplied by Acoreus (and Lucan) are ultimately something of a let-down. This pattern seems to replicate the promise held out by Erictho, which is similarly unfulfilled. Caesar's love of 'knowledge' contrasts with Cato's devotion to *virtus*.

l. 291 **And . . . low:** The idea of a former, more secretive, priesthood is strengthened by Rowe, perhaps reflecting his distaste for the Catholic church.

ll. 298–300 **Know . . . given:** 'The planets, which, according to the astronomy of the Romans at that time, were carried round in every twenty-four hours by the eighth sphere, or Primum Mobile' (Rowe). For an account of the astronomical matters discussed in the lines which follow see Housman 1926, 334–7.

ll. 313–22 **When . . . divide:** 'Upon this occasion Lucan enumerates the several different opinions that were then held concerning the increase and decrease of the Nile. The first he gives is the presence of the planet Mercury upon the fountains of the Nile, which he supposes to lie under the sign of Cancer. The fact is that the river begins to swell after midsummer, comes to its height in August, and falls again about the Autumnal equinox in September' (Rowe).

l. 317 **Maia's son:** Mercury.

l. 334 **Dog:** Sirius: the Dog Star.

l. 362 **Airy brethren:** winds.

l. 364 **Head:** source.

l. 374 **Disembogues:** pours forth, discharges.

l. 393 **Less:** lesser.

l. 407 **Philip's great son:** Alexander the Great.

ll. 407–14 **Philip's . . . beheld:** Acoreus describes how Alexander sought the source of the Nile. Caesar's desire is again linked with tyranny.

ll. 415–20 **Fierce ... Rhone:** Sesostris, an Egyptian king, also tried to discover the source.

ll. 419–20 **But ... Rhone:** Even though Sesostris never visited Gaul or Italy, and thus could never have discovered these rivers' sources, they would have been easier to discover than that of the Nile.

l. 421 **Cambyses:** a sixth-century Persian king who invaded Egypt.

l. 422 **Where ... head:** This is a reference to the Macrobii, a mythical Ethiopian tribe whose average life span was 120 years. Rowe probably derived this detail from Herodotus, III.17.26 for it is not included by Lucan.

l. 433 **Records, demonstrate:** both accented on the second syllable.

ll. 434–5 **Than ... know:** Cf. Raphael's advice to Adam in *Paradise Lost* VIII.66–178.

l. 439 **Northern Wain:** the Great Bear.

l. 442 **Seres:** a nation envisaged in the south of Africa, later identified with the Chinese.

l. 476 **Erythraean:** the Arabian Sea.

ll. 495–517 **In ... bleed:** Pothinus now plots to murder Caesar.

l. 497 **Infest:** attack.

l. 500 **Distained:** stained.

l. 502 **Within ... dwell:** The Furies stir up rage in Pothinus, as the Fury Allecto incited Amata to mad hostility against the Trojans in Book VII of the *Aeneid*.

l. 506 **Prevent:** anticipate. The reference is to the possibility of a slave anticipating the exemplary assassination of Caesar by Brutus.

l. 518 **Feeble boy:** Ptolemy.

l. 528 **The former rule:** 'The king's authority' (Rowe).

l. 530 **Dost ... state:** 'This is meant scornfully and ironically' (Rowe).

ll. 546–7 **On ... power:** They would be crucified or burnt alive.

l. 553 **By ... spilt:** Pothinus refers to the murder of Pompey which found them no favour in the eyes of Caesar.

l. 555 **For:** in place of.

l. 555 **Hymen:** god of marriage (ironically of Caesar's union with Cleopatra).

l. 575 **Crime:** the murder of Pompey.

l. 581 **Devoted:** doomed.

l. 584 **Ye Romans:** Pothinus addresses the Roman mercenaries.

ll. 591–629 **Nor ... head:** Achillas surrounds the palace with troops, among whom are many Roman mercenaries, in the pay of Egypt.

ll. 605–7 **For ... away:** 'That is, they do not kill Caesar for the wrongs he had done to Rome, but at the command of that Egyptian master whom they obey and serve for hire' (Rowe).

ll. 612–13 **What ... son:** Egypt could have done no more against Caesar if she had welcomed Pompey rather than destroying him.

ll. 630–1 **But ... hands:** Ptolemy is in the palace with Caesar.

l. 639 **Life:** Caesar's.

l. 643 **Lucifer:** the planet Venus.

l. 674 **Ind:** the Indus.

ll. 676–7 **From ... dread:** 'The original is,

> *Non Scytha, non fixus qui ludit in hospite Maurus;*

alluding to a piece of cruelty practised among those barbarians, to take strangers and set them up for marks to dart their javelins at. I can't think the omission of this circumstance in the translation of any great consequence' (Rowe).

l. 682 **Still ... bears:** Caesar holds Ptolemy hostage.

l. 688 **So ... fled:** When Medea fled from Colchis with Jason, she killed her brother Absyrtus and tore him to pieces in order to delay the pursuit of her father Aeëtes.

ll. 692–5 **Yet ... disclaim:** Caesar tries to bargin with the attacking forces.

l. 703 **Prodigies:** 'As the murder of ambassadors, whose persons and characters are sacred amongst the most barbarous nations' (Rowe).

l. 704 **Purple:** bloodstained.

l. 705 **Pharnaces:** Pharnaces led a revolt against his father, Mithridates, though Rowe's note shows no awareness of the fact.

l. 705 **Moor:** Juba.

l. 714 **More than:** more firmly than.

ll. 716–59 **On . . . death:** Caesar fights off the naval attack and takes Pharos. He then kills Pothinus.

l. 724 **Phalaric darts:** A *falarica* is the Latin for a missile bound with tow and smeared with pitch, which was thrown from a catapult after being ignited.

l. 726 **Unctuous sides:** The ships were caulked with wax.

l. 730 **Strowed:** strewed.

ll. 738–9 **Soon . . . turn:** The famous library of Alexandria was burned in the fire.

l. 742 **Involving:** enveloping.

l. 744 **In . . . reign:** In Herodotus and Euripides Proteus, normally the Old Man of the Sea, is a virtuous Egyptian king.

l. 751 **Watery field:** sea.

l. 759 **And . . . death:** He is killed in the same way as Pompey.

ll. 760–82 **Meanwhile . . . sword:** Arsinoë was the younger sister of Cleopatra and Ptolemy. She puts her tutor, Ganymede, a eunuch, in charge of the army and gives orders for Achillas to be slain. Ganymede then continues the attack on Caesar.

l. 775 **Him:** Achillas.

ll. 783–5 **While . . . passed:** Caesar fights to protect his men while they board the ships.

l. 793 **Vulgar period:** ordinary death.

l. 796 **Renown:** make famous.

ll. 806–11 **At . . . held:** Caesar is inspired by the thought of the valiant Scaeva, whose death is described in Book VI.

l. 811 **And . . . held:** 'This is the last line of the translation, the death of Lucan having left his work thus abrupt and imperfect here. What follows to the end of this book is a supplement of my own, in which I have only endeavoured to finish the relation of this very remarkable action, with bringing Caesar to safety to his own fleet, with the circumstances in which all authors who have writ on this subject agree' (Rowe). Thomas May also provided a short conclusion to Book X in which Caesar is carried safely to his fleet, bearing his papers, while he is shot at by a cloud of darts. This doubtless influenced Rowe's conclusion to the translation, although the more interesting features – the criticism of divine machinery and, of course, the Miltonic echo – are not derived from May.

ll. 830-1 Her . . . head: The sea (Tethys) protects Caesar who swims to safety.

l. 846 Thrilling: piercing.

l. 860 Looser Muse: A poet in the Virgilian manner would have here inserted a scene in which Venus pleads for her supposed descendant Caesar (so in *Aeneid* I Venus appeals to Jupiter on behalf of Aeneas). By contrast 'the just recording Roman' – whether Lucan himself or any writer opposed to 'the looser muse' – reads and depicts the scene very differently. By implication Rowe contrasts Virgil and Lucan, myth and history, Caesarism and liberty. The vocabulary (fancy, feign) recalls Milton's hostility, in *Paradise Lost*, to classical myth as opposed to Christian truth.

l. 861 Devious: Rambling, circuitous and perhaps also with a pun (deceitful).

l. 869 Nemesis: This goddess personified righteous anger, especially that of the gods at human presumption.

GLOSSARY

Abatos	A rock in the Nile near Philae.
Absyrtos	An island in the Adriatic near Illyria.
Actium	A promontory in the south of Epirus, and the site of the famous sea battle in 31 BC when Octavian defeated the fleets of Antony and Cleopatra.
Aeas	A river in Epirus.
Aeolidae	A people of Aeolia in Asia Minor.
Alani	A people of Scythia.
Alba	A town in Latium, home of the house-gods brought by Aeneas.
Alexandria	A city on the north coast of Egypt, built by Alexander the Great.
Allia	A tributary of the Tiber.
Almo	A small river near Rome.
Alpheus	The chief river of Peloponnese.
Amanus	A mountain in Cilicia.
Ambracia	A town in the south of Epirus.
Amphisa	A town in Phocis, north-west of Delphi.
Amphrysus	A small river of Phthiotis.
Anauros	A river in Thessaly.
Anio	A tributary stream of the Tiber.
Ancon	A city in Picenum.
Anxur	A town in Latium on the Appian Way.
Apidanus	A river in Thessaly, tributary of Peneus.
Aponus	A hot spring near Padua.
Apsus	A river in Macedonia.
Apulia	A province in Lower Italy, now Puglia.
Arar	A river in Gaul, now the Saône.
Araxes	A river in Armenia.
Areians	A people of Persia.
Argos	The capital of the province Argolis, in the Peloponnese.
Aricia	A town on the Appian Way.
Arimaspians	A people of Scythia.

Ariminum	A city on the Adriatic coast, about 9 miles (14 kilometres) south of the Rubicon, modern Rimini.
Arisbe	A small town in the Troad.
Asopas	A river of Boeotia.
Asturia	A Spanish province.
Atax	The river Aude in southern France.
Athamans	A people who lived in the mountains in Epirus.
Athos	A mountain in Macedonia.
Atlas	A mountain-range in north Africa.
Atur	The river Adour in south-west France.
Aufidus	A river in Apulia.
Aulis	A seaport of Boeotia.
Ausonia	Italy.
Autololes	A people of Mauretania.
Auximon	A town of the Piceni.
Averni	A people from modern Auvergne who were sometimes thought to claim brotherhood with the Romans.
Bactros	A river of Bactriana in Central Asia.
Baetis	A river in southern Spain.
Bagrada	A river in Africa, near Utica.
Batavians	A Germanic people.
Bebrycians	A tribe of Asia Minor.
Bistones	A Thracian people.
Bituriges	A people who lived around Bourges.
Boebeis	A lake south of Mount Ossa.
Boreas	The north wind.
Bosporus	The Straits of Constantinople.
Brundisium	Brindisi.
Caicus	A river of Greater Mysia in Asia Minor.
Calpe	One of the Pillars of Hercules in Gibraltar.
Calydon	A town in Aetolia.
Campania	A province in central Italy.
Candavia	A mountain range separating Illyricum from Macedonia.
Cannae	A village in Apulia where Hannibal inflicted a great defeat on the Romans in 216 BC.
Canopus	A town on the western mouth of the Nile.
Cantabrians	A Spanish people.
Cappadocia	A country of Asia Minor.
Capua	A town in western Italy, which was punished for going over to the Carthaginian side during the Punic wars.
Carmania	A country to the north of the Persian Gulf.

Carystos	A town on the south coast of Euboea.
Casius	A mountain on the Egyptian coast.
Cauci	A people from northern Germany.
Celenae	A city of southern Phrygia.
Celtiberians	A people of central Spain.
Cephisus	A river in central Greece.
Ceraunia	A rocky coastal range near Oricum.
Chalcis	The chief town of Euboea.
Chaldeans	A people of Assyria.
Chaonia	A region in the north-west of Epirus.
Chios	An island in the Aegean sea.
Cilicia	A province in the southern part of Asia Minor.
Cimbri	A people from northern Germany.
Cimmerians	A Thracian people who lived on both sides of the Dnieper.
Cinga	A river in Spain.
Cirrha	A city in Phocis, serving as the harbour for Delphi.
Clitumnus	A river in Umbria.
Cnidos	A city on the coast of Asia Minor.
Coastrians	A Scythian people.
Colchis	A province of Asia, east of the Black Sea.
Colophon	A city on the coast of Asia Minor.
Cone	An island at the mouth of the Danube.
Corcyra	An island in the Ionian sea, opposite Epirus; modern Corfu.
Corfinium	A City in the Abruzzo.
Corinth	A city in the Peloponnese.
Corus	The north-west wind.
Corycus	A city in the Cilicia.
Cos	An island in the Aegean sea.
Crustumium	A river in Umbria.
Cumae	A colony in Campania.
Curicta	An island off the coast of Illyricum.
Cyllene	A mountain in Arcadia, birthplace of Mercury.
Cyrene	A city in Libya.
Cythera	An island south-west of Cape Malea.
Dacians	A people of the Lower Danube.
Dahae	A Scythian nomad tribe.
Damascus	A city in Syria.
Dirce	A spring near Thebes.
Dodona	A city in Epirus.
Dolopes	A people of Thessaly.
Dryopes	A people of Thessaly.

Dyrrachium	A city on the coast of Illyricum.
Egae	A port in Cilicia.
Emathia	A synonym used for Thessaly or Pharsalia.
Encheliae	A tribe from Illyria.
Enipeus	A river in Thessaly flowing into the Peneus.
Ephesus	A city on the coast of Asia Minor.
Epidamnus	A Greek city on the Adriatic coast in Illyria.
Epirus	A province in the north of Greece.
Eridanus	The Po.
Erythraean	The Red Sea.
Eryx	A mountain in Sicily.
Euboea	An island in the Aegean Sea.
Euphrates	A river in Syria.
Eurus	The east or south-east wind.
Euxine	The Black Sea.
Evenos	A river of Aetolia.
Gades	Cadiz, a Carthaginian colony.
Garamantines	A tribe from the interior of Africa.
Garganus	A mountain in northern Apulia.
Gaurus	Mountains in Campania.
Gaza	A city on the sea-coast of Palestine.
Gebenna	A French mountain range, the modern Cévennes.
Geloni	A people from east of the Tanaïs.
Genusus	A river in Macedonia.
Getulians	A people from north-west Africa.
Haemus	A mountain-range in Thrace.
Halys	A river between Lydia and Media.
Hellespont	The Dardanelles.
Heniochi	A people of Asiatic Sarmatia.
Hermus	A Lydian river.
Hesperia	Latin for 'the western land' and used here to denote Italy, or sometimes Spain.
Hircania	A mountainous region south-east of the Caspian Sea.
Hybla	A mountain in Sicily.
Hydaspes	A tributary of the Indus.
Hydrus	A port in Calabria.
Iberus	A river in Spain, the modern Ebro.
Icaria	An island in the Aegean sea.
Idalium	A mountain-city in Cyprus.
Idume	A region in Palestine.
Ilerda	A city in Spain, the modern Lerida.

Inarime	An island on the coast of Campania, the modern Ischia.
Indus	The river Indus, which falls into the Indian ocean.
Iolcos	A town and harbour in Thessaly.
Isara	The river Isère.
Isaurus	A river of Picenum.
Ister	The lower part of the Danube.
Istrians	A people of the Danube.
Ituraeans	A Syrian people.
Lacinium	A promontory in southern Italy, modern Capo di Colonne.
Larisa	A city in Thessaly.
Lelegians	A tribe in Asia Minor.
Leman	Lake Geneva.
Lemnos	An island in the Aegean sea.
Leptis Minor	A city on the African coast, south of Carthage.
Lesbos	A large Greek island off the coast of Asia Minor.
Leuca	A town in Calabria.
Leucadian	The adjective derived from Leucas.
Leucas	A promontory near where the battle of Actium was fought.
Leuci	A people of the Upper Moselle.
Liburnians	An Illyrian people.
Ligures	A people of the Maritime Alps.
Lingones	A people who lived in north-east France.
Lissus	A town on the coast of Macedonia.
Liris	The modern Garigliano.
Luceria	A town in Apulia.
Luna	Lucca, a town near Pisa.
Lydia	A country in the centre of western Asia Minor.
Macra	A river between Liguria and Etruria.
Maeander	A Phrygian river.
Maenalus	A mountain in the Peloponnese.
Maeotis	The sea of Azov.
Magnetes	A people of Thessaly.
Malea	A promontory at the south-east point of the Peloponnese.
Malian gulf	The Malaic gulf between Thessaly and Achaia.
Mallus	A port in Cilicia.
Mareotis	A large lake near Alexandria.
Marmaridans	An African people.
Massagetes	A Scythian people.
Massilia	Marseilles.
Massyli	A people of Africa.
Mazacs	A people of Numidia.

Melas	A river of Sicily.
Meliboea	A town in Thessaly.
Memphis	A town in Egypt.
Meroë	An island of the Nile, in Ethiopia.
Metaurus	A river in Umbria, the site of the defeat of Hannibal's brother Hasdrubal.
Mevania	A town in Umbria, Mevagna.
Minyae	A people of Thessaly.
Monoechus	A promontory and harbour in Liguria, the modern Monaco.
Moschi	A people from between the Black and the Caspian Seas.
Munda	A town in Spain where Caesar won a battle in 45 BC.
Mutina	Modena, near Bologna, which resisted Pompey in 78 BC and Antony in 43 BC.
Mytilene	The principal city of Lesbos.
Nar	The Nera, a river in central Italy.
Nasamones	A Libyan people.
Nemossus	A city of Aquitanian Gaul, now Clermont.
Nervii	A people from north of Cambrai.
Nesis	An island on the coast of Campania.
Ninos	Generally thought to be Nineveh, although other cities have also been associated with Lucan's Ninos.
Niphates	A river in Armenia.
Numidians	A people from North Africa.
Nymphaeum	A port on the coast south of Lissus.
Nysa	A place associated with Bacchus, of unknown origin.
Oeta	A mountain in Thessaly.
Opitergium	A Roman colony near Venice.
Oricos	A town on the coast of Epirus.
Orontes	The river Asi.
Ossa	A mountain in Thessaly.
Pachynus	The south-eastern promontory of Sicily.
Pactolus	A Lydian river.
Palaeste	A town on the coast of Epirus.
Pamphylia	An area along the southern coast of Asia Minor.
Pangaea	A mountain overlooking Philippi.
Pannonia	A country lying between Dacia, Noricum and Illyria.
Paphos	A city in Cyprus.
Parnassus	A mountain above Delphi, associated with the Muses.
Paros	One of the Cyclades, famous for its marble.
Pelion	A mountain in Thessaly.

Pelorus	A promontory in Sicily.
Pelusium	A marshy area along the Egyptian coast.
Peneus	A river in Thessaly.
Perusia	An Etruscan hill city which was besieged during the Perusine war in 41 BC.
Petra	A hill near Dyrrhachium.
Peuce	An island near the mouth of the Danube.
Pharsalia	A territory in Thessaly and the site of Caesar's final victory over Pompey in 48 BC.
Phaselis	A city and port of Lycia.
Phasis	A river in Colchis, the modern Rioni.
Philae	An island on the Nile near Syene.
Phlegra	A country of Macedonia.
Phocis	An area of central Greece.
Phoenix	A river of Thessaly.
Pholoe	A mountain in Arcadia, also a mountain in Thessaly.
Phycus	A town on the coast of Cyrenaica in Africa.
Pindus	A mountain range in northern Greece.
Pitane	A sea-port of Mysia.
Po	A river in Italy.
Pomptine	The Pomptine marshes lie south-east of Rome.
Pontus	A region of northern Asia Minor.
Punic	Carthaginian. The three Punic wars took place in the third and second centuries BC.
Remi	A people from the region of Rheims.
Rhipaei	A Scythian mountain-range.
Rhodes	An island off Asia Minor.
Rubicon	A small river in north Italy which separated Gallia Cisalpina from Italy.
Rutheni	A people of Aquitanian Gaul.
Rutuba	A river in Liguria.
Saba	A town in Arabia.
Salamis	An island in the Saronic Gulf.
Salapia	A town in northern Apulia.
Salonae	A city in Illyria, the capital of Dalmatia.
Samos	An island in the Aegean sea off the coast of Asia Minor.
Sarmatians	A nomad tribe from the Danube region.
Santones	A people who lived in south-west France.
Sapis	A river in Umbria.
Sarmatia	An area of south Russia.
Sarnus	A river of Campania.

Sason	A rocky island half-way to Epirus.
Scythians	Nomadic tribes from the north of Europe and Asia.
Selloi	A people of Epirus.
Sena	A town on the coast of Umbria.
Sequani	A people from Besançon.
Seres	The Chinese.
Sicoris	A river in Spain, the modern Segre.
Sidon	A city near Tyre.
Sigeum	A promontory near Troy.
Siler	A river bordering Lucania and Campania.
Sipus	A town in Apulia.
Sithonians	A Thracian people.
Sophene	An area on the left bank of the upper Euphrates.
Spercheos	A river in Thessaly.
Stoechades	A group of islands in the Mediterranean, east of Massilia.
Strymon	A river of Thrace.
Suebi/Suevi	A people who lived east of the Elbe in Germany.
Suessons	A people of northern France and Belgium.
Susa	The capital city of the Achaemenids.
Syedra	A small town in Cilicia.
Syene	A town in upper Egypt.
Taenarus	A town in Laconia.
Tagus	A river in Lusitania.
Tanais	The river Don.
Taras	A town in Italy, the modern Taranto.
Tarbelli	The Landes region in south-west France.
Tarpeia	A rock at the south-west corner of the Capitoline hill.
Tarsos	A city in Cilicia.
Taulantii	A people of Illyria, near Dyrrachium.
Taurus	A mountain-range in the south-eastern part of Asia Minor.
Telmessus	A city on the southern coast of Asia Minor.
Tempe	A valley in Thessaly.
Thebes	1) The principal city of Boeotia in Greece. 2) Greek name of a city in Upper Egypt.
Tigris	A river in Mesopotamia.
Timavus	A river near Trieste.
Titaresis	A river in Thessaly which joins the Peneus.
Trachis/Trachyn	A town in southern Thessaly.
Trebia	A river in Cisalpine Gaul where Hannibal defeated the Romans in 218 BC.

Treviri	A people through whose territory flowed the Moselle.
Triton	A lake near the Lesser Syrtis.
Tyre	A city on the coast of Syria.
Tyrrheni	A Pelasgian people who migrated to Italy.
Vangiones	A German people from near Worms.
Varus	The river Var in southern France.
Vectones/Vettones	A Portuguese people.
Veii	An ancient city in Etruria.
Vestini	A people of Italy on the Adriatic sea.
Vosegus	A mountain-chain dividing Lorraine and Alsace, the modern Vosges.
Vultur	A mountain in Apulia.
Vulturnus	A river of Campania.
Xanthus	A river near Troy.
Zeugma	A town on the Euphrates, boundary of the Parthian and Roman empires.

TEXT SUMMARY

In the first edition of the poem each book was prefaced by a brief argument. These are printed below to provide a summary of the contents.

Book One
In the first book, after a proposition of his subject, a short view of the ruins occasioned by the civil wars in Italy and a compliment to Nero, Lucan gives the principal causes of the civil war, together with the characters of Caesar and Pompey. After that the story properly begins with Caesar's passing the Rubicon, which was the bound of his province towards Rome, and his march to Ariminum. Thither the tribunes and Curio, who had been driven out of the city by the opposite party, come to him, and demand his protection. Then follows his speech to his army, and a particular mention of the several parts of Gaul from which his troops were drawn together to his assistance. From Caesar the poet turns to describe the general consternation at Rome, and the flight of great part of the Senate and people at the news of his march. From hence he takes occasion to relate the foregoing prodigies (which were partly an occasion of those panic terrors) and likewise the ceremonies that were used by the priests for purifying the city and averting the anger of the gods, and then ends this book with the inspiration and prophecy of a Roman matron, in which she enumerates the principal events which were to happen in the course of the civil war.

Book Two
Amidst the general consternation that fore-ran the civil war, the poet introduces an old man giving an account of the miseries that attended on that of Marius and Sulla, and comparing their present circumstances to those in which the commonwealth was when that former war broke out. Brutus consults with Cato, whether it were the duty of a private man to concern himself in the public troubles, to which Cato replies in the affirmative. Then follows his receiving Marcia again from the tomb of Hortensius. While Pompey goes to Capua, Caesar makes himself master of the greatest part of Italy, and among the rest of Corfinium, where Domitius, the governor for Pompey, is seized by his garrison and delivered to Caesar, who pardons and dismisses him.

Pompey in an oration to his army makes a trial of their disposition to a general battle, but, not finding it to answer his expectation, he sends his son to solicit the assistance of his friends and allies, then marches himself to Brundisium, where he is like to be shut up by Caesar, and escapes at length with much difficulty.

Book Three

The third book begins with the relation of Pompey's dream in his voyage from Italy. Caesar, who had driven him from thence, after sending Curio to provide corn in Sicily, returns to Rome. There disdaining the single opposition of L. Metellus, then tribune of the people, he breaks open the temple of Saturn, and seizes on the public treasure. Then follows an account of the several different nations that took part with Pompey. From Rome Caesar passes into Gaul, where the Massilians, who were inclinable to Pompey, send an embassy to propose a neutrality; this Caesar refuses, and besieges the town. But meeting with more difficulties than he expected, he leaves C. Trebonius his lieutenant before Massilia, and marches himself into Spain, appointing at the same time D. Brutus admiral of a navy which he had built and fitted out with great expedition. The Massilians likewise send out their fleet, but are engaged and beaten at sea by Brutus.

Book Four

Caesar, having joined Fabius, whom he had sent before him into Spain, encamps upon a rising ground near Ilerda, and not far from the river Sicoris. There the waters being swollen by great rains endanger his camp, but, the weather turning fair and the floods abating, Pompey's lieutenants, Afranius and Petreius, who lay over against him, decamp suddenly. Caesar follows, and encamps so as to cut off their passage, or any use of the river Iberus. As both armies lay now very near to each other, the soldiers on both sides knew and saluted one another, and, forgetting the opposite interest and factions they were engaged in, ran out from their several camps, and embraced one another with great tenderness. Many of Caesar's soldiers were invited into the enemy's camp, and feasted by their friends and relations. But Petreius, apprehending this familiarity might be of ill consequence to his party, commanded them all (though against the rules of humanity and hospitality) to be killed. After this he attempts in vain to march back towards Ilerda, but is prevented and enclosed by Caesar, to whom both himself and Afranius, after their army had suffered extremely for want of water and other necessaries, are compelled to surrender, without asking any other conditions than that they might not be compelled to take on[1] in his army. This Caesar, with great generosity, grants, and dismisses them. In the meanwhile, C. Antonius, who commanded for Caesar near Salonae on the coast of Dalmatia, being shut up by Octavius, Pompey's admiral, and destitute of provisions, had attempted by help of some vessels, or floating machines of a new invention, to pass through Pompey's fleet. Two of them by advantage of the tide found means to escape, but the third, which carried a thousand Opitergians commanded by Vulteius, was intercepted by a boom laid under the water. These when they found it impossible to get off, at the persuasion and by the example of their leader, ran upon one another's swords and died. In Africa the poet introduces Curio enquiring after the story of Hercules and Antaeus, which is recounted to him by one of the natives, and afterwards relates the particulars of his being circumvented, defeated and killed by Juba.

Book Five

In Epirus the consuls assemble the Senate, who unanimously appoint Pompey general of the war against Caesar, and decree public thanks to the several princes and states who assisted the commonwealth. Appius, at that time praetor of Achaia, consults the oracle of Delphos concerning the event of the civil war. And, upon this occasion, the poet goes into a digression concerning the origin, the manner of the delivery and the present silence of that oracle. From Spain, Caesar returns into Italy, where he quells a mutiny in his army, and punishes the offenders. From Placentia, where this disorder happened, he orders them to march to Brundisium where, after a short turn to Rome, and assuming the consulship, or rather the supreme power, he joins them himself. From Brundisium, though it was then the middle of winter, he transports part of his army by sea to Epirus, and lands at Palaeste. Pompey, who then lay about Candavia, hearing of Caesar's arrival and being in pain for Dyrrachium, marched that way. On the banks of the river Apsus they met and encamped close together. Caesar was not yet joined by that part of his troops which he had left behind him at Brundisium, under the command of Mark Antony, and, being uneasy at his delays, leaves his camp by night, and ventures over a tempestuous sea in a small bark to hasten the transport. Upon Caesar's joining his forces together, Pompey perceived that the war would now probably be soon decided by a battle, and, upon that consideration, resolved to send his wife to expect the event at Lesbos. Their parting, which is extremely moving, concludes this book.

[1] Take on: enlist.

Book Six

Caesar and Pompey lying now near Dyrrachium after several marches and countermarches, the former with incredible diligence runs a vast line, or work, round the camp of the latter. This Pompey, after suffering for want of provisions, and a very gallant resistance of Scaeva, a centurion of Caesar's, at length breaks through. After this Caesar makes another unsuccessful attempt upon a part of Pompey's army, and then marches away into Thessaly. And Pompey, against the persuasion and counsel of his friends, follows him. After a description of the ancient inhabitants, the boundaries, the mountains and rivers of Thessaly, the poet takes occasion from this country, being famous for witchcraft, to introduce Sextus Pompeius inquiring the event of the civil war from the sorceress Erictho.

Book Seven

In the seventh book is told, first, Pompey's dream the night before the battle of Pharsalia, after that the impatient desire of his army to engage, which is reinforced by Tully. Pompey, though against his own opinion and inclination, agrees to a battle. Then follows the speech of each general to his army, and the battle itself, the flight of Pompey, Caesar's behaviour after his victory, and an invective against him and the very country of Thessaly, for being the scene (according to this and other authors) of so many misfortunes to the people of Rome.

Book Eight

From Pharsalia Pompey flies, first to Larisa, and after to the seashore, where he embarks upon a small vessel for Lesbos. There, after a melancholy meeting with Cornelia, and his refusal of the Mitylenians' invitations, he embarks with his wife for the coast of Asia. In the way thither he is joined by his son Sextus, and several persons of distinction, who had fled likewise from the late battle, and among the rest by Deiotarus, king of Gallo-Graecia. To him he recommends the soliciting of supplies from the king of Parthia and the rest of his allies in Asia. After coasting Cilicia for some time, he comes at length to a little town called Syhedra, or Syhedrae, where great part of the Senate meet him. With these he deliberates upon the present circumstances of the commonwealth, and proposes either Mauritania, Egypt or Parthia, as the proper places where he may hope to be received, and from whose kings he may expect assistance. In his own opinion he inclines to the Parthians, but this Lentulus, in a long oration, opposes very warmly, and in consideration of young Ptolemy's personal obligations to Pompey prefers Egypt. This advice is generally approved and followed, and Pompey sets sail accordingly for Egypt. Upon his arrival on that coast, the king calls a council, where at the instigation of Pothinus, a villainous minister, it is resolved to take his life, and the execution of this order is committed to the care of Achillas, formerly the king's governor, and then general of the army. He, with Septimius, a renegado Roman soldier, who had formerly served under Pompey, upon some frivolous pretences persuades him to quit his ship and come into their boat, where, as they make towards the shore, he treacherously murders him, in the sight of his wife, his son, and the rest of his fleet. His head is cut off, and his body thrown into the sea. The head is fixed upon a spear, and carried to Ptolemy, who, after he has seen it, commands it to be embalmed. In the succeeding night one Cordus, who had been a follower of Pompey, finds the trunk floating near the shore, brings it to land with some difficulty, and, with a few planks that remained from a shipwrecked vessel burns it. The melancholy description of this mean funeral, with the poet's invective against the gods and fortune for their unworthy treatment of so great a man, concludes this book.

Book Nine

The poet, having ended the foregoing book with the death of Pompey, begins this with his apotheosis; from thence, after a short account of Cato's gathering up the relics of the battle of Pharsalia and transporting them to Cyrene in Africa, he goes on to describe Cornelia's passion upon the death of her husband. Amongst other things she informs his son Sextus of his father's last commands to continue the war in defence of the commonwealth. Sextus sets sail for Cato's camp, where he meets his elder brother Cn. Pompeius, and acquaints him with the fate of their father. Upon this occasion the poet describes the rage of the elder Pompey, and the disorders that happened in the camp, both which Cato appeases. To prevent any future inconvenience of this kind, he resolves to put them upon action, and in order to that to join with Juba. After a description of the Syrtes and their dangerous passage by them follows Cato's speech to encourage the soldiers to march through the deserts of Libya, then an account of Libya, the deserts, and their march; in the middle of which is a beautiful digression concerning the temple of Jupiter-Ammon, with Labienus' persuasion to Cato to enquire of the oracle concerning the event of the war, and Cato's famous answer. From thence, after a warm eulogy upon Cato, the author goes on to the account of the original of serpents in Afric, and this, with the description of their various kinds and the several deaths of the soldiers by them, is perhaps the most poetical part of this whole work. At Leptis he leaves Cato, and returns to Caesar, whom he brings into Egypt, after having shown him the ruins of Troy, and from thence taken an occasion to speak well of poetry in general and himself in particular. Caesar, upon his arrival on the coast of Egypt, is met by an ambassador from Ptolemy with Pompey's head. He receives the present (according to Lucan) with a feigned abhorrence, and concludes the book with tears, and a seeming grief for the misfortune of so great a man.

Book Ten

Caesar, upon his arrival in Egypt, finds Ptolemy engaged in a quarrel with his sister Cleopatra, whom, at the instigation of Pothinus and his other evil counsellors, he had deprived of her share in the kingdom, and imprisoned. She finds means to escape, comes privately to Caesar and puts herself under his protection. Caesar interposes in the quarrel, and reconciles them. They in return entertain him with great magnificence and luxury at the royal palace in Alexandria. At this feast Caesar, who at his first arrival had visited the tomb of Alexander the Great and whatever else was curious in that city, enquires of the chief priest Acoreus, and is by him informed of the course of the Nile, its stated increase and decrease, with the several causes that had been till that time assigned for it. In the meantime Pothinus writes privately to Achillas, to draw the army to Alexandria and surprise Caesar; this he immediately performs, and besieges the palace. But Caesar, having set the city and many of the Egyptian ships on fire, escapes to the island and tower of Pharos, carrying the young king and Pothinus, whom he still kept in his power, with him; there having discovered the treachery of Pothinus, he puts him to death. At the same time Arsinoë, Ptolemy's youngest sister, having by the advice of her tutor, the eunuch Ganymedes, assumed the regal authority, orders Achillas to be killed likewise, and renews the war against Caesar. Upon the mole between Pharos and Alexandria he is encompassed by the enemy, and very near being slain, but at length breaks through, leaps into the sea, and with his usual courage and good fortune swims in safety to his own fleet.

SUGGESTIONS FOR FURTHER READING

Texts and Commentaries, etc.

The best text remains that of A. E. Housman, Oxford: Basil Blackwell, 1926 (this is also the text used by J. D. Duff for his Loeb translation, London and New York: Heinemann 1928).

The only complete commentary in English is C. E. Haskins, London, 1887, with an important introduction by W. E. Heitland. Individual commentaries exist for Book I (R. J. Getty, Cambridge: Cambridge University Press, 1940; reprinted Bristol Classical Press, 1992); Book II (Elaine Fantham, Cambridge: Cambridge University Press, 1992); Book III (Vincent Hunink, Amsterdam: J. C. Gieben, 1992); Book V (Pamela Barratt, Amsterdam: Adolf Hakkert, 1979); Book VII (O. A. W. Dilke, Cambridge University Press: Cambridge, 1960, a revision of J. P. Postgate, 1913); Book VIII (Roland Mayer, Warminster: Aris and Phillips, 1981). Editions of Books VI and IX would be particularly welcome.

Recent verse translations have no great literary merit, giving little sense of the *Pharsalia*'s poetic power: most helpful perhaps is Susan H. Braund (*World's Classics*, Oxford and New York: Oxford University Press, 1992), with informative introduction and notes, which could usefully be read in conjunction with Rowe's much freer version.

Studies

Ahl, Frederick M. (1976), *Lucan: An Introduction*. Ithaca and London: Cornell University Press.

Aubrey, John (1950), *Brief Lives*, ed. O. L. Dick. London: Secker and Warburg.

Bartsch, Shadi (1997), *Ideology in Cold Blood: A Reading of Lucan's Civil War* Cambridge, Mass. and London: Harvard University Press.

Blissett, William (1956), 'Lucan's Caesar and the Elizabethan Villain', *Studies in Philology* 53, pp. 553–75.

Bramble, J. C. (1982), 'Lucan', in E. J. Kenney and W. V. Clausen, eds., *The Cambridge History of Latin Literature: vol 2. Latin Literature*, pp. 533–57. Cambridge: Cambridge University Press.

Burrow, Colin (1993), *Epic Romance: Homer to Milton*, pp. 180–99. Oxford: Clarendon Press.

Chester, Allen Griffith (1930), *Thomas May: Man of Letters, 1595–1650*. Philadelphia.

Conte, Gian Biagio (1994), *Latin Literature: A History*, translated by Joseph B. Solodow, 'Lucan', pp. 440–52. Baltimore and London: Johns Hopkins University Press.

Dick, B. (1967), '*Fatum* and *Fortuna* in Lucan's *Bellum Civile*', *Classical Philology* 62, pp. 235–42.

Dilke, O. A. W. (1972), 'Lucan and English Literature', in D. R. Dudley, ed., *Neronians and Flavians: Silver Latin 1*, pp. 83–112. London and Boston: Routledge and Kegan Paul.

Feeney, Denis (1986), ' "Stat magni nominis umbra": Lucan on the Greatness of Pompeius Magnus', *Classical Quarterly* ns 36, pp. 239–43.

Feeney, Denis (1991), *The Gods in Epic: Poets and Critics of the Classical Tradition*, ch. 6 'Epic of History', pp. 250–312. Oxford: Clarendon Press.

Gillespie, Stuart (1988), *The Poets on the Classics: An Anthology*, 'Lucan', pp. 139–49. London and New York: Routledge.

Gordon, Richard (1987), 'Lucan's Erictho' in M. and M. Whitby, P. Hardie, eds., *Homo Viator: Classical Essays for John Bramble*, pp. 231–41. Bristol: Bristol Classical Press.

Hardie, Philip (1993), *The Epic Successors of Virgil: A Study in the Dynamics of a Tradition*. Cambridge: Cambridge University Press.

Henderson, John (1988), 'Lucan / The Word at War', in A. J. Boyle, ed., *The Imperial Muse; Ramus Essays on Roman Literature of the Empire To Juvenal Through Ovid*, pp. 122–64. Victoria: Aureal Publications.

Hesse, Alfred William (1950), *Nicholas Rowe's Translation of Lucan's Pharsalia 1703–1718: A Study in Literary History* (dissertation). Philadelphia: University of Pennsylvania Press.

Johnson, Samuel (1932), *Lives of the English Poets*, ed. Arthur Waugh, 2 vols. Oxford: Oxford University Press.

Johnson, W. R. (1987), *Momentary Monsters: Lucan and his Heroes*. Ithaca and London: Cornell University Press.

Lapidge, M. (1979), 'Lucan's Imagery of Cosmic Dissolution', *Hermes* 107, pp. 344–70.

Martindale, Charles (1976), 'Paradox, Hyperbole and Literary Novelty in Lucan's *De Bello Civili*', *Bulletin of the Institute of Classical Studies* 23, pp. 45–54.

Martindale, Charles (1984), 'The Politician Lucan', *Greece and Rome* 31, pp. 71–80.

Martindale, Charles (1986), *John Milton and the Transformation of Ancient Epic*, ch. 5 'Lucan', pp. 197–224. London and Sidney: Croom Helm.

Martindale, Charles (1993), *Redeeming the Text: Latin Poetry and the Hermeneutics of Reception*, pp. 48–53, 64–72. Cambridge: Cambridge University Press.

Masters, Jamie (1992), *Poetry and Civil War in Lucan's 'Bellum Civile'*. Cambridge: Cambridge University Press.

Masters, Jamie, and Elsner, Jas, eds. (1994), *Reflections of Nero: Culture, History and Representation*. London: Duckworth.

Morford, M. P. O. (1967), *The Poet Lucan: Studies in Rhetorical Epic*. Oxford: Basil Blackwell.

Norbrook, David (1994), 'Lucan, Thomas May, and the Creation of a Republican Literary Culture', in Kevin Sharpe and Peter Lake, eds., *Culture and Politics in Early Stuart England*, pp. 45–66. London and Basingstoke: Macmillan.

Quint, David (1993), *Epic and Empire: Politics and Generic Form from Virgil to Milton* (especially introduction and ch 4). Princeton, NJ: Princeton University Press.

Rowe, Nicholas (1929), *Three Plays: Tamerlane, The Fair Penitent, Jane Shore*, ed. J. R. Sutherland, London: The Scholartis Press.

Sanford, E. M. (1931), 'Lucan and his Roman Critics', *Classical Philology* 26, pp. 233–57.

Sherburn, George, ed. (1956), *The Correspondence of Alexander Pope*, 2 vols. Oxford: Clarendon Press.

Smith, Nigel (1994), *Literature and Revolution in England 1640–1660*, ch. 7, 'Heroic Work'. New Haven and London: Yale University Press.

Rosner-Siegel, J. A. (1983), 'The Oak and the Lightning: Lucan *BC* 1.135–57', *Athenaeum* ns 61, pp. 165–77.

Thompson, L., and Bruère, R. T. (1968), 'Lucan's Use of Vergilian Reminiscence', *Classical Philology* 63, pp. 1–21.

Williams, Gordon (1978), *Change and Decline: Roman Literature in the Early Empire*. University of California Press: Berkeley and Los Angeles.